This Book Belongs To:

BALFOUR.

A SCOTTISH COLLECTION

The Maiden's Bequest
The Minister's Restoration
The Laird's Inheritance

BETHANY HOUSE PUBLISHERS

Minneapolis, Minnesota 55438

The Novels of George MacDonald Edited for Today's Reader

Edited Title	Original Title
The two-volume story of Malcolm:	
The Fisherman's Lady	*Malcolm*
The Marquis' Secret	*The Marquis of Lossie*
Companion stories of Gibbie and his friend Donal:	
The Baronet's Song	*Sir Gibbie*
The Shepherd's Castle	*Donal Grant*
Companion stories of Hugh Sutherland and Robert Falconer:	
The Tutor's First Love	*David Elginbrod*
The Musician's Quest	*Robert Falconer*
The Maiden's Bequest	*Alec Forbes of Howglen*
Companion stories of Thomas Wingfold:	
The Curate's Awakening	*Thomas Wingfold*
The Lady's Confession	*Paul Faber*
The Baron's Apprenticeship	*There and Back*
Stories that stand alone:	
A Daughter's Devotion	*Mary Marston*
The Gentlewoman's Choice	*Weighed and Wanting*
The Highlander's Last Song	*What's Mine's Mine*
The Laird's Inheritance	*Warlock O'Glenwarlock*
The Landlady's Master	*The Elect Lady*
The Minister's Restoration	*Salted with Fire*
The Peasant Girl's Dream	*Heather and Snow*
The Poet's Homecoming	*Home Again*

MacDonald Classics Edited for Young Readers

Wee Sir Gibbie of the Highlands
Alec Forbes and His Friend Annie
At the Back of the North Wind
The Adventures of Ranald Bannerman

George MacDonald: Scotland's Beloved Storyteller by Michael Phillips
Discovering the Character of God by George MacDonald
Knowing the Heart of God by George MacDonald
A Time to Grow by George MacDonald
A Time to Harvest by George MacDonald

GEORGE MACDONALD

The Maiden's Bequest
The Minister's Restoration
The Laird's Inheritance

EDITED FOR TODAY'S READER BY
MICHAEL R. PHILLIPS

BETHANY HOUSE PUBLISHERS
MINNEAPOLIS, MINNESOTA 55438

The
Maiden's
Bequest

Contents

Introduction

When George MacDonald wrote *Alec Forbes of Howglen* in 1865 (here titled *The Maiden's Bequest*), one cannot help but think he enjoyed himself. The setting for Glamerton is the Scottish village of Huntly where MacDonald himself grew up. As is the case in most of MacDonald's books, a good deal of autobiography found its way into the pages. How many of the escapades of Alec and his friends had their roots in MacDonald's own childhood, we have no way of knowing. But we sense pure delight at the whole idea of being young. In *Alec Forbes*, MacDonald offers his readers a picture of the love he had for the young at heart, those who could find a way to enjoy life whatever their surroundings.

It is no secret that MacDonald often sought to convey his attitudes and even spiritual doctrines through his writing. Thus in their original editions his novels often contained cumbersome digressions from the actual story. But little of these doctrinal treatises are to be found in *Alec Forbes*. Indeed, it is the smoothest flowing, most cohesive of all MacDonald's novels. Every character is crucial to the development of the plot; every incident follows the next in logical progression. Therefore, *Alec Forbes* might be termed more entirely "story" than most of the other books. There is less point, more plot; less meaning, more movement; fewer lessons, more laughs. In short, though the principles of truth are reflected just as strongly, it is not as *heavy* a book as, for instance, *The Musician's Quest*. One imagines the author taking great pleasure in the task of piecing it together, without attempting any particular message and concerned merely to offer his readers an enjoyable source of entertainment.

This new edition of *Alec Forbes* has—similarly to the other books in the Bethany House MacDonald Reprint Series—been edited and trimmed for publication. In addition, the Scottish dialect of the original has been "translated" into more current usage. As a sample, here is a random selection from the original—perhaps for some of you not impossible to decipher, but sure to slow down the text.

> "Gin it hadna been for the guid wife here, 'at cam' up, efter the clanjamfrie had ta'en themsel's aff, an' fand me lying upo' the hearthstane, I wad hae been deid or noo. Was my heid aneath the grate, guidwife?"
>
> "Na, nae freely that, Mr. Cupples; but the blude o't was. Mr. Forbes, ye maun jist come doon wi' me. I'll jist mak' a cup o' tay till him."
>
> "Tay, guidwife! Deil slocken himsel' wi' yer tay! Gie me a sook o' the tappit hen."
>
> " 'Deed, Mr. Cupples, ye's hae neither sook nor sipple o' that spring."
>
> "Ye rigwiddie carlin!" grinned the patient.
>
> "Never a glaiss sall ye hae fra my han', Mr. Cupples. It wad be the deid

o' ye. And forbye, thae ill-faured gutter-partans toomed the pig afore they gaed."

"Gang oot o' my chaumer wi' yer havers," cried Mr. Cupples, "and lea' me wi' Alec Forbes. He winna deave me wi' his clash."

It is interesting to note that the original *Alec Forbes of Howglen* was of average length compared with MacDonald's other novels. However, in edited form it is the longest by a substantial amount. The reason for this is as already mentioned, there are fewer extraneous digressions. Thus, in one sense *The Maiden's Bequest* is nearer its original *Alec Forbes* than the others in this series, precisely because the first edition was so skillfully woven together, every part playing its own integral role in the whole.

Alec Forbes of Howglen epitomizes a great range and depth of distinctive features. It was MacDonald's second Scottish novel (following *David Elginbrod,* 1863—*The Tutor's First Love*), along with *Robert Falconer,* 1868 (*The Musician's Quest*), that formed the triad for which MacDonald was best known as a novelist. MacDonald's reputation as a 19th-century literary figure was largely based on these three works and they were considered by most as MacDonald's best fiction. They established the cornerstone of his achievement. In discussing this period of his life and these particular novels as they related to his broadening literary talents, Ronald MacDonald commented that his father was "well into his stride" in *Alec Forbes* and "fully extended" by the time of *Robert Falconer.*

Of course one can scrutinize *Alec Forbes* like any work, and there are a good many things that can fruitfully be discussed. But on the other hand, this book can be viewed as a good, fun story. One of MacDonald's great skills as a writer was his ability to work in many diverse genres with equal mastery, from fantasy to poetry, from essays to literary criticism, from romance to history to children's stories. We know, in addition, that together with his wife he wrote for, and acted upon the stage. In *Alec Forbes* MacDonald tried his hand at good old-fashioned theatrical soap opera. Here is melodrama at its finest, complete with villain, mortgage, humor, inheritance, tragedy, foreclosure, romance, and . . . but of course I can't tell you the ending!

Whether you enjoy it better or not as well as other MacDonald's you may have read will depend primarily upon the story itself. But looking at it purely from a literary standpoint, those familiar with the body of MacDonald's work praise its unity as a piece of literature because of the tight consolidation of its elements. Rolland Hein calls it "the most delightful of all the novels." Richard Reis says, "I consider *Alec Forbes of Howglen* MacDonald's best novel." And MacDonald's son Greville calls it "perhaps the most successful, as fiction, of all his efforts."*

---

*Quoted are: Ronald MacDonald, author of the Scottish reminiscence *From a Northern Window* (London: James Nisbet, 1911); Greville MacDonald, author of *George MacDonald and His Wife* (London: George Allen & Unwin, 1924); Richard Reis, author of the Twayne English Authors Series volume *George MacDonald* (New York: Twayne Publishers, 1972), and; Rolland Hein, author of *The Harmony Within: The Spiritual Vision of George MacDonald* (Grand Rapids: Eerdmans Pub. Co., 1982).

Therefore, sit back and enjoy the story of little Annie Anderson and her childhood friend Alec Forbes. This is the stuff of which rainy nights and crackling fires and cozy chairs are made—if you have a cup of tea beside you, so much the better! Here is the sparkle of life—the pains and wonders of childhood, the delights of the seasons, the exuberance and sheer pleasure of youth, the awe of dawning maturity, the uncertainty of spiritual yearnings, the heart-tugging agony of first loves.

As always, I sincerely hope you enjoy your experience with my friend of a century past, George MacDonald. Both I and the publisher welcome your comments.

Michael Phillips
One Way Book Shop
1707 E Street
Eureka, CA 95501

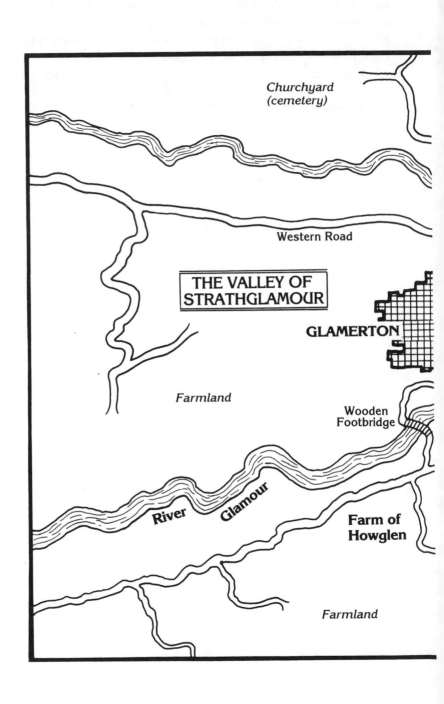

*Churchyard
(cemetery)*

Western Road

THE VALLEY OF
STRATHGLAMOUR

GLAMERTON

Farmland

Wooden
Footbridge

River Glamour

**Farm of
Howglen**

Farmland

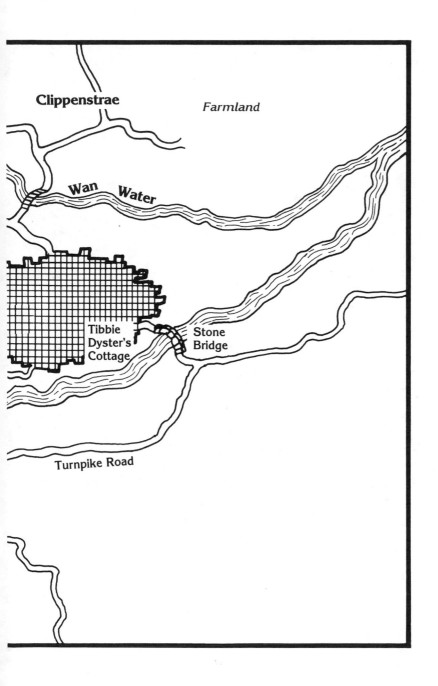

Clippenstrae

Farmland

Wan Water

Tibbie
Dyster's
Cottage

Stone
Bridge

Turnpike Road

1

••••••••••••••••••

Burying Day

The farmyard was full of the light of a summer noonday. Not a living creature was to be seen in all the square enclosure, though barns and stables formed the greater part of it, while one end was occupied by a house. Through the gate at the other end, far off in the fields, might be seen the dark forms of cattle. And on a road nearer by, a cart crawled along, drawn by one sleepy horse. An occasional weary low came from some imprisoned cow, but not even a cat crossed the yard. The door of the empty barn was open and through the opposite doorway shone the last year's ricks of corn, standing golden in the sun.

Although a farmyard is rarely the liveliest of places about noon in the summer, there was a peculiar cause rendering this one, at this moment, exceptionally deserted and dreary. There were, however, a great many more people about the place than usual. But they were all gathered in the nicest room of the house—a room of tolerable size, with a clean, boarded floor, a mahogany table black with age, and chairs with high straight backs. Every one of these chairs was occupied by a silent man whose gaze was either fixed on the floor or lost in the voids of space. Most were clothed in black and each wore a black coat. Their hard, thick, brown hands—hands evidently unused to idleness—grasped their knees or, folded in each other, rested upon them. Apparently, the meeting was not entirely for business purposes, for some bottles and glasses, with a plate of biscuits, sat on a table in a corner. Yet there were no signs of any sort of enjoyment. Nor was there a woman to be seen in the company.

Suddenly another man appeared at the open door, his shirtsleeves very white against his other clothing, which, like that of the rest, was black.

"If any o' ye want t' see the corpse, noo's yer time," he said to the assembly.

No one responded to his offer, and with a slight air of discomfiture the carpenter—for such he was—turned on his heel and re-ascended the narrow stairs to the upper room where the corpse lay waiting for its final dismissal.

"I reckon they've all seen him afore," he remarked as he rejoined his companion. "Poor fellow! He's sure some worn. There'll be not much o' *him* to rise again."

"George, man, don't jest in the face o' the corpse," returned the other. "Ye don't know when yer own turn may come."

"It's not disrespect to the dead, Thomas. I was only pityin' his worn face. I just don't like t' put the lid over him."

"Hoot! Let the Lord look after His own. The lid o' the coffin hides nothin' from His eye."

The last speaker was a stout, broad-shouldered man, a stonemason by trade, powerful but somewhat asthmatic. He was regarded in the neighborhood as a very religious man, but was more respected than liked because his forte was rebuke.

Together they lifted the last covering of the dead, laid it over him, and fastened it down. And now there was darkness about the dead; but he knew it not, because he was full of light. For this man was one who all his life had been full of goodness and truth.

Meantime, the clergyman having arrived, the usual religious ceremonial of a Scottish funeral—the reading of the Word and prayer—was going on below. When the prayer was over, the company again seated themselves, waiting till the coffin, now descending the stairs, should be placed in the hearse, which stood at the door. One after another of them slowly rose and withdrew from the interior of the house. They watched the scene unravel in silence, and at last fell in behind the body which moved in an irregular procession from the yard. They were joined by several more men in gigs and on horseback; and thus they crept, a curious train, away toward the resting place of the dead.

When the last man had disappeared down the road, the women began to come out. The first to enter the deserted room was a hard-featured woman, the sister of the departed. She instantly began to put the place in order, as if she expected to have her turn on the morrow. In a few moments more a servant-girl appeared and began to assist her. She had been crying and the tears continued to come, in spite of her efforts to suppress them. She vainly attempted to dry her eyes with the corner of her apron and nearly dropped one of the chairs which she was both dusting and restoring to its usual place. Her mistress turned upon her with a cold kind of fierceness.

"Is that how ye show yer regard for the dead, by breaking the chairs he left behind him? Let it sit and go out and look for that poor, little, good-for-nothing Annie. If it had only been the Almighty's will t' have taken her and left him, honest man."

"Don't say a word against the child, mem," the girl remonstrated with quiet intensity. "The dead'll hear ye and not lie still."

"Go and do what I tell ye this minute! What business do ye have t' go crying about the house? He was not a drop o' blood o' yers."

To this the girl made no reply but left the room in quest of Annie. When she reached the door, she stood for a moment on the threshold and called, *"Annie!"* But, apparently startled at the sound of her own voice where the unhearing dead had so recently passed, she let the end of the call die away and set off to find the missing child by the use of her eyes alone.

First she went into the barn, and then through it into the field, round the ricks one after another, then into the grain loft—but all to no avail. At length she came to the door of one of the cow-houses. She looked round the corner into the stall next to the door. This stall was occupied by a favorite cow—brown with large white spots—called Brownie. Her manger was full of fresh-cut grass. Half buried in the grass at one end, with her back against the wall, sat Annie, holding one of the ears of the hornless Brownie with one hand and stroking the creature's nose with the other.

She was a delicate child, about nine years old, with blue eyes half full of tears, hair somewhere between dark and fair, and a pale face on which a faint smile was glimmering. The old cow continued to hold out her nose to be stroked.

"Isn't Brownie a fine cow, Emma?" asked Annie, as the maid went on staring at her. "Poor Brownie! Nobody minded me and so I came to you, Brownie."

She laid her cheek—white, smooth, and thin—against the broad, flat, hairy forehead of the friendly cow. Then turning again to Emma, she said, "Don't tell Auntie where I am, Emma. Let me be. I'm best here with Brownie."

Emma said not a word but returned to her mistress.

"Where's the bairn, Emma? At some mischief or other?"

"Hoot, mem! The bairn's well enough. Bairns mustn't be followed like calves."

"Where is she?"

"I can't just downright exactly take it upon me to say," answered Emma, "but I have no fear about her. She's a wise child."

"*Ye're* not the lassie's keeper, Emma. I see I must seek her out myself. Ye're aiding and abetting as usual."

So saying, Auntie Meg went out to look for her niece. It was some time before the natural order of her search brought her at last to the byre. By that time Annie was almost asleep in the grass, though the cow was gradually pulling it away from under her. Through the open door the child could see the sunlight lying heavy upon the hot stones that paved the yard. But where she was it was so dark and cool, and the cow was such good, kindly company, and she was so safe hidden from Auntie, so she thought—for no one had ever found her there before and she knew Emma would not tell—that, as I say, she was nearly asleep with comfort, half buried in Brownie's dinner.

But she was roused all at once to a sense of exposure and insecurity. She looked up, and at that moment the hawk nose of her aunt came round the door. Auntie's temper was none the better than usual. After all, it had pleased the Almighty to take the brother whom she loved and to leave behind this child whom she regarded as a painful responsibility. The woman's small, fierce eyes, and her big, thin nose—both red with suppressed crying—did not appear to Annie to embody the maternal love of the universe.

"Ye plaguesome brat!" she cried. "Emma has been looking for ye and I have been looking for ye far and near, in the very rat holes, and here ye are on yer own father's burying day taking up with a cow!"

The causes of Annie's preference for the society of Brownie to that of Auntie might have been tolerably clear to an onlooker. For to Annie and her needs there was comfort in Brownie's large, mild eyes and her hairy, featureless face, which was all nose and no nose. Indeed, she found more of the divine in Brownie than in the human form of Auntie Meg. And there was something of an indignation quite human in the way the cow tossed her head and neck toward the woman that darkened the door, as if warning her off her premises.

Without a word of reply, Annie rose, flung her arms around Brownie's head, kissed the white star on her forehead, disengaged herself from the grass, and got out of the manger. Auntie seized her hand with a rough but not altogether ungentle action, and led her away to the house.

The stones felt very hot to her little bare feet.

2

· · · · · · · · · · · · · · · · · · · ·

Two Conversations

By this time the funeral was approaching the churchyard. All along the way the procession had been silently joined by others, and as they drew near, their pace slowed to hardly more than a crawl. They stopped at the gate of the yard, and from there it was the hands of friends and neighbors, not undertakers or hired helpers, that bore the dead man to his grave. When the body had been settled into its final place of decay, the last rite to be observed was the silent uncovering of the head, as a last token of respect and farewell.

Before the grave was quite filled the company had nearly gone. Thomas Crann, the stonemason, and George Macwha, the carpenter, alone remained behind, for they had some charge over the arrangements and were now taking a share in covering the grave. At length the last sod was laid upon the mound and stamped into its place, where soon the earth's broken surface would heal, as society would flow together again, closing over the place that had known the departed and would know him no more. Then Thomas and George sat down opposite each other, on two neighboring tombstones, and wiping their brows, each gave a sigh of relief, for the sun was hot.

" 'Tis a weary world," murmured George.

"What right have ye t' say it, George?" answered Thomas. "Ye've never fought wi' it, never held the sword o' the Lord. And so, when the Bridegroom comes, ye'll be ill-off for a lamp wi' which to greet Him."

"Hoot, man! Don't speak such things in the very churchyard."

"Better hear them in the churchyard than at the closed door of heaven, George!"

"Well," rejoined Macwha, anxious to turn the current of the conversation, "just tell me honestly, Thomas Crann, do ye believe that the dead man—God be with him . . ."

"Not prayin' for the dead in my hearin', are ye, George? As the tree falleth, so it shall lie. The same it is with a man. There is no changin' after death."

"Well, I didn't mean anything."

"That I verily believe. Ye seldom do!"

"But I just wanted to ask," resumed George, rather nettled at his companion's persistent discourtesy, "if ye believe that James Anderson here, honest man beneath our feet, crumblin' away—do ye believe that his honest face will one day part the mounds and come up again, just here, in the face of the light, the very same as it vanished when we put the lid over him? Do ye believe that, Thomas Crann?"

"No, no, George, man. Ye know little about what ye're sayin'. It'll be a glorified body that he'll rise with. 'Tis sown in dishonor and raised in glory. Hoot! Ye *are* ignorant, man!"

Macwha got more nettled still at his companion's tone of superiority.

"Would it be a glorified wooden leg he'd raise with if he had been buried with one?" he asked.

"His own leg would be buried somewhere."

"Ow, ay! No doubt. And it would come hoppin' over the Pacific or the Atlantic to join its original stump, would it? But supposin' the man had been born *without* a leg—eh, Thomas?"

"George! George!" Thomas shook his head with great solemnity, "look after yer own soul and the Lord'll look after yer body—legs and all. Man, ye're not converted, so how can ye understand the things o' the Spirit? Aye, jeering and jeering!"

"Well, well, Thomas," rejoined Macwha, soothed in perceiving that he had not altogether gotten the worst in the tilt of words, "I would only take the liberty of thinkin' that when He was about it, the Almighty might as well make a new body altogether as go patchin' up the old one. So I'll just be makin' my way home now."

"Mind yer immortal part, George," said Thomas with a final thrust, as he likewise rose to go home with him on the box of the hearse.

"If the Lord takes such good care of the body, Thomas," retorted Macwha with less irreverence than appeared in his words, "maybe He wouldn't object to give a look t' my poor soul as well. For they say it's worth more. I wish He would, for He knows better than me how t' set about the job."

So saying, he strode briskly over the graves and out of the churchyard to the hearse, leaving Thomas to follow as fast as suited his unwieldy strength.

Meantime, another conversation was going on in one of the gigs, as it bore two of the company from the place of the tombs. One of the two, Robert Bruce, was a cousin of the deceased. The other was called Andrew Constable and was a worthy elder of the church.

"Well, Robert," began the latter, after they had gone on in silence for half a mile or so, "what's to be done with little Annie Anderson and her Auntie Meg, now that the poor man's gone home and left them here?"

"They can't have much left after the doctor and all's settled for."

"I'm sure you're right there. It's long since he was able to do a day's work."

"James Dow looked well after the farm, though."

"No doubt. He's a good servant. But there can't be much money left."

A pause followed.

"What do you think, Andrew?" recommended Bruce. "You're well known as an honest and levelheaded man. Do you think that folk would expect anything of me if the worst came to the worst?"

"Well, Robert, I don't think there's much good in looking to what folk might or might not expect of you."

"That's just what I was thinking myself. For you see, I have my own small family and a hard enough time already."

"No doubt, no doubt. But—"

"Ay, ay, I know what you would say. I mustn't altogether disregard what folk might think because of my shop. If I once got—not to say a bad name—but just the wind of not being so considerate as I ought to have been, there's no saying but that folk might start walking on past my door and cross over to Jamie Mitchell's yonder."

"Do what's right, Robert Bruce."

"But a body must take care of his own, else who's to do it?"

"Well," rejoined Andrew with a smile, for he understood Bruce well enough, although he pretended to have mistaken his meaning, "then if the bairnie falls to you, no doubt you must take charge of her."

"I didn't mean James Anderson's bairns—I mean my own."

"Robert, whatever way you decide, I hope it may be such a decision that will allow you to cast your care upon *Him*."

"I know all about that, Andrew. But my opinion on that text is just this— that every vessel has to hold what fills it by itself, and what runs over may be committed to Him, for you can hold it no longer. Them that won't take care of what they have will be destroyed. It's a lazy, thoughtless way to be going to the Almighty with every little thing. You know the story about my namesake and the spider?"

"Ay, well enough," answered Andrew.

But he did not proceed to remark that he could see no connection between that story and the subject in hand. Bruce's question did not take him by surprise. Bruce was in the habit of making all possible references to his great namesake of ancient Scotland. Indeed, he wished everybody to think, though he seldom ventured to assert it plainly, that he was lineally descended from the king. Nor did Andrew make further remark of any sort with regard to the fate of Annie or the duty of Bruce. He saw that his companion wanted no advice—only some talk and possibly some sympathy as to what the world might think of him.

But with this perplexity Andrew could accord Bruce very little sympathy indeed. He did not care to buttress a reputation quite undermined by widely reported acts of petty meanness and selfishness. Andrew knew well that it would be a bad day for poor Annie if she came under Bruce's roof, and he therefore silently hoped that Auntie Meg might find some way of managing without having to part with the child. For he knew too that, though her aunt was fierce and hard, she had yet a warm spot somewhere about her heart.

Margaret Anderson had known perfectly well for some time that she and Annie must part before long. The lease of the farm would expire at the close of the autumn of next year. And as it had been rather a losing affair for some time, she had no desire to request a renewal. When her brother's debts were paid, there would not remain, even after the sale of the livestock, more than a hundred and fifty pounds. For herself, she planned to take a job as a maid—which would hurt her pride more than it would alter her position in the world, for her hands were used to doing more of the labor than those of the maid who had assisted her on the farm. But what was to become of Annie she could not yet see.

Meantime there remained for the child just a year more of the native farm, with all the varieties of life which had been so dear to her. Auntie Meg made sure she prepared her for the coming change. But it seemed to Annie so long in coming that it never would arrive. While the year lasted she gave herself up to the childish pleasures of the place without thinking of their approaching separation.

And why should Annie think of the future when the present was full of such delights? If she did not receive much tenderness from Auntie, at least she was not afraid of her. The pungency of her temper acted as salt and vinegar to bring out the true flavor of the other numberless pleasures around her. Were her excursions far afield, perched aloft on Dowie's shoulder, any less delightful because Auntie was scolding at home? And if she was late for one of her meals and Auntie declared she should have to fast, there still remained rosy-faced Emma who connived to surreptitiously bring the child the best of everything that was at hand, and put cream in her milk and butter on her oatcake. And Brownie was always friendly; ever ready for a serious emergency, when Auntie's temper was less than placid, to yield a corner of her stall as a refuge for the child. And the cocks and hens, and even the peacock and turkey, knew her perfectly and would come when she called them—if not altogether out of affection for her, at least out of hope in her bounty. And she would ride the horses to water, sitting sideways on their broad backs like a barefooted lady.

And then there were the great delights of the harvest field. With the reapers she would remain from morning till night, sharing in their meals and lightening their labor with her gentle frolic. Every day after the noon meal she would go to sleep on the shady side of a stook of straw, on two or three sheeves which Dowie would lay down for her in a choice spot.

Indeed, the little mistress was very fond of sleep and would go to sleep anywhere; this habit being indeed one of her aunt's chief grounds of complaint. Before haytime, for instance, when the grass in the fields was long, if she came upon any place that took her fancy she would tumble down at once and fall asleep on it. On such occasions it was no easy task to find her in the midst of the long grass that closed over her. But in the harvest field, at least, no harm could come of this habit, for *Dooie,* as she always called him, watched over her like a mother.

The only discomfort of the harvest field was that the sharp stubble forced her to wear shoes. But when the grain had all been carried home and the potatoes had been dug up and heaped in warm pits for the winter, and the mornings and evenings grew cold, then she had to put on both shoes and socks, which she did not like at all.

So through a whole winter of ice and snow, through a whole spring of promises slowly fulfilled, through a summer of glory, and another autumn of harvest joy, the day drew nearer when they must leave the farm. And still to Annie it seemed as far off as ever.

3

•••••••••••••••••••

Robert Bruce

One lovely evening in October, when the shadows were falling from the western sun and a keen little wind was just getting ready to come out the moment the sun would be out of sight, Annie saw a long shadow coming in at the narrow entrance of the yard. She continued to fasten up the cows for the night, drawing iron chains around their soft necks. But at length she found that the cause of the great shadow was only a little man, none other than her father's cousin, Robert Bruce. Alas! how little a man may cast a great shadow!

He came up to Annie and addressed her in the smoothest voice he could find, fumbling at the same time in his coat pocket.

"How are you tonight, Annie? Are you well? And how's your auntie?"

He waited for no reply to any of these questions, but went on, "See what I have brought you from the shop."

So saying, he put into her hand about a half dozen sweet candies, wrapped up in a bit of paper. With this gift he left her and walked on to the open door of the house, which as a cousin he considered himself privileged to enter, unannounced even by a knock. He found the mistress in the kitchen, looking over the cooking of supper.

"How are you tonight, Margaret?" he said in a tone of conciliatory smoothness. "You're busy as usual, I see. Well, the hand of the diligent maketh rich, you know."

"That portion o' the Word must be o' limited application," returned Margaret. Withdrawing her hand from her cousin's, she turned again to the pot hanging over the fire. "No man would dare to say that my hand hasn't been the hand of the diligent. But God knows I'm none the richer for it."

"We mustn't complain, Margaret. Right or wrong, it's the Lord's will."

"It's easy for you, Robert Bruce, with yer money in the bank, to speak that way to a poor, lonely body like me that has to work for her bread when I'm not so young as I might be. Not that I'm about to die o' old age either."

"I haven't so much in the bank as some folk may think; though what there is is safe enough. But I have a good business down yonder, and it might be better yet if I had more money to put into it."

"Take it oot o' the bank then, Robert."

" 'The bank,' did you say? I can't do that."

"And why not?"

" 'Cause I'm like the hens, Margaret. If they don't see one egg in the nest, they have no heart to lay another. I dare not meddle with the bank."

"Well, let it sit then, and lay away at yer leisure. How's the mistress?"

"Not that well, and not that bad. The family's rather hard upon her. But even with all that I can't keep her out of the shop. She's like me—she would always be turning a coin. But what are you going to do yourself, Margaret?"

"I'm going to my uncle and aunt—ol' John Peterson and his wife. They're old and frail now and they want someone to look after them."

"Then you're well provided for. Praise be thanked, Margaret."

"Ow ay, no doubt," replied Margaret with bitterness, of which Bruce took no notice.

"And what's to come of the bairnie?" he pursued.

"I'll just have to get some decent person in the town to take her in and let her go to the school. It's time. The ol' folk wouldn't be able to put up with her for a week."

"And what'll that cost you, Margaret?"

"I don't know. But the lassie's able to pay for her own upbringing."

"It's not far that a hundred and fifty pounds will go in these times, and it would be a pity to take from the principal. She'll be marrying some day."

"Oh, indeed, maybe. Bairns will be fools."

"Well, couldn't you lend it out at five percent, and then there would be something coming from it? That would be seven pounds ten in the year, and the bairnie might almost—not easily I grant—be brought up on that."

Margaret lifted her head and gaped at him.

"And who would give five percent for her money when he can get four and a half from the bank, on good security?"

"Just myself, Margaret. The poor orphan has nobody but you and me to look to. And I would willingly do that much for her. I'll tell you what—I'll give her five percent for her money; and for the little interest I'll take her in with my own bairns and she can live and eat and go to school with them, and then—after a while—we'll see what comes next."

To Margaret this seemed a very fair offer. It was known to all that the Bruce children were well enough dressed and looked well fed. And although Robert had the character of being somewhat mean, she did not regard that as the worst possible fault, or one likely to injure the child. So she told her cousin she would think about it, which was quite as much as he could have expected. He left all but satisfied that he had carried his point and was optimistic about his prospects.

Was it not a point worth carrying—to get both the money and the owner of it into his hands? Not that he meant conscious dishonesty to Annie. He only rejoiced to think that he would thus satisfy any expectations the public might have on him and would enjoy besides a splendid increase of capital for his business. And he was more than certain that he could keep the girl on less than the interest would come to. And then, if anything should happen to her—she had always been rather delicate—the result was worth waiting for. If she did well, he had three sons growing up, one of whom might take a fancy to the young heiress and would have the means to marry her. Grocer Robert was as deep in his foresight and scheming as King Robert of time past.

But James Dow was not pleased when he heard of the arrangement—which was completed in due time. "I can't abide that Bruce," he said. "He wouldn't fling a bone to a dog before he'd taken a poke at himself." He agreed, however, with his mistress that it would be better to keep Annie unaware of her destiny as long as possible. This consideration sprang from the fact that her aunt, now that she was on the eve of parting with Annie, felt a delicate growth of tenderness sprouting over the old stone wall of her affection for the child. It arose partially because she doubted whether Annie would be entirely comfortable in her hew home.

4
•••••••••••••••••

Little Gray Town

A day that is fifty years off comes as certainly as if it had been next week; and Annie's feelings of infinite duration did not stop the sandglass of Old Time. The day arrived when everything was to be sold by public auction. A great company of friends, neighbors and acquaintances gathered and much drinking of whisky-punch went on in the kitchen, as well as in the room where, a year earlier, the solemn funeral assembly had met.

Little Annie now understood what all the bustle meant. The day of desolation so long foretold by her aunt had actually arrived; all the things she knew so well were vanishing from her sight forever.

She was in the barn when the sound of the auctioneer's voice in the grainyard made her look over the half door and listen. The truth dawned on her, and she burst into tears over an old rake that had just been sold, which she had been accustomed to call hers because she had always dragged it during the harvest time. Then, wiping her eyes hastily, she fled to Brownie's stall; she buried herself in the manger and began crying again. After a while the fountain of tears was for the time exhausted. She sat disconsolately gazing at the old cow feeding away as if food were everything and an auction nothing at all. Soon footsteps approached the stable and, to her further dismay, two men she did not know untied Brownie and actually led her away before her eyes. She continued to stare at the empty space where Brownie had stood. But how could she sit there without Brownie! She jumped up and, sobbing so that she could hardly breathe, she rushed across the yard into the crowded and desecrated house, and up the stairs to her own little room. There she threw herself on the bed, buried her eyes in the pillow, and, overcome with grief, fell fast asleep.

When she awoke in the morning she remembered nothing of Emma's undressing her and putting her to bed. The day that was gone seemed only a dreadful dream. But when she went outside she found that yesterday would not stay among her dreams. Brownie's stall was *empty*. The horses were all gone and most of the cattle. Those that remained looked like creatures forgotten. The pigs were gone, too, and most of the poultry. Two or three favorite hens were left, which Auntie was going to take with her. But of all the living creatures Annie had loved, not one had been kept for her. Her life seemed bitter with the bitterness of death.

In the afternoon her aunt came up to her room where she sat in tearful silence. Auntie told her that she was going to take her into the town and then proceeded, without further explanation, to put all her little personal effects into an old trunk which Annie called her own. Along with some trifles that lay about the room, she threw into the bottom of the box about a dozen old books which had been on the chest of drawers since long before Annie could remember. The poor child let her do as she pleased and asked no questions, for the shadow in which she stood was darkening and she did not care what came next.

For an hour the box stood on the floor like a coffin. Then Emma came, with red eyes and red nose, and carried it downstairs. Auntie came up again, dressed in her Sunday clothes. She dressed Annie in her best frock and bonnet—adorning the victim for sacrifice—and led her down to the door. There stood a horse and cart in which was some straw and a sack stuffed with hay. As Annie was getting into the cart, Emma rushed out from somewhere, grabbed her up, kissed her in a disorderly manner, and before her mistress could turn round in the cart, gave her into James Dow's arms and vanished with strange sounds of choking.

Dowie thought to put her in with a kiss, for he dared not speak, but Annie's arms went round his neck and she clung to him sobbing—clung till she roused the indignation of Auntie, at the first sound of whose voice Dowie was free and Annie was lying in the cart with her face buried in the straw. Dowie then mounted in front. The horse—one Annie did not know—started off gently, and Annie was borne away, helpless, to meet the unknown.

She had often been along this road before, but it had never looked as it did now. The first half mile went through fields whose crops were gone. The stubble was sticking through the grass and the potato stalks, which ought to have been gathered and burned, lay scattered about the brown earth. Then came two miles of moorland country, high and bleak and barren with hillocks of peat. In all directions one could see black mounds standing beside the black holes where the peat had been dug out. Next came some scattered, ragged fields, the outskirts of cultivation which seemed to draw closer and closer together while the soil grew richer and more hopeful, till after two miles more they entered the first straggling precincts of the gray market town.

By this time the stars were shining clear in the cold, frosty sky, and candles or train-oil lamps were burning in most of the houses—for this was long before gas had been heard of in those parts. A few faces were pressed close to the windowpanes as the cart passed and some rather untidy women came to their doors to look.

By and by the cart stopped at Robert Bruce's shop door. Dowie got down and went into the shop. The house was a low one, although of two stories, built of gray stone with thatched roof. Inside the windowed door burned a single tallow candle, revealing to the gaze of Annie what she could not but regard as a perfect mine of treasures. For besides calico and sugar and all the varied stock in the combined trades of draper and grocer, Robert Bruce sold penny toys and halfpenny picture books and every kind of candy which had as yet been revealed to the young generations of Glamerton.

But Annie did not have long to contemplate these wonders from the outside, for Bruce came to the door and, having greeted his cousin and helped her down, turned to take Annie. Dowie was there before him, however, and now held the pale child silent in his arms. He carried her into the shop and set her down on a sack before the counter. From her perch Annie drearily surveyed the circumstances.

Auntie was standing in the middle of the shop. Bruce was holding the counter open and inviting her to enter.

"You'll come in and take a cup o' tea after your journey, Margaret?" he said.

"No, I thank ye, Robert Bruce. James and I must just turn right away and go back home again. There's a lot to look after yet, and we mustn't neglect our work. The house gear's all to be picked up in the morning."

Turning to Annie, she continued: "Now Annie, lass, ye'll be a good bairn and do as ye're told. An' mind ye don't disturb things in the shop."

A smile of peculiar significance glimmered over Bruce's face at the sound of this injection. Annie made no reply but stared at Mr. Bruce.

"Good-bye to ye, Annie!" said her aunt, rousing the girl a little from her stupor.

She then gave her a kiss—the first, as far as the child knew, that Auntie had ever given her—and went out. Bruce followed Auntie out and Dowie came in. He took her up in his arms and whispered, "Good-bye to ye, my bonnie bairn. Be a good lass and ye'll be taken care of. Don't forget that. Mind ye say yer prayers."

Annie kissed him with all her heart but could not reply. He set her down again and went out. She heard the harness rattle and the cart roll off. She was left sitting on the sack.

Presently Mr. Bruce came in and, passing behind his counter, proceeded to make an entry in a book. It was a memorandum of the day and hour when Annie was put down on that very sack—so methodical was he. And yet it was some time before he seemed to awake to remembrance of the presence of the child. Looking up suddenly at the pale, weary thing as she sat with her legs hanging lifelessly down the side of the sack, he asked—pretending to have forgotten her—"O child, are you still there?"

Going round to her he set her feet down on the floor and led her by the hand through the mysterious gate of the counter and through a door behind it. Then he called in a sharp, decided tone, "Mother, you're wanted."

Immediately a tall, thin, anxious-looking woman appeared, wiping her hands in her apron.

"This is little Miss Anderson," said Bruce. "She has come to stay with us. Give her a biscuit and take her up the stairs to her bed."

As it was the first, so it was the last time he called her Miss Anderson, at least while she was one of the household. Mrs. Bruce took Annie by the hand in silence and led her up two narrow stairs into a small room with a skylight. There by the shine of the far-off stars, she helped her unpack. But she forgot the biscuit and, for the first time in her life, Annie went supperless to bed.

In order to get rid of the vague fear she felt at being in a strange place without light, she lay for a while trying to imagine herself in Brownie's stall among the grass and clover, for she did not like not knowing what was next to her in the dark. But the fate of Brownie and everything else she had loved came back upon her. The sorrow drove away the fear, and she cried till she could cry no longer, and then she slept. It is by means of sorrow sometimes that He gives His beloved His restful sleep.

5

● ● ● ● ● ● ● ● ● ● ● ● ● ● ● ● ●

The Robert Bruces

The following morning Annie woke early and dressed herself. But there was no water to wash with and she crept down the stairs to look for some. Nobody, however, was awake. She looked wistfully at the back door of the house, for she longed to get outside into the fresh air. But seeing she could not open it she went back up to her room. She sat on the side of her bed and gazed round the cheerless room. At home she had had checkered curtains; here there were none of any kind, and her eyes rested on nothing but bare rafters and boards. And there were holes in the roof and floor, which she did not like. They were not large holes, but they were dreadful. For they were black and she did not know where they might go. She grew very cold.

At length she heard some noise in the house. It grew and was presently enriched by a mixture of baby screams and the sound of the shop shutters being taken down. At last footsteps approached her door. Mrs. Bruce entered, and finding her sitting dressed on her bed, exclaimed: "Ow! You're already dressed, are you?"

"Ay, well enough," answered Annie as cheerily as she could. "But," she added, "I would like some water to wash myself with."

"Come down to the pump then," said Mrs. Bruce.

Annie followed her to the pump where she washed in a tub. She then ran dripping into the house for a towel, but was dried by the hands of Mrs. Bruce in her dirty apron. By this time breakfast was nearly ready, and in a few minutes more Mrs. Bruce called Mr. Bruce from the shop and the children from the yard, and they all sat round the table in the kitchen—Mr. Bruce to his tea and oatcake and butter and Mrs. Bruce and the children to badly made oatmeal porridge and sky-blue milk. This poor quality milk was remarkable seeing that they had cows of their own. But then they sold milk. And if any customer had accused her of watering it, Mrs. Bruce's best answer would have been to show how much better what she sold was than what she retained. She put twice as much water in what she used for her own family—with the exception of the portion destined for her husband's tea.

There were three children, two boys with great jaws—the elder a little older than Annie—and a very little baby. After Mr. Bruce had prayed for the blessing of the Holy Spirit upon their food, they gobbled down their breakfasts with a variety of inarticulate noises. When they finished, the Bible was brought out; a psalm was sung, in a fashion quite unextraordinary to the ears of Annie; a chapter was read—it happened to tell the story of Jacob's speculations in the money market of his day and generation. The exercise concluded with a prayer of a quarter of an hour, in which the God of Jacob was especially invoked to bless the Bruces, His servants, in their store, and to prosper the labors of that day in particular. The prayer would have been much longer but for the click of the latch of the shop door which brought it to a speedy close. And almost before the *amen* was out of his mouth, Robert Bruce was out of the kitchen.

When he had served the early customer, he returned and, sitting down, drew Annie toward him and addressed her with great solemnity.

"Now, Annie," he said, "you'll get today to play by yourself. But you must go to school tomorrow. We can have no idle folk in this house, so we must have no words about it."

Annie was not one to argue about that or anything. She was only too glad to get away from him. Indeed, the prospect of school, after what she had seen of the economy of her home, was rather enticing. So she answered, "Very well, sir."

Seeing her so agreeable, Mr. Bruce added, in the tone of one conferring a great favor and knowing so, "You can come into the shop for the day and see what's going on. When you're more of a woman you may be fit to stand behind the counter yourself—who knows?"

Robert Bruce regarded his shop as his battleground where all his enemies, namely customers, were to be defeated that he might be enriched with their spoils. It was, therefore, a place of such consuming interest in his eyes that he thought it must be interesting to everybody else. Annie followed him into the shop and saw quite a wonderful wealth of good things around her. Lest she should put forth her hand and take, however, the militant eyes of Robert Bruce never ceased watching her with quick recurring glances, even when he was cajoling some customer into a doubtful purchase.

Long before the noon mealtime arrived, Annie was heartily sick of the monotony of buying and selling in which she had no share. Not even a picture book was taken down from the window for her to look at. Mr. Bruce looked upon them as far below the notice of his children, although he derived a keen enjoyment from the transfer—by their allurements—of the halfpence of other children from their pockets into his till.

"Nasty trash of lies," he remarked, apparently for Annie's behalf, as he hung the fresh bait up in his window, "only fit for dirty laddies and lassies."

He stood ever watchful in his shop like a great spider that ate children, and his windows were his web.

They dined at noon on salt herrings and potatoes—much better fare than bad porridge and watered milk. Robert Bruce the younger, who inherited his father's name and disposition, made faces at Annie across the table as often as he judged it prudent to run the risk of discovery. But Annie was too stupefied with the change in menu to mind it much. Indeed, it required all the attention she could command to stop the herring bones on the way to her throat.

After dinner, business was resumed in the shop, with the resemblance of an increase in vigor, for Mrs. Bruce went behind the counter and gave her husband time to sit down at the desk to write letters and make out bills. Not that there was much of either sort of clerkship necessary, but Bruce was so fond of business that he liked to seem busier than he was. As it happened to be a half holiday, Annie was sent with the rest of the children into the yard to play.

"And mind," said Bruce, "that you keep away from the dog."

Outside, Annie soon found herself at the mercy of those who had none. It is marvelous what an amount of latent torment there is in boys, ready to come out the minute an object presents itself. It is not exactly cruelty. They are unaware, for the most part, of the suffering brought on by their actions. So children, even ordinarily good children, are ready to tease any child who simply looks teasable. Now the Bruces, as one would naturally expect, were not good children. And they despised Annie because she was a girl and because she had no self-assertion. If she had shown herself aggressively disagreeable, they would have made some attempt to be friendly with her; but as it was, she became at once the object of whatever they could devise to torment her with. At one time they satisfied themselves with making faces at her; at another, they rose to rubbing her face with dirt. Their persecution bewildered her and the resulting stupor was a kind of support to her for a while. But at last she could endure it no longer, being really hurt by a fall one of the boys had engineered, and ran crying into the shop, where she sobbed out, "Please, sir, they won't let me be."

"Don't come into the shop with your stories. Make it up among yourselves."

"But they won't make it up."

Robert Bruce rose indignant at such an interruption of his high calling and strode outside with the air of much parental grandeur. He was instantly greeted with a torrent of assurances that Annie had fallen and then laid the blame on them. He turned sternly to her and said, "Annie, if you tell lies, you'll go to hell."

But paternal partiality did not prevent him from addressing them with a lesson also, though of quite a different tone.

"Mind, boys," he advised in a condescending tone, "that poor Annie has neither a father nor a mother, and you must be kind to her."

He then turned and left them for the more important concerns within doors. The persecution began anew, though in a somewhat subdued form. The little wretches were willing to temporarily abstain from such intense pleasure until a more suitable occasion.

Somehow the day passed, although I must not close my account of this first day without mentioning something which threatened yet more suffering.

After worship the boys crawled away to bed, half-asleep, or, I should say, only half-awake from their prayers. Annie lingered behind.

"Can't you take off your own clothes as well as put them on, Annie?" asked Mrs. Bruce.

"Ay, well enough. Only I would so like a little candle," was Annie's trembling reply, for by now she had a foreboding instinct.

"Candle! No, no child," proclaimed Mrs. Bruce. "You'll get no candle here. You would have the house in a flame around our ears. I can't afford candles. You can just feel your way up the stairs. There's thirteen steps to the first landing, and twelve to the next."

With choking heart, but without reply, Annie left.

Groping her way up the steep ascent, she found her room without difficulty. As it was again a clear, starlit night, she was able to find everything she wanted. She soon got into bed and, as a precautionary measure, buried her head under the covers before she began to say her prayers. But her prayers were suddenly interrupted by a terrible noise of scrambling and scratching and scampering in the very room beside her.

The child's fear of rats amounted to a frenzied horror. She dared not move a finger. To get out of bed with those creatures running about the room was as impossible as it was for her to cry out. But Annie's heart did what her frozen tongue could not do—it cried out with a great and bitter cry to one who was more ready to hear than Robert or Nancy Bruce. And what her heart cried was this: "O God, take care of me from the rats."

There was no need to send an angel from heaven in answer to this little one's prayer: the cat would do. Annie heard a scratch and a mew at the door. The rats made one frantic scramble and were still.

"It's pussy!" she cried, recovering in joy the voice that had failed her for fear.

Fortified by the cat's arrival and still more by the feeling that it was a divine messenger sent in direct answer to her prayer, Annie sprang out of bed, darted across the room, and opened the door to let it in. A few minutes more and Annie was fast asleep, guarded by God's angel, the cat. Ever after she took care to leave the door ajar to allow pussy's entrance.

Though it is always ready to shut, there are also ways of keeping the door of the mind open.

6

••••••••••••••••••

School

"Now, Annie, put on your bonnet and go to the school with the rest; and be a good girl."

This was Robert Bruce's parting address to Annie before he left the kitchen for the shop, after breakfast and prayers had been duly observed. It was quarter to ten and the school was some five minutes distant.

With a flutter of fearful hope Annie obeyed. She ran upstairs, made herself as tidy as she could, smoothed her hair, put on her bonnet, and was waiting at the door when her companions joined her. She was very excited and looked forward to something that might not be disagreeable.

As they sauntered off, the boys got one on each side of her in a rather sociable manner. They had gone half the distance and not a word had been spoken when Robert Bruce junior opened the conversation abruptly.

"You'll get it!" he declared as if he had been brooding upon the fact for some time and now it had broken out.

"What'll I get?" asked Annie timidly, for his tone had already filled her with apprehension.

"Such lickin's," he answered with apparent relish at the thought. "Won't she, Johnny?"

"Ay, will she," answered Johnny, following his leader with confidence.

Annie's heart sank within her; the poor little heart was used to sinking now. But she said nothing, resolved—if possible—to avoid all occasions for "getting it."

Not another word was spoken before they reached the school, the door of which was not yet open. A good many boys and girls were assembled, waiting for the master, filling the street with the musical sound of children's voices. None of them took any notice of Annie, so she was left to study the outside of the school. It was a long, low, thatched building, of one story and a garret, with five windows toward the street and some behind. From the thatch some of the night's frost was dripping in slow, clear drops.

Suddenly a small boy cried out: "The master's coming!" and instantly the noise sank to a low murmur.

Looking up the street, Annie saw the figure of the descending dominie. He was dressed in what seemed to be black but was in reality dark gray. He came down the hill of the street swinging his arms and marching at a rapid pace. With the door key in his hand already pointing toward the key hole, he swept through the little crowd, which cleared a wide path for him, without word or gesture of greeting on either side. In he strode, followed at the heels by the troop of boys, big and little, and lastly by the girls—and the very last of all, a short distance back, by Annie, like a motherless lamb that followed the flock because she did not know what else to do. She found she had to go down a step into a sunken passage and then up another step, through a door on the left and into the school. There she saw a double row of desks, with a clear space down the middle between the rows. Each scholar was hurrying to his place at one of the desks, where each then stood.

Murdoch Malison had already taken his position as master in solemn posture at the front of the class, prepared to commence the extempore prayer, which was printed in a kind of blotted stereotype upon every one of their brains. Annie had barely succeeded in reaching a vacant place among the girls when he began. The boys were silent as death while the master prayed; but a spectator might easily have discovered that the chief good some of them got from the ceremony was a perfect command of the organs of sound. For their restraint was limited to those organs. But projected tongues, deprived of their natural exercise, turned themselves into the means of telegraphic dispatches to all parts of the room throughout the ceremony, along with winking eyes, contorted features, and a wild use of hands. The master, afraid of being himself detected in the attempt to combine prayer and vision, kept his eyelids tight and played the spy with his ears alone. The boys and girls, understanding the source of their security perfectly, believed that the eyelids of the master would keep faith with them, and so sported themselves without fear in the delights of their dumb show.

As soon as the prayer was over, they dropped with noise and bustle into their seats. But presently Annie was rudely pushed out of her seat by a girl who, arriving late, had stood outside the door till the prayer was over and then entered unnoticed during the subsequent confusion. Some little ones on the opposite side, however, liking the look of her, made room beside them. The desks were double, so that the two rows at each desk faced each other.

"Bible class, come up," were the first words of the master ringing through the room and resounding in Annie's ears.

A moment of chaos followed during which all the boys and girls considered capable of reading the Bible arranged themselves in one great crescent across the room in front of the master's desk. Each read a verse—neither more nor less—often leaving half of a sentence to be taken up by another; thus perverting what was intended as a help to *find* the truth into a means of hiding it.

Not knowing what to do, Annie had not dared to stand up with the class, although she could read fairly well. A few moments after the readers were dismissed, she felt herself overshadowed by an awful presence, and looking up she saw the face of the master bending down over her. He proceeded to question her, but for some time she was too frightened to give a rational account of her learning. The best of her education was certainly not of a kind to be appreciated by the master even if she had understood it enough to set before him. Thus she was put into the spelling book, which excluded her from the Bible class. She was also condemned to copy with an uncut quill, over and over again, a single straight stroke. Dreadfully dreary she found it, and over it she fell fast asleep. Her head dropped on her outstretched arm and the quill dropped from her sleeping fingers. But she was soon roused by the voice of the master. "Ann Anderson!" it called in a burst of thunder; and she awoke to shame and confusion, amidst the titters of those around her.

Before the morning was over she was called up, along with some children considerably younger than herself, to read and spell. The master stood before them, armed with a long, thick strap of horsehide. The whip had been prepared by steeping in brine, cut into fingers at one end and then hardened in the fire.

Now there was a little pale-faced, delicate-looking boy in the class who blundered a good deal. Every time he did so the cruel serpent of leather went at him, coiling round his legs with a sudden, hissing *swash*. This made him cry and his tears blinded him so that he could not even see the words which he had been unable to read before. He still attempted to go on, and still the instrument of torture went at his thin little legs, raising upon them plentiful blue welts.

At length either the heart of the master was touched by the sight of his sufferings and repressed weeping, or he saw that he was demanding the impossible; for he staid execution and passed on to the next, who was Annie.

It was no wonder after such an introduction to the ways of school that the trembling child, who could read tolerably well, should fail utterly in making anything like coherence of the sentence before her. Had she been left to herself, she would have taken the little boy in her arms and cried with him. As it was, she struggled mightily with her tears but did not read to much better purpose than the poor boy who was still busy wiping his eyes with his sleeve. But being a newcomer as well as a girl, and her long dress ill-suited to this kind of incentive to learning, she escaped for the time.

That first day at school was a dreadful experience of life. Well might the children have prayed with David: "Let us fall into the hands of the Lord, for his mercies are great, and not into the hands of men."

At one o'clock they were dismissed and went home to dinner, to return at three.

In the afternoon Annie was made to write figures on a slate. She wrote till her back ached. The monotony was relieved only by the execution of criminal law upon various offending boys; for the master was a hard man with a severe, if not an altogether cruel, temper and a savage sense of duty. The punishment was mostly in the form of blows, delivered generally with the full swing of the *tawse*, as it was called, thrown over the master's shoulder and brought down with the whole strength of his powerful right arm on the outstretched hand of the culprit.

Annie shivered and quaked. Once she burst out crying but managed to choke her sobs, even if she could not hide her tears.

A fine-looking boy, three or four years older than herself, was called up to receive chastisement, merited or unmerited, as the case might be. The master was fond of justice, and justice according to him consisted of vengeance. He did not want to punish the innocent, it is true; but I doubt whether the discovery of a boy's innocence was not occasionally a disappointment to him.

Without a word of defense the boy held out his hand with his arm at full length, received four stinging blows upon it, grew very red in the face, and returned to his seat with the suffering hand sent into retirement in his pocket. Annie's admiration of his courage caused her to make up her mind to bear more patiently her persecutions. And if ever her turn should come to be punished—as no doubt it would—she resolved to take the whipping as she had seen Alec Forbes take it.

At five the school was dismissed for the day, but not without another prayer. A succession of jubilant shouts arose as the boys rushed out into the street. Every day to them was a cycle of strife, suffering, and deliverance. Birth and death, with the life struggle between, were shadowed out in it. The difference was this: the stone-hearted God of popular theology in the person of Murdoch Malison ruled that world, and not the God revealed in the man Christ Jesus. Most of them, having felt the day more or less a burden, were now going home to heaven for the night.

Annie, having no home, was among the few exceptions. Dispirited and hopeless—a terrible condition for a child—she wondered how Alec Forbes could be so merry. She had but one comfort left: hopefully, no one would prevent her from creeping up to her own desolate garret, which was now the dreary substitute for Brownie's stall. There the persecuting boys were not likely to follow her. And if the rats were in the garret, so was the cat—or at least the cat knew the way to it. There she might think in peace about some things she had never had to think about before.

7
....

A New Friend

*Th*us Annie's days passed. She became interested in what she had to learn, if not from the manner in which it was presented to her. Happily or unhappily she began to get used to the sight of the penal suffering of her schoolfellows. Nothing of the kind had yet come upon her, for it would have been hard even for one more savage than Mr. Malison to punish the nervous, delicate, anxious little orphan who was so diligent and as quiet as a mouse. She had a scared look, too, that may have moved the heart of Malison. The loss of human companionship, the loss of green fields and of country sounds and smells, and a constant sense of oppression were quickly working sad effects on her. The little color she had slowly died out of her cheek. Her face grew even more thin and her blue eyes looked wistful and large. Not often were tears to be seen in them now, and yet they looked well acquainted with tears—like fountains that had been full yesterday. She never smiled, for there was nothing to make her smile.

But she gained one thing by this desolation: the thought of her dead father came to her, as it had never come before, and she began to love him with an intensity she had known nothing of till now. Her mother had died at her birth and she had been her father's treasure. But in the last period of his illness she had seen progressively less of him, and the blank left by his death had, therefore, come upon her gradually. Before she knew what death was, she had begun to forget. In the minds of children the grass grows very quickly over their buried dead. But now she learned what death meant, or rather what love had been. It was not, however, an added grief; it comforted her to remember how her father had loved her. And she said her prayers oftener because they seemed to go somewhere near the place where her father was. She did not think of her father being where God was, but of God being where her father was.

The winter was drawing nearer and the days were now short and cold. A watery time began, and for many days in a row the rain kept falling without interruption. I almost think Annie would have died without her dead father to think about. On one of those rainy days, however, she began to find that it is in the nature of good things to reveal themselves in odd ways. It had rained the whole day, not tamely in a drizzle but in real earnest—dancing and rebounding from the pools. Now and then the school became silent, just to listen to the great noise made by the thunderous torrent of the heavens. But the boys thought only of the fun of dabbling in the puddles as they went home or the delights of fishing in the swollen and muddy rivers.

The afternoon was waning. It was nearly time to go, and still the rain was *pouring*. In the gathering gloom there had been more than the usual amount of wandering from one part of the school to another, and the elder of the Bruce boys had stolen toward a group of little boys, next to which Annie sat with her back toward them. If it was not the real object of his expedition, at least he took the opportunity to give Annie a spiteful dig with his elbow which forced from her an involuntary cry.

Now the master occasionally indulged in throwing his tawse at the offender, not so much for the sake of hurting—though that happened as well—as of humiliating; for the culprit had to bear the instrument of torture back to the hands of the executioner. He threw the tawse at Annie, half, let us suppose, in thoughtless cruelty, half in evil jest. It struck her rather sharply, even before she had recovered her breath after the blow Bruce had given her. In pain and terror she rose, pale as death, and staggered up to the master, carrying the whip with something of the horror she would have felt had it been a snake. With a grim smile he sent her back to her seat. The moment she reached it her self-control gave way and she burst into despairing, silent tears. The desk was still shaking with her sobs, and some of the girls were still laughing at her grief as the master dismissed his pupils.

There could be no better fun for most of the boys and some of the girls than to wade through the dirty water running between the schoolhouse and the street. Many of them dashed through it at once, shoes and all. But as it was too wide to cross in a single bound, some of the boys and almost all the girls took off their shoes and socks and carried them across the steadily rising rivulet. But the writhing and splashing water looked so ugly that Annie shrank from fording it. She was still standing looking at it in perplexity and dismay, with the forgotten tears still creeping down her cheeks, when she was suddenly caught up from behind by a boy who was carrying his shoes and socks in his other hand.

She glanced timidly around to see who it was, and the brave, brown eyes of Alec Forbes met hers, lighted by a kind, pitying smile. In that smile the cloudy sky of the universe gently opened and the face of God looked out upon Annie. It gave her, for that brief moment, all the love and understanding she had been dying for during the last weeks—weeks that seemed as long as years. She could not help herself; she threw her arms round Alec Forbe's neck and sobbed as if her heart would break. She did not care about the Bruces or the rats or even the schoolmaster now.

Alec clasped her tighter and vowed in his heart that if ever that brute Malison lifted his hand toward her again, he would fly at his throat. He would have carried her farther, but as soon as they were onto the street, Annie begged him to set her down and he complied. Then bidding her good night, he turned and ran home barefoot through the flooding town.

The two Bruces had gone on ahead with the only two umbrellas, one of which Annie had shared in coming to school. Needless to say, she was very wet before she got home. But no notice was taken of the condition she was in; though it brought a severe cold and cough, which, however, were not regarded as any ob-stacles to her going to school the next day.

That night she lay awake for a long time, and when at last she fell asleep, she dreamed she took Alec Forbes home to see her father. She told him how kind Alec had been to her and how happy she was going to be now. And her father had put his hand out of the bed and laid it on Alec's head, and said: "Thank ye, Alec, for being kind t' my poor Annie." And then she cried, and woke crying—strange tears out of dreamland, half of sorrow and half of joy.

What changed feelings she had the next day as she seated herself in school. After the prayer, she glanced around to catch a glimpse of her new friend. There he was, radiant as usual. He took no notice of her and she had not expected he would. But now that he had befriended her, it was not long before he found out that her cousins were by no means friendly to her.

In the afternoon, while she was busy over an unusually obstinate addition sum, Robert came up stealthily behind her, licked his finger, watched for his op-portunity, and then rubbed the answer from her slate. The same moment he re-ceived a box on the ear, which no doubt filled his head with more noises than that of the impact. He yelled with rage and pain and, catching sight of the ad-ministrator of justice as he was returning to his seat, bawled out in a tone of fierce contempt: "Sanny Forbes!"

"Alexander Forbes! Come up," resounded the voice of the master. Forbes, not being a first-rate scholar, was not a favorite with him, for Mr. Malison had no sense for what was fine in character or disposition. Had the name reaching his ears been that of one of his better Latin scholars, Bruce's cry would most likely have passed unheeded.

"Hold up your hand," he said without requesting an explanation.

Alec obeyed. Annie gave a smothered shriek and, tumbling from her seat, rushed up to the master. When she found herself face to face with the tyrant, however, she could not speak a single word. She opened her mouth but throat and tongue refused to comply with their offices and she stood gasping. The master stared, his arm arrested in the act to strike, and his face turned toward her over his left shoulder. All the blackness of his anger at Forbes he was now lowering upon Annie.

He stood thus for one awful moment; then, motioning her aside with a sweep of his head, he brought down the tawse on Alec's hand. Annie gave a choking cry, and Alec, so violent was the pain, involuntarily withdrew his hand. But instantly, ashamed of his weakness, he presented it again and received the remainder of his punishment without flinching. The master then turned to Annie. Finding her still speechless he gave her a push and said: "Go to your seat, Ann Anderson. The next time you do that I will punish you severely."

Annie sat down and neither sobbed nor cried. But it was days before she re-covered from the shock.

8

. . . .

A Visit from Auntie

$\mathcal{F}$or some time neither of the young Bruces ventured to make even a wry face at her at school, but their behavior to her at home was only so much the worse.

Two days after the rainstorm, as Annie was leaving the kitchen after worship to go up to bed, Mr. Bruce called her.

"Annie Anderson," he said, "I want to speak to you."

Annie turned, trembling.

"I see you know what it's about," he went on, staring full in her pale face. "You can't even look me in the eye. Where're the sugar candies? I know well enough where they are, and so do you."

"I know nothing about it," answered Annie with a sudden revival of energy.

"Don't lie, Annie. It's enough to steal, without lying."

"I'm not lying," she protested, starting to cry. "Who said I took the candies?"

"That's not the point. You wouldn't cry that way if you were innocent. I never missed anything before. And you know well enough there's an eye that sees all things, and you can't hide from it."

Bruce could hardly have intended her to believe it was by inspiration from on high that he had discovered the thief of his sweets. But he thought it better to avoid mentioning that the informer was his own son. Johnnie, on his part, had thought it better not to mention that he had been incited to the act by his brother Robert. And Robert had thought it better not to mention that he did so partly to shield himself, and partly out of revenge for the box on the ear which Alec Forbes had given him. The information had been yielded to the inquisition of the parent who said with truth that he had never missed anything before. I suspect, however, that the boys had long since begun a course of petty and cautious pilfering. This day it had passed the narrow bounds within which it could be concealed from the keen eyes of the boys' father.

"I don't want to hide from it!" cried Annie. "God knows," she went on in desperation, "I wouldn't touch a grain of salt without permission."

"It's a pity, Annie, that some folk don't get their share of Mr. Malison's discipline. I don't want to lick you myself 'cause you're other folks' bairn. But I can hardly hold my hand off you."

It must not be supposed from this statement that Robert Bruce ever ventured to lay hands on his own children. He was too much afraid of their mother, who, perfectly submissive ordinarily, would have flown into the rage of a hen with chicks if even her own husband had dared to chastise one of *her* children. The shop might be more Robert's than hers, but the children were more hers than Robert's.

Overcome with shame and righteous anger, Annie burst out in the midst of fresh tears.

"I wish Auntie would come and take me away! It's an ill house to be in."

These words had a visible effect upon Bruce. He was expecting a visit from Margaret Anderson within a day or two, and he did not know what the effect of whatever stories Annie might tell her would be. The use of Annie's money had not been secured to him for any lengthened period. Dowie, anxious to take all precautions for his little mistress, consulted a friendly lawyer on the subject to make sure Annie should not be left defenseless in the hands of a man of whose moral qualities Dowie had no exalted opinion. The sale had turned out better than expected and the sum committed to Bruce was two hundred pounds. To lose this now would seem to him nothing short of ruin. Though convinced Annie was the guilty person, he thought it better to count the few pieces of candy he might lose as additional interest and not quarrel with his creditor for extorting it. So with the weak cunning of his kind he went to the shop, brought back a bit of sugar candy about the size of a pigeon's egg, and said to the still-crying child: "Don't cry, Annie. I can't stand to see you crying. If you want a bit of candy any time, just tell me and don't help yourself. That's all. Here."

He thrust the lump into Annie's hand, but she dropped it on the floor and rushed upstairs to her bed as fast as the darkness would let her. In spite of her indignation she was soon sound asleep.

Bruce searched for the rejected candy until he found it. He then restored it to the drawer he had taken it from and resolved to be more careful in the future of offending little Annie Anderson.

When the Saturday arrived upon which he expected Margaret's visit, Bruce was on the watch the whole afternoon. From his shop door he could see all along the street and a good way beyond it. Being very quick sighted, he recognized Margaret when she was yet a great distance away as she sat in an approaching cart.

"Annie!" he called, opening the inner door as he returned behind the counter.

Annie, who was upstairs in her own room, immediately appeared.

"Annie," he said, "run out at the back door and through the yard and over to Logan Lumley's and tell him to come over to see me directly. Don't come back without him. That's a good child!"

He sent her off with this message, knowing well enough that the man had gone to the country that day and there was no one at his house who was likely to know where he had gone. He hoped that Annie would go and look for him about town and so be gone during her aunt's visit.

"Well, Margaret," he said with his customary greeting, in which the foreign oil sought to overcome the home-bred vinegar, "how are you today?"

"Oh, not that bad," answered Margaret with a sigh.

"And how's Mr. and Mistress Peterson?"

"Just brawly. How's Annie coming on?"

"Not that bad. She's still some riotous."

He thought to please her with the remark because she had been in the habit of saying the same thing herself. But distance had made Annie dearer and her aunt's nose took fire with indignation as she replied: "The lassie's well-mannered enough. I saw nothing o' the sort about her. If ye can't guide her, that's *yer* fault!"

Bruce was abashed, but not confounded. He was ready in a moment.

"I never knew any good to come of being too hard on children," he said. "She's as easy to guide as a cow going home at night, only you must just let her know that you're there, you know."

"Ow, ay," said Margaret, a little bewildered in her turn.

"Would you like to see her?"

"What else did I come for?"

"Well, I'll go and look for her."

He went to the back door and called aloud, "Annie, your auntie's here and wants to see you."

"She'll be here in a minute," he said to Margaret as he reentered the shop.

After a little more random conversation, he pretended to be surprised that Annie did not make her appearance, and went once more to the door and called her name several times. He then pretended to search for her in the yard and all over the house and returned with the news that she was nowhere to be seen.

"She's afraid that you're come to take her with you and she's run away somewhere. I'll send the laddies to look for her."

"No, no, never mind. If she doesn't want to see me, I'm sure I don't need to see her. I'll be off to the town," said Margaret, her face growing red as she spoke.

She bustled out of the shop, too angry with Annie to say farewell to Bruce. She had not gone far, however, before Annie came running out of a narrow alley, almost into her aunt's arms. But there was no refuge for her there.

"Ye little limmer!" cried Margaret, seizing her by the shoulder, "what made ye run away? I don't want ye, ye brat!"

"I didn't run away, Auntie."

"Robert Bruce called ye to come in himself."

"It was him that sent me to Logan Lumley's to tell him to come to the shop."

Margaret could not make heads or tails of it. But as Annie had never told her a lie, she could not doubt her. So taking time to think about it, she gave her some rough advice and a smooth penny and went away on her errands. She was not long in coming to the conclusion that Bruce wanted to part her and the child, and this offended her so much that she did not go near the shop for a long time. Thus Annie was forsaken and Bruce had what he wanted.

He needed not have been so full of scheming, though. Annie never said a word to her aunt about their treatment of her. It is one of the marvels in the constitution of children how much they can bear without complaining. Parents have no right to suppose all is well in the nursery or schoolroom merely from the fact that the children do not complain. Servants and tutors may be cruel, and children will be silent—partly, I presume, because they forget so soon.

But vengeance of a sort soon overtook Robert Bruce the younger. For the evil spirit in him—derived from no such remote ancestor as the king—would not allow him a long respite from evildoing, even in school. He knew Annie better than his father did, that she was not likely to complain of anything, and that the only danger lay in the chance of being discovered in the deed.

One day when the schoolmaster had left the room to confer with some visitor at the door, Robert saw Annie stooped over tying her shoe. Perceiving, he thought, that Alec Forbes was looking in the other direction, he gave Annie a strong push from behind. She fell on her face in the middle of the floor. But Alec caught sight of the deed and was down upon him in a moment. Having already proved that a box on the ear was of no lasting effect, Alec gave him a downright good thrashing. Robert howled vigorously, partly from pain, partly in the hope that the same consequences as before would overtake Forbes. He was still howling when Mr. Malison reentered.

"Robert Bruce, come up," he commanded, the moment he opened the door.

And Robert Bruce went up and, notwithstanding his protests, received a second and more painful punishment from the master. For the master there was no fixed principle as to the party on whom the punishment should fall. Punishment, in his eyes, was enough in itself. He was not capable of seeing that *punishment* falling on the wrong person was not punishment at all, but only *suffering*.

If Bruce howled before, he howled ten times worse now and went home howling, too. Annie was sorry for him and tried to say a word of comfort to him, but he repelled her advances with hatred and blows. As soon as he reached the shop, he told his father that Forbes had beaten him without his having said a word to him, which was as correct as it was untrue, and that the master had taken Forbes' part and had licked him soundly, an assertion which showed proof enough on his body. Robert the elder was instantly filled with smoldering wrath, and from that moment he hated Alec Forbes. For like many others of similar nature, he had yet some animal affection for his children, combined with an endless amount of prejudice on their behalf. Indeed, for nothing in the world but money would he have sacrificed what seemed to him their interests.

A man must learn to love his children, not because they are his, but because they are *children,* otherwise his love will scarcely be a better thing in the end than the party spirit of the faithful politician.

9

•••••••••••••••••••

The Shorter Catechism

$\mathscr{I}$n her innermost heart Annie now dedicated herself to the service of Alec Forbes. And it was not long before she had an opportunity to help him.

One Saturday the master made his appearance in black stockings instead of his usual white, a bad omen in the eyes of his scholars. And on this occasion at least their prognostications were justified. The joy of the half day off which Saturday afternoon afforded was balanced by the terrible weight of the study of the Shorter Catechism. This of course made them hate the Catechism.

Every Saturday Murdoch Malison's pupils had to learn a certain number of questions from the Shorter Catechism, with their corresponding proofs from Scripture. Whoever failed in the task was condemned to imprisonment for the remainder of the day or until the task was accomplished. On one Saturday each month, moreover, the students were tested on all the questions and proofs that had been covered during the previous month.

The day in question was one of those of accumulated labor, and the only proofs Alec Forbes had succeeded in displaying was proof of his inability for the task. In consequence he was condemned to be kept in—a trial hard indeed for one whose chief delights were the open air and the active exertion of his growing body.

Seeing his downcast expression filled Annie with such concern that she lost track of the class and did not know when her turn came until suddenly the master was standing before her in silent expectation. He had approached soundlessly and then stood till the universal silence had at length aroused Annie's consciousness. Then with a smile on his thin lips, but a lowering thundercloud on his brow, he repeated the question: "What doth every sin deserve?"

Annie, bewildered and burning with shame at finding herself the core of the silence, could not recall a word of the answer given in the Catechism. So in her confusion she fell back on her common sense and experience.

"What doth every sin deserve?" repeated the tyrant.

"A lickin'," whispered Annie, her eyes filling with tears.

The master seemed much inclined to consider her condemned out of her own mouth and to give her a whipping at once. But reflecting, perhaps, that she was a girl, and a little one, he instead gave a side wave of his head, indicating the culprit's doom to be kept in for the afternoon. Annie took her place among the condemned with a flutter of joy in her heart that Alec Forbes would not be left without a friend in trial. A few more boys made up the unfortunate party, but they were younger ones and so there was no companion for Forbes who evidently felt the added degradation of being alone. The hour arrived and the school was dismissed. The master strode out, locking the door behind him; and the defaulters were left alone to chew the bitter cud of ill-cooked theology.

For some time there was a dreary silence in the room. Alec sat with his elbow on his desk, biting his nails. Annie divided her silent attention between her book and Alec. The other boys seemed to be busy with their catechisms, in the hope of getting out as soon as the master returned. At length Alec took out his knife, and out of sheer boredom, began to whittle away at the desk in front of him. When Annie saw that, she crept across the floor and sat down at the opposite desk. Alec looked up at her, smiled, and went on with his whittling. Annie slid a little nearer and then asked him to hear her say her Catechism. He consented and she repeated the lesson perfectly.

"Now let me hear you, Alec," she said.

"No, thank you, Annie. I can't say it. And I won't say it for all the teachers in creation."

"But he'll lick you, Alec, and I can't stand it," said Annie, the tears rising to her eyes.

"Well, I'll try—to please you, Annie," said Alec, seeing that the little thing was in earnest.

How her heart bounded with delight! That great boy, so strong and so brave, learning a lesson to please her!

But it would not work.

"I can't remember a word of it, Annie. I'm dreadful hungry besides. I was in too big a hurry with my breakfast. If I had known what was coming, I would have laid in a better stock," he added, laughing rather drearily.

As he spoke he looked up and his eyes wandered from one window to another for a few moments.

"No, it's no use," he resumed at last. "I have eaten too much to escape that way anyway."

Annie was as sad over Alec's hunger as any mother over her child's. She felt it pure injustice that he should ever be hungry. But unable to think of any way to help him, she could only respond, "I don't know what you mean, Alec."

"When I was no bigger than you I could squeeze out of a smaller hole than that," he answered, pointing to the open windowpane in an upper corner of the windows; "but I've eaten too much since then."

Annie sprang to her feet.

"If you could get through it once, I can get through it now, Alec. Just hold me up a bit. You *can* lift me, you know."

She looked at him shyly and gratefully.

"But what'll you do when you *are* out, Annie?"

"Run home and get a loaf of bread to bring back with me."

"But Rob Bruce'll see your head between your feet before he'll give you a loaf of bread; and it's too far to run to my mother's. Murdoch would be back long before that."

"Just help me out and leave the rest to me," said Annie confidently. "If I don't fetch a loaf of white bread, never trust me again."

The idea of bread, a rarity and consequently a delicacy to Scottish country boys, was too much for Alec's imagination. He jumped up and put his head out of one of the open panes to see if the coast was clear. He saw a woman approaching whom he knew.

"I say, Lizzie," he called.

The woman stopped.

"What do you want, Master Alec?"

"Just stand there and pull this lassie out. We're kept in together and nearly starving."

"The Lord preserve us! I'll go for the key."

"No, no. *We* would have to pay for that. Take her out—that's all we want."

"He's a coarse creature, that master of yours. I would go to see him hanged."

"That'll come in good time," said Alec. "But never mind 'Murder' Malison. Just pull out the little lassie, will you?"

"Where is she?"

Alec jumped down and held Annie up to the open window, less than a foot square. He told her to put her arms through first. Then between them they got her head through, at which point Lizzie caught hold of her—the school was so low—and dragged her out and set her on her feet. But a windowpane was broken in the process.

"Now, Annie," cried Alec, "never mind the window. Run!"

She was off like a live bullet.

She scampered home prepared to encounter whatever dangers were necessary, the worst to her mind being the danger of not succeeding and thus breaking faith with Alec. She had sixpence of her own in coppers in her box. But how was she to get into the house and out again without being seen? With the utmost care she managed to get in the back door unnoticed and up to her room. In a moment more the six pennies were in her hand and she was back in the street. She dashed straight for the baker's shop.

"A six-penny loaf," she panted out.

"Who wants it?" asked the baker's wife.

"There's the coins," answered Annie, laying them on the counter.

The baker's wife gave her the loaf with the biscuit, which from time immemorial had always graced a purchase in the amount of sixpence, and Annie sped back to the school like a runaway horse to his stable.

As she approached, out popped the head of Alec Forbes. He had been listening for the sound of her feet. She held up the loaf as high as she could and he stretched down as low as he could and so their hands met on the loaf.

"Thank you, Annie," said Alec. "I won't forget this. How did you get it?"

"Never mind that, but I didn't steal it," answered Annie. "Alec, how shall I get in again?" she added, suddenly waking up to that difficult necessity, looking up at the window above her head.

"I'm a predestined idiot!" said Alec with an impious allusion to the Catechism as he scratched his helpless head. "I never thought of that."

It was clearly impossible.

"You'll catch it," said one of the urchins to Annie, with his nose flattened against the window.

The roses of Annie's face turned pale, but she answered stoutly: "Well, I care little as the rest of you, I'm thinkin'."

By this time Alec had made up what was often a bullheaded mind.

"Run home, Annie," he said. "And if Murder tries to lay a finger on you Monday, *I'll* murder *him*. Faith! Run home before he comes and catches you at the window."

"No, Alec," pleaded Annie.

"Hold your tongue," interrupted Alec, "and run, will you?"

Seeing he was quite determined, Annie—though not wanting to leave him and in terror of what was implied in the threats he uttered—obeyed him and turned to walk leisurely home, avoiding the quarters where there might be a chance of meeting her jailer.

She found that no one had observed her former visit, and the only remarks made were those concerned with the disgrace of being kept in.

When Mr. Malison returned to the school about four o'clock, he found all quiet as death. The boys appeared totally absorbed in the Catechism. But to his additional surprise the girl was absent.

"Where is Ann Anderson?" he demanded in a condescending voice.

"Gone home!" cried two of the little prisoners.

"Gone home!" echoed the master in a tone of savage incredulity. Although not only was it plain enough that she was gone, from former experience he probably knew well enough how her escape had been made.

"Yes," said Forbes; "it was me who made her go. I put her out at the window. And I broke the window," he added, knowing it would be found out sooner or later, "but I'll get it mended on Monday."

Malison turned white as a sheet with rage. Indeed, the hopelessness of the situation had made Alec speak with too much nonchalance.

Anxious to curry favor, the third youngster called out, "Sanny Forbes made her go and fetch him a loaf of white bread."

The little informer still had some of the crumbs sticking to his jacket. How corrupting is a reign of terror! The bread was eaten, and now the giver was being betrayed by the urchin in the hope of gaining a little favor with the tyrant.

"Alexander Forbes, come up."

Beyond this point I will not here carry the narrative.

After he had spent his wrath, the master allowed them all to part without further reference to the Shorter Catechism.

10

· · · · · · · · · · · · · · · · · · ·

The Next Monday

The Sunday following was anything but a day of rest for Annie—she looked with such frightful anticipation to the coming Monday. The awful morning dawned. When she woke and the thought of what she had to meet came back to her, she turned sick, not metaphorically but physically. Yet breakfast time would come, and worship did not fail to follow, and then to school she must go. There all went on as usual for some time. The Bible class was called up, heard, and dismissed; and Annie was beginning to hope that the whole affair was somehow or other going to pass by. She had heard nothing of Alec's fate after she had left him imprisoned, and except for a certain stoniness in his look, his face gave no sign. She dared not lift her eyes from the spelling book in front of her to look in the direction of the master. No murderer could have felt more keenly as if all the universe were one eye and that eye were fixed on him than poor Annie.

Suddenly the awful voice resounded through the school, and the words it uttered—though even after she heard them it seemed too terrible to be true—were: "Ann Anderson, come up."

For a moment she lost consciousness. When she recovered herself she was standing before the master. She vaguely remembered being asked two or three unanswered questions. What they were she had no idea. But presently he spoke again and, from the tone, what he said was evidently the repetition of a question—probably put more than once before.

"Did you, or did you not, go out at the window on Saturday?"

She did not see that Alec Forbes had left his seat and was slowly lessening the distance between them and him.

"Yes," she answered, trembling from head to foot.

"Did you, or did you not, bring a loaf of bread to those who were kept in?"

"Yes, sir."

"Where did you get it?"

"I bought it, sir."

"Where did you get the money?"

Every eye in the school was fixed upon her, those of her cousins sparkling with delight.

"I got it out of my own chest, sir."

"Hold up you hand."

Annie obeyed, her face pleading with a most pathetic dumb terror.

"Don't touch her," said Alec Forbes, stepping between the executioner and his victim. "You know well enough it was all my fault. I told you so on Saturday."

Murder Malison, as the boys called him, answered him with a hissing blow of the tawse over his head, followed by a succession of furious blows upon every part of his body as the boy twisted and writhed and doubled. At length, making no attempt to resist, he was knocked down by the storm. He lay on the floor under continued fierce lashes, the master holding him down with one foot. Finally Malison stopped, exhausted, and turned white with rage toward Annie, who was almost in a fit of agony, and repeated the order: "Hold up your hand."

But as Malison turned, Alec bounded to his feet, his face glowing and his eyes flashing. He scrambled round in front and sprang at the master's throat just as the tag was descending. Malison threw him off, lifted his weapon once more and swept it with a stinging lash round his head and face. Alec, feeling that this occasion was no longer accountable to the rules of a fair fight, lowered his head like a ram and rushed full tilt against the pit of Malison's stomach. The tall man doubled up and crashed backward into the peat fire which was glowing on the hearth. In his attempt to save himself, he thrust his right hand into it.

Alec rushed forward to drag him off the fire, but he was up before Alec reached him, his face concealing the pain.

"Go home!" he shouted to the scholars throughout the room, and sat down at his desk to hide his suffering.

For one brief moment there was silence. Then a tumult arose, a shouting and screeching, and the whole school rushed to the door, as if the devil had been after them to catch whoever was last through it. Strange was the uproar that invaded the ears of Glamerton—strange, that is, at eleven o'clock in the morning on Monday, for it was the uproar of jubilant freedom.

But the culprits, Annie and Alec, stood and stared at the master, whose face was covered with one hand, while the other hung helpless at his side. Annie stopped, partly out of pity for the despot and partly because Alec stopped. Alec stopped because he was the author of the situation—at least he never could give any better reason.

At length Mr. Malison lifted his head and made a movement toward his hat. He started when he saw the two still standing there. But the moment he looked at them their courage failed them.

"Run, Annie!" said Alec.

Away she bolted, and he was after her as well as he could, which was not with his usual fleetness by any means. When Annie had rounded a corner, she stopped and looked back for Alec. He was a good many paces behind her, and now she first discovered the condition of her champion. The excitement over, he could scarcely walk; he was a mass of wales and bruises from head to foot. He put his hand on her shoulder to help steady himself and made no opposition to her accompanying him as far as the gate of his mother's garden, which was nearly a mile from the town on the farther bank of one of the rivers which watered the valley plain. Then she went slowly home, bearing with her the memory of the smile which, in spite of pain, had illuminated his face as she left him.

When she got home she saw at once, from the black looks of the Bruces, that the story—whether in its true form or not—had arrived before her.

Nothing was said, however, till after worship that evening. Then Bruce gave her a long lecture on the wickedness and certain punishment of "takin' up with loons like Sanny Forbes." But he came to the conclusion, as he confided to his wife that night, that the lassie was already growing hardened; she had not shed even a single tear of remorse as a result of his lecture. The moment Annie lay down on her bed she fell to weeping over the sufferings of Alec. She was asleep a moment after, however. If it had not been for the power of sleep in the child, she would undoubtedly have given way long before now to the hostile influences around her and died.

There was considerable excitement about the hearths of Glamerton that night from the news carried home by the children of the master's defeat. Various were the judgments elicited by the story. The religious portion of the community seemed to their children to side with the master; the worldly—namely, those who did not profess to be particularly religious—all sided with Alec Forbes, with the exception of a fish-cadger who had one son, the plague of his life.

Among the religious there was, at least, one exception too. He had no children of his own, but he had a fancy for Alec Forbes. That exception was Thomas Crann, the stonemason.

11

A Visit to Howglen

Thomas Crann was building a house, for he was both a contractor and a day laborer. He had arrived at the point in the process where the assistance of a more skilled carpenter was necessary. Therefore, he went to George Macwha, whom he found planing at his workbench. This bench was in a workshop with two or three more benches in it, some pine boards set up against the wall, a couple of cartwheels sent in for repairs, and the tools and materials of his trade all about. The floor was covered with shavings. After a short and gruff greeting on the part of Crann, and a more cordial reply from Macwha, who stopped his labor to attend to his visitor, they began to discuss the business at hand. Once that had been satisfactorily completed, the conversation took a more general scope, accompanied by the sounds of Macwha's busy instrument.

"A terrible laddie, that Sanny Forbes!" remarked the carpenter. "They say he licked the dominie an' almost killed him."

"I've known worse laddies than Sanny Forbes," was Thomas's curt reply.

"Ow, indeed! I know nothin' against the laddie. Him and our Willie's always together."

Thomas's sole answer was a grunt, and a silence of a few seconds followed before he spoke.

"I'm not sure that thrashin' the schoolmaster is such a bad sin. He's a dour creature that Murdoch Malison wi' his fair face and smooth words. I don't doubt that the children hae the worst o' it in general. An' for Alec I hae great hopes. He comes o' good stock. His father, honest man, was one o' the Lord's own. An' if his mother's been some too soft on him an' has given the lad too long a tether, he'll come right afore long, for he's worth lookin' after."

"I don't rightly understand ye, Thomas."

"I don't think the Lord'll lose the grip o' such a father's son. He's not converted yet, but he's well worth convertin', for there's good stuff in him."

Thomas did not consider how his common sense was running away with his theology. But Macwha was not the man to bring him to task on that score. His only reply lay in the *whishk, whashk* of his plane. Thomas resumed: "He just needs what ye need yerself, George Macwha."

"What's that, Thomas?" asked George, with a grim attempt at a smile, as if to say: "I know what's coming but I'm not going to mind it."

"He just needs to be well shaken over the mouth o' the pit. He must smell the brimstone o' the overlastin' burnin'. He's none o' yer soft boards that ye can smooth with a sweep o' yer arm. He's a blue whunstane that's hard to dress; but once dressed, it stands up against the weather. I like to work on such hard boards myself. None o' yer soft wood that ye could cut with a knife for me!"

"Well, I dare say ye're right, Thomas."

"And besides, they say he took his own licks without sayin' a word, an' flew at the master only when he was goin' to lick the poor orphan lassie—James Anderson's lassie, you know."

"Ow, ay! 'Tis the same tale they all tell. I have no doubt it's correct."

"Well, let him take it then, an' be thankful! For it's no more than was well spent on him."

With these conclusive words Thomas departed. He was no sooner out of the shop than out came, from behind the stack of deal boards standing against the wall, Willie, the eldest hope of the house of Macwha—a dusky-skinned, black-eyed, curly-headed, roguish-looking boy, Alec Forbes' companion and occasional accomplice. He was more mischievous than Alec and sometimes led him into unseen scrapes; but whenever anything extensive had to be executed, Alec was always the leader.

"What are ye hiding for, ye rascal?" said his father. "What mischief are ye up to now?"

"Nothing," was Willie's cool reply.

"What made ye hide then?"

"Tom Crann never sets eye on me but he accuses me o' something."

"Ye get no more than ye deserve, I don't doubt," returned George. "Here, take the chisel and cut that beading into lengths."

"I'm going over the river to ask after Alec," replied the lad, in the hope of excusing himself.

"Ay, ay! there's always something!—What ails Alec now?"

"Mr. Malison's nearly killed him. He hasn't been to school for two days."

With these words Willie bolted from the shop and set off at full speed. The latter part of his statement was perfectly true.

The day after the fight Mr. Malison came to the school as usual, but with his arm in a sling. To Annie's dismay, Alec did not make his appearance.

It had of course been impossible to conceal his physical condition from his mother. The heart of the widow so yearned over the suffering of her son, though no confession of suffering escaped Alec's lips, that she vowed in anger that he should never cross the door of that school again. For three days she held immovably to her resolution, much to Alec's annoyance and to the consternation of Mr. Malison, who feared that he had not only lost a pupil but made an enemy. For Mr. Malison had every reason for being as smooth-faced with the parents as possible: he had ulterior hopes in Glamerton. The clergyman was getting old, and Mr. Malison was a licentiate of the Church. Although the people had no direct voice in the filling of the pulpit, it was very desirable that a candidate should have none but friends in the parish.

Mr. Malison made no allusion whatever to the events of Monday, and things went on as usual in the school, with just one exception: for a whole week the tawse did not make its appearance. This was owing in part at least to the state of his hand; but if he had ever wished to be freed from the necessity of using the lash, he might have derived hope from the fact that somehow or other the boys were no worse than usual during this week.

As soon as school was over on that first day of Alec's absence, Annie darted off on the road to Howglen where he lived and never slowed to a walk until she reached the garden gate. Fully conscious of her inferior position, she went to the kitchen door. The door was opened to her knock before she had recovered breath enough to speak. The servant saw a girl with shabby dress and a dirty bonnet, which partially covered a disorderly mass of hair—for Annie was not kept so tidy on the interest of her money as she had been at the farm. The girl, I say, seeing this, and finding besides that Annie had nothing to say, took her for a beggar, returned to the kitchen and brought her a piece of oatcake, the common dole to the young beggars of the time. Annie's face flushed crimson, but she said gently, having by this time got her runaway breath a little more under control: "No, I thank you; I'm no beggar. I only wanted to know how Alec was today."

"Come in," said the girl, "an' I'll tell the mistress."

Annie followed the maid into the kitchen and sat down on the edge of a wooden chair, like a perching bird, until she should return.

"Please, mem, here's a lassie wanting to know how Master Alec is," said Mary, with her hand on the handle of the parlor door.

"That must be little Annie Anderson, Mamma," said Alec, who was lying on the sofa.

Alec had told his mother all about the affair. Some of her friends from Glamerton, who likewise had sons at the school, had called and given their versions of the story, in which the prowess of Alec was made more of than in his own account. Indeed, all his fellow scholars except the young Bruces sang his praises aloud; for whatever the degree of their affection for Alec, every one of them hated the master. So the mother was proud of her boy—far prouder than she was willing for him to see. Therefore, she could not help feeling some interest in Annie and some curiosity to see her. She had known James Anderson, her father, and he had been her guest more than once when he had called on business. Everybody had liked him; and this general approval owed itself to no lack of character but to his genuine kindness of heart. So Mrs. Forbes was prejudiced in Annie's favor—but far more by her own recollections of the father than by her son's representations of the daughter.

"Tell her to come up, Mary," she said.

So Annie, with all the disorganization of school about her, was shown, considerably to her discomfort, into Mrs. Forbes' dining room.

There was nothing remarkable in the room; but to Annie's eyes it seemed magnificent, for carpet and curtains, sideboard and sofa, were luxuries altogether strange to her eyes. She entered very timidly and stood close to the door. But Alec scrambled from the sofa, and taking hold of her by both hands, pulled her up to his mother.

"There she is, Mamma!" he said.

And Mrs. Forbes, although not gratified at seeing her son treat with familiarity a girl so neglectedly attired, yet received her kindly and shook hands with her.

"How do you do, Annie?" she said.

"Quite well, I thank you, mem," answered Annie.

"What's going on at school today, Annie?" asked Alec.

"Not much out of the ordinary," answered Annie. "The master's a bit quieter than usual. I fancy he's the better behaved for his burnt fingers. But, oh, Alec!"

And here the little maiden burst into a passionate fit of crying.

"What's the matter, Annie?" said Mrs. Forbes, as she drew nearer, genuinely concerned at the child's tears.

"Oh, mem! You didn't see how the master licked him."

Tears from some mysterious source sprang to Mrs. Forbes' eyes. But at that moment Mary opened the door and said, "Master Bruce is here, mem, wantin' t' see ye."

"Tell him to walk up, Mary."

"Oh no, no, mem! Don't let him come till I'm gone. He'll take me with him," cried Annie.

Mary stood waiting the result.

"But you must go home, you know, Annie," said Mrs. Forbes kindly.

"Ay, but not with *him*," pleaded Annie.

From what Mrs. Forbes knew of the manners and character of Bruce, she was not altogether surprised at Annie's reluctance. So turning to the maid, she asked, "Have you told Mr. Bruce that Miss Anderson is here?"

"Me tell him! No, mem."

"Then take the child into my room till he is gone." Turning to Annie she said, "But perhaps he knows you are here, Annie?"

"He can't know that, mem. He jumps at things sometimes, though. He's sharp enough."

"Well, we shall see."

So Mary led Annie away to the sanctuary of Mrs. Forbes' bedroom.

Bruce was not upon Annie's track at all. But his visit will need a few words of explanation.

Bruce's father had been a faithful servant to Mrs. Forbes' father-in-law, who had held the same farm before his son, both having been what are called gentlemen farmers. The younger Bruce, being anxious to set up a shop, had—for his father's sake—been loaned the money by the elder Forbes. This money he had repaid before the death of the old man, who had never asked any interest on it. Before many more years had passed, Bruce, who had a wonderful capacity for petty business, was known to have accumulated some savings in the bank. Now the younger Forbes, being considerably more enterprising than his father, had spent all his capital upon improvements about the farm—draining, fencing, and the like. Just then his younger brother, to whom he was greatly attached, applied to him in an emergency. As he had no cash of his own he thought of Bruce. To borrow from him for his brother would not involve exposing the fact that he was in a temporarily embarrassing financial position—an exposure very undesirable in a country town like Glamerton.

After a thorough investigation of the solvency of Mr. Forbes, Bruce supplied him with a hundred pounds upon personal bond, at the usual rate of interest, for a certain term of years. Mr. Forbes died soon thereafter, leaving his affairs somewhat strained because of his outlay. Mrs. Forbes had paid the interest of the debt now for two years. But as the rent of the farm was heavy, she found this additional sum a burden. She had good reason to hope for better times, thinking that the farm must soon increase its yield. Mr. Bruce, on his part, regarded the widow with somewhat jealous eyes, because he very much doubted whether, when the day arrived when the note came due, she would be able to pay him the money she owed him. That day, however, was not yet at hand. It was this diversion of his resources, and the moral necessity for a nest egg for Annie, as he had represented the case to Margaret Anderson, which had urged him to show hospitality to Annie Anderson and her little fortune.

So neither was he in pursuit of Annie nor was it anxiety for the welfare of Alec that induced him to call on Mrs. Forbes. Indeed, if Malison had killed the boy outright, Bruce would have been more pleased than otherwise. But he was in the habit of reminding the widow of his existence by an occasional call, especially when the time approached for the half yearly payment of the interest.

And now the report of Alec's condition gave him a suitable pretext for looking in upon his debtor without appearing too greedy after his money.

"Well, mem, how are you today?" he said as he entered, rubbing his hands.

"Quite well, thank you, Mr. Bruce. Take a seat."

"And how's Mr. Alec?"

"There he is to answer for himself," said Mrs. Forbes, looking toward the sofa.

"How are you, Mr. Alec, after all this?" said Bruce.

"Quite well, thank you," answered Alec, in a tone that did not altogether please either of his listeners.

"I thought you had been rather sore," returned Bruce in an acid tone.

"I've got a bruise or two, that's all," said Alec.

"Well, I hope it'll be a lesson to you."

"To Mr. Malison, you should say, Mr. Bruce. I am perfectly satisfied, for my part."

His mother was surprised to hear him speak like a grown man, as well as annoyed by his behavior to Bruce, in whose power she feared they might one day find themselves. But she said nothing. Bruce, likewise, was rather nonplussed. He grinned and was silent.

"I hear you have taken James Anderson's daughter into your family now, Mr. Bruce."

"Oh, ay, mem. There was nobody to look after the wee lassie. So, though I could but ill-afford it, with my own small family growing up, I was in a manner obliged to take her, James Anderson being a cousin of my own, you know, mem."

"Well, I'm sure it was very kind of you and Mrs. Bruce. How does the child get on?"

"Middling, mem . . . middling. She's just some the worse for taking up with loons."

Here he glanced at Alec with an expression of successful spite. He certainly had the best of it now.

Alec restrained the reply that rushed to his lips. A little small talk followed, and the visitor departed with a laugh from between his teeth as he took leave of Alec, a laugh which I can only describe as embodying an *I told you so* sort of satisfaction.

Almost as soon as he was out of the house, the parlor door opened and Mary brought in Annie. Mrs. Forbes' eyes were instantly fixed on her with mild astonishment, and something of a mother's tenderness awoke in her heart toward the little child. What she would not have given for such a daughter! During Bruce's call Mary had been busy with the child. She had combed and brushed Annie's thick brown hair, washed her face and hands and neck, made the best she could of her poor, dingy dress, and put one of her own Sunday collars upon her.

Annie had submitted to it all without question, and thus adorned, Mary had introduced her again into the dining room. Mrs. Forbes was captivated by the pale, patient face, and the longing blue eyes that looked at her as if the child felt that she ought to have been her mother but somehow they had missed each other.

They gazed out of the shadows of the mass of dark brown wavy hair that fell to her waist. But Mrs. Forbes was speedily recalled to a sense of propriety by observing that Alec too was staring at Annie with a mingling of amusement, admiration and respect.

"What have you been about, Mary," she said in a tone of attempted reproof. "You have made a fright of the child. Take her away."

When Annie was once more brought back with her hair restored to its net, silent tears of mortification were still flowing down her cheeks. When Annie cried the tears always rose and flowed without any sound or convulsion. Rarely did she sob. This completed the conquest of Mrs. Forbes' heart. She drew the little one to her and kissed her, and Annie's tears instantly ceased, while Mrs. Forbes wiped away those still lingering on her face. Mary then went to get the tea, and Mrs. Forbes having left the room for a moment to recover her composure, the loss of which is peculiarly objectionable to a Scotswoman, Annie was left seated on a footstool before the bright fire while Alec lay on the sofa looking at her.

"I wouldn't want to be grand folk," mused Annie aloud, forgetting that she was not alone.

"We're not grand folk, Annie," said Alec.

"Ay, you are," returned Annie persistently.

"Well, why wouldn't you like it?"

"You must always be afraid of spoiling things."

"Mamma would tell you a different story," rejoined Alec, laughing. "There's nothing here to spoil."

Mrs. Forbes returned. Tea was brought in. Annie behaved herself like a lady, and after tea ran home with mingled feelings of pleasure and pain. For notwithstanding her assertion to Alec, the Bruces' kitchen fire, small and dull, the smelling shop, and her own dreary attic room, did not seem more desirable after her peep into the warmth and comfort of the house at Howglen.

Questioned as to what had delayed her return from school, she told the truth; she had gone to ask after Alec Forbes and they had kept her to tea.

"I told them that you ran after the loons!" said Bruce triumphantly. Then stung with the reflection that *he* had not been asked to stay to tea, he added: "It's not for the likes of you, Annie, to go to gentlefolk's houses where you're not wanted. So don't let me hear of it again."

But it is wonderful how Bruce's influence over Annie, an influence of distress, was growing gradually weaker. He could make her uncomfortable enough. But as to his opinion of her, she had almost reached the point of not caring a straw for that. And she had faith enough in Alec to hope that he would defend her from whatever Bruce might have said against her.

Whether Mary had been talking in the town, as is not improbable, about little Annie Anderson's visit to her mistress, and so the story of the hair came to be known, or not, I cannot tell. But it was a notable coincidence that a few days later Mrs. Bruce came to the back door with a great pair of shears in her hand,

and calling Annie, said: "Come here, Annie! Your hair's too long. I must just cut it. It's giving you sore eyes."

"There's nothing the matter with my eyes," said Annie gently.

"Don't talk back. Sit down," returned Mrs. Bruce, leading her into the kitchen.

Annie cared very little for her hair, and well enough remembered that Mrs. Forbes had said it made a fright of her; so it was with no great reluctance that she submitted to the operation. Mrs. Bruce chopped it short all the way around. This permitted what there was of it to fall about her face, there being too little to confine in the usual prison of the net. Thus, her appearance did not bear such marks of deprivation; or in other Scottish words, "she didna lulk sae dockit," as might have been expected.

But wavy locks of rich brown were borne that night by the careful hands of Mrs. Bruce to Rob Guddle, the barber. Nor was the hand less careful that brought back their equivalent in money—for such long and beautiful hair commanded a good sum. With a smile to her husband, half loving and half cunning, Mrs. Bruce dropped the amount in the till.

12
....

Alec and Thomas

Although Alec Forbes was not a boy of quick receptivity as far as books were concerned, and therefore had never been a favorite with Mr. Malison, he was not by any means a common or stupid boy. His own eyes could teach him more than books could, for he had a very quick observation of things about him, both in nature and in humanity. He knew all the birds, all their habits, and all their eggs. Not a boy in Glamerton could find a nest quicker than he, nor treated a nest with such respect. For he never took young birds and seldom more than half the eggs. Indeed, he was rather an uncommon boy, having, along with more than the usual amount of activity even for a boy, a tenderness of heart altogether rare in those his age. He was as familiar with the domestic animals and their ways of feeling and acting as Annie herself. He detested cruelty in any form; and yet, as the occasion required, he could execute stern justice. With the world of men around him he was equally at home. He knew the simple people of the town wonderfully well and took to Thomas Crann more than to anyone else, even though Thomas often read him long lectures. To these lectures Alec would listen seriously enough, believing Thomas to be right, though he could never make up his mind to give any attention to what was required of him as a result.

The first time Alec met Thomas after the affair with the dominie was on the day before he was to go back to school; for his mother had yielded at last to his desire to return. Thomas was building an addition to a water mill on the banks of the Glamour not far from where Alec lived, and Alec walked there to see how the structure was progressing. He expected a sharp rebuke for his behavior to Mr. Malison, but somehow he was not afraid of Thomas despite his occasional gruffness. The first words Thomas said, however, were: "Weel, Alec, can ye tell me the name o' King David's mither?"

"I cannot, Thomas," answered Alec. "What was it?"

"Find out. Look in yer Bible. Hae ye been back to the school yet?"

"No. I'm going tomorrow."

"Ye're not goin' to fight wi' the master before the day's over, are ye?"

"I don't know," answered Alec. "Maybe he'll pick a fight with me. But you know, Thomas," he continued, defending himself from what he supposed Thomas was thinking, "King David himself killed the giant."

"Ow, ay! I'm not thinkin' o' that. Maybe ye did right. But take care, Alec"—here Thomas paused from his work, and turning toward the boy with a trowelful of mortar in his hand, spoke very slowly and solemnly—"take care that ye bear no malice against the master. Justice done for the sake o' a private grudge will bounce back on the doer. I hae little doubt the master'll be the better for it. But if ye be the worse, it'll be an ill job, Alec, my man."

"I have no ill will at him, Thomas."

"Weel, jist watch yer own heart an' beware o' it. I would counsel ye to try an' please him a grain more than usual. It's not that easy to the carnal man, but ye know we ought to crucify the old man, with his affections an' lusts."

"Well, I'll try," said Alec, to whom it was not nearly so difficult as Thomas imagined.

And he did try. And the master seemed to appreciate Alec's efforts and to accept them as a peace offering, thus showing that he really was the better for the punishment he had received.

It would be a great injustice to judge Mr. Malison too harshly by the customs of his day. It was the feeling of the time and the country that the tawse should be used unsparingly. *Law* was, and in great measure still is, the highest idea of the divine generated by the ordinary mind. It had to be supported at all risks, even by means of the leather strap. In the hands of a wise and even-tempered man, no harm could result from the use of this instrument of justice. But in the hands of a fierce-tempered and changeable man of small moral stature, and liable to prejudices and offense, it became the means of unspeakable injury to those under his care.

Mr. Malison had nothing of the childlike in him, and consequently he never saw the mind of the child whose body he was assailing with a battery of excruciating blows. A *man* ought to be able to endure wrongful suffering and be none the worse; but who dares demand that of a child? It is indeed well for such cruel masters that even they are ultimately judged by the heart of a father, and not by the law of a king (this is the worst of all the fictions of an ignorant and low theology). And if they must receive punishment in the end, at least it will not be like the heartless punishment which they inflicted on the boys and girls under their law but will be a punishment springing from an even greater Love.

Annie began to be regarded as a protégé of Alec Forbes, and as Alec was a favorite with most of his classmates, and was feared where he was not loved, even her cousins began to look upon her with something like respect and to lessen their persecutions. But she did not therefore become much more reconciled to her position; for the habits and customs of her home were distasteful to her, and its whole atmosphere uncongenial. Nor could it have been otherwise in any house where the entire aim was, first, to make money, and next, not to spend it.

The heads did not in the least know that they were unkind to her. On the contrary, Bruce thought himself the very pattern of generosity if he gave her a scrap of string. And Mrs. Bruce, when she said to inquiring neighbors, "The bairn's just like other children—she's good enough," thought herself a pattern of justice and even forbearance. But neither cared for her as their own children. When Alec's mother sent for her one Saturday, soon after her first visit, they hardly concealed their annoyance at the preference shown her by one who was under such great obligation to them, the parents of children every way superior to her.

13

· · · · · · · · · · · · · · · · · · · ·

Juno

The winter drew on—a season as different from the summer in those northern latitudes as if it belonged to another solar system. Cold and stormy, it is yet full of delight for all beings who can either romp, sleep, or think it through. But alas for the old and sickly, in poor homes, with scanty food and provisions for fire!

The winter came. One morning all awoke and saw a white world around them. Alec jumped out of bed in delight. It was a sunny, frosty morning. The snow had fallen all night, and no wind had interfered with the gracious alighting of the feathery water. Every branch, every twig was laden with its sparkling burden of flakes. The only darkness in the outstretched glory of white was the line of the winding river; all the snow that fell on it vanished. It flowed on, black, through its banks of white.

From the door opening into this fairyland Alec sprang into the untrodden space. He had discovered a world without even the print of human foot upon it. The keen air made him happy; and the peaceful face of nature filled him with jubilance. He was at the school door before a human being had appeared in the streets of Glamerton. Its dwellers all lay still under those sheets of snow, which seemed to hold them asleep in its cold enchantment.

Before any of his fellows made their appearance, he had kneaded and piled a great heap of snowballs and stood by his pyramid prepared for the offensive. He attacked the first that came, and soon there was a great troop of boys pelting away at him. But with his store of balls at his feet, he was able to pay pretty fairly for what he received. By and by the little ones gathered, but they kept away for fear of the flying balls, for the boys had divided into two equal parties and were pelting away at each other. At length the woman who had charge of the schoolroom finished lighting the fire and opened the door, and Annie and several other of the smaller ones made a run for it during a lull in the fury of the battle.

"Stop!" cried Alec; and the flurry ceased. One boy, however, just as Annie was entering the room, threw a snowball at her. He missed, but Alec did not miss him; for scarcely was the ball out of his hand when the attacker received another, right between his eyes. Over he went amidst a shout of satisfaction.

When the master appeared at the top of the lane, the fight came to an end; and as he entered the school, the group round the fire broke up and dispersed. Alec had entered close behind the master and overtook Annie as she went to her seat, for he had observed as she ran into the school that she was limping.

"What's the matter with you, Annie?" he said.

"Juno bit me," she answered.

"Ay! Very well!" returned Alec in a tone that had more meaning than the words themselves.

Soon after the Bible class was over and they had all taken their seats, a strange quiet stir and excitement gradually arose, like the first motions of a whirlpool at the turn of the tide. The master became aware of more than the usual flitting to and fro among the boys, just like the coming and going which precludes the swarming of bees. But as he had little or no inductive power, he never saw beyond symptoms. These were to him mere isolated facts, signifying disorder.

"John Morison, go to your seat!" he cried.

John went.

"Robert Rennie, go to your seat."

Robert went. And this continued till, six having been thus passed by, the master could stand it no longer. The *tag* was thrown and a licking followed, making matters a little better from the master's point of view.

Now I will try to give, from the scholar's side, a peep of what passed.

As soon as he was fairly seated, Alec said in a low voice across the double desk to one of the boys on the opposite side, calling him by his nickname, "I say, Divot, do you know Juno?"

"Maybe not!" answered Divot. "But if I don't, my left leg does."

"I thought you knew the shape of her teeth, man. Just give Scrumpie there a dig in the ribs."

"What are ye after, Divot? I'll give ye a clout on yer ear!" growled Scrumpie.

"Hoot, man! The General wants ye." "General" was Alec's nickname.

"What is it, General?"

"Do you know Juno?"

"Hang the beast! I know her too well. She took her dinner off one of my hips last year."

"Just creep over to Cadger there and ask if he knows Juno. Maybe he's forgotten her."

Cadger's reply was interrupted by the interference of the master, but a pantomimed gesture conveyed to the General sufficient assurance of Cadger's memory in regard to Juno and her favors. Such messages and replies, notwithstanding more than one licking, kept passing the whole of the morning.

Juno was Robert Bruce's dog. She had the nose and legs of a bulldog but was not by any means purebred, and her behavior was worse than her breed. She was a great favorite with her master who ostensibly kept her chained in his backyard for the protection of the house and store. But she was not by any means popular with the rising generation, for she was given to biting, with or without provocation, and every now and then she got loose. Complaint had been made to her owner but without avail. Various vows of vengeance had been made by certain of the boys. But now Alec Forbes had taken up the cause of humanity and justice; for the brute had bitten Annie, and *she* could have given no provocation.

It was soon understood throughout the school that war was to be made upon Juno, and that every able-bodied boy must be ready when called out by the General. The minute they were dismissed the boys gathered in a knot at the door.

"What are ye goin' t' do, General?" asked one.

"Kill her," answered Alec.

"How?"

"Stone her to death, like the man who broke the Sabbath."

"Broken bones for broken bones, eh? Ay!"

"But there's no stones to be gotten in the snow, General," argued Cadger.

"You simpleton! We'll get more stones than we can carry from the side of the road up yonder."

A confused chorus of suggestions and exclamations now arose, in the midst of which Willie Macwha, whose obvious nickname was Curly, came up.

"Here's Curly!"

"Well, is it all settled?" he asked.

"She's condemned but not executed yet," said Grumpie.

"How will we get at her?" asked Cadger.

"That's just the problem," said Divot.

"We can't kill her in her own yard," said Houghie.

"No. We must just bide our time and take her when she's out and about," said the General.

"But who's to know that? And how are we to gather?" asked Cadger, who seemed both of a practical and a despondent turn of mind.

"Just hold your tongues and listen to me," retorted Alec.

The excited assembly was instantly silent.

"The first thing is to store plenty of ammunition."

"Ay, ay, General."

"Where had we best stow the stones, Curly?"

"In our yard. They'll never be noticed there."

"That'll do. Some time tonight, you'll all carry what stones you can—and make sure they're of a serviceable nature—to Curly's yard. He'll be watching for you. And, I say, Curly, you have an old gun, don't you?"

"Ay, I have; but she's an old one."

"Load her to the mouth. But stand well back from her when you fire if you can. It will be our signal."

"I'll take care, General."

"Scrumpie, you don't live that far from the dragon's den. You just keep your eye on her comings and goings. As soon as you see her loose in the yard, you be off to Willie Macwha. Then, Curly, you fire your gun, and if I hear the signal I'll be over in seven minutes and a half. Every one of you that hears must look after the nest, and we'll gather at Curly's. Bring your bags for the stones, them that has bags."

"But what if you don't hear, for it's a long road, General?" interposed Cadger.

"If I'm not at your yard in seven and a half minutes, Curly, send Linkum after me. He's the only one that can run. It's all that he can do, but he does it well. Once Juno's out, she's not in a hurry to get back in again."

The boys separated and went home in a state of excitement to their dinners. The sun now set between two and three o'clock and there were no long evenings to favor the plot. Perhaps their hatred of the dog would not have driven them to such extreme measures—even though she had bitten Annie Anderson—had her master been a favorite or even generally respected. But Alec knew well enough that the townspeople were not likely to sympathize with Bruce on any ill treatment of his cur.

When the dinner and the blazing fire had filled him so full of comfort that he was once more ready to encounter the cold, Alec rose to leave the house again.

"Where are you going, Alec?" inquired his mother.

"Into the yard, Mamma."

"What can, you want in the yard—it's full of snow?"

"It's just the snow I want, Mamma."

And in another moment he was under the clear blue night-heaven, with the keen, frosty air blowing on his warm cheek, busy with a wheelbarrow and shovel, slicing and shoveling in the snow. He was building a hut with it, after the fashion of the Eskimo hut, with a very thick circular wall, which began to lean toward its own center as soon as it began to rise. Often he paused in his work and turned toward the town, but no signal came. When called in to tea he gave a long wistful look townwards. Out he went again afterward but there came no news that Juno was ranging the streets, and he was forced to go to bed at last and take refuge from his disappointment in sleep.

The next day he strictly questioned all his officers as to the manner in which they had fulfilled their duty and found no just cause of complaint.

"What are you in such a state about, Alec?" asked his mother that night.

"Nothing very particular, Mamma," answered Alec, ashamed at his lack of self-command.

"You've looked out at the window twenty times in the last half hour," she persisted.

"Curly promised to burn a blue gaslight, and I wanted to see if I could see it."

Suspecting more, his mother was forced to be content with his answer.

But that night also passed without sight of the light, which Curly had said he would ignite before firing the gun. Juno kept safe in her barrel, little thinking of the machinations against her in the wide snowcovered country all around. Alec finished his Eskimo hut and with the snow falling again that night, it looked as if it had been there all winter. As it seemed likely that a long spell of white weather had set in, Alec resolved to enlarge his original ice-dwelling and was hard at work in the execution of this project on the third night, or rather late afternoon (they called it *forenight* there).

"What can that be, over at the town there?" said Mary to her mistress, as in passing she peeped out of the window.

"What is it, Mary?"

"That's just what I don't know, mem. It's a curious kind of blue light.—It's not canny.—And, preserve us all! It's cracking as well," cried Mary, as the subdued sound of a far-off explosion reached her.

This was of course no other than the roar of Curly's gun. But at the moment Alec was too busy in the depths of his snow-vault to hear or see the signals.

By and by a knock came to the kitchen door. Mary went and opened it.

"Where's Alec? Is he at home?" said a rosy boy, almost breathless from past speed and present excitement.

"He's in the yard."

The boy turned immediately and Mary shut the door.

Linkum sought Alec's snow house, and as he approached he heard Alec whistling a favorite tune as he shoveled away at the snow.

"General!" cried Linkum in ecstasy.

"Here!" answered Alec, flinging his spade down and bolting in the direction of the call. "Is it you, Linkum?"

"She's out, General."

"The devil have her if she ever gets in again, the brute! Did you go to Curly?"

"Ay, did I. He fired the gun and burned his light, and waited seven minutes and a half; and then he sent me for ye, General!"

"Confound it!" cried Alec and tore through the shrubbery and hedge, the nearest way to the road, followed by Linkum, who even at full speed was not a match for Alec. Away they flew like the wind, along the well-beaten path to the town, over the footbridge that crossed the Glamour, and full speed up the hill to Willie Macwha, who was anxiously awaiting the commander with a dozen or fifteen more. They all had their book bags, pockets, and arms filled with stones. One bag was filled and ready for Alec.

"Now," said the General, in the tone of Gideon of old, "if any of you are afraid of the brute, just go home now."

"Ay, ay, General."

But nobody stirred.

"Who's watching her?"

"Doddles, Gapey, and Goat."

"Where was she last seen?"

"Taking up with another tyke on the square."

"Come along then. This is how you're to go. We mustn't all go together. Some of you—you three—down the Back Wynd; you six up Lucky Hunter's Close; and the rest by Gowan Street; and the first at the pump waits for the rest."

"How are we to make the attack, General?"

"I'll give my orders as the case may demand," replied Alec.

And away they shot.

The muffled sounds of the feet of the various companies, as they thundered past upon the snow, roused the old wives dozing over their knitting by their fires, causing various remarks: "Some mischief o' the loons!" "Some ploy o' the laddies!" "Some devilry o' the rascals from Malison's school!"

They reached the square almost together and found Doddles at the pump, who reported that Juno had gone down into the innyard, and Gapey and Goat were watching her. Now she would have to come out to get home again, for there was no back way. So by Alec's orders they dispersed a little to avoid observation and drew gradually between the entrance of the innyard and the way Juno would take to go home.

The town was ordinarily lighted at night with oil lamps, but moonlight and snow had rendered them for some time unnecessary.

"There she is! There she is!" cried several at once in a hissing whisper of excitement.

"Hold still!" cried Alec. "Wait till I tell you. Don't you see that there's Long Tom's dog with her, and he's done nothing. We mustn't punish the innocent with the guilty."

A moment later the dogs took their leave of each other and Juno went off at a slow slouching trot in the direction of her own street.

"Close in!" cried Alec.

Juno found her way barred in a threatening manner, and sought to pass meekly by.

"Let at her, boys!" cried the General.

A storm of stones was their answer to the order, and a howl of rage and pain burst from the animal. She turned, but found that she was the center of a circle of enemies.

"Let at her! Hold at her!" yelled Alec.

And thick as hail the well-aimed stones flew from the practiced hands; though of course in the frantic rushes of the dog to escape, not half of them took effect. She darted first at one and then at another, snapping wildly, and meeting with many a kick and blow in return.

The neighbors began to look out at their shop doors and windows; for the boys, rapt in the excitement of the sport, no longer laid any restraint upon their cries. But none of the good folks cared so much to interfere, for flying stones are not pleasant to encounter. And indeed they could not clearly make out what was the matter. In a minute more a sudden lull came over the hubbub. They saw all the group gather together in a murmuring knot.

The fact was this. Although cowardly enough now, the brute, infuriated with pain, had made a determined rush at one of her antagonists, and a short hand-to-teeth struggle was now taking place, during which the stoning ceased.

"She has a grip of my leg," muttered Alec, "and I have a grip of her throat. Curly, put your hand in my jacket pocket and take out a bit of twine you'll find there."

Curly did as he was bid and drew out a yard and a half of garden line.

"Put it in a single turn round her neck, and two or three of you take a hold at each end, and pull for your lives!"

They hauled with hearty vigor, and Juno's teeth relaxed their hold of Alec's calf. In another minute her tongue was hanging out of her mouth, and when they ceased the strain she lay limp on the snow. With a shout of triumph they started off at full speed, dragging the brute by the neck through the street. Alec tried to follow them, but found his leg too painful and was forced to go limping home.

When the victors had run till they were out of breath, they stopped to confer. The result of their conference was that in solemn silence they drew the dog home to the back gate, and finding all quiet in the yard, delegated two of their company to lay the dead body in its kennel.

Curly and Linkum drew her into the yard, tumbled her into her barrel, which they set up on end, undid the string, and left Juno lying neck and tail together in ignominious peace.

Before Alec reached home his leg had swollen very large and was so painful that he could hardly limp along; for Juno had taken no passing snap but a great, strong mouthful. He concealed his condition from his mother for that night; but next morning his leg was so bad that there was no longer a possibility of hiding it. To tell a lie would have been too hard for Alec, so there was nothing for it but confession. His mother scolded him to a degree considerably beyond her own estimation of his wrongdoing, telling him he would get her into disgrace in the town as the mother of a lawless son who meddled with other people's property in a way little better than stealing.

"I fancy, Mamma, a loun's legs are aboot as muckle his ain property as the tyke was Rob Bruce's. It's no the first time she's bitten half a dizzen legs that were neither her ain nor her maister's."

Mrs. Forbes could not well answer this argument; so she took advantage of the fact that Alec had, in the excitement of self-defense, lapsed into Scottish.

"Don't talk so vulgarly to me, Alec," she said; "keep that for your ill-behaved companions in the town."

"They are no worse than I am, Mamma. I was at the bottom of it."

"I never said they were," she answered.

But in her heart she thought if they were not, there was little amiss with them.

14

•••••••••••••••••

Revenge

*A*lec was once more condemned to the sofa, and Annie had to miss him and wonder what had become of him. She always felt safe when Alec was there and grew timid when he was not, even though whole days would sometimes pass without either speaking to the other.

About noon, when all was tolerably harmonious in the school, the door opened and the face of Robert Bruce appeared, with gleaming eyes of wrath.

"God preserve us!" said Scrumpie to his neighbor. "Such a lickin' as we're gonna get! Here's Rob Bruce! Who's gone and told him?"

Some of the gang of conspirators, standing in a group near the door, stared in horror. Among them was Curly. His companions declared afterward that had it not been for the strength of the curl, his hair would have stood upright. For, following Bruce and led by the string, came an awful apparition—Juno on her own feet, a pitiable mass of caninity—looking like the resuscitated corpse of a dog that had been nine days buried.

"She's not dead after all! Devil take her, for he's in her," whispered Doddles hoarsely.

"We didn't kill her enough," murmured Curly.

And now the storm began to break. The master had gone to the door and shaken hands with his visitor, glancing with a puzzled look at the miserable animal which had just enough shape left to show that it was a dog.

"I'm very sorry, Mr. Malison, to come to you with my complaints," said Bruce; "but just look at the poor dumb animal! She couldn't come herself, so I had to bring her. Stand still, you brute!"

For Juno, having caught sight of some boy's legs, began to tug at the string with feeble earnestness—no longer, however, regarding the said legs as made for dogs to bite but as fearful instruments of vengeance, in league with stones and cords. So her straining and pulling was all homeward. But her master had brought her as chief witness against the boys and she must remain.

"Eh, lass!" he said, hauling her back by the string; "if you had but the tongue of the prophet's ass, you would soon point out the rascals that mistreated you.

But here's the just judge that'll give you your rights, and that without fee or reward.—Mr. Malison, she was one of the bonniest bicks you could ever set your eyes upon—"

A smothered laugh gurgled through the room.

"—till some of your loons—no offense, sir—I know well enough they're not yours, nor a bit like you—some of your pupils, sir, have just driven the soul out of her with stones."

"Where does the soul of a bitch live?" asked Goat, in a whisper, of the boy next to him.

"The devil knows," answered Gapey; "if it doesn't live in the bottom o' Rob Bruce's belly."

The master's wrath, ready enough to rise against boys and all their works, now showed itself in the growing redness of his face. This was not one of his worst passions—in those times he grew white—for this injury had not been done to himself.

"Can you tell me which of them did it?"

"No, sir. There must have been more than two or three at it, or she would have frightened them away. The best-natured beast in all the town!"

A decisive murmur greeted his last comment.

"William Macwha!" cried Malison.

"Here, sir."

"Come up."

Willie ascended to the august presence. He had made up his mind that, seeing so many had known all about it and some of them had already turned cowardly, it would be of no use to deny the deed.

"Do you know anything about this cruelty to the poor dog, William?" said the master.

Willie gave a Scotchman's answer, which, while evasive, was yet answer and more. "She bit me, sir."

"When? While you were stoning her?"

"No, sir. A month ago."

"You're a lying wretch, Willie Macwha, as you well know in your own conscience!" cried Bruce. "She's the quietest, kindliest beast that ever was born. See, sir; just look here. She'll let me put my hand in her mouth and take no more notice than if it were her own tongue."

Now, whether it was that the said tongue was still swollen and painful, or that Juno disapproved of the whole proceeding, I cannot tell; but the result of this proof of her temper was that she made her teeth meet through Bruce's hand.

"Curse the bitch!" he roared, snatching the hand away with the blood beginning to flow.

A laugh, not smothered this time, billowed and broke through the whole school. The fact that Bruce should be caught speaking so in public, added to the yet more delightful fact that Juno had bitten her master, was altogether too much.

"Eh! Isn't it good we didn't kill her after all?" exulted Curly.

"Good doggie," said another, patting his own knee as if to entice her to come and be petted.

"At him again, Juno!" cheered a third.

Bruce, writhing with pain and mortified at the result of his would-be proof of Juno's incapability of biting, still more mortified at having so far forgotten himself as to utter an oath, and altogether unnerved by the laughter, turned away in confusion.

"It's their fault, the bad boys! She never did the like before. They have ruined her temper," he said as he left the school, following Juno who was tugging away at the string as if she had been a blind man's dog.

"Well, what have you to say for yourself, William?" demanded Malison.

"She began it, sir."

This best of excuses could not, however, satisfy the master. The punishing mania had possibly taken fresh hold upon him. But he would ask more questions first.

"Who besides you tortured the animal?"

Curly was silent. He had neither a very high sense of honor, nor many principles to govern his behavior, but he had a considerable amount of devotion to his party, which is the highest form of conscience to be found in many.

"Tell me their names!"

Curly was still silent.

But a white-haired urchin, whom innumerable whippings, not bribe, had corrupted, cried out in a wavering voice: "Sanny Forbes was one o' them; an' he's not here, 'cause Juno bit him."

The poor creature gained little by his treachery; for the smallest of the conspirators fell on him when school was over and gave him a thrashing, which he deserved more than even one of Malison's.

But the effect of Alec's name on the master was amazing. He changed his manner at once, sent Curly to his seat, and nothing more was heard of Juno or her master.

The following morning, the neighbors across the street stared in bewildered astonishment at the place where the shop of Robert Bruce had been. Had it been possible for an avalanche to fall like a thunderbolt from the heavens, they would have supposed that one had fallen in the night and overwhelmed the house. Door and window were invisible, buried in a mass of snow. Spades and shovels in boys' hands had been busy for hours, during the night, throwing it up against the house, the door having first been blocked up with a huge snowball, which they had rolled in silence the whole length of the long street.

Bruce and his wife slept in a little room immediately behind the shop, that they might watch over their treasures; and Bruce's first movement in the morning was always into the shop to unbolt the door and take down the shutters. His astonishment when he looked upon a blank wall of snow may well be imagined. He did not question that the whole town was similarly overwhelmed. Such a snowstorm had never been heard of before, and he thought with uneasy recollection of the oath he had uttered in the schoolroom. He imagined for a brief moment that the whole of Glamerton lay overwhelmed by divine wrath, because he, under the agony of a bite from his own dog, had consigned her to a quarter where dogs and children are not admitted. In his bewilderment, he called aloud: "Nancy! Robbie! Johnnie! We're buried alive!"

"Preserve us all, Robert! What's happened?" cried his wife, rushing from the kitchen.

"*I'm* not buried that I know of," cried Robert the younger, entering from the backyard.

His father rushed out to the back door and, to his astonishment and relief, saw the whole world about him. It was a private judgment, then, upon him and his shop. And so it was—a very private judgment. It was probably because of his thoughts upon it that he never after carried complaints to Murdoch Malison.

Alec Forbes had nothing to do with this revenge. But Bruce always thought he was at the bottom of it and hated him all the more. He disliked all loons but his own, but Alec Forbes he hated above the rest. For in every way Alec was the very opposite to Bruce himself. Mrs. Bruce always followed her husband's lead, being capable only of two devotions—the one to her husband and children, and the other to the shop. Of Annie they highly and righteously disapproved, partly because they had to feed her and partly because she was friendly with Alec. This disapproval rose into dislike after their sons had told them that it was because Juno had bitten her that the boys of the school, with Alec for a leader, had served her as they had.

For the rest of Juno's existence, the moment she caught sight of a boy she fled as fast as her four bowlegs would carry her, not daring even to let her tail stick out behind her, lest it should afford a handle against her.

When Annie heard that Alec had been bitten she was miserable. She knew that his bite must be worse than hers, or he would not be kept at home. The modesty of the maidenly child made her fear to intrude, but she could not keep herself from following the path to his house to see how he was. But when she arrived she could not quite make up her mind to knock at the door, for despite the lady's kindness she was a little afraid of Mrs. Forbes. So she wandered around the side of the house until she came upon the curious heap of snow with the small round tunnel opening into it. She examined Alec's Eskimo hut all around, and then, seeing that the tunnel into it was hollow, she entered. It was dark, with a faint light from the evening glimmering through the roof, but not so cold as in the outer air where a light, frosty wind was blowing. Annie seated herself and before long, as was her custom, fell fast asleep.

In the meantime, Alec was sitting alone by the light of the fire, finishing the last of a story. His mother had gone into town. When he was through reading he got a candle and went out into the descending darkness to see how his little snow room looked in candlelight. As he entered he could hardly believe his eyes. A figure was there—motionless—dead perhaps. If he had not come then, Annie might indeed have slept on till her sleep was too deep for any voice of the world to rouse her.

Her face was pale and deathly cold, and it was with difficulty that he woke her. He took hold of her hands, but she did not move. He sat down, took her in his arms, spoke to her—became frightened when she did not answer, and began shaking her. Still she would not open her eyes. But he knew she was not dead yet, for he could feel her heart beating. At length she lifted her eyelids, looked up in his face, gave a low happy laugh, like the laugh of a dreaming child, and was fast asleep again the next moment.

Alec hesitated no longer. He tugged her out of the chamber, then rose with her in his arms and carried her into the parlor and laid her down on the rug before the fire with a pillow under her head. When Mrs. Forbes came home, she found Alec reading and Annie sleeping beside the fireside. Before his mother had recovered from her surprise, Alec had the first word. "Mamma!" he said, "I found her sleeping in my snow hut outside; and if I hadn't brought her in, she would have been dead by this time."

Poor little darling, thought Mrs. Forbes. She stooped and drew the child back from the fire; after making the tea, she proceeded to take off Annie's bonnet and shawl. By the time she had got rid of them, Annie was beginning to move and Alec rose to go to her.

"Let her alone," said his mother. "Let her come to herself slowly. Come to the table."

Alec obeyed. They could see that Annie had opened her eyes and lay staring at the fire. What was she thinking about? She had fallen asleep in the snow hut and here she now was by a bright fire!

"Annie, dear, come to your tea," were the first words she heard. She rose and went, and sat down at the table with a smile, taking it all as the gift of God, or a good dream, and never asking how she had come to be so happy. She carried that happiness with her across the bridge, through the town and up to her garret. Pleasant dreams came naturally that evening.

15

· · · · · · · · · · · · · · · · · ·

Alec's Boat

The spirit of mischief had never been so thoroughly aroused in the youth of Glamerton as it was this winter. The snow lay very heavy and thick, while almost every day a fresh fall added to its depth and the cold strengthened their impulses to muscular exertion.

"The loons are jist growin' t' be perfect deevils," growled Charlie Chapman, the wool carder, as he bolted into his own shop, the remains of a snowball melting down the back of his neck. "We must hae another constable to hald them in order," he muttered.

The existing force of law was composed of one long-legged, short-bodied, middle-aged man who was so slow in his motions that the boys called him "Stumpin' Steenie" and stood in no more awe of him than they did of his old cow—which, her owner being a widower, they called *Mrs. Stephen*. So there was some ground for the wool carder's remark. How much a second constable would have helped, however, is doubtful.

"I never saw such gallows birds," chimed in a farmer's wife who was standing in the shop. "They had a rope across the Wast Wynd in the snow an' down I came on my knees as sure's yer names Charles Chapman—wi' more o' my legs oot o' my coats than was altogether to my credit."

"I'm sure ye can hae no reason t' take shame o' yer legs," was the gallant rejoinder; to which their owner replied with a laugh, "They weren't made fer public inspection, anyway."

"Hoot! Nobody saw 'em. I'll warrant ye didn't lie there long! But the loons—they're jist past all! Did ye hear what they did t' Rob Bruce?"

"Fegs! They tell me they all but buried him alive."

"Ow! Ay! But there's a later story."

Here Andrew Mellon, the clothier, dropped in and Chapman turned to him, "Did ye hear what the loons did t' Robert Bruce the night afore last?"

"No. What was that? They hae a spite at puir Rob, I believe."

"Weel, it didn't look altogether like respect, I must allow. I was standin' at the counter o' his shop an' Robert was servin' a little bairn wi' a pennyworth o' candy, when all at once there came such a blast an' a reek fit t' smother ye oot o' the fire an' the shop was full o' the reek an' smoke afore ye knew it. 'Preserve us all!' cried Rob; but before he could say another word, from inside the house, scushlin in her old shoes, comes Nancy runnin' an' opens the door wi' a screech: 'Preserve's all!' yelled she, 'Robert, the chimneys' plugged!' An' fegs! The house was as full as it could be, from cellar t' attic, o' the blackest smoke that ever burned from coal. Out we ran, an' it was a sight t' see the creature Bruce wi' his long neck lookin' up at the chimneys. But not a spark came out o' them—or smoke either, for that matter. It was easy t' see what was amiss. The loons had been up the riggin' an' flung a handful o' blastin' powder down each smokin' chimney an' then covered them wi' a big divot o' turf upon the mouth o' them. Not one o' them was in sight, but I doubt if any o' them was far away. There was nothin' for it but t' get a ladder an' jist go up an' take off the pot lids. But eh! Poor Robert was jist rampin' wi' rage! Not that he said much, for he dared not open his mouth for fear o' swearin'; an' Robert wouldn't swear, ye know."

"What laddies were they, Charles, do ye know?" asked Andrew.

"There's a heap o' them up to tricks. If I don't hae the rheumateese houndin' away between my shoulders tonight, it won't be because o' them. For as I came over from the ironmonger's there, I jist got a ball in the back o' my neck that almost sent me a fallin' with my snoot in the snow. An' there it stuck, an' at this present moment it's runnin' down the small o' my back as if it were a stream down a hillside. We must hae another constable!"

"Hoot, hoot, Charles! Ye don't need a constable t' dry yer back. Go t' yer wife with it," said Andrew. "She'll give ye a dry shirt. Let the laddies work it off. As long as they keep their hand from what doesn't belong to them, I don't mind a little mischief now an' then. They'll not turn out the worse for a prank or two."

The fact was, none of the boys would have dreamed of interfering with Andrew Mellon. Everybody respected him, not because he was an elder in the church but because he was a good-tempered, kindly, honest man.

While Alec was confined to the house with his wounded leg, he had been busy inventing all kinds of gainful employment for the period of the snow; his lessons never occupied much of his thoughts. The first day of his return to society, when school was over, he set off rejoicing in his freedom, still revolving in his mind what he was to do next, for he wanted some steady employment with an end in view. In the course of his solitary walk he came to the Wan Water, the other river that flowed through the wide valley—and wan enough it was now with its snow-sheet over it. As he stood looking at its still, dead face, all at once a summer vision of live water arose in his mind. He thought of how delightful it would be to go sailing down the rippling river with the green fields all about him and the hot afternoon sun over his head. His next thought was both an idea and a resolve. Why shouldn't he build a boat? He *would* build a boat. He would set about it at once. Here was work for the rest of the winter!

His first step must be to go home and have his dinner; his next—to consult George Macwha, who had been a ship carpenter in his youth. He would run over in the evening before George had finished his work and commit the plan to his judgment.

It was a still, lovely night, clear and frosty. Alec walked on till the windows of the town began to throw shadows across the snow. The street was empty. From end to end nothing moved but an occasional shadow. As he came near to Macwha's shop he had to pass a row of cottages which stood with their backs to a steep slope. Here too all was silent as a frozen city.

But when he was about opposite the middle of the row, he heard a stifled laugh and then a kind of muffled sound as of hurrying steps. In a moment more, every door in the row was torn open and out bolted the inhabitants—here an old woman, there a shoemaker with an awl in his hands, here a tailor with his shears, and there a whole family of several trades and ages. Everyone rushed into the middle of the road, turned around, and looked up. Then arose such a clamor of tongues that it broke on the still air like a storm.

"What's up, Betty?" asked Alec of a decrepit old creature, bent almost double with rheumatism, who was trying hard to see something or other in the air or on the roof of her cottage.

But before she could speak, the answer came to him in another form, addressing itself to his nose instead of his ears. For out of the cottages floated clouds of smoke, pervading the air with a variety of scents—burning oak bark, burning leather cuttings, damp firewood and peat, the cooking of red herrings, the boiling of porridge, the baking of oatcake, etc. Happily for all the inhabitants, "the deevil loons" had used no powder here.

But the old woman, looking round when Alec spoke and seeing that he was one of the obnoxious schoolboys, broke out upon him. "Go an' take the divot off my chimney, Alec, like a good lad! Ye shouldn't play such tricks on poor old folks like me. I'm jist in tears from the smoke in my old eyes." She wiped her eyes with an apron.

Alec did not wait to clear himself of an accusation so gently put, but was on the roof of Lucky Lapp's cottage before she had finished her appeal to his generosity. He pitched the divot halfway down the hillside at the back of the cottage. Then he scrambled from one chimney to the other and went on pitching the sods down the hill. At length two of the inhabitants, who had climbed up at the other end of the row, met him, and taking him for a repentant sinner at best made him their prisoner, much to his amusement, and brought him down, saying that it was too bad of gentlefolks' sons to persecute the poor in that way.

"I didn't do it," Alec assured them.

"Don't lie," came the curt rejoinder.

"I'm not lying."

"Who did it then?"

"I can guess. And it shan't happen again if I can help it."

"Tell us who did it."

"I won't say names."

"He's one o' them!"

"The fowl thief, take him! I'll give him a hidin'," said a burly shoemaker coming up. "The loons are not to be borne with any longer." He caught Alec by the arm.

"I didn't do it!" persisted Alec.

"Who killed Rob Bruce's dog?" asked the shoemaker, squeezing Alec's arm to point the question.

"I did," answered Alec, "and I will do yours the same good turn if he bites children."

"And quite right too!" put in the shoemaker's wife. "Let him go. I'll be bound he's not one o' them."

"Tell us about it, then. How did ye come t' be here?"

"I went up to take the divot off Lucky Lapp's chimney. Ask her. Once up I thought I might give the rest of you a good turn, and this is what I get for it."

"Well, well! Come in an' warm ye, then," said the shoemaker, convinced at last.

So Alec went in, had a chat with them, and then went on to George Macwha's.

The carpenter took to his scheme at once. Alec was a fair hand at all sorts of work, and being on the friendliest terms with Macwha, it was soon arranged that the vessel should be laid in the end of the workshop and that, under George's directions and what help son Willie chose to render, Alec should build his boat himself. Just as they concluded their discussion, in came Willie, wiping some traces of blood from his nose. He pantomimed a gesture of vengeance at Alec.

"What have ye been after now, laddie?" asked his father.

"Alec's jist given me a bloody nose," said Willie.

"What do you mean, Curly?" asked Alec in amazement.

"That divot that ye flung off Lucky Lapp's chimney," said Curly, "came right onto the back o' my head as I lay on the hillside. Ye pretend ye didn't see me, no doubt."

"I say, Curly," said Alec, putting his arm around his shoulders and leading him aside, "we must have no more of this kind of work. It's shameful. Don't you see the difference between choking an ill-fared tyke of a dog and choking a poor widow's chimney?"

"'Twas only for fun."

"It's no fun that both sides can't laugh at, Curly."

"Rob Bruce wasn't laughing when he brought the bick to the school, nor yet when he went home again."

"That wasn't for fun, Curly. That was downright earnest."

Curly paused a moment to mull it over in his mind. "Well, well, Alec; there is a difference. Say no more aboot it."

"No more will I. But if I was you, Curly, I would take Lucky a sack of kindling in the morning."

"I'll take them tonight, Alec. Father, hae ye an old sack?"

"There's one up in the loft. What do ye want with a sack?"

But Curly was in the loft almost before the question had left his father's lips. He was down again in a moment and on his knees filling the sack with shavings and all the chips he could find. And in a few moments more Curly was off to Widow Lapp with his bag of firing.

"He's a fine boy, that Willie of yours, George," said Alec to Willie's father. "He only needs to have a thing well put before him and he acts upon it directly."

"It's good for him he makes a cronie o' you, Alec. There's a heap o' mischief in him.—Where's he off wi' that bag?"

Alec told the whole story, much to the satisfaction of George, who could appreciate the repentance of his son. From that day on he thought even more of young Alec, and of Willie as well.

"Now, Curly," said Alec as soon as he reappeared with the empty sack, "your father's going to let me build a boat, and you must help me."

"What's the use of a boat in this weather?" said Curly.

"Ye buffoon!" returned his father. "Ye never look an inch past the point o' yer nose. Ye wouldn't think o' a boat afore the spring. The summer would be over an' the water frozen again afore ye had it built. Look at Alec there. He's worth ten o' ye!"

"I know that every bit as well as ye do, Father. Jist start us off with it, Father."

"I can't attend to it just now, but I'll get ye started tomorrow morning."

So here was an end to the troubles of the townsfolk from the loons, and without any increase of the constabulary force; for Curly being withdrawn from the ranks there was no one else of sufficiently inventive energy to take the lead. Curly soon had both this hands quite occupied with boat building.

16

....

Dowie

*E*very afternoon now, the moment dinner was over, Alec set off for the workshop and did not return till eight o'clock or sometime later. Mrs. Forbes did not at all relish this change in his habits, but had the good sense not to interfere.

One day he persuaded her to go with him and see how the boat was getting on. This caused in her some sympathy with his work. For there was the boat—a skeleton it is true, and not nearly ready for the clothing of its planks or its final skin of paint—yet an undeniable boat to the motherly eye of hope. And there were Alec and Willie working away before her eyes. The little quiet chat she had with George Macwha in which he lauded the praise of her boy also went a long way to reconcile her to his nightly desertion of her.

But Mrs. Forbes never noticed the little figure lying in a corner half-buried in wood shavings and fast asleep. It was, of course, Annie Anderson. Having heard of the new occupation of her hero, she had one afternoon three weeks before found herself at George's shop door. It seemed that she had followed her feet and they had taken her there before she knew where they were going. Peeking in, she had watched Alec and Willie for some time at their work without showing herself. But George, who had come up behind her as she stood, took her by the hand and led her in, saying kindly: "Here's a new apprentice, Alec. She wants to learn boat buildin'."

"Annie, is that you?" said Alec. "Come on in. There's a fine heap of spales you can sit on and see what we're about."

And so saying he seated her on the shavings and half-buried her with an armful more to keep her warm.

"Close the door, Willie," he added. "She'll be cold. She's not working, you see."

Whereupon Willie shut the door, and Annie found herself very comfortable indeed. There she sat, in perfect contentment, watching the progress of the boat—a progress not very perceptible to her inexperienced eyes. But after she had sat for a good while in silence, she looked up at Alec and said: "Is there nothing I can do to help you, Alec?"

"Nothing, Annie. Lassies can't saw or plane, you know."

Again she was silent for a long time, and then with a sigh she looked up and said: "Alec, I'm so cold!"

"I'll bring my plaid to wrap you in tomorrow."

Annie's heart bounded with delight, for here was what amounted to an express invitation to return.

"But come with me," Alec went on, "and we'll soon get you warm again. Give me your hand."

Annie gave Alec her hand, and he lifted her out of the heap of spales and led her away. She never thought of asking where he was leading her. They had not gone far down the street when a roaring sound fell upon her ear, growing louder and louder as they went on till they turned a sharp corner, and there saw the smithy fire. The door of the smithy's shop was open, and they could see the smith at work some distance off. The fire glowed with gathered rage at the impudence of the bellows blowing in its face. The huge smith, with one arm flung over the shoulder of the bellows, urged the insulting party to the contest while he stirred up the other to increased ferocity by poking a piece of iron into the very middle of it.

Annie was delighted to look at it, but there was a certain fierceness about the whole affair that made her shrink from going nearer. She could not help feeling a little afraid of the giant smith with his brawny arms that twisted and tortured iron bars all day long—and his black, fierce-looking face. Again he stooped, caught up a great iron spoon, dipped it into a tub of water, and poured the spoonful on the fire—a fresh insult, at which it hissed and sputtered, like one of the fiery flying serpents of which she had read in her Bible—gigantic, dragon-like creatures to her imagination. But not the slightest motion of her hand lying in Alec's indicated reluctance as he led her into the shop and right up to the wrathful man.

"Peter Whaup, here's a lassie that's most frozen to death with cold. Will you take her in and let her stand by your fire and warm herself?"

"I'll do that, Alec. Come in, my bairn. What do they call ye?"

"Annie Anderson."

"Ow, ay! I know all about ye well enough. Ye can leave her with me, Alec; I'll look after her."

"I must go back to my boat, Annie," said Alec apologetically, "but I'll come back for you again."

So Annie was left with the smith, of whom she was not the least afraid now that she had heard him speak. With his leather apron he swept a space on the front of the elevated hearth of the forge, clear of dust and cinders. Then, having wiped his hands on the same apron, he lifted the girl as tenderly as if she had been a baby and set her down on this spot, about a yard from the fire and on a level with it. And there she sat in front of the smith, looking back and forth between the smith and the fire. He asked her a great many questions about herself and the Bruces, and her former life at home; and every question he asked he put in a yet kindlier voice. Sometimes he would stop in the middle of blowing, lean forward with his arm on the handle of the bellows, and look full in the child's face till she was through answering him.

"Ay, ay!" he would say, resuming his blowing slowly, with eyes that shone in the light of the fire. For this terrible smith's heart was just like his fire. He was a dreadful fellow for quarreling when he got a drop too much to drink. But to this little woman-child his ways were as soft and tender as a mother's.

"An' ye say ye liked it at the farm best?" he said.

"Ay. But, you see, my father died—"

"I know that, my bairn. The Lord hold tight to ye!"

It was not often that Peter Whaup indulged in a pious ejaculation. But this was a genuine one, and may be worth recording for the sake of Annie's answer.

"I'm thinking He holds tight to us all, Mr. Whaup."

Then she told him about the rats and the cat. For hardly a day passed at this time without Annie not merely retelling it but reflecting on it. And when she was done the smith drew the back of his hand across both his eyes and then pressed both eyes hard with the thumb and forefinger of his right hand. But he hardly needed to do so, for Annie would never have noticed his tears and the heat from the fire would have quickly dried them. Then he pulled out the red-hot iron bar which he seemed to have forgotten ever since Annie came in, and standing with his back to her to protect her from the sparks, he put it on his anvil and began to lay on it as if in a fury while the sparks flew from his blows. Then, as if anxious to hear the child speak again, he put the iron once more in the fire, proceeded to rouse the wrath of the coals, and said: "Ye knew James Dow, then?"

"Ay, well that. I knew Dowie as well as Brownie."

"Who was Brownie?"

"Ow, nobody but my own cow."

"An' James was kind to ye?"

To this question no reply followed. But Peter, who stood looking at her, saw her lips and the muscles of her face quivering an answer, which if uttered at all could come only in sobs and tears.

But the sound of approaching steps and voices restored her composure. Over the half door of the shop appeared two men, each bearing on his shoulder the shares of two plows to be sharpened. The instant she saw them she tumbled off her perch, and before they had got the door opened she was halfway to it, crying, "Dowie! Dowie!" In another instant she was lifted high in Dowie's arms.

"My little mistress!" he exclaimed kissing her. "How do ye come to be here?"

"I'm safe enough here, Dowie. Don't be afraid. I'll tell you all about it. Alec's in George Macwha's shop yonder."

"And who's Alec?" asked Dowie.

Leaving them to their private communications, James Dow's young companion and the smith set to work sharpening the blades of the plows. In about fifteen minutes Alec returned to the shop.

Addressing herself to Dowie, who still held her in his arms, Annie said, "This is Alec, that I told you about. He's right good to me. Alec, here's Dowie, that I like better than anybody in the world."

She turned and kissed the bronzed face, which was a clean face notwithstanding the contrary appearance given it by a beard of three days' growth, which Annie's kiss was too full of love to mind.

Later, Dowie carried Annie home in his arms, and on the way she told him all about the kindness of Alec and his mother. He asked her many questions about the Bruces. But her patient nature, and the instinctive feeling that it would make Dowie unhappy, caused her to withhold representing the hardships of her position in too strong colors. Dowie, however, had his own thoughts on the matter.

"How are ye tonight, Mr. Dow?" said Robert, who treated him with oily respect because he was not only acquainted with all Annie's affairs but was a kind of natural if not legal guardian of her and her property. "And where did you fall in with this stray lammie of ours?"

"She's been with me all this time," answered Dow, declining with Scottish instinct to give an answer before he understood the drift of the question. A Scotsman would always like the last question first.

"She's some ill for running out," said Bruce, with soft words addressed to Dow, and a cutting look flung at Annie, "without asking permission, and we don't know where she goes. That's not right for such small girls."

"Never ye mind, Mr. Bruce," replied Dow. "I know her better than ye, not meanin' any offense, seein' she was in my arms afore she was a week old. Let her go where she likes, an' if she does what she shouldn't do, I'll bear all the blame for it."

Now there was no great anxiety about Annie's welfare in the minds of Mr. and Mrs. Bruce. The shop and their own children—chiefly the former—occupied their thoughts. The less trouble they had from the presence of Annie the better pleased they were—provided they could always escape the judgment of neglect. Hence it was that Annie's absences were but little inquired into.

But Bruce did not like the influence that James Dow had with her; and before they retired for the night, he had another lecture ready for Annie.

"Annie," he told her, "it's not becoming for one in your station to be so familiar. You'll be a young lady someday, and it's not right to take up with servants. There's James Dow, just a laboring man, and beneath your station altogether, and he takes you up in his arms as if you were a child of his own. It's not proper."

"I like James Dow better than anybody in the whole world," said Annie, "except—"

Here she stopped short. She would not expose her heart to the gaze of this man.

"Except who?" urged Bruce.

"I'm not going to say," returned Annie firmly.

"You're a perverse lassie," said Bruce, pushing her away with forceful acidity in the combination of tone and action.

She walked off to bed, caring nothing about his rebuke. Since Alec's kindness had opened to her a well of water of life, she had almost ceased to suffer from the ungeniality of her guardians. She forgot them as soon as she was out of their sight. And certainly they were better to forget than to remember.

17
Ballads

*A*s soon as she was alone in her room, Annie drew from her pocket a parcel which Dowie had brought for her on their way home. When undone it revealed two or three tallow candles! But how would she get a light? For this was long before matches had risen upon the horizon of Glamerton. There was but one way.

She waited, sitting on the edge of her bed in the cold and darkness, until every sound in the house had ceased. Then she stepped cautiously down the old stairs, which would crack now and then, however gentle she attempted to be.

It was the custom in all the houses of Glamerton to *rest* the fire; that is, to keep it gently alive all night by the help of a *truff,* sod cut from the top of a peat moss—a coarse peat in fact, more loose and porous than the proper peat—which they laid close down upon the fire, destroying most of the draught for its live coals. To this sealed fountain of light the little maiden was creeping through the dark house with one of her candles in her hand.

A pretty study she would have made for an artist, her face close to the grate, mouth puckered up to do its duty as a bellows, one hand holding a twisted piece of paper between the bars, while she blew at the live but reluctant fire, a glow spreading over her face at each breath and then fading as the breath ceased till at last the paper caught.

Thus she lit her candle and again with careful steps made her way back up to her own room. Setting the candle in a hole in the floor left by the departure of a knot, she opened her box in which lay the few books her aunt had thrown into it when she left her old home. One of these contained poems of a little-known Scottish poet her father had been fond of reading. She had read him now and then too when she discovered a poem which happened to strike her fancy. It was very cold work at midnight in winter, and in a garret too, but she feared that the open enjoyment of such a book in the sight of any of the Bruces would only lead to its being confiscated as "altogether unsuitable for one so young."

When she entered George Macwha's workshop the next evening, she found the two boys already busy at their work. Without interrupting them she took her place on the heap of shavings which had remained undisturbed since the previous night. As she sat, unconsciously from her mouth began to come fragments of one of the ballads she had read several times from her father's book. The boys did not know what to make of it at first, hearing something come all at once from Annie's lips which broke upon the silence like an alien sound. But they said nothing until she had finished all she could remember:

"O lat me in, my bonny lass!
    It's a lang road ower the hill;
And the flauchterin' snaw began to fa',
    As I cam' by the mill."

She continued for several more stanzas until her memory failed her.

George Macwha, who was at work in the other end of the shop when she began, had drawn near, chisel in hand, and joined the listeners.

"Well done, Annie!" he exclaimed as soon as she had finished, feeling very shy and awkward at what she had done.

"Say it over again, Annie," encouraged Alec.

This was music to her ears! Could she have wished for more?

So she repeated it again, this time adding still another verse that came back to her.

"Eh, Annie! That's real bonnie. Where did you get it?" he asked.

"In an old book of my father's."

"Is there any more like it."

"Ay, several," replied the lassie.

"Just learn another, will you, before tomorrow?"

"I'll do that, Alec."

"Didn't you like it, Curly?" asked Alec, for Curly had said nothing.

"Ay, fegs!" was Curly's emphatic and uncritical reply.

Such a reception to her verses motivated Annie wonderfully, and she continued her midnight reading with heightened enthusiasm. Now she also carried the precious volume, which she hoped would bind her yet more closely to the boat and its builders, to and from school. Practicing verses the whole way as she went, Annie began taking a roundabout road that her cousins might not interrupt her or discover her pursuit.

A rapid thaw set in, and up through the vanishing whiteness dawned the dark colors of mire and dirt on the wintry landscape. But once the snow had vanished a hard black frost set it. The surface of the slow-flowing Glamour and of the swifter Wan Water were chilled and stiffened to ice, which grew thicker and stronger every day. And now, there being no coverlet of snow upon it, the boys came out in troops. In their ironclad shoes and their clumsy skates, they skimmed along those floors of delight that the winter had laid for them. Alec and Willie left their boat—almost forgot it for a time—repaired their skates, joined their schoolfellows, and shot along the solid water with the banks flying past them.

For many afternoons and into the early night, Alec and Curly held on to the joyful sport, and Annie was for a time left lonely. But she was neither disconsolate nor idle. To the boat and to her they must eventually return. She still went to the shop now and then to see George Macwha, who, of an age beyond the seduction of ice and skates, kept on steadily at his work. To him she would repeat a ballad or two at his request, and then go home to learn another. This was becoming, however, a work of some difficulty, for her provision of candles was exhausted and she had no money with which to buy more. The last candle had come to a tragic end. Hearing footsteps approaching her room one morning, before she had put her candle away in its usual safety in her box, she hastily poked it into one of the holes of the floor and forgot it. When she sought it at night it was gone. Her first dread was that she had been found out; but hearing nothing of it, she concluded that her enemies the rats had carried it off and devoured it.

"Devil choke them on the wick o' it!" exclaimed Curly when she told him the next day, seeking a partner in her grief.

But she soon faced a greater difficulty. It was not long before she had exhausted the contents of the little book of her father's. There being no more of that type among the contents of her chest, she thought where she might find another, and at last came to the resolution of applying to Mr. Cowie, the clergyman. Without consulting anyone, she knocked at Mr. Cowie's door the very next afternoon.

"Could I see the minister?" she said to the maid.

"I don't know. What do you want?" was the maid's reply.

But Annie was Scottish too and perhaps perceived that she would have but a small chance of being admitted if she revealed the object of her request to the servant. So she only replied, "I want to see himself, if you please."

"Well, come in and I will tell him. What's your name?"

"Annie Anderson."

"Where do you live?"

"At the Bruces', in the Wast Wynd."

The maid went and presently returned with the message that she was to go up the stairs. She conducted her up to the study where the minister sat—a room, to Annie's amazement, filled with books from the top to the bottom of every wall. Mr. Cowie held out his hand to her and said, "Well, my little maiden, what do you want?"

"Please, sir, would you lend me a songbook?"

"A psalm book?" said the minister, supposing he had not heard correctly.

"No, sir, I have a psalm book at home. It's a songbook that I want, a book of poems and ballads."

Now the minister was one of the old school—a very worthy, kindhearted man. He knew what some of his Lord's words meant, and among them certain words about little children. In addition he had an instinctive feeling that to be kind to little children was an important branch of his office. So he drew Annie close to him as he sat in his easy chair, and said in the gentlest way: "And what do you want a songbook for, dawtie?"

"To learn bonnie songs out of it, sir. Don't you think they're the bonniest things in the world?"

For Annie had by this time learned to love ballad verse above everything but Alec and Dowie.

"And what kind of poems do you like?" the clergyman asked, instead of replying.

"I like them best that make you cry, sir."

At every answer she looked up in his face with her open, clear-blue eyes. And the minister began to love, not merely because she was a child, but because she was this child.

"Do you sing them?" he asked, after a little pause spent gazing into the face of the child.

"Na, na. I only say them. I don't know the tunes."

"And do you say them to Mr. Bruce?"

"Mr. Bruce, sir! Mr. Bruce would say I was daft. I wouldn't say them to him, sir, for all the sweeties in his shop."

"Well, who do you say them to?"

"To Alec Forbes and Willie Macwha. They're building a boat, sir; and they like to have me by them to say songs to them while they work. And I like it right well."

"It'll be a lucky boat, surely," declared the minister, "to rise to the sound of rhyme, like some old Norse warship."

"I don't know, sir," responded Annie, who certainly did not know what he meant.

"Well, let's see what we can find for you, Annie," said the minister, rising from his chair and taking her by the hand.

He led her into the dining room to ask his daughters' assistance in finding a suitable book. There tea was all laid out. He led Annie to the table and she went without a questioning thought or a feeling of doubt. It was a profound pleasure to her not to know what was coming next, provided someone whom she loved knew. So she sat down to the tea with the perfect composure of submission to a superior will. It never occurred to her that she had no right to be there, for had not the minister himself led her there? And his daughters were very kind and friendly. In the course of the meal, Mr. Cowie told them the difficulty before him, and one of his daughters said that she might be able to find what the girl wanted. After tea she left the room and returned presently with two volumes of ballads of all sorts—some old, some new, some Scottish, some English. She put the books in Annie's hands. The child eagerly opened one of the volumes and glanced at a page: it sparkled with just the right ore of ballad words. The color of delight grew in her face. She closed the book as if she could not trust herself to look at it while the others were looking at her, and said with a sigh: "Eh, mem! You won't trust me with *both* of them?"

"Yes, I will," assured Miss Cowie. "I am sure you will take care of them."

"That—I—will," returned Annie with an honesty and determination of purpose that made a great impression on Mr. Cowie. She ran home some time later with a feeling of richness such as she had never before experienced.

Her first business was to scamper up to her room and hide the precious treasures in her chest, there to wait all night like the buried dead for the coming morning.

When she confessed to Mr. Bruce that she had had tea with the minister, he held up his hands in the manner which commonly expresses amazement. But what the peculiar character or ground of the amazement was would have to remain entirely unrevealed, for he said not a single word to explain the gesture.

The next time Annie went to see the minister, it was on a very different quest than the loan of a songbook.

18

Murdoch Malison

One afternoon as Alec went home to dinner, he was considerably surprised to find Mr. Malison leaning on one of the rails of the footbridge over the Glamour, looking down on its frozen surface. There was nothing so unusual in this, but what was surprising was that the scholars seldom encountered the master anywhere except in school. Alec thought to pass, but the moment his foot was on the bridge the master lifted himself up from the railing and turned toward him.

"Well, Alec," he said, "and where have you been?"

"To get a new strap for my skates," answered Alec.

"You're fond of skating, are you, Alec?"

"Yes, sir."

"I used to be when I was a boy. Have you had your dinner?"

"No, sir."

"Then I suppose neither has your mother?"

"She never does until I get home, sir."

"Then I won't intrude on her. I did mean to call this afternoon."

"She will be very glad to see you, sir. Come and take a share of what there is."

"I think I had better not, Alec."

"Do, sir. I'm sure she will make you welcome."

Mr. Malison hesitated. Alec pressed him. He yielded, and they went along the road together.

The school portion of Mr. Malison's life was, both inwardly and outwardly, very different from the rest. The moment he was out of school, the whole character—certainly the conduct—of the man changed. He was now as meek and gentle in speech and behavior as any mother could have desired.

Nor was the change a hypocritical one. He was glad enough to accept utter responsibility for that part of his time spent in the schoolroom. On the other hand, the master rarely interfered with what the boys did out of school, only when pressure from without was brought to bear upon him—as in the case of Juno. Therefore, between the two parts of the day, as they passed through the life of the master, there was almost as little connection as between the waking and sleeping hours of a sleepwalker.

But as he leaned over the rail of the bridge where a rare impulse to movement had driven him, his thoughts had turned upon Alec Forbes and his antagonism. Out of school he could not help feeling that the boy had not been very far wrong, however subversive of authority his behavior had been. But it was not therefore the less mortifying to recall how he had been treated by the lad. He was compelled to acknowledge to himself that it was a mercy Alec was not one to follow up his advantage by turning the rest of the school against him, which would have been ready enough to follow such a victorious leader. So there was but one way of setting matters right, as Mr. Malison had generosity enough left within him to perceive; and that was to make a friend of his adversary. Indeed, in the depths of every human breast, reconciliation is the only victory which can give true satisfaction. Nor was the master the only one to gain by the resolve which thus arose in his mind the very moment before he felt Alec's footsteps upon the bridge.

They walked together to Howglen, talking kindly the whole way; to which talk, and most likely to which kindness between then, a little incident had contributed as well. Alec had that day translated a passage of Virgil with remarkable accuracy, greatly pleasing to the master, who, however, had no idea what had caused this isolated success. The passage had reference to the setting of sails, and Alec could not rest till he had satisfied himself about its meaning. So he had with some difficulty cleared away the mists that clung about the words, till at length he pictured in his mind and understood the facts found in the section.

Alec had never had praise from Mr. Malison before—at least none that had made any impression on him—and he found it very sweet. And through the pleasure dawned the notion that perhaps he might be a scholar after all if he put his mind to it. Mrs. Forbes, seeing the pleasure on Alec's face, received Mr. Malison with more than the usual cordiality, forgetting once he was present before her eyes the former bitterness she had felt toward him.

As soon as dinner was over Alec rushed off to the river and his boat, leaving his mother and the master together. Mrs. Forbes brought out a bottle of wine and Mr. Malison filled a glass for himself and his hostess.

"We'll make a man of Alec someday yet," the schoolmaster offered.

"Indeed!" returned Mrs. Forbes, somewhat irritated at the suggestion of any difficulty in the way of Alec's ultimate manhood. Perhaps she was glad for the opportunity of speaking her mind at last. "Indeed, Mr. Malison, you made him a bonnie monsieur a month ago! It would do you well to try your hand at making a man of him now."

For a moment the dominie was taken aback and sat over his wineglass growing red. The despotism he exercised in the school, even though exercised with a certain sense of justice and right, made the autocrat, out of school, cower before the parents of his helpless subjects. With this quailing in his heart he perceived that his only chance was to throw himself on the generosity of a woman. He said: "Well, ma'am, if you had to keep seventy boys and girls quiet, and hear their lessons at the same time, perhaps you would feel yourself in danger of doing in haste what you might repent at leisure."

"Well, well, Mr. Malison, we'll talk no more about it. My laddie's none the worse for it. And I hope you *will* make a man of him someday, as you say."

"He translated a passage of Virgil today in a manner that surprised me."

"Did he though? He's not a dunce, I know. If it weren't for that stupid boat he and William Macwha are building, he might be made a scholar. George should have more sense than to encourage such a waste of time and money. He's always wanting something or other for the boat, and I confess I can't find it in my heart to refuse him, for whatever he may be at school, he's a good boy at home, Mr. Malison."

But the schoolmaster did not reply at once, for a light had dawned on him: this was the secret of Alec's translation—a secret worth his finding out. One can hardly believe that this was his first revelation that a practical interest is the strongest incitement to learning. But such was the case.

He answered after a moment's pause, "I suspect, ma'am, on the contrary, that the boat, of which I had heard nothing till now, was Alec's private tutor in the passage of Virgil."

"I don't understand you, Mr. Malison."

"I mean, ma'am, that his interest in his boat made him take an interest in those lines about ships and their rigging. So the boat taught him to translate them."

"I see . . ."

"And that makes me doubt whether we shall be able to make him learn anything to good purpose that he does not take an interest in."

"Well, what *do* you think he is fit for, Mr. Malison? I should like him to be able to be something other than a farmer, whatever he may settle down to at last."

Mrs. Forbes thought, whether wisely or not, that as long as she was able to manage the farm, Alec might as well be otherwise employed. And she had ambition for her son as well. But the master was able to make no definite suggestion. Alec seemed to have no special qualification for any profession; for the mechanical and constructive faculties alone had reached a high point of development in him as yet. So after a long talk, his mother and the schoolmaster had come no nearer than before to a determination of what he was fit for. The interview, however, restored a good understanding between them.

19
• • • • • • • • • • • • • • • • • •

Religious Talk

It was upon a Friday night that the frost finally broke up. A day of wintry rain followed, dreary and depressing. But the two boys, Alec and Willie, had a refuge from the weather in their boat building. In the early evening of the following Saturday, they were in close conversation about a doubtful point in their labor. George Macwha entered the shop in conversation with Thomas Crann, the mason, who, being quite interrupted by the rain, had the more leisure to bring his mental powers to bear upon the condition of his neighbors.

" 'Tis a sad pity, George," he was saying as he entered, "that a man like ye wouldn't once take a thought an' consider the end o' everything the sun shines upon."

"How do ye know, Thomas, that I don't take such thought?"

"Do ye say that ye *do*, George?"

"I'm a bit o' a Protestant, though I'm no Missionary."

"Well, well. I can only say that I hae seen no signs o' a savin' seriousness about ye, George. Ye're too taken up wi' the world."

"How do ye come to think that? Ye build houses, an' I make doors for them. And they'll both be standin' after both ye and me's laid in the ground. It's well known that ye have a bit o' money in the bank, and I hae none."

"Not a penny hae I, George. I can pray for my daily bread with an honest heart. For if the Lord doesn't send it, I hae no bank t' fall back on."

"I'm sorry to hear it, Thomas," said George—"But God guide us!" he exclaimed, "there's the two laddies listening to every word we say!"

He hoped thus to turn the current of the conversation, but hoped in vain.

"All the better," persisted Thomas. "They need t' be reminded as well as yersel' an' me that the ways o' this world passeth away.—Alec, my man, Willie, my lad, can ye build a boat t' take ye over the river o' Death? No, ye can't do that. But there's an Ark o' the Covenant that'll carry ye safe over, an' that's a worse flood to boot.—'Upon the wicked he shall rain fire and brimstone—a furious tempest.'—We had a grand sermon on the Ark o' the Covenant from young Mr. Mirky last Sabbath night. Why won't ye come an' hear the Gospel for once at least, George Macwha? Ye can sit in my seat."

"I'm obliged t' ye," answered George; "but the Muckle Kirk does well enough for me."

"The Muckle Kirk!" repeated Thomas in a tone of contempt. "What do ye get there but the dry bones o' morality upon which the wind o' the Word has never blown to put life into the poor skeleton. Come to our kirk an' ye'll get a rousin', I can tell ye, man. Eh! man, if ye were once converted, ye would know how to sing."

Before the conversation had reached this point another listener had arrived. The blue eyes of Annie Anderson were fixed upon the speaker from over the half door of the workshop. The drip from the thatch eaves was soaking her shabby little shawl as she stood, but she was utterly heedless of it in listening to Thomas Crann. He talked with authority and a kind of hard eloquence of persuasion.

I ought to explain here that the *Muckle Kirk* meant the parish Presbyterian church. The religious community to which Thomas Crann belonged was an independent body which commonly went by the name of *Missionaries* in that district, a name arising apparently from the fact that they were among the first in that neighborhood to advocate sending missionaries out to the heathen.

"Are ye not goin' t' get a minister o' yer own, Thomas?" resumed George after a pause, still wishing to turn the cartwheels of the conversation out of the deep ruts in which the stiff-necked Thomas seemed determined to keep them moving.

"No. We'll wait a while and try the spirits. We're not like you—forced to swallow any jabble o' lukewarm water that's been standin' in the sun from year's end t' year's end just because the patron pleases t' stick a pump in it and call it the well o' salvation. We'll know where the water comes from. We'll taste them all, an' choose accordingly."

"Well, I wouldn't like the trouble nor the responsibility o' that."

"I dare say not."

"No. Nor the shame o' pretendin' to judge my betters," added George, now a little nettled, as was generally the end result of Thomas's sarcastic tone.

"George," declared Thomas solemnly, "none but them that has the Spirit can know the Spirit."

With these words he turned and strode slowly and gloomily out of the shop— no doubt from dissatisfaction with the result of his attempt.

Annie was perfectly convinced that Thomas was possessed of some divine secret, the tone of his voice having a greater share in producing this conviction than anything he had said. As he passed out the door, she looked up reverently at him, as one to whom deep things lay open. Thomas had a kind of gruff gentleness toward children which they found very attractive. And this meek maiden he could not threaten with the vials of wrath. He laid his hard, heavy hand kindly on her head, saying: "Ye'll be one o' the Lord's lambs, won't ye, now? Ye'll go into the fold after Him, won't ye?"

"Ay, will I," answered Annie, "if He'll let in Alec and Curly too."

"Ye must make no bargains with Him; but if they'll go in, He'll not hold them out."

Somewhat comforted, the honest stonemason strode away through the darkness and then ran to his own rather cheerless home where he had neither wife nor child to welcome him. An elderly woman took care of his house, whose habitual attitude toward him was half of awe and half of resistance.

By this time Alec and Curly were in full swing with their boat building. But the moment Thomas went, Alec took Annie to the forge to get her well dried out before he would allow her to occupy her place on the heap of shavings.

"Who's preaching at the Missionary kirk in the morn, Willie?" asked the boy's father. For Willie knew everything that took place in Glamerton.

"Mr. Brown," answered Curly.

"He's a good man anyway," returned his father. "There's not many like him. I think I'll turn Missionary myself for once, and go hear him tomorrow night."

At the same instant Annie entered the shop, her face glowing with the heat of the forge and the pleasure of rejoining her friends. Her appearance turned the current and no more was said about the Missionary church. Only a few minutes had passed before she had begun to repeat to the eager listeners one of the two new poems which she had gotten ready for them from the book Miss Cowie had loaned her.

20

Hellfire

*W*hatever effect the arguments of Thomas might or might not have had upon the rest, Annie had heard enough to make her want to go to the Missionary church. Was it not plain that Thomas Crann knew something that she did not know? And where could he have learned it but at the said kirk? So without knowing that George Macwha intended to be there, and with no expectation of seeing Alec or Curly, and without having consulted any of the Bruce family, she found herself, a few minutes after the service had commenced, timidly peering through the inner door of the chapel.

Annie started back, with mingled shyness and awe, from the huge solemnity of the place. She withdrew in dismay to go up into the gallery upstairs, where, entering from behind, she would see fewer faces than she had when opening the door below from right behind the preacher. She stole to a seat as a dog might steal across the room to creep under the master's table. When she ventured to lift her head, she found herself in the middle of a sea of heads. The minister was reading, in a solemn voice, a terrible chapter of denunciation out of the prophet Isaiah, and Annie was soon seized with a deep awe. The severity of the chapter was, however, considerably softened by the gentleness of an old lady sitting next to her who put into her hand a Bible, smelling sweetly of dried leaves, in which Annie followed the reading word for word.

For his sermon, Mr. Brown chose for his text these words of the Psalmist:

"The wicked shall be turned into hell, and all the nations that forget God." His message consisted of two parts: "Who are the wicked?" and "What is their fate?" The answer to the first question was, "The wicked are those that forget God"; the answer to the latter, "The torments of everlasting fire." Upon Annie the sermon produced the immediate conviction that she was one of the wicked and that she was in danger of hellfire. The distress generated by the sermon, however, like that occasioned by the chapter of prophecy, was considerably lessened by the kindness of the unknown hand, which kept up a counteractive ministration of peppermint lozenges. But the preacher's explanations grew so horrifying as the sermon approached its end that when at last it was over and Annie drew one long breath of exhaustion, she became aware that the peppermint lozenge which had been given her a quarter of an hour before was still lying undissolved in her mouth.

When all had ceased—when the prayer, the singing, and the final benediction were over—Annie crept out into the dark street as if into the outer darkness of eternity. She felt the rain falling upon something hot, but she hardly knew that it was her own cheeks being wet by the heavy drops. Her first impulse was to run to Alec and Curly, put her arms around their necks and entreat them to flee from the wrath to come. But she must not look for them tonight. She must go home. For herself she was not too much afraid. For there was a place where her prayers were heard as certainly as in the Holy of Holies in the old Jewish temple—a little garret room namely, with holes in the floors out of which came rats, but with a door as well, in through which came the prayed-for cat.

But alas for Annie and her chapel going! For as she was creeping up from step to step in the dark, the feeling came over her that it was no longer against the rats that she needed to pray. A spiritual terror was seated on the throne of the universe, and was called God—and to whom should she pray against it? Amidst the nighttime darkness, a deeper darkness fell.

She knelt by her bedside but she could not lift up her heart; for was she not one of them that had forgotten God, and was she not therefore very wicked? And was not God angry with her every day?

But there was Jesus Christ. She would cry to Him. But did she believe in Him? She tried hard to convince herself that she did. At last she laid her weary head on the bed and groaned in despair. At that moment a rustling in the darkness broke the sad silence with a throb of terror. She jumped to her feet. She was exposed to all the rats in the universe now, for God was angry with her, and she could not pray. The cat would not help now!

With a stifled scream she darted to the door and half tumbled down the stairs in an agony of fear.

"What makes you make such a din in the house on the Sabbath night?" shouted Mrs. Bruce.

But little did Annie feel the reproof. And as little did she know that the dreaded rats had this time been messengers of God to drive her from a path in which lies madness. She was forced at length to go to bed, where God made her sleep and forget Him, and the rats did not come near her again that night.

Curly and Alec had been in the chapel too, but they were not of a temperament to be disturbed by Mr. Brown's discourse.

21

Truffey

*L*ittle as Murdoch Malison knew of the worlds of thoughts and feelings which lay within those young faces assembled as usual the next day, he knew almost as little of the mysteries that lay within himself.

Annie was haunted all day with the thought of the wrath of God. When she forgot it for a moment it would return again with a sting of actual physical pain, which seemed to pierce her heart. Before school was over she had made up her mind what to do.

And before school was over, Malison's own deed had opened his own eyes, had broken through the crust that lay between him and the vision of his own character.

There could not be found a more thorough impersonation of his own theology than a Scottish schoolmaster of the rough, old-fashioned type. His pleasure was law, irrespective of right or wrong. He had his favorite students in various degrees, whom he chose according to inexplicable directions of feeling. These found it easy to please him, while those with whom he was not primarily pleased found it impossible to please him.

Now there had come to the school about two weeks before, two unhappy-looking little twin orphans, with thin white faces and bones in their clothes instead of legs and arms. They had been committed to the mercies of Mr. Malison by their grandfather. Bent into all the angles of a grasshopper, and lean with ancient poverty, the old man tottered away with his stick in one hand after saying in a quavering, croaking voice, "Now ye jist give them their whips well, Master Malison, for ye know that he that spareth the rod spoileth the bairn."

Thus authorized, Malison certainly did "give them their whips well." Before that day was over, they had both lain shrieking on the floor under the torture of the lash. And such poor half-clothed, half-fed creatures they were, and looked so pitiful and cowed, that one cannot help thinking it must have been for his own glory rather than their good that he treated them thus.

But in justice to Malison, another fact must be mentioned which, although inconsistent with the one just recorded, was in perfect consistency with the theological subsoil from whence both sprang. After about a week, during which they had been whipped almost every day, the orphans came to school with a cold and a terrible cough. Then his observant pupils saw the man who was both cruel judge and cruel executioner feeding his victims with licorice till their faces were stained with its exuberance.

The old habits of severity, which had in some measure been interrupted, had returned upon him with gathered strength, and this day Annie was to be one of the victims. Although he would not dare to whip her, he was about to incur the shame of making this day, pervaded as it was with the aura of the sermon she had heard the night before, the most wretched day that Annie's sad life had yet seen. The spirits of the pit seemed to have broken loose and filled Murdock Malison's schoolroom with the stench of their fire and brimstone.

She sat longing for school to be over that she might follow a plan which had a glimmer of hope in it. Stupefied with her laboring thoughts, she fell fast asleep. She was roused by a stinging blow from the tawse, flung with unerring aim at the back of her bare neck. She sprang up with a cry and, tottering between sleep and terror, proceeded at once to take the leather snake back to the master. She would have fallen halfway had not Alec caught her in his arms. He reseated her and, taking the tawse from her trembling hand, carried it himself to the tyrant. Upon him Malison's fury broke loose, expelling itself in a dozen blows on the right hand which Alec held up without flinching. As he walked to his seat, burning with pain, the voice of the master sounded behind him.

"Ann Anderson," he bawled, "stand up on your seat."

With trembling limbs Annie obeyed. She could scarcely stand at first and her knees shook beneath her. For some time her color kept alternating between crimson and white, but at last settled into a deadly pallor. Indeed, it was to her a most terrible punishment to be exposed to the looks of all the boys and girls in the school. The elder of the two Bruces tried hard to make her see one of his vile grimaces, but feeling as if every nerve in her body were being stung with eyes, she never dared to look away from the book which she held upside down before her. This was the punishment for falling asleep, as hell was the punishment for forgetting God. There she had to stand for a whole hour.

"The devil catch you, Malison!" and various other subdued exclamations were murmured about the room. Annie was a favorite with most of the boys, and yet more because she was "the General's sweetheart," as they said. But these expressions of popular feeling were too faint to reach her ears and comfort her isolation and exposure. Worst of all, she soon witnessed from her elevated vantage point an outbreak of the master's temper far more painful than she had yet seen, both from its cruelty and its consequences.

A small class of mere children, among whom were the Truffey orphans, had been committed to the care of one of the bigger boys while the master was engaged with another class. Every boy in the latter had already had his share of punishment, when a noise in the younger children's class attracted the master's attention. He turned and saw one of the Truffeys hit another boy in the face. He strode upon him at once. Asking not a single question as to the reason for the provocation, he took the boy by the neck, fixed it between his knees, and began to lash him with stinging blows. In his agony the little fellow managed to twist his head about and get a mouthful of the master's leg, inserting his teeth in a most canine and pain-inducing manner. The master caught him up and threw him on the floor. There the child lay, motionless. Alarmed and cooled off as a result, Malison proceeded to lift him. He was apparently lifeless, but he had only fainted with pain. When he came to himself a little, it was found that his leg was hurt. It appeared afterward that the kneecap was greatly injured. Moaning with pain, he was sent home on the back of a big parish scholar.

Annie stared at all this with horror. The feeling that God was angry with her grew upon her, and Murdoch Malison became for a time inseparably associated with her idea of God.

The master still looked uneasy, threw the tawse into his desk, and beat no one else that day. Indeed, only half an hour of school time was left. As soon as it was over, he set off at a rapid pace for the old grandfather's cottage.

What passed there was never known. The other Truffey came to school the next day as usual and told the boys that his brother was in bed. In that bed he lay for many weeks, and many were the visits the master paid him. This did much with the townsfolk to wipe away his reproach. They spoke of the affair as an unfortunate accident, and pitied the schoolmaster even more than they did the victim.

When at length the poor boy was able to leave his bed, it became apparent that he would be a cripple for life.

The master's general behavior was certainly modified by this consequence of his fury, but it was some time before the full reaction was known.

22
• • • • • • • • • • • • • • • •

Mr. Cowie Again

When Annie descended from her hateful position just before the final prayer, it was with a deeper sense of degradation than any violence of the tawse on her poor little hands could have produced. Nor could the attentions of Alec, anxiously offered as soon as they were out of school, console her as they once might have; for such was her sense of condemnation that she dared not take pleasure in anything. The thought of having God against her took the heart out of everything. Nothing else was worth minding till something was done about that. As soon as Alec left her, she walked straight to Mr. Cowie's door.

She was admitted at once and shown into the library where the clergyman sat in the red, dusky glow of the fireplace. "Well, Annie, my dear," he said, "I am glad to see you. How does the boat get on?"

Deeply touched by his kindness which fell like dew upon the parching misery of the day, Annie burst into tears. Mr. Cowie was greatly distressed. He drew her between his knees, laid his cheek against hers, and said with soothing tenderness: "What's the matter with my dawtie?"

After some vain attempts at speech, Annie succeeded in giving the following account of the matter, much interrupted with sobs and fresh outbursts of weeping.

"You see, sir, I went last night to the Missionary kirk to hear Mr. Brown. And he preached a grand sermon. But I haven't been able to bide myself since then. For I'm one of the wicked that God hates, and I'll never get to heaven, for I can't help forgetting Him sometimes. And the wicked'll be turned into hell and all the nations that forget God. And I can't stand it."

In the heart of the good man rose a gentle indignation against the overly pious who had thus terrified and bewildered that precious being, a small child. He thought for a moment and then gave in to his common sense.

"You haven't forgotten your father, have you, Annie?" he began.

"I think about him most every day," she answered.

"But there comes a day now and then when you don't think much about him, doesn't there?"

"Yes, sir."

"Do you think he would be angry with his child because she was so much taken up with her books or her play—"

"I never play with anything, sir."

"Well, with learning poems and songs to recite to Alec Forbes and Willie Macwha? Do you think he would be angry that you didn't think about him that day, especially when you can't see him?"

"Indeed no, sir. He wouldn't be so sore upon me as that."

"What do you think he would say?"

"If Mr. Bruce were to get after me for it, my father would say: 'Let the lassie alone. She'll think about me another day—there's time enough!'"

"Well, don't you think your Father in heaven would say the same?"

"Maybe He might, sir. But, you see, my father was my own father, and would make the best of me."

"And is not God kinder than your father?"

"He couldn't be that, sir. And there's the Scripture besides."

"He sent His very own Son to die for us."

"Ay—for those who are chosen, sir," returned the little theologian.

Now this was more than Mr. Cowie was well prepared to meet, for certainly this doctrine was perfectly developed in the creed of his own Scottish church as well—the assembly of divines had sat upon the Scripture egg till they had hatched it in their own likeness. Poor Mr. Cowie! There were the girl's eyes, blue and hazy with tearful questions, looking up at him hungrily—and the result of his efforts to find a suitable reply was that he lost his temper—not with Annie, but with the popular interpretation of the doctrine of election.

"Go home, Annie, my bairn," he said, "and don't trouble your head about election and all that. No mortal man can ever get to the bottom of it. I'm thinking we maybe shouldn't have much to do with it. Go home, dawtie, and say your prayers to be preserved from the wiles of Satan. There's a sixpence to you."

His kind heart was sorely grieved that he had no more comfort to give her. She had asked for bread, and he had but a stone, as he thought, to offer. But for my part I think the sixpence had more bread in it than any theology he might have been expected to have at hand. For, so given, it was the symbol and the sign of love, which is the heart of divine theology.

Annie, however, drew back from the proffered gift.

"No, thank you, sir," she said. "I couldn't take it."

"Will you not take it to please an old man, child?"

"Indeed I will, sir. I would do a lot more than that to please you."

And again the tears filled her blue eyes as she held out her hand—receiving in it a shilling which Mr. Cowie, for more relief to his own burdened heart, had substituted for the sixpence.

"It's a shilling, sir!" she said, looking up at him with the coin lying on her open palm.

"Well, why not? Isn't a shilling a sixpence?"

"Ay, sir. It's two of them."

"Well, Annie," said the old man, suddenly elevated into prophecy for the child's need, "when God offers us a sixpence, it may turn out to be two. Good night, my bairn."

But Mr. Cowie was sorely dissatisfied with himself. For not only did he perceive that the heart of the child could not thus be satisfied, but he began to feel something new stirring in his own heart. The fact was that in her own way Annie was further along than Mr. Cowie. She was a child searching hard to find the face of her Father in heaven: he was but one of God's babies, who had been receiving contendedly and happily the good things God gave him but never looking up to find the eyes of Him from whom the good gifts came. And now the heart of the man, touched by the motion of the child's heart—yearning after the truth about her Father in heaven, and yet scarcely believing that He could be so good as her father on earth—began to stir uneasily within him. He went down on his knees and hid his face in his hands.

Annie, though not satisfied, went away comforted. After such a day of agony and humiliation, Mr. Cowie's kiss came with gracious restoration and blessing. It had something in it which was not in Mr. Brown's sermon. And yet if she had gone to Mr. Brown, she would have found him kind also—very kind; but solemnly kind, severely kind. His long, saintly face would beam with religious tenderness—not human cordiality, not sympathy with the distress his own one-sided teaching had produced; nay, inclined rather to rejoice over this unhappiness as the sign of grace bestowed and an awakening conscience.

But notwithstanding the comfort Mr. Cowie had given her—the best he had, poor man!—Annie's distress soon awoke again. To know that she could not be near God in peace and love without fulfilling seemingly unreachable conditions filled her with an undefined but terribly real misery, only the more distressing that it was vague.

It was not, however, the strength of her love to God that made her unhappy in being thus barred away from Him. It was rather the check thus given to the whole upward tendency of her being, with its multitude of undefined hopes and longings now drawing nigh to the birth. It was in her ideal self rather than her conscious self that her misery arose. And now, dearly as she loved Mr. Cowie, she began to doubt whether he knew much about the matter. He had put her off without answering her questions, either because he thought she had no business with such things, or because he had no answer to give. This latter possibility added greatly to her unhappiness, for it gave birth to a fearful doubt as to the final safety of kind Mr. Cowie himself.

But there was one other man who knew more about such secret things, she fully believed, than any other man alive; and that man was Thomas Crann. Thomas was a rather dreadful man, with his cold eyes, high shoulders, and wheezing breath; and Annie was afraid of him. But she would have encountered the terrors of the Valley of the Shadow of Death to get rid of the demon nightmare that lay upon her heart, crushing the life out of it. So she plucked up courage, and resolved to set out for the house of the Interpreter. Judging, however, that he could not yet be home from his work, she thought it better to go home first herself.

After eating a bit of oatcake with a mug of blue milk, she went up to her garret and waited drearily, but did not try to pray.

23

•••••••••••••••••

Thomas Crann

It was very dark by the time she left the house, for the night was drizzly. But she knew the windings of Glamerton almost as well as the way up her garret stair. Thomas's door was half open and a light was shining from the kitchen. She knocked timidly. Her knock was too gentle and was not heard inside. But as Jean was passing the door a moment later, she saw Annie standing alone on the threshold. She stopped with a start.

"The Lord preserve us, lassie!" she cried.

"Jean, what are ye swearin' at?" cried Thomas angrily.

"At Annie Anderson," answered Jean simply.

"Why are ye swearin' at *her*? I'm sure she's a respectable lassie. What does the bairn want?"

"What do ye want, Annie?"

"I want to see Thomas, if you please," answered Annie.

"She wants to see ye, Thomas," shouted Jean, remarking in a low voice, "He's as deaf as a doornail, Annie Anderson."

"Let her come in," bawled Thomas.

"He's tellin' ye to come in, Annie," said Jean, as if she had been interpreting his words. "Go in there, Annie," she directed, throwing open the door of the room adjoining the kitchen where Thomas was sitting in the dark, which was often his custom.

The child entered and stood just inside, not knowing even where Thomas sat. But a voice came to her out of the gloom. "Ye're not feared at the dark, are ye, Annie? Come in."

"I don't know where I'm going."

"Never mind that. Come straight ahead. I'm watchin' ye."

Thomas had been sitting in the dark till he could see in it (which, however, is not a certain result in the spiritual realm). But she obeyed the voice and went straight forward into the dark, evidently much to the satisfaction of Thomas. Seizing her arm with one hand, he laid the other, calloused and heavy, on her head, saying: "Now, my lass, ye'll know what faith means. When God tells ye to go into the dark, go!"

"But I don't like the dark," said Annie.

"No human soul can," responded Thomas. "Jean, bring a candle directly."

The candle was brought and set on the table, showing two or three geranium plants in the window. Why her eyes should have fixed upon these, Annie tried to discover afterward, when she was more used to thinking. But she could not tell, except it were that they were so scraggy and wretched, half-drowned by the one who must water in the darkness and half-blanched by the miserable light, and therefore must have been very like her own feelings as she stood before the ungentle but not unkind stonemason.

"Well, lassie," he said when Jean had retired, "what do you want with me?"

Annie burst into tears.

"Jean, go into the kitchen directly!" cried Thomas, on the mere chance of his attendant having lingered at the door. And the sound of her retreating footsteps, though managed with all possible care, immediately justified his suspicion. This interruption turned Annie's tears aside, and when Thomas spoke next, she was able to reply.

"Now, my bairn," he said, "what's the matter?"

"I was at the Missionary kirk last night," faltered Annie.

"Ay! An' the sermon took a grip o' ye?—No doubt, no doubt. Ay?"

"But I can't help forgetting *Him,* Thomas."

"But ye must try an' not forget Him, lassie."

"So I do. But it's dour work, and almost impossible."

"So it must ever be; to the old Adam impossible; to the young Christian a weary watch."

Hope began to dawn upon Annie.

"A body might have a chance then," she asked, "even if she did forget Him sometimes?"

"No doubt, lassie. The nations that forget God are them that don't care, that never bother their heads or their hearts about Him—them that were never called, never chosen."

Annie's troubles returned like a sea wave that had only retired to gather strength.

"But how's a body to know whether she *be* one of the elect?" she asked, quaking.

"That's a hard matter. It's not necessary to know now. Just let that alone in the meantime."

"But I can't let it alone. It's not altogether for myself, either. Could *you* let it alone, Thomas?"

This home-thrust prevented any questioning about the second clause of her answer. And Thomas dearly loved plain dealing.

"Ye hae me there, lassie. No, I couldn't let it alone. An' I never did let it alone. I plagued the Lord night an' day till He let me know."

"I tried hard last night," said Annie, "but the rats were too many for me."

"Satan has many wiles," said the mason reflectively.

"Do you think they weren't rats?" asked Annie.

"Ow! No doubt. I dare say."

" 'Cause if I thought they were only devils, I wouldn't care a periwinkle for them."

"It's much the same whatever ye call them if they keep ye from God's throne o' grace, lassie."

"What am I to do then, Thomas?"

"Ye must keep trustin' lassie, like the poor widow did with the unjust judge. An' when the Lord hears ye, ye'll know ye're one o' the elect, for it's only His own elect that the Lord does hear. Eh! lassie, little ye know about prayin' an' not faintin'."

Alas for the parable if Thomas's theories were to be carried out in its exposition! For they would lead to the conclusion that the Lord and the unjust judge were one and the same person. To Thomas's words Annie's only reply was a fixed gaze which he answered thus, resuming his last words: "Ay, lassie, little ye know about watchin' an' prayin'. Say what they like, 'tis my firm belief that there is, an' can be, but one way o' comin' to the knowledge o' the secret whether ye be one o' the chosen."

"And what's that?" entreated Annie, whose life seemed to hang upon his lips.

"Jist this. Get a sight o' the face o' God. It's my own belief that no man can get a glimpse o' the face o' God but one o' the chosen. I'm not sayin' that a man's not one o' the elect that hasn't had that favor vouchsafed to him; but this I do say, that he can't *know* his election without that. Try ye to get a sight o' the face o' God, lassie: then ye'll know an' be at peace. Even Moses himself couldn't be satisfied without that."

"What is it like, Thomas?" said Annie, with an eagerness which awe made very still.

"The Holy Spirit will tell ye, an' when He does, ye'll know it. There's no fear o' mistakin' *that*."

Teacher and scholar were silent. Annie was the first to speak. She had gained her quest. "Am I to go home now, Thomas?"

"Ay, go home, lassie, t' yer prayers. But I don't doubt it's dark. I'll go wi' ye.— Jean, my shoes!"

"No, no. I could go home blindfolded."

"Hold yer tongue. I'm goin' home wi' ye, bairn.—Jean, my shoes!"

"Hoot, Thomas! I've just cleaned them!" shrieked old Jean from the kitchen at the second call.

"Fetch them here directly."

Jean brought them and sulkily put them down before him. In another minute the great shoes, full of nails half an inch long, were replaced on the tired feet. With her soft little hand clasped in the great calloused hand of the stonemason, Annie trotted home by his side. With Scottish caution, Thomas, as soon as they had entered the shop, instead of turning to leave, went up to the counter and asked for an ounce of tobacco, as if his appearance along with Annie was merely accidental. Annie, with perfect appreciation of the reticence, ran through the gap in the counter.

She was so comforted and so much tired that she fell asleep at her prayers by the bedside. Presently she awoke in terror. It was Pussy, however, that had waked her, as she knew by the green eyes. She then closed her prayers rather abruptly, clambered into bed, and was soon fast asleep.

And in her sleep she dreamed that she stood in the darkness in the midst of a great field full of peat bogs. She thought she was kept in there, unable to move for fear of falling into one of the hundred quagmires about her on every hand, until she should pray enough to get herself out of it. And she tried hard to pray, but she could not. And she fell down in despair, overcome with the terrors of those frightful holes full of black water which she had seen on her way to Glamerton. But a hand came out of the darkness, laid hold of hers, and lifting her up, led her through the bog. And she dimly saw the form that led her, and it was that of a man who walked looking down upon the ground. She tried to see His face but she could not, for He walked always a little in front of her. And He led her to the old farm, where her father came to the door to meet them. And he looked just the same as in the old happy days; only, his face was strangely bright. And with the joy of seeing her father, she awoke to a gentle sorrow that she had not seen also the face of her deliverer.

The next evening she wandered down to George Macwha's and found the two boys at work. She had no poetry to give them, no stories to tell, no answer to their questions as to where she had been the night before. She could only stand in silence and watch them. The skeleton of the boat grew beneath their hands, but it was on the workers and not on their work that her gaze was fixed. For her heart was burning within her and she could hardly restrain herself from throwing her arms about their necks and imploring them to seek the face of God! Oh! If only she were sure that Alec and Curly were of the elect! But they alone could find that out. There was no way for her to peer into that mystery. All she could do was watch their wants, have the tool they needed next ready to their hand, clear away their shavings from before the busy plane, and lie in wait for any chance of putting her little strength to help. Perhaps they were not of the elect! She would minister to them, therefore, all the more tenderly.

"What's come over Annie?" said the one to the other when she had gone.

But there was no answer to the question to be found. Could they have understood her if she had told them what had come over her?

24
●●●●●●●●●●●●●●●●●●
The Schoolmaster's New Friend

And so the time went on, slow-paced, with its silent destinies. Annie said her prayers, read her Bible, and tried not to forget God. Ah, could she have only known that God never forgot her. Whether she forgot Him or not, He gave her sleep in her dreary garret, gladness even in Murdoch Malison's schoolroom, and the light of life everywhere! He was now leading on the blessed season of spring, when the earth would be almost heaven to those who had passed through the fierceness of the winter. Even now, the winter, old and weary, was halting away before the sweet approaches of the spring—a symbol of that eternal spring before whose slow footsteps death itself, "the winter of our discontent," shall vanish.

I have been lengthy in my account of Annie's first winter at school because what impressed her should impress those who read her history. But by degrees the school became less difficult for her. She grew more interested in her work. A taste for reading began to wake in her. If ever she came to school with her lesson unprepared, it was because some book of travel or history had had attractions too strong for her. And all that day she would go about with a guilty sense of neglected duty.

With Alec it was very different. He would often find himself in a similar situation. But the neglect would make no impression on his conscience. Or if it did, he would struggle hard to keep down the sense of dissatisfaction which strove to rise within him and enjoy himself in spite of it.

Still Annie haunted George Macwha's workshop where the boat soon began to reveal the full grace of its lovely outlines. As I have said, reading became a delight to her, and Mr. Cowie threw open his library, with very few restrictions, to her. She carried every new book home with a sense of richness and a feeling of upliftedness which I cannot describe. Now that the days were growing longer she had plenty of time to read; for although her so-called guardians made cutting remarks upon her idleness, they had not yet compelled her to needlework. With the fear of James Dow before their eyes, they let her alone. As to her doing anything in the shop, she was far too much an alien to be allowed to minister in even the lowest office in that sacred temple of Mammon. So she read anything she could lay her hands on, and as often as she found anything particularly interesting she would take the book to the boat, where the boys were always ready to listen to whatever she brought them. And this habit made her more discerning.

Before I leave the school, however, I must give one more scene out of its history.

One midday in spring, just as the last of a hail shower was passing away and one sickly sunbeam was struggling out, the schoolroom door opened and in came the long-absent Andrew Truffey with a smile on his worn face, which shone in touching harmony with the watery gleam of the sun between the two hailstorms, for another was close at hand. He swung himself on his new pivot of humanity, namely his crutch. He looked very long and deathly, for he had grown several inches while lying in bed.

The master rose hurriedly from his desk and advanced to meet him. A deep stillness fell upon all the scholars. They dropped all their work and gazed at the meeting between the two. The master held out his hand. With awkwardness and difficulty Andrew presented the hand which had been holding the crutch; and not yet thoroughly used to the management of it, he staggered and would have fallen. But the master caught him in his arms and carried him to his old seat beside his brother.

"Thank ye, sir," said the boy with another smile, through which his thin features and pale eyes told plainly of his sad suffering—all the master's fault, as the master knew.

"Look at the dominie," whispered Curly to Alec. "He's cryin'."

For Mr. Malison had returned to his seat and had laid his head down on the desk, evidently to hide his emotion.

"Hold your tongue, Curly," returned Alec. "Don't look at him. He's sorry for poor Truffey."

Everyone behaved to the master that day with marked respect. And from that day forward Truffey was in universal favor.

Let me once more assert that Mr. Malison was not a *bad* man. The misfortune was that his notion of right fell in with his natural fierceness. Along with that, theology had come in and wrongly taught him that his pupils were all hopelessly bad—the only remedy he knew or could introduce was blows. Independent of any remedial quality that might be in them, these blows were an embodiment of justice. "Every sin," as the Catechism teaches, "deserveth God's wrath and curse both in this life and that which is to come." The master therefore was, he thought, only a co-worker with God in every blow he inflicted on his pupils.

I do not mean that he reasoned thus but that such were the principles he had to act upon. And I must add, that with all his brutality, he was never guilty of such cruelty as one reads about occasionally perpetuated by certain English schoolmasters. Nor were the boys ever guilty of such cruelty to their fellows as is not only permitted but excused in the public schools of England.

And now the moderation which had at once followed upon the accident was confirmed. Punishment became less frequent still, and when it was inflicted its administration was considerably less severe. Nor did the discipline of the school suffer in consequence. If one wants to make a hard-mouthed horse more responsive to the rein, he must relax the pressure and friction of the bit and make the horse feel that he has to hold up his own head. If the rider supports himself by the reins, the horse will pull.

But the marvel was to see how Andrew Truffey haunted and dogged the master. There was no hour of a day off from school in which Truffey could not tell where the master was about town. If one caught sight of Andrew hobbling down a street or leaning against a building, he could be sure the master would pass within a few minutes. And the haunting of little Truffey worked so on the master's conscience that if the better nature of him had not asserted itself in love to the child, he would have been compelled to leave the town. For think of having a visible sin of your own, in the shape of a lame-legged little boy, peeping at you round every corner!

But he did learn to love the boy; and therein appeared the divine vengeance—ah, how different from human vengeance!—that the outbreak of unrighteous wrath reacted on the wrongdoer in shame, repentance and love.

25

Launching the Boat

At length the boat was calked, tarred and painted.

One evening as Annie entered the workshop, she heard Curly cry, "Here she is, Alec!" And Alec answer, "Let her come. I'm just done."

Alec stood at the stern of the boat with a pot in one hand and a paintbrush in the other. When Annie came near, she discovered to her surprise, and not a little to her delight, that he was finishing off the last E of "T-H-E B-O-N-N-I-E A-N-N-I-E."

"There," he said, "that's her name. How do you like it, Annie?"

Annie was much too pleased to reply. She looked at it for a while with a flush on her face; and then turning away, sought her usual seat on the heap of shavings.

How much that one winter, with its dragons and heroes, its boat-building and its poetry, its discomforts at home and its consolations abroad, its threats of future loss and comforts of present hope, had done to make the wild country child into a thoughtful little woman.

Now, who should come into the shop at that moment but Thomas Crann— the very man of all men not to be desired on this occasion. The boys had contemplated a certain ceremony of christening, which they dared not carry out in the presence of the stonemason—without which, however, George Macwha was very doubtful the little craft would prove a lucky one. By common understanding they made no allusion to the matter, thus postponing it for the present.

"Ay! ay! Alec," said Thomas; "so yer boat's built at last!"

He stood contemplating it for a moment, not without some perceptible signs of admiration, and then said: "If ye had her out on a lake o' water, do ye think ye would jump out over the side if the Savior told ye, Alec Forbes?"

"Ay, would I, if I were right sure He wanted me."

"Ye would stand and parley with Him, no doubt?"

"I'd be behooved to be right sure it was His own self, ye know, and that *He* did call me."

"Ow, ay, laddie! That's all right. Well, I hope ye would. Aye, I had good hopes o' ye, Alec, my man. But there may be such a thing as leapin' into the sea, out o' the ark o' salvation. An' if ye leap in when He doesn't call ye, or if ye don't get a grip o' His hand when He does, ye're sure t' drown, as sure as one o' the swine that ran headlong in and perished in the water."

Alec had only a dim sense of his meaning, but he had faith that it was good and so listened in respectful silence. Surely enough of sacred as well as lovely sound had been uttered over the boat to make her faithful and fortunate.

At length the day arrived when *The Bonnie Annie* was to be launched. It was a bright Saturday afternoon in the month of May, full of a kind of tearful light which seemed to say: "Here I am, but I go tomorrow." Though there might be plenty of cold weather and hail and snow still to come, yet there would be no more frozen waters and the boughs would be bare and desolate no more. A few early primroses were peeping from the hollows damp with moss and shadow along the banks, and the trees by the stream were in small, young leaf. There was a light wind full of memories of past summers and promises for the new one at hand, one of those gentle winds that blow the eyes of the flowers open that the earth may look at the heaven. In the midst of this baby-waking of the world, the boat was to glide into her new life.

Alec got one of the men on the farm to yoke a horse to bring the boat to the river. With George's help she was soon placed in the cart, and Alec and Curly climbed in beside her. The little creature looked very much like a dead fish as she lay jolting in the hot sun, with a motion irksome to her delicate sides, her prow sticking awkwardly over the horse's back, and her stern projecting as far beyond the cart behind.

When they had got about halfway, Alec said to Curly: "I wonder what's come of Annie, Curly? If would be a shame to launch the boat without her."

" 'Deed it would. I'll just run and look for her, an' ye can look after the boat."

So saying, Curly was out of the cart with a bound. Away he ran over a field of potatoes as straight as the crow flies, while the cart went slowly on toward the Glamour.

"Where's Annie Anderson?" he cried as he burst into Robert Bruce's shop.

"What's *your* business with her?" asked Bruce—a question which, judging from his tone, wanted no answer.

"Alec wants her."

"Well, he can keep wanting her," retorted Robert, shutting his jaws with a snap and grinning a smileless grin from ear to ear, like the steel clasp of a purse.

Curly left the shop at once and went around the house into the yard, where he found Annie loitering up and down with the Bruces' baby in her arms and looking very tired. This was in fact the first time she had had to carry the baby, and it fatigued her dreadfully. Till now Mrs. Bruce had had the assistance of a ragged child whose father owed them money for groceries: he could not pay it and they had taken his daughter instead. Long ago, however, she had slaved it out and had gone back to school. The sun was hot, the baby was heavy, and Annie felt all arms and back—they were aching so with the unaccustomed duty. She was all but crying when Curly darted to the gate, his face glowing from his run and his eyes sparkling with excitement.

"Come, Annie," he cried; "we're goin' to launch the boat!"

"I can't, Curly. I have the bairn to mind."

"Take the bairn into its mither."

"I don't dare."

"Lay it down on the table an' run."

"No, no, Curly. I couldn't do that. Poor little creature!"

"Is the beastie heavy?" asked Curly with deceitful interest.

"Dreadful."

"Let me try."

"You'll drop her."

" 'Deed no. I'm not so weak as that. Give me a hold o' her."

Annie yielded her charge; but no sooner had Curly possession of the baby than he bounded away with her toward a huge sugar cask. The cask, having been converted into a reservoir, stood under a spout and was at this moment half full of rainwater. Curly, having first satisfied himself that Mrs. Bruce was at work in the kitchen and would therefore be sure to see him, climbed a big stone that lay beside the barrel and pretended to lower the baby into the water, as if trying to see how much she would endure without crying. In a moment he received such a box on the ear that, had he not been prepared for it, he would have in reality dropped the child into the barrel. The same moment the baby was in its mother's arms, and Curly was sitting at the foot of the barrel, nursing his head and pretending to suppress a violent attack of weeping. The angry mother sped into the house with her rescued child.

No sooner had she disappeared than Curly was on his feet scudding back to Annie, who had been staring over the garden gate in utter bewilderment at his behavior. She could no longer resist his pleading; off she ran with him to the banks of the Glamour, where they soon came upon Alec and the man in the act of putting the boat on the slip, which in this case was a groove hollowed out of a low part of the bank, so that she might glide in more gradually.

"Hurrah! There's Annie!" cried Alec. "Come on, Annie. Here's a glass of whisky I got from my mother to christen the boat. Fling it at her name."

Annie did as she was told, to the perfect satisfaction of all present, particularly of the long, spare, sinewy farm servant who had helped move the boat. When Alec's back was turned, he had swallowed the whisky and true swan-self when sitting gracefully in the water.

"Isn't she bonnie?" cried Annie, clapping her hands in delight.

And indeed she was, in her green and white paint, lying like a great water beetle ready to scamper over the smooth surface. Alec sprang on board, nearly upsetting the tiny craft. Then he held it by a bush on the bank while Curly handed in Annie, who sat down in the stern. Curly then got in himself and he and Alec each seized an oar.

But what with their inexperience and the nature of the channel, they found it hard to get along. The river was so full of great stones that in some parts it was not possible to row. They knew nothing about the management of a boat and were no more at ease than if they had been afloat in a tub. Alec having stronger arms than Curly, they went round and round for some time, as if in a whirlpool. At last they gave it up in weariness, and allowed *The Bonnie Annie* to float along the stream, taking care only to keep her off the rocks. Past them went the banks— here steep and stony but green with moss where little trickling streams found their way into the channel; there spreading into low shores covered with lovely grass full of daisies and buttercups, from which there rose a willow whose low boughs swept the water. A little while ago they had skated down its frozen surface and had seen a snowy land shooting past them. Now with an unfelt gliding they floated down, and the green meadows dreamed away as if they would skim past them forever. Suddenly, as they rounded the corner of a rock, a great roar of falling water burst on their ears and they started in dismay.

"The sluice is up!" cried Alec. "Take to your oar, Curly."

Along this part of the bank, some twenty feet above them, ran a millstream, which a few yards lower down poured by means of a sluice into the river. This sluice was now open, for, from the late rains, there was too much water and the surplus rushed from the stream into the Glamour in a foaming cataract. Seeing that the boys were uneasy, Annie got very frightened and, closing her eyes, sat motionless. Louder and louder grew the tumult of the waters till their sound seemed to fall in a solid thunder on her brain. The boys tried hard to row against the river but without success. Slowly and surely it carried them down into the very heart of the boiling fall; for on this side alone was the channel deep enough for the boat, and the banks were too steep and bare to afford any hold on branches or shrubs. At length the boat, drifting rear end first, entered the fall. A torrent of water struck Annie and tumbled into the boat as if it would beat the bottom out of it. Annie was tossed about in fierce waters and ceased to know anything.

When she came to herself she was in an unknown bed, with Mrs. Forbes bending anxiously over her. She would have risen, but Mrs. Forbes told her to lie still, which indeed Annie found much more pleasant.

As soon as they had gotten under the fall, the boat had filled and floundered. Alec and Curly could swim like otters and were out of the pool at once. As they went down, Alec had made a plunge to lay hold of Annie, but had missed her. The moment he got his breath he swam again into the boiling pool, dived, and got hold of her. But he was so stupefied by the force of the water falling upon him and beating him down that he could not get out of the raging depth—for here the water was many feet deep—and as he would not let go of his hold on Annie, was in danger of being drowned.

Meantime Curly had scrambled on shore and climbed up to the millstream where he managed to shut the sluice down hard. In a moment the tumult had ceased and Alec and Annie were in still water. In a moment more he had her on the bank, apparently lifeless, and he then carried her home to his mother in terror. She immediately resorted to one or two of the usual restoratives and was presently successful.

As soon as Annie had opened her eyes, Alec and Curly hurried off to get out their boat. They met the miller in an awful rage. The sudden doubling of water on his overshot wheel had set his machinery off as if it had been bewitched, and one old stone, which had lost its iron girdle, had flown into pieces, to the frightful danger of the miller and his men.

"Ye ill-designed villains!" he cried at them, "what made ye close the sluice? I'll teach ye to mind what ye're about. Devil take ye rascals!"

He seized one in each brawny hand.

"Annie Anderson was drownin' in the waste water," answered Curly promptly.

"The Lord preserve us!" cried the miller, relaxing his hold. "How was that? Did she fall in?"

The boys told him the whole story. In a few minutes more the backfall was again turned off, and the miller was helping them get their boat out. *The Bonnie Annie* was found uninjured. Only the oars and cushions had floated down the stream and were never seen again.

Alec had a terrible scolding from his mother for getting Annie into such mischief. Indeed, Mrs. Forbes did not like the girl's being so much with her son; but she comforted herself with the probability that by and by Alec would go to college and forget her. Meantime, she was very kind to Annie and took her home herself, in order to excuse her absence, the blame of which she laid entirely on Alec, not knowing that thereby she greatly aggravated any offense of which Annie might have been found guilty. Mrs. Bruce solemnly declared her conviction that a judgment had fallen upon Annie for Willie Macwha's treatment of her baby.

"If I hadn't just gotten a glimpse of him in time, he would have drowned the bonny infant before my very eyes!"

This first voyage of *The Bonnie Annie* may seem like a bad beginning; but I am not sure that many good ends have not had such a bad beginning. Perhaps the world itself may be received as a case in point. Alec and Curly went about for a few days with a rather subdued expression. But as soon as the boat was refitted, they got George Macwha to go with them for cockswain, and under his instructions they made rapid progress in rowing and sculling. Then Annie was again their companion; and the boat being by this time fitted with a rudder, she had several lessons in steering in which she soon became proficient. Many a moonlight row they now had on the Glamour; and many a night after Curly and Annie had gone home would Alec again unmoor the boat and float down the water alone—not always sure that he was not dreaming himself.

26

. . . .

Changes

*M*y story must have shown already that, although several years younger than Alec, Annie had more character than he. Alec had not yet begun to look realities in the face. The very nobility and fearlessness of his nature had preserved him from many actions which give occasion for looking within oneself and asking where things are leading. Full of life and restless impulses to activity, all that could be properly required of him as yet was that the action into which he rushed should be innocent, and if mischievous then usually harmless, unless he was taking action against injustice, as in the case of the Bruces' dog.

Comfortless at home and gazing all about her to see if there was a rest anywhere for her, Annie had been driven by the outward desolation away from the window of the world to that other window which opens on the regions of silent being where God is, and into which His creatures enter. Alec, whose home was happy, knew nothing of that sense of discomfort which for many is the herald of a greater need. But he was soon to take a new start in his intellectual development; nor in that alone, seeing the changes which were about to come upon him also bore a dim sense of duty. The fact of his not being a scholar in the mind of Murdoch Malison arose from no deficiency of intellectual *power*, but only of intellectual *capacity*—the enlargement of which requires only a fitting motivation from without.

The season went on, and the world, like a great flower afloat in space, kept opening its thousandfold blossoms. Hail and sleet were things lost in the distance of the year—storming away in some far-off region of the north, unknown to the summer generation. The butterflies, with wings looking as if all the flower painters of fairyland had wiped their brushes upon them in freakful yet artistic sport, came forth in the freedom of their wills and the faithful ignorance of their minds. The birds, the poets of the animal creation, awoke to utter their own joy and awake a similar joy in others of God's children. Then the birds grew silent, because their history had laid hold upon them, compelling them to turn their words into deeds, keep eggs warm and hunt for worms. The butterflies died of old age and delight. The green life of the earth rushed up in corn to be ready for the time of need. The corn grew ripe and therefore weary, hung its head, died, and was laid aside for a life beyond its own. The keen, sharp old mornings and nights of autumn came back as they had come so many thousand times before, and made human limbs strong and human hearts sad and longing. Winter would soon be near enough to stretch out a long forefinger once more, and touch with the first frosty shiver some little child that loved summer and shrank from the cold.

There had been growing in Alec, though it was still a vague sense in his mind, that he was not doing as well as he might, that the mischief of boyhood—which, notwithstanding the maturity wrought by the building and care of the boat, had continued throughout the summer with the rest of his less-noble companions—had already begun to extend further than it ought toward manhood. Several rebukes from Thomas Crann served to bring such notions toward the light of Alec's own consciousness. Therefore, once the harvest was past and school begun afresh, Alec began to work better. Mr. Malison saw the change and acknowledged it. This in turn reacted on Alec's feelings for the master. During the following winter, he made three times the scholastic progress he had made in any winter preceding it.

For the sea of summer had ebbed away and the rocky channels of the winter had appeared, with its cold winds, its ghostlike mists, and the damps and shiverings that clung about the sepulcher in which Nature lies sleeping. The boat was carefully laid up across the rafters of the barn, well wrapped in a shroud of tarpaulin. It was buried up in the air; and the Glamour on which it had floated so gayly would soon be buried under the ice. Summer alone could bring them together again—the one from the dry gloom of the barn, the other from the cold seclusion of its wintry sleep.

Meanwhile, Mrs. Forbes was somewhat troubled in her mind as to what should be done with Alec, and she often talked to the schoolmaster about him. Of higher birth socially than her late husband, she had the ambition that her son should be educated. She was less concerned about his exercise of some profession as that he simply obtain an education, for she was not at all willing that the farm which had been in her husband's family for hundreds of years should pass into the hands of strangers, especially as Alec himself had the strongest attachment to the ancestral soil.

At length his increased diligence, which had not escaped her observation and was confirmed by Mr. Malison, strengthened her determination that he should at least go to college. Whether the university beyond that would remain to be seen. He would be no worse a farmer for having an A.M. after his name, and the curriculum was common to all the professions. So it was resolved that in the following winter he should compete for a bursary.

The communication that his fate lay in that direction roused Alec still more. Now that a future object made his studies more attractive, he turned his attention to them with genuine earnestness. After another circuit of the seasons on a cloudy day toward the end of October—several months before his sixteenth birthday— Alec found himself on the box seat of the Royal Mail coach, with his trunk on the roof behind him, bound for a certain city where his future—at least for the present—lay.

27

In the City

As no one but Alec had come to the college from Glamerton that year, he did not know even one of his fellow students. There were very few in the first class indeed who had had any previous acquaintance with each other. But before many days had passed like had begun to draw to like and opposites to their natural opposites. Some of the youths were of the lowliest origin—the sons of plowmen and small country shopkeepers. Some, on the other hand, showed themselves at once the aristocracy of the class by their carriage, dress, and social qualifications. Alec belonged to the middle class. Well dressed, he yet knew that his clothes had a country air and that beside some of the others he cut a poor figure. A certain superiority of manner distinguished these others, indicating that they had been accustomed to more of the outward refinements of life than he.

The competition was held within the first week. Alec gained a small scholarship, and then the lectures commenced. One morning about two months after the beginning of the session, the professor of the Greek class looked up at the ceiling with sudden discomposure. There had been a heavy fall of snow in the night and one of the students had tightly packed a large snowball and, before the arrival of the professor, had thrown it against the ceiling with such forceful precision that it stuck right over the center of his chair. When the air in the room had warmed, the snow began to drip on the head of the old professor.

The moment he looked up, seeing what was the matter, Alec sprang from his seat, rushed out of the classroom and returned with a long broom which the groundskeeper had been using to clear footpaths across the quadrangle. The professor left his chair, Alec jumped up on the desk and swept the snow from the ceiling. He then wiped the seat with his handkerchief and returned to his place. The gratitude of the old man shone in his eyes.

"Thank you, Mr. Forbes," he stammered; "I am ek-ek-ek-exceedingly obliged to you."

The professor was a curious, kindly little man—lame, with a brown wig, a wrinkled face, and a long mouth, of which he made use of the half on the right side to stammer out humorous and often witty sayings. Somehow Professor Fraser's stutter never interfered with the point of the joke. He seemed, while hesitating on some unimportant syllable, to be arranging what was to follow and strike the blow with a sudden rush.

"Gentlemen," he continued upon this occasion, "the Scripture says you're to heap c-c-coals of fire on your enemy's head. When you are to heap drops of water on your friend's w-w-wig, the Scripture doesn't say."

The same evening Alec received a note asking him to breakfast with the professor the following morning, which was Saturday and consequently a holiday. It was usual with the professors to invite a dozen or so of the students to breakfast on Saturdays, but on this occasion Alec was the sole guest.

As soon as Alec entered the room, Mr. Fraser hobbled to meet him with outstretched hand of welcome and a kindly smile on his face.

After some conversation while Mr. Fraser began to fill the teacups, Alec said, "My mother told me in a letter I had from her yesterday that your brother, sir, had married a cousin of hers."

"What! Are you a son of Mr. Forbes of Howglen?"

"Yes, sir."

"You young rascal! Why didn't your mother send you straight to me when you arrived?"

"She didn't want to trouble you, I suppose, sir."

"People like me that haven't any relatives must make the most of the relatives they do have. I am in no danger of being troubled that way. You've heard of my poor brother's death?"

"No, sir."

"He died last year. He was a clergyman, you know. When you begin the new session next year, I hope to show you his daughter—your cousin, you know. She is coming to live with me. People that don't marry don't deserve to have children. But I'm going to have one after all. She's in school now. What are you thinking of going into, Mr. Forbes?"

"I haven't thought much about it yet, sir."

"Ah, I dare say not. If I were you, I would be a doctor. If you're honest you're sure to do some good. I think you're just the man to be a doctor—you respect your fellowmen. And you don't laugh at old age, Mr. Forbes."

And so the kind, garrulous old man went on, talking about everything except Greek. This was the first time Alec's thoughts had been turned toward a profession. The more he thought about it the better he liked the idea of being a doctor. At length, after one or two talks about it with Mr. Fraser, he resolved to pursue it and to get into the anatomy course for the rest of the session. The Greek and Latin were relatively easy for him, and it would be that much time gained if he entered the first medical class at once. His mother was more than satisfied with the proposal. Mr. Fraser smoothed the way with the medical professor, and he, with a hard study of the books for the course, was soon busy making up the two months he had lost.

The first day of his attendance in the anatomy room was a memorable one. He had considerable misgivings about the new experience and tried to mentally prepare himself with calmness. When he entered the room he found the group already gathered. He drew timidly toward the table on the far wall, not daring to glance at something which lay on the table—something very pale and white. He felt as if all the others were looking at him as he kept staring, or trying to stare, at other things in the room. But all at once, from an irresistible impulse, he faced round and looked at the table.

There lay the dead body of a woman with a young, sad face. Alec's lip quivered and his throat swelled with a sensation of choking. He turned away and bit his lip hard to keep down his emotion.

One of the students, sneering at his discomposure, made a brutal jest. Try as he might to hold it in, Alec let escape one sob in a vain effort to master the conflicting emotions of pity for the woman and anger at the youth. It reverberated in the laugh which burst from the students. Above the laugh he heard further words of sarcastic contempt against "the young clodhopper"—meaning himself— who had just come from herding his father's cows and was not yet fit for a *man's* occupation. His face blazed, his eyes flashed, his fists clenched and he had begun to step forward when the professor arrived.

After this, as often as Patrick Beauchamp and he passed each other in walking up and down the arcade, Beauchamp's high, curved upper lip would curve yet higher. Beauchamp was no great favorite even in his own set, though there were many who would follow his lead at his jests; for there is one kind of religion in which the more devoted a man is, the fewer proselytes he makes; it is the worship of himself.

Alec remained in his room on holidays to read and study his medical and anatomical books. One day his landlady asked, "Have ye been up the stairs to visit Mr. Cupples yet?"

"I didn't know you had anybody up the stairs. Who's Mr. Cupples?"

"Weel, he knows that best himsel'! But he's a strange one, he is. He's some scholar though, folk say—grand at the Greek an' mathematics. Only ye mustn't be frightened at him."

"I'm easily frightened," said Alec with a laugh, recalling his first day in the anatomy room. "But I would like to see him."

"Go up then, an' clap at the garret door."

"But what reason am I to give for disturbing him?" asked Alec.

"Ow, none at all. Jist take a mouthful o' Greek with ye to ask the right meanin' of."

"That will do first rate," said Alec, "for I have just been puzzling over a sentence for the last half hour." He caught up his book and bounded away up the garret stairs. At the top he found himself under the bare roof with only boards and slates between him and the clouds. The landing was lighted by a skylight, across which diligent and undisturbed spiders had woven their webs for years. He stood outside for a moment or two, puzzled as to which door he ought to try, for all the doors about looked like closed doors. At last, with the aid of his nose, he made up his mind, and knocked.

"Come in!" cried a voice.

He opened the door and entered, assailed at once by the full force of the odor which had aided his decision at which door to knock.

"What do you want?" demanded the voice, its source almost invisible in the thick fumes of genuine pigtail tobacco from his pipe.

"I want you to help me with a bit of Homer, if you please, Mr. Cupples— I'm not up to Homer yet."

"Do you think I have nothing else to do than to grind the grandeur of an old heathen into little pieces for a young sinner like you?" he rasped out.

"You don't know what I'm like, Mr. Cupples," returned Alec, remembering his landlady's injunction not to be afraid of this man.

"You young dog! There's stuff in you!" Then composing himself a little, he said, "Come through the smoke and let's get a look at you."

Alec obeyed and found the speaker seated by the side of a little fire in an old easy chair. Mr. Cupples was a man who might have been almost any age between twenty-five and fifty—at least Alec's experience was insufficient for the task of determining to what decade of human years he belonged. He was a little man, in a long, black coat much too large for him, and dirty gray trousers. He had no shirt collar visible, although a loose rusty stock revealed the whole of his brown neck. His hair was long, thin, and light, mingled with gray, and his ears stood far out from his large head. His eyes were rather large, well-formed, bright and blue. His hand, small and dirty, grasped a tumbler of toddy, while his feet, in un-matched slippers, balanced themselves on a small table.

"Well, you look like one of the right sort," he said at length. "I'll do what I can for you. Where's your Homer?"

So saying, he rose with care and went toward a cupboard in the corner. Glancing around the little garret room, Alec saw a bed and a small chest of drawers, a painted table covered with papers, and a chair or two. An old broadsword leaned against a wall in a corner. A half-open cupboard revealed bottles, glasses, and a dry-looking cheese. To the corresponding cupboard on the other side of the fire, which had lost a corner by the descent of the roof, Mr. Cupples now dragged his slippers, feeling in his waistcoat pocket as he went for the key. There was another door, partly sunk in the slope of the ceiling.

When he opened the cupboard, a dusky glimmer of splendid bindings filling the whole recess shone out upon the dingy room. From a shelf he took a volume of Homer, bound in leather with red edges and, having closed the door again, resumed his seat in the easy chair. He found the passage and read it through aloud. Then pouncing at once upon the shadowy word which was the key to the whole, he laid open the construction and meaning in one sentence of explanation.

"Thank you! thank you!" exclaimed Alec. "I see it all now as plain as English."

"Stop, stop, my young bantam!" said Mr. Cupples. "Don't think you're going to break into my privacy and get off with the booty so cheaply. You must now construe the whole sentence to me."

Alec did so reasonably well. Mr. Cupples put several questions to him, which gave him more insight into Greek than a week's work in the class would have done, and ended with a small lecture suggested by the passage, drinking away at his toddy all the time. The lecture and the toddy ended together. Laying his head back against the chair, he said sleepily: "Go away—I don't know your name.— Come and see me tomorrow night. I'm drunk now."

Alec rose, making some attempts at thanks. Receiving no syllable of reply, he went out, closing the door behind him and leaving Mr. Cupples to his dreams.

28

Annie in Glamerton

*M*eantime, at Glamerton the winter passed very much like former winters to all but three—Mrs. Forbes, Annie Anderson, and Willie Macwha. To these the loss of Alec was dreary. So they were in a manner compelled to draw closer together. At school, Curly assumed the protectorship of Annie which had naturally fallen upon him, although there was now comparatively little occasion for its use. And Mrs. Forbes, finding herself lonely in her parlor during the long forenights, got into the habit of sending Mary at least three times a week to fetch Annie. This was not agreeable to the Bruces, but the kingly creditor awaited his hour; and Mrs. Forbes had no notion of the amount of offense she gave with her invitations.

That parlor at Howglen was to Annie a little heaven hollowed out of the winter. The warm curtains drawn, the fire blazing defiantly—the angel with the flaming sword to protect their Paradise from the frost—it was indeed a contrast to the sordid shop and the rat-haunted garret.

After tea they took turns to work and to read. There were more books in the house than usual even in that of a gentleman farmer; and several of Sir Walter's novels, besides some travels and a little Scottish history, were read between them that winter. In poetry, Annie had to forage for herself. Mrs. Forbes could lend her no guiding hand in that direction.

The bond between them grew stronger every day. Annie was to Mrs. Forbes an outlet for her maternity, which could never have outlet enough without a girl as well as a boy to love. Annie, as a result, was surrounded by many wholesome influences, which, operating at a time when she was growing fast, had their full effect upon both her mind and body. In a condition of rapid change, mass is more yielding and responsive.

One result in her was that she began to manifest a certain sober grace in her carriage and habits. Mrs. Forbes came to Annie's aid with dresses of her own, which they altered and remade together. It will easily be believed that no avoidable expense remained unavoided by the Bruces. Indeed, but for the feeling that she must be decent on Sundays, they would have let her go yet shabbier than she was when Mrs. Forbes thus partially adopted her. Now that she was warmly and neatly dressed, she began to feel and look more like the lady-child she really was. No doubt the contrast was very painful to her when she returned from Mrs. Forbes' warm parlor to sleep in her own garret with the snow on the roof, scanty covers on the bed, and rats in the floor. It is wonderful how one gets through what one cannot avoid.

Robert Bruce was making money, but not so fast as he wished, which led to a certain change in the Bruces' habits with important results for Annie. The returns of the shop came only in small purchases, although the profits were great, for his customers were chiefly of the poorer classes of the town and neighborhood. They preferred his shop to the more showy establishments of some of his rivals. A sort of confidentially flattering way that he had with them pleased them and contributed greatly to keeping them true to his counter. And as he knew how to buy as well as how to sell, the poor people, if they had not their money's worth, had at least good merchandise. But, as I have said, although he was making haste to be rich, he was not succeeding fast enough. So he began thinking about the Missionary church and how it was getting rather large and successful.

A month or two before this time the Missionaries had made choice of a very able man for their pastor—a man of genuine and strong religious feeling who did not allow his theology to interfere with the teaching given him by God's Spirit more than he could help. If he had been capable of choosing sides at all, he would have made it with the poor against the rich. This man had gathered about him a large congregation of the lower classes of Glamerton, and Bruce had learned with some uneasiness that a considerable number of his customers was to be found in the Missionary kirk on Sundays, especially in the evenings.

There was a grocer among the Missionaries who, he feared, might draw some of his subjects away from their allegiance to him. Should he join the congregation, he would not only retain the old but also have a chance to gain new customers as well. So he took a week to think about it, a Sunday to hear Mr. Turnbull alone in order that the change might not seem too abrupt, and the next Sunday he and his family were seated in a pew under the gallery, adding greatly to the prestige both of the place and himself in the eyes of his Missionary customers.

Although Annie found the service more wearisome than good Mr. Cowie's, lasting as it did three quarters of an hour longer, yet, occasionally when Mr. Turnbull testified of that which he himself had seen and known, the honest heart of the maiden recognized the truth and listened, absorbed. The young Bruces, for their part, would gladly have gone to sleep, which would perhaps have been the most profitable use to which they could put the time. But they were kept upright and in a measure awake by the constant application of the paternal elbow and the judicious administration, on the part of the mother, of the unfailing peppermint lozenges, to which in the process of ages a certain sabbatical character has attached itself. To Annie, however, no such ministration extended, for it would have been a downright waste, seeing she could keep awake without it.

One bright frosty morning, the sermon appeared to have no relation to the light around or within them, but only to the covenant made with Abraham. Annie, neither able to enter into the subject nor to keep from shivering with the cold, tried to amuse herself by gazing at one brilliant sun streak on the wall. She discovered it to be gradually shortening itself and retreating toward the window by which it had entered the room. Wondering how far it would move before the sermon was over, and whether it would have shone so bright if God had made no covenant with Abraham, she was earnestly watching it pass from spot to spot, from cobweb to cobweb, when she caught sight of a very peculiar face turned in the same direction—that is, not toward the minister, but toward the traveling light. She thought the woman was watching it as well as she, and wondered whether she too was hoping for a bowl of hot broth as soon as the sunbeam had gone a certain distance—broth being the Sunday fare with the Bruces. The face was very plain, seamed and scarred as if the woman had fallen into a fire when a child, and Annie had not looked at her two seconds before she realized that the woman was perfectly blind. But she saw too that there was a light on the face, a light which neither came from the sun in the sky nor the sunbeam on the wall. Though it was the ugliest of faces, over it, as over the rugged channel of a sea, flowed the transparent waves of a heavenly light.

When the service was over, almost before the words of the benediction had left the minister's lips, the people hurried out of the chapel as if they could not possibly endure one word more. But Annie stood staring at the blind woman. When at length she followed the woman out into the open air, Annie found her standing by the door, turning her sightless face on all sides as if looking for someone and trying hard to open her eyes that she might see better. Annie watched her till, seeing her lips move, she knew half by instinct that she was murmuring, "The bairn's forgotten me!" Thereupon she walked up to her and said gently: "If you'll tell me where you live, I'll take you home."

"What do they call *you,* bairn?" returned the blind woman in a gruff, almost manlike voice, no more pleasant to hear than her face was to look at.

"Annie Anderson," answered Annie.

"Ow, ay! I thought as much. I know about ye. Give me a hold o' yer hand. I live in that wee house down at the bridge, between the dam an' the Glamour, ye know. Ye'll keep me away from the stones?"

"Ay, I will," answered Annie confidently.

"I could go alone, but I'm growin' some old now, an' I'm jist rather feared for fallin'."

"Well, what made you think it was I? I never spoke to you before," commented Annie as they walked on together.

"Well, 'tis jist half guessin', an' half a kind o' judgment—puttin' things together, ye know, my bairn. Ye see, I know all the bairns that come to our kirk already. An' I heard tell that Master Bruce was come. So when a lassie spoke to me that I never heard afore, I jist kind o' knew it must be yersel'."

All this was spoken in the same harsh voice, but the woman held Annie's hand kindly and yielded like a child to her guidance, which was as careful as that of the angel that led Peter.

It was a new delight to Annie to have someone to whom she, a child, could be a kind of mother, to whom she could fulfill a woman's highest calling—that of ministering. And it was with something of a sacred pride that she safely led her through the snowy streets and down the steep path that led from the level of the bridge, with its three high stone arches, to the little meadow where her cottage stood. Before they reached it, the blind woman, whose name was Tibbie (Isobel) Dyster, had put many questions to her and had come to a tolerably correct knowledge of her character, circumstances and history.

As soon as they entered the cottage, Tibbie was entirely at her ease. The first thing she did was to lift the kettle from the fire and feel the fire with her hands in order to find out in what condition it was. She would not allow Annie to touch it—she could not trust the creature that had nothing but eyes to guide her with such a delicate affair. The very hands looked like blind eyes trying to see, as they went wandering over the tops of the live peats. She rearranged them, put on some fresh pieces, blew a little at them all astray and to no purpose, was satisfied, coughed, and then sank in a chair.

Her room was very bare, but was as clean as it was possible for a room to be. Her bed was in the wall which divided it from the rest of the house, and this one room was her whole habitation.

Annie looked all about the room, and seeing no signs of any dinner for Tibbie was reminded thereby that her own chances had considerably diminished.

"I must go home," she said with a sigh.

"Ay, lassie; they'll be waitin' their dinner for ye."

"No fear of that," answered Annie, adding with another sigh, "I doubt there'll be much of the broth left when I get home."

"Well, jist stay, bairn, an' take a cup o' tea with me. It's all I hae to offer ye. Will ye stay?"

"Maybe I would be in your way," objected Annie feebly.

"Na, na; no fear o' that. Ye'll read a bit to me afterward."

"Ay, will I."

And Annie stayed all the afternoon with Tibbie and went home with the Bruces after the evening service.

It soon grew into a custom for Annie to escort Tibbie home from the chapel— a custom to which the Bruces could hardly have objected had they been so inclined. But they were not so inclined, for it saved the broth—that is, each of them got a little more in consequence, and Annie's absence was therefore a Sabbath blessing.

Much as she was neglected at home, however, Annie was steadily gaining a good reputation in the town. Old men said she was a *gude bairn* and old women said she was a *douce lassie*, while those who enjoyed finding fault more than giving praise turned their silent approbation of Annie into expressions of disapproval of the Bruces—"lettin' her go like a beggar, as if she was no kin o' theirs, when 'tis well known whose heifer Rob Bruce is plowin' with."

But Robert nevertheless grew and prospered all day, and dreamed at night that he was the king, digging the pits for the English cavalry and covering them again with the treacherous turf. Somehow the dream never went further. The field and the kingship would vanish and he would remain Robert Bruce, the general dealer, plotting still, but in his own shop.

29

•••••••••••••••••••

Alec and Mr. Cupples

The next evening Alec knocked at Mr. Cupples's door and entered. The strange creature was sitting in the same position as before, looking as if he had not risen since the previous night. But there was a certain Sunday look about the room which Alec could not account for. The same pictures were on the wall, the same tumbler of toddy was steaming on the table amidst the same little array of books and papers covered with the same dust and marked with the same circles from the bottoms of wet glasses. The same black pipe reposed between the teeth of Mr. Cupples.

After he had been seated for a few moments, however, Alec all at once discovered the source of the reformation of the place: Mr. Cupples had on a white shirt and collar. Although this was no doubt the chief cause of the change of expression in the room, in the course of the evening Alec discovered further signs of improvement: one, that the hearth had been cleared of a great heap of ashes and now looked as if belonging to an old maid's cottage instead of a bachelor's garret.

"More Greek, laddie?" inquired Mr. Cupples.

"No, thank you," answered Alec. "I only came to see you. You told me to come again tonight."

"Did I then? Well, I protest against being made accountable for anything that fellow Cupples may choose to say when I'm not at home."

Here he emptied his glass of toddy and filled it again from the tumbler.

"Shall I go away?" asked Alec, half bewildered.

"No, no; sit still. You're a good sort of innocent, I think. I won't give you any toddy though. You needn't look so greedy at it."

"I don't want any toddy, sir. I never drank a tumbler in my life."

"For God's sake!" exclaimed Mr. Cupples with sudden eager energy, leaning forward in his chair, his blue eyes flashing—"for God's sake, never drank a drop!"

He sank back in his chair and said nothing for some time. Alec thought he was drunk again and rose to go.

"Don't go yet," insisted Mr. Cupples authoritatively. "You come at your will; you must go at mine.—If I could but get a kick at that fellow Cupples! But I declare I can't help it. If I were God, I would cure him of drink. It's the very first thing I would do."

Alec could not help being shocked at the irreverence of the words. But the solemnity of Mr. Cupples's face speedily dissipated the feeling. Suddenly changing his tone, he went on: "What's your name?"

"Alec Forbes."

"Alec Forbes. I'll try to remember it. I seldom remember anybody's name, though. I sometimes forget my own."

"I see something like poetry lying about the table, Mr. Cupples," Alec said. "Would you let me look at it?"

Mr. Cupples glanced at him sharply, then replied: "Broken bits of them! Let them sit there—bridges over nothing, with no road over the top of them, like the stone bridge of Drumdochart after the flood. Keep your hands and eyes off them.—Ay, ay, you can look at them if you like. Only don't say a word to me about any of them. I'm going to fill my pipe again. But I won't drink more tonight 'cause it's the Sabbath, and I'm going to read my book. So hold your tongue."

So saying, he proceeded to get the tobacco out of his pipe by knocking it on the hob while Alec took up the paper that lay nearest. He found it contained a fragment of a poem in the Scottish language; and searching among the rest of the scattered sheets, he soon got the whole of it together.

Now, although Alec had but little acquaintance with verse, he was able, thanks to Annie Anderson, to enjoy a ballad very heartily. There was something in this one which, associating itself in his mind with the strange being before him, moved him more than he could account for.

When he had finished reading it, he found himself gazing at the man who had penned it. He could not quite get the verses and Mr. Cupples into harmony. Not daring to make any observation, however, he sat with the last sheaf still in his hand and a reverential stare on his face. Suddenly lifting his eyes, Mr. Cupples exclaimed, "What are you glaring at me for? I'm neither ghost nor warlock!" He cursed. "Get out, if you're going to stick me through with your eyes that way!"

"I beg your pardon, Mr. Cupples. I didn't mean to be rude," replied Alec humbly.

"Well, I've had enough of you for one night. I can't stand glaring eyes, especially in the heads of idiots and innocents like you."

I am sorry to have to record what Alec learned from the landlady afterward that Mr. Cupples went to bed that night, notwithstanding it was the Sabbath, more drunk than she had ever known him. Indeed, he could not properly be said to have gone to bed at all, for he had tumbled on the floor in his clothes and clean shirt, where she had found him fast asleep the next morning, with his book terribly crumpled under him.

"But," asked Alec, "what *is* Mr. Cupples?"

"That's a question he couldn't well answer himself," was the reply. "He does a heap o' things—writes for the lawyers sometimes; buys an' sells strange books; gives lessons in Greek an' Hebrew—but he doesn't like that—he can't stand to be contradicted, an' laddies is always that way; helps anybody that wants help in the way o' numbers when their books go wrong. He's a kind o' librarian at yer own college, Mr. Forbes. The old man's dead an' Mr. Cupples is jist doin' the work. They won't give him the run o' the place—'cause he has a reputation for drinkin'. But they'll get as much work out o' him as if they did, and for half the money. He can do most anything all day, but the minute he comes home, out comes the drink and he jist sits down an' drinks till he turns the world over on top o' him."

The next day about noon, Alec went into the library where he found Mr. Cupples busy rearranging the books and the catalogue, both of which had been neglected for years. This was the first of many visits to the library, or rather to the librarian.

There was a certain confusing sobriety of demeanor about Mr. Cupples all day long, as if in the presence of such serious things as books he was bound to be upon his good behavior and confine his debauchery to taking snuff in prodigious quantities. He was full of information about books and opinions besides. For instance, one afternoon when Alec picked up a book of which Cupples disapproved, the librarian snatched it from his hand and put it back on the shelf.

"A palace of dirt and impudence and spiritual stink," he said. "Let it sit there and rot. You don't need to be reading the likes of that!"

Mr. Cupples never would remain in the library after the day began to ebb. The moment he became aware that the first filmy shadow had fallen from the coming twilight, he grabbed his hat, locked the door, gave the key to the sacrist, and hurried away.

The friendly relations between the two struck its roots deeper and deeper during the school session, and when it drew to a close after winter was past, it was with regret that Alec bade him good-bye.

30

Homecoming

*W*inter had begun to withdraw its ghostly troops and Glamerton began to grow warmer. Annie, who had been very happy all that season, began to be aware of something more at hand. A flutter scarcely recognizable, as of the wings of awaking delight, now stirred her heart occasionally with a sensation of physical presence and motion. She would find herself giving an involuntary skip as she walked along, and now and then humming a bit of a psalm tune. A hidden well was throbbing in the child's soul. Its waters had been frozen by the winter; and the spring, which sets all things springing, had made it flow and swell anew, soon to break forth bubbling. But her joy was gentle, for even when she was merriest, it was in a sober and maidenly fashion, testifying that she had already walked with Sorrow and was not afraid.

Robert Bruce's last strategical move against the community had been tolerably successful, even in his own eyes; and he was enough satisfied with himself that he could afford to be in good humor with other people. Annie, too, came in for a share of this humor. Although she knew him too well to have anything like regard for him, it was yet a comfort to her to be on such terms with him as not to have to dread a bitter word every time she chanced to meet him. This comfort, however, stood on a sandy foundation.

At length, one bright day in the end of March, Alec came home, not the worse to friendly eyes for having been at college. He seemed the same cheery, active youth as before. The chief visible differences were that he had grown considerably and that he wore a coat. There was a certain indescribable alteration in tone and manner, a certain crystallization and polish, which the same friends regarded as an indubitable improvement.

The day after his arrival, crossing the square of Glamerton, he saw a group of men talking together, among them his old friend Thomas Crann. He went up and shook hands with him and with Andrew Constable, the clothier.

"Hasn't he grown into a long child?" remarked Andrew to Thomas, regarding Alec kindly.

"Humph!" returned Thomas, "he'll jist need the longer a coffin."

Alec laughed, but Andrew said, "Hoot!"

Thomas and Alec walked away together. But scarcely a sentence had been exchanged before the stonemason, with a delicacy of perception of which his rough manner and calloused hands gave no indication, felt that a film of separation had come between the youth and himself. Anxious to break through it, he said abruptly: "How's yer immortal part, Alec? Mind ye, there's a knowledge that worketh death."

Alec laughed—not scornfully—but he laughed.

"Ye may laugh, Alec, but 'tis the truth," said the mason.

Alec held out his hand, for here their way diverged. Thomas shook it kindly, but walked away gloomily. When he arrived at home, he shut his bedroom door and went down on his knees by his bedside.

In order to prepare for the mathematical studies of the following year, Alec went to the school again in the morning on most days, Mr. Malison being well able to give him the assistance he required. The first time he made his appearance at the door, a momentary silence as of death was the sign of his welcome. But a tumult presently arose and discipline was for a time suspended.

Annie sat still, staring at her book, and turning red and pale alternately. But he took no notice of her, and she tried to be glad of it. When school was over, however, he came up to her in the lane and addressed her kindly.

But the delicate little maiden felt as the rough stonemason had felt, that a change had passed over the old companion and friend. True, the change was only a breath—a mere shadow. Yet it was a measureless gulf between them. Annie went to her garret that night with a sense of sad privation.

But her pain sprang from a source hardly so deep as that of the stonemason. For the change she found in Alec was chiefly of an external kind, and if she had a vague feeling of a deeper change, it had scarcely yet come into her consciousness. When she saw the *young gentleman,* her heart sank within her. Her friend was lost; and a shape was going about, *looking* like the old Alec who had carried her in his arms through the invading torrent. But to complete her confusion of feelings, she felt also a certain added reverence for the apparition.

Mrs. Forbes never asked her to the house now, and it was well for her that her friendship with Tibbie Dyster had begun. But as she saw Alec day after day at school, the old colors began to revive out of the faded picture. And when the spring had advanced a little, the boat was got out. Alec could not go rowing in *The Bonnie Annie* without thinking of its godmother and inviting her to join them. Indeed, Curly would not have let him forget her, for he felt that she was a bond between him and Alec, and he loved Alec the more devotedly since the rift between their social positions had begun to show itself. The devotion of the schoolboy to his superior in schoolboy arts had begun to change into something like the devotion of clansman to his chief. And not infrequently would an odd laugh of consciousness between Annie and Curly reveal the fact that they were both watching for a peep or word from Alec.

In due time harvest came; and Annie could no more keep from haunting the harvest than the crane could keep from flying south when the summer was over. She watched all the fields around Glamerton; she knew what response each made to the sun and which would first be ripe for reaping. And the very day that the sickle was put in, there was Annie to see and share in the joy. Unquestioned as uninvited, she became one of the company of reapers, gatherers, binders, and stookers, assembled to collect the living gold of the earth from the early fields of the farm of Howglen. Sadly her thoughts went back to the old days when Dowie was master of the field and she was Dowie's little mistress. Not that she met with anything but kindness—only it was not the same kindness she had had from Dowie. But the pleasure of being once more near Alec almost made up for every loss. And he was quite friendly, although, she must confess, not quite so kindly as of old. But that did not matter, she assured herself.

The laborers all knew her well and themselves took care that she should have the portion of their food which her assistance had well earned. She never refused anything that was offered her except money. That she had taken only once in her life—from Mr. Cowie, whom she continued to love the more dearly, although she no longer attended his church.

But again the harvest was safely lodged and the sad old age of the year sank through the rains and frosts to his grave.

The winter came and Alec went.

He had not been gone a week when Mrs. Forbes' invitations began again. And, as if to make up for the neglect of the summer, they were more frequent than before. No time was so happy for Annie as the time she spent with her. And this winter she began to make some return in the way of household assistance.

31

Kate

Hello, bantam!" exclaimed Mr. Cupples to Alec, as the youth entered the garret within an hour of his arrival in his old quarters. As he spoke he emptied his glass and refilled it from the tumbler. "How are you getting on with the mathematics?"

"Middling only," answered Alec.

"I don't doubt that. Small preparations do well enough for Professor Fraser's Greek, but you'll find it's another story with the mathematics. You must just come to me with it as you did with the Greek."

"Thank you, Mr. Cupples," said Alec heartily. "I don't know how to repay you."

"Repay me! I want no repayment. Only ask me no questions and leave me when I'm drunk."

After all his summer preparation, Alec was still behind in mathematics, but his medical studies interested him more and more all the time.

Not many days after his arrival Alec resolved to pay a visit to Mr. Fraser. He was sure of a welcome from the old man; for although Alec gave less attention to his Greek now, Mr. Fraser would be delighted that he was doing his best to make himself a good doctor. The professor's friendliness toward him had, in fact, increased; for the man thought he saw in Alec noble qualities and enjoyed having such a youth near him.

Alec was shown into the professor's drawing room, which was unusual. The professor was seated in an easy chair with one leg outstretched before him.

"Excuse me, Mr. Forbes," he said, holding out his left hand without rising. "I am laid up with the gout—I don't know why. The port wine my grandfather drank, I suppose. I never drink it. I'm afraid it's old age. And yon's my nurse.— Mr. Forbes, your cousin, Kate, my dear."

There at the other side of the fire sat a girl, half smiling and half blushing as she looked up from her work. Alec advanced and she rose and held out her hand. She might have been a year older than he, perhaps seventeen or eighteen.

"So you are a cousin of mine, Mr. Forbes," she said when they were all seated by the blazing fire—she with a piece of plain needlework in her hands, he with a very awkward nothing in his, and the professor contemplating his swathed leg on the chair before him.

"So your uncle says," he answered, "and I am happy to believe him. I hope we shall be good friends."

Alec was recovering himself after his initial modesty.

"I hope we shall," she responded with a quick, shy, asking glance from her fine eyes.

Those eyes were worth looking into, if only as a study of color. They were of many hues marvelously blended. Their glance rather discomposed Alec. He had not yet learned that ladies' eyes are sometimes very disquieting. Yet he could not keep his own from wandering toward them; and the consequence was that he soon lost the greater part of his senses. After sitting speechless for some moments, he was suddenly seized by a horrible conviction that if he remained silent an instant longer, he would be driven to do or say something absurd. So he did the latter at once by bursting out with the stupid question, "What are you working at?"

"A duster," she answered instantly—this time without looking up.

Now the said "duster" was of the finest cambric material; so that Alec could see that she was making game of him. This banished his shyness and plucked up his vigor.

"I see," he said, "when I ask you questions, you—"

"Tell lies," she interposed, without giving him time even to hesitate, adding, "Is your mother nice, Mr. Forbes?"

"She's the best woman in the world," he answered with feeling, almost shocked at having to answer such a question.

"Oh, I beg your pardon," returned Kate, laughing; and the laugh revealed very pretty teeth, with a semi-transparent pearly-blue shadow in them.

"I am glad she is nice," she went on. "I should like to know her. Mothers are always nice."

Mr. Fraser sat watching the two with his amused old face, one side of it twitching in the effort to suppress the smile which sought to break from the useful half of his mouth. The gout could not have been very bad just then.

"I see, Katie, what that long chin of yours is thinking," he said.

"What is my chin thinking, Uncle?" she asked.

"That uncles are not always so nice. They snub little girls, sometimes, don't they?"

"I know one who *is* nice, all except for one naughty leg."

She rose as she said this and, going round to the back of the chair, leaned over it and kissed his forehead. The old man looked up to her gratefully.

"Ah, Katie!" he said, "you may make game of an old man like me. But don't try your tricks on Mr. Forbes. He won't stand them."

Alec blushed. Kate went back to her seat, and took up her "duster" again.

Not until she had drawn nearer in approaching her uncle had Alec realized how pretty Kate was. He found too that her great mass of hair was full of glints and golden hints, as if she had twisted up a handfull of sunbeams with it in the morning. Before she got back to her seat, he was very nearly in love with her. And if he had talked stupidly before, he talked worse now; at length he went home with the conviction that he had made a great donkey of himself.

When he arrived home he found he could neither read nor think. At last he threw his book to the other side of the room and went to bed, where he found it not half so difficult to go to sleep as it had been to study.

The next day things went better, for he was not yet so lost that a night's sleep could do him no good. But he was fortunate that there was no Greek class and that he was not called up to read Latin.

As he left his final class of the day, he said to himself that he would just look in and see how Mr. Fraser was. He was shown into the professor's study.

Mr. Faser smiled as he entered with a certain grim comicality.

"I hope your gout is better today, sir," he said, sending his glance wide astray of his words.

"Yes, thank you, Mr. Forbes," answered Mr. Fraser, "it is better. Won't you sit down?"

Warned by his earlier smile, Alec was astute enough to decline and presently took his leave. As he shut the study door, he thought he would just peep into the dining room, the door of which stood open opposite the study. There she was, sitting at the table writing.

Who can that be a letter to? thought Alec, for already the early signs of jealousy had begun to take root.

"How do you do, Mr. Forbes?" said Kate, holding out her hand.

Could it be that he had seen her only yesterday? Or had he simply forgotten what she was like? She was so different from how he had been imagining her.

The fact was merely this—she had been writing to an old friend, and her manner for the time, as well as her expression, was affected by her mental proximity to that friend. Indeed, Alec was not long in finding out that one of her witcheries was that she was never the same.

"I am glad to find your uncle much better," he said.

"Yes. You have seen him then?"

"Yes. I was very busy in the dissecting room, till—"

He stopped, for he saw her shudder.

"I beg your pardon," he hastened to substitute. "We are so used to saying those things that—"

"Don't say another word about it," she said hastily. Then, in a vague kind of way, "Won't you sit down?"

"No, thank you. I must go home," answered Alec, feeling that she did not want him. "Good night," he added, advancing a step.

"Good night, Mr. Forbes," she returned in the same manner, without extending her hand.

Alec checked himself, bowed, and went with a feeling of mortification and the resolution not to repeat his visit too soon. She interfered with his studies throughout the following week, notwithstanding, and sent him wandering out in the streets many times when he ought to have been reading at home.

32

Alec and Kate

The Saturday after the next Alec received a note from Mr. Fraser, hoping that his new cousin had not driven him away, and inviting him to dine that same afternoon.

He went. After dinner the old man fell asleep in his chair.

"Where were you born?" Alec asked Kate.

She was more like his first impression of her.

"Don't you know?" she replied. "In the north of Sutherlandshire—near the foot of a great mountain, from the top of which, on the longest day, you can see the sun, or a bit of him at least, all night long."

"How glorious!" said Alec.

"I don't know. I never saw him. And the winters are so long and terrible. Nothing but snowy hills about you, and great clouds always coming down with fresh loads of snow to scatter over them."

"Then you don't want to go back?"

"No. There is nothing to make me wish to go back. There is no one there to love me now."

She looked very sad for a few moments.

"Yes," said Alec thoughtfully, "a winter without love must be dreadful. But I like the winter, and we have plenty of it where I come from too."

"Where is your home?"

"Not many miles north of here."

"Is it a nice place?"

"Yes, of course—I think so."

"Ah! You have a mother. I wish I knew her."

"I wish you did. True, the whole place is like her to me. But I don't think everybody would admire it. There are plenty of bare, snowy hills there too in winter. But I think the summers and the harvests are as delightful as anything can be, except—"

"Except what?"

"Don't make me say what will make you angry with me."

"Now you must, else I shall think something that will make me more angry."

"Except your face," Alec confessed, frightened at his own boldness, but glancing at her shyly.

She flushed a little, but did not look angry.

"I don't like that," she said. "It makes one feel awkward."

"At least," rejoined Alec boldly, "you must admit it is your own fault."

"I can't help my face," she said, laughing.

"Oh! You know what I mean. You made me say it."

"Yes, after you had half said it already. Don't do it again."

And there followed more of such foolish talk, uninteresting to my readers.

"Where were you at school?" asked Alec after a pause. "Your uncle told me you were at school."

"Near London," she answered.

"Ah, that accounts for your beautiful speech."

"There again. I declare I will wake my uncle if you go on in that way."

"I beg your pardon," protested Alec; "I forgot."

"But," she went on, "in Sutherlandshire we don't talk so horribly as they do around here."

"I dare say not," returned Alec.

"I don't mean you. I wonder how it is that you speak so much better than all the people here."

"I suppose because Mother speaks well."

"She does not speak with the accent?"

"She never lets me speak broad Scot around her."

"Your mother again!"

Alec did not reply.

"I should like to see her," pursued Kate.

"You must come and see her then!"

"See whom?" asked Mr. Fraser, rousing himself from his nap.

"My mother, sir," answered Alec.

"Oh, I thought you had been speaking of Katie's friend," said the professor, and fell asleep again.

"Uncle means Bessie Warner who is coming by the steamer from London on

Monday. Isn't it kind of him to ask her to come and see me?"

"He is always kind. Was Miss Warner a schoolfellow of yours?"

"Yes—no—not exactly. She was one of the governesses. I must go and meet her at the steamer. Will you go with me?"

"I shall be delighted. When does she arrive?"

"They say about six."

"I will come and fetch you before that."

"Thank you. I suppose I may, Uncle?"

"What, my dear?" said the professor, rousing himself again.

"Have my cousin to take care of me when I go to meet Bessie."

"Yes, certainly. I shall be much obliged to you, Mr. Forbes. I am not quite so agile as I was at your age, though my gouty leg is better."

This conversation would hardly have been worth recording had it not led to the walk and the waiting on Monday. They found when they reached the region of steamers that she had not yet arrived. So Alec and Kate walked out along the pier, to pass the time. The pier runs down the side of the river, and a long way into the sea. It had begun to grow dark and Alec had to take great care of Kate among the tramways, coils of rope and cables that crossed their way. At length they got clear of these and found themselves upon the pier, built of great rough stones tapering away into the dark.

"It is a rough season of the year for a lady to come by sea," said Alec.

"Bessie is very fond of the sea," answered Kate. "I hope you will like her, Mr. Forbes."

"Do you want me to like her better than you?" rejoined Alec. "Because if you do—"

"Look how beautiful that red light is on the other side of the river," interrupted Kate. "And there is another farther out."

"When the man at the helm gets those two lights in a line," said Alec, "he may steer straight in, in the darkest night."

"Look how much more glorious the red shine is on the water below!" said Kate.

"It looks so wet," returned Alec—"just like blood."

He almost cursed himself as he said so, for he felt Kate's hand stir as if she would withdraw it from his arm. But after fluttering like a bird for a moment, it settled again upon its perch and there rested.

The day had been quite calm, but now a sudden gust of wind from the northeast swept across the pier and made Kate shiver. Alec drew her shawl closer about her, and her arm farther within his. They were now close to the sea. On the other side of the wall which rose on their left they could hear the sound of the breaking waves. It was a dreary place. Clouds hung above the sea; and above the clouds two or three disconsolate stars.

"Here is a stair!" exclaimed Alec. "Let's go up on the top of the sea wall, and then we shall catch the first glimpse of the light from the steamer."

They climbed the steep, rugged steps and stood on the broad wall, hearing the sea pulses lazily fall at its foot. Feeling Kate draw a deep breath like the sigh of the sea, Alec looked round in her face. There was still light enough to show it frowning and dark and sorrowful and hopeless. It was in fact a spiritual mirror, which reflected in human forms the look of that weary waste of waters. She gave a little start, gathered herself together, and murmured something about the cold.

"Let us go down again," said Alec. "The wind has risen considerably, and the wall will shelter us down below."

"No, no" she answered; "I like it. We can walk here just as well. I don't mind the wind."

"I thought you were afraid of falling off."

"No, not in the dark. I should be, I dare say, if I could see how far we are from the bottom."

So they walked on. The waves no longer fell at the foot of the wall, but now leaned against it as the level of the water steadily rose and fell. The wind kept coming in gusts, tearing a white gleam now and then on the dark surface of the sea. Behind them shone the dim lights of the city; before them all was dark as eternity, except for the one light at the end of the pier. At length Alec spied another out at sea.

"I believe that is the steamer," he said. "But she is a good way off. We shall have plenty of time to walk to the end—that is, if you would like to."

"Certainly; let us go on. I want to stand on the very point," answered Kate.

They soon came to the lighthouse on the wall and there descended to the lower part of the pier, the end of which now plunged with a steep descent into the sea. It was constructed of great stones clamped with iron, and built into a natural foundation of rock.

They stood looking out into the great dark before them, dark air, dark sea, dark sky, watching the one light which grew brighter as they gazed. Neither of them saw the dusky figure watching them from behind a great cylindrical stone standing on the end of the pier, close to the wall.

A wave rushed up, almost to their feet.

"Let us go," said Kate, with a shiver. "I can't bear it longer. The water is calling me and threatening me. There! See how that wave rushed up as if it wanted me at once!"

Alec again drew her closer to him, and, turning, they walked slowly back. He was silent with the delight of having that lovely creature all to himself, leaning on his arm in the enfolding and protecting darkness, and Kate was likewise silent.

By the time they reached the quay at the other end of the pier, the steamer had crossed the bar, and they could hear the thud of her paddles treading the water beneath them eagerly, as if she knew she was now near her rest. After a few struggles she lay quiet in her place, and they went on board.

Alec saw Kate embrace a girl perhaps a little older than herself and he helped her find her luggage. After putting them into a carriage, he took his leave of them, and went home.

He did not know that all the way back along the pier he and Kate had been followed by Patrick Beauchamp.

33
·······················

Alec and Beauchamp

I should mention an event that occurred soon after the commencement of the new session which greatly influenced Alec's future at the college.

One evening Alec determined to attend a meeting of the Magistrand Debating Society. Though under the control of the members of the fourth class, the society was open on equal terms in most other respects to the members of the lower classes. At seven o'clock, curious and expectant, he arrived at the place of meeting and found that some two hundred others were also present.

After the discussion of various preliminary matters the debate began. At length a certain third classman stood up whom Alec immediately recognized as his anatomy classmate Patrick Beauchamp. He proceeded to give his opinion on some subject in dispute but eventually his well-ordered and fashionable speech gave way to hemming and stammering till the weary assembly booed him with a torrent of hisses and animal exclamations. Filled with indignation, he poured forth a torrent of sarcastic contempt on the young clodhoppers (many freshmen were present), who, having just come from herding their fathers' cows, could express their feelings in no more suitable language than that of the bovine animals. As he sat down his eyes rested with scorn upon Alec Forbes. Now it must be mentioned that each class level carried a nickname, that of Beauchamp's coincidentally being *sheep*. Alec immediately stood in the midst of the din, but finding it impossible to speak so as to be heard, contented himself with uttering a sonorous *ba-a-a-a*, and instantly dropped to his seat, all the other outcries dissolving in shouts of laughter at Beauchamp's expense.

After this Alec was popular but was disdained more than ever by Beauchamp, with whom he continued to share medical studies. But Beauchamp never forgot the incident and vowed to make Alec Forbes pay for his public humiliation. Thus he often haunted his footsteps, seeking some opportunity, as had been the case the night Alec and Kate had walked along the pier.

"Beware of the man," Mr. Cupples had warned him. "He'll do you mischief yet if you don't keep a sharp eye out." For Mr. Cupples was well acquainted with him. "I know his breed. I've seen him watching you like a hungry devil at the library."

Mr. Cupples then launched into a somewhat rambling account of Patrick Beauchamp's antecedents, indicating by his detail that there must have been personal relations of some kind between them or their families. Perhaps he hinted at something of the sort when he said that old Beauchamp was a hard man even for a lawyer.

Beauchamp's mother, he said, was the daughter of a Highland chief, whose pedigree went back to an Irish king of remote date. Mrs. Beauchamp had all the fierceness without much of the grace belonging to the Celtic nature. She grew to despise, then hate, her husband while giving her son every advantage her position could afford, molding and modeling him after her own heart.

"So you see, Mr. Forbes, if the rascal takes after his mother, you have made a dangerous enemy," said Mr. Cupples in conclusion.

"What do you want me to do?" asked Alec.

"Take care about Beauchamp. And meantime, mind what you're about with the Fraser lassie."

Alec glanced up, wondering how Mr. Cupples could be so well-informed about his personal life. But the man went on paying no heed to Alec's look of shock and mild embarrassment.

"She's pretty enough, but you could get into trouble by no fault of your own. Mind I'm telling you, if you take my advice you'll give yourself a dose of mathematics, especially Euclid. It's a fine alternative, as well as antidote."

There was more ground for Mr. Cupples's warning than Alec realized. Beauchamp had in fact been dogging him from the very commencement of the session. In the anatomical class, where they continued to meet, he attempted to keep up the old look of disdain. Beauchamp's whole consciousness was poisoned by the galling recollection of being humiliated in front of, as he considered it, the entire school. Incapable of regarding anything except in relation to *himself*, the supreme effort of his life had been to maintain his feeling of superiority. For destroying that in the eyes of his fellows, he hated Alec passionately.

Now hate keeps its object present even more than the opposite passion. Love makes everything lovely; hate concentrates itself on the one thing hated. The very sound of Alec's voice became to the ears of Beauchamp what a filthy potion would have been to his palate.

No way of gratifying his hatred, however, had presented itself—though he had been brooding over it all the previous summer—till now. Now he saw the possibility of working a dear revenge indeed. Beauchamp had an unlimited confidence in some gifts which he supposed himself to possess by nature and to be capable of using with unequaled art.

But the time was not yet ripe. He would delay, let Alec fall still deeper into the descent where he was already heading, and thus the revenge would be all the sweeter. For true hate, as well as true love, knows how to wait.

34

·······················

Tibbie's Cottage

𝒜nnie's visits to Tibbie Dyster increased, and she began to read regularly to the blind woman. One Saturday evening, after she had been reading for some time, interrupted frequently by the harsh old woman, the latch of Tibbie's door was lifted and in walked Robert Bruce. He stared when he saw Annie, for he thought her at Howglen and said in a sharp tone, "You're everywhere at once, Annie Anderson. A downright runabout!"

"Let the bairn be, Master Bruce," said Tibbie. "She's doin' the Lord's will, whether ye may think so or not. She's visitin' them that's in the prisonhouse o' the dark. She's ministerin' to them that hae many preevileges na doubt, but hae room for more."

"I'm not saying anything," said Bruce defensively.

"Ye are sayin'. Ye're offendin' one o' His little ones. Take ye hold o' the mill-stone."

"Hoot, toot, Tibbie. I was only wishing that she would keep a small part of her ministrations for her own home and her own folk who help her. There's the mistress and me just martyrs to that shop! And there's the baby in need of some ministration now and then, if that be what you call it."

A grim compression of the mouth was all Tibbie's reply. She did not choose to tell Robert Bruce that although she was blind—and possibly because she was blind—she heard rather more gossip than anybody else in Glamerton, and that consequently his appeal to her sympathy had no effect upon her. Finding she made no answer, Bruce turned to Annie.

"Now, Annie," he said, "you're not wanted here any longer. I have a word or two to say to Tibbie. Go home and learn your lessons for tomorrow."

"It's Saturday night," answered Annie.

"But you have your lessons to learn for the Monday."

"Ow, ay. But I have a book or two to take home to Mistress Forbes. I think I'll stay with her and come to church with her in the morning."

Now, although all that Bruce wanted was to get rid of her, he went on to oppose her. Common-minded people always feel they give the enemy an advantage if they show themselves content.

"It's not safe for you to run about in the dark."

"I know the road to Mrs. Forbes like the back of my hand."

"No doubt!" he answered with a sneer peculiar to him. "And there's dogs about," he added, remembering Annie's fear of dogs.

But by this time Annie, gentle as she was, had got a little angry.

"The Lord'll take care of me from the dark and the dogs and the rest of you, Mr. Bruce," she said.

And bidding Tibbie good night, she took up her books and departed to wade through the dark and the snow, trembling lest some unseen dog should lay hold of her as she went.

As soon as she was gone, Bruce proceeded to make himself agreeable to Tibbie by retelling all the bits of gossip he could think of. While thus engaged he kept peering earnestly about the room from door to chimney, turning his head on every side, and surveying everything as he turned it. Tibbie perceived from the changes in his voice that he was thus occupied.

"So your old landlord's dead, Tibbie?" he said at last.

"Ay, honest man. He always had a kind word for a poor body."

"Ay, ay, no doubt. But what would you say if I told you I had bought the little house and was your new landlord, Tibbie?"

"I would say that the doorsill wants mendin' to keep the snow oot; an' the poor place is in sore need o' new thatch."

"Well, that's very reasonable, no doubt, if all is as you say."

"Be as I say, Robert Bruce?"

"Ay, ay. You see, you're not altogether like other folk. I don't mean you any offense, you know, Tibbie. But you don't have the sight of your eyes."

"Maybe I don't hae the feelin' o' my old bones either, Master Bruce? Maybe I'm too blind to hae rheumatizm, or to smell the old wet thatch when there's been a scatterin' o' snow or a drop o' rain on the riggin'!"

"I didn't want to anger you, Tibbie. All that deserves attention. It would be a shame to let an old person like you—"

"Not that old, Mr. Bruce, if you knew the truth."

"Well, you're not too young not to need to be well taken care of—are you, Tibbie?"

Tibbie grunted.

"Well, to come to the point. There's no doubt that the house needs a lot of doctoring."

"Indeed it does," interposed Tibbie. "It needs a new door."

"No doubt you're right, Tibbie. But seeing that I have to lay out so much, I'll be compelled to add another threepence onto the rent."

"Another threepence, Robert Bruce! That's three threepence in the place o' two. That's a big rise! Ye can't mean what ye say! 'Tis all I'm able to do to pay my sixpence! An old, blind body like me doesn't fall in with sixpence when she goes lookin' about with her long fingers when she's dropped somethin'."

"But you do a heap of spinning, Tibbie, with those long fingers. No one in Glamerton spins like you."

"Maybe ay and maybe no. It's not much that comes to. I wouldna spin so well if it weren't that the Almighty put some sight into the points o' my fingers 'cause there was none left in my eyes. An' if ye make another threepence a week out o' that, ye'll be turnin' the weather that He sent to run my mill into your dam; and I wouldn't doubt that it will play bad ill water with your wheels."

"Hoot, hoot! Tibbie. It hurts my heart to appear so hard-hearted."

"I have no doubt ye don't want to *appear* so. But do ye know that I make so little by the spinnin' that the kirk gives me a shillin' a week to make up with? An' if it weren't for kind friends, 'tis an ill living I would have in dour weather like this. Don't ye imagine, Mr. Bruce, that I hae anythin' put away excep' sevenpence in a stockin'. An' it would hae to come off my tea or something else I would ill miss."

"Well, that may be very true," rejoined Bruce, "but a body must have their just rewards for all that. Wouldn't the church give you the other threepence?"

"Do ye think I would take it from the kirk to put into yer till?"

"Well, say sevenpence rent then, and we'll be quits."

"I tell ye what, Robert Bruce: rather than pay ye one penny more than the sixpence, I'll go out in the snow an' let the Lord look after me."

Robert Bruce went away and did not purchase the cottage, which was on the market at a low price. He had intended Tibbie to believe, as she did, that he had already bought it; and if she had agreed to pay even the sevenpence, he would have left her to go and buy it.

There was no day yet in which Annie did not think of Alec with the same feeling of devotion she had always had, although all her necessities, hopes, and fears were now beyond any assistance he could render. She was far on in a new path toward light and truth: he was loitering behind, out of hearing. He would not have dared to call her thoughts and feelings nonsense; but he would have rejected all such religious matters as belonging to women and not to youths such as himself just beginning in the ways of the world. He never thought now about the lessons of Thomas Crann. He began to look down upon all his past, and even upon his old companions. Since knowing Kate, who had more delicate habits and ways than he had ever seen, he had begun to refine his own behavior. While he became more polished in his anxiety to be like her, he became less genial and wide-hearted.

But none of his old friends forgot him. I believe not a day passed in which Thomas did not pray for him in secret, naming him by his name and lingering over it mournfully: "Alexander Forbes—the young man that I thought would hae been plucked frae the burnin' afore noo. But thy time's the best, O Lord. It's all thy work; an' there's no good thing in us. An' thou canst turn the heart o' man as the rivers o' water. An' maybe thou hast given him grace to repent already, though I know nothin' aboot it."

35

• • • • • • • • • • • • • • • • •

Annie and Thomas

*T*his had been a sore winter for Thomas, and he had had plenty of time for prayer. He had gone up on a scaffold one day to see that the wall he was building was properly protected from the rain, and his foot slipped on a wet pole. He fell to the ground and one of his legs was broken. Not a moan escaped him—a complaint was out of the question. They carried him home, and the surgeon did his best for him.

Annie went every day to ask about him and every day had a kind reception from Jean. At length one day Jean asked her if she would not like to see him.

"Ay, would I, right well," answered Annie.

Jean led her into Thomas's room where he lay in bed. He held out his hand. Annie put hers into his, saying timidly, "Is your leg very sore, Thomas?"

"Ow no, dawtie. The Lord's been very merciful—jist like himsel'. It was hard to bide for a while when I couldn't sleep. But I jist sleep now like one o' the beloved."

"I was right sorry for you, Thomas."

"Ay. Ye've a kind heart, lassie. Ye're surely one o' the Lord's bairns—"

"Eh! I don't know," cried Annie, half-terrified at such an assurance from Thomas, and yet delighted at the same time.

"Ay, ye are," continued Thomas confidently. "Now sit ye doon aside me and open the Bible there an' read that hunner an' seventh psalm. Eh, lassie! but the Lord is good. What right hae I to praise Him?"

"You have the best right, Thomas, for hasn't He been good to you?"

"Ye're right, lassie, ye're right . . . It's wonnerful the common sense o' bairns."

Thomas's sufferings had made him more gentle—and more sure of Annie's eternal salvation. Annie saw him often after this, and he never let her go without reading a chapter to him, his remarks upon which were always of some comfort and application to her.

Although the framework of Thomas was roughly hewn, he had always been subject to fluctuations of feelings as are more commonly found among women. Sometimes he would be lifted to the very "mercy seat of God," as he would say; at others he would fall into fits of doubting whether he was indeed "one of the elect." At such latter times he was subject to a great temper, alternately the cause and effect of his misery. If Jean, who had no idea what he happened to be thinking, dared to interrupt his devotions at such a time by calling through the bolted door, the saint who had been kneeling before God in utter abasement and self-contempt would suddenly throw it open wrathful and boiling over with angry words. Having driven the enemy away in confusion, he would bolt his door again and return to his prayers in twofold misery, the guilt from his anger raising yet another wall of separation between him and God.

This weakness all but disappeared during the worst of his illness, but returned with increased force when his recovery had advanced far enough to allow him out of bed. A deacon of the church, a worthy little weaver, had been unofficially appointed to visit Thomas and find out—which was not an easy task—if he was in want of anything. When James Johnstone arrived Jean was out. He lifted the latch, entered, and tapped gently at Thomas's door—too gently, for he received no answer. With hasty yet hesitating carelessness, he opened the door and peeped in. Thomas was on his knees by the fireside with his plaid blanket over his head. Startled by the weaver's entrance, he raised his head, and his rugged face, red with wrath, glared out of the thicket of his plaid upon the intruder.

"James, ye're takin' the part o' Satan, drivin' a man from his prayers!" he cried fiercely.

"Hoot, Thomas! I beg yer pardon," answered the weaver, rather flurried. "I thought ye might hae been asleep."

"Ye had no business to think for yersel' in such a manner. What do ye want?"

"I jist came to see whether ye was in want o' anythin', Thomas."

"I'm in want o' nothin'. Good night to ye."

"But really, Thomas," expostulated the weaver, "ye shouldn't be doon on yer knees like that, with yer leg in such a weak condition."

"What do ye know aboot my leg? An' what's the use o' knees, but to go doon upon them? Go home, an' go doon upon yer own, James, an' don't disturb other folk who know what theirs was made for."

Thus admonished, the weaver dared not linger. As he turned to shut the door, he wished the mason good night but received no answer. Thomas had sunk forward on the chair in front of him and had already drawn his blanket back over his head.

But the sacred place of the Most High will not be entered in this fashion. It is not by driving away our brother that we can be alone with God. Thomas's plaid could not isolate him with his Maker, for communion with God is far more than isolation. The chamber with the shut door may shut out God too and leave the supplicant alone with only himself. The love of brethren opens the door into God's chamber, which is within ours. So Thomas—who was far from hating his brother, and who would have, in fact, struggled to his feet and limped out to do him a service, though he did not hold out his hand to *receive* one—Thomas, I say, felt worse than ever.

At length another knock came, which although very gentle, he heard and knew well enough.

"Who's there?" he asked, notwithstanding with a fresh dose of anger.

"Annie Anderson," was the answer through the door, in a tone which at once soothed the ruffled waters of Thomas's spirit.

"Come in," he said.

She entered, quiet as a ghost.

"Come in, Annie. I'm glad to see ye. Jist come and kneel down aside me an' we'll pray together, for I'm sore troubled with an ill temper."

Without a word of reply, Annie knelt down by the side of his chair. Thomas drew the blanket over her head and took her hand, which was swallowed up in his. After a solemn pause, he began to pray in an outbursting agony of his heart: "O Lord, don't let us cry to ye in vain, this thy lambie, an' me, thy old sinner. Forgive my sins an' my vile temper, an' help me to love my neighbor as mysel'. Let Christ dwell in me, an' then I shall do right—not from mysel', for I hae no good thing in me, but from thy Spirit that dwelleth in us."

After this prayer, Thomas felt refreshed and hopeful. He rose slowly from his knees, sank into his chair, and drew Annie toward him and kissed her. Then he said, "Will ye go on a small errand for me, Annie?"

"That I will, Thomas."

"I would be obliged to ye if ye would jist run down to James Johnstone, the weaver, and tell him that I'm sorry I spoke to him as I did. An' I would take it right kind o' him if he would come an' take a cup o' tea with me in the mornin', an' then we could hae worship together. An' tell him to think no more o' the way I spoke to him, for I was troubled in my mind, an' I'm an ill-natured man."

"I'll tell him all that you say," answered Annie, "as well as I can remember it. Would you like me to come back and tell you what he says?"

"No, no, lassie. It'll be time for ye to go home to yer bed. An' it's a cold night. I know that by my leg. An' ye see, James Johnstone's not an ill-natured man like me. He's a douce man, an' he's sure to be well-pleased an' come to tea. No, no, ye needn't come back. Good night to ye, my dawtie. The Lord bless ye for comin' to pray with an ill-natured man."

36

• • • • • • • • • • • • • • • • • •

The Arrival of the Coach

*N*ow that Kate had a companion, Alec never saw her alone. Miss Warner was a nice, open-eyed, fair-faced English girl, with pleasant manners and though more shy than Kate was yet ready to take her part in conversation. Alec soon perceived that the two girls were both interested in poetry. By making use of the library of the college, he studied with great earnestness those poets they talked about so he would be able to keep up with them.

I will not weary my readers with the talk of the three young people enamored of Byron. In Kate's eyes Alec gained considerably from being able to talk about her favorite author, while she appeared to him more beautiful than ever. He began to discover now what I have already alluded to, that is the *fluidity* of her facial expression; for he was almost startled every time he saw her, by finding her different from what he had expected to find her. She behaved the same to him, but always looked slightly different, so that Alec felt as if he could never quite know her fully.

Had it not been for the help Mr. Cupples gave him toward the end of the session, he would have done poorly in both Greek and mathematics because of the time taken for his new pursuit of poetry. But Alec was so captured by the phantasy of Kate Fraser that, although not totally insensitive to his obligation to Mr. Cupples, he regarded it lightly. Ready to give his life for a smile from Kate, he took all the man's kindness and drunken wisdom as a matter of course.

And when he next visited home for the summer and saw Annie and Curly, he did not speak to them quite so heartily as on his former return.

In one or two of his letters home, which were never very long, Alec had merely mentioned Kate, and now Mrs. Forbes had many inquiries to make about her. Old feelings and thoughts awoke in her mind and made her wish to see the daughter of her old cousin. She wrote to Mr. Fraser asking him to allow his niece to pay her a visit of a few weeks, but she said nothing about it to Alec. The arrangement happened to be convenient to Mr. Fraser, who wished to accept an invitation himself. It was now the end of April and he proposed that the time should be set for the beginning of June.

When this favorable response arrived, Mrs. Forbes gave Alec the letter to read and watched the flush of delight rise in his face. The observation was gratifying to her; that Alec should at length marry one of his own people was a pleasing idea.

Alec ran off into the fields. To think that all these old familiar places would one day soon be glorified by *her* presence! That the daisies would bend beneath the foot of the goddess! It was more than he could do to contain his joy and harness his expectation into the carrying out of day-to-day affairs for the month of waiting that followed.

When the day at last arrived, Alec could not rest. He wandered about all day, haunting his mother as she prepared his room for Kate, hurrying away with a sudden sense of the propriety of indifference, and hurrying back on some cunning pretext. All the while his mother smiled to herself at his eagerness and the transparency of his wiles. At length, as the hour drew near, he could restrain himself no longer. He rushed to the stable, saddled his pony, and galloped off to meet the mail coach. The sun was nearing the west; a slight rain had just fallen, and the wind was too gentle even to shake the drops from the trees.

At last as he turned a corner of the road, there was the coach coming toward him. He had just time to wheel his pony around before it was up with him. A little gloved hand greeted him with a wave out the window, and the face he had been longing for shone out lovelier than ever. There were no passengers inside other than Kate. He rode alongside till they drew near the place where the gig was waiting for them. He gave his pony to the man, helped Kate down from the coach and into the small carriage, and then drove her home in triumph to his mother.

On the opposite side of the road from where the coach stopped, a grassy field sloped up to the shoulder of a hill which was crowned with firs. The rays of the sun, now red with rich age, flowed in a wide stream over the grass and shone on an old Scotch fir making its bark glow. At the foot of the tree sat Tibbie Dyster. From her the luminous red steamed up the trunk and along the branches of the glowing fir, and over the radiant grass of the upsloping field away toward the western sun.

Alec would have found it difficult to say whether or not he had seen the red cloak of the sunset. But from the shadowy side of it there were eyes shining upon him with a deeper and truer, though calmer, devotion than that with which he regarded Kate. Annie sat by Tibbie's side, the side away from the sun. There they were seated side by side: old, scarred, blind Tibbie and cold, gentle Annie with her dark hair, blue eyes, and the sad wisdom of her pale face. Tibbie had come out to bask a little in the warmth of the setting sun, and to breathe the air which, through her prison bars of darkness, spoke to her of freedom.

"What did the coach stop for, Annie, lass?" asked Tibbie as soon as it had driven on.

"It's a lady going to Mistress Forbes' at Howglen."

"How do ye know that?"

" 'Cause Alec Forbes rode out to meet her and then took her home in the gig."

"Ay! ay! I thought I heard more than the ordinary nummer o' horse feet as the coach came up. He's a fine lad, that Alec Forbes, isn't he?"

"Ay, he is," answered Annie sadly—not from jealousy, for she still admired Alec from afar, but as looking up from her purgatorial exclusion to the paradise of Howglen where the beautiful lady would have Mrs. Forbes, and Alec too, all to herself.

The old woman caught the tone, but misinterpreted it.

"I doubt," she said, "he won't get any good at that college."

"Why not?" returned Annie. "I was at school with him and never saw anything to find fault with."

"Ow, no, lassie. Ye had nothin' to do findin' fault with him. His father was a douce man, an' maybe a God-fearin' man, though he made but few words about it. I think we're sometimes too hard on them that promises little, but maybe *does* more. Ye remember what ye read to me afore we came out together, about the lad that said to his father, *I go not*, but afterward he repented and went."

"Ay."

"Weel, I think we'll go home now."

They rose and went, hand in hand, over the bridge and round to the end of the parapet, and down the steep descent to the cottage at its foot.

"Now," said Tibbie after they had arrived, "ye'll jist read a chapter to me, lassie, afore ye go home, an' then I'll go to me bed. Blindness is a painful way to save candles."

She forgot that it was summer when, in those northern regions, the night has no time to gather before the sun is flashing again in the east.

The chapter happened to be the ninth of John's Gospel, about Jesus curing a man blind from his birth. When she had finished, Annie asked: "Might not He cure you, Tibbie, if you asked Him?"

"Ay, might He, an' ay He will," answered Tibbie. "I'm only jist bidin' His time. But I'm thinkin' He'll cure me better than He cured the blind man. He'll jist take the body off o' me altogether an' then I'll see, no with eyes like yers, but with my whole speeritual body. I wish Mr. Turnbull would take it into his head to preach aboot that sometime afore my time comes, which won't be that long, I'm thinkin'. The wheels'll be stoppin' at my door before long."

"What makes you think that, Tibbie? There's no sign of death about you, I'm sure," protested Annie.

"Well, ye see, I can't well say. Blin' folk somehow know more than other folk about things that the sight o' the eye has little to do with. But never mind. I'm willin' to bide in the dark as long as He likes."

When their talk was over, Annie went home to her garret. It was a remarkable experience the child enjoyed in the changes that came to her with the seasons. The winter with its frost and bitter winds brought her a home at Howglen with kind Mrs. Forbes; the summer, whose airs were molten kisses, took it away and gave her the face of nature instead of the face of a human mother. In place of the snug little room in Howglen—in which she heard with quiet exultation the fierce rush of the hail-scattering tempest against the window of the fluffy fall of the snowflakes—she now had the garret room with its curtainless bed and through whose roof the winds easily found their way. But the winds were warmer now, and through the skylight the sunbeams illuminated the room. It also showed all the rat holes and wretchedness of decay.

There was comfort out of doors in the daytime—in the sky and the fields and all the goings-on of life. And this night, after her talk with Tibbie, Annie did not much mind going back to the garret. Nor did she lie awake to think about the beautiful lady Alec had taken home with him.

She dreamed instead that she saw the Son of Man. There was a veil over His face like the veil that Moses wore in the scripture she had recently read to Tibbie. But the face was so bright that it almost melted the veil away, and what she saw made her love that face more than the presence of Alec, more than the kindness of Mrs. Forbes or Dowie, and even more than the memory of her father.

37

·················

Kate in Howglen

$\mathcal{A}$lec did not fall asleep so soon. The thought that Kate was in the house—asleep in the next room—kept him awake. Yet he woke the next morning earlier than usual. There were bands of golden light upon the wall, though Kate would not be awake for hours yet.

He sprang out of bed and ran to the banks of the Glamour. He plunged in and washed the dreams from his eyes with a dive and a swim under the water. Then he rose to the surface and swam slowly about under the overhanging willows. He dressed himself and lay down on the meadow grass, each blade shadowing its neighbor in the slant sunlight. Cool as it still was with the coldness of the vanished twilight, it yet felt warm to his bare feet, fresh from the waters that had crept down through the night from the high mountains. He fell fast asleep, and the sheep came and fed about him as if he had been one of themselves. When he woke, the sun was high; and when he reached the house he found his mother and Kate already seated at breakfast—Kate in the prettiest of cotton dresses, looking as fresh and country-like as the morning itself. The window was open, and through the encircling ivy the air came in fresh and cool.

"What are you going to do with Kate today, Alec?" said his mother.

"Whatever Kate likes," answered Alec.

"I have no choice," returned Kate. "I don't know yet what I have to choose between. I am in your hands, Alec."

It was the first time she had called him by his first name, and a spear of sunshine seemed to quiver in his heart. He was restless as a hyena till she was ready. He then led her to the banks of the river, here low and grassy, with plenty of wild flowers, and a low babblement everywhere.

"This is delightful," said Kate. "I will come here as often as you like, and you shall read to me."

"What shall I read? Would you like one of Sir Walter's novels?"

"Just the thing."

Alec started for the house at full speed.

"Stop!" cried Kate. "You're not going to leave me alone beside this—talking water?"

"I thought you liked the water," said Alec.

"Yes. But I don't want to be left alone beside it. I will go with you and get some handwork."

She turned away from the stream with a strange backward look, and they walked home.

But after Alec had found the book, Kate showed some disinclination to return to the riverside, so Alec made a seat for her near the house, in the shadow of a silver birch, and threw himself on the grass at her feet to begin reading. At noon Mrs. Forbes sent them a dish of curds and a great jug of cream, with oatcakes and butter soft from the churn. The rippling shadow of the birch played over the white curds and the golden butter as they ate.

Those among my readers who have had the happiness to lead innocent boy lives will know what a marvelous delight it was to Alec to have this girl near him in his own home and his own haunts. He never speculated on her character or nature, for his own principles existed within him only in a latent condition.

The next day saw Alec walking by the side of Kate mounted on his pony, up a steep path to the top of one of the highest hills surrounding the valley. It was a wild hill, with hardly anything growing on it but heather, which would make it regal with purple in the autumn. No tree could stand the blasts that blew over that hill in winter. Having climbed to the topmost point, they stood and gazed. The country lay outstretched beneath in the glow of a June day, while around them flitted the cool airs of heaven. Above them rose the soaring blue of the summer sky, with a white cloud or two floating in it, and a blue peak or two leaning its color against it. Through the green grass and the green corn below crept two silvery threads, meeting far away and floating as one—the two rivers which watered the valley of Strathglamour. Between the rivers lay the gray stone town, with its roofs of thatch and slate. One of its main streets stopped suddenly at the bridge with the three arches above Tibbie's cottage, and at the other end of the bridge lay the green fields.

The landscape was not one of the most beautiful, but it had a beauty of its own, which is all a country or a woman needs. Kate sat gazing about her in evident delight. She had taken off her hat to feel the wind, letting her hair fall in golden heaps upon her shoulders, in which the wind and the sunbeams played hide-and-seek.

In a moment the pleasure vanished from her face. It clouded over, while the country lay full in the sun. Her eyes no longer looked wide about her, but expressed defeat and retirement. Listlessly she began to gather her hair together.

"Do you ever feel as if you could not get room enough, Alec?" she said wearily.

"No, I don't," he answered, honestly and somewhat stupidly. "I have always as much as I want. I should have thought you would too—up here."

"I did feel satisfied for a moment, but it was only a moment. It is gone now."

Alec had nothing to say in reply. He never had anything to give Kate but love; and now he gave her more love. It was all he was rich in. But she did not care for his riches. And so, after gazing a while, she turned to descend. Alec picked up her hat and took his place at the pony's head. He was not so happy as he thought he should be. Somehow she was of another order, and he could not understand her—he could only worship her.

The whole of the hot afternoon they spent on the grass. After tea they leaned together over the gate and watched the weary sun, who in this region works long after hours in the summer, go down.

"What a long shadow everything throws," said Kate. "Look how the light creeps about the roots of the grass on the ridge, as if it were looking for something between the shadows."

The sun diminished to a star, and vanished. As if it had sunk into a pool of air and made it overflow, a gentle ripple of wind blew from the sunset over the grass. They could see the grass bending and swaying and bathing in the wind's coolness before it came to them. It blew on their faces at length, and whispered something they could not understand, making Kate think of her mother, and Alec of Kate.

That same breeze blew upon Tibbie and Annie as they sat in the patch of meadow by the cottage. It made Tibbie think of death, the opener of sleeping eyes. For Tibbie's darkness was the shadow of her grave, on the further border of which the light was breaking in music.

When the gentle, washing wind blew upon Annie, she remembered, "The wind that bloweth where it listeth"; and thought that if ever the Spirit of God blew upon her, she would feel it just like that wind of summer sunset—so cool, so blessed, so gentle, so living! And was it not God who breathed that wind upon her? Was He not even then breathing His Spirit into the soul of that woman-child?

It blew upon Andrew Constable, as he stood in his shopdoor, the easy labor of his day all but over. And he said to his little weasel-faced, douce, old-fashioned child who stood leaning against the other doorcheek: "That's a fine little blast, Isie! Don't ye like to feel it blowin' on yer hot cheeks, dawtie?"

And she answered, "Ay, I like it weel, Daddie; but it min's me some o' the winter."

It blew upon Robert Bruce, who had just run out into the yard to see how his potatoes and cabbages were coming on. He said, "It's some cold," and ran in again to put on his hat.

Alec and Kate stood looking into the darkening field. A great flock of rooks, which filled the air with their rooky gossip, was flying straight home to an old, gray ruin just visible among some ancient trees. Hearing them rejoicing far over-head, Kate searched for them in the darkening sky, found them, and watched their flight till the black specks were dissolved in the distance. They are not the most poetic of birds, but in a darkening country twilight, over silent fields, they blend into the general tone till even their noisy caw suggests repose. But it was room Kate wanted, not rest. She would know one day, however, that room and rest are the same, and that the longings for both spring from the same need.

"What place is that in the trees?" she asked.

"The old castle of Glamerton," answered Alec. "Would you like to go and see it?"

"Yes, very much."

"We'll go tomorrow, then."

"The dew is beginning to fall, Kate," Mrs. Forbes called as she now joined them. "You had better come in."

Alec lingered behind. An unknown emotion drew his heart toward the earth. He would watch her go to sleep in the twilight, which was now beginning to brood over her, as with the brown wings of a hen. The daisies were all asleep, spotting the green grass with stars of color; for their closed red tips, like the finger points of two fairy hands, tenderly joined together, pointed up in little cones to keep the yellow stars warm within, that they might shine bright when the great star of day came to look for them again. The trees stood still and shadowy as clouds but breathing out mysterious odors. The stars overhead, half-dimmed away in the ghostly twilight that would not go away, were yet busy at their night-time work. There was no moon. A wide stillness and peace, as of a heart at rest, filled the space. Now and then a bird sprang out with a sudden tremor of leaves. All was marvel. And Alec, too, went to his rest.

In the morning, great sun-crested clouds with dark sides hung overhead; and while they sat at breakfast, one of those glorious showers, each of whose great drops carries a sun-spark in its heart, fell on the earth with a tumult of gentle noises. The leaves of the ivy, hanging over the windows, quivered and shook. And between the drops darted and wound a great bumble bee.

Kate and Alec went to the open window and looked out on the rainy world, breathing the odors released from the grass and the ground. Alec turned from the window to Kate's face and saw upon it a keen yet solemn delight. But as he gazed he saw a cloud come over it. Instinctively he glanced out again for the cause. The rain had become thick and small, and a light opposing wind had disordered its descent with broken and crossing lines.

This change from a summer rain to a storm had altered Kate's mood, and her face was now, as always, a reflex of the face of nature.

"Shut the window, please, Alec," she said with a shiver.

"We'll have a fire directly," said Alec.

"No," returned Kate, trying to smile. "Just fetch me a shawl from the closet in my room."

Alec had not been in his own room since Kate had come. He entered it with a kind of gentle awe, and stood gazing just within the door. From a pair of tiny shoes under the dressing table radiated a whole roomful of femininity. He was almost afraid to go farther, and would not have dared to look in the mirror. In less than three days her mere presence had made the room marvelous.

Recovering himself, he hastened to the closet, got the shawl, and went down the stairs three steps at a time.

"Couldn't you find it, Alec?" said Kate.

"Oh, yes; I found it at once," answered Alec, blushing.

I wonder whether Kate guessed what made the boy blush. But it does not matter much now, though she did look curiously at him for a moment.

"Just help me with my shawl," she said.

38

....

Annie's Kitten

*D*uring all this time, Annie had scarcely seen a thing of her aunt, Margaret Anderson. Ever since Bruce had offended her on her first visit, she had taken her business elsewhere and had never even called to see her niece. Annie had met her several times in the street and that was all. Hence, on one of the beautiful after-noons of that unusually fine summer, and partly perhaps from missing the kind-ness of Mrs. Forbes, Annie took a longing to see her old aunt and set out for Clippenstrae to visit her. It was a walk of two miles, chiefly along the high road, bordered in part by vegetation. Through this she loitered along, enjoying the few wild flowers and the many lights and shadows, so that it was almost evening before she reached her destination.

"Preserve us all! Annie Anderson, what brings ye here this time o' night?" exclaimed her aunt.

"It's a long time since I saw you, Auntie, and I wanted to visit you."

"Weel, come in the house. Ye're growin' into a great muckle queen," said her aunt, inclined to a favorable consideration of her by her growth.

Margaret "didna like bairns—thoughtless craturs—aye wantin' ither folk to do for them!" But growth was a kind of regenerating process in her eyes, and when a girl began to look like a woman, she regarded it as an outward sign of conversion, or something equally valuable. So she conducted Annie into the pres-ence of her uncle, a little old man, worn and bent, with gray locks peeping out from under a Highland bonnet.

"This is my brother James's bairn," she told him.

The old man received Annie kindly, called her his dawtie, and made her sit down by him on a three-legged creepie stool, talking to her as if she had been quite a child, while she, capable of high conversation as she was, replied in cor-responding terms. Her great-aunt was confined to her bed with rheumatism. Sup-per was preparing and Annie was not sorry to have a share, for indeed, during the summer her meals were often scanty enough. While they ate, the old man kept helping her to the best, talking to her all the time.

"Will ye no come and bide with me, dawtie?" he said, meaning little by the question.

"Na, na," interposed Margaret. "She's at the school, ye know, Uncle, an' we mustn't interfere with her schoolin'.—How does that lyin' Robert Bruce carry himsel' to ye, child?"

"Ow, I just never mind him," answered Annie.

"Weel it's all he deserves from ye. But if I were you, I would let him know that if he plants yer corn, ye have a right to more than his gleanin's."

"I don't know what you mean," responded Annie.

"Ow, na, I dare say not. But ye may jist as well know. Robert Bruce has two hunner pound odd o' yer own, lassie. An' if he doesn't treat ye well, ye can jist tell him that I told ye so."

This piece of news did not have the overpowering effect on Annie which her aunt had expected. No doubt the money seemed in Annie's eyes a limitless fortune; but, then, Bruce had it. She might as well think of robbing a bear of her cubs as getting her money from Bruce. Besides, what could she do with it if she had it? And she had not yet acquired the faculty of loving money for its own sake. When she rose to go home, she felt little richer than when she entered, except for the kind words of John Peterson, the uncle.

"It's too late for ye to go home alone, dawtie," said the old man.

"I'm not that scared," answered Annie.

"Weel, if ye walk with Him, the dark'll be light about ye," he said. "Be a good lass, an' run home as fast as ye can. Good night to ye, dawtie."

Rejoicing as if she had found her long-lost home, Annie went out into the twilight feeling it impossible that she should be frightened at anything. But when she came to the part of the road bordered with trees, she could not help thinking she saw a figure flitting along from tree to tree just within the deeper dusk of the wood, and as she hurried on, her fancy turned to fear.

Presently she heard awful sounds, like the subdued growling of wild beasts. She would have taken to her heels in terror, but she reflected that thereby she would only ensure pursuit, whereas if she continued to walk slowly she might slip away unnoticed. As she reached a gate leading into the wood, however, a dusky figure came bounding over it and came straight toward her. To her relief it went on two legs, and when it came nearer she recognized some traits of old acquaintance about it. When it was within a couple yards of her, she stopped and cried out joyfully: "Curly!"—for it was her old vice-champion.

"Annie!" was the equally joyful response.

"I thought you were a wild beast!" said Annie.

"I was only growlin' for fun to mysel'," answered Curly, who would have done it all the more if he had known there was anyone on the road. "I didn't know I was scaring anybody. How are ye, Annie? An' how's Blister Bruce?" Curly was dreadfully prolific in nicknames.

Annie had not seen him for six months. He had continued to show himself so full of mischief, though of a comparatively innocent sort, that his father thought it better at last to send him to a town at some distance to learn the trade of a saddler, for which he had shown a preference.

This was his first visit to his home. Up to now his father had received no complaints of his behavior, and had now asked for a holiday for him.

"Ye're some grown, Annie," he said.

"So are you, Curly," answered Annie.

"An' how's Alec?"

"He's very well."

Whereupon much talk followed. At length Curly asked: "An' how's the rats?"

"Over well and thriving."

"Jist put yer hand in my coat pocket an' see what I hae brought ye."

Knowing Curly's natural bent, Annie refused.

"It's a wild beast," said Curly.

So saying, he pulled out of his pocket the most delicately colored kitten, not half the beauty of which could be seen in the gloaming.

"Did you bring this all the way from Spinnie for me, Curly?"

"Ay, did I. Ye see, I don't like rats either. But ye must keep it out o' their way for a few weeks, or they'll tear it all to bits. It'll soon be a match for them though, I'll warrant. She comes o' a killin' breed."

Annie took the kitten home, and it shared her bed that night.

"What's that meowin'?" asked Bruce the next morning, the moment he rose from the genuflexion of morning prayers.

"It's my kitten," answered Annie. "I'll let you see it."

"We have too many mouths in the house already," Bruce rasped out as she returned with the little, peering kitten in her arms. "We have no room for more. Here, Rob, take the creature and put a bag around its neck and a stone in the bag and fling it into the Glamour."

Annie, not waiting to parley, darted from the house with the kitten.

Rob bolted after her, delighted with his commission. But instead of finding her at the door, as he had expected, he saw her already a long way up the street, flying like the wind. He launched out in keen pursuit. He was now a great lumbering boy, and although Annie's wind was not equal to his, she was faster. She took the direct road to Howglen and Rob kept floundering after her. Before she reached the footbridge, she was nearly breathless and he was gaining quickly upon her. Just as she turned the corner of the road, leading up on the other side of the water, she met Alec and Kate. Unable to speak, she passed without a word. But there was no need to ask the cause of her pale, agonized face, for there was young Bruce at her heels. Alec collared him instantly.

"What are you up to?" he demanded.

"Nothin'," answered the panting pursuer.

"If you be after nothing, you'll find that nearer home," retorted Alec, twisting him round in that direction and giving him a kick to expedite his return. "Let me hear of you troubling Annie Anderson, and I'll take a piece out of your skin the next time I lay my hands on you. Now go home."

Rob obeyed like a frightened dog, while Annie pursued her course to Howglen as if her enemy were still on her track. Rushing into the parlor, she fell on the floor before Mrs. Forbes, unable to speak. The kitten sprang out of her arms and took refuge under the sofa.

"Ma'am," she gasped at length, "take care of my kitten. They want to drown it! It's my own. Curly gave it to me."

Mrs. Forbes comforted her and readily undertook the assignment. Annie was very late for school, for Mrs. Forbes made her have another good breakfast before she went. Fortunately, Mr. Malison was in a good humor that day and said nothing. Not surprisingly, Rob Bruce looked devils at her. What he had told his father I do not know; but whatever it was, it was all written down in Bruce's mental books to the debit of Alexander Forbes of Howglen.

Mrs. Forbes' heart grieved her when she found what persecution her little friend was exposed to during those times when she did not have her over for daily visits. But she did not see how she could well remedy the situation. She was herself in the power of Bruce, so protest from her would be worth little; while to have Annie in the house as before would involve consequences unpleasant to all concerned. She resolved to make up for it by being kinder to her than ever as soon as Alec had followed Kate back to the university. For the present she comforted both herself and Annie by telling her to "be sure to come when you find yourself in any trouble."

But Annie was not one to apply to her friends except she was in great need of their help. The present case had been one of life and death. She found no further occasion to visit Mrs. Forbes that summer before Kate and Alec had both gone.

39

Tibbie and Thomas

On one of those sleepy summer afternoons, just when the sunshine had begun to turn yellow, Annie was sitting with Tibbie on the grass in front of her little cottage, whose door looked up the river. Tibbie's blind face was turned toward the sun and her fingers busy as ants with her knitting needles, for she was making a pair of heavy stockings for Annie for the winter.

"Who's that comin', lassie?" she asked.

Annie, who had heard no one, glanced round and said, "It's Thomas Crann."

"That's not Thomas Crann," rejoined Tibbie. "I don't hear his cough."

Thomas came up pale and limping a little.

"That's not Thomas Crann!" repeated Tibbie before he had time to address her.

"Why not, Tibbie?" returned Thomas.

" 'Cause I can't hear you breathin'."

"That's a sign that I hae all the more breath, Tibbie. I'm so much better o' that asthma that I think the Lord must hae blown into my nostrils another breath o' that life He breathed into Adam an' Eve."

"I'm right glad to hear it, Thomas. Breath must come from Him one way or the other."

"No doubt, Tibbie."

"Will ye sit down beside us, Thomas? It's long since I've seen ye." Tibbie always spoke of seeing people.

"Ay, will I, Tibbie. I haven't much work on my hands these days."

"Annie and me's just been talking about this thing and that thing, Thomas," said Tibbie, dropping her knitting on her knees and folding her palms together. "Maybe *you* can tell me whether there be any likeness between the light that I can't see and the sound o' the water running that I like so well to hear."

"Weel, ye see, Tibbie," answered Thomas, "it's almost as hard for the likes o' us to unnerstan' yer blindness as it may be for ye to unnerstan' our sight."

" 'Deed maybe neither o' us know much about oor own gift. Say anything ye like, as long as ye don't tell me, as the bairn here once did, that I couldn't tell what the light was. I don't know what yer sight may be, and I'm thinking I care as little. But I well know what light is."

"Tibbie, don't be ill-natured like me. Ye have no call to be that way. I'm tryin' to answer yer question. An' if ye interrupt me again, I'll rise an' go home."

"Say away, then, Thomas. Don't heed me. I'm just cantankerous sometimes. I know that well enough."

"Ye hae no business to be, Tibbie."

"No more or less than other folk."

"Less, Tibbie."

"How do ye make that oot?" asked Tibbie defensively.

"Ye don't see the things to anger ye that other folk sees. As I came down the street just now, I came upon the two laddies—ye know them—they're twins, one o' them a cripple—"

"Ay, that was Murdoch Malison's work!" interposed Tibbie with indignant reminiscence.

"The man's been sorry for it ever since," said Thomas, "so we mustn't go over it again, Tibbie."

"Very well, Thomas. I'll hold my tongue. What about the laddies?"

"They were fightin' in the street, hitting one another's heads an' punchin' at one another's noses, an' doin' their best to destroy the very image o' the Almighty. So I thrashed them both."

"An' what became o' the image o' the Almighty then?" asked Tibbie with a grotesque contortion of her mouth and a roll of her veiled eyeballs. "I don't doubt, Thomas, that ye angered yersel' more than ye quieted them with the thrashing. The wrath o' man, ye know, Thomas, worketh not the righteousness o' God."

There was not a person in Glamerton who would have dared to speak thus to Thomas Crann but Tibbie Dyster, perhaps because there was not one who had such a respect for him. Possibly the darkness about her made her bolder; but I think it was her truth, which is another word for *love*, however unlike love the outcome may look, that made her able to speak in this fashion.

There was silence for a long minute. Then he said: "Maybe ye're in the right, Tibbie. Ye anger me, but I would rather have a body anger me by telling me the truth than I would have all the fair words in the dictionary. It's a strange thing, woman, but ay when a body's tryin' hardest to go upright, he's sure to catch a dreadful fall. Here I hae been wrestlin' with my bad temper harder than in all my life; an' yet I never in all my days licked two laddies for lickin' one another till jist this very day. I can't seem to get to the bottom o' it."

"There's worst things than an ill temper, Thomas. Not that it's a good thing. And it's none like Him that was meek an' lowly of heart. But, as I say, there's worse faults than a bad temper. It would be no gain to ye, Thomas, and no glory to Him if you were to overcome yer temper and then think a heap o' yersel' that ye had done it. Maybe that's why ye're not allowed to be victorious in yer endeavors."

" 'Deed, maybe, Tibbie," said Thomas solemnly. "I don't doubt the fault's not so much in my temper as in my heart. It's more love I need, Tibbie. If I loved my neighbor as myself, I couldn't be so ill-natured."

"Resist the devil, Thomas. He's sure to run in the end. But I'm afraid ye're going to go away without telling me aboot the light and the water. When I'm sitting here listening to the water as it comes murmuring and gurgling down the river, it puts me in the mind o' the scripture that says, 'His voice was as the sound o' many waters.' Now His face is light—ye know that, don't ye—and if His voice be like the water, there must be somethin' alike between light and water. That's what made me ask ye, Thomas?"

"Weel, I don't rightly know how to answer ye, Tibbie. But at this moment the light's playin' bonnie upon the little dam down there by the mill—shimmerin' on the water. Eh! it's bonnie, woman; an' I wish ye had the sight o' yer eyes to see with, though ye do pretend to think little o' it."

"Well, well, my time's comin', Thomas. I must jist wait till it comes. Ye can't help me, I can see that. If only I could open my eyes for a minute, I would know all aboot it and be able to answer mysel'."

All the time they were talking Annie was watching Alec's boat, which had come down the river and was floating in the sunshine above the dam. Thomas must have seen it too, for it was in the very heart of the radiance reflected to them from the watery mirror. But Alec was a painful subject with Thomas, for when they chanced to meet now, nothing more than the passing nod of ordinary acquaintance was exchanged. And certain facts in Thomas's nature, as well as certain articles in his creed, made him unable to be indulgent to young people.

So, being one of those who never speak of what is painful to them if they can avoid it, he talked about the light and said nothing about the boat that was in the middle of it. Had Alec been rowing, Tibbie would have heard the oars; but he only paddled enough to keep the boat from drifting onto the dam by the dyer's mill. Kate sat in the stern looking at the water with half-closed eyes, and Alec sat looking at Kate, as if his eyes were made only for her. And Annie sat in the meadow, and she too looked at Kate. She thought how pretty Kate was, and how she must like being rowed about in the old boat. It seemed quite an old boat now. An age had passed since her name had been painted on it. She wondered if *The Bonnie Annie* was worn off the stern yet; or if Alec had painted it out and put the name of the pretty lady instead. When Tibbie and Thomas rose and walked away into the house, Annie lingered behind on the grass.

The sun sank lower and lower till at length Alec leaned back with a stronger pull on the oars and the boat crept away up the stream, growing smaller with each sweep of the oars, and turning a curve in the river, was lost to sight.

Still Annie sat, one hand lying listlessly in her lap and the other plucking blades of grass and making a little heap of them beside her till she had pulled a spot quite bare and the brown earth peeped through between the roots. Then she rose, went to the door of the cottage, called a good night to Tibbie and took her way home.

40

•••••••••••••••••••

The Castle Ruin

*T*hough my story has primarily to do with the slow-paced life of a country region where growth and change occur imperceptibly, like the ripening of a harvest, there will yet come clouds and rainbows, adventures and coincidences, even in the quietest village. Such unexpected occurrences often bring change that is unpredictable, unsought, and even unwelcome.

As Kate and Alec walked along the street, having finally arranged for a visit to the castle, one of the coaches from the county town drove up with its four thoroughbreds.

"What a handsome fellow the driver is!" remarked Kate.

Alec looked up at the box. There sat Beauchamp with the reins in his grasp, handling the horses with composure and skill. Beside him sat the owner of the coach, a laird of the neighborhood. Beauchamp had at last judged the time ripe and this was the first evidence of his closer approach.

A pain shot through Alec's heart. Certainly Beauchamp was a handsome fellow, but it was the first time Alec had compared himself with another. That she should admire Beauchamp more than him! If his rival were never seen again, he would already have worked a bitter revenge for Alec's humiliation of him at the debate. For the memory of that moment and Kate's remark made Alec writhe on his bed years afterward. But alas, Patrick Beauchamp had only begun to exact his avenging pound of flesh from the country boy, Alec Forbes of Howglen!

Alec's face fell. They walked on in silence in the shadow of a high wall. Kate looked up at the top of the wall and stopped. Alec looked at her. Her face was as full of light as a diamond in the sun. He forgot all his jealousy. The fresh tide of his love swept it away, or at least covered it.

They walked up to the ruined walls of the castle. Long grass grew about them, close to the very door, which was locked. If old Time could not be kept out, younger destroyers might. Alec had borrowed a key from the caretaker, and they entered by a door in the great tower, under the spiky remnants of the spiral stair projecting from the huge circular wall. To the right, a steep descent led down to the cellars and the dungeon—a terrible place, which needed no popular legends such as Alec had been telling Kate of a walled-up door and lost room, to add to their influence. It was no wonder that when he held out his hand to lead her down into the darkness, she shrank and drew back. A few rays came through the decayed planks of the door which Alec had tried to push closed behind them. One larger ray from the keyhole fell upon Kate's face and showed it blanched with fear.

At that moment a sweet, low voice came from somewhere out of the darkness, saying: "Don't be frightened, mem, to go where Alec wants you to go. You can trust him."

Staring in the direction of the sound, Kate saw the pale face of a slender girl— half child, half maiden—glimmering across the gulf that led to the dungeon. She stood in the midst of a faint light, a dusky and yet radiant creature, seeming to throw off from her a faint brown light—a lovely, earth-stained ghost.

"Oh, Annie! is that you?" said Alec.

"Ay, it is," answered Annie.

"This is an old schoolfellow of mine," he said, turning to Kate who was look- ing at the girl.

"Oh! Is it?" said Kate with a hint of condescension in her tone.

Between the two maidens, each looking ghostly to the other, lay a dark cavern mouth that seemed to go down to Hades.

"Won't you go down, mem?" said Annie.

"No, thank you," answered Kate decisively.

"Alec'll take good care of you, mem."

"Oh, yes! I dare say; but I would rather not."

Alec said nothing. So Kate would not trust him. Would she have gone with Beauchamp if he had asked her? Ah! If he had asked Annie, she too would have turned pale, but she would have laid her hand in his and gone with him.

"If you want to go up, then," she said, "I'll show you the easiest path. It's round this way."

She pointed to a narrow ledge between the descent and the circular wall, by which they could cross to where she stood. But Alec, having no desire for Annie's company, declined her guidance and took Kate up a nearer, though more difficult ascent, to the higher level. Here all the floors of the castle lay in dust beneath their feet. The whole central space lay open to the sky.

Annie remained standing on the edge of the dungeon slope. She had been on her way to see Tibbie when she caught a glimpse of Kate and Alec as they passed.

Since watching them in the boat the evening before, she had been longing to speak to Alec, longing to see Kate nearer. She guessed where they were going, and across the fields she bounded like a fawn. She did not need a key, for she knew a hole on the level of the grass, wide enough to let her creep through the two-yard-thick wall. So she had crept in and taken her place near the door.

After they had rambled over the lower part of the building, Alec took Kate up a small winding stair, past a succession of empty doorways, each leading nowhere because the floors had fallen. Kate was so frightened by coming suddenly upon one after another of these defenseless openings that by the time she reached the broad platform which ran around the top of the tower, she felt quite faint.

Alec saw that she was ill, comforted her as well he could, and by degrees got her to the bottom. There was a spot of grass inside the walls where he had her lie down to rest, and as the sun shone on her through one of the ruined windows, Alec stood so that his shadow fell across her eyes. After standing thus for some time gazing upon the sleeping beauty—for Kate had indeed fallen asleep—on the grass beneath him, he turned his eyes up to the tower from which they had just descended. Looking down upon them from one of the isolated doorways, he saw the pale face of Patrick Beauchamp. Alec bounded to the stair, rushed to the top and round the platform, but found nobody. Beginning to doubt his eyes, he glanced down from whence he had come, only to see Beauchamp standing over the sleeping girl. He darted down the screw of the stair, but when he reached the bottom Beauchamp had again disappeared.

The same moment Kate began to wake. Alec returned to her side, and they left the place, locked the door behind them, took the key back to the caretaker at the lodge, and went home. After tea, believing he had locked Beauchamp into the castle, Alec returned and searched the building from top to bottom. Getting a candle and a ladder, he went down into the dungeon. Still finding no one, he went home bewildered.

While Alec was searching the vacant ruin, Beauchamp was comfortably seated on the box of a coach halfway back to the house of the laird, its owner. The laird, or landholder, whom he was visiting was a relative of his mother. Beauchamp had seen Kate and Alec take the way to the castle, had followed them, and found the door unlocked. Watching them about the place he ascended the stair from another approach. The moment Alec looked up at him he ran down again and had just dropped into a sort of well-like place, which the stair had used to fill on its way to a lower level, when he heard Alec's feet thundering over his head. Determined then to see what the lady was like, for he had never seen her close, he scrambled out and approached her cautiously. He had only a few moments to contemplate her before he saw that Alec had again caught sight of him, and he immediately fled to his former refuge.

The sound of the rusty bolt rather alarmed him, for he had not expected their immediate departure. His first impulse was to see whether he could not get the bolt loose from the inside. This he soon found to be impossible. He next turned to the windows in the front, but there the ground fell away so suddenly that he was many feet from it—an altogether dangerous leap. He was beginning to feel seriously concerned when he heard a voice: "Do you want to get out, sir? They locked the door."

He turned and could see no one. Approaching the door again, he saw Annie in the dark twilight, standing on the edge of the descent to the vaults. He had passed the spot not a minute before and she was not there then. But instead of taking her for a ghost, he accosted her with easy insolence.

"Tell me how to get out, my pretty girl, and I'll give you a kiss."

Seized with a terror she did not understand, Annie darted into the cavern between them and sped down its steep descent into the darkness. A few yards down she turned aside through a low doorway, into a small room. Beauchamp rushed after her, passed her, and fell over a great stone lying in the middle of his way. Annie heard him fall, sprang forth again, and flew to the upper light. She found her way out the same way she had entered and left the discourteous knight a safe captive, fallen upon that horrible stair.

Annie told the keeper that there was a gentleman shut up in the castle, and then ran a mile and a half to Tibbie's cottage without stopping. But she did not say a word to Tibbie about her adventure.

41

The Spirit of Prophecy

A spirit of prophecy, whether from the Lord or not, was abroad this summer in Glamerton. Those who read their Bibles took to reading the prophecies, all the prophecies, and scarcely anything but the prophecies. Either for himself or following in the track of his spiritual instructor, every man exercised his individual powers of interpretation upon these shadowy glimpses into the future. Whatever was known, whether about ancient Assyria or modern Tahiti, found its theoretical place. Of course the Church of Rome received her due share of the curses from all parties. And neither the Church of England, the Church of Scotland, nor either of the dissenting sects went without its portion freely dealt, each of the last finding something that applied to all the rest. One might have thought they were reveling in the idea of vengeance, instead of striving for the rescue of their neighbors from the wrath to come. Among these were Thomas Crann and his minister, Mr. Turnbull. To them Glamerton was the center of creation, providence, and revelation. Every warning finger in the Book pointed to it; every burst of indignation from the laboring heart of the holy prophets was addressed to its sinners. Thomas was ready to fly at the meekest or the greatest man in Glamerton with terrible denunciations of the wrath of the Almighty for their sins. All the evildoers of the place feared him—the rich manufacturer and the strong horsedoctor included. They called him a wheezing, canting hypocrite, and would go streets out of their way to avoid him.

In the midst of this commotion, the good Pastor Cowie died. He had taken no particular interest in what was going on. Ever since Annie's petition for counsel, he had been thinking, as he had never thought before, about his own relationhip to God. Now he had carried his thoughts into another world.

He was gently regarded by all—even by Thomas.

"Ay, ay," Thomas said with slow emphasis, "he's gone is he, honest man? Weel, maybe he had the root o' faith an' truth in him, although it made little enough show about the yard. There was small flower an' less fruit. But judgment dinna belong to us, ye see, Jean."

Thomas would judge the living from morning to night; but the dead—he would leave them alone in better hands.

Except for his own daughters there was no one who mourned so deeply the loss of Mr. Cowie as Annie Anderson. She had left his church and gone to the Missionaries, but she could never forget his kisses, or his gentle words, or his shilling; for by them Mr. Cowie had given her a more trusting notion of God and His tenderness than she could have found in a hundred sermons put together. What greater gift could a man give? Was that not worth ten bookfuls of sound doctrine?

When she had last entered his room and found him supported with pillows in his bed, he stretched out his arms to her feebly, held her close to him, and wept.

"I'm going to die, Annie," he said.

"And go to heaven, sir, to the face of God," returned Annie, not sobbing but with tears streaming silently down her face.

"I don't know, Annie."

"If God loves you half as much as I do, sir, you'll be well off in heaven. And I'm thinking He must love you more than me. For, you see, sir, God is love itself."

"I sometimes don't know what God thinks of me anymore, Annie. But if ever I do get there, which'll be more than I deserve, I'll tell Him about you and ask Him to give you the help I couldn't give you."

Love and death make us all children.

Annie had no answer but what lay in her tears. He called his daughter, who stood weeping in the room. She came near.

"Bring my study Bible," he said to her feebly.

She went and brought it.

"Here, Annie," said the dying man, "here's my Bible that I've made too little use of myself. Promise me that if ever you have a house of your own, you'll read out of that book every day at worship. I want you not to forget me, as, if all's well, I shall never forget you."

"I will, sir," responded Annie earnestly.

"And you'll find a new five-pound note between the pages. Take it for my sake."

"Yes, sir," answered Annie, feeling this was no time for objecting to anything.

"And good-bye, Annie. I can't speak anymore."

He drew her to him again and kissed her for the last time. Then he turned his face to the wall, and Annie went home weeping, with the great Bible in her arms.

In the inadvertence of grief, she ran into the shop.

"What have you got there, lassie?" demanded Bruce, as sharply as if she might have stolen it.

"Mr. Cowie gave me this Bible, 'cause he's dying himself and doesn't want it any longer," answered Annie.

"Let me look at it."

Annie gave it up with reluctance.

"It's a fine book, and pretty boards. We'll just lay it upon the room table, and we'll have worship out of it when anybody wants."

"I—I want it myself," objected Annie in dismay, for although she did not think of the money at the moment, she had better reasons for not liking the thought of parting with the book.

"You can have it when you want it. That's enough, surely."

Annie could hardly think his saying so to be much comfort. The door to *the room* was kept locked, and Mrs. Bruce, patient woman as she was, would have boxed anyone's ears whom she met coming from within the sacred precincts.

Before the next Sunday Mr. Cowie was dead; and through some mistake or mismanagement there was no one to preach. So the congregation did each as seemed right in his own eyes. Mrs. Forbes went to the Missionary church in the evening to hear Mr. Turnbull. Kate and Alec accompanied her.

By this time Robert Bruce had become a great man in the community—in his own judgment at least. He had managed to secure one of the most fashionable pews in the chapel; and now when Mrs. Forbes' party entered, and a little commotion rose in consequence—they being more of gentlefolk than the place was accustomed to—Bruce was the first to rise and walk from his seat and request them to occupy his pew. Alec would have passed on, for he disliked the man, but Mrs. Forbes had reasons for being agreeable and accepted his offer. Colds had kept the rest of the Bruces at home, and Annie was the only other occupant of the pew. She crept to the end of it, like a shy mouse, to be as far out of the way as possible.

"Come out, Annie," said Bruce in a loud whisper.

Annie came out, a warm flush over her pale face, and Mrs. Forbes entered, then Kate, and last of all Alec, much against his will. Then Annie reentered, and Bruce resumed his place as guardian of the pew door. So Annie was seated next to Alec, as she had never been before, either in church or in school. But Annie felt no delight and awe like that with which encompassed Alec as he sat close to his beautiful cousin. Annie had a feeling of pleasure, no doubt, but the essence of that pleasure was faith. She trusted him and believed in him as much as she ever had. In the end, those who trust most will find they are nearest the truth.

Soon after the sermon was over, venturing a look around, Alec saw the eyes of Thomas Crann fixed on him. Alec's conscience told him, stung by that glance, that he had behaved ill to his old friend. Nor did this lessen the vague feeling which the sermon had awakened in his mind that something ought to be done, that something was wrong in him somewhere, that it ought to be set right somehow.

A special prayer meeting had been set to be held after the sermon, and Robert Bruce remained to join in intercession for the wicked town and its wicked neighborhood. He even "engaged in prayer" for the first time in public, astonishing some of the older members by his gift of devotion. He had been officially received into the church only a week or two before. There had been one or two murmurs against his reception, and he had been visited and talked with several times before the church was satisfied as to his conversion. But nothing was known specifically against him; and having learned many of their idioms, he had succeeded in persuading his examiners, and possibly himself at the same time, that he had passed through all the phases of conversion—including conviction, repentance, and final acceptance of offered mercy on the terms proposed—and was now undergoing the slow and troublesome process of sanctification. Many of those who admitted him to their communion were good people, fully believing that none but conscious Christians should enjoy that privilege. Yet his reputation for wealth had something to do with it. Probably they thought if the gospel proved mighty in this new disciple, more of his money might be accessible and by and by for good missionary purposes. And now he had been asked to pray, and had prayed with much propriety and considerable fervor. To be sure, Tibbie Dyster did sniff disdainfully a good deal during the performance; but then that was a way she had of relieving her feelings, next best to that of speaking her mind.

When the meeting was over, Robert Bruce, Thomas Crann, and James Johnstone, who was one of the deacons, walked away together. Very little conversation took place between them, for no subject but a religious one was admissible; and the religious feelings of those who had any were pretty nearly exhausted. Bruce's, however, were not in the least exhausted. On the contrary, he was so pleased to find that he could pray as well as any of them, and the excitement of doing so before judges had been so new and pleasant to him that he thought he should like to try it again. He thought too of the grand Bible lying up there on the room table.

"Come in, sirs," he beckoned as they approached his door, "and take a part in our family worship."

Neither of his companions felt much inclined to accede to his request, but they both yielded nevertheless. He conducted them upstairs, unlocked the musty room, pulled up the blinds, and admitted enough of lingering light for the concluding devotions of the day. He then proceeded to gather his family together, calling them one by one.

"Mother," he cried from the top of the stair.

"Yes, Father," answered Mrs. Bruce.

"Come to worship.—Robert!"

"Ay, Father."

"Come to worship.—Johnnie!"

And so he went through the family roll call. When all had entered and seated themselves, the head of the house went slowly to the side table, took from it reverently the late minister's study Bible, sat down by the window, laid the book on his knees, and solemnly opened it.

Now a five-pound note is not thick enough to make a big Bible open between the pages where it is laid. But the note might very well have been laid in a place where the Bible was in the habit of opening. Without an instant's hesitation, Robert slipped it away, and, crumpling it up in his hand, gave out the twenty-third psalm, over which it had lain, and read it through. Finding it too short, however, for the respectability of worship, he went on with the twenty-fourth, turning the leaf with thumb and forefinger, while the rest of the fingers clasped the note tight in his palm, and reading as he turned: "He that hath clean hands and a pure heart—"

As soon as he had finished this psalm, he closed the book with a snap, immediately regretting such improper noise and behavior. He put an additional compensating solemnity into the tone in which he said: "Thomas Crann, will you engage in prayer?"

"Pray yersel'," answered Thomas gruffly.

Whereupon Robert rose, and, kneeling down, did pray himself.

But Thomas, instead of leaning forward on his chair when he kneeled, glanced sharply round at Bruce. He had seen him take something from the Bible and crumple it up in his hand. He would not have felt any inclination to speculate about it had it not been for the peculiarly keen expression of eager surprise and happy greed which came over Bruce's face in the act. Having seen that, and being always more or less suspicious of Bruce, he wanted to know more.

He saw Bruce take advantage of the posture of devotion which he had assumed to put something into his pocket unseen of his guests, as he believed.

When worship was over, Bruce did not ask them to stay to supper. Prayers did not involve expense; supper did.

Thomas went home pondering. The devotions of the day were not to be concluded for him with any social act of worship. He had many anxious prayers yet to offer before his heart would be quiet in sleep. Especially there was Alec to be prayed for, and his dawtie Annie; and in truth the whole town of Glamerton, and the surrounding parishes—and Scotland, and the whole world. Indeed, sometimes Thomas went further, and although it is not reported of him that he ever prayed for the devil, he yet did something very like it once or twice when he prayed for "the haill universe o' God, an' a' the being's in 't, up an' doon, that we ken unco little aboot."

42

· · · · · · · · · · · · · · · · · · · ·

"The Stickit Minister"

*T*he next morning Kate and Alec rose early to walk before breakfast to the top of one of the hills, through a young larch wood which covered it from head to foot. The morning was cool and the sun exultant. The dew diamonds were flashing everywhere. The young explorers came to the gentle twilight of green, flashed with streaks of gold. A forest of delicate young larches crowded them in, their rich brown cones hanging like the knobs that looped up their dark garments fringed with paler green.

And the scent! What a thing to *invent*—the smell of a larch wood! It is the essence of the earth odor, distilled in the thousandfold leaves of those feathery trees. And the light winds that awoke blew murmurous music, so sharply and sweetly did that keen foliage divide the air.

Having gazed their fill on the morning around them, they returned to breakfast and afterward went down to the river. They stood on the bank over one of the deepest pools, in the bottom of which the pebbles glimmered brown. Kate, abstracted, gazed into it, swinging her neckerchief in her hand. Something fell into the water.

"Oh!" she cried, "what shall I do? It was my mother's!"

The words were scarcely out of her mouth when Alec was in the water. Bubbles rose and broke as he vanished. Kate stood pale, with parted lips, staring into the pool. With a boiling and heaving of the water, after a few moments he rose triumphant, holding the brooch.

"Oh, Alec!" she cried. "You shouldn't have frightened me so."

"I didn't mean to frighten you. It was your mother's brooch."

"Yes, but we could have got it out somehow."

"No other way I know of. Besides, I am almost a water rat."

"But what will your mother say? Now you'll get your death of cold. Come along."

Alec laughed. He was in no hurry to go home. But she seized his hand and half dragged him all the way. He had never been so happy in his life.

That night they walked in the moonlight, and the silence and the dimness of the world sank into Alec's soul. The only sound was the noise of the river. Kate sat down at the foot of an old tree which stood alone in one of the fields. Alec threw himself on the grass and looked up in her face.

"Oh, Kate, I love you!" he burst out at length.

Kate started. She was frightened. Her mind had been full of other thoughts.

Yet she laid her hand on his arm and accepted the love.

"You dear boy!" she said.

Perhaps Kate's answer was the best she could have given. But it stung Alec to the heart, and they went home in a changed silence.

The resolution Kate came to along the way was not so good as her answer. She did not love Alec as he did her. But he was only a boy, and therefore he would not suffer much, she thought. He would forget her as soon as she was out of his sight. Therefore, as he was a very dear boy, she would be as kind to him as she could, for she was going away soon.

She did not realize that Alec would take the kindness she gave as meaning more than she intended by it.

When they reached the house, Alec recovered himself a little and requested her to sing. She complied at once, and was foolish enough to sing a ballad from one lover to another. Alec sat listening, as if Kate were meaning the song for him and the rosy glow within his heart grew all the brighter. But despite the scent of sweet peas stealing like love through the open window, and despite the throbbing in Alec's chest, and despite the radiance of her own beauty, Kate was only singing a song. And alas for Alec's poor heart!

The following Sunday Murdoch Malison, the schoolmaster, was appointed to preach in the parish church. Though he had always aspired to the pulpit, it was not without some misgivings that he accepted the opportunity now given him. He came to two resolutions: the first, that he would not read his sermon but would commit it to memory and deliver it as extemporaneous; the second, to follow in the current fashion of preaching—to wield the forked lightning of the law against the sins of Glamerton.

So on the appointed day he ascended the pulpit stairs, and, conscious of a strange timidity, read the psalm. He cast one hasty glance around as he took his seat for the singing and saw a number of former as well as present pupils gathered to hear him, among whom were the two Truffeys, with their grandfather seated between them. He got through the prayer very well, for he was accustomed to that kind of thing in the school. But when he came to the sermon, he found that to hear boys repeat their memorized lessons and punish them for failure did not necessarily stimulate the master's own memory.

He gave out his text from the prophet Joel and then began. Now if he could have read his sermon, it would have shown itself a most creditable invention. It had a general introduction upon the present punishment of sin, with two heads, each of which had a number of horns called particulars. Then there was a tail called an application in which the sins of his hearers were duly chastised, with vague and awful threats of some vengeance not confined to the life to come.

But he had resolved not to read his sermon. So he began to repeat it, with sweeps of the hands, pointings of the fingers, and other such tricks of second-rate actors, to aid the self-delusion of his hearers that it was a genuine present outburst from the soul of Murdoch Malison. But as he approached the second head, the fear suddenly flashed through his own that he would not be able to recall it; and suddenly at that moment all the future of the sermon stammered, stared, did nothing, thought nothing. Long moments passed.

At length, roused by the sight of the faces of his hearers growing more expectant at the very moment when he had nothing more to give them, he gathered what remained of his wits, and as a last resort, resolved to read the remainder. He had a vague recollection of putting his manuscript in his pocket, but in order to give the change of mode an appearance of the natural, he managed with a struggle to bring out the words: "But, my brethren, let us betake ourselves to the written testimony."

Everyone concluded he was going to quote from Scripture; but instead of turning over the leaves of the Bible, he plunged his hand into the folds of his coat. Horror of horrors!—the pocket was as empty as his own memory. The cold dew of agony broke over him. He turned deadly pale. His knees knocked one another. A man of strong will, he made yet a frantic effort to bring his discourse down the inclined plane of a conclusion.

"In summary," he stammered, "my beloved brethren, if you do not repent and be converted and return to the Lord, you will—you will—you will have a very bad harvest."

Having uttered this solemn prediction, Murdoch Malison sat down, a failed minister. His brain was a vacuum, and the thought of standing up again to pray was intolerable. But he couldn't just sit there, for if he sat, the people would sit too. Something must be done, and there was nobody to do anything. He must get out and then the people would go home. But how could he escape? He cared no more for his vanished reputation. His only thought was how to get out.

Meanwhile, the congregation was variously affected. Some held down their heads and laughed immoderately. These were mostly Mr. Malison's scholars. Others held their heads down in sympathetic shame. Andrew Truffey was crying bitterly. His sobs were heard through the church, and some took them for the sobs of Murdoch Malison, who had shrunk into the pulpit like a snail into its shell so that not an atom of his form was to be seen except from the side galleries.

At length the song leader, George Macwha, who had for some time been turning over the leaves of his psalm book, came to the rescue. He rose in the lectern and announced the hundred and fifty-first psalm. The congregation could find only a hundred and fifty, and took the last of the psalms for the one meant. But George, either from old spite against the tormentor of boys and girls, or from mere coincidence—he never revealed which—had in reality chosen a part of the *fifty-first* psalm.

"The hunner an' fifty-first psalm," repeated George, "from the fifteent' verse. An' then we'll all go home. 'My closed lips, O Lord, by thee, let them be opened.' "

As soon as the singing was over, George left the lectern, and the congregation following his example went straggling out of the church toward home.

When the sounds of retiring footsteps were heard no more in the great echoing church, the form of Murdoch Malison slowly rose up above the edge of the pulpit. With his face drained as that of a corpse, he gave a frantic look around and, not seeing little Truffey concealed behind one of the pillars, concluded the place empty. He half crawled, half tumbled down the stair to the vestry, where the sexton was awaiting him. It did not restore his lost composure to discover, in searching for his handkerchief, that the encumbrance of the pulpit gown over his suit had made him put his hand into the wrong pocket, and that in the other his manuscript lay as safe as it had been useless.

He took the gown off quietly, bade the old sexton a quiet good day, and stole away home through the streets. He had wanted to get out, and now he wanted to get in; for he felt very much as Lady Godiva would have felt if her heroism had given way.

Poor Murdoch had no mother and no wife—he could not go home and be comforted. Nor was he a youth to whom a first failure might be of small consequence. He was forty-five, and his head was sprinkled with gray. He was a schoolmaster and everybody knew him. Some of his students had witnessed the debacle. As he walked along the deserted streets, he felt that he was running the gauntlet of scorn. But everyone who saw him coming along with his head sunk on his chest drew back from the window till he had gone by. Returning to the window to watch him out of sight, they saw a solitary little figure about twenty yards behind him, with tears running down its face, stumping slowly step by step, and keeping the same distance from the dejected master.

But however silently Truffey might use his third leg, the master heard the *stump-stump* behind him, and felt that he was followed home every foot of the way by the boy whom he had crippled. He felt, too, in some dim degree which yet had practical results, that the boy was taking divine vengeance upon him, heaping on his head the coals of that consuming fire which is love, which is our God. And when the first shame was over, the thought of Truffey came back with healing on his lonely heart.

When he reached his own door, he hurried in and closed it behind him as if to shut out the whole world through which he had passed with that burden of contempt upon his degraded shoulders. He was more ashamed of his failure than he had been sorry for the lamenting Truffey. But the shame would pass; the sorrow would endure.

Meantime, two of his congregation, elderly sisters, were going home together. They were distantly related to the schoolmaster, whom they regarded as the honor of the family and as their bond with the world above them. So when Elspeth addressed Meg with reference to the sermon in a manner which showed her determination to acknowledge no failure, Meg took her cue directly.

"Eh! it's a sore outlook for poor folk like us if things be goin' that way!"

" 'Deed it's that. If the harvest be goin' to the moles an' the bats, it's time we were away home; for it'll be a cold winter."

"Ay, that it will! The minister was so o'ercome at the prospect, honest man, that it was all he could do to get to the end o' his discoorse."

"He sees into the will o' the Almighty. He's been far wi' Him—that's very clear."

"Ay."

And hence, in the middle of the vague prophecies of vengeance there gathered a more definite kernel of prediction—believed by some, disbelieved yet feared by others—that the harvest would be eaten by the worm that dieth not, that bread would be up to famine prices and the poor would die of starvation.

But still the flowers came out and looked men in the face and went in again. And still the sun shone on the evil and on the good, and still the rain fell on the just and on the unjust.

And still the denunciations from the pulpits went on. But the human souls thus exposed to the fires seemed only to harden under their influences.

43

* * * * * * * * * * * * * * * *

The Hypocrite

On the Monday morning after his terrible failure, Mr. Malison felt almost too ill to go to the school. But he knew that if he gave in he would have to leave the town. And he had a good deal of that form of courage which enables a man to face the inevitable. So he went, keeping a calm exterior over the shame and mortification that burned and writhed within him. He prayed the morning prayer, falteringly but fluently, and called up the Bible class. He corrected their blunders with an effort for, in truth, the hardest task he had ever had was to find fault that Monday. In short, he did everything as usual, except bring out the tawse. How could he punish failure when he had failed so shamefully in the sight of them all? And to the praise of the students of Glamerton, let it be recorded that there had never been a quieter day, one of less defiance, than that day of the master's humiliation. In the afternoon Andrew Truffey laid a splendid bunch of flowers on his desk, and the next morning it was so crowded with offerings of the same sort that he had quite a screen behind which to conceal his emotion.

Wonderful is the divine revenge! The *children* would wipe away the humiliation of their tyrant! His desk, the symbol of merciless law, became an altar heaped with offerings, behind which the shamed divinity bowed his head and acknowledged a power greater than that of stripes. His boys, who hated spelling and figures, hated even more the Shorter Catechism, and could hardly be brought to read the book of Leviticus with decency, chose to forget it all, loving the man beneath whose lashes they had writhed in torture.

In his heart the master made a vow, with a new love that loosed the millstone of many offenses against the little ones, the weight for years had been hanging about his neck. He vowed that he would never leave them, but would spend his days making up for the hardness of his heart and hand; vowed that he himself would be good, and so make them good; that he would henceforth be their friend and let them know it.

Blessed failure that ends in such a victory! Blessed pulpit of cleansing and healing, into which he entered full of self, and from which he came down disgusted with that paltry self as well as with its deserved defeat. The gates of its evil fortress were now undefended, for Pride had left them open in scorn; and Love, in the form of flower-bearing children, rushed into the citadel. The heart of the master was forced to yield, and the last state of the man was better than the first.

Before the end of Kate's visit, a letter arrived from Professor Fraser which was to Alec like a reprieve from execution. He asked that if Mrs. Forbes did not mind keeping his niece a little longer, he would be greatly indebted to her. And the little longer lengthened into the late harvest season.

The summer shone on and the corn grew, green and bonnie. And Alec's love grew with the corn. Kate liked him better and better but was not a bit more inclined to fall in love with him.

Summer flowed into autumn and there was no sign of the coming vengeance of heaven. The green grain turned pale at last before the gaze of the sun. The life within had done its best and now shrank back to the earth. Anxious farmers watched their fields and joyfully noted every shade of progress. All day the sun shone strong, and all night the moon leaned down from heaven to see how things were going and to keep the work gently moving. At length the new revelation of ancient life was complete, and the grain stood in living gold, and men began to put it to the sickle because the time of harvest was come.

But the feelings with which the master longed for the harvest holiday were sadly different from those of his boys. It was a delight to his students to think of having nothing to do on those glorious hot days but to gather blueberries or lie on the grass or swim in the Glamour and dry themselves in the sun ten times a day. For the master, he only hoped to get away from the six thousand eyes of Glamerton. Not one allusion had been made in his hearing to his dismal degradation, but he knew that was only because it was too dreadful to be alluded to. The tone of additional kindness and consideration with which many addressed him only made him think of what lay behind, and refuse every invitation given him. If he could only get away from everyone's sight, his oppressed heart would begin to revive and he might gather strength to calmly face the continuous pressure in the performance of his duty to the boys and girls of Glamerton.

At length the slow hour arrived. Longing thoughts had almost obliterated the figures upon Time's dial and made it look a hopeless, undivided circle of eternity. But at length twelve o'clock on Saturday came; and the delight would have been almost unendurable to some had it not been calmed by the dreary closeness of the Sabbath lying between them and freedom. Almost the moment the *amen* of the final prayer was out of the master's mouth, the first boys were shouting jubilantly in the open air. Truffey, who was always the last, was crutching it out after the rest when he heard the master's voice calling him back. He obeyed it with misgiving, so much had fear become a habit.

"Ask your grandfather, Andrew, if he will allow you to go down to the seaside with me for two or three weeks," said the master.

"Yes, sir," Truffey meant to say, but the attempt produced instead an unearthly screech of delight, with which he went off in a series of bounds worthy of a kangaroo, lasting all the way to his grandfather's and taking him there in half the usual time.

And the master and Truffey did go down to the sea together. The master borrowed a gig and hired a horse and driver. They all three sat in the space meant for two. To Truffey a lame leg or two was hardly to be compared with the exultant glory of that day. Was he not the master's friend from now on? And was he not riding with him in a gig—bliss supreme? Truffey was prouder than Mr. Malison could have been if he had been judged to surpass Mr. Turnbull himself in every pulpit gift. And if there be joy in the universe, what is the difference how it be divided?—whether the master be raised from the desk to the pulpit, or Truffey have a ride in a gig?

About this time Tibbie caught a bad cold and cough and for two weeks was confined to bed. Annie became her constant companion.

"I told ye I would hae the light before long," she said the first time Annie came to her."

"Hoots, Tibbie! It's only a cold," said Annie. "You mustn't be downhearted."

"Downhearted! Who dares to say I'm downhearted within sight o' the New Jerusalem?"

"I beg your pardon, Tibbie. But you see, however willing you may be to go, we're none so willing to lose you."

"Ye'll be better off without me, lass."

Annie's quiet squeeze of her hand disputed the words. She waited on Tibbie day and night. And that year, for the first time since she had come to Glamerton, the harvest began without her. But when Tibbie got a little better, Annie ran out now and then to see what progress the reapers were making.

One bright morning Tibbie, feeling better, said to her, "Noo, bairn, I'm much better today. Ye must jist run out an' play yersel'. So jist run oot an' don't let me see ye afore dinnertime."

At Howglen there happened to be a field of oats not far from the house, the reaping of which was to begin that day. It was very warm, glorious with sunshine. So after a few stooks had been set up, Alec went out with his mother and Kate. Sheltered from the sun by a stook, he lay down on some sheaves and watched. He fell into a doze, not realizing that his mother and Kate had left him, and at length the sun rose till the stook could shelter him no more. Too lazy to move, Alec lay with eyes closed, wishing that someone would come to shade him.

Suddenly a shadow came over him. When he looked up to find the source of the grateful relief, he could see nothing but an apron held up—hiding both the sun and the face of the helper.

"Who's there?" he asked.

"It's me—Annie Anderson," came the voice from behind the apron.

"Don't bother, Annie," he said. "I don't want the shade. My mother will be here in a minute. I see her coming."

Annie dropped her arms and turned away in silence. If Alec could have seen her face, he would have been sorry he had refused her service. She vanished in a moment so that Mrs. Forbes and Kate never saw her. They sat down beside him so as to shelter him, and he again fell fast asleep. When he woke he found his head in Kate's lap and her parasol casting a cool green shadow over him. His mother had gone again. Having made these discoveries, he closed his eyes and pretended to be still asleep. But Kate soon saw that his face was awake, although his eyes were closed.

"I think it is time we went into the house, Alec," she said. "You have been asleep nearly an hour."

"Happy so long and not knowing it," he returned, looking up at her from where he lay.

Kate blushed a little. I think she began to realize that he was not quite a boy. But he obeyed her like a child, and they went in together.

When Annie vanished among the stooks after the rejection of her offered shadow, a throbbing pain at her heart kept her from returning to the reapers. She wandered away up the field toward a little old cottage in which some of the farm servants resided. She knew that Thomas Crann was at work there and found him busy rough-casting the outside of it with plaster.

"You're busy working, Thomas," said Annie, for the sake of something to say.

"Ay, jist helpin' to make a hypocrite," answered Thomas, with a nod and a smile as he threw a trowelful of mortar against the wall.

"What do you mean by that?" asked Annie.

"If ye knew this old place as well as I do, ye wouldn't need to ask that question. It should hae been pulled down from the riggin' to the foundation a century ago, An' here we're puttin' a clean face on it."

"It *looks* well enough."

"I told ye I was makin' a hypocrite," and he chuckled.

Thomas went on whitening his "hypocrite" in silence for a few moments, then resumed, "Where did Robert Bruce get that gran' Bible, Annie, do ye know?"

"That's my Bible, Thomas. Old Mr. Cowie gave it to me when he was lying close to death."

"Hmm, ay! An' how came it that ye didn't take it an' put it in yer own room?"

"Mister Bruce took it and laid it in his room as soon as I brought it home."

"Did Master Cowie say anythin' to ye aboot anythin' that was in it?"

"Ay, he did. He spoke of a five-pound note that he had put in it. But when I looked for it, I couldn't find it."

"Ay! When did ye look for it?"

"I forgot it for two or three days—maybe a week."

"Do ye remember that Sunday night that two or three o' us came home with Bruce an' had worship with him an' ye?"

"Ay, well enough. It was the first time he read out of my Bible."

"Was it afore or after that when ye looked for the money?"

"It was the next day; for the sight of the Bible put it in my mind. I ought not to have thought about it on the Sabbath, but it came of itself. I didn't look till the Monday morning, before they were up. I reckon Mr. Cowie forgot to put it in after all."

"Hmm! hmm! Ay! ay! Weel, ye see, riches takes to themsel's wings an' flies away; an' so we must not set oor hearts upon them. The worst bank a man can lay up his own money in is his own heart."

Soon Annie had forgotten her own troubles in Thomas's presence, for to her, and even in some ways to Tibbie, he was a shelter—as a river in a dry place, as a shadow of a great rock in a weary land. He was certainly not felt to be such by all whom he encountered, however; for his ambition was to rouse men from the sleep of sin; to set them face to face with the terrors of the Ten Commandments and Mount Sinai; to "shake them ower the mou' o' the pit" till they were all choked with the fumes of the brimstone.

"How's Tibbie today?" inquired Thomas.

"A wee bit better," answered Annie.

"It's a great privilege, lassie, to be so much with one o' the Lord's elect as ye are with Tibbie Dyster. She's some twisted sometimes, but she's a good honest woman who has the glory o' God in her heart. An' she's told me my duty an' my sins in a manner worthy o' Deborah the prophetess."

Annie did not return to the harvest field again that day. She did not want to go near Alec again. So, after lingering a while with Thomas, she wandered slowly across some fields of barley stubble through which the fresh young clover was already spreading its soft green. She then went over the Glamour by the bridge with the three arches, down the path at the other end, over the single great stone that crossed the dyer's dam, and so into Tibbie's cottage.

Had Annie been Robert Bruce's own, she would have had to mind the baby, to do part of the housework, and, being a wise child, to attend in the shop during meals. But Robert Bruce was ignorant of how little Annie knew about the investment of her money. He took her freedom of action for the result of the knowledge that she paid her way, whereas Annie followed her own impulse and never thought about the matter. Indeed, in tight-lipped Scottish fashion, none of her Glamerton friends had given her any information about her little fortune. Had Bruce known this, he would have found no work too constant for her and no liberty small enough.

Thomas did not doubt that Robert Bruce had stolen the note. But he did not see yet what he ought to do about it. The thing would be hard to prove, and the man who would steal would lie. But he bitterly regretted that such a man should have found his way into their congregation.

44

. . . .

Kate's Going

*A*t length the oats and wheat and barley was gathered in all over the valley of the two rivers. The master returned from the seacoast, bringing Truffey, radiant with life, with him. Nothing could lengthen that shrunken limb, but in the other and the crutch together he had more than the function of the two.

The master was his idol, and the master was a happier man. The scene of his late failure had begun to fade a little from his brain. He had been loving and helping; and the love and help had turned into a great joy, whose tide washed from out of his heart the bitterness of his remembered sin. When we love God and man truly, all the guilt and oppression of past sin will be swept away.

So the earth and all that was in it did the master good. And he came back able to look the people in the face—humble still, but no longer humiliated. And when the children gathered again on a Monday morning with the sad feeling that the holidays were over, the master's prayer was different from what it used to be, and the work was not so bad as before, and school was not so hateful after all.

But the cool, bright mornings, and the frosty evenings with the pale green sky after sundown, spoke of a coming loss to Alec's heart. Kate never had shown that she loved him, so he felt a restless trouble even in her presence. Yet as he lay in the gathering dusk and watched the crows flying home, he felt that a change was near and that for him winter was coming before its time.

And, indeed, on one of those bright mornings, the doom fell in its expected form, a letter from the Professor. He was home at last and wanted his niece to mix his toddy and scold his servants for him. Alec's heart sank within him.

Her departure was fixed in but a few days, and his summer would go with her.

The day before her departure they were walking together along one of the dirt roads leading to the hills.

"Oh, Kate!" exclaimed Alec all at once in an outburst of despair, "what will I do when you are gone?"

"Oh, Alec!" objected Kate, "I shall see you again in November."

"Oh, yes, you shall see me. But shall I see *you*—this very you? Oh, Kate, I feel you will be different then. You will not look at me as you do now. Oh, won't you love me, Kate? I don't deserve it. But I've read so often of beautiful women loving men who do not deserve it. Perhaps I may be worthy of it someday. But by that time you will have loved someone else!"

He turned away and walked toward home. But recovering himself instantly, he turned back and put his hand on Kate's arm. Like a child praying to its mother, he repeated: "*Won't* you love me, Kate?—just a little?"

"I do love you dearly. You know that, Alec. Why do you always press me to say more?"

"Because I do not like the way you say it."

"You want me to speak your way, not my own, and be a hypocrite?"

"Kate, Kate! I understand you all too well."

They walked home in silence.

When the last night arrived, after it was late, he quietly walked up the stairs and knocked at her door to see her once again, and make one more appeal. Now an appeal has only to do with justice or pity. With love it is of no use. With love it is as unavailing as wisdom or gold or beauty. But no lover believes this.

There was no answer to the first gentle knock, his inarticulate appeal. He lost his courage and dared not knock again; and while Kate was standing with her head cocked to one side and her dress half off, wondering if anyone had knocked, he crept away to his bed, ashamed. There was only a partition of lath and plaster between the two, neither of whom could sleep but neither of whom could have given the other any comfort.

At length the dawn came; it was the dreariest dawn Alec had ever known. Kate appeared at breakfast with the indisputable signs of preparation about her. The breakfast was cheerless. The inevitable gig appeared at the door. Alec was not even to drive it. He could only help her into it, kiss her gloved hand on the rail, and see her vanish behind the shrubbery.

He turned in stern endurance and rushed up into the very room he had thought it impossible ever to enter again. He caught up a handkerchief she had left behind her, pressed it to his face, threw himself on her bed, and—well, he fell fast asleep.

He woke not quite so miserable as he had expected. He tried hard to make himself more miserable, but his thoughts would not obey him. They would take their own way, fly where they pleased, and alight where they would. And the meeting in November was the most attractive object in sight. So easily is hope born.

Alec soon found that Grief will not come when she is called; but if you leave her alone, she will come of herself. Before the day was over the whole vacant countryside rushed in upon him with a ghostly sense of emptiness and desolation. He wandered about the dreary house. The flowers no longer had anything to say. The sunshine was hastening to have done with it and let the winter come as soon as it liked, for there was no more use in sunshine like this. Alec could feel all this, for the poetic element has its share in all men, especially those in love. For when a man is in love, what of poetry there is in him as well as what there is of any sort of good thing will rise to the surface. In love every man shows himself better than he is, though, thank God, not better than he is meant to become.

Eventually Alec found his way out, breathed the air of life of which he had been fond even before he knew Kate, and managed to renew a few old acquaintances.

The first project he undertook was to superintend the painting and laying up of his boat for the winter. It was placed across the rafters of the barn and wrapped in tarpaulins.

The light grew shorter and shorter. A few rough, rainy days stripped the trees of their foliage. Although the sun shone out again and made lovely weather, it was plain to all the senses that the autumn was drawing to a close.

All the prophetic rumors of a bad harvest had proved themselves false. Never a better harvest had been gathered. But the passion for prophetic warnings over the whole district had not abated.

Suddenly one day there appeared in the streets of Glamerton a man who cried with a loud voice: "Yet forty days, and Glamerton shall be destroyed."

This cry he repeated at intervals of about a minute, walking slowly through every street of the town. The children followed him in awe-struck silence; the women stared fearfully from their doors as he passed. The insanity which gleamed in his eyes and his pale, long-drawn countenance heightened the effect of the terrible prediction. His words took the town by storm.

The men outwardly smiled to each other and said that he was a madman. But as prophets have often been taken for madmen, so madmen often pass for prophets. Even Stumpin' Steenie, the town constable, had too much respect for either his prophetic claims or his lunacy, perhaps both, to take him into custody. So through Glamerton he went with his bare feet and tattered garments, proclaiming aloud the coming destruction. He walked in the middle of the street and turned aside for nothing. The coachman of the Royal Mail Coach had to pull up his four gray horses on their haunches to keep them off the defiant prophet and leave him to pursue the straight line of his mission. The ministers warned the people on the following Sunday against false prophets, but did not say that this man was a false prophet, while with their own denunciations they continued as well. The chief effects of it all were excitement and fear. There was little sign of repentance. The prophet appeared one day. He vanished the next. But the spiritual physicians did not, therefore, doubt their exhibition. They only increased the dose.

But within a few days, a still more awful prediction rose, cloudlike, on the spiritual horizon. A placard was found affixed to the door of every place of worship in the town, setting forth in large letters that according to certain irrefutable calculations from "the number of man" and other such of the more definite utterances of Daniel and St. John, the day of judgment must fall without fail the next Sunday.

Glamerton was variously affected by this condensation of the vapor of prophecy into a definite prediction.

"What do ye think o' it, Thomas Crann?" asked Andrew Constable. "The calculation seems to be all correct. Yet somehow I canna believe in't."

"Dinna bother yer head aboot it, Andrew. There's a heep o' judgments atween this an' the other end. The Lord'll come when nobody's lookin' fer Him. An' so we must aye be ready. But I don't think the man that made that 'calculation' as ye call it is jist altogether infallible. Fer one thing, he's forgotten to make allooance fer the leap years."

"The day's already by then!" exclaimed Andrew, in a tone contrasting strongly with his previous expression of unbelief.

"Or else it's not comin' so soon as the prophet thought. I'm not clear at this moment aboot that. But it's a small matter."

Andrew's face fell and he looked thoughtful.

"How do ye make that oot?" he inquired.

"Hoots man!" answered Thomas. "Don't ye see that if the man was capable o' makin' such a mistake as that, he could hardly hae been intended by Providence for an interpreter o' dark sayin's of old?"

Andrew burst into a laugh.

"Who would hae thought, Thomas, that ye could hae such wisdom!"

And so they parted, Andrew laughing and Thomas with a curious smile.

45

Rain

Toward the middle of the following week the sky grew gloomy and a thick, small, incessant rain brought the dreariest weather in the world. There was no wind, and miles and miles of mist were gathered in the air. After a day or two the heavens grew lighter but the rain fell as steadily as before, and in heavier drops. Still there was little rise in either rivers, the Glamour or the Wan Water, and the weather could not be said to be anything but seasonable.

On Saturday afternoon, weary of some poor attempts at Greek and Latin, weary of the rain, and weary with wishing to be with Kate, Alec could stay in the house no longer and went out for a walk. Along the bank of the river he wandered, with the rain above and the wet grass below. He stood for a moment gazing at the muddy Glamour which now came down bank full.

"If this holds, we'll have a flood," remarked Alec to himself when he saw how the water was beginning to invade the trees upon the steep banks below. The scene was in harmony with his feelings. The delight of the sweeping waters entered his soul and filled him with joy and strength. He thought how different it was when he had walked along this way with Kate, when the sun was bright and the trees were covered with green. But he would rather have it this way, now that Kate was gone.

That evening, in the schoolmaster's lodgings, little Truffey sat at the tea table triumphant. The master had been so pleased with an exercise which the lad had written for him that he had taken the boy home to tea with him, dried him well at his fire, and given him as much buttered toast as he could eat. Oh, how Truffey loved his master!

"Truffey," said Mr. Malison, after a long pause, during which he had been staring into the fire, "how's your leg?"

"Quite well, thank ye, sir," answered Truffey, unconsciously putting out the foot of the good leg on the fender, "There wasna anything the matter with it."

"I mean the other leg, Truffey—the one that I—that I—hurt."

"Perfectly well, sir. It's not worth asking about. I wonder that ye take such pains with me, sir, when I was such a mischievous nickum."

The master could not reply. But he was more grateful for Truffey's generous forgiveness than he would have been for the richest estate in Scotland. Such forgiveness gives us back ourselves—clean and happy. And for what gift can we be more grateful? He vowed all over again to do all he could for Truffey. Perhaps the failure of a minister might have a hand in making a minister that would not fail.

"It's time to go home, Andrew Truffey. Put on my cloak—there. And keep out of the puddles as much as you can."

"I'll put the small foot in," answered Truffey cheerfully, holding up the end of his crutch as he stretched it forward to make one bound out of the door. For he delighted in showing off his agility to the master.

When Alec looked out of his window the next morning, he saw a broad yellow expanse below. The Glamour was rolling, a mighty river, through the land. A wild waste of foamy water, it swept along the fields where only recently the grain had bowed to the autumn winds. But he had seen it this high before. And all the grain was safely in the barns. Neither he nor his mother regretted much that they could not go to church.

All night Tibbie Dyster had lain awake in her lonely cottage, listening to the rising water. She was still far from well and was more convinced than ever that the Lord was going to let her see His face. Annie would have stayed with her that Saturday night, as she often did, had she not known that Mrs. Bruce would make it a pretext for giving her no change of linen for another week.

The moment Bruce entered the chapel—for no weather deprived him of his Sabbath custom—Annie, who had been his sole companion, darted off to see Tibbie. When Bruce found that she had not followed him, he hurried back to the door only to see her halfway down the street. He returned in anger to his pew, which he was ashamed of showing thus empty to the eyes of his brethren. But there were many pews in like condition that morning.

The rain having moderated a little in the afternoon, the chapel was crowded in the evening. Mrs. Bruce was the only one of the Bruce family absent. The faces of the congregation wore an expectant look, for Mr. Turnbull always sought to give his sermons added clout by allowing Nature herself to give effect to his persuasions.

The text he had chosen was: "But as the days of Noah were, so shall also the coming of the Son of Man be." He made no allusion to the paper which the rain was busy washing off the door of the chapel. Nor did he wish to remind the people that this was the very day foreseen by the bill-posting prophet as appointed for the coming of judgment. But when, in the middle of the sermon, a flash of lightning cracked, followed by an instant explosion of thunder and a burst of rain as if a waterspout had broken over their heads, the general start and pallor of the congregation showed that they had not forgotten the prediction.

Was this then the way in which judgment was going to be executed—a second flood about to sweep them from the earth? Although all stared at the minister as if they drank in every word of his representation of Noah's flood—with its despairing cries, floating carcasses, and lingering deaths on the mountaintops as the water crept slowly up from peak to peak—yet in reality they were much too frightened at the little flood in the valley of two rivers to care for the terrors of the great deluge of the world, in which, according to Mr. Turnbull, eighty thousand millions of the sons and daughters of men perished. Nor did they heed the practical application which he made of his subject.

When the service was over, they rushed out of the chapel.

Robert Bruce was the first to step from the threshold up to his ankles in water. The rain was falling—not in drops, but in little streams.

"The Lord preserve us!" he exclaimed. "It's risen a foot on Glamerton already. And there's sugar in the cellar! Children, run home yourselves! I can't wait for you."

"Hoots man!" cried Thomas Crann, who came behind him, "ye're so taken up with the world that ye hae no room fer ordinary common sense. Ye're only standin' in water up to the mouths o' yer shoes. Ye turned yer dry stone dyke into a byre wall that'll keep two feet more water than this oot."

Robert held his tongue. At that moment Annie was slipping past him to run back to Tibbie. He made a pounce on her and grabbed her by the shoulder.

"No more of this, Annie!" he ordered. "Come home and don't be running about nobody knows where."

"Everybody knows where," returned Annie. "I'm only going to stay with Tibbie Dyster, poor blind body!"

"Let the blind sleep with the blind, and come home with me," said Robert, abusing several texts of Scripture in a breath and pulling Annie away with him.

Heartily vexed and disappointed, Annie made no resistance. And how the rain did pour as they went home! They were all wet to the skin in a moment, except Mr. Bruce, who had a fine umbrella and reasoned with himself that his Sabbath clothes were more expensive than those of the children.

By the time they reached home Annie had made up her mind what to do. Instead of going into her room, she waited on the landing, listening for the cessation of footsteps. The rain poured down on the roof with such a noise that she found it difficult to be sure. There was no use in changing her clothes only to get them wet again, and it was well for her that the evening was warm. But at length she was satisfied that her keepers were at supper, whereupon she stole out of the house as quietly as a kitten and was out of sight as quickly. Not a creature was to be seen. The gutters were all choked and the streets had become riverbeds. But through it all she dashed fearlessly to Tibbie's cottage.

"Tibbie!" she cried as she entered, "there's going to be a terrible flood."

"Let it come!" cried Tibbie. "The bit hoosie's founded upon a rock, an' the rains may fall an' the winds may blow, an' the floods may beat against the hoosie, but it won't fall, it canna fall, for it's founded on a rock."

Perhaps Tibbie's mind was wandering a little, for when Annie arrived she found Tibbie's face flushed and her hands moving restlessly. But what with this assurance of her confidence and the pleasure of being with her again, Annie thought no more about the waters of the Glamour.

"What kept ye so long, lassie?" said Tibbie after a moment's silence, during which Annie had been arranging the peats to get some light from the fire.

She told her the whole story.

"An' ye hae had no supper?"

"No. But I don't want any."

"Take off yer wet clothes then, an' come to yer bed."

Annie crept into the bed beside her—not dry even then, for she was forced to retain her last garment. Tibbie was restless and kept moaning, so that neither of them could sleep. And the water kept sweeping on faster, rising higher up the rocky mound on which the cottage stood. The old woman and the young girl lay within and listened, fearless.

46

· · · · · · · · · · · · · · · ·

The Flood

*A*lec, too, lay awake and listened to the untiring rain. In the morning he rose and looked out of the window. The Glamour spread out and rushed on like a torrent of a sea forsaking its old bed. Down its course swept many dark objects which were too far away to distinguish. He dressed himself and went down to its edge: not its bank: that lay far beneath its torrent. Past him swept trees torn up by the roots; sheaves went floating by, then a cart with a drowned horse. Next came a great waterwheel. This made him think of the mill, and he hurried off to see what the miller was doing.

Truffey went stumping through the rain and the streams to the morning school. Gladly would he have waited on the bridge, which he had to cross on his way, to look at the water instead. But the master would be there, and Truffey would not be late. When Mr. Malison arrived, Truffey was standing in the rain waiting for him. Not another student was there. The master sent him home. And

Truffey went back to the bridge over the Glamour and there stood watching the awful river.

Mr. Malison sped away westward toward the Wan Water. On his way he found many groups of the inhabitants going in the same direction. The bed of the Wan Water was considerably higher than that of the Glamour here, although by a rapid descent it reached the same level a few miles below the town. Its waters had never, to the knowledge of any of the inhabitants, risen so high as to overflow the ridge between it and the town. But now people said the Wan Water would be down upon them in the course of an hour or two, and then Glamerton would be in the heart of a torrent, for the two rivers would be one. So instead of going to school, all the boys had gone to look, and the master followed them. Nor was the fear without foundation; for the stream was still rising, and a foot more would overtop the ground between it and the Glamour.

But while the excited crowd of his townsmen stood in the middle of a stubble field watching the progress of the enemy at their feet, Robert Bruce was busy in his cellar making final preparations for its reception. In spite of Sabbath restrictions, upon hurrying home from chapel the day before he had carried the sugar up the cellar stairs in the coal scuttle, while Mrs. Bruce, in a condition very unfit for such efforts, had toiled behind him with a smaller load. This morning he was making sure he had missed nothing of any consequence which could be moved to safety. As soon as he had finished his task, he hurried off to join the watchers of the water.

James Johnstone's workshop was not far from the Glamour. When he went into the shop that Monday morning he found the treadles under water and realized there could be no work done that day.

"I'll jist take a stroll doon to the bridge to see the flood go by," he said to himself and, putting on his hat, he went out into the rain.

As he came near the bridge, he saw the small, crippled Truffey leaning over the parapet with a horror-stricken face. The next moment the boy bounded to his one foot and his crutch, and gamboled across the bridge toward the other side as if he had been gifted with six legs.

When James reached the parapet he could see nothing to account for the terror and eagerness on Truffey's pale face, nor for his precipitate flight. But being shortsighted and inquisitive, he set off after Truffey as fast as the dignity proper to an elderly weaver and a deacon of the Missionaries would permit.

Alec, on his way to the mill, saw two men standing together on the verge of the brown torrent, the miller and Thomas Crann. Thomas had been up all night, wandering along the shore of the Wan Water, sorely troubled about Glamerton and its spiritually careless people. Toward morning he had found himself in the town again, and, crossing the Glamour, had wandered up the side of the water. He had come upon the sleepless miller contemplating his mill in the embrace of the torrent.

Alec joined the two and their talk continued. But it was soon turned into another channel by the appearance of Truffey, who, despite frantic efforts, made but little speed across the field to reach them, so deep did his crutch sink into the soaked earth. He had to pull it out at every step, and seemed mad in his foiled anxiety to reach them. He tried to shout, but nothing was heard beyond a crow like that of a hoarse chicken. Alec, finally noticing, started off to meet him, but just as he reached him Truffey's crutch broke in the earth, and he fell and lay unable to speak a word. With slow and ponderous arrival, Thomas Crann came up.

"Annie Anderson!" panted out Truffey at length.

"What about her?" said both in alarm.

"Tibbie Dyster!" sobbed Truffey in reply.

"Here's James Johnstone!" said Thomas; "he'll tell us all aboot it."

"What's this?" he cried fiercely as James came within hearing.

"Yes, what is it?" returned the weaver eagerly.

If Thomas had been a swearing man, what a terrible oath he would have sworn in the wrath which this unhelpful response of the weaver roused in his apprehensive soul. But Truffey was again trying to speak. They bent their ears to listen.

"They'll all be droont! They'll be taken away. They can't get oot!"

Thomas and Alec turned and stared at each other.

"The boat!" gasped Thomas.

Alec made no reply. That was a terrible water to look at. And the boat was small.

"Can ye guide it, Alec?" asked Thomas, his voice trembling and the muscles of his face working.

Still Alec made no reply. He was afraid.

"Alec!" shouted Thomas in a voice that might have been heard across the roar of the Glamour. "Will ye let the women droon?"

The blood shot into Alec's face. He turned and ran.

"Thomas," said James Johnstone, laying a hand on the stonemason's broad chest, "have ye considered what ye're drivin' the young man to?"

"Ay, weel enough, James. I would rather see my friend hanged than see him deserve hanging, or droon rather than be a coward to save himsel'. But don't ye worry aboot Alec. If he doesn't go, I'll go mysel', an' I never was in a boat in my life!"

"Come on, Thomas!" cried Alec, already across three or four ridges of the field; "I can't carry the boat alone."

Thomas followed as fast as he could, but before he reached the barn, he met Alec and one of the farm servants with the boat on their shoulders.

It was a short way to the water. They had her afloat in a few minutes, below the footbridge. At the edge the water was still as a pond.

Alec seized the oars and the men shoved him off.

"Pray, Alec!" shouted Thomas.

"I haven't time. Pray yourself!" shouted Alec in reply, and gave a stroke that shot him far toward the current. Before he reached it, he shifted his position and sat facing the bow. There was little need for pulling, nor was there much fear of being overtaken by any floating mass; but there was great necessity for looking out ahead. The moment Thomas saw the boat laid hold of by the current, he turned his back to the Glamour, fell upon his knees in the grass, and cried in an agony: "Lord, let not the curse o' the widow an' the childless be upon me."

Thereafter he was silent.

Johnstone and the farm lad who had helped with the boat ran down the riverside. Truffey had started for the bridge again, having bound his crutch with a string. Thomas remained kneeling.

Alec did not find it so hard as he had expected to keep the boat from capsizing. But the rapidity with which the banks swept past him was frightful. The cottage lay on the other side of the Glamour, lower down, and all that he had to do for a while was to keep the bow of his boat down the stream. When he approached the cottage, he attempted to draw a little out of the center of the current, which, confined within higher banks, was here fiercer than anywhere above where the fields allowed the river to spread out.

But out of the current he could not go, for the cottage lay between the channel of the river and the stream through the mill—now joined as one. He would hardly have known where to guide his tiny craft, the look of everything was so altered by the flood, except for the relation of Tibbie's cottage to the bridge. It was now crowded with anxious spectators watching as Alec sped toward the doomed little hovel.

Alec could see as he approached that the water was already more than halfway up the door. He resolved to send his boat right through the doorway, but was doubtful whether it was wide enough to let him through. But he saw no other way of doing it; for if he could not get inside the flooding house the current would sweep him instantly past it and there would be no hope of his rowing upstream to make a second run at it. There was no dry ground anywhere around the place and no other possible way for Annie and Tibbie to escape.

He hoped his momentum would be enough to force the door open and carry him inside. If he failed, no doubt both he and the boat would be in danger, but he would not make any further resolutions until necessity demanded it. As he drew near his mark, therefore, he resumed the seat of a rower, kept taking good aim at the door, gave a few vigorous pulls with the oars, then drew them in, bent his head forward, and prepared for the shock.

Crash went *The Bonnie Annie;* away went the door and posts; and the lintel came down on Alec's shoulders.

But I will now tell how the night had passed with Tibbie and Annie.

Tibbie's moaning grew gentler and less frequent, and both fell into a troubled slumber. Annie awoke at the sound of Tibbie's voice. She was talking in her sleep.

"Don't wake Him," she said, "don't wake Him; He's too tired an' sleepy. Let the wind blow, lads. Do ye think He can't see when His eyes are closed? If the water meddles with ye, He'll soon let it know it's in the wrong."

A pause followed. It was clear that she was in a dreamboat with Jesus in the back asleep. The sounds of the water outside had stolen through her ears and made a picture in her brain. Suddenly she cried out: "I told ye so! I told ye so! Look at it! The waves go doon as if they were so many little pups!"

She woke with the cry—weeping.

"I thought I had the sight o' my eeys," she said, sobbing, "an' the Lord was blin' with sleep."

"Do you hear the water?" said Annie.

"Who cares for *that* water!" she answered in a tone of contempt. "Do ye think He canna manage *it*!"

But there was a noise in the room beside them, and Annie heard it. The water was lapping at the foot of the bed.

"The water's in the house!" she cried in terror, rising.

"Lie still, bairn," said Tibbie authoritatively. "If the water be in the hoose, there's no getting oot. It'll be doon afore the mornin'. Lie still."

Annie lay down again and in a few minutes more she was asleep again. Tibbie slept too.

But Annie woke from a terrible dream—that a dead man was pursuing her, and had laid a cold hand upon her. The dream was gone, but the cold hand remained.

"Tibbie!" she cried. "The water's in the bed."

"What say ye, lassie?" returned Tibbie, waking up.

"The water's in the bed!"

"Weel, lie still. We canna sweep it oot."

It was pitch dark. Annie, who lay at the front, stretched her arm over the side. It sunk to the elbow. In a moment more the bed beneath her was like a full sponge. She lay in silent terror, longing for the dawn.

"I'm terrible cold," said Tibbie.

Annie tried to answer her, but the words would not leave her throat. The water rose. They were lying half-covered with it. Tibbie broke out singing. Annie had never heard her sing, and it was not very musical. "Savior, through the desert lead us. Without thee we can not go."

"Are ye awake, lassie?"

"Ay," answered Annie.

"I'm terrible cold, an' the water's up to my throat. I can't move. I'm so cold. I dinna think water hae been so cold."

"I'll help you to sit up a bit. You'll have dreadful rheumatism after this, Tibbie," said Annie, as she got up on her knees and proceeded to lift Tibbie's head and shoulders and draw her up in the bed.

But the task was beyond her strength. She could not move the helpless weight, and, in her despair, she let Tibbie's head fall back with a dull splash upon the pillow.

Seeing that all she could do was sit and support her, she got out of bed and waded across the floor to the fireside to find her clothes. But they were gone. Chair and all had floated away. She returned to the bed and, getting behind Tibbie, lifted her head on her knees and sat.

An awful dreary time followed. The water crept up and up. Tibbie moaned a little, and then lay silent for a long time, drawing slow and feeble breaths. Annie was almost dead with cold.

Suddenly in the midst of the darkness, Tibbie cried out, "I see light! I see light!"

A strange sound in her throat followed, after which she was quite still. Annie's mind began to wander. Something struck her gently on the arm and kept bobbing against her. She put out her hand to feel what it was. It was round and soft. She said to herself: "It's only somebody's head that the water's torn off," and she put her hand under Tibbie again.

In the morning she found it was a drowned hen.

At length she saw motion rather than light. The first of the awful dawn was on the yellow flood that filled the floor. There it lay throbbing and swirling. The light grew. She strained her eyes to see Tibbie's face. At last she saw that the water was over her mouth and that her face was like the face of her father in his coffin. She knew that Tibbie was dead. She tried nevertheless to lift her head out of the water, but she could not. So she crept out from under her with painful effort, and stood up in the bed. The water almost reached her knees. The table was floating near the bed. She got hold of it, and, scrambling onto it, sat with her legs in the water. The table went floating about for another long space, and she dreamed that she was having a row in *The Bonnie Annie* with Alec and Curly. In the motions of the water, she had passed close to the window and Truffey had seen her from the bridge above.

Suddenly wide awake, she started from her stupor at the terrible *crash* with which the door burst open. She thought the cottage was falling, and that her hour was come to follow Tibbie down the dark water.

But in shot the sharp prow of *The Bonnie Annie* and in glided after it the stooping form of Alec Forbes. She gave one wailing cry, and forgot everything.

That cry, however, had not ceased before she was in Alec's arms. In another moment, wrapped in his coat, she was lying in the bottom of the boat.

Alec was now as cool as any hero should be, for he was doing his duty. He looked all about for Tibbie, and at length saw her drowned in her bed.

"I wish I had been in time," he said.

But what was to be done next? Down the river he must go, yet they would reach the bridge in two minutes after leaving the cottage.

He would have to shoot for the middle arch, for that was the highest. But even should he escape being dashed against the bridge before he reached the arch, and even if he had time to get in a straight line for it, the risk was still a terrible one, for the water had risen to within a few feet of the peak of the arch, and the current was swift and torturous.

But when he shot *The Bonnie Annie* again through the door of the cottage, neither arch nor bridge was to be seen, and the boat went down the open river like an arrow.

Approaching the cottage down the current, Alec had not been aware that the wooden bridge upstream had given way just minutes after he had entered the water with his boat. It floated down the river after him. As he turned to row into the cottage, on it came and swept past him toward the other bridge.

The stone bridge was full of spectators, eagerly watching the boat, for Truffey had spread the report of the attempt. When news of the situation of Tibbie and Annie reached the Wan Water, those who had been watching it were now hurrying toward the bridge of the Glamour.

The moment Alec disappeared into the cottage, some of the spectators caught sight of the wooden bridge coming down full tilt upon them. Already fears for the safety of the stone bridge had been talked about, for the weight of the water rushing against it was tremendous. And now that they saw this ram coming down the stream, a panic, with cries and shouts of terror, arose. A general rush left the bridge empty just at the moment when the floating mass struck one of the principal piers. Had the spectators remained upon it, the bridge might have stood.

But one of the crowd was too much absorbed in watching the cottage to heed the sudden commotion around him. This was Truffey. Leaning wearily on the edge with his broken crutch at his side, he was watching anxiously through the cottage window. Even when the bridge struck the pier, and he must have felt the mass on which he stood tremble, he still kept staring at the cottage. Not till he felt the bridge begin to sway, I presume, had he an inkling of his danger. Then he sprang up and made for the street. Half of the bridge crumbled away behind him, and vanished in the seething yellow-brown abyss.

At this moment the first of the crowd from the Wan Water reached the foot of the bridge, among them the schoolmaster. Truffey was making desperate efforts to reach the bank. His mended crutch had given way and he was hopping wildly along. Murdoch Malison saw him, and rushed upon the falling bridge. He reached the cripple, caught him up in his strong arms, turned, and was halfway back to the street when, with a swing and a sweep and a great splash, the remaining half of the bridge reeled into the current and vanished. Murdoch Malison and Andrew Truffey left the world each in the other's arms.

Their bodies were never found.

A moment after the fall of the bridge, Robert Bruce, gazing with the rest at the triumphant torrent, saw *The Bonnie Annie* go darting past. Alec was in his shirt sleeves, facing down the river, with his oars level and ready to dip. But Bruce did not see Annie in the bottom of the boat.

"I wonder how old Margaret is," he murmured to his wife the moment he reached home.

But his wife could not tell him. Then he turned to his two younger children.

"Bairns," he said, "Annie Anderson's drowned. Ay, she's drowned," he continued, as they stared at him with frightened faces. "The Almighty's taken vengeance upon her for her disobedience, and for breaking Sabbath. See what you'll come to, children, if you take up with loons and don't mind what's said to you."

Mrs. Bruce cried a little. Robert would have set out at once to see Margaret

Anderson, but there was no possibility of crossing the Wan Water.

Fortunately for Thomas Crann, James Johnstone reached the bridge just before the alarm rose and sped to the nearest side, which was the one away from Glamerton. So, having seen the boat go past with Alec still safe in it, he was able to set off with the good news for Thomas. After searching for him at the miller's and at Howglen, he found him where he had left him, still on his knees with his hands in the grass.

"Alec's safe, man!" he cried.

Thomas fell on his face and gave still more humble thanks.

There was no getting to Glamerton. So James took Thomas, emotionally exhausted, to the miller's for shelter. The miller made Thomas take a glass of whisky and get into his bed.

Down the Glamour and down the Wan Water—for the united streams went by the latter name—the terrible current bore *The Bonnie Annie*. Nowhere could Alec find a fit place to land till they came to a small village, fortunately on the same side as Howglen, into the streets of which the river was now flowing. He bent to his oars, got out of the current, and rowed up to the door of a public house. The fat, kind-hearted landlady had certainly expected no guests that day. In a few minutes Annie was in a hot bath and before an hour had passed, was asleep, breathing peacefully. Alec got his boat into the coach's house, and hiring a horse from the landlord, rode home to his mother. She had heard only a confused story, and was getting terribly anxious about him when he made his appearance. As soon as she learned that he had rescued Annie and where he had left her, she had the horse put to the gig, and drove off to see after her neglected favorite.

From the moment the bridge fell the flood began to subside. Tibbie's cottage did not fall, and those who entered the next day found her body lying in the wet bed, its face still shining with the reflex of the light which broke upon her spirit as the windows were opened for it to pass.

"She sees noo," said Thomas Crann to James Johnstone as they walked together at her funeral. "The Lord sent that flood to wash the scales from her eyes."

Mrs. Forbes brought Annie home to Howglen as soon as she was fit to be moved.

Alec left for the city again, starting off a week before the commencement of the winter session.

47

· · · · · · · · · · · · · · · ·

The University Again

$\mathscr{I}$t was a bright, frosty evening in the end of October that Alec entered once more the streets of the city. The moment he had succeeded in satisfying his landlady's questions, he rushed up to Mr. Cupples's room. He was not there. So Alec wandered out and along the seashore toward the wall of the pier, his thoughts full of Kate. When he returned he ascended the garret stairs and again knocked at Mr. Cupples's door.

"Come in," came the reply in a strange, dull tone. Mr. Cupples had shouted into his empty tumbler while just about to swallow the last few drops without the usual intervention of the wine glass. Alec hesitated, but the voice came again with its usual ring, tinged with irritation, and he entered.

"Hello, bantam!" exclaimed Mr. Cupples, holding out a grimy hand that many a lady might have been pleased to possess and keep clean and white. "How's the cocks and hens?"

"Brawly," returned Alec. "Are you still acting as librarian?"

"Ay. I'm acting *as* librarian," returned Mr. Cupples dryly. "And I'm thinking that the books are beginning to know by this time what they're about, for such a thoroughly dilapidated collection of books I've never seen. Are you going to take the chemistry along with the natural philosophy?"

"Ay."

"Well, just come to me as you have done before. I'm not so good at those things as I am at the Greek; but I know more already than you'll know when you know all that you will know. And that's no flattery either to you or me."

With beating heart, Alec knocked the next day at Mr. Fraser's door and was shown into the drawing room, where Kate sat alone. The moment he saw her he knew there was a gulf between them as wide as the Glamour in a flood. She received him kindly and there was nothing in her manner or her voice which indicated the change, yet with that instinctive self-defense with which maidens are gifted, she had set up such a wall between them that he knew he could not approach her. With a miserable sense of cold exhaustion and aching disappointment, he left her. She shook hands with him warmly, was very sorry her uncle was out, and asked him whether he would not call again tomorrow. He thanked her in a voice that seemed not his own, while her voice seemed to come out of some far-off cave of the past. The cold, frosty air received him as he stepped from the door, and its breath was friendly. If the winter would only freeze him to one of its icicles.

And still, that heart of his insisted on going on throbbing, although there was no reason for it to beat anymore!

He wandered through the old burgh, past its once mighty cathedral, down to the bridge with its one Gothic arch, across the river, and into the wintry woods. On he wandered, seeing nothing, thinking nothing, almost feeling nothing, when he heard a voice behind him.

"Hello, bantam!" it cried and Alec did not need to turn around.

"I thought I saw you come out of Professor Fraser's," said Cupples, "and I decided a walk in the cold air would do me no harm; so I came after you."

Then changing his tone, he added, "Alec, man, get hold of yourself. Let go of *anything* before you lose yourself."

"What do you mean?" asked Alec, not altogether willing to understand him.

"You know well enough what I mean. There's trouble upon you. I'm asking no questions. We'll just have a walk together."

And so he began a lengthy, humorous travesty of a lecture on physics. It was evident from the things he said that he not only was attempting to take Alec's mind off whatever was troubling him but also had some perception of the real condition of Alec's feelings. After walking a couple of miles into the open country, they retraced their footsteps. As they approached the college, Mr. Cupples said: "Now, Alec, you must go home to your dinner. I'll be home before night. If you like, you can come with me to the library in the morning and I'll give you something to do."

Glad of anything to occupy his thoughts, Alec went to the library the next day. Mr. Cupples was making a catalogue and at the same time a thorough change in the arrangement of the books, and he found plenty for Alec to do. Alec soon found his own part in the work very agreeable. There was much to be done in mending old covers, mounting worn title pages, and such like. But in this department Mr. Cupples accepted very limited assistance; books were his gold and jewels and furniture and fine clothes, and whenever Alec ventured to pick up a book destined for repair, he was conscious of two possessive eyes watching his every move.

In a few days the opening of the session began. Appearing with the rest was Patrick Beauchamp—claiming now the title and dignity of his grandfather's estate, for the old man had died. He was even more haughty than before and after classes went about everywhere in Highland costume. Beauchamp no longer attended the anatomical lectures; and when Alec observed his absence, he could not help but recall the fact that Kate could not even bear the slightest mention of that branch of study. The thought of anyone handling a corpse sent her into an immediate faint.

Had it not been for the good influences of Mr. Cupples, whether or not Alec would have continued with this aspect of his medical studies with any heartiness himself this session is more than doubtful. But the garret scholar gave him constant aid—sometimes praise, sometimes rebuke, sometimes humor—and Alec succeeded in making progress.

Fortunately for the designs of Beauchamp, during the summer Mr. Fraser had been visiting in the neighborhood of Beauchamp's mother. Nothing was easier for one who possessed more than the ordinary power of ingratiating than to make himself agreeable to the old man. When he took his leave to return to the college, Mr. Fraser begged the young man to call upon him when he returned to the city. With a cunning attempt at modesty, Beauchamp declared that he would be only too pleased to honor the professor's request.

Soon after the commencement of the session, a panic seized the townspeople from certain reports connected with the school of anatomy, which stood by itself in a low neighborhood. They were to the effect that great indignities were practiced upon the remains of the subjects, and that occasionally the nearby graveyard was not safe from looting when a body happened to be needed.

Now whether Beauchamp had anything to do with what followed I cannot tell, but his innocence was doubtful at best.

Alec was occupied one evening at the college when he was roused by a yell outside. Looking down from the window he saw the unmistakable signs of gathering commotion of a most dubious nature. He quickly extinguished his candle and bolted down the backstairs and out a side door which was seldom used. But the moment he had let himself out and turned to go home, he heard an urchin who had peeped around a corner screech to the crowd—many of them drunk—across the yard: "He's oot at the backdoor! He's oot at the back and away!"

Another yell arose, followed by the sound of trampling feet.

Alec knew his only chance lay in his heels, and he took to them faithfully. The narrow streets rang with the pursuing shouts. Alec, however, easily eluded them and was before long recovering in his apartment.

But within ten minutes the mob was thundering at the door below. And the fact that they knew where Alec lived adds to my suspicion of Beauchamp. The landlady wisely let them in, and for a few minutes they were busy searching the rooms. It was some time before Alec, from his vantage point on the roof to which he had safely retreated just moments before the heavy footsteps had reached the floor of his room, saw the small mob leave the house again. When the tumult in the street had gradually died away, he crept back down the way he had come. As he passed the garret landing, to his dismay he saw that Mr. Cupples's door was ripped off its hinges and lay on the floor. He entered the room and saw Mr. Cupples on his bed, holding a bloody bandage to his head. Trying to defend himself against the angry citizens, he had been shoved, had fallen against the fender, and had a bad cut as the result.

"Bantam," he said feebly, "I thought you would have your neck broken by this time. How the devil did you get out of their grasp?"

"By playing the cat on the roof," answered Alec. "I'll get the landlady."

But just as he turned to leave the room, she arrived carrying water and a fresh bandage.

" 'Deed, bantam," said Mr. Cupples, "if it hadn't been for the gudewife here chasing them off and picking me up off the hearthstone, I would have been dead before now."

"Not that likely, Mr. Cupples," she said. "Now just hold your tongue and lie still. I'll bring you a cup of tea directly."

"Tea, gudewife! The devil can have your tea! Give me a drink from my tumbler."

" 'Deed, Mr. Cupples, you'll have no drink at my hand."

"Ye rigwiddie carlin!" grumbled the patient.

"If you don't hold your tongue, I'll go for the doctor."

"I'll fling him down the stairs. Here's doctor enough!" Then he added, looking at Alec, "Give me half a glass."

"You'll have nothing," interposed the landlady again. "It would be the death of you. I've taken everything out of here, Mr. Cupples."

"Get out of my room!" he cried. "Leave me with Alec Forbes. He'll give me what I need."

" 'Deed, I'll leave no two such fools together. Come down the stairs directly, Mr. Forbes."

Alec saw that it would be better to obey. He went back up on the sly in the course of the evening, however, but, seeing his friend asleep, came down again. He insisted on sitting up with him though, to which their landlady consented after repeated vows of prudence and caution. Mr. Cupples was restless and feverish during the night. Alex gave him some water. He drank it eagerly. In the morning he was better, but quite unable to get up.

Leaving him in the hands of the landlady, Alec set off for the college to do what he could in the way of preserving Mr. Cupples's good standing at the library before any false rumors should have started regarding his absence.

The moment he was out of the room, Mr. Cupples got out of bed and crawled to the cupboard. To his mortification, he found that what his landlady had said was true and there was not a spoonful of whisky left in the house. He drained the few drops which had gathered in the sides of his tumbler, and crawled back to bed.

After the morning classes were over, Alec went to tell Mr. Fraser about his adventure and of the consequences of the librarian's fate; he was most anxious that Mr. Cupples's good standing not be jeopardized because of him.

"I was uneasy about you, Mr. Forbes," said the professor, "for I heard from your friend Beauchamp that you had got into a row with the blackguards, but he did not know how you had come off."

His "friend" Beauchamp! How did he know about it?

But at that moment Kate entered and Alec forgot Beauchamp. She hesitated but advanced and held out her hand. Alec took it, but felt it tremble in his with a backward motion of reluctance.

"Will you stay and have tea with us?" asked the professor. "You so rarely come to see us now."

Alec stammered out an unintelligible excuse.

"Your friend Beauchamp will be here," continued Mr. Fraser.

"I fear Mr. Beauchamp is no friend of mine," said Alec.

"Why do you think that? He speaks very kindly of you—always."

Alec made no reply. Ugly things were vaguely showing themselves through a fog.

Alec went home with such a raging jealousy in his heart that he almost forgot Mr. Cupples. Why should Kate hesitate to shake hands with him? He recalled how her hand had trembled and fluttered on his arm when he spoke of the red stain on the water; and how on another occasion she had declined to shake hands with him when he told her he had come from the dissecting room. The conviction suddenly seized him that Beauchamp had been working on her morbid sensitiveness—taking revenge by making the girl whom he worshiped shrink from him with loathing. But in the lulls of his rage and jealousy, he had some faint glimpses, perhaps for the first time, into Kate's character. Not that he was capable of thinking about it; but flashes of reality came now and then across the vapors of passion.

Poor Alec! If he that same evening had seen Kate looking up into Beauchamp's face as she had never looked into his, with her face aglow at the sight of his Highland dress which set off to full advantage his broad shoulders and commanding height—as I said, if Alec had seen her face, he may have died on the spot.

Beauchamp had quite taken her by storm, and yet not without well-laid schemes. Having discovered her admiration for poets, he made himself her pupil with regard to Byron, listening to everything she had to say as to a new revelation. At the same time he began to study Shelley and to introduce her to writings of which she had scarcely heard. And the cunning Celt, perceiving her emotional sensitivities, used his insights against him whose rival he had become. Both to uncle and niece he had always spoken of Alec in a familiar and friendly manner. But now he began to occasionally drop a word with reference to him and break off with a laugh.

"What *do* you mean, Mr. Beauchamp?" asked Kate on one of these occasions.

"I was only thinking how Forbes would enjoy some lines I found in Shelley yesterday."

"What are they?"

"Ah, I must not repeat them to you. You would turn pale and shudder again, and it would kill me to see your white face."

Whereupon Kate pressed the question no further, and an additional feeling of discomfort associated itself with the name of Alec Forbes.

48

•••••••••••••••••

The Coming of Womanhood

*F*or several months Annie lay in her own little room at Howglen. Mrs. Forbes was dreadfully anxious about her, often fearing that her son's heroism had only prolonged the process of dying, that despite his efforts that awful night might yet take its toll. At length on a morning in February the first wave of the feebly returning flow of the life-tide visited her heart. She looked out her window and saw the country wrapped in a sheet of snow. A thrill of gladness, too pleasant to be borne without tears, made her close her eyes. It was not gladness for any specific reason, but the essential gladness of *being* that made her weep. There lay the world, white over green; and here she lay, faint and alive.

As the spring advanced, her strength increased till she became able to move about the house again. Nothing was said of her returning to the Bruces. What Robert Bruce's reaction was to the news that she was alive after all, I will not venture to speculate. But suffice it to say that they were not more desirous of having her than Mrs. Forbes was of parting with her.

If there had ever been any danger of anyone falling in love with Annie, there was much more now. For as her health returned it became evident that a change had passed upon her. She had always been a womanly child; now she was a childlike woman. Her eyes had grown deeper and the outlines of her form more graceful; and a flush as of sunrise dawned oftener over the white roses of her cheeks. She had not grown much taller, but her shape produced the impression of tallness. When Thomas Crann saw her after her illness, he held her at arm's length and gazed at her.

"Eh! lassie," he said, "ye're grown a woman! Ye'll have the bigger heart to love the Lord with. I thought He would hae taken ye away a bairn before we had seen how ye would turn oot. An' sadly would I hae missed ye! An' all the more that I hae lost old Tibbie. A man canna do weel without some woman or other to tell him the truth. I sadly wish I hadn't been so cantankert with her."

"I never heard her say that you were, Thomas."

"No, I dare say not. She wouldn't say't. She was a kindhearted old body."

"But she didn't like to be called old," interposed Annie with a smile.

"Aweel, she's not that old now!" he answered. "Eh, lassie! it must be a fine thing to have the wisdom o' age along with the light heart an' strong bones o' youth. I was once proud o' that arm"—and he stretched out his right arm whose muscles still indicated great power—"an' there was no man within ten miles o' Glamerton who could lift what I could lift when I was twenty-five. But any lad in the mason trade could best me at liftin' noo; for I'm stiff in the back and my arm's jist red-hot sometimes with rheumatism.—Ye'll be goin' back to Robert Bruce before long, I'm thinkin'."

"I don't know. The mistress has said nothing about it. And I'm in no hurry, I can tell you that, Thomas. Ay, it's a fine thing to have thick milk for your porridge instead of sky-blue water," said Annie with another smile.

Thomas glanced at her. *What could ail the lassie?* he worried. The truth was that under the genial influences of home tenderness and early womanhood, a little spring of gentle humor had begun to flow softly through the quiet fields of Annie's childlike nature.

The mason gazed at her doubtfully. Annie saw his discomposure and took his great hand in her two little ones, looked full into his cold, gray eyes, and asked, still smiling, "Eh, Thomas, would you have a body never make fun of something when it just comes of itself?"

"We don't hear that the Savior himsel' ever so much as smiled," he returned.

"Well, that would have been little wonder with all the burdens He had upon Him. But I'm not sure that He didn't, for all that. Folk don't always say when someone laughs. I'm thinking that if one of the bairnies that He took upon His knees had held up his wee toy horse with a broken leg, and had prayed Him to work a miracle and mend the leg, He wouldn't have worked a miracle maybe, but He would have smiled or maybe laughed a bit, I dare say, and then He would have mended the leg some way or other to please the bairnie. And if it were I upon His knee, I would rather have had the mending of His own two hands, with a knife to help them maybe, than twenty miracles upon it."

Thomas gazed at her for a moment in silence. Then with a slow shake of the head, and a full-flown smile on his rugged face, he said: "Ye're a curious cratur', Annie. I don't rightly know what to make o' ye sometimes. Ye're like a tiny bairn an' a grandmother both in one. But I'm thinkin' that between the two, ye're mostly in the right."

Meantime, a great pleasure dawned on Annie. James Dow came to visit her not long after this conversation with Thomas Crann. He had a long interview with Mrs. Forbes, the result of which Annie did not learn till some time later. One of Mrs. Forbes' farm servants who had been at Howglen for some years was going to leave at the next term, and she had asked Dow whether he knew of anyone to take his place. Whereupon he offered himself, and they arranged everything for his taking the position of foreman, the post he had occupied with James Anderson and was at present occupying some ten or twelve miles up the hill country.

Few things would have pleased Mrs. Forbes more, for James Dow was recognized throughout the country as the very pattern of what a foreman ought to be. One factor was his reputation for saving his employers all possible expense. Of late Mrs. Forbes had found it increasingly more difficult to meet her current expenses; for Alec's requirements at college were heavier this year. Much to her annoyance she had been compelled to delay the last half-yearly payment of Bruce's interest. She could not easily bear to recall the expression on his keen, weasel-like face when she informed him that it would be more convenient to pay the money a month hence. That month had passed, and another, before she had been able to do so. For although the home expenses upon a farm in Scotland are very small, yet even in the midst of plenty, money is often scarce enough.

Now, however, she hoped that with James Dow's management things would go better, and she would be able to hold her head a little higher in her own presence. So she was happy, knowing nothing of the cloud that was gathering over the far-off university, soon to sweep northward and envelop Howglen in its dusty folds.

49

In the Library

To ease Mr. Cupples's uneasiness about the books and catalogue, Alec offered to spend an hour or two every evening in carrying out his work in the library. This was a great relief to the librarian, and his health improved more rapidly thereafter.

"Mr. Forbes," said Mr. Fraser, looking at Alec kindly one morning after the lecture, "you are a great stranger now. Won't you come and spend tomorrow evening with us? We are going to have a little party. It is my birthday, though I'm sure I don't know why an old man like me should have any birthdays. But it's not my doing. Kate found it out, and she would have a merrymaking. Myself, I think after a man is forty he should go back to thirty-nine, thirty-eight, and so on, indicating his progress toward none at all. That gives him a good sweep before he comes to two, one, and zero—at that rate I shall be thirteen tomorrow," and he smiled at his own cleverness as he chattered on.

Whether the old man knew the real cause of Alec's gloom, I cannot tell. But with a feeling like that which makes one irritate a smarting wound or urge on an aching tooth, Alec resolved to go and have his pain in earnest.

He was the first to arrive.

Kate was in the drawing room at the piano, radiant in white—lovelier than ever. She rose and met him with some embarrassment, which she tried to cover under more than usual kindness.

"Oh, Kate!" blurted Alec, overpowered with her loveliness.

Kate took it for reproach and, making no reply, withdrew her hand and turned away. Alec saw as she turned that all the light had gone out of her face. But that instant Beauchamp entered, and as she turned once more to greet him, the light flashed full from her face and her eyes. Beauchamp was magnificent, clad in his tartan kilt, fully decorated with silver, jewels, brooch, and dirk. Not observing Alec, he advanced to Kate with the confidence of an accepted suitor; but some motion of her hand or glance from her eyes warned him in time. He looked around, started a little, and greeted Alec with a slight bow. He then turned to Kate and began to talk in a low tone. As Alec watched, the last sickly glimmer of his hope died out in darkness. Beauchamp now had his revenge of mortification, and with it power enough over Kate's sensitive nature to draw her into the sphere of his flaunted triumph. Had Alec then been able to see his own face, he would have seen upon it the very sneer that he hated so much upon Beauchamp's.

Other visitors arrived, and Alec found a strange delight in behaving as if no hidden wound existed. Some music and a good deal of provincial talk followed. At length, Beauchamp urged Kate to sing, and she complied. It was a ghostly and eerie ballad from the Shetland Isles, and as Kate neared its completion her face grew pale. As the last wailing sounds of the accompaniment ceased, she gave one glance into Beauchamp's face and left the room.

Alec's heart swelled with indignant sympathy. But what could he do? The room became oppressive to him and he made his way to the door. As he opened it he could not help glancing at Beauchamp. Instead of the dismay he expected, he saw the triumph of power in the curl of his lip. Alec flew from the house. Seeking refuge he rushed to the library, where he lay on the floor, alone with the heap of books he had that morning arranged for binding. He felt even darker than the night around him.

It was a bitter hour. He had lain a long time when suddenly he started and listened. He heard the sound of an opening door, but not one of those in ordinary use. Thinking the noises those of thieves, he kept still. There was a door in a corner of the library which was never opened. It led into a part of the quadrangle buildings which had been formerly used as a students' dormitory but which had been abandoned now for many years. Alec knew this, but he did not know that there was also access between this empty region and some of the houses and apartments of the faculty, among them Mr. Fraser's. Nor did he know that the library had been used before as a tryst by Beauchamp and Kate.

The door closed and the light of a lantern flashed to the ceiling.

"Why were you so unkind, Patrick?" said Kate. "You know it kills me to sing that old ballad."

"Why should you mind singing an old song?"

"Oh, Patrick! What *would* my mother say if she knew I met you this way? You know I can refuse you nothing; you shouldn't make such demands on me."

Alec could not hear his answer, and he knew why. The thought of Kate's lips caressing his enemy's filled Alec with loathing.

Of course he should not have listened. But the fact was that for the time, all consciousness of free will and capability of action had vanished from his mind. His soul was but a black gulf.

"Ah, yes, Patrick. Kisses are easy. But you hurt me terribly sometimes. And I know why. You hate my cousin, poor boy—and you want me to hate him too. I wonder if you love me as much as he does. Surely you are not jealous of him."

"Jealous of *him*! I should think not!"

"But you hate him."

"I don't hate him. He's not worth hating—the awkward clown."

"His mother has been very kind to me. I wish you would make up with him for my sake, Patrick. I love you so—though you are unkind sometimes. Patrick, don't make me do things in front of my cousin that will hurt him."

Alec knew that she pressed closer to Beauchamp, and offered him her face.

"Listen, my Kate," said Beauchamp. "I know there are things you cannot bear to hear; but you must hear this."

"No, no, not now!" answered Kate, shuddering.

"You must, Kate, and you shall," said Beauchamp. "I have tried to shield you from the knowledge of what goes on in that dissecting room during the evenings after classes are over. And he—that cousin of yours—is the ringleader. That is why I discontinued anatomy. I once rebuked him, the first day he walked into class, for his unmanly behavior, and—"

"Liar!" shouted Alec, springing into the light of their lantern.

Beauchamp's hand flew to the hilt of his dirk. Alec laughed with bitter contempt.

"Do so if you dare!" he cried. "Even you, I believe, know I am no coward."

Kate stood staring and trembling. Beauchamp's presence of mind returned. He thrust his half-drawn knife back into its sheath, and said coldly, "Eavesdropping?"

"Lying?" retorted Alec.

"You brute!" answered Beauchamp. "You will answer me for this!"

"When you please," returned Alec. "Meantime, you will leave this room, or I will make you."

"Go to the devil!" said Beauchamp, again laying his hand on his dirk.

"I have only to ring this bell and the watchman will be here."

"That is your regard for your cousin! You would expose her like that."

"I would expose her to anyone rather than to you," said Alec. "I have held my tongue too long."

By this time Kate was no longer leaning against the bookcase, but had slipped to the floor.

"And you will leave her lying here?"

"*You* will leave her lying here."

"That is your revenge, is it?"

"I want no revenge, even on you, Beauchamp. Now go."

"I will certainly not forget mine," said Beauchamp as he turned and left the library.

Alec could not understand the ease of his victory. But above all things, Beauchamp hated to find himself in an awkward position, which certainly would have been his case if Alec had rung the bell. Nor did he like to act on the spur of the moment. He was one who must have plans, those he would carry out remorselessly. So he went away to contemplate further revenge.

Alec found Kate moaning, and he supported her head as she had done for him in that old harvest field. Before her senses had quite returned, she began to talk, and after several inarticulate attempts, her murmured words became plain.

"Never mind, dear," she said; "the boy is wild. He doesn't know what he says. Oh, Patrick, my heart is aching with love for you. You must be kind to me and not make me do what I don't like to do. And you must forgive my poor cousin, for he did not mean to tell lies. He fancies you bad because I love you so much more than him."

Alec felt as if a green flame were consuming his brain. He had to get Kate home before she discovered she was not talking to her lover—and before he himself went mad! There was only one way to do it, and that lay in a bold venture. Mr. Fraser's door lay just across a corner of the quadrangle. He would carry her to her own room. The guests would be gone and it was a small household, so the chance of effecting it undiscovered was a good one.

Alec swooped her up, and within three mintues she was on her own bed and he was speeding out of the house as fast and quietly as he could.

Before he reached home his heart felt like a burned-out volcano.

Meantime, Mr. Cupples had been fretting over his absence, for he had come to depend very much on Alec. At last he rang the bell, knowing that the landlady was out. He bribed the little girl who answered it, and she ran to the grocer's for him.

When Alec came home he found his friend fast asleep in bed, the room smelling strongly of toddy—the ingredients for which the girl had purchased for him—and the bottle standing on the table beside the empty tumbler. Faint in body, mind, and spirit, Alec grabbed the bottle, poured the tumbler full, and raised the drink to his lips recklessly. A cry rang from the bed, and the same instant the tumbler was struck from his hand. It flew in fragments against the grate, and the spirit rushed in a roaring flame of demoniacal wrath up the chimney.

"Curse you!" half-shrieked Mr. Cupples, still under the influence of the same spirit he had banned on its way to Alec Forbes' empty house. "Curse you, bantam! You've broken my father's tumbler. Devil take you! I've a good mind to wring your neck!"

Seeing that Mr. Cupples was only two-thirds of Alec's height, and only one-half of his thickness, the threat was rather ludicrous. Miserable as he was, Alec could not help laughing.

"You may laugh, bantam! But I want no companion in hell to cast his damnation in my teeth. If you touch that bottle again, I'll brain you and send you into the other world without that handle for Satan to catch a grip of you. And there *may* be a handle somewhere on the right side of you for some soft-hearted angel to lay a hand on and give you a lift where you don't deserve to go, you buckie! After all that I have said to you—you fool!"

Alec burst into a roar of laughter. For there was the little man standing only in his shirt, shaking a trembling fist at him, stammering with eagerness, and half-choked with excitement.

"Go to your bed, Mr. Cupples, or you'll catch your death of cold. I'll put the bottle away." Alec seized the bottle once more.

Mr. Cupples flew at him and would have knocked the bottle on the floor had not Alec held it high above his reach.

"Toots, man! I'm going to put it away. Go to your bed and trust me."

"You give me your word you won't put it to your mouth?"

"I do," answered Alec.

Mr. Cupples lay down and a violent fit of coughing, the consequence of the exertion, overtook him.

Alec sat down in his easy chair and stared into the fire.

"The laddie's going to the dogs for want of being looked after," muttered Mr. Cupples. "This won't do any longer. I must be up tomorrow. It's the women! The women!"

Alec sat, still staring helplessly into the fire. The world was very black and dismal.

Then he rose to go to bed, for Mr. Cupples did not require him now. Finding him fast asleep under the covers, Alec made him as comfortable as he could. Then he locked the closet where the whisky was, and took the key with him.

Their mutual care in this respect was comical indeed.

50

●●●●●●●●●●●●●●●●●●●

The Lady's Laugh

The next morning Alec saw Mr. Cupples in bed before he left. His surprise therefore was great when, entering the library after morning lectures, he found him seated in the usual place, hard at work on his catalogue. Except that he was yet thinner and paler than before, the only difference in his appearance was that his eyes were brighter and his complexion clearer.

"You here, Mr. Cupples!" he exclaimed.

"What made you lock the cupboard last night, you devil?" returned the librarian, paying no attention to Alec's expression of surprise. "But I say, bantam," he continued, not waiting for a reply, "you have done your work well—very near as well as I could have done myself."

"I'm sure, Mr. Cupples, it was the least I could do."

"You impudent cock! It was the very best you could do, or you wouldn't have come within sight of me. I may not be much at thrashing attorneys or cutting up dead corpses, but I defy you to come up to me in anything connected with books."

"Faith! Mr. Cupples, you may go further than that. After what you have done for me, if I were a general, you should lead the Forlorn Hope."*

"Ay, ay. It's a forlorn hope, all that I'm fit for, Alec Forbes," returned Cupples sadly.

This struck Alec so near his own grief that he could not reply with even seeming cheerfulness. He said nothing. Mr. Cupples resumed, "I have but two or three words to say to you, Alec Forbes. Can you believe in a man as well as you can in a woman?"

"I can believe in you, Mr. Cupples. That I'll swear to."

"Well, just sit down there and carry on with the books from where you left off yesterday. Then after the three o'clock lecture—what is it that you're attending this session?—we'll go down to Luckie Cumstie's and have a mouthful of dinner—she'll do her best for me—and I'll have just one tumbler of toddy, but not a devil's drop shall you have, bantam! And then we'll come back here in the evening, and I'll give you a little episode of my life.—Episode did I call it? Faith, it's my life itself, and not worth much either. You'll be the first man that ever I told it to. And you may judge my high regard for you from that fact."

Alec worked away at his cataloguing and then attended the afternoon lecture. Dinner at Luckie Cumstie's followed—plain but good. And just as the evening was fading into night, they went back to the library. The two friends seated themselves on the lower steps of an open, circular oak staircase which wound up to a gallery running around the walls.

"After I had taken my degree," began Mr. Cupples, "I heard of a great library in the north—I won't say where—that needed the hand of a man that knew what he was about to put it in decent order. Don't imagine that it was a public library. No. It belonged to a great house. So I took the job, and liked the work very well, for books are the bonniest things in the world. One day as I was working away, I heard a kind of rustling. I thought it was mice, to which I've been a deadly enemy ever since they ate half of a first edition of mine of the *Fairy Queen*. But when I looked up, what should I see but a lady in a pale, pink gown standing in front of the bookshelves at the farther end of the room. I had good eyesight and had just put the books in that part of the shelves away, and I saw her put her hand on a book that was not fit for her. I won't say what it was but it was written by some evil creature who had no respect for man or woman and whose neck should have been broken by the midwife.

" 'Don't touch that book, my bonny lady!' I cried.

"She started and looked around, and I rose and went across the floor to her. And her face grew prettier and prettier the nearer I came. Her eyes went right through me and made of my life what it is and what I am. They went through every fiber of my being, twisting it up just as a spider does a fly before it sucks the life out of it.

---

*Forlorn Hope comes from the Dutch phrase *verloren hoop*. It signifies an attack force of volunteers ahead of the main body which would attempt some perilous service.

" 'Are you the librarian?' she asked, soft and small.

" 'That I am, ma'am,' I answered. 'My name's Cupples—at your service.'

" 'I was looking, Mr. Cupples,' she said, 'for some book to help me learn Gaelic. I want very much to read Gaelic.'

" 'Well, ma'am,' I said, 'if it had been any of the Romance languages I might have given you some help. But you'll have to wait till you go to Edinburgh or Aberdeen, where you'll easily fall in with some student that'll be proud to instruct you and count himself more than well paid with the sight of your bonny face.'

"She turned red at that and I was afraid I had angered her. But she gave a small laugh and out the door she went. Well, that was the first time I saw her. But in a day or two there she was again. She began coming to the library nearly every day, asking me questions and wanting to see books. She seemed prettier every time, wearing long silk dresses and with diamonds for buttons. Well, to make a long story short, she came oftener and oftener and before long every time she left, I went after her—in my thoughts, I mean—all through the house.

"You may say I was a gowk. And you may laugh at me for crying after the moon. But better cry for the moon than not be capable of crying for the moon. And I must confess that I could have licked the very dust off the floor where her foot had been. Man, I never saw anything like her! She was just perfection itself and I was out of my wits in love with her.

"Well, one night my eyes were suddenly dazed with the glimmer of something white. At first I thought I had seen a ghost. But there she was, in a fluffy cloud of whiteness, with her bonny bare shoulders and arms, and just one white rose in her black hair.

" 'It's so hot in the drawing room,' she said. 'And they're talking such nonsense there. There's nobody speaks to me but you, Mr. Cupples.'

" 'Indeed, ma'am,' I said, 'I don't know where it's to come from tonight. For I have only one sense left, and that's almost "with excess of brightness blind." Old Spenser says something like that, doesn't he, ma'am?' I added, seeing that she looked a little grave.

"But what she might have said or done, I don't know. For I swear to you, bantam, that delirium came upon me and I know nothing that happened afterward, till I came to myself at the sound of a laugh from outside the door. I knew it well enough, though it was a light, fluttering laugh. I sprang to my feet, but the place reeled round and I fell. It was the laugh that killed me, bantam. She killed me with her laugh. She had never loved me at all! And why shouldn't she laugh? And such a one as her that was no light-headed lassie but could read and understand with the best? I suppose I had gone down upon my knees to her, and then like the rest of the celestials, she took to her feathers and flew.

"But I know more than this, that for endless ages I went following her through the halls, knowing that she was behind the next door, and opening that door to an empty room, to be equally certain that she was behind the next. And so I went on and on, behind a thousand doors, always hearing the laugh, till I began to see the poor old walls of my mother's little house on the edge of the bog, and she was hanging over me, as I lay feverish, saying her prayers. How or when I had got there I don't know, but when she saw me open my eyes, she dropped upon her knees and went on praying. And I wonder that those prayers weren't listened to. I could never understand that."

"How do you know they weren't listened to?" asked Alec.

"Look at me! Do you call this listening to a prayer? Look what she got me back for. Do you call that an answer to prayers like my old mother's? Faith! I'll be forced to repent some day for her sake. But man! I would have repented long ago if I could have gotten a glimpse of the possible justice of putting a heart like mine into such a contemptible, scrimpit body as this. Man, the first thing I did when I came to myself was justify my angel before God for laughing at me. How could anybody help laughing at me? It wasn't her fault. But I won't let you laugh at me, bantam. I tell you that."

"Laugh at you! I would rather be a doormat to the devil!" exclaimed Alec.

"Thank you, bantam. Well, you see, once I had made up my mind about why she laughed at me, I just began following after her again like a hungry pup that stops the minute you look round at him—in my thoughts, you know—just as I had been following her all the time of my fever through the halls of heaven—of heaven as I imagined. When I grew some better and got up—would you believe it?—the kindness of the old, warped, brown, wrinkled woman that brought me forth—me, with the big heart and small body—began to console me for the laugh of that queen of white-skinned ladies. My mother thought a heap of me. But it was small honor I brought her name, with my eyes burned out for crying at the moon.—But I'll tell you the rest after we go home. I can't stand to be here in the dark. It was in the midst of books, in the dark, that I heard that laugh. The first time I let evening come down upon me in this library, all at once I heard a small snicker of a woman's laugh from somewhere. I grew fiery hot as brimstone and was out the door in an instant. And sure as death, I'll hear it again if I stay a minute longer."

They left the library and walked home. Mr. Cupples set the kettle boiling for his toddy, and resumed his story.

"As soon as I was able I left my mother crying—God bless her!—and came to this town. The first thing I took to was teaching. Now that's a braw thing, when the laddies and lassies want to learn and have questions of their own to ask. But when they don't care, it's the very devil. Before long everything grew gray. I cared for nothing and nobody. My very dreams went from me, or came to torment me.

"Well, one night I came home, worn out with wrestling to get bairns to eat that had no hunger, and saw on the table a bottle of whisky a friend of mine had sent to me. I opened the bottle and drank a glass. Then another. And before long the colors began to come out again and I said to myself with pride: 'My lady can't with all her breeding and bonny skin keep me from loving her!' And I followed her about again through all the outs and ins of the story, and the past was restored to me.—That's how it appeared to me that night. Was it any wonder that the first thing I did the next night was to have another two or three glasses from the same bottle? I wanted nothing from God or Nature but just that the color might not be taken out of my life. The devil was in it, that I couldn't stand up to my fate like a man. If my life was to be gray, I ought to have just taken up my cloak about me and gone on content. But I couldn't. I had to see things as bonny, or my strength left me. But you can't slink in at back doors that way. I was put out, and out I must stay. It wasn't long before I began to discover that it was all a delusion and a snare. When I fell asleep I would sometimes dream that, opening the doors into one of the halls of light, there she was laughing at me. And she might have gone on laughing to all eternity for anything I cared. And—ten times worse—I would sometimes come upon her crying and repenting and holding her hand out to me, and me caring no more for her than the beard of a barley stalk.

"But after a while all the whisky in Glenlivat* couldn't console me.—Look at me now. You see what I am. Look at my hand, how it trembles. Look at my heart, how it's burned out. There's no living creature but yourself that I have any regard for, since my old mother died. If it weren't for books, I would almost cut my throat. Man, better lay hands on a torpedo than upon a cunning and beautiful woman, for she'll make you spin till you don't know your thumb from your big toe. And when I saw you pour out the whisky in that mad-like manner, as if you were going to have a drink of penny ale, it just drove me insane with anger."

"Well, Mr. Cupples," Alec ventured to say, "why don't you send the bottle to the devil?"

"What!" exclaimed Mr. Cupples, with a sudden reaction from the seriousness of his recent mood. "No, no. My old toddy maker won't go to the devil till we go together. Eh! We'll both have dry insides before we can get away from him, I don't doubt. That drought's an awful thing to contemplate. But speak of getting over the drink, don't think I haven't made that attempt. And why should I go to hell before my time? No, no. Once you have learned to drink, you can't do without it. For God's sake, for your mother's sake, for *any* sake, don't let a drop of the hell-broth pass your throat, or you'll be damned like me forever. It's as good as signing away your soul with your own hand and your own blood."

Mr. Cupples lifted his glass, emptied it, and, setting it down on the table with a gesture of hatred, proceeded to fill it yet again.

---

*Glenlivat is a city in Banffshire, Scotland, renowned for its whisky.

51

· · · · · · · · · · · · · · · · · · ·

It Comes to Blows

Several days later Alec was walking along the pier, renewing his grief by the sea. His was a young love and his sorrow was yet interesting to him. He crossed to the desolate, sandy shore and then wandered back to the old city, standing at length over the middle of the bridge and looking down into the dark water below the Gothic arch.

He heard a footstep behind him on the bridge. Looking round he saw Beauchamp. Without reason he walked up boldly to him. Beauchamp drew back.

"Beauchamp," said Alec, "you are my devil."

"Granted," said Beauchamp, coolly, but on his guard.

"What are you about with my cousin?"

"What is that to you?"

"She is my cousin."

"I don't care. She's not mine."

"If you play her false, as you have played me—by heavens!—"

"Oh, I'll be very kind to her! You needn't be afraid. I only wanted to take down your brazen arrogance. You may go to her when you like."

Alec's answer was to attempt a blow, which Beauchamp was prepared for and avoided. Alec pursued the attack with a burning desire to give him the punishment he deserved. But suddenly he turned sick, and, although he afterward recalled a wrestle on the bridge, the first thing he was aware of was the cold water of the river closing over him. The shock restored him. When he rose to the surface he swam down the stream, for the banks were very high near the bridge. At length he succeeded in landing, dragged himself ashore, and set out for home.

He had not gone far, however, before he grew very faint and had to sit down. He discovered that his arm was bleeding and realized that Beauchamp had stabbed him. But he managed to reach home without much further difficulty. Mr. Cupples had not come in. So he got his landlady to tie up his arm for him, and then he changed his clothes. Fortunately the wound, although long and deep, ran lengthwise between the shoulder and the elbow, on the outside of the arm, and so was not serious. Feeling better, he eventually went back out.

Fierce as the struggle had been, I do not think Beauchamp intended murder, for the consequences of murder would be a serious consideration to every gentleman. He came of a wild race with whom a word and a steel blow had been linked for ages. And habits transmitted become almost instincts. Whether Beauchamp tried to throw him from the bridge must also remain in doubt, for when the bodies of two men are locked in the wrestle of hate, their own souls do not know what they intend.

In any case, Beauchamp must have run home with the conscience of a murderer, thinking that he had stabbed Alec fatally. And yet when Alec made his appearance in class the following day, a revival of hatred was his first mental experience.

Soon after Alec had left the house, Cupples came home with a hurried inquiry whether the landlady had seen anything of him. She told him as much as she knew, whereupon he went upstairs.

The moment Alec entered the garret two hours later, Mr. Cupples, who had already consumed his nightly potion, saw that Alec had been drinking. He looked at him with wide-opened blue eyes, dismay and toddy combining to render them of uncertain vision.

"Eh, bantam! bantam!" he said, and sank back in his chair. "You've been at it in spite of me."

Mr. Cupples burst into silent tears—a phenomenon not unusual in men under the combined influences of emotion and drink.

"I want to tell you about it," said Alec.

Mr. Cupples took little notice, but Alec began his story notwithstanding, and as he went on his friend became attentive, inserting here and there an expletive to the disadvantage of Beauchamp.

When Alec had finished, Cupples said solemnly: "I warned you against him, Alec. But a worse enemy than Beauchamp has gotten hold of you, I don't doubt. Do what he like, Beauchamp's dirk couldn't hurt you so much as your own hand when you lift the first glass to your own mouth. You've despised my warnings. And sorrow and shame'll come of it. Your mother'll hate me. Go away to your bed. I can't stand the sight of you."

Alec went to bed, rebuked and distressed. But not having taken enough to hurt him much, he was unfortunately able, the next morning, to regard Mr. Cupples's lecture from a ludicrous point of view. *And what danger am I in,* he asked himself, *when I drank less than most of the rest of the fellows?*

And although the whisky had done him no great immediate injury, yet its reaction, combined with the loss of blood, made him restless all that day. When the afternoon came, instead of going to Mr. Cupples in the library, he joined some of the same set he had been with the evening before. And when he came home, instead of going upstairs to visit Mr. Cupples, he went straight to bed.

The next morning, while he was at breakfast, Mr. Cupples made his appearance in his room.

"What became of you last night, bantam?" he asked kindly, but with evident uneasiness.

"I came home tired and went straight to bed."

"But you weren't home very early."

"I wasn't that late."

"You have been drinking again. I know by the look of your eye."

Alec had a very even temper. But a headache and a sore conscience together were enough to upset it. To be out of temper with oneself is to be out of temper with the universe.

"Did my mother commission you to look after me, Mr. Cupples?" he demanded, and could have dashed his head against the wall the next moment. But the look of pitying concern in Mr. Cupples's face fixed him so that he could say nothing.

Mr. Cupples turned and walked slowly away, with only the words: "Eh! bantam! bantam! The Lord have pity on you—and me too!"

He went out at the door bowed like an old man.

I need hardly depict the fine gradations by which Alec sank after this. He was not fond of whisky. He could take it or leave it. And so he took it; and finding that there was some comfort in it, took it again, and again. The vice laid hold of him like a serpent and his life slowly ebbed away from him.

Mr. Cupples, unseen, haunted his steps. The strong-minded, wise-headed, weak-willed little poet, wrapped in a coat of darkness, dogged the footsteps of a handsome, good-natured, sinking student friend who had now withdrawn all affection of their common friendship in order that he might go the downward road unchecked. Distracted by his own guilt, Cupples drank harder than ever, but only grew more miserable over Alec. He thought of writing to Alec's mother, but with the indecision of a drunkard, could not make up his mind. He pondered over every side of the question till he was lost in a maze of incapacity.

52

From Bad to Worse

*A*ndrew Constable, with his wife and small daughter Isie, was seated at tea in the little parlor opening from their shop when he was called into the shop by a customer. He remained longer than was to be accounted for by the transaction of business at that time of the day. And when he returned his honest face looked troubled.

"Who was that?" asked his wife.

"Only James Johnstone, wantin' a bit o' flannel for his wife's coat."

"An' what did he hae to say that kept ye till yer tea's not fit to drink?"

"Ay, woman," replied Andrew, "it'll be sore news to the lady o'er the water."

"Ye mean Mistress Forbes?"

"'Deed, I mean jist her."

"Is't her son? What's happened? Is he drowned or killed? The Lord preserve us!"

"No, it's worse than that. Ay, woman, ye know little o' the wickedness o' great towns—how they lie in wait at every corner, with their snares an' their pits to catch the unwary youth," said Andrew, with something of the pride of superior knowledge in spite of his dire assessment.

He was presently pulled down from this elevation in a rather ignominious fashion by his more plain-spoken wife.

"Andrew, don't try to speak like a chapter o' the Proverbs o' Solomon. Say straight oot what's gotten a grip o' the bonnie lad."

Therewith, Andrew proceeded to tell what he knew, but not without the continual use of heavy scriptural symbolism, mixing in grotesque fashion the imagery of St. John's Revelation with denunciations of modern city life. The little ears of Isie grew longer and longer with curious horror as the words flowed into her ears, until at length she could not disassociate the face of Alec Forbes from certain of the more graphic woodcuts in Fox's *Book of Martyrs,* three folio volumes which lay in the adjoining room, imagining Alec's fate to be along similar lines to the saints of old.

"But ye must hold a quiet tongue, gudewife," advised Andrew at last.

"I'll warrant it's all over Glamerton afore it comes to yer ears, Andrew. But I would sorely like to know who sent home the word o' it."

"I'm thinkin' it must hae been the young Bruce."

"The Lord be praised for a lie!" exclaimed Mrs. Constable. "I hae told ye before that Rob Bruce has a spite at that family for takin' such a heap o' notice o' Annie Anderson. An' I wouldn't wonder if he has set his heart on marryin' her to his own young Rob an' so keepin' her money in the family."

" 'Deed, maybe. But he's a burnin' an' shinin' light among the Missionaries. An' ye mustn't speak ill o' him or he'll hae ye up afore the church."

"Ay, 'deed he is! He's a burnin' shame an' a stinkin' lamp!"

"Hoot, lass! Ye're o'er hard on him. But it's very true that if the story came from that end o' town, there's room for rizzonable doobts."

What rendered it probable that the rumor came from "that end of town" was that Bruce the younger was this year a freshman at Alec's college, the only other scion of Glamerton there grafted. Bruce the elder had determined that in his son he would fully restore the fortunes of the family. He was giving his son such an education as would entitle him to hold up his head with the best, and especially with that proud upstart Alec Forbes.

The recent news had reached Thomas Crann and filled him with concern. As was his custom, he had immediately fallen on his knees before "the throne of grace" and "wrestled in prayer" with God to restore the prodigal to his mother. What would Thomas have thought if he had been told that his love, true as it was, did not come near the love and anxiety of another man who spent his evenings in drinking whisky and reading heathen poets and who never opened his Bible from one end of the year to the other? If he had been told that Mr. Cupples had more than once, after the first tumbler of toddy but before the second, gone to his prayers for his poor Alec Forbes and begged God Almighty to do for him what he could not do, though he would die for his young friend—if he had heard this, he would have said it was a sad pity, but such prayers could not be answered, seeing that the one that prayed was himself in the bond of iniquity.

There was many a shaking of the head among the old women over Alec's fall, and many a word of tender pity for his poor mother floated forth on the frosty air of Glamerton. But no one ventured to go and tell her the sad tidings. The men left it to the women; and the women knew too well how the bearer of such ill news would appear in her eyes. So they said to themselves she must know it just as well as they did; or if she did not, poor woman, she would know enough soon enough, for all the good it would do her. And that was what came of sending sons to college! And so it went.

Meanwhile, Mr. Cupples's distress over Alec grew. While not abating his own drinking, he yet grew more and more anxious to find a way to put a stop to Alec's. Nightly he haunted his footsteps, seeking an opportunity. He tried to talk to his young friend, but without avail, for Alec had grown distant from him. With mingled love and anger, and not a little self-reproach, he lay awake in his garret listening for the sound of Alec's late-returning footsteps trudging heavily and unsteadily up the stairs. Then, seeking to drown his own guilt over his friend, he would stretch forth his hand to his own bottle, which now rarely found its way back into the cupboard from one night to the next.

One night, late, Mr. Cupples again followed Alec through the streets. It was midnight and the youth had just been turned out of Luckie Cumstie's. But he and the friend he was with had not had enough of revelry yet. They went to another public house with worse reputation, but just as Alec was about to follow his companion inside, he was suddenly seized in the dark and pulled backwards away from the door. Recovering himself he pivoted and raised his arm to strike. Before him stood a little man whose hands were in the pockets of his trousers; the wind was blowing about the tails of his old and dirty dresscoat.

"*You*, Mr. Cupples!" he exclaimed. "I didn't expect to see you here."

"I was never across the doorsill of such a place in my life," said Mr. Cupples, "nor please God, will either you or me ever cross such a doorsill."

"Hooly, hooly, Mr. Cupples. Speak for yourself. I'm going in right now."

"Man!" implored Cupples, laying hold of Alec's coat.

"Don't stand preaching to me! I'm past that."

"Alec, you'll wish to God you hadn't when you see your mother, when you come to marry a bonnie wife."

It was an ill-timed argument. Alec flared up wildly.

"Wife!" he cried, "there's no wife for me. Get out of my way! Don't you see I've been drinking? And I won't be stopped."

"Drinking!" exclaimed Mr. Cupples. "Little you know about drinking. I've drunk three times as much as you. If that be any argument for me keeping out of your way, it's more argument for you to keep out of *my* path. I swear to God I won't stand this any longer. You come home with me from this mouth of hell!"

And with that the brave little man placed himself squarely between Alec and the door.

But the opposition of Mr. Cupples had increased the action of the alcohol upon Alec's brain, and he blazed up in a fury. He took one step toward Mr. Cupples, who had restored his hands to his pockets and backed a few paces toward the door of the house to guard against Alec's passing him.

"Get out of my way, or I'll strike you," he said fiercely.

"I will not," answered Mr. Cupples, and the next instant he lay senseless on the stones of the court.

It was some time later when by slow degrees Mr. Cupples came to himself. He was half dead with cold and his head was aching frightfully. A pool of blood already frozen lay on the stones. He crawled on his hands and knees till he reached a wall, by which he raised and steadied himself. Feeling along this wall he got into the street; but he was so confused and benumbed that if a policeman had not come up, he would have died on someone's doorstep. The man knew him and got him home. Mr. Cupples allowed both the policeman and his landlady to suppose that his condition was the consequence of drink; and so was helped up to his garret and put to bed.

53

. . . .

A Solemn Vow

All night Isie Constable lay dreaming about Alec Forbes and the terrible trouble he was in at the city. If her parents or no one else would not tell Mrs. Forbes, then her duty was clear to seven-year-old Isie. But it had snowed all night and therefore it was many days before she could contrive to be about her important mission. At length she was allowed to go out and no sooner was she alone than she darted through the back gate and was headed across the rude temporary bridge over the Glamour on her way to Howglen.

Mrs. Forbes and Annie Anderson were sitting together when Mary put her head in at the door and told her mistress that the daughter of Mr. Constable, the clothier, wanted to see her.

"Why, she's a mere infant, Mary!" exclaimed Mrs. Forbes. "How could she have come all this way?"

" 'Deed, mem. But nonetheless she's doon the stairs in the kitchen."

"Bring her up, Mary. Poor little thing! What can she want?"

Presently Isie entered the room, looking timidly about her.

"Well, my dear, what do you want?"

"It's aboot Alec, mem," said Isie, glancing toward Annie.

"What about him?" asked Mrs. Forbes, considerably bewildered.

"Hae ye heard nothin' aboot him, mem?"

"Nothing particular. I haven't heard from him for several weeks. Speak out, Isie."

"Well, mem, I don't rightly know everythin'. But they hae taken him into a dreadful place an' whether they hae left a whole inch o' skin on his body I can't tell; but they hae racked him an' pulled his nails off, maybe them all, an'—"

"Good heavens!" exclaimed Mrs. Forbes with a most unusual inclination to break out in laughter. "What *do* you mean, child?"

"I'm tellin' ye it as I heard it, mem. I hope they haen't burnt him yet. Ye must go an' take him oot o' their han's."

"Whose hands, child? Who's doing all this to him?"

"They stand aboot the corners o' the streets, mem, in big cities, an' they catch a hold o' young lads, an' they jist torment the life oot o' them."

"Where did you hear all this, Isie, dear?"

"I heard my father an' my mither lamentin' o'er him."

Mrs. Forbes rose and paced to and fro. Her spirit was troubled, notwithstanding the child's unlikely tale.

"I must go by the mail coach this afternoon," she said at length.

"Wouldn't it be better to write first?" suggested Annie.

Before Mrs. Forbes could reply, Mrs. Constable appeared at the door. She was in hot pursuit of her child, whose footsteps she had traced through the melting snow.

"Ye ill-contrived smatchit! What have ye been aboot?" she said to Isie.

"I don't see what better you could expect of your own child, Mrs. Constable, if you go spreading rumors against other people's children," reproached Mrs. Forbes.

"It's a lie, whatever she said," retorted Mrs. Constable.

"Where else could the child have heard such reports then?"

"I only telled Mistess Forbes hoo ill they were to Alec," Isie defended herself.

"The bairn's a curious child, mem," said Mrs. Constable appeasingly. "She's overheard her father an' me speakin' together."

"But what right had you to talk about my son?"

"Well, mem, what's already proclaimed from the housetops may surely be spoken of in the closets. If ye think that folk'll hold their tongue aboot yer son any more than any other body's, ye're mistaken, mem. But no one heard it from me, or my man either."

"What are you talking about, Mrs. Constable?" Mrs. Forbes asked. "I am quite ignorant. What do they say?"

"Ow, jist that he's consortin' with the worst o' ill company, mem, an' turnin' to the drink now an' then."

Mrs. Forbes sank on the sofa and buried her face in her hands. Annie turned white and escaped from the room. When Mrs. Forbes lifted her head, Mrs. Constable and her strange child had vanished.

When Annie had recovered somewhat from the shock, she returned to the sitting room and she and Mrs. Forbes wept together. Then the mother sat down and wrote, begging Alec to deny the terrible charge, after which they both felt better. But when the return mail brought no reply day after day after day, Mrs. Forbes resolved to go to the hateful city herself.

When Alec awoke the morning after the night last recorded, it rushed upon his mind that he had had a terrible dream. He reproached himself that even in a dream he should be capable of striking to the earth the friend who was trying to save him from disgrace. But as his headache began to yield to cold water, discomposing doubts rose upon his clearing mental horizon. They were absurd, but still they were unpleasant. It *must* be only a dream! How could he have knocked down a man twice his age and only half his size, and his friend besides? Horrible thought! Could it be true?

Haggard, he rushed out of his room toward the stairs, but was met by his landlady.

"Mr. Forbes, if you and Mr. Cupples go on this way, I'll be forced to give you both warning to leave. It's a sad thing when young lads take to drink and turn reprobates in a jiffie."

"I don't go to your church. You needn't preach to me. But what's the matter with Mr. Cupples? He hasn't taken to drink in a jiffie, has he?"

"He came home last night bleeding at the head and in the care of a kind policeman. He was an awful sight, poor man! They say there's a special Providence watches over drunks and bairns. He could hardly get up the stairs."

"What did he say about it?" asked Alec.

"Ow, nothing. But don't go near him, for I left him fast asleep. Go back to your own room and I'll be back with your breakfast in ten minutes. Eh, but you would be a fine lad if only you would give up the drink."

Alec obeyed, ashamed of himself and full of remorse. The only thing he could do was attend to Mr. Cupples's business in the library. He worked at the catalogue till the afternoon lecture was over. Nobody had seen Beauchamp, and walking through the quadrangle Alec could see that Kate's windows were drawn down.

All day Alec's heart was full of Mr. Cupples. He knew that his conduct had been as vile as it was possible for conduct to be. Because a girl could not love him, he had ceased to love his mother, had given himself up to Satan, and had returned his friend's devotion with a murderous blow. Because he could not have a bed of roses, he had thrown himself down in the pigsty. He rushed into a public house and swallowed two glasses of whisky. That done, he went straight home and ran up to Mr. Cupples's room.

Mr. Cupples was sitting in front of the fire, his hands on his knees and his head bound in white, bloodstained bandages. He turned a ghastly face and tried to smile. Alec's heart gave way utterly, and he burst into tears.

"Eh, bantam, bantam!"

"Mr. Cupples, forgive me. I'll cut my throat if you like."

"You would do better to cut the devil's throat."

"Tell me how, and I'll do it."

"Break the whisky bottle, man. That's at the root of it. It's not you. It's the drink. And, eh! Alec, we might be right happy together after that. I would make a scholar of you."

"Well, Mr. Cupples, you have a right to demand of me what you like."

"Bantam," said Mr. Cupples, with the solemnity of resolution, "I swear to God, if you'll give up the drink and the rest of your ill ways, I'll give up the drink as well. I have nothing else to give up.—But it won't be so easy," he added with a sigh, stretching his hand toward his glass.

With a sudden influx of energy, Alec reached his hand toward the same glass. Laying hold of it as Mr. Cupples was raising it to his lips, he cried: "I swear to God as you request—and now," he added, letting go of the glass, "you dare not drink that."

Mr. Cupples threw the filled glass into the fire.

"That's my farewell libation," he said. "But, eh, it's a terrible undertaking. Bantam, I have sacrificed myself to you. Hold to your part, or I can't hold to mine."

It was indeed a terrible undertaking. I doubt whether either of them would have had courage to take up such a vow had they not both been under its exciting influences even then. For them the battle was yet to come.

With Alec the struggle would soon be over. His nervous system would speedily recover its healthy operations. But for Cupples—from whose veins alcohol had nearly expelled the blood—delirium would surely follow.

Alec's habits of study had been quite broken up of late. Even his medical lectures and the hospital classes had been neglected. But Cupples, remembering Jesus' admonition, felt that if no good spirit came into the empty house, sweeping and putting things to right would only incite seven to take the place of the one. So he tried to interest his pupil once again in his old studies; and by frequent changes succeeded in holding tedium at bay.

But all his efforts would have resulted in nothing had not both their hearts already been opened to Love which, when it is pure, at long last will expel whatever opposes it. While Alec felt that he must do everything to please Mr. Cupples, he, on his part, felt that all the future of the youth lay in his hands. He ignored the pangs of alcoholic desire in his fear that Alec should not be able to endure the tedium of abstinence. And Alec's gratitude and remorse made him humble as a slave to the little, big-hearted man whom he had injured so cruelly.

"I'm tired and must go to bed, for I have a sore head," said Mr. Cupples that first night.

"That's my doing," confessed Alec sorrowfully.

"If this new repentance of yours and mine turns out to have anything in it, we'll both have reason to be thankful that you dented my skull. But eh me! I'm afraid I won't sleep much tonight."

"Would you like me to sit up with you?" offered Alec. "I could sleep in your chair well enough."

"No, no. We both have need to say our prayers, and right now we couldn't do that together as well as alone. Go to your own bed, and mind your vow to God and to me. And don't forget your prayers, Alec."

Neither of them forgot his prayers. Alec slept soundly—Mr. Cupples not at all.

"I think," he said, when Alec appeared in the morning, "that I won't take such a hardship upon me another night. Just open the door of my cupboard and fling the bottle into the yard. I hope it won't cut anyone's feet."

Alec ran to the cupboard and pulled out the offending object.

"Now," said Mr. Cupples, "open the two doors of the window wide and fling it far."

Alec did as he was desired and the bottle fell on the stones of a little court. The clash rose sweetly to the ears of Mr. Cupples.

"Thank God," he said with a sigh.—"Alec, no man that hasn't gone through the same can guess what I have gone through this past night with that devil in the cupboard there crying, 'Come taste me! come taste me!' But I heard and did not hearken to it. And yet sometime in the night, although I'm sure I didn't sleep a wink, I thought I was fumbling away at the lock of the cupboard and couldn't get it opened. And the cupboard was a coffin set up on end and I knew that there was a corpse inside it, and yet I tried so hard to get it open. But I'm better now, and I would so like a drop of that fine beverage they call water."

Alec ran down and brought it cold from the pump.

"Now, Alec," said Mr. Cupples, "I don't doubt but that it'll be a sore day. Bring me my books over there, and I won't get out of bed till you come home. So be no longer than you can help. But eh, Alec, you must be true to me."

Alec promised, and set off with a heart lighter than it had been for months. Beauchamp was at none of the classes. And the blinds of Kate's windows were still drawn down.

For a whole week Alec came home as early as possible and spent the rest of the day with Mr. Cupples. Many dreary hours passed over them both. The sufferings of Mr. Cupples and the struggle which he sustained are perhaps indescribable to one who has not lived through such agony himself. But true to his vow, he endured manfully. Still it was with a rueful-comical look and a sigh, sometimes, that he would sit down to his tea and remark, "Eh, man! this is miserable stuff— a pagan invention altogether!"

But the tea comforted his half-scorched nerves, and by slow degrees they began to gather tone and strength. His appetite improved, and at the end of the week he resumed his duties in the library. He and Alec spent most of their time together and occasionally broke out laughing as the sparks of life revived.

Inquiring after Miss Fraser, Alec learned that she was ill. The maid asked in return if he knew anything of Mr. Beauchamp. Alec didn't know what to make of this.

54

· · · · · · · · · · · · · · · · · ·

The End of the Session

*A*s soon as his classes were over, Alec would go to the library to assist Mr. Cupples. On other days Mr. Cupples would linger near the medical school or hospital till Alec came out, and then they would go home together. They both depended greatly on the other.

They were hard at work one afternoon in Mr. Cupples's room—the table covered with books and papers—when a knock was heard at the door and the landlady ushered in Mrs. Forbes.

The two men sprang to their feet, and Mrs. Forbes stared with gratified amazement. The place was crowded with signs of intellectual labor; not even a pack of cards was visible.

"Why didn't you answer my last letter, Alec?" she asked.

In the disarray of those previous weeks, it had been misplaced beneath some books, and he had never seen it.

"What is the meaning, then, of some reports I have heard about you?" she resumed.

Alec looked confused, grew red, and was silent.

Mr. Cupples replied for him. "You see, mem, from the time of Adam, the human individual must learn to refuse the evil and choose the good. The choice to eat butter and honey does not *require* the contrast of eating ashes and dirt; but now my pupil here, mem, your son, has eaten that dirt and made the right choice. And I'll be security for him that he'll never more return to wallow in that mire. It's three weeks, mem, since a single drop of whisky has passed his mouth."

"Whisky!" exclaimed the mother. "Alec! Is it possible?"

"Mem, mem! It would better become you to fall down on your knees and thank the God who's brought him out of the fearful pit. If you fall to upbraiding him, you may make him clean forget his washing."

But Mrs. Forbes was a proud lady and did not like this interference between her and her son. Had she found things as bad as she had expected, she would have been humble. Now that her fears had abated, her natural pride resumed control.

"Take me to your own room, Alec," she announced.

With a nod and smile to Cupples, Alec led the way.

He would have told his mother everything if she had been genial. As she was, he contented himself with a general confession that he had been behaving very badly and would have grown ten times worse but for Mr. Cupples, who was the best friend he had on earth.

"He ought to have behaved more like a gentleman to me," she complained, jealousy putting her on her guard.

"Mother, you don't understand Mr. Cupples. He's a strange creature."

"I don't think he's fit company for you anyhow.—We'll change the subject, if you please."

So Alec was yet more annoyed, and the interaction between mother and son was forced and uncomfortable. As soon as she lay down to rest, Alec bounded up the stairs.

"Never mind my mother," he said. "She's a good woman, but she's vexed with me and took it out on you."

"Mind her!" answered Mr. Cupples. "She's a fine woman and she may say what she likes to me. A woman with one son is like a cow with one horn—a bit ticklish, you know."

The next day mother and son went to call on Professor Fraser. He received them kindly, and thanked Mrs. Forbes for her attentions to his niece. But he seemed oppressed and troubled. His niece was far from well, he said—had not left her room for some weeks, and could see no one.

Mrs. Forbes associated Alec's recent conduct with Kate's illness, but said nothing about her suspicions. After one day more, she returned home, reassured but not satisfied by her visit. She guessed that Alec had outgrown his former relation to her and had a dim perception that her pride had prevented them from entering into a closer relation. It is their own fault when mothers lose by the growth of their children.

Meantime, it had been a dreadful shock to Annie to hear such things reported of her hero, her champion. He had been to her the center of all that was noble and true. And yet now he had erred and had reveled in company of which she knew nothing except far-off hints of unapproachable pollution! Her idol of silver was tarnished and the world became dark.

In this mood she went to the evening service at Mr. Turnbull's chapel. There she sat listlessly, looking for no help and caring for none of the hymns or prayers. At length Mr. Turnbull began to read the story of the Prodigal Son. And during the reading her distress vanished. For she took upon herself the part of the elder brother, prayed for forgiveness, and came away loving Alec Forbes more than she had ever loved him before. If God could love the Prodigal, might she not, *ought* she not to love him too? The deepest source of her misery, though she did not know it, had been the fading of her love toward him.

As she walked home through the dark, the story grew into another comfort. A prodigal might see the face of God, then! The Divine One was no distant monarch, no unapproachable and wrathful king after all, but a kind and loving Father! He would receive Alec one day, and let him look in His face.

From that day her trouble did not return anymore to her. Nor was there ever a feeling of repugnance mingled with her thought of Alec. For such a one as he could not help repenting, she said. He would be sure to rise and go back to his Father.

When Mrs. Forbes came home, she entered into no detail and was not inclined to talk about the matter at all, probably as much from dissatisfaction with herself as with her son. But Annie's heart blossomed into a quiet delight when she learned that the facts were not so bad as the reports. Yet with the delight also came the knowledge that the evil time was drawing nigh when she would have to return to the Bruces for the spring and summer.

Meanwhile, Mrs. Forbes received a letter from Mr. Cupples.

Dear Madam,
After all the efforts of Mr. Alec, aided by my best endeavors and his diligent study, but hindered by the grief of knowing that his cousin, Miss Fraser, entertained a regard for a worthless class-fellow of his—after all our united efforts, Mr. Alec has not been able to pass more than two of his examinations. I am certain he would have done better but for the unhappiness to which I have referred, combined with the illness of Miss Fraser. In a day or two he will be returning to you in Howglen. If you can succeed, as none but mothers can, in restoring him to some composure of mind and strength of body, he will be perfectly able during the vacation to make up for lost time.
I am, dear madam, your obedient servant,

C. Cupples

Angry with Kate, annoyed with her son, vexed with herself, and indignant at the mediation of "that dirty, vulgar, little man," Mrs. Forbes forgot her usual restraint. She threw the letter across the table with the words, "Bad news, Annie," and left the room. But the letter produced a very different effect upon Annie.

Up till now she had looked up to Alec as a great, strong creature. Her faith in him had been unquestioning and unbounded. But now that he had been rejected and disgraced and his mother dissatisfied, his friend disappointed, and himself foiled in the battle of life, he had fallen upon evil days, and all the woman in Annie rose to his defense. Suddenly they had changed places. The strong youth was weak and defenseless; the gentle girl opened her heart to shelter him. A new tenderness took possession of her, and all the tenderness of her tender nature gathered about her fallen hero. Annie was indignant with Kate, angry with the professors, and ready to kiss the hand of Mr. Cupples. Alec had been a bright star beyond her sphere. But now the star lay in the grass, shorn of its beams, and she took it to her bosom.

Two days passed. On the third evening in walked Alec, pale and trembling, evidently too ill to even be questioned. His breathing was short.

"If I hadn't come at once, Mother," he gasped out, "I should have been laid up there. It's pleurisy, Mr. Cupples says."

"My poor boy! You've been working too hard."

Alec laughed bitterly.

"I did work, Mother; but it doesn't matter. She's dead."

"Who's dead?"

"Kate's dead. And I couldn't help it. I tried hard. And it's my fault too. I might have saved her."

He leaped up from the sofa and went pacing about the room, his face flushed and his breath coming faster and shorter. His mother got him to lie down again and asked no more questions. The doctor came and bled him at the arm, and sent him to bed.

When Annie saw him worn and ill, her heart swelled till she could hardly bear the aching of it. She would have been his slave, and yet she could do nothing. She must leave him instead. She went to her room, put on her bonnet and cloak, and was leaving the house when Mrs. Forbes caught sight of her.

"Annie, what are you doing, child! You're not going to leave me?"

"I thought you wouldn't want me here anymore, now that Alec is home."

"You silly child!"

Annie ran back to her room, hardly able to contain her disparate emotions.

When Mr. Cupples and Alec had begun to place some confidence in each other's self-denial, they had dogged each other less and less through the mornings and afternoons. One day in the early evening, Alec had wandered out to his former refuge of misery, that long desolate stretch of barren sand between the mouths of the two rivers of the city. A sound as of one singing came to him. He turned in the direction of it, for something in the tones reminded him of Kate; he almost believed the song was the ghostly ballad she had sung the night of her uncle's party. The singing rose and fell, and he ran toward it. Suddenly a wild cry came from the sea where the waves were far out and ebbing from the shore. He dashed along the glimmering sands, thinking he saw something white, but there was no moon to give any certainty. As he advanced he became surer there was something in the water. He rushed in. The water grew deeper and deeper. He plunged in and swam farther away from the shore. Before he had reached the spot, with another cry the figure vanished, probably in one of the deep pits which abound beneath the surface along that shore. Still he kept on, diving many times, but in vain. His strength was not what it had once been, and at length he was so exhausted that when he came to himself, he was lying on his back on the dry sands. He would have rushed again into the water, but he could hardly move his limbs. He crawled part of the way back to the college. There he inquired if Miss Fraser was in the house. The maid assured him that she was in her own room. But scarcely had he turned to leave for home when they discovered that her room was deserted and she was nowhere to be found. The shock of this news made it impossible for him to throw off the effects of the cold and exposure and he lingered on until Mr. Cupples compelled him to go home. Not even then, however, had her body been discovered. It washed ashore a few days after his departure, and it was well he did not see it.

It soon became known that she had been out of her mind for some time. The exact cause was not known, but suspicions pointed to factors having to do with

Beauchamp. One strange fact in the case was her inexplicable aversion to water—either a prevision of her coming fate or the actual cause of it. The sea, visible from her window, may have fascinated her and drawn her to her death.

During the worst period of Alec's illness, he always felt he was wandering along that shore or swimming in those deadly waters. Sometimes he had laid hold of the drowning girl and was struggling with her to the surface. Sometimes he was drawing her in an agony from the terrible quicksand lurking in the bottom of the underwater pits.

Annie took her turn in the sick chamber, watching beside the half-conscious lad. The feeling with which she had received the prodigal home into her heart spread its roots deeper and wider. It seemed to the girl that she had loved him so always, only she had not thought about it. He had fought for her and endured for her at school; he had saved her life from the greedy waters of the Glamour at the risk of his own. She would be the most ungrateful of girls if she did not love him.

Never had she had happier hours than those in which it seemed only the stars and the angels were awake beside herself. And if while watching him at night she grew sleepy, she would kneel down and pray to God to keep her awake so that no harm should come to Alec. Then she would wonder if even the angels could do without sleep always, or whether they sometimes lie down on the warm fields of heaven between their own shadowy wings. She would wonder next if it would be safe for God to close His eyes for one minute—safe for the world, she meant. Then she would nod, and wake up with a start, flutter silently to her feet and go and peep at the slumberer.

Sometimes in those terrible hours after midnight that belong neither to the night nor the day, the terrors of the darkness would seize upon her, and she would sit trembling. But the lightest movement of the sleeper would rouse her, and a glance at the place where he lay would dispel her fears.

55
· · · · · · · · · · · · · · · · ·

Mr. Cupples in Howglen

*O*ne night Annie heard a rustling among the bushes in the garden and the next moment a subdued voice began to sing a wild and wailing tune.

"I didn't know you cared about psalm-tunes, Mr. Cupples," murmured Alec from his bed.

The scratchy voice went on and he grew more restless.

It was an eerie thing to go outside, but she must stop the singing for the sake of Alec's sleep. Annie rose and slowly opened the door. The dark figure of a little man stood leaning against the house, singing gently.

"Are you Mr. Cupples?" she said.

The man started and answered, "Yes, my lass. And who are you?"

"I'm Annie Anderson. Alec's disturbed with your singing. You'll wake him up."

"I won't sing another note. How's Alec?"

"Some better. When did you come, Mr. Cupples?"

"Earlier this very night. But you were all in your beds and I dared not disturb you. So I sat down to smoke my pipe and look at the stars, and after a while I was singing to myself. But I'll come back tomorrow."

"But do you have a bed?" asked the thoughtful Annie.

"Ay, at the house of a jabbering creature they call King Robert the Bruce."

Annie knew that he must be occupying her own room and was on the point of expressing a hope that he wouldn't be disturbed with the rats, when she realized her comment would lead to new explanations and would delay her return to Alec.

"Good night, Mr. Cupples," she said, holding out her hand.

"Good night—what do they call you again? I forget names dreadful."

"Annie Anderson."

"Ay; Annie Anderson. I've surely heard that name before. Well, I won't forget *you*, whether I forget your name or not."

Mr. Cupples was partial to garrets. He could not be comfortable if any person was over his head. He could breathe, he said, when he got next to the stars.

It had been a sore trial for him to keep his vow after Alec was gone. In his loneliness it was harder to do battle with his deep-rooted desires. He would never drink as he had before, he assured himself. But might he not have just one tumbler? That one tumbler he did not take, however. And the rewards soon began to blossom within him. The well of song returned to his lips, beauty returned to the sunsets, and the world turned green again.

Another reward was that he had money in his pocket; with this money he would go and see Alec Forbes. He had written two or three times to Mrs. Forbes asking about his young friend but received no satisfactory answer, and he had grown anxious about him. His resources were small, however, and he saved them by walking. Hence it came that he arrived in Glamerton late and weary. Entering the first shop he came to, he asked about a cheap lodging. For he said to himself that the humblest inn was no doubt beyond his means. Robert Bruce scrutinized him keenly from under his eyebrows, and debated within himself whether the applicant was respectable—that is, whether he could pay. Mr. Cupples was such an odd blend of scholar and vagrant that Bruce was slow with an answer.

"Are you deaf, man?" demanded Mr. Cupples, "or are you afraid to take a chance by giving a fair answer to a fair question?"

The arrow went too near the mark not to irritate Bruce.

"Go your way," he said. "We want no tramps in this town."

"Well, I am a tramp, no doubt," returned Cupples, "for I have come every step of the way on my own two feet. But I have read of several tramps that were respectable enough. If you won't give me anything in this shop—even information—at least will you sell me an ounce of tobacco?"

"I'll sell it if you can pay for it."

"There you are," said Cupples, laying the orthodox pence on the counter. "And now will you tell me where I can get a respectable, decent place to lie down in? I'll want it for a week, at any rate."

Before he finished the question, the door behind the counter opened and young Bruce entered. Mr. Cupples knew him well enough by sight from the college, and they greeted one another.

"This gentleman is the librarian of our college, Father."

Bruce took off his hat. "I beg your pardon," he said. "I'm terribly shortsighted in the candlelight."

"I'm used to being mistaken," answered Cupples, beginning to perceive that he had gotten hold of a character. "Make no apologies, but just answer my question."

"Well, to tell you the truth, seeing you're a gentleman, we have a room ourselves. But it's a garret room, and maybe—"

"Then I'll take it, whatever it be, if you don't want too much for it."

"Well, you see, sir, your college is a great expense to humble folk like ourselves, and we have to make it up the best we can."

"No doubt. How much do you want?"

"Would you think five shillings too much?"

"Indeed, I would."

"Well, we'll say three then—for *you,* sir."

"I won't give you more than half a crown."

"Hoot, sir. That's too little."

"Well, I'll look further," said Mr. Cupples, moving toward the door.

"No, no, sir. You'll do no such thing. Do you think I would let the librarian of my son's college go out my door at this time of night? Just have your price, and welcome. You'll have your tea and sugar and pieces of cheese from me, you know?"

"Of course—of course. And if you could get me some tea at once, I should be obliged to you. I have been walking some distance."

"Mother," cried Bruce through the house door, and held a momentary whispering with the partner of his throne.

"So your name's Bruce, is it?" resumed Cupples, as the shopkeeper returned to the counter.

"Robert Bruce, at your service."

"It's a grand name," remarked Cupples.

"Indeed it is, and I have a right to bear it."

"You'll be a descendant, no doubt, of the Earl of Carrick?" said Cupples, guessing at his weakness.

"Of the king, sir. Folk may think little of me; but I come of him that freed Scotland. If it hadn't been for him, where would Scotland be today?"

"Almost civilized under the fine influences and cultivation and manners of the English, no doubt."

After further private consultation, Mr. and Mrs. Bruce came to the conclusion that it might be politic, for Rob's sake, to treat the librarian with consideration. Consequently, Mrs. Bruce invited him, after he was settled in his room, to come down to his tea in *the room*. Descending before it was quite ready, Mr. Cupples looked about him. The only thing that attracted his attention was a handsomely bound Bible. He took it up, thinking to get some amusement from the births of the illustrious Bruces. But the only inscription he could find beyond the name of *John Cowie* was the following in pencil: *"Super Davidis Psalmum tertium vicesimum, syngrapham pecuniariam centum solidos valentem, quae, me mortuo, a Annie Anderson, mihi dilecta, sit, posui."*

Then came some figures, and then the date, with the initials *J.C.* So it was earlier in the evening that Mr. Cupples had thought he had heard the name of Annie Anderson before.

"It's a grand Bible," he said as Mrs. Bruce entered.

"Ay, it is. It belonged to our parish minister."

Nothing more passed, for Mr. Cupples was hungry.

After a long sleep in the morning, Mr. Cupples called on Mrs. Forbes, and was rather kindly received. But it was a great disappointment to him to find that he could not see Alec. As he was in the country, he resolved to make the best of it and enjoy himself for a week. Every day he climbed to the top of one of the hills which enclosed the valley and was rewarded with fresh vigor and renewed life. He, too, was a prodigal returned at least into the vestibule of his Father's house. The Father sent the servants out to minister to him; and Nature, the housekeeper, put the robe of health upon him, and gave him new shoes of strength. The delights of those spring days were endless to him whose own nature was budding with new life. Familiar with all the cottage ways, he would drop into any house he came near about dinnertime, and asking for a piece of oatcake and a mug of milk, would make his dinner from them and leave a trifle behind in acknowledgment. But as evening began to fall he was always careful to be near Howglen that he might ask about his friend.

Mrs. Forbes gradually began to understand him better. Before the week was over, there was not a man or woman about Howglen whom he did not know, including their names; for, to his surprise, even his forgetfulness was fast vanishing.

On the next to last day of his intended stay, he went to the house and heard the happy news that Alec insisted on seeing him. Mrs. Forbes had at last consented, and the result was that Cupples sat up with him that night, and Mrs. Forbes and Annie both slept. In the morning he found a bed ready for him, to which he reluctantly went and slept for a couple of hours. The end of it was that he did not go back to Mr. Bruce's except to pay his bill. And he did not leave Howglen for many weeks.

One lovely morning when the sun shone into the house and the deep blue sky rose above the earth, Alec opened his eyes and suddenly became aware that life was good and the world was beautiful. Cupples propped him up with pillows and opened the window that the warm air might flow in upon him. He smiled and lay with his eyes closed, looking so happy that Cupples thought he must be praying. But he was only blessed. So easily can God make a man happy!

The past had dropped from him like a wild and weary dream. He had received divine life and was reborn into a new family and a beautiful world. One of God's lyric prophets was pouring out a vocal summer of jubilant melody. The lark thought nobody was listening; but God heard in heaven, and the young prodigal heard on the earth. He would be God's child from this moment on, for one bunch of the sun's rays was enough to be happy upon!

His mother entered and saw the beauty on her son's worn countenance. She saw the noble, watching love on that of his friend; and her own face filled with light as she stood silently looking at the two. Annie entered and gazed for a moment, then fled to her own room and burst into tears.

She *had* seen the face of God, and that face was Love—love like a mother's, only deeper, tenderer, lovelier, stronger. She could not recall what she had seen or how she had known it; but the conviction remained that she had seen His face, and that it was infinitely beautiful.

He has been with me all the time, she thought. *He gave me my father, and sent Brownie to take care of me, and Dooie, and Thomas Crann, and Mrs. Forbes, and Alec. And He sent the cat when I prayed to Him about the rats. And He's been with me—I don't know how long, and He's with me now. And I have seen His face, and I'll see His face again. And I'll try hard to be good. Eh! It's just wonderful! And God's just . . . nothing but God himself!*

56

●●●●●●●●●●●●●●●●●

Annie Returns to Glamerton

Within another few weeks Annie began to perceive that it was time for her to go, and this she communicated to Alec's mother. She had two major reasons for leaving. First, with Alec better, she was no longer needed so much. Second, she was finding in herself certain feelings which she did not know what to do with.

"Annie's coming back to you in a day or two, Mr. Bruce," said Mrs. Forbes, having called to pay some of her interest and to prepare the way for her return. "She has been with me a long time, but you know she was ill, and besides I could not bear to part with her."

"Well, mem," answered Bruce, "we'll be very happy to take her home again, as soon as you have had all the use you want of her."

He had never assumed this tone before, either to Mrs. Forbes or with regard to Annie. But she took no notice of it.

Both Mr. and Mrs. Bruce received the girl so kindly that she did not know what to make of it. Mr. Bruce especially was all sugar and butter—rancid butter, to be sure. When she went up to her old rat-haunted room, her astonishment was doubled. The holes in floor and roof had been mended; the skylight was as clean as glass a hundred years old could be; a square of carpet lay in the middle of the floor; and checked curtains adorned the bed. She concluded that these luxuries had been procured for Mr. Cupples, but could not understand how they came to be left for her.

Nor did the consideration shown her decrease after the first novelty of her return had worn off; and altogether her former discomforts had ceased. The baby had become a sweet-tempered little girl; Johnnie was at school all day; and Robert was comparatively well-behaved, though still a sulky youth. He gave himself great airs to his former companions, but to Annie he was condescending. He was a good student, and had the use of *the room* for a study.

Robert Bruce the elder had disclosed his designs for Annie to his heir, and his son had naturally declined all efforts to help his father. But he began at length to observe that Annie had grown very pretty. Then, too, he thought it would be a nice thing to fall in love with her, since, from his parents' wishes to that end, she must have some money.

Annie, however, did not suspect anything till one day she chanced to hear the elder say to the younger, "Don't push her. Just go into the shop and get a piece of red candy-sugar and give her that next time you see her alone. The likes of her knows what that means. And if she takes it from you, you may have the run of the shop drawer. It's worthwhile, you know. Those that won't sow, won't reap."

From that moment she was on her guard.

Meantime, Alec got better and better, went out with Mr. Cupples in the gig, ate like an ogre, drank water, milk and tea like a hippopotamus, and was rapidly recovering his former strength.

One evening over their supper he was for the twentieth time opposing Mr. Cupples's departure. At length the latter said: "Alec, I'll stay with you till the next session on one condition."

"What is that, Mr. Cupples?" said Mrs. Forbes. "I shall be delighted to know it."

"You see, mem, this young rascal here made a fool of himself at the last session and didn't pass; and—"

"Let bygones be bygones, if you please, Mr. Cupples," returned Mrs. Forbes pleasantly.

" 'Deed no, mem. What's the use of bygones but to learn from them how to meet the bycomes? Just hear me out."

"Fire away, Mr. Cupples," said Alec.

"I will. For them that didn't pass at the end of last session, there's another examination at the beginning of the next—if they want to take it. If they don't, they have to go through the same classes over again, and take the examination at the end again—that is, if they want their degree. And that's a terrible loss of time. Now, if Alec'll set to work like a man, I'll help him all I can. By the time the session's ready to begin, he'll be up with the rest of the fleet. And I'll sit with him and blow into his sails!"

That very day Alec resumed with Mr. Cupples again as his mentor. But the teacher would not let the student work a moment after he began to show symptoms of fatigue. This limit was moved further and further every day till at length he could work four hours. His tutor would not hear of any further extention, and declared that he would pass triumphantly.

The rest of each summer day they spent in wandering about or lying in the grass, for it was hot and dry, and the grass was a very bed of heath. Then came all the pleasures of the harvest. And when the evenings grew cool, there were the books for pleasure that Mr. Cupples foraged for in Glamerton—he seemed to locate them by the scent.

Annie would perhaps have benefited more than either of the two men from those books, and Mr. Cupples missed her very much. He went often to see her, taking what books he could. With one or the other of these books, she would wander along the banks of the clear, brown Glamour, now reading a page or two, now seating herself on the grass beside the shadowy pools. Even her new love did not more than occasionally ruffle the flow of her inward river. She had long cherished a deeper love, which kept it very calm. Her stillness was always wandering into prayer; but never did she offer a petition that associated Alec's fate with her own; though sometimes she would find herself holding up her heart like an empty cup. She missed Tibbie Dyster dreadfully.

One day, thinking she heard Mr. Cupples walking up the stairs, she ran down with a smile on her face, which fell off it like a withered leaf when she saw that it was but Robert the student. Taking her smile as meant for himself, he approached her, demanding a kiss. An ordinary Scottish maiden of Annie's rank would have answered such a request from a man she did not like with a box on the ear, tolerably delivered. But Annie was too proud even to struggle, and stood like a marble statue, except that she could not help wiping her lips afterward. The youth walked away more discomfited than if she had made angry protests and a successful resistance.

Annie sat down and cried. Her former condition in this house was enviable to this. That same evening, without saying a word to anyone, for there was a curious mixture of outward lawlessness with perfect inward obedience in the girl, she set out for Clippenstrae, on the opposite bank of the Wan Water. It was a gorgeous evening. The sun was going down in purple and crimson, divided by faint bars of gold. A faint rosy mist hung its veil over the hills about the sunset. The air was soft and the light sobered with a sense of the coming twilight.

When she reached Clippenstrae, she found that she had been directed there by a Higher hand. Her aunt came from the inner room as she opened the door, and Annie knew at once by her face that death was in the house. For its expression recalled the sad vision of her father's departure. Her great-uncle, the little gray-haired old cottar in the Highland bonnet, lay dying. He has had nothing to do with our story, except that once he made our Annie feel that she had a home. And to give that feeling to another is worth living for.

Auntie Meg's grief was plainly visible. She led the way into the deathroom, and Annie followed. By the bedside sat an old woman with more wrinkles in her face than moons in her life. She was perfectly calm, and looked like one already half across the river, watching a friend as he passed her toward the opposite bank. The old man lay with his eyes closed.

"Ye're come in time," said Auntie Meg, and whispered to the old woman—"my brither James's bairn."

"Ay, ye're come in time, lassie," responded the great-aunt kindly, and said no more.

The dying man heard the words, opened his eyes, glanced once at Annie, and closed them again.

"Is that one o' the angels come?" he asked, for his wits were gone a little way before.

"No, it's Annie Anderson, James Anderson's lass."

"I'm glad to see ye, dawtie," he said, still without opening his eyes. "I hae wanted to see more o' ye, for ye're jist such a bairn as I would hae liked to hae mysel' if it had pleased the Lord. Ye're a douce, God-fearin' lassie, an' He'll take care o' His own."

Here his mind began to wander again.

"Margaret," he said, "is my eyes closed, for I think I see angels?"

"Ay, they are."

"Weel, that's very weel. I'll hae a sleep noo."

He was silent for some time. Then he reverted to the fancy that Annie was the first of the angels come to carry away his soul, and murmured brokenly: "Be careful hoo ye handle it, for it's weak an' not too clean. I know mysel' there's a spot o'er the heart o' it which came o' an ill word I gave a bairn for stealin' from me once. But they did steal a lot that year. An' there's another spot on the right hand which came o' a good bargain I made with old John Thompson o'er a horse. An' it would never come oot with all the soap an' water . . . Hoots! I'm haverin'! It's on the hand o' my soul, where soap an' water can never come. Lord, make it clean, an' I'll give him it all back when I see him in thy kingdom. An' I'll beg his pardon too. But I didn't cheat him altogether. I only took more than I would hae given for the colt mysel'."

He went on thus, with wandering thoughts that in their wildest whimsies were yet tending homeward; and when too soft to hear, were yet busy with the wisest of mortal business—repentance. By degrees he fell into a slumber, and from that, about midnight, into a deeper sleep.

The next morning Annie went out. She could not feel oppressed or sorrowful at such a death, and she walked up the river to the churchyard where her father lay. The Wan Water was shallow and full of dancing talk about all the things that were deep secrets when its bosom was full. She went up a long way, and then crossing some fields, came to the churchyard. She did not know her father's grave, for no stone marked the spot where he sank in this broken earthly sea. There was no church; even its memory had vanished. She lingered a little and then set out on her slow return.

Sitting down to rest about halfway home, she sang a song which she had found in her father's old songbook. She had said it once to Alec and Curly, but they did not care much for it, and she had not thought of it again till now.

"Ane by ane they gang awa'.
The gatherer gathers great an' sma'.
Ane by ane maks ane an' a'.

"Aye whan ane is ta'en frae ane,
Ane on earth is left alane,
Twa in heaven are knit again.

"Whan God's harvest is in or lang,
Golden-heidit, ripe, an' thrang,
Syne begins a better sang."

She looked up and Curly was walking through the broad river to where she sat.

"I knew ye a mile off, Annie," he said.

"I'm glad to see you, Curly."

"I wonder if ye'll be as glad to see me the next time, Annie."

Then Annie perceived that Curly looked earnest and anxious.

"What do you say, Curly?"

"I hardly know what I say, Annie. They say the truth always comes oot, but I wish it would without a body sayin' it."

"What can be the matter, Curly?" Annie was growing frightened. "It must be ill news or you wouldn't look like that."

"I don't doubt it'll be worse news to them that it's news to."

"You speak in riddles, Curly."

He tried to laugh, but succeeded badly, and stood before her with downcast eyes. Annie waited in silence, and that brought it out at last.

"Annie, when we were at the school together, I would hae given ye anythin'. Noo I hae given ye all things, an' my heart to boot in the bargain."

"Curly," murmured Annie, and said no more, for she felt as if her heart would break.

"I liked you at the school, Annie; but noo there's nothin' in the world but you."

Annie rose gently, came close to him, and laying a hand on his arm, said, "I'm sorry, Curly."

He half turned his back, was silent a moment, and then said in a distant but trembling voice, "Don't distress yersel'. We can't help it."

"But what'll you do, Curly?" asked Annie in a tone full of compassion, and with her hand still on his arm.

"God knows. I must jist wrestle through it. I'll go back to the pig-skin saddle I was working at," said Curly, with a smile at the bitterness of his fate.

"It's not that I don't like you, Curly. You know that. I would do anything for you that I could do. You have been a good friend to me."

And here Annie burst out crying.

"Don't cry. The Lord preserve us! Don't cry. I won't say another word aboot it. What's Curly that such a one as you should cry for *him*? Faith! It's almost as good as if ye loved me," said Curly in a voice ready to break with emotion.

"It's a sad thing that things won't go right!" said Annie at last, after many vain attempts to stop the fountain by drying the stream of her tears. "It's my fault, Curly," she added.

"Deil a bit o' 't!" cried Curly. "An' I beg yer pardon for my words. Yer fault! I was a fool. But maybe," he added, brightening a little, "I might hae a chance— someday, someday far away ye know, Annie?"

"No, Curly. Don't think of it."

His face flushed red.

"That lick-the-dirt Bruce's not goin' to make ye marry his college brat?"

"Don't be worried that I'll marry anybody I don't like, Curly."

"Ye don't like him, I hope to God!"

"I can't abide him."

"Weel, maybe—who knows. I dare not despair."

"Curly, Curly. I must be honest with you as you were with me. When once a body's seen one, he can't see another, you know. Who could have been at the school as I was so long, and then taken out of the water, you know, and then—?"

Annie stopped.

"If ye mean Alec Forbes—" said Curly, and stopped too. But presently went on again, "If I were to come atween Alec Forbes an' you, hangin' would be too good for me. But has Alec—?"

"No, not a word. But hold your tongue, Curly. Once is all with me. It's not many lasses would have told you such a thing. But I know it's right. You're the only one that has my secret. Keep it, Curly."

"Like Death himsel'," said Curly. "Ye *are* a braw lass."

"You mustn't think ill of me, Curly. I've told you the truth."

"Just let me kiss yer bonnie hand an' I'll go content."

Wisely done or not, it was truth and tenderness that made her offer her lips instead. He turned in silence, comforted for the time, though the comfort would evaporate long before the trouble would sink.

"Curly!" cried Annie, and he came back.

"I think I see young Robert Bruce. He's come to Clippenstrae to ask after me. Don't let him come farther. He's an uncivil fellow."

"If he gets by me, he must have feathers," retorted Curly and walked toward the village.

Annie followed slowly. When she saw the young men meet, she sat down.

Curly spoke first as he came up to Bruce. "A fine day, Robbie," he said.

Bruce made no reply, for relations had altered since school days. It was an unwise moment, however, to carry a high chin to Willie Macwha, who was out of temper with the whole world except Annie Anderson.

"I said it was a fine day," he repeated loudly. "An' it is the custom in this country to give an answer when ye're spoken to civily."

"I consider you uncivil."

"That's jist what the bonnie lassie sittin' yonder said aboot you when she asked me not to let ye go a step nearer to her."

Curly found it at the moment particularly agreeable to quarrel. Moreover he had always disliked Bruce, and this feeling was some aggravated because Annie had complained about him.

"I have as much right to walk here as you or anyone else," challenged Bruce.

"An' Annie Anderson has a right not to be disturbed when her uncle, honest man, is jist lyin' waitin' for his coffin in the house yonder."

"I'm her cousin."

"And small comfort any o' yer breed ever brought her. Cousin or no, ye'll not go near her."

"I'll go where I please," answered Bruce, moving to pass.

Curly moved right in front of him.

"I'll see the devil take you!" shouted Bruce.

"Maybe ye may, bein' likely to arrive at the spot first."

Further angered, Bruce moved forward again, attempting to shove Curly aside with another oath. But the sensation he instantly felt in his nose astonished him, and the blood beginning to flow cowed him at once. He put his handkerchief to his face, turned, and walked back to Glamerton. Curly followed him at a safe distance and then went to his own father's shop for a visit.

After a short greeting, very short on Curly's part, his father said, "Hoot, Willie! What's come o'er ye. Ye look as if some lass said *no* to ye."

"Some lasses' *no's* better than other lasses' *ay*, Father."

" 'Deed maybe, laddie," said George, adding to himself, *That must hae been Annie Anderson—an' no other.*

Had Annie been compelled to return to the garret over Robert Bruce's shop after this incident, she would not indeed have found the holes in the floor and the roof reopened, but she would have found that the carpet and the curtains were gone.

The report went through Glamerton before week's end that she and Willie Macwha were *courtin'*.

57

· · · · · · · · · · · · · · · · · ·

Deception Revealed

*H*aving been in the precincts of Glamerton and Howglen now for some months, Mr. Cupples had become rather well acquainted with most of the men of the place, including James Dow, whom he saw upon many occasions about the farm, and Thomas Crann. More surprising perhaps is the fact that he and Thomas, as different as they each were peculiar in their own way, should have become fast friends.

The appetite for prophecy having assuaged with the passing of the flood the previous winter, the people of Glamerton had no capacity for excitement left. In consequence, the congregations began to diminish, especially those in the evening. Having ceased to feel anxiety about some impending vengeance, comparatively few chose to be chastised any longer about their sins. In addition, the novelty of Mr. Turnbull's style had worn off and he himself was not able to preach with the same fervor as before; the fact being that he had exhausted the electric region of the spiritual brain. Even his greatest admirers were compelled to acknowledge that Mr. Turnbull had "lost much of his anointing," and unless the Spirit was poured down upon them from on high, their prospects were very disheartening.

Pondering over the signs of disfavor and decay of his church, Thomas Crann concluded that there must be a contamination in the camp. And indeed, if an infestation of defilement had somehow penetrated their ranks, it could be none other than the money-loving, mammon-worshiping Robert Bruce. But he did not see what could be done. Had he been guilty of any open fault, such as getting drunk, they could have gotten rid of him with comparative ease. For one solitary instance of drunkenness they had already excluded one of their best men. But who was so free from visible fault as Bruce? True, he was guilty of overreaching whenever he had the chance, and of cheating when there was no risk of being found out, but he had no *faults*. Yet Thomas Crann knew his duty.

"James Johnstone," he said one day, "the kirk's makin' no progress. It's not as in the time o' the apostles when the saved were added to daily."

"But that wasna *oor* kirk exactly, an' it wasna Mr. Turnbull that was the head o' it," returned the deacon.

" 'Tis all the same; the principle's the same. 'Tis the same gospel. Yet here's the congregation dwindlin' away. An' I'm thinkin' there's an Achan in the camp— a son o' Saul in the kingdom o' David, a Judas among—"

"Hoots! Thomas Crann; ye're not talking aboot that poor, useless body, Rob Bruce, are ye?"

"He's none useless for the devil's work or for his own, which is one an' the same. Out he must go."

"Don't jest, Thomas, aboot such a dangerous thing." James was mildly happy for a lone opportunity of rebuking the granite-minded mason.

"I'm far from jestin'. Ye don't know fervor from jokin', James."

"He might take the law upon us for defaming his character, an' that would be an awful thing."

"The Scripture's clear; I'm only bidin' my time till I see what's to be done."

"Ye needn't burn the whole hoose to get rid o' the rats. I don't doubt ye'll get us into hot water. A body doesn't need to take the skin off for the sake o' cleanliness. Jist take care what ye're aboot, Thomas."

Having thus persisted in opposing Thomas to a degree he had never dared before, James took his departure, pursued by the words, "Take care, James, that in keepin' the right hand from hurt, ye don't send the whole body to hell."

"There's more virtues in the Bible than courage, Thomas," retorted James, holding the outer door open to throw the sentence in, and shutting it instantly to escape with the last word.

Abandoned to his own resources, Thomas meditated long and painfully. But all he could arrive at was the resolution to have a talk with his new friend Mr. Cupples. He might not be a Christian man, but he was honest and trustworthy, with a greater than average amount of what Thomas recognized as good sense. From his scholarship he might be able to give him some counsel. So he walked to Howglen the next day and found him with Alec in the harvest field. And Alec's reception of Thomas showed what a fine thing illness is for bringing people together. Mr. Cupples walked beside Thomas through the field and Thomas told him the story of Annie Anderson's five-pound note along with his concern for the Missionary church. As he spoke, Cupples was tormented as with the flitting phantom of a half-forgotten dream. All at once light flashed upon him.

"An' so what am I to do?" Thomas was saying as he finished his tale. "I can prove nothin'. But I'm certain in my own mind, knowin' the man's nature, that it was the note he took oot o' the Bible."

"I'll put the proof of it into your hands, or I'm badly mistaken," asserted Cupples.

"You, Mr. Cupples?"

"Ay, me, Thomas Crann. But maybe you wouldn't take proof from such a sinner against such a saint."

"If ye can direct me to the purification o' oor wee temple, I'll listen humbly. I only wish ye would repent an' be one o' us."

"I'll wait till you've gotten rid of Bruce, anyway. I care little for all your small separatist churches. You're all so divided from each other it's a wonder you don't pray for a darkening of the sun that you might do without the common daylight. But I do think it's a shame for such a sneak to be in the company of honest folk, as I take the most of you to be. So I'll do my best. You'll hear from me in a day or two."

Cupples had remembered the inscription on the fly-leaf of the big Bible, which, according to Thomas Crann, Mr. Cowie had given to Annie. He now went to James Dow.

"Did Annie ever tell you about a Bible Mr. Cowie gave her, James?"

"Ay, she did."

"Could you get hold of it?"

"Eh, I don't know. The creature has laid his own claws upon it. It's a sad pity that Annie's oot o' the house or she could take it hersel'."

"Truly being her own, she might. But you're a kind of guardian to her, aren't you?"

"Ay. I hae made mysel' that in a way. But Bruce would be looked upon as the proper guardian."

"Do you have hold of the money?"

"I made him sign a lawyer's paper aboot it."

"Well, just go and demand the Bible, along with the rest of Annie's property. You know she's had trouble about her chest and can't get it from him. And if he makes any difficulty, just drop a hint of going to the lawyer about it. The likes of him's as afraid of a lawyer as a cat is of cold water. But get the Bible we must."

Dow was a peaceable man and did not much relish the commission. Cupples, thinking he too was a Missionary, told him the story of the note.

"Well," said Dow, "he can sit there in the congregation for all I care. Maybe they'll keep him from doin' more mischief!"

"I thought you were one of them."

"No, no. But I'll hold my tongue. An' I'll do what ye want."

So after his day's work, which was hard enough at this season of the year, James Dow put on his blue Sunday coat and set off to the town. He found Robert Bruce dickering with a country girl over some butter, for which he wanted to give her less than the market value. This roused Dow's indignation and put him in a much fitter mood for an altercation.

"I won't give you more than fivepence. How are you today, Mr. Dow?—I tell you, it has the taste of turnips, or something worse."

"How can that be, Mr. Bruce, at this season o' year, when there's plenty o' grass for man an' beast?" asked the girl.

"It's not for me to say how it can be. That's not my business.—Now, Mr. Dow?"

Bruce, whose very life lay in driving bargains, had a great dislike to any interruption of the process. So he turned to James Dow, hoping to get rid of him before concluding his bargain with the girl, whose butter he was determined to have even if he must pay her own price for it. But while doing business that his soul cherished, he could not tolerate the presence of any third person.

"Now, Mr. Dow?" he repeated.

"My business'll keep," replied Dow.

"But you see we're busy tonight."

"Weel, I don't want to hurry ye. But I wonder why ye would buy bad butter to please anybody, even a bonnie lass like that."

"Some folk like the taste of turnips, though I don't like it myself," answered Bruce. "But the fact is that turnips is not a favorite in the marketplace with most folk, and that brings down the price."

"Turnips is neither here nor there," retorted the girl and, picking up her basket, she turned to leave the shop.

"Wait a minute, my lass," cried Bruce. "The mistress would like to see you. Just go into the house to her with your basket and see what she thinks of the butter. I may be wrong, you know."

So saying he opened the inner door and ushered the young woman into the kitchen.

"Now, Mr. Dow?" he said once more. "Is it tobacco or snuff, or what?"

"It's Annie Anderson's chest an' gear."

"I'm surprised at you, James Dow. There's the lassie's room up the stairs, fit for any princess whenever she wants to come back to it. But she always was a riotous lassie."

"Ye lie, Rob Bruce!" exclaimed Dow, surprised by his own proprieties. "Don't say such a thing to me!"

Bruce was anything but a quarrelsome man with anyone other than his inferiors. He pocketed the lie very clamly.

"Don't lose your temper, Mr. Dow. It's a bad fault."

"Jist deliver the bairn's effects, or I'll go to them that will."

"Who might that be, Mr. Dow?" asked Bruce, wishing first to know how far Dow was prepared to go.

"Ye have no right whatever to keep that lassie's clothes, as if she owed ye anything for rent."

"Have *you* any right to take them away? How do I know what will come of them?"

"Weel, I'll jist be off to Mr. Gibb an' we'll see what can be done there. It's well known all over Glamerton, Mr. Bruce, in what manner ye an' yer whole house hae carried yersel's to that orphan lassie. An' I'll go into every shop down the street an' jist tell them where I'm goin', an' why."

The thing beyond all others which Bruce dreaded was profit-shrinking notoriety.

"Hoots! James Dow, you don't know joking from jesting. I never was a man to oppose anything unreasonable. I just didn't want it said about us that we drove the poor lassie out of the house and then flung her things after her."

"The one ye have done; the other ye shall not do, for I'll take them. An' I'll tell ye what folk'll say if ye don't give up the things. They'll say that ye both drove her away and kept her duds. I'll see to that—*and more besides.*"

Bruce understood that he referred to Annie's money. His object in refusing to give up her box had been to retain as long as possible a chance of persuading her to return to his house. For should she leave it completely, her friends might demand the interest in money, which at present he was obligated to pay only in food and shelter, little of either of which she required at his hands. But here was a greater danger still.

"Mother," he cried, "put up Miss Anderson's clothes in her box to go with the carrier tomorrow morning."

"I'll take them with me now," said Dow resolutely.

"You can't. You have no cart."

"Ye get them ready an' I'll fetch a wheelbarrow," said James, leaving the shop.

He borrowed a wheelbarrow from Thomas Crann and found the box ready for him when he returned. The moment he lifted it, he was certain from the weight of the poor little property that the Bible was not there.

"Ye haven't put in Mr. Cowie's Bible."

"Mother! Did you put in the Bible?" cried Bruce, for the house door was open.

" 'Deed no, Father. It's better where it is," said Mrs. Bruce from the kitchen in a shrill voice.

"You see, Mr. Dow, the Bible's lain so long there, that it's become like our own. And the lassie can't want it till she has a family to have worship with. And then she'll be welcome to take it."

"Ye go up the stairs for the book, or I'll go mysel'."

Bruce went and fetched it, with bad enough grace, and handed it over with the last tattered remnants of his dignity into the hands of James Dow.

Mr. Cupples made a translation of the inscription and took it to Thomas Crann.

"Do you remember what Bruce read that night as you saw him take something out of the book?" he asked as he entered.

"Ay. He began with the twenty-third psalm, an' went on to the next."

"Well, read that. I found it on a blank leaf of the book."

Thomas read: *Over the twenty-third psalm of David I have laid a five-pound note for my dear Annie Anderson, after my death.* Then lifting his eyes, he stared at Mr. Cupples, his face slowly brightening with satisfaction. Then a cloud came over his brow—for was he not rejoicing in iniquity? At least he was rejoicing in coming shame.

"How could it be that Bruce didn't see this as well as yersel', Mr. Cupples?"

" 'Cause it was written in Latin. Since it said nothing *to* him, he never thought it could say anything *about* him."

"It's a fine thing to be a scholar, Mr. Cupples."

"Ay, sometimes. But there's one thing more I would ask you. Can you tell me the day of the month that you went home with your praying friend?"

"It was the night o' a special prayer meetin' for the state o' Glamerton. I can find oot the date from the church books. What am I to do with it when I hae it?"

"Go to the bank the man deals with, and ask whether a note bearing the number of those figures was paid into it on the Monday following that Sunday, and who paid it. That'll tell you everything."

For various reasons Thomas was compelled to postpone the carrying out of his project. And Robert went on buying and selling and getting gain, all unaware of the pit he had dug for himself.

58

· · · · · · · · · · · · · · · · · ·

The Unmasking

The autumn months wore on. Alec's studies progressed and he grew confident. In October he and Mr. Cupples returned to their old quarters. Alec passed his examinations triumphantly, and he continued his studies with greater vigor than before. He made his rounds in the hospital with much greater attention and interest toward his patients.

Mr. Fraser declined seeing him. The old man was in a pitiable condition, and indeed never lectured again. Alec no more frequented his old dismal haunt by the seashore. He feared the cry of a sea gull or the washing of the waves on the shore would be enough to bring back the memory of the girl in white vanishing before his eyes. But the further the pain receded into the background of his memory, the more heartily he worked.

Annie's great-aunt took to her bed for a while directly after her husband's funeral. Finding there was much to do about the place, Annie felt no hesitation about remaining with Auntie Meg. She worked harder than she had ever worked before, blistered her hands, and browned her face and neck. Later, she and her aunt together reaped the little field of oats, dug up the potatoes and covered them in a pit with a blanket of earth, looked after the one cow and calf, fed the pigs and the poultry, and went with a neighbor and his cart to dig their winter store of peats.

Before the winter came there was little left to be done, and Annie saw by her aunt's looks that she wanted to be rid of her. Hence, as soon as Alec was gone, with the simplicity belonging to her childlike nature, Annie bid Margaret goodbye at Clippenstrae and returned to Mrs. Forbes. The repose of the winter was a sharp contrast with the events of Annie's fall. But the rainy, foggy, frosty, snowy months passed away much as they had done before, fostering even more the growth of Mrs. Forbes' love for her semi-protégé.

One event of considerable importance in its results to the people of Howglen took place this winter among the Missionaries of Glamerton.

So entire was Thomas Crann's notion of discipline that it could not be satisfied merely by ridding the congregation of Robert Bruce. A full disclosure to the entire membership was necessary. But afraid of opposition, either on the part of the minister or deacons or his friend James Johnstone, he communicated his design to no one ahead of time.

Therefore, when the business meeting arrived at which Thomas had determined in advance to state his case, and when the matters of discussion had been concluded and the minister was preparing to give out a hymn, Thomas Crann arose from the rear of the assembly. Mr. Turnbull stopped to listen and there fell an expectant silence.

"Brethren an' office bearers o' the church, it's upon discipline that I want to speak. Discipline is one o' the main objects for which a church is gathered by the Spirit o' God. An' we must work discipline among oorsel's or else the rod o' the Almighty'll come doon on oor backs. But I won't hold ye from the particulars any longer. On a certain Sabbath night last year, I went into Robert Bruce's house to hae worship with him. When he opened the book, I saw him slip somethin' oot from atween the pages an' crunkle it up in his hand. Then he read the twenty-third psalm. I couldn't help watchin' an' I saw him put whate'er it was in his pocket. Afterward I found oot that the book belonged to Annie Anderson an' that old Mr. Cowie had given it to her upon his deathbed an' told her that he'd put a five-poun' note atween the pages for her to remember him by. What say ye to that, Robert Bruce?"

"It's a lie!" cried Robert, "gotten up between yourself and that ungrateful cousin of mine, James Anderson's lass, who I've cared for like one of my own."

Bruce had been sitting trembling; but when Thomas put the question to him, believing that he had heard all that Thomas had to say and that there was no proof against him, he resolved at once to meet the accusation with a stout denial.

Thomas resumed: "Ye hear him deny't. Weel, I hae seen the Bible mysel', an' there's this inscription on one o' the blank pages: 'Over the twenty-third psalm o' David, I hae laid a five-poun' note for my dear Annie Anderson, after my death!' Then followed the nummer o' the note, which I can show them that wants to see. Noo I hae the banker's word that on the very Monday mornin' after that Sunday, Bruce paid into his account a five-poun' note o' that very same nummer. What say ye to that, Robert Bruce?"

A silence followed. Thomas broke it himself with the words: "Do ye not call that a breach o' the eighth commandment, Robert Bruce?"

But now Robert Bruce rose. He spoke with solemnity and pathos. "It's a sad thing that among Christians, who call themselves a chosen priesthood and a peculiar people, a member of the church should meet with such an accusation as I have at the hands of Mr. Crann. To say nothing of his not being ashamed to confess being such a hypocrite in the sight of God as to look about him while on his knees in prayer, lying in wait for a man to do him hurt when he pretended to be worshiping with him before the Lord his Maker. But the worst of it is that he beguiles a young thoughtless child, who has been the cause of much discomfort in our house, to join him in the plot. It's true enough that I took the bank note from the Bible, which was a very unsuitable place to put the unrighteous mammon, and it's true that I put it into the bank the next day—"

"What made ye deny it, then?" interrupted Thomas.

"Wait a minute, Mr. Crann, and settle down. You have been listened to without interruption, and I must have fair play here whatever I get from you. I don't deny the fact that I took the note. Who could deny the fact? But I deny the light of wickedness and thieving that Mr. Crann casts upon it. *I* saw that inscription and read it with my own eyes the very day the lassie brought home the book and knew as well as Mr. Crann that the money was hers. But I said to myself, 'It'll turn the lassie's head, and she'll just fling it away in crumbs on sweets and such,' for she was greedy; 'so I'll just put it into the bank with my own and account for it afterward with the rest of her money.'"

He sat down, and Mr. Turnbull rose.

"My Christian brethren," he said, "it seems to me that this is not the proper place to discuss such a question. It seems to me ill-judged of Mr. Crann to make such an accusation in public against Mr. Bruce, who, I must say, has met it with a self-restraint most creditable to him, and has answered it in a very satisfactory manner. Now let us sing the hundreth psalm."

"Hooly unfairly, sir!" exclaimed Thomas, forgetting his manners in his eagerness. "I'm not finished yet. An' where would be the place to discuss such a question but before a meetin' of the church? Wasn't the church instituted for the sake o' discipline? The Lord's withdrawn His presence from us, an' the cause o' His displeasure is the accursed thing which the Achan in oor camp has hidden in the County Bank."

"All this is nothing to the point, Mr. Crann," said Mr. Turnbull in displeasure.

"It's very to the point," returned Thomas, equally displeased. "If Robert Bruce saw the inscription the day the lassie brought home the book, will he tell me how it was that he came to leave the note in the book till that Sabbath night?"

"I looked for it, but I couldn't find it, and I thought she had taken it out on her way home."

"Couldn't ye find the twenty-third psalm?—But jist one thing more, Mr. Turnbull, and then I'll hold my tongue," resumed Thomas. "James Johnstone, will ye run o'er to my house an' fetch the Bible.—Jist hae patience till he comes back, sir, an' then we'll see how Mr. Bruce'll read the inscription. Mr. Bruce is a scholar, an' he'll read the Latin to us."

By this time James Johnstone was across the street.

"There's some foul play in this!" cried Bruce. "My enemy has to send for an outlandish speech and a heathen tongue to ensnare one of the brethren!"

Profound silence followed as all sat expectantly. Every ear was listening for the footsteps of the returning weaver. But they had to wait a full five minutes before the messenger returned, bearing the large volume of the parish clergyman in both hands in front of him.

The book was laid out on the desk before Mr. Turnbull, and Thomas called out from the back region of the chapel, "Now, Robert Bruce, go up an' find this inscription that ye know so weel aboot an' read it to the church that they may see what a scholar they hae among them."

But there was no movement nor voice.

After a pause, Mr. Turnbull spoke.

"Mr. Bruce, we're waiting for you," he said. "Do not be afraid. You shall have justice."

A dead silence followed.

Presently some of those farthest back spoke in scarcely audible voices.

"He's not here, sir. We can't see him."

"Not here!" cried Thomas.

They searched the pew where he had been sitting, and the neighboring pews, and the whole chapel, but he was nowhere to be found.

"That would have been him, when I heard the door bang," said one to another.

And so it was. Perceiving that things had gone against him, he had slipped down in his pew and crawled on all fours to the door. In the darkness of the candlelight meeting, Bruce had got out of the place unseen.

A formal sentence of expulsion was passed upon him by a show of hands.

"Thomas Crann, will you engage in prayer?" said Mr. Turnbull.

"Not tonight," answered Thomas. "I've been doin' necessary but foul work an' I'm not in a right spirit to pray in public. I must get home to my own prayers. I must ask the Lord to keep me from doin' somethin' mysel' before long that'll make it necessary for ye to dismiss me next. But if that time should come, I beseech ye not to spare me."

So after a short prayer from Mr. Turnbull, the meeting separated in a state of considerable excitement. Thomas half expected to hear of action against him for libel, but Robert knew better than to venture such a thing. Besides, there were no monetary damages that could be got out of Thomas.

When Bruce was once outside the chapel, he again assumed erect posture and walked home by circuitous ways.

"Preserve us, Robert! what's come over you?" exclaimed his wife.

"I had such a headache, I was forced to come home early," he answered. "I don't think I'll go there anymore. They don't conduct things altogether to my liking."

His wife looked at him, perhaps with some vague suspicion of the truth; but she said nothing, and I do not believe the matter was ever alluded to between them. Of the two, however, perhaps Thomas Crann was the more unhappy as he went home that night. He felt nothing of the elation which commonly springs from success in a cherished project. He had been the promoter in the downfall of another man. Although the fall was a just one, and it was better for the man to be down than standing on a false pedestal, Thomas could not help feeling the reaction of a fellow human's humiliation. Now that the thing was done, and the end gained, the eternal brotherhood asserted itself, and Thomas pitied Bruce and mourned over him.

Scarcely any of the members henceforth traded with Bruce, and the modifying effect upon the weekly return was very perceptible. This was the only form in which a recognizable vengeance could have reached him. To escape from it, he had serious thoughts of leaving the place and setting up his trade in some remote village.

59

Alec's Plans

*D*espite his diligence and the genial companionship of Mr. Cupples, Alec occasionally found himself asking, "What is the use of it all?" Whether this thought rose from the death of Kate, or his own illness, or the reaction of his shame after his sojourn with the dark places of life, I cannot tell. The moments of such vague uneasiness were infrequent, however, and usually dispelled by a reviving interest in his studies or a merry talk with Mr. Cupples.

What made these questionings develop into a more definite self-condemnation began with a letter he had written to his mother for money to buy better instruments and new chemical apparatus. She had replied sadly that she was unable to send it. She hinted that his education had cost more than she had expected. She was in debt to Robert Bruce for a hundred pounds and had lately been compelled to delay the payment of its interest. She informed him also that, even under James Dow's conscientious management, there seemed little hope that the farm would ever make a profit to justify the large outlay his father had made upon it.

This letter stung Alec to the heart. That his mother should be in the power of such a man as Bruce was bad enough. But that she should be exposed, for the sake of his education, to ask Bruce to put off payment—that was unendurable.

He wrote a humble letter to his mother, and worked still harder. For although he could not make a shilling while he was still in school, the future contained a great deal of hope.

Meantime, Mr. Cupples got a new hat and coat. His shirt became clean and white and it was evident to all at the college that a great change had passed upon him. These signs of improvement led to inquiries on the part of the governing staff. As a result, before three months of the session were over, he was formally installed as the permanent librarian. His first impulse on receiving the good news was to rush down to Luckie Cumstie's and have a double tumbler. But conscience was too strong for Satan, and sent him home instead to his pipe—which, it must be confessed, he smoked twice as much as before his reformation.

From the moment of his appointment, he seemed to regard the library as his own private property, or rather as his own family. All the books he gave out with injunctions as to care, and special warnings against forcing the backs, crumbling or folding the pages, and making thumbmarks.

"Now," he would say to some country freshman, "take the book in your hand not as if it were a turnip, but as if it were the soul of a newborn child. Remember that it has to serve many a generation after your own bones are lying bare in the ground, and you must have respect to them that come after you. So I beg you not to mangle it."

The freshmen used to laugh at him. But long before they had graduated, the best of them had a profound respect for the librarian. Not a few of them went to him with their difficulties with classes; and such a general favorite was he that any story of his humor or oddity was sure to be received with a roar of laughter. Indeed, I don't doubt that within the course of four years, Mr. Cupples had become the real center of intellectual and moral life in that college.

One evening, as he and Alec were sitting together speculating on the quickest way of Alec earning some money from his schooling, their landlady entered.

"My cousin's here," she said, "Captain McTavish of the ship the *Sea-horse,* Mr. Forbes, who says that before long he'll be wanting a young doctor to go and keep the scurvy from his men while they're whale fishing. I thought of you and came up the stairs to see you. It'll be fifty pounds in your pouch, and plenty of rough ploys that the likes of you young fellows like, though I can't say I would like such things myself."

"Tell Captain McTavish that I'll go," answered Alec, who did not hesitate for a moment. He rose and followed her down the stairs.

He soon returned, his eyes flashing with delight. Adventure! And fifty pounds to send to his mother!

"The captain has promised to take me, Mr. Cupples, if my testimonials are good," he said. "I think they will be. If it weren't for you, I would be lying in the gutter by now instead of walking the quarterdeck."

"Well, bantam. There's two sides to most obligations—I'm librarian!"

Having always been fond of anything to do with water and boats, Alec was nearly beside himself with delight. The *Sea-horse* may not be *The Bonnie Annie,* but it would take him across the real sea! His enthusiasm continued until he heard from his mother. She had too much sense to oppose him in this, but she could hardly hide her anticipation of loss and loneliness. This quelled Alec's exuberance, but could not alter his resolve. He would return in the fall of the year, bringing with him what would ease her mind of half its load.

He passed all his examinations at the end of the session.

Mrs. Forbes became greatly perplexed about Annie. She could not bear the thought of turning her out this spring. She did not see where she could go, for she could not be in the same house with young Bruce. But notwithstanding her financial obligation to the elder Bruce, Mrs. Forbes was a landowner, clearly aware of the impropriety of a union between her son and an orphan maiden who, despite her charm and character, was of a different class altogether. With Alec due home for a time before his departure, she could not help feeling the dangerous sense of worldly duty to prevent the so-called unsuitable match, the chance of which was now more threatening than ever. Annie had grown very lovely, and having taken captive the affections of the mother, must put the heart of the son in dire jeopardy.

Alec arrived two days before he was expected and delivered his mother from her perplexity by declaring that if Annie were sent away, he too would leave the house. Mrs. Forbes contented herself with the realization that Alec's visit would be brief. She would not have to face an ultimate decision until his return at the end of the year. So Annie remained where she was, much, I must confess, to her inward delight.

Alec's college life had interposed a gulf between him and his previous history. As his approaching departure into places unknown and a life untried worked on his mind and spiritual condition, he felt an impulse to strengthen all the old bonds which had been stretched thin by time and absence.

He took a day to see Curly and spent a pleasant afternoon with him, recalling the old times and the old stories and the old companions. For the youth with a downy chin has a past as ancient as that of the man with the gray beard. Curly told him the story of his encounter with young Bruce and over and over again Annie's name came up, but Curly never hinted at her secret.

The next evening Alec went to see Thomas Crann. Thomas received him with a cordiality amounting even to a gruff form of tenderness.

"I'm right glad to see ye," he said, "an' I take it kindly o' ye with all yer learnin' to come an' see an ignorant man like me. But, Alec, my man, there's some things I know better than ye know them yet. Him that made the whales is better worth seeking than the whales themsel's. Come doon upon yer knees with me an' I'll pray for ye."

Yielding to the spiritual power of Thomas, whose gray-blue eyes were flashing with fervor, Alec kneeled down as he was desired, and Thomas said: "O thou who madest the whales to play in the great waters, be round aboot this youth, an' when thou seest his ship go sailin' into the far north, put doon thy finger, O Lord, an' strike a track afore it through the hills o' ice, that it may go through in safety, even as thy chosen people went through the Red Sea. For, Lord, we only want him home again in thy good time. But above all, O Lord, save him by thy grace an' let him know the glory o' God, even the light o' thy face. Spare him, O Lord, an' give him time for repentance, if he has a chance; but if he has none, take him at once that his doom may be lighter."

Alec rose with a very serious face and went home with a mood more in tune with his mother's than the lightheartedness with which he generally tried to laugh away her apprehensions.

He even called on Robert Bruce, at his mother's request. It went terribly against his grain, but he was surprised to find him pleasant. Bruce's civility came from two sources—hope and fear. Alec was going away and might never return. That was the hope. For although Bruce had spread the report of Annie's engagement to Curly, he believed that Alec was the real obstacle to his ultimate plans. At the time he was afraid of Alec, believing in his cowardly mind that Alec would not stop short of brutal physical reprisals if he should offend him. Alec was now a great six-foot fellow, of whose prowess at college confused and exaggerated stories were floating about the town.

"Ay, ay! Mr. Forbes—so you're going away among the fish, are you? Have you any share of the take?"

"I don't think the doctor has any share," answered Alec.

"But I imagine you'll put your hand to it and help at the catching."

"Very likely."

"Well, if you come in for a barrel or two, you may count upon me to take it off your hands, at the ordinary price—to the wholesale merchant, you know—with maybe a small discount for ordering before the whale was taken."

The day drew near. He had bidden all his friends farewell. He must go just as the spring was coming. His mother would have traveled to the harbor with him to see him on board, but he prevailed on her to say good-bye to him at home. She kept her tears till after he was gone. Annie bade him farewell with a pale face and a smile that was sweet but not glad. She did not weep afterward. A gentle cold hand pressed her heart down, so that no blood reached her face and no water reached her eyes. She went about everything just as before, because it had to be done. But it seemed foolish to do anything. The spring might as well stay away for any good that it promised.

As Mr. Cupples was taking his farewell on board, Alec said, "You'll go to see my mother?"

"Ay, bantam; I'll do that. Now take care of yourself, and don't take any liberties with behemoth. Put a ring in its nose if you like, but keep away from its tail. He's not to be meddled with!"

So away went Alec northwards, over the blue-gray waters, surgeon of the strong ship *Sea-horse*.

60

· · · · · · · · · · · · · · · · · ·

The Summer

Two days after Alec's departure, Mr. Bruce called at Howglen to see Annie.

"How are you, Mistress Forbes? How are you, Miss Anderson? I was just coming over the water for a walk, and I thought I might as well bring the little bit of money that I owe you."

Annie's eyes opened wide. She did not know what he meant.

"It's been twelve months that you have had neither bite nor sup beneath my humble roof, and as that was to make up for the interest, I must pay you the one seeing that you wouldn't accept the other. I have just brought you the ten pounds to put in your own pocket in the meantime."

Annie could hardly believe her ears. Could she be the rightful owner of such untold wealth? Without giving her time to say anything, Bruce went on, still holding in his hand the bunch of dirty one-pound notes.

"But I'm thinking the best way of disposing of it would be to let me put it with the rest of the principal. So I'll just take it to the bank as I go back. I cannot give you anything for it, for that would be breaking the law against compound interest, you know, but I can make it up to you in some other way, you know."

But Annie had been too much pleased at the prospect of possession to let the money go so easily.

"I have plenty of ways of spending it," she asserted, "without wasting it. So I'll just take it myself, and thank you, Mr. Bruce."

She rose and took the notes from Bruce's unwilling hand. He had been on the point of replacing them in his trousers pocket when she rescued them. Discomfort was visible in his eyes and in the little tug of retraction with which he loosed his hold upon the notes. He went home feeling mortified and poverty-stricken, but yet having gained a step toward a further end.

Annie begged Mrs. Forbes to take the money, but she would not—partly from the pride of beneficence, partly from fear of involving it in her own straits. How Annie longed for Tibbie Dyster! But not having her, she went to Thomas Crann who helped her distribute it among the poor of Glamerton.

After three months Bruce called again with the quarter's interest. Before the next period he had an interview with James Dow. He told Dow that since he was now paying Annie's interest out in cash, he should not have to be exposed to the inconvenience of being called upon at any moment to pay back the principal, but should have the money secured to him for ten years. After consultation James Dow consented to a three-year loan, beyond which he would not yield. Papers to this effect were signed and one quarter's more interest was placed in Annie's willing hand.

In the middle of summer Mr. Cupples made his appearance and was warmly welcomed. He had at length completed the catalogue of the library, had got the books arranged to his satisfaction, and was a brimful of enjoyment. He ran about the fields like a child; gathered bunches of white clover; made a great kite and bought an unmeasurable length of string, with which he flew it the first day the wind was worthy of the honor. He got out Alec's boat and capsized himself in the Glamour—fortunately, in shallow water; was run away with by one of the plow horses in the attempt to ride him to the water, and was laughed at and loved by everybody about Howglen. But in a fortnight he began to settle down into his more usual sobriety of demeanor.

Calling one day on Thomas Crann, he found him in one of his gloomy moods.

"How are you, old friend?" asked Cupples.

"Old as ye say, an' not much further on than when I began. I sometimes think I have profited less than anybody I know. But I would be sorry, if I was you, to die afor I had gotten a glimpse o' the face o' God."

"How do you know I haven't gotten a glimpse of it?"

"You would be more solemn."

"Maybe so," responded Cupples.

"Man, strive to get it. Give Him no rest day or night till ye get it. Knock till it be opened to ye."

"Well, Thomas, you don't seem so happy yourself. Don't you think you're like one that's trying to see through a crack in the door instead of having patience till it's opened?"

But the suggestion was quite lost upon Thomas, who after a gloomy pause, went on, "Sin's such an awful thing," he began, when the door was opened and in walked James Dow.

His entrance did not interrupt Thomas, however.

"Sin's such an awful thing! An' I have sinned so often an' so long that maybe He'll be forced to send me to the bottomless pit."

"Hoot, Thomas! don't speak aboot such awful things," said Dow. "I'll warrant He's at least as kindhearted as yersel'."

James had no reputation for piety, though much for truthfulness and honesty. Nor had he any idea how much lay in the words he had hastily uttered.

"I said He might be *forced* to send me after all."

"What, Thomas!" cried Cupples. "He *couldn't* save you? With both His Son and the Spirit to help Him? And your willing heart besides? Fegs! You have a greater opinion of Satan than I would have thought."

"It's not Satan. It's mysel'."

"But what of repentance, Thomas? You've repented."

Thomas was silent for a few moments. Then he said, "Go away, an' leave me to my prayers."

The two men obeyed. Mr. Cupples could wait. Thomas could not.

Among those who sit down at the gate till One shall come and open it are to be found both the wise and the children.

61

· · · · · · · · · · · · · · · · · · ·

Bruce

*M*r. Cupples returned to his library, and autumn came and lengthened toward winter. The time drew nigh when the two women began watching the mail coach for the welcome letter announcing Alec's return from his sea voyage. At length one morning Mrs. Forbes said: "We may look for him any day now, Annie."

But the days went on and Alec did not come. While they imagined the *Seahorse* full-sailed, stretching herself homeward toward the hospitable shore, she in fact lay a frozen mass, trapped immobile in a glacier of ice. The *Sea-horse* would not return this year and the winds and snows would go whistling and raving through it in the wild waste of the north all winter long.

What had been a longing hope under the roof of Howglen began to make the heart sick. Dim anxiety passed into vague fear and finally deepened into the dull conviction that the *Sea-horse* was lost and Alec would never return. Each would find the other wistfully watching the windows. But finally the moment came when their eyes met and they burst into tears, each accepting the other's confession of hopeless grief as the seal of doom.

I will not follow them through the slow shadows of gathering fate. I will not describe the silence that closed in upon their days, nor the visions of horror that tormented them. I will not detail how they heard his voice calling to them for help from the midst of the winter storm, or how through the snowdrifts they saw him plodding wearily home. His mother forgot her debt and ceased to care what became of herself. Annie's anxiety settled into an earnest prayer that she might not rebel against the will of God.

But the anxiety of Thomas Crann was not limited to the earthly fate of the lad. It extended to his fate in the other world—all too probable, in Thomas's view, that endless fate of separation from his Maker. Terrible were his agonies in wrestling with God for the life of the lad, and terrible his fear lest his own faith should fail him if his prayers should not be heard. Alec Forbes was to Thomas Crann the representative of all the unsaved brothers and sisters of the human race, for whose sake he, like the Apostle Paul, would have gladly undergone what he dreaded for them. He went to see Alec's mother and inquired, "How are ye, mem?" There he sat down; never opened his lips, except to offer a few commonplaces; rose and left her—a little comforted.

As she ministered to her friend, Annie's face shone—despite her full share in the sorrow—a light that came not from the sun or the stars, a suppressed, waiting light. And Mrs. Forbes felt the holy influences that proceeded both from her and from Thomas Crann.

How much easier it is to bear a trouble that comes on the heels of another than one which comes suddenly into the midst of merrymaking. Thus Mrs. Forbes scarcely felt it a trouble when she received a note from Robert Bruce informing her that, as he was on the point of leaving to another place which offered greater opportunities for the little money he possessed, he would be obliged to her to pay as soon as possible the hundred pounds she owed him, along with certain back interest specified. She wrote that it was impossible for her at present, and forgot the whole affair. Within three days she received a formal application for the debt from a new lawyer. To this she paid no attention, just wondering what would come next. After about three months a second application was made, according to a legal form. In the month of May a third arrived, with the hint from the lawyer that his client was now prepared to proceed to the extremity of foreclosure on her farm. She now felt for the first time that she must do something.

She sent for James Dow and handed him the letter.

James took it and read it slowly. Then he stared at his mistress. He read it over again. At length, with a bewildered look, he said, "Give him the money; ye must pay it, mem."

"But I can't."

"The Lord preserve us! What's to be done? I hae saved up aboot thirty pounds, but that wouldn't go far."

"No, no, James," returned his mistress. "I am not going to take your money to pay Mr. Bruce."

"He's an awful creature."

"Well, I must see what can be done. I'll go and consult Mr. Gibb."

James took his leave, dejected. Going out he met Annie. "Eh, Annie!" he said; "this is awful."

"What's the matter, Dooie?"

"That mean Bruce is threatenin' to destroy the mistress for a bit o' money she owes him."

"He dare not!" exclaimed Annie.

"He'll dare anything but lose money. Eh, lassie, if only we hadn't lent him yours!"

"I'll go to him directly. But don't tell the mistress. She wouldn't like it."

"I'll hold my tongue," promised Dowie.

He turned and walked away, murmuring as he left, "Maybe she'll persuade the ill-faured tyke."

When Annie entered Bruce's shop, the big spider was unoccupied and ready to devour her. He therefore put on his most gracious reception.

"How are you, Miss Anderson! I'm glad to see you. Come into the house."

"No, thank you. I want to speak to you, Mr. Bruce. What's all this about Mrs. Forbes and you!"

"Great folk mustn't ride over the top of poor folk like me, Miss Anderson."

"She's a widow, Mr. Bruce"—Annie could not frame the words "and childless," though the thought filled her mind—"and lays no claim to be great folk. It's not a Christian way of treating her."

"Folk has a right to their own. The money's mine and I must have it. There's nothing against that in the Ten Commandments. There's no gospel for not giving folk their own. I'm not a Missionary now. I don't hold with such things. I can't turn my family into beggars just to hold up her big house. She must pay me or I'll take it."

"If you do, Mr. Bruce, you'll not have my money one minute after the time's up; and I'm sorry you have it till then."

"That's neither here nor there. You would be wanting it before that time anyhow."

Now actually Bruce had given up the notion of leaving Glamerton, for he had found that the patronage of the evangelicals of his former congregation was not essential to a certain measure of success. Neither did he have any intention of proceeding to a foreclosure auction of Mrs. Forbes' farm and possessions. He saw that would put him in a worse position with the public than any amount of quiet practice in lying and stealing. But there was every likelihood of Annie's being married someday; and then her money would be recalled, and he would be left without the capital necessary for carrying on his business upon the same enlarged scale—seeing that he now supplied many of the little country shops. It would be a grand move then, if by far-sighted generalship copying his great ancestor the king, he could get a permanent hold of some of Annie's property. Hence had come his descent upon Mrs. Forbes, and here came its success.

"You have as much of mine to yourself as'll clear Mrs. Forbes," said Annie.

"Well, very well.—But you realize that it's mine for two and a half more years anyway. That would only amount to losing her interest for two and a half years altogether. That won't do."

"What *will* do, then, Mr. Bruce?"

"I don't know. I want my own money."

"But you mustn't torment her, Mr. Bruce. You know that."

"Well, I'm open to anything reasonable. There's the interest for two and a half—call it three years—and what I could make on it—say eight percent—twenty-four pounds. Then there's her back interest, then there's the loss of the turnover, and then there's the loss of the money that you won't have to lend me. If you'll give me a quittance for a hundred and fifty pounds, I'll give her a receipt, though it'll be a sore loss to me."

"Anything you like," replied Annie.

Bruce immediately brought out papers already drawn up by his lawyer, one of which he signed and she the other.

"You'll remember," he added, as she was leaving the shop, "that I have to pay you no interest now except on fifty pounds?"

He had paid her nothing for the last half year at least.

He would not have dared to fleece the girl thus had she had any legally constituted guardians; or had those who would gladly have interfered had the power to protect her. Seeing that he paid her only five percent interest and had not paid her even that for the last two quarters, his computations with regard to their arrangement were favorable to him to say the least. To cancel Mrs. Forbes' note of one hundred pounds in exchange for a reduction in Annie's of a hundred and fifty netted Bruce a handsome profit of half a year's wages. He took care to word the quittance so that in the event of anything going wrong, he might yet claim his hundred pounds from Mrs. Forbes.

Annie begged Bruce not to tell Mrs. Forbes and he was ready enough to consent. He did more. He wrote to Mrs. Forbes to the effect that, upon reflection, he had resolved to drop further proceedings for the present. He said nothing about the cancellation of her note and all back interest. When she took him a half-year's interest not long thereafter, he took it in silence, justifying himself on the ground that the whole transaction was doubtful anyway, and he must therefore secure what he could.

62

·················

Homecoming

𝒯t was a dreary summer for all at Howglen. Why should the ripe grain wave in the gold of the sunbeams when their dear Alec lay frozen beneath fields of ice or sweeping about under them like broken seaweed in the waters so cold? Yet the work of the world must go on. The grain must be reaped. Things must be bought and sold. Even the mourners must eat and drink. And the dust to which Alec had gone down must be swept from the floor.

So things did go on—of themselves, for no one cared much about them, although it was the finest harvest year that Howglen had ever borne. Annie grew paler but did not relax her efforts of kindness in the small community. She told the poor friends she had befriended that she had no money now, but most were nearly as glad to see her as before. One of them, who had never liked receiving alms from a girl in such a lowly position, loved her even better when she had nothing to give but herself. She renewed her acquaintance with Peter Whaup, the blacksmith, through his wife who was ill. And in all eyes the maiden grew in favor. Her beauty, both inward and outward, was that of the twilight, of a morning cloudy with high clouds, or of a silvery sea: it was an inward, spiritual beauty. And her sorrow gave a quiet grace to her demeanor, peacefully ripening it into what is loveliest in ladyhood. She always looked like one waiting—sometimes like one listening, attune to melodies unheard.

One night toward the end of October, James Dow was walking by the side of his cart along a lonely road. He was headed to the nearest seaport for a load of coal. The moon was high and full. Approaching a solitary milestone in the midst of a desolate heathland, he drew near an odd-looking figure seated on it. He was about to ask him if he would like a lift when the figure rose and cried joyfully, "Jamie Dow!"

Dow staggered back, for the voice was Alec Forbes'. He gasped for breath. All he was capable of in the way of an utterance was to cry *whoa!* to his horse.

There stood Alec in rags, his face thin but brown—healthy, bold, and firm. He looked ten years older standing there in the moonlight.

"The Lord preserve us!" cried Dow, and could say no more.

"He has preserved me, you see, Jamie. How's my mother?"

"She's brawly, just brawly, Mr. Alec. The Lord preserve us! She's been terrible upset aboot ye. Ye mustn't walk in on her in her bed. It would kill her."

"I'm awful tired, Jamie. Can you turn your cart around and take me home?

I'll be worth a load of coal to my mother anyway. And then you can break the news to her."

Without another word, Dow turned his horse, helped Alec into the cart, covered him with his coat and some straw, and walked back along the road, half thinking himself in a dream. Alec fell fast asleep and did not wake up till the cart was standing still, about midnight, at his mother's door. He started up.

"Lie still, Mr. Alec," said Dow in a whisper. "The mistress'll be in her bed. I'll go to her first."

Alec lay down again and Dow went to Mary's window on the other side to try to wake her. Just as he returned to the cart, they both heard Alec's mother's window open.

"Who's there?" she called.

"Nobody but me—James Dow," answered James. "I was halfway to Portlokie when I had a mishap on the road. Bettie put her foot on a sharp stone an' fell doon an' broke both her legs."

"How did she come home, man?"

"She *had* to come home, mem."

"On broken legs!"

"Hoot, mem—her knees. I don't mean the bones, ye know, mem; only the skin. But she wasn't fit to go on. An' so I brought her back."

"What's that in the cart? Is it anything dead?"

"No, mem, de'il a bit o't! It's livin' enough. It's a stranger lad that I gave a lift to on the road. He's mighty tired."

But Dow's voice trembled, or something or other revealed all to the mother's heart. She gave a great cry. Alec sprang from the cart, rushed into the house, and was in his mother's arms.

Annie was asleep in the next room, but she half awoke with a sense of his presence. She had heard his voice through the folds of sleep. And she half-dreamed that she was lying on the rug in front of the dining room fire with Alec and his mother at the table, as on that night when he brought her in from the snow hut. As wakefulness gradually came upon her, she all at once knew that she was in her own bed and that Alec and his mother were talking in the next room.

She rose, but could hardly dress herself for trembling. When she was dressed she sat down on the edge of the bed to think.

Her joy was almost torture, but it had a certain quality of the bitter in it. Ever since she had believed him dead, Alec had been so near to her. She had loved him as much as ever she would. But Life had come in suddenly, and divided those whom death had joined. Now he was again a great way off, and she dared not speak to him whom she had cherished in her heart. Ever since her confession to Curly, she had been making fresh discoveries in her own heart. And now the tide of her love swelled so strong that she felt it would break out in an agony of joy and betray her if she just once looked into Alec's face. Not only this. What she had done about his mother's debt must come out sooner or later, and she could not bear the thought that he might feel under some obligation to her. These things and many more so worked in the sensitive maiden that as soon as she heard Alec and his mother go into the dining room, she put on her bonnet and cloak, stole like a wraith to the back door, and let herself out into the night.

She avoided the path and went through the hedge into a field of stubble at the back of the house, across which she made her way to the turnpike road and the new bridge over the Glamour. Often she turned back to look at the window of the room where he who had been dead was alive and talking with his widowed mother. Only when trees finally rose up between her and the house did she begin to think of what she should do. She could think of nothing but to go to her aunt once more, and ask her to take her in for a few days. So she walked on through the sleeping town.

Not a soul was awake and the stillness was awful. In the middle of the large square of the little gray town, she stood and looked around her. All one side lay in shade, the other three lay in moonlight. She walked on, passed over the western road and through the trees to the bridge over the Wan Water. Everything stood so still in the moonlight! The smell from the withering fields, laid bare of the harvest and breathing out their damp odors, came to her mixed with the chill air from the dark hills around, already spiced with keen atoms of frost. She was not far from Clippenstrae, but she could not go there in the middle of the night, for her aunt would be frightened first, and angry next. So she wandered up the stream to the old churchyard, and sat on one of the tombstones. It became very cold as the morning drew on. The moon went down; the stars grew dim; the river ran with a livelier murmur; and through all the fine gradations of dawn she sat until the sun came forth rejoicing.

The long night was over. It had not been a weary one, for Annie had thoughts of her own to keep her company. Yet she was glad when the sun came. She rose and walked through the long shadows of the graves down to the river which shone in the morning light like a flowing crystal of delicate brown—and so to Clippenstrae, where she found her aunt still in her nightcap. She was standing at the door, however, shading her eyes with her hand, looking abroad as if for someone that might be crossing toward her from the east. She did not see Annie approaching from the north.

"What are you looking for, Auntie?"

"Nothin'. Not for you, anyway, lassie."

"Well, I'm come without being looked for. But you were looking for somebody, Auntie."

"No, I was only just lookin'."

Even Annie did not then know that it was the soul's hunger, the vague sense of a need which nothing but the God of human faces can satisfy, that sent her money-loving, poverty-stricken, pining, grumbling old aunt out staring toward the east. It is this formless idea of something at hand that keeps men and women striving to tear from the bosom of the world the secret of their own hopes. How little they know that what they look for is in reality their God!

"What do ye want so early as this, Annie?"

"I want you to take me in for a while," answered Annie.

"For an hour or two? Ow, ay."

"For a week or two maybe?"

"'Deed no. I'll do nothing o' the kind. Let them that made ye proud keep ye proud."

"I'm not so proud, Auntie. What makes you say that?"

"So proud that ye wouldn't take a good offer when it was in yer power. An' then yer grand friends turn ye oot when it suits them. I'm not goin' to take ye in. There's Davie Gordon wants a lass. Ye can jist go look for work like other folk."

"I'll go and see about it directly. How far is it, Auntie?"

"Goin' an' givin' away yer money to beggars as if it were dust jist to be a grand lady! Ye're none so grand, I can tell ye. An' then comin' to poor folk like me to take ye in for a week or two!"

Auntie had been listening to evil tongues—so much easier to listen to than just tongues. With difficulty Annie kept back her tears. She made no defense, tried to eat the porridge her aunt set before her, and then departed. Before three hours were over she had been given the charge of the dairy and cooking at Willowcraig for the next six months of coming winter and spring. Protected from suspicion, her spirits rose all the cheerier for their temporary depression, and she soon was singing about the house.

As she did not appear at breakfast, and was absent from dinner as well, Mrs. Forbes set out with Alec to inquire after her. Not knowing where else to go first, they went to Robert Bruce. He showed more surprise than pleasure at seeing Alec, smiling with his own acridness as he said: "I doubt you've brought home that barrel of oil you promised me, Mr. Alec? It would have cleared off a good sheave of your mother's debts."

Alec answered cheerily, although his face flushed.

"All in good time, I hope, Mr. Bruce. I'm obliged to you for your forbearance about the debt, though."

"It can't last forever, you know," rejoined Bruce, happy to be able to bite, although his poison bag was gone.

Alec made no reply.

"Have you seen Annie Anderson today, Mr. Bruce?" asked his mother.

"Indeed no, mem. She doesn't often trouble herself with our company. We're not grand enough for her."

"Hasn't she been here today?" repeated Mrs. Forbes, with discomposure in her look and tone.

"Have you lost her, mem?" rejoined Bruce. "This *is* a pity. She's be away with that vagabond Willie Macwha, I don't doubt. He was in town last night. I saw him go by with Bobby Peterson."

They made him no reply, understanding well enough that though the one premise might be true, the conclusion must be as false as it was illogical and spiteful. They did not go to George Macwha's, but set out for Clippenstrae. When they reached the cottage, they found Meg's nose in full vigor.

"No. She's not here. Why should she be here? She has no claim upon me, although it pleases ye to turn her oot—after bringin' her up with notions that hae jist ruined her with pride."

"Indeed, I didn't turn her out, Miss Anderson."

"Weel, ye should never hae taken her in."

There was something in her manner which made them certain she knew where Annie was, but she avoided their every attempt to draw it out of her, and they departed foiled. Meg knew well enough that Annie's refuge could not long remain concealed, but she found it pleasant to annoy Mrs. Forbes.

Indeed it was not many days before Mrs. Forbes did learn where Annie was. But she was so taken up with her son that two weeks passed before that part of her nature which needed a daughter's love began again to assert itself.

Alec had to go away once more to the great city. He had certain remnants of study to gather up at the university before he could obtain his surgeon's license. The good harvest would put a little money in his mother's hands, and the sooner he was ready to practice medicine, the sooner he could relieve her of her debt.

The very day after he went, Mrs. Forbes drove to Willowcraig to see Annie. She found her clad like any other girl at the farmhouse. Annie was rather embarrassed at the sight of her friend. Mrs. Forbes could easily see, however, that there was no breach in the mutual affection of their friendship. She found that winter very dreary without Annie.

63

·····················

Alec Forbes of Howglen

Annie spent the winter in housework, combined with the feeding of pigs and poultry and some milking of the cows. There was little real hardship in her life. She had plenty of wholesome food to eat and she lay warm at night. The old farmer, who was rather overbearing with his men, was kind to her because he liked her, and when his wife scolded her she never meant anything by it.

Annie cherished her love for Alec, but was quite peaceful as to the future. When her work for the day was done she would go out on long, lonely walks in the countryside.

One evening toward the end of April she went out to a certain meadow which was haunted by wild flowers and singing birds. It had become one of her favorites. As she was climbing over a fence, a horseman came round the corner of the road. She saw at a glance that it was Alec, and stepped down beside the road.

Change had passed on them both since they had last seen one another. He was a full-grown man with a settled look. She was a lovely woman, even more delicate and graceful than her childhood had promised.

As she got down from the fence, he got down from his horse. Without a word on either side, their hands joined, and still they stood silent for a minute, Annie with her eyes on the ground, Alec gazing in her face, which was pale with more than its usual paleness.

"I saw Curly yesterday," said Alec at length, with what seemed to Annie a look of meaning.

Her face flushed as red as fire. Could Curly have betrayed her?

She managed to stammer out as she dropped his hands, "Oh! Did you?"

And silence fell again.

"We never thought we would see you again, Alec," she said at length, taking up the conversation again.

"I thought that too," answered Alec, "when the great iceberg came down on us in the snowstorm and flung the ship onto the ice floe with her side crushed in. How I used to dream about the old school days, Annie, and finding you in my hut! And I did find you in the snow, Annie."

But a figure came round the corner—for the road made a double sweep at this point—and cried, "Annie, come home directly. Ye're wanted."

"I'm coming to see you again soon, Annie," said Alec. "But I must go away for a month or two first."

Annie replied with a smile and an outstretched hand—nothing more. She could wait well enough.

How lovely the flowers in the dyke sides looked as she walked home. But the thought that perhaps Curly had told him something was like a thorn in her joy. Yet somehow she had become so beautiful before she reached the house that her aunt, who was there to see her, called out, "Losh, lassie! What hae ye been aboot? Yer face is full o' color!"

"That's easily accounted for," said her mistress roguishly. "She was standin' talkin' with a bonnie young lad on a horse. I won't hae such doin's aboot my house, I can tell ye, lass."

Margaret Anderson flew into a passion and abused her with many words, which Annie, far from resenting, scarcely even heard. At length her aunt ceased and then departed almost without an adieu. But what did it matter? What did any earthly thing matter *if only Curly had not told him*?

But all that Curly had told Alec was that Annie was not engaged to him.

So the days and nights passed. Annie re-engaged herself at the end of six months and gradually spring changed into summer, but still Alec did not come.

One evening, when a wind that seemed to smell of the roses of the sunset was blowing from the west and filling her rosy heart with joy, Annie sat down to read in a rough little garden. It was of the true country order, containing the old-fashioned glories of sweet peas, larkspur, poppies, and peonies along with gooseberry and currant bushes, as well as potatoes and other vegetables. She sat with her back to a low stone wall, reading aloud the sonnet by Milton, *Lady that in the prime of earliest youth.* As she finished it, a low voice said, almost in her ear, "That lady's you, Annie."

Alec was looking over the garden wall behind her.

"Eh, Alec!" she cried, startled and jumping to her feet, both shocked and delighted, "don't say that. But I wish I was a little like her."

"Well, Annie, I think you're just like her. But come out with me. I have a story to tell you. Give me your hand, and put your foot on the seat."

She was over the wall in a moment and before long they were seated under the trees of the meadow near where Annie had met him before. The brown twilight was coming on, and a warm sleepy hush pervaded earth and air, broken only by the stream below them, cantering away over its stones to join the Wan Water.

Time unmeasured by either passed without speech.

"They told me," said Alec at length, "that you and Curly had made it up."

"Alec!" exclaimed Annie, looking up in his face as if he had accused her of infidelity, but, instantly dropping her eyes, said no more.

"I would have found you before the first day was over if it hadn't been for that."

Annie's heart beat violently, but she said nothing. After a silence, Alec went on, "Did my mother ever tell you how the ship was lost?"

"No, Alec."

"It was a terrible, wind-blown snowstorm. We couldn't see more than a few yards ahead. The sails were down but we couldn't keep from drifting. All of a sudden a huge, ghastly thing came out of the evening to windward, bore down on us like a specter, and dashed us on a floating field of ice. The ship was thrown upon it with one side crushed in, but, thank God, nobody was killed. It was an awful night, Annie; but I'm not going to tell you about it now. We made a rough sledge, and loaded it with provisions, and set out westward, and were carried westward at the same time on the ice floe till we came near land. Then we launched our boat and got to the shore of Greenland. There we set out traveling southwards. Many of our men died, do what I could to keep them alive. But I'll tell you all about it another time if you like. What I want to tell you now is this: Every night, as sure as I lay down in the snow to sleep, I dreamed I was at home. All the old stories came back. I woke once, thinking I was carrying you through the water in the street by the school and that you were crying on my face. And when I woke up, my face was wet. I don't doubt but that I'd been crying myself. All the old faces came around me every night, Thomas Crann and James Dow and my mother—sometimes one and sometimes another—but you were *always* there.

"One morning when I woke up, I was alone. I don't rightly know how it happened. I think the men were nearly dazed with the terrible cold and the weariness of the travel, and I had slept too long and they forgot about me. And what do you think was the first thought in my head when I came to myself in the terrible white desolation of cold and ice and snow? I wanted to run straight to you and lay my head upon your shoulder. For I had been dreaming all night that

I was lying in my bed at home, terribly ill, and you were going about the room like an angel, with the glimmer of white wings about you, which I reckon was the snow coming through my dream. And you would never come near me, and I couldn't speak to cry for you to come. At last, when my heart was ready to break because you wouldn't look at me, you turned with tears in your eyes, and came to the bedside and leaned over me, and—"

Here Alec's voice failed him.

"So you see it was no wonder that I wanted you when I found myself all alone in the dreadful place, the very beauty of which was deadly . . .

"Well, that wasn't all. I was given more that day than I ever thought I'd get. Annie, I believe what Thomas Crann used to say must be true. Annie, I think a person may someday get a kind of a sight of the face of God. I was so downcast when I saw myself left behind that I sat down on a rock and stared at nothing. It was awful. And it grew worse and worse till the only comfort I had was that I couldn't live long. And, with that, the thought of God came into my head, and it seemed as if I had a right to call upon Him. I was so miserable." Alec's voice again trailed away.

"And there came over me a quietness, like a warm breath of spring air." His tone was stronger as he again took up the account. "I don't know what it was, but it set me upon my feet, and I started to follow the rest. Snow had fallen so I could hardly see their tracks. I never did catch up with them, and I haven't heard of them since then.

"The silence at first had been fearful; but now, somehow or other—I can't explain it—the silence seemed to be God himself all about me.

"And I'll never forget Him again, Annie."

She watched his face in wonder.

"I came upon tracks," he continued, "but not of our own men. They were the folk of the country. And they brought me where there was a schooner lying ready to go to Archangel. And here I am."

Was there ever a gladder heart than Annie's? She was weeping as if her life would flow away in tears. She had known that Alec would come back to God someday.

He ceased speaking, but she could not cease weeping. If she had tried to stop the tears, she would have been torn with sobs. They sat silent for a long time. At length Alec spoke again: "Annie, I don't deserve it—but *will* you be my wife someday?"

And all the answer Annie made was to lay her head on his chest and weep on.

64

·····················

Ending Fragments

The farm of Howglen prospered. Alec never practiced further in his profession, but he did become a first-rate farmer. Within two years Annie and he were married, and began a new chapter of their history.

When Mrs. Forbes found that Alec and Annie were engaged, she discovered that she in reality had been wishing it for a long time, and that the opposing sense of "duty" had been worldly.

Mr. Cupples came to see them every summer, and generally remained over the harvest. He never married. But he wrote a good book.

Thomas Crann and Cupples had many long disputes, and did each other much good. Thomas grew gentler as he grew older. And he learned to hope more for other people. And then he hoped more for himself too.

The first time Curly saw Annie after the wedding, he was astounded at his own presumption in ever thinking of marrying such a lady. When about thirty, by which time he had a good business of his own, he married Isie Constable—still little and still wise.

Margaret Anderson was taken good care of by Annie Forbes but kept herself clear of all obligation by never acknowledging any.

In the end Robert Bruce was forced to refund Mrs. Forbes the interest he had taken from her and had to pay back the last fifty pounds he owed to Annie. He died worth a good deal of money anyway, which must have been some comfort to him at the last.

Young Robert is a clergyman, has married a rich wife, hopes to be Moderator of the Church Assembly someday, and never alludes to his royal ancestor.

Afterword
A Closer Look At *The Maiden's Bequest*

Richard Reis, author of the very well-done analytical study entitled *George MacDonald* (Twayne Publishers, 1972), writes: "The author of 29 novels may be expected to produce at least one which is better than commonplace; such is MacDonald's *Alec Forbes of Howglen*. In plot especially, this work is intriguing, well-motivated, tightly integrated, and more original than most of MacDonald's realistic tales." Whatever your personal reaction to the story you have just completed, the mere fact that many critics such as Reis laud it shows that it deserves some special attention.

Reis summarizes his own view: "There are several aspects of *Alec Forbes of Howglen* which set it apart . . . especially in plot. Every incident is effectively integrated into the story."

If your familiarity with MacDonald has been primarily through the edited novels, you may at first not readily grasp the enormous significance of that statement; for a large percentage of my own editorial work addresses the difficulty of tangential material usually found in the originals. I prune and trim in order to more tightly weave the progress of the story line. But when one comes to *Alec Forbes,* the need for such editing is greatly diminished. For each character is laced in and throughout the story from beginning to end. Every incident furthers the story and enhances character development.

In addition, the main characters, Annie and Alec, grow, travel, mature and change while still maintaining their roots and earlier relationships. In *The Musician's Quest* we observe just the opposite. As Robert leaves Rothieden, so do we as readers, almost never to set eyes on it again. When Donal (*The Shepherd's Castle*) leaves home for Auchars, we never see Janet and Robert and the region of Gormgarnet again. This does not necessarily weaken these books; it simply points out the uniqueness of *The Maiden's Bequest*. From beginning to end we stay fully in tune with both Alec and Annie.

Robert Wolff, author of *The Golden Key* (Yale University Press, 1961), says:

> *Alec Forbes* does not fall apart because important characters vanish from the scene; instead they remain and grow and develop. When the hero goes off to the University, the author manages to follow his adventures there while simultaneously keeping his reader in touch with the fortunes of those left behind in Glamerton. *Alec Forbes* is all of [one] piece.

And Reis:

> . . . one never gets the feeling that material is forced into the story for mere

excitement. . . . At [one] point the reformed Murdoch Malison tries to become a minister instead of a schoolteacher, but fails when he forgets his sermon, which he had tried to memorize. . . . But the appearance in the story . . . is far from irrelevant; it serves admirably to engage our sympathy for the changed Malison, preparing for the pathos of the scene in which he dies trying to rescue his own crippled victim. Some of the characters, too, are remarkably effective. . . . Alec himself, Malison, Bruce, and especially Cupples, are complex, fascinating persons, clearly not "taken out of stock" but powerfully alive and real.

But perhaps the most striking aspect of *Alec Forbes of Howglen* is the fact that its happy ending is as compromised as life itself. The hero does not, as in so many Victorian novels . . . rise in the world and obtain . . . worldly "success"; instead, Alec's reform is rewarded by a good though not brilliant wife, and an honorable but humble career as a farmer.

Indeed, is there not a great satisfaction when Alec forsakes the potential honor and acclaim—and the wealth which accompany them—that could undoubtedly have been his in the social life of the city, and instead returns to his roots, and to Annie, the friend of his youth, to live out his days as a small-town farmer? This is one of MacDonald's most gratifying conclusions, not only because Alec finally discovers that he loves Annie, but also because of the career and status he lays down in the process. Similarly, Annie's monetary "bequest" to save the farm cements her love for Alec far above any earthly gain. This is not a "rags-to-riches" fairy tale, but something far better.

Somewhat unique to *The Maiden's Bequest* is MacDonald's approach to the religiosity of the community. His ordinary custom throughout many of his books is to clearly differentiate between hypocritically narrow Calvinists and their churches and his "saints" who ascribe to no doctrine other than a daily living out of the truth. (See Introductions to *The Shepherd's Castle* and *The Musician's Quest*.) However, this time MacDonald introduces two distinct churches of Glamerton, both Calvinist in their outlook and neither "right" nor "wrong." Modified are his slashing attacks on untrue doctrine and sham which find their way into most of his other novels. Here it seems MacDonald finds himself able to appreciate both the strengths and weaknesses in each of the worshiping bodies, allowing room for humanness and growth. There are no faultless saints here, just real people with both blind spots and human qualities which endear them to us. George Macwha, the carpenter, says the "muckle kirk does well enough for him," but his friend Thomas Crann, a dedicated and staunch member of the evangelical sect of Missionaries, views Macwha's shallowness with scorn. Yet with all his narrowness and inability to see beyond the confines of his own system of belief, we cannot help but like Crann. Indeed, he is one of the book's principal characters. And poor Mr. Cowie hasn't the faith or understanding to help Annie through her troubles about eternal hell-fire. And yet he has the compassion to offer help to her on another level (which Crann doesn't), and we love him for it. In the same way, we find ourselves drawn to Malison and Mr. Cupples through all their faults. In *The*

Maiden's Bequest MacDonald has presented a wide range of diverse and believable characters.

"Best of all," according to Wolff, "is . . . Cupples, the little weasened scholar who occupies the garret at the top of Alec Forbes' lodging house in Aberdeen, learned in all the disciplines, a poet, but a slave to alcohol. He stays sober all day, but as soon as he comes home at night, out comes the whisky bottle, and he drinks himself slowly to sleep."

Yet it is through Mr. Cupples that Alec ultimately finds the strength to stem the tide of his own drinking habits. Mr. Cupples's restoration in Glamerton, his friendships there, and his renewed acquaintance with nature prove to be one of the most delightful sections of the entire story.

One of the factors in MacDonald's own life which has long puzzled biographers concerns his cataloguing of a great library during the summer of 1842 when he was seventeen. Even his son Greville is uncertain about the facts surrounding the event. He writes in his *George MacDonald and His Wife:* ". . . he spent some summer months in a certain castle or mansion in the far North, the locality of which I have failed to trace, in cataloguing a neglected library." Though many have speculated, the location of this library has never been confirmed, nor any of the details of MacDonald's stay there. But the experience clearly had a profound impact on the growth of the young man, for mention of such material is found in at least seven of his novels.

Many have imagined, from *Alec Forbes, The Portent,* and others, the distinct possibility that MacDonald himself fell in love with a beautiful young lady of the house. Given the impressionable age of the youth, and the possible circumstances surrounding his brief months as librarian, it is not difficult to theorize that the lady of the mansion formed the basis for many of MacDonald's later heroines. Do we not see many common threads running through the personalities of Florimel, Euphra, Arctura—the beauty, the sly coyness, eyes hinting at hidden subtle design, the occasional impishness? In his development of each of these women, MacDonald seems to be trying to convey a certain duplicity—a surface shyness, motives that hint of subtle seduction and cunning, and yet on the other hand a deeper, true-hearted desire to grow and leave behind the masquerade which society and upbringing has, in a sense, forced them to wear. All his women progress from the one initial state to the other. Are we not, in fact, obtaining a picture of the woman MacDonald may have fallen in love with, an enchanting vision whom MacDonald wanted to believe was good and true (and so convinced himself in his youthful innocence) but who, in matter of fact, left him heartbroken at seventeen? The lady he fell in love with in the library in the North did not ultimately reveal her truth-loving nature, and MacDonald perhaps lamented, through Mr. Cupples, that if he had not been so foolish and blind in his youth, he would have been able to see the insincerity of her motives.

How much of Mr. Cupples's stirring story in chapter 50 is in fact autobiographical, we cannot even conjecture. But most intriguing of all is the fact that the falsehood of the girl's flirtation toward the young Cupples is revealed to the reader without Cupples even himself seeing it. She immediately reminds us of Euphra and Florimel and—can one assume?—MacDonald's own enchantress during that summer of '42. A single laugh at her triumph over helpless Cupples is the only evidence of her venom. But it is enough, and Cupples is undone. As Wolff perceptively notes:

> MacDonald makes Cupples himself reveal the girl's falseness without realizing it: is it not unlikely that an intelligent and well-educated young woman would *un*intentionally reach for a wicked book on the library shelf? Rather, are we not supposed to realize something that Cupples himself has never realized: the corrupt girl came to the library, unaware of the presence of the librarian, to find the book by the [evil creature], and when Cupples saw what she was doing she produced the excuse that she was looking for a book that would help her learn Gaelic?

Alec's story is fun. Spiritual growth within the characters is certainly an integral part of the book's development, for such is the essence of George Mac-Donald fiction. And nuggets of truth regarding God's character are imbedded throughout the text, as always. But the portentous weight of intensity is left for other books. For example, *The Musician's Quest* opens with Robert in a solitary mood—alone, meditative. The scene is cold, lonely, and introspective. And this melancholy feeling permeates the book all the way through.

But *The Maiden's Bequest* rings with a lighter sense of gladness. Winter comes to Glamerton just as bitterly as it does to Rothieden. Times are cruel for Annie in her garret. And school is a harsh place indeed, far worse for Annie and Alec than for Robert and Shargar. Yet the whole mood of *The Maiden's Bequest* remains one of joy and discovery.

Feel the difference between winter in Rothieden:

> . . . how drearily the afternoon had passed. He had opened the door again and looked out. There was nothing alive to be seen, except a sparrow picking up crumbs. . . . At last he had trudged upstairs . . . [and] remained there till it grew dark. . . . There was even less light than usual in the room . . . for a thick covering of snow lay over the glass of the small skylight. A partial thaw, followed by a frost, had fixed it there. It was a cold place to sit, but the boy had some faculty for enduring cold when that was the price to be paid for solitude. . . . [Outside] what was to be seen . . . could certainly not be called pleasant. A broad street with low houses of cold, gray stone, as uninteresting a street as most any to be found in the world. . . . The sole motion was the occasional drift of a film of white powder which the wind would lift like dust from the snowy carpet that covered the street. Wafting it along for a few yards, it would drop again to its repose, foretelling the wind on the rise at sundown—a wind cold and bitter as death—which would rush over the street and raise a denser cloud of the white dust to sting the face of any improbable person who might meet it in its passage.

And in Glamerton:

The winter came. One morning all awoke and saw a white world around them. Alec jumped out of bed in delight. It was a sunny, frosty morning. The snow had fallen all night, and no wind had interfered with the gracious alighting of the feathery water. Every branch, every twig was laden with its sparkling burden of flakes. . . . From the door opening into this fairyland Alec sprang into the untrodden space. He had discovered a world without even the print of human foot upon it. The keen air made him happy; and the peaceful face of nature filled him with jubilance. He was at the school door before a human being had appeared in the streets of Glamerton. Its dwellers all lay still under those sheets of snow, which seemed to hold them asleep in its cold enchantment.

As much as any other factor, perhaps, MacDonald's flexibility as a fictional craftsman stands among his most appealing attributes. Every book is uniquely its own. Therefore, I love *The Musician's Quest* precisely because it is so weighty. Its serious mood is in perfect harmony with the character of Robert Falconer. On the other hand, I delight in *The Maiden's Bequest* because it is *not* so ponderous. Its altogether different flavor fits its characters just as thoroughly.

What remain in my memory the longest are the pleasures of the summer and winter, the building and sailing of *The Bonnie Annie*, the snow, the flood, the blacksmith's forge whose heat provided such a haven of warmth for Annie in the middle of a wintry rain, the boyish shenanigans. As Wolff explains:

As the seasons follow each other at Glamerton, MacDonald catches their rhythm in his disciplined descriptions of the changes in the sky and the landscape: the northern lights flickering over the icy earth, the river in flood brawling against the bridges, the heat and beauty of the harvest-time, and the dismal endless rains of autumn.

Standing out among the many features of *The Maiden's Bequest* is MacDonald's portrayal of his people. While the story itself is perhaps not the most original or dramatic, the personalities painted are striking. The gradual changes MacDonald weaves into our sympathies for Malison and Cupples catch us almost unaware. It takes a master in the art of characterization to create such tenderness in our hearts toward a man like the schoolmaster whom we had every reason to hate such a short time earlier. Who can read of his experience in the pulpit without empathy and pity? And his poignant relationship with sad little Truffey sets us up for such a rush of tears when the bridge gives way. In addition, Mr. Cupples is far from the standard MacDonaldian counselor and spiritual advisor. No David Elginbrod, Andrew Comin, or Graham the schoolmaster here, only a failed scholar who seems little more than a wretched drunkard. And yet in his very weakness (following sound scriptural principle), Alec in the end is enabled to become strong. Do we not delight all the more when the reformed and rejuvinated Cupples dances about Glamerton, invigorated with the joy of life once again?

And of course there is the maiden heroine of our story, Annie herself. Is she not in fact the embodiment of what makes *The Maiden's Bequest* so intriguingly unique? She is attractive but not stunning—somewhat ordinary, shy, possessed of no riches or remarkable gifts. Her personality is subdued, slow to show itself, waiting to flower. Alongside Florimel, Arctura, and Clementina, she is positively unremarkable. Annie is not the usual leading lady. She is simplicity itself. "O God," she prays at night, "tak care o' me frae the rottans (rats)." School for Annie is sheer torment as she is "condemned to follow with an uncut quill, over and over again, a single straight stroke set by the master," or to give "Scripture proofs" of the various assertions of the Shorter Catechism. Her hand is stung by the master for her failures. She watches in speechless terror the punishments meted out around her. Paralyzed with fear, when Malison asks the question, "What doth every sin deserve?" she answers so simply, "A lickin'."

And even as she grows and matures, Annie's true nature remains dormant, sleeping. She faces life without airs or hint of sophistication. As she begins to realize her true feelings for Alec, she dares not reveal them to anyone, hardly dares admit them to herself. She is meekness itself, of the godly sort which will inherit the earth: innocence personified. As a result Annie stands distinct from any of MacDonald's other women—an atypical heroine.

Many of George MacDonald's novels take place, at least in part, in the genteel surroundings of aristocratic families, complete with formal drawing rooms, wealth, great mansions, titles and inheritances. If the hero is poor when the story opens, chances are he will become a nobleman before it is over. Not so in *The Maiden's Bequest.* We never see London, we meet no lairds or ladies, we hear of no castles or mansions within sight of Glamerton. The whole of the narrative takes place in humble surroundings and involves simple folk. And when Alec ultimately realizes his own feelings for Annie, when his eyes behold the blossoming of the flower that had been before him all along, we are left with a great sense of fulfillment that everything turned out "just as it should have." This is a down-to-earth romance, and therein lies its genius.

In summary, perhaps a brief quote from Lewis Carroll will capsulize our thoughts. In the entry for January 16, 1866, from *The Diaries of Lewis Carroll,* the creator of *Alice in Wonderland* wrote, "*Alec Forbes* . . . is very enjoyable, and the character of Annie Anderson is one of the most delightful I have ever met with in fiction."

—Michael Phillips

The Minister's Restoration

Contents

Introduction

The year was 1896. George MacDonald—Scottish novelist, poet, preacher, essayist, and lecturer—was reaching the end of a long and highly successful literary career. At 71 years of age, he had authored 51 books of a singularly diverse nature that had sold in the many millions of copies. He was held in the highest esteem as a scholar, a man of letters, and a gifted writer, as well as a spiritual sage. Some would have ventured to call him a prophet. Others spoke of his imaginative powers as genius.

Only a year previously his eerie *Lilith* had been released—that book which would come to be viewed by the critics as the crowning achievement to cap his distinguished life, that chilling fictional fantasy of death which various commentators have in retrospect viewed as a prelude to his own.

But now, a year later, the force of his imagination and concentration was gradually diminishing. He was able to travel but little. His days of teaching, lecturing, and writing were largely past. Many of the ailments which had stalked him throughout life were at last taking their toll. Three years later he would suffer the stroke that would effectively signal an end to his active life.

What then was left for this man, who had already done so much, to give to the world—a world that would in a very short time be able to remember him only through his books?

The answer to that question lies in the pages you are about to read. In that period between *Lilith* and the stroke which came at age 74, during the year 1896, George MacDonald sat down to write one last novel, which he called *Salted With Fire*.

A simple story, neither so long nor complex of plot and description as most of his earlier and lengthier novels, *Salted With Fire* somehow provides a fitting climax to MacDonald's historic and controversial career. Its essential themes echo in concise and straightforward manner those elements of fundamental spirituality that MacDonald had been conveying through his books, his characters, his poems, his sermons, and his very life for over forty years.

Many aspects of the faith MacDonald so cherished found their way onto these pages, and from a whole variety of perspectives, *Salted With Fire* typifies the fiction of George MacDonald. Here again we encounter a minister (like Wingfold, Drake, Bevis, Cowie) wrestling with the truth and claims of the gospel as he must evaluate the foundations of his own relationship with God. As he does so, other familiar themes come to bear upon his troubled but searching heart—what is the nature of repentance, how exhaustive is God's forgiveness, what is the path to restoration with God and man, and what is the nature of the Love which will spare no pain to break through into an individual heart?

Here too we encounter the dialect of the best of MacDonald's Scottish novels. With delight we meet another memorable, aging humble saint (reminding us particularly of Donal Grant's cobbler friend Andrew, as well as David Elginbrod, Alexander Graham, and Joseph Polwarth) who acts as spiritual mentor to those in need. There is the hearkening back to MacDonald's personal roots in Scotland; only six or seven miles southwest of MacDonald's hometown of Huntly is a tiny village called Tillathrowie which is quite possibly the setting for this story. The people and themes are agrarian, and we are strongly reminded of the intrinsic link in MacDonald's personal faith between his love for his homeland and his love for the Lord. And the final chapters of *Salted With Fire* provide a grand and victorious statement of the essence of faith, as MacDonald, now at the end of his life, viewed it—practical, living, growing, honest, and humble—rooted in the love of God that man must learn to choose as the best, indeed the only pathway into life.

The title of the book, perhaps as much as the contents themselves, gives us a window into George MacDonald's mind at the time he penned his tale. From the earliest stages of his career, George MacDonald found himself in theological difficulty with the fundamental Calvinist wing of Christendom because of his view of God's character. To the Calvinists, a sinner was lost, both in this life and in the life to come. To MacDonald, however, God's love was infinite, and extended itself toward all of creation, even potentially onto the other side of death if necessary, using whatever extremes of discipline and purposeful suffering as will open the eyes of repentance and cause His love to break through.

The very phrase "salted with fire" in so many ways capsulizes and provides a final and powerful statement of MacDonald's view of God's purifying and inescapable repentance-producing fire, which comes to bear in this story on young Blatherwick. Salt has long been both a practical and a spiritual symbol for and expression of purification. Thus, the very title of this book captures the theme of the whole, as does the quote from chapter fourteen: "There was no way around the purifying fire! He could not escape it; he must pass through it!"

Purification (salt) of the spirit comes through pain, through godly discipline, through searing repentance, through spiritual fire. Jesus said, "Everyone will be salted with fire," echoing the prophets Zechariah and Malachi, who said: "I will bring them into the fire: I will refine them like silver and test them like gold. They will call on my name and I will answer them" (Zech. 13:9) and, "But who can endure the day of his coming? . . . For he will be like a refiner's fire. . . . He will sit as a refiner and purifer of silver; he will purify the Levites and refine them like gold and silver" (Mal. 3:2–3).

It was scriptures such as these that George MacDonald felt revealed the true extent of God's love, harsh as they seemed on the surface, and the far-reaching purposefulness of His nature in all of life and even beyond death. Those who have attempted to categorize MacDonald through the years as a "liberal" (which he was to some) or a "conservative" (which he was to others) or a "universalist" (which he appeared to those who did not study his writings in sufficient depth), or a "heretic" (which he seemed to the staunch Calvinists of his day) have all largely missed the point in their attempts to pigeonhole him according to their pre-set standards. They overlook the intense hunger of his heart after God. They overlook the obedience and fruit of his life. For MacDonald, to this day, steadfastly resists all attempts to categorize him. His views do not fall neatly into any doctrinal "camp." He forged new theological ground by proposing entirely new and bold interpretations of many aspects of God's character, including: the purpose of the afterlife, of God's redemptive plan, of the deeper meaning of God's justice, of the limitlessness of the atonement, of the divine intent behind the purifying fire spoken of by the Old Testament prophets, and of the extent of God's ultimate victory over sin.

The title of this present book, therefore, as well as that of one of his well-known published sermons dealing with similar themes ("Our God Is a Consuming Fire"), in a sense pinpoints one of the key topics MacDonald felt keenly driven to communicate and which remained focal for him all his life. From his earliest days as a child, when he questioned God's condemnation of sinners, young George MacDonald grappled to come to grips with God's character and what His love entailed. As a youth he searched to integrate these questions into a consistent picture of God's love in harmony with His anger and justice. Finally as an adult he presented to the world a fully matured vision of a God of infinite love who was prepared to go to any lengths (even through the use of the purifying fire of His love) to redeem a man, to bring about repentance in the utter depths of his heart, and ultimately to heal and restore him and bring him back into fellowship with Him. It was convictions such as these that gave MacDonald such a victorious and visionary outlook concerning God's purposes, a vision communicated through his novels.

On an altogether different level, *Salted With Fire* speaks to the twentieth-century church about a problem as contemporary as today's newspapers and national events—sin, not only within the individual heart, but within the public ministry. Indeed, it is uncanny how prophetic MacDonald's subject matter is, written almost one hundred years ago, with respect to events that have rocked evangelicalism in America in recent years. And through the characters of George MacDonald's creation can be found properly scriptural solutions. Here we find no leveling of charges by fellow Christians and fellow ministers, no breakdown of unity within the body over issues that make the ministry a mockery in the eyes of a watching world, no attempts to hide and deceive and twist the truth, no plays for power, no motives rooted in money, no national scandal, no conditional repentance.

One hundred years ago, George MacDonald offered a simple solution to sin according to the biblical standard that today's church would do so well to heed. A definite order exists toward a total and godly resolution. *Repentance* for the wrong done must precede all else. Following repentance comes *forgiveness,* of a threefold nature—forgiveness by God, forgiveness on the part of others, and forgiveness of self. Once these two vital foundation stones have been laid, there can come *healing,* which is based in stepping down and humbly laying aside all claim to position, wealth, influence, and reputation. Then at last can come, in God's time and God's way, *restoration*. How greatly could today's church learn how to apply these basic truths as taught in the nineteenth century by the author of *Salted With Fire*.

Working on *Salted With Fire* presented both unique challenges as well as unique rewards. I found this book more difficult in certain ways than perhaps any of the other MacDonald novels I have edited to date. Part of this may be due to MacDonald's age at the time the book was written. Though I have no way of ascertaining this, some of his linguistic powers may have been fading. I seemed to detect more frequent rambling sentences, more organizational incongruities, less vivid descriptive passages. However, none of this in any way diminished the clarity of the truths that emerged.

Adding to this challenge was the fact that I had before me two editions of the original, both first editions—one American, one British, both published in 1897, and yet *different* textually. This made it difficult to tell (something Bible translators always face) which was the "truest" mode of expression or turn of phrase according to MacDonald's mind at the time of writing. By far the majority of the sentences in each of the two books were distinct. Sometimes one seemed more clear, sometimes the other, but generally I found the British edition to be preferable; it seemed slightly more lucid, and it is my guess that it was indeed the most recent draft of the book.

Neither of MacDonald's two bibliographers (John Malcolm Bulloch, Aberdeen, 1924; and Mary Nance Jordan, Wheaton, 1984), who have extensively catalogued all known published editions of MacDonald's original works, mention this discrepancy. My own conjecture is that when the book first appeared for serialization in the *Glasgow Weekly* magazine during the latter months of 1896, it was taken exactly as it was for the American edition, which was published the following year by Dodd-Mead. However, in final preparation for the British edition which was to follow the magazine's run, MacDonald no doubt did further editing of the manuscript. This would account for the Hurst and Blackett edition, also released in 1897, showing slightly more refinement.

One of the particular rewards in being able to share this book with you is the simple fact that this is my wife Judy's favorite of George MacDonald's novels. She has read it over and over, every time coming away with her deep hunger after God rekindled, and thirsting anew to have that purifying fire of God's love continue its surgical work in her heart.

She was quicker than I to perceive the spiritual content in *Salted With Fire*. She had read it, tearfully, three times, describing to me its impact on her, and all the while I was stalled with it. The difficulties of the original obscured for me the fundamental truths MacDonald was attempting to convey. But at every step, when I listened to what she was saying, I discovered her instincts to be true. She has always had an ear keenly tuned to MacDonald's essential themes. We all owe her our thanks for being an inspired encouragement to me, both with this book and many of the others.

Thus, this is a project which has been a double-edged labor of love on my part, both toward MacDonald, and toward her. All along I have felt as though I have been fulfilling a debt of gratitude to Judy for at last bringing into the attention of the public this book she had loved for so many years.

The novels containing Scottish dialect have been most meaningful to Judy. Somehow, the earthy and picturesque language, coming from the mouths of David Elginbrod, Andrew Comin, Janet Grant, or John MacLear, speaking in humble and simple terms about the things of God, has given the dialect itself a feel almost of holiness. To hear it in her mind's ear was to be transported to a simpler time, among simple people, who loved God with all the heart, soul, mind, and strength of their humble yet powerful lives.

Because of this it seemed only fitting to retain a good deal of that dialect while editing *Salted With Fire.* My objectives here have been just as they were in *The Laird's Inheritance,* in the Introduction to which I described the process of how and why I did what I did to the original Scots. For anyone interested I would refer you to that source, and I have here included a brief glossary for your added convenience. For those of you interested in the man MacDonald himself, there is now available a full-length biography, entitled *George MacDonald: Scotland's Beloved Storyteller,* also published by Bethany House. It is out of the flow of the spiritual themes of his life that his books can best be understood, and it is this flow which I have tried to capture in the biography. *Salted With Fire,* especially, takes on a poignant reality in light of the later years of MacDonald's life, knowing as you read that these are among the final words for which he will be remembered.

Finally, I enjoy hearing from you. Many have written me, and both I and the publishers continue to welcome your responses. In addition to the biography, I have prepared a small pamphlet on MacDonald which I would be happy to send you upon request. I hope you will get the pamphlet, will read the biography, and will write to let us know how MacDonald has been used of the Lord in your life.

God bless you all!
Michael Phillips
One Way Book Shop
1707 E Street
Eureka, CA 95501

Glossary

aboot—about
ahind—behind
ain—own
ale—give
an'—and
atween—between
ben-end—inner part of house
ben—inside
bide—abide, stand, stay
body—person
bonny—pretty
brose—oats, or oatmeal
burn—stream
canna—can't
cottar—farmer
couldna—couldn't
dautie—daughter
didna—didn't
differ—difference
dinna—don't
disna—doesn't
fer—for
frae—from
hae—have
haena—haven't
hasna—hasn't
hoo—how
jist—just

ken—know
kirk—church
kist—chest
limmer—rascal, rogue, fool
mains—farmhouse
mirk—darkness
mither—mother
muckle—much, great
nae—no
nicht—night
oot—out
o'er—over
o'—of
ony—any
sae—so
sich—such
soutar—cobbler
stourum—liquid gruel
toon—town
wee—little
weel—well
whaur—where
wi'—with
winna—won't
wi'oot—without
wouldna—wouldn't
ye—you
yer—your

1
. . . .
The Cobbler

The day would be a hot one, and the fragrant scents throughout the land had already come to life, borne on the wings of the warm morning's breezes. The subtle perfume, which spoke of oats and cattle, sheep and potatoes, and greening heather, saving its explosive bloom for fall, gave the eastern Scottish countryside its essential character and its people a contentment of spirit. The night had passed, the dawn had come, and still the earth gave of itself to feed those who dwelt upon it.

Outside the rural village small farms dotted the landscape, some but an acre of rocky ground where poor cottars struggled with a cow or two and a garden of potatoes to carve out a meager living. Others, such as the holdings of Stonecross, were of considerable extent.

But size and apparent means notwithstanding, all was not as it once had been for the Blatherwicks of that estate—a family whose dawn was not yet at hand despite the coming of a new day to the land. For the son and heir of Stonecross had left home—a statement sadly reflecting truth in both the physical and spiritual realms—and within the house where hope once reigned a certain cloud of uneasiness had descended. However, the burning of liberating sorrow lying on the distant horizon was not visible to Marion and Peter Blatherwick. Their only son, James, studying in Edinburgh with hopes for the ministry, was one of whom they had been proud and for whom they had cherished dreams of a strong character. And though vague hints had grown perceptible, in their occasional disquiet they yet had little inkling to what degree he had left the home of his heavenly Father as well. Like the prodigal, but with no inheritance in hand, he had turned from both his fathers, thinking to make his mark in the world by his intellect, not his honor. But the purifying fires of his redemptive trial had not yet begun.

In God's kingdom, however, a man's salvation rarely comes without the prayers of another who labors unseen. In the village of Tiltowie, two or three miles distant, stood another house—a humble dwelling—where the householder remained in the light of loving fellowship with his Father above. John MacLear, the town's cobbler, who lived with his daughter, Margaret, dwelt in a spiritual atmosphere so unlike that which surrounded young Blatherwick that few in the world—gazing upon mere appearances—would have imagined that the poor village soutar was miles farther along the road of life than the well-placed seminarian. Neither would any have guessed that the prayerful ordeal of the old man on behalf of the young childhood friend of his daughter's had been underway long before

James knew there was anything within him requiring the salting of God's fire, or the prayers of a righteous man.

But though one was growing in light while the other groped in darkness, the whole story was far from told. For there is always hope even for the most wayward of God's children. The shepherd's staff of his Son never ceases seeking the lost of his Father's sheep, whatever cleansing afflictions that salvation may require.

In the house of light, both old and young had risen with the sun, and now Margaret was preparing to leave her father as he glanced up from the shoes upon which his deft and careful hands had been working.

"Whaur are ye off to this bonny mornin', Maggie, my dear?" said the cobbler, looking toward his daughter as she stood in the doorway with her own shoes in her hand.

"Jist o'er t' Stonecross, wi' yer permission, Father, to ask the mistress for a few handfuls o' chaff; yer bed's grown a mite hungry for more."

"Hoot, the bed's weel enough, lassie!"

"It's anything but weel enough. 'Tis my part t' look after my ain father, an' see that there be nae knots in either his bed or his porridge."

"Ye're jist like yer mither all o'er again, lass! Weel, I winna miss ye that much, for the minister Pethrie'll be in this mornin'."

"Hoo do ye know that, Father?"

"We didna agree very weel last night, an' I'm certain he'll be back, nae jist for his shoes, but t' finish his argument."

"I canna bide that man—he's such a quarrelsome body!"

"Toots, bairn! I dinna like t' hear ye speak scornful o' the good man that has the care o' oor souls."

"It would be more t' the purpose if ye had the care o' his!"

"An' see I have. Hasna everybody the care o' every other's'?"

"Ay. But he presumes upon it—an' ye dinna; there's the difference!"

"But ye see, lassie, the man has nae insight—none t' speak o', that is. An' it's pleased God t' make him a wee bit slow an' some twisted in what he thinks. Why, we canna yet see, but 'tis for the man's own good, o' that we can be sure. He has nae notion even o' the work I put into this shoe o' his—that I'm this moment laborin' over. But his time t' see'll come. The Lord'll make sure o' that!"

"Yer work's sorely wasted on him 'at canna see the thought in it."

"Is God's work wasted upon you an' me except when we see all o' it an' understan' it, Maggie?"

The girl was silent. Her father resumed.

"There's three concerned in the matter o' the work I may be at: first, my own duty t' the work—that's me. Then him I'm workin' for—that's the minister. An' then Him that sets me t' the work—an' ye ken who that is. Noo, which o' the three would ye hae me leave oot o' the consideration?"

For another moment the girl continued silent; then she said: "Ye must be right, Father. I believe it, though I canna jist see all o' it. A body canna like everybody, an' the minister's jist the one man I canna bide."

"Ay, ye could, if ye loved the *one* as He ought t' be loved, an' as ye must learn t' love him."

"Weel, I'm not come t' that wi' the minister yet!"

"It's the truth—but 'tis a sore pity, my dautie."

"He provokes me the way he speaks to you, Father—him that's not fit t' tie the thong o' yer shoe."

"The Master would let him tie his, an' say thank ye."

"It aye seems t' me that he has such a scanty way o' believin'! It's hardly like believin' at all. He winna trust him for nothin' that he hasna his own word, or some other body's for. Do ye call that trustin' him?"

It was now the father's turn to be silent for a moment. Then he said, "Leave the judgin' o' him to his own master, lassie. I hae seen him sometimes sorely concerned fer other folk."

"Concerned that they wouldna agree wi' him, an' were condemned in consequence—wasna that it?"

"I canna answer ye that, bairn."

"Weel, I ken he doesna like you—not one wee bit. I ken he's talkin' against ye t' other folk."

"Maybe. Then more's the need I should love him."

"But hoo *can* ye, Father? The more I was t' try, the more I jist couldna."

"Ye could try, an' the Lord could help ye."

"I dinna ken. I only ken that ye say it, an' I must believe ye. None the more can I see hoo it's ever t' be brought aboot."

"No more can I, though I ken it can be. But jist think, my own Maggie, hoo would anybody else ever ken that one o' us was his disciple if we were disputin' aboot the holiest things—at least what the minister counts the holiest, though maybe I ken better? It's when two o' us strive against each other that what's called a schism begins, an' I jist winna, please God—an' it does please him. He never said, Ye must all think the same way, but he did say, Ye must all love one another, an' no strive amoong yersel's."

"Ye dinna go to his kirk, Father."

"Na, for I'm afraid sometimes lest I should stop lovin' him. It matters little aboot going t' the kirk every Sunday, but it matters a heap aboot lovin' one another."

"Weel, Father, I dinna believe that I can love him any day, so wi' yer leave, I'll be off to Stonecross afore he comes."

"Go yer way, lassie, an' the Lord go wi' ye, as once he did wi' them that was goin' t' Emmaus."

With her shoes in her hand, the girl was leaving the house when her father called after her, "Hoo'll folk ken that I provide for my own when my bairn goes unshod? If ye like, take off yer shoes when ye're oot o' the toon."

"Are ye sure there's no hypocrisy about such a false show, Father?" asked Maggie, laughing. "I must jist hide them better."

As she spoke she put them in the empty bag she carried for the chaff.

"There—that's a hidin' o' what I have—not a pretendin' t' have what I haven't! I'll be home in good time for yer tea, Father. I can walk so much better withoot them," she added as she threw the bag over her shoulder. "I'll put them on when I come t' the heather."

"Ay, ay, go yer way, an' leave me t' the work ye haena the grace t' advertise by wearin' it."

As she passed it on her way, Maggie looked in at the window and got a last sight of her father. The sun was shining into the little bare room, and her shadow fell upon him as she passed. But his form lingered clear in the chamber of her mind after she had left him far behind her. There it was not her shadow, but rather the shadow of a great peace that rested upon him as he bent over the shoe, his mind fixed indeed upon his work, but far more occupied with the affairs of quite another region.

Mind and soul were each so absorbed in their accustomed labor that never did either interfere with that of the other. His shoemaking lost nothing when he was deepest sunk in some one or other of the words of his Lord which he was seeking to understand. In his leisure hours he was an intense reader, but it was nothing in any book that now occupied him; it was instead the live Good News, the man Jesus Christ himself. In thought, in love, in imagination, that man dwelt in him, was alive in him, and made him alive. For the cobbler believed absolutely in the Lord of Life, was always trying to do the things he said, and strove to keep his words abiding in him. Therefore he was what the parson called a mystic, yet was at the same time the most practical man in the neighborhood. Therefore, he made the best shoes, because the work of the Lord did abide in him.

Not many more minutes passed when the door opened and the minister came into the kitchen. The cobbler always worked there that he might be near his daughter, whose presence never interrupted either his work or his thought, or even his prayers, which at times seemed involuntary as a vital automatic impulse.

"It's a grand day," said the minister. "It seems to me that on just such a day will the Lord come, nobody expecting him, and the folk all following their various callings, just as when the flood came and surprised them all."

Without realizing it, the man was reflecting on what the soutar had been saying during their previous discussion. Neither did he happen to think, at the moment, that it was the Lord himself who had said it first.

"An' I was thinkin', this very minute," returned the cobbler, "that it would be a bonny day for the Lord t' go aboot among his own folk. I was thinkin' that maybe he was walkin' wi' Maggie up the hill t' Stonecross—closer t' her, maybe, than she could see or think."

"You're a good deal taken up with vain imaginings, MacLear," returned the minister. "What scripture do you have for such a notion that has no practical value?"

"Indeed, sir, what scripture hae I for takin' my breakfast on this or any mornin'? Yet I ne'er look for a judgment t' fall upon me for eatin' it! I think we do more things in faith than we ken—yet still not enough! I was thankful for what

I ate, though, I know that, an' maybe that'll stan' for faith. But if I go on this way, we'll be beginnin' as we left off last night! An' we hae t' love one anither, not accordin' t' what the one thinks, but accordin' as each kens the Master loves the other, for he loves the two o' us t'gither."

"But how do you know he's pleased with you?"

"I said nothin' aboot that. I said he loves us."

"For that he must be pleased with you."

"I dinna think aboot that. I jist take my life in my han', an' give it t' him. An' he's ne'er turned his face from me yet. Eh, sir! think what it would be if he did!"

"But we mustn't think of him other than he would have us think."

"That's why I'm hangin' aroun' his door, an' lookin' aboot for him."

"Well, I don't know what to make of you. I must just leave you to him."

"Ye couldna do a kinder thing! I desire nothin' better from man or minister than t' be left t' him."

"Well, well, see to yourself."

"I'll see t' him, an' try t' love my neighbor—that's you, Mr. Pethrie. I'll hae yer shoes ready by Saturday. I trust they'll be worthy o' the feet God made, an' that hae t' be shod by me. I trust an' believe they'll not distress ye, or interfere wi' yer preachin'. I'll bring them to ye mysel'."

"No, no don't do that! Let Maggie come with them. You would only be putting me out of humor for the Lord's work with your foolish carrying on."

"Weel, I'll sen' Maggie, then—only ye might oblige me by not talkin' t' her, for ye might put *her* oot o' humor, an' then she mightna give yer sermon fair play the next mornin'."

The minister closed the door with some sharpness.

2

·······················

The Student

In the meantime Maggie was walking shoeless and bonnetless up the hill to the farm she sought. The June morning was now hot, tempered by a wind from the northwest. The land was green with the slow-rising tide of the young grain, among which the cool wind made little waves, showing the brown earth between them on the dry face of the hill. A few fleecy clouds shared the high blue realm with the keen sun.

As she rose to the top of the road, the gable of the house came suddenly into her sight, and near it was a sleepy old gray horse, treading his ceaseless round at the end of a long lever, too listless to feel the weariness of a labor that to him must have seemed unprogressive. It did not seem to give the horse any consolation to listen to the commotion he was causing on the other side of the wall, where an antiquated threshing machine was in full response with many diverse movements to the monotony of his circular motion. Nearby a peacock, as conscious of his glorious plumage as indifferent to the ugliness of his feet, kept time with his swaying neck to the motion of those same feet, as he strode with stagey gait across the cornyard, now and then stooping to spitefully pick up a stray grain, and occasionally erecting his neck to give utterance to a hideous cry of satisfaction at his own beauty, as unlike it as ever discord was to harmony.

Just as the sun touched the meridian the old horse stopped and stood still; the hour of rest and food had come, and he knew it. The girl passed one of the green-painted doors of the farmhouse and stopped at the kitchen one. It stood open, and a ruddy maid answered her knock, with question in her eyes and a smile on her lips at sight of the shoemaker's daughter, whom she knew well. Maggie asked if she might see the mistress.

"Here's the soutar's Maggie wantin' ye, mem!" called the maid, and Mrs. Blatherwick, who was close at hand, came forward and Maggie humbly but confidently made her request. It was kindly granted, and Maggie at once proceeded to the barn to fill the bag she had brought with the light plumy covering of the husk of the oats, the mistress of Stonecross helping her, and talking away to her as she did so, for both the soutar and his daughter were favorites with her and her husband, and she had not seen either of them for some time.

"Ye used t' know oor James in the old days, Maggie," she went on, for the two had played together as children at school, although growth and difference of station had gradually put an end to their friendship. As much as she liked Maggie, the mother now referred to her son somewhat guardedly, seeing that James was now on his way to becoming a great man since he was a divinity student. For in the Scotch church every minister, until he has discredited himself at least, is regarded with quite a high degree of respect, and therefore her son was prospectively to his mother a man of no little note.

Maggie remembered how, when a boy, he had liked to talk to her father, who listened to him with a curious look on his rugged face, while he set forth the commonplaces of a lifeless theology. But she remembered also that she had never heard her father make the slightest attempt to lay open to the youth his stores of what one or two in the place counted wisdom and knowledge. He only listened, and, until young James should ask for his insight, seemed content to say little on his own side.

"He's a clever laddie," he had once said to Maggie, "an' if he gets his eyes open in the course o' his life, he'll doubtless see somethin'. But he disna yet ken that there's anything real t' be seen ootside or inside o' him." When he had heard that James was going to study divinity, he shook his head and was silent.

"I'm jist home from payin' him a short visit," Mrs. Blatherwick went on. "I came home but two nights ago. He's lodgin' wi' a decent widow in Arthur Street, in a room up a long stair. She looks after his clothes an' sees t' the washin' an' does her best t' keep him tidy. But Jeamie was always particular aboot his appearance! So I was weel pleased wi' the old woman."

The conversation gradually moved into other channels until Maggie's bag was full, and with hearty thanks she took her leave of Mrs. Blatherwick and returned to her father, to whom she passed on the news of James she had received. The cobbler received it with a somber expression, turned away from his work for a few moments, and was silent. Maggie always knew when he was praying, and left him alone. She did not altogether understand the deep concern he had shown of late for the young Blatherwick, but she respected it because she knew it originated out of his heart of compassion.

In her conveyance of the news concerning her son, however, Mrs. Blatherwick did not open the discussion in the direction that should have been of most concern. For there was another in the Edinburgh lodging who did not appear more often than she must, at least so long as Mrs. Blatherwick was there, and of whom the mother had made no mention to her husband upon her return, any more than she did on this day to Maggie MacLear. Indeed, at first she had taken so little notice of her that she could hardly be said to have seen her at all.

This was a girl of about sixteen, who did far more for the comfort of her aunt's two lodgers than her aunt who reaped all the advantage. If Mrs. Blatherwick had let her eyes rest upon her but for a moment, she would probably have looked again, and would certainly have discovered that she was a good-looking and graceful little creature, with blue eyes and hair as black and fine and plentiful as could be imagined. She might have discovered as well a certain look of devotion which, when it came to her relation to her son James, Mrs. Blatherwick would assuredly have counted dangerous. But seeing her poorly dressed and looking untidy, the mother took her for an ordinary servant girl and gave her no particular attention. And she did not for a moment doubt that her son saw the girl just as she did.

He was her only son, and her heart was full of ambition for him, and she thought long about the honor he would eventually bring her and his father. The father, however, caring much less for his good looks, had neither the same satisfaction in him nor an equal expectation from him. In fact, neither of his parents had as yet reaped much pleasure from his existence, however full their hopes might be for the time to come. There were two things working against such parental satisfaction—the first, that James had never been open-hearted and communicative of his feelings or doings toward them; and the second, and the worse, he had come to feel a certain unexpressed claim of superiority over them. It would surely have done nothing to comfort their uneasiness about him had they noted that the existence of such a feeling of superiority was more or less evident in all his relationships with most everyone he met. This conceit showed itself in a stiff incommunicative reluctance, a contempt for any sort of manual labor, by the affectation of a ridiculously proper form of English, from all of which his simple and old-fashioned father shrank with dislike.

He was glad enough that his son should be better educated than himself, but he could not help feeling that his son's ways of asserting himself were but signs of foolishness, especially as conjoined with his wish to be a minister. Peter was full of simple paternal affection, yet it was completely quenched by the behavior of his son. He was continually aware of something that seemed an impassable gulf between son and parents. Peter himself was profoundly religious and full of a great and simple righteousness—that is, of a loving sense of fair play, a very different thing, indeed, from what most of those who count themselves religious mean when they talk of the righteousness of God.

However, James was little able to yet see this or other great qualities in his father. It was not that he was consciously disrespectful to either of his parents, or even that his behavior was unloving. He honored their character, but shrank from the simplicity of their manners. He had never been disobedient and had done what he could to be outwardly religious enough to convince himself that he was a righteous youth, or at least enough to nourish his ignorance of the fact that he was far from being the person of moral strength that he imagined himself. The person he saw in the mirror of his self-consciousness was a very fine and altogether trustworthy young man; the reality so twisted in its reflection was but a decent lad, as lads go, who had not the slightest notion of his true self.

James was one of the many bound up in the slavery of reverencing the judgments of society. Often without knowing it, such judge life, and truth itself, by the falsest of all measures—that is, the judgment of others falser than themselves. They do not ask what is true or right, but what folk will think and say about this or that. James, for instance, completely missed the point of what being a gentleman was, but his habit was of always asking, in such and such a circumstance, how a gentleman would behave. Thinking himself a man of honor, he would never tell a lie or break a promise. But he did not mind raising expectations that he had not the least intention of fulfilling, a more subtle misapplication of the same virtue.

Being a Scot lad, it is hardly to be wondered at that he should turn to theology as a means of livelihood. Neither is it surprising that he should have done so without any conscious love for God, for it is not in Scotland alone that men take refuge in the church when they have no genuine call to it. James's ambition was nonetheless contemptible that it was a common one—that, namely, of distinguishing himself in the pulpit.

Mr. Pethrie, the local minister whom it cost the cobbler so much care and effort to love, was yet far removed from James in this regard. Personal ambition did not count a great deal with him, which surely one day would be counted to his credit. Though intellectually small, he was a good man and certainly not a coward where he judged people's souls in danger. He sought to save the world by preaching a God eminently respectable to those who could believe in such a God, even though the God he preached was not a particularly grand one. Through his life, nevertheless, he showed himself in many ways a believer in him who revealed a grand and larger God indeed—which did not, however, prevent him from looking down on the cobbler as one whose notions were in rebellion against God.

But young Blatherwick was cut out of a different cloth even than old and good Mr. Pethrie. He had already, as a result of his theological studies, begun to turn his back upon several of the special tenets of Calvinism. This in itself, of course, made of him neither a better nor a worse man. He had cast aside, for instance, the doctrine of an everlasting hell for the unbeliever. But in so doing, as with other doctrines, he did not fill himself instead with a heart after truth and a love for the Man of Truth, but left his fields fallow for the cultivation of nothing but weeds and half-baked notions of men. Sweeping his empty house clean, he made of it all the more suitable a home for the demons of falsehood because he did not seek doctrines of truth with which to replace those he repudiated.

Mr. Pethrie, on the other hand, held to the aforementioned doctrine as absolutely fundamental, as with all those of Scottish Calvinism, while the cobbler, who had discarded it almost from his childhood, positively refused to enter into any argument on the matter with the disputatious little man. Long ago he had learned that the minister was unable to perceive any force in the cobbler's argument that to tell a man he must one day give in and repent would have greater force with the unbeliever than to tell him that the hour would come when repentance itself would do no good.

In the meantime, as James studied his Scotch theology, he kept his changing views to himself. He knew the success of his probation and ministerial license depended on his skillfully concealing any hint of his freer opinions. He must not jeopardize his career until his position was secure.

He was in his final year, and the close of his studies in divinity was drawing close at hand.

3

• • • • • • • • • • • • • • • • • •

The Sin

The day was a stormy one in the great northern city, and young James Blatherwick sat in the same shabbily furnished room where his mother had visited him in the ancient house, preparing for what he regarded as his career. The great clock of a church in the neighboring street had just begun to strike five of a wintry afternoon, dark with snow—falling and still to fall—when a gentle tap came to his door. He opened it to the same girl I have already mentioned, who came in with a tray and the makings for his most welcomed meal of coffee and bread and butter. She set it down in silence, which seemed to contain more than the mere silence of a servant, gave him one glance of devotion, and was turning to leave the room when he looked up from the paper he was writing, and said, "Don't be in such a hurry, Isy. Haven't you time to pour out my coffee for me?"

Isy was a small, dark, neat little girl, with finely formed features, and a look of childlike simplicity, not altogether different from childlikeness. She answered him first with her blue eyes full of love and trust, and then with her voice.

"Plenty of time. What else do I have to do than to see you're comfortable?"

He shoved aside his work, looked up at her with some intent consideration in his gaze, pushed his chair back a little from the table, and replied, "What's the matter with you this last day or two, Isy? You've not been like yourself."

She hesitated a moment, then answered, "It's nothing, I suppose, but just that I'm growing older and beginning to think about things."

She stood near him. He put his arm round her little waist and tried to draw her down to sit upon his knees, but she resisted.

"I don't see what difference that can make all at once, Isy. We've known each other so long there can be no misunderstanding between us. You have always been good and modest, and most attentive to me all the time I have been in your aunt's house."

"That's but been my duty. But it's almost over now!" she said with a sigh that indicated tears somewhere, and yielded to the increased pressure of his arm.

"What makes you say that?" he returned, giving her a warm kiss, plainly neither unwelcome nor the first.

"Don't you think it would be better to drop that kind of thing now?" she said, and tried to rise from his lap, but he held her fast.

"Why now, more than at any other time? What is the difference with today all of a sudden? What has put this idea into your pretty little head?" he asked.

"It has to come someday, and the longer from now the harder it'll be."

"But tell me, what has set you to thinking about it all at once?"

She burst into tears. He tried to soothe and comfort her, but in struggling not to cry she only sobbed the worse. At last, however, she succeeded in faltering out an explanation.

"Auntie's been telling me that I should look after my heart so I won't lose it altogether! But it's gone already," she went on with a fresh outburst, "and it's no use crying to it to come back to me! I might as well cry on the wind as it blows by me. I can't understand it. I know well enough you'll soon be a great man with all the town wanting to hear you. And I know just as well that I'll have to sit still in my seat and look up to where you stand—not daring to say a word, not even daring to think a thought lest somebody sitting beside me should hear what I'm thinking. For it would be impudent then for me to think that once I was sitting where I'm sitting now—and right in the very church."

"Didn't you ever think, Isy, that maybe I might marry you someday?" said James jokingly, confident in the social gulf between them.

"No, not once. I knew better than that! I never even wished it. For that would be no friend's wish; you would never get on if you did. I'm not fit to be a minister's wife—nor worthy of it. I might not do that badly in a tiny little place—but among grand folk, in a big town—for that's where you're sure to be—eh me, me! All the last week or two I haven't been able to help seeing you drifting away from me, out and out to the great sea where never a thought of Isy would come near you again; and why should there? You didn't come into the world to think about me or the likes of me, but to be a great preacher and leave me behind you, like a sheaf of corn you have just cut and left in the field!"

Here came another burst of bitter weeping, followed by words whose very articulation was a succession of sobs.

"Eh me! Now I've clean disgraced myself!"

As to young Blatherwick, I doubt that anything of evil intent was passing through his mind during this confession, and yet what was it but utterly selfish that he found a certain gratification in the fact that this simplehearted and very pretty girl loved him unsought, and had told him unasked? A truehearted man would have at once perceived what he was bringing upon her and taken steps to stop it. But James's vanity got the upper hand over him. And while his ambition made him think of himself as so much her superior that there could be no thought of marrying her, it did not prevent him from yielding to the delight of being so admired. Isy left the room not a little consoled and with a new hope in her innocent imagination. James remained to exult over his conquest and indulge a more definite pleasure than before in the person and devotion of the girl. As to any consciousness of danger to either of them, it was no more than the uneasy stir on the shore of a storm far out at sea.

As to her fitness to be a minister's wife, he had never asked himself a question concerning it. But in truth, she could very soon have grown far fitter for the position than he was now for that of a minister. In character she was much beyond him, and in breeding and consciousness far more of a lady than he of a gentleman. Her manners were immeasurably better than his, because they were simple and aimed at nothing; she had no hidden motives. Instinctively she avoided anything she would have recognized as uncomely. She did not know that simplicity was the purest breeding, yet from mere truth of nature practiced it without knowing it. If her words were old-fashioned, her tone was less so. James would, I am sure, have admired her if she had been dressed on Sundays in something more showy than a simple cotton gown. But her aunt was poor, and she even poorer, for she had no fixed wages. And I fear that her poverty had its influence in the freedoms he allowed himself with her.

Isy's aunt was a weak as well as unsuspicious woman, who had known better days, and pitied herself because they were past and gone. She gave herself no anxiety about her niece's prudence. It would have required a man, not merely of greater goodness than James, but of greater insight into the realities of life as well, to perceive the worth of the girl who waited upon him with a devotion far more angelic than servile.

Thus things went on for a while, with a continuous strengthening of the pleasant yet not altogether easy bonds in which Isobel walked, and a constant increase in the power of the attraction that drew the student to the self-yielding girl. At last the appearance of another lodger in the house, with the necessary attentions he began to demand as well on Isy's time, was the means of opening young Blatherwick's eyes to the state of his own feelings. Realizing that he was dangerously in peril of falling in love with one of such low station, he knew that if he did not mean to go further, here it must stop. He therefore began to change a little in his behavior toward her whenever she came into his room to serve him.

Poor Isy was immediately aware of the change but attributed it to a temporary absorption in his studies. Soon, however, she could not doubt that not merely was his voice changed toward her, but that his heart had also grown cold to her. For there was more at work than mere jealousy; what concerned the minister-to-be more than anything was the danger into which he was drifting of irrecoverably damaging his prospects for the future with an imprudent marriage. "To be saddled with a wife," as he expressed it to himself, before he had the opportunity to distinguish himself and before a church was attainable to him was a thing he could not contemplate even for a moment. So when one day Isobel sorrowfully asked him some indifferent question, the uneasy knowledge that he was on the verge of wrecking her happiness all the more by his rejection made him answer her roughly. White as a ghost she stood silently staring at him for a moment, sick at heart, and then fainted on the floor.

He was suddenly seized with an overpowering remorse that brought back all the tenderness he had felt for her earlier. James sprang to her, lifted her in his arms, laid her on the sofa, and cast all his previous cautions to the wind by lavishing caresses and kisses upon her, until she recovered sufficiently to know that she lay in the false paradise of his arms, while he knelt over her in a passion of regret, the first such passion of love he had felt for her. He poured into her ear words of incoherent dismay, which, taking shape as she revived, soon became promises of love and vows to remain with her forever. Thereupon, worse consequences followed. Dreamily coming to herself, before she was fully master of her emotions again, Isy returned his affections heatedly, with the result that her fervid lover lost control of his altogether. At the moment when self-restraint had become most imperative, his trust in his own honor became the last loop of the snare about to entangle his and her very life. At the moment when a genuine love would have stopped, in order to surround her with arms of safety rather than passion, he ceased to be his sister's keeper. Cain ceased to be his brother's when he slew him.

But the vengeance on his unpremeditated treachery came close upon its heels. The moment Isy left the room weeping and pallid, conscious of no love but rather of a miserable shame, James threw himself down, writhing as in the claws of a hundred demons. He had done the unthinkable!

And the day after the next he was to preach his first sermon in front of his class, in the presence of his professor of divinity! His immediate impulse was to rush from the house and home to his mother on foot. It would probably have been well for him had he indeed done so, confessed everything, and turned his back on the church and his paltry ambition altogether. But he had never been open with his mother, and he feared his father, not knowing the tender righteousness of his heart, or the springs of love that would at once have opened to meet the sorrowful tale of his sliding-back son.

But instead of fleeing at once to that city of refuge, he fell to pacing the room in helpless bewilderment. And it was not long before he was searching every corner of his reviving consciousness—not exactly for any justification, but for what rationalization of his "fault" might be found. And it was not long before a multitude of sneaking arguments, imps of Satan, began to come at the cry of the agony of this lover of self.

But in that agony there came no detestation of himself because of his humiliation of the trusting Isobel. He did not yet loathe his abuse of her confidence by his miserable weakness—the hour of a true and good repentance was not yet come. The only shame he felt was in the failure of his own fancied strength; there was as yet no shame in the realization of what he was. All he could think of was what contempt would come to him if the thing should ever come to be known. The pulpit, the goal of his ambition, the field of his imagined triumphs, the praise he had dreamed of all these years—had he thrown it all away in a moment of folly? The very thought of it made him sick!

Still, there yet lay the chance that no one might hear a word of what had happened. Isy would surely never tell anyone—least of all her aunt! He had promised to marry the poor girl, and that possibly he would have to do. But it could be managed, though certainly nothing was to be contemplated any time soon. There could at the moment be no necessity for such an extreme measure.

He would wait and see. He would be guided by events. As to the sin of the act—how many countless others had fallen like him, and no one had ever been the wiser! Never would he so offend womankind again. And in the meantime, he would let it go, and try to forget it—in the hope that Providence now, and at some future time, would bury it from all men's sight. He would go on the same as if the ugly thing had not so cruelly happened, had cast no such cloud over the fair future that lay before him.

And by the time his rationalizations had progressed this far, they had—as they often do—become justifications, and his selfish regrets came to be mingled with a certain annoyance that Isy should have yielded so easily. Why had she not aided him to resist the weakness that had wrought his undoing? She was as much to blame as he. And for her unworthiness was he to be left to suffer?

Within half an hour he had returned to the sermon he had in hand, revising it for the twentieth time, to have it perfect before finally committing it to memory; for the orator would have it seem the very thing it was not—the outcome of extemporaneous feeling—so the lie of his life be crowned with success. During what remained of the next two days he spared no labor, and at last delivered it with considerable unction and felt he had achieved his end. On neither of those days did Isy make any appearance. Her aunt told him that she was in bed with a bad headache.

The next day she was about her work as usual, but never once looked up. He imagined that she was mad at him and did not venture to say a word. But indeed, he had no wish to speak to her, for what was there to be said? A cloud was between them; a great gulf seemed to divide them. He found he was no longer attracted to her, and wondered how he could have so delighted in her presence only a short while earlier.

It was not that his resolve to marry her wavered; he fully intended to keep his promise to her. But he would have to wait for the proper time, the right opportunity to reveal his engagement to his parents. But after a few days, during which there had been no return to their former familiarity, it was with a fearful kind of relief that he learned she was gone to pay a visit to an old grandmother in the country. He did not care that she had gone without saying goodbye to him; he only wondered if she could have said anything to incriminate him. The school session came to an end while she was still gone. He formally moved out of her aunt's house and went home to Stonecross.

His father at once felt a wider division between them than before, and his mother was now compelled also to acknowledge that they were not one with their son. At the same time he carried himself with less arrogance, and seemed almost humbled rather than uplifted by his success with his schooling.

During the year that followed he made several visits to Edinburgh, but never did he inquire or hear anything about Isy. Before long he received a position in a somewhat stylish parish, by way of a gift from a certain duke who had always been friendly with his father as an unassuming tenant of one of his largest farms in the north. With a benefice in hand whereby he could put to use his less than modest ecclesiastical gifts, he might now have taken steps to fulfill his promises to Isy. But even then he could not quite persuade himself that the right time had come for revealing it to his parents. He knew it would be a great blow to his mother to learn he had so handicapped his future, and he feared the silent face of his father listening to the announcement of it.

It is hardly necessary to say that he made no attempt to establish any correspondence with the poor girl. But this time he was not unwilling to forget her, and found himself hoping that she had, if not forgotten, at least dismissed from her mind all that had taken place between them. Now and then in the night he would have a few tender thoughts about her, but in the morning they would all be gone, and he would drown painful reminiscence in the care with which he would polish and repolish his sentences, trying to imitate the style of the great orators of the day. Apparent richness of composition was his principal aim, not truth of meaning or clarity of utterance.

I can hardly be presumptuous in adding that, although thus growing in a certain popularity, he was not growing in favor with God, for who can that makes the favor of man his aim? And as he continued to hear nothing about Isy, the hope at length awoke in him, bringing with it a keen shot of pleasure, that he was never to hear any more of her. For the praise of men, and the love of that praise, had now restored him to his own good graces, and he thought more highly of himself than ever. His continued lack of inquiry about her, despite the predicament in which he might possibly have placed her in, was a worse sin, being deliberate, than his primary wrong to her. And it was that which now recoiled upon him in his increase of hardness and self-satisfaction.

He had not been in his parish more than a month or two when he was attracted by a certain young woman in his congregation. She was of some inborn refinement and distinction of position, and he quickly became anxious to win her approval, and, if possible, her admiration.

So in preaching—if the word used for the lofty utterance of divine messengers may be misapplied to his paltry memorizations—his main thought was always whether she was justly appreciating the eloquence and wisdom with which he meant to impress her. Even though her deep natural insight penetrated him and his pretensions, in truth she encouraged him, thus making him all the more eager after her good opinion. He came at last to imagine himself thoroughly in love with her—a thing at present impossible to him with any woman.

Finally, encouraged by the fancied importance of his position, and his own fancied distinction in it, he ventured an offer of his feeble hand and feebler heart—only to have them, to his surprise, definitely and absolutely refused. He turned from her door a good deal disappointed, but severely mortified. And judging it impossible for any woman to keep silence concerning such a refusal, and unable to endure the thought of the gossip that would come of it and to be the object of what snickers would inevitably follow, he began at once to look about for some place to hide. Very frankly, he told his patron the whole story.

It happened to suit the duke's plans, and he speedily came to his assistance with the offer of his native parish. From that post the cobbler's argumentative friend, Mr. Pethrie, had recently been elevated to a position, probably not a very distinguished one, in the kingdom of heaven. Thus, it seemed a thing most natural, and even rather pious, when James Blatherwick exchanged his parish to become minister in the one where he was born, and where his father and mother continued to occupy the old farm of Stonecross.

4

• • • • • • • • • • • • • • • • • •

The Daughter

The village soutar John MacLear was still meditating on spiritual things, still reading the Gospels, still making and mending shoes, and still watching the development of his daughter. She had now unfolded into what many of the neighbors counted nothing less than beauty. The farm laborers in the vicinity were nearly all more or less her admirers, and many a pair of shoes was carried to her father for the sake of a possible smile from Maggie. But a certain awe of her kept them from presuming beyond a word of greeting or farewell. Her dark and in a way mysterious look had a great deal to do with it, for it seemed to suggest behind it a beauty her face itself was unable to reveal.

She was a little short in stature, being of a strong active type, well proportioned, with a calm and clear face, and quiet but keen dark eyes. Her complexion owed its white rose tinge to a strong but gentle life, and its few freckles to the pale sun of Scotland and the breezes she met bonnetless on the hills when she accompanied her father on his walks, or when she delivered some piece of work he had finished.

Her father rejoiced in her delight with the wind, thinking that it indicated a sympathy with the Spirit whose symbol it was. He loved to think of that Spirit folding her about, more closely and more lovingly than his own soul.

Almost from the moment of her mother's death, she had given herself to his service, first in doing all the little duties of the house, and then, as her strength and abilities grew, in helping him more and more in his trade. By degrees she had grown so familiar with the lighter parts of it that he could leave them to her with confidence. As soon as she had cleared away the few things necessary for their breakfast of porridge and milk, Maggie would hasten to join her father stooping over his workbench, for he was a little near-sighted.

When he lifted his head you might see that, despite the ruggedness of his face, he was a good-looking man, with strong, well-proportioned features, in which, even on Sundays, when he scrubbed his face unmercifully, there would still remain lines suggestive of ingrained rosin and heelball. On weekdays he was not so careful to remove every sign of the labor by which he earned his bread, but when his work was over till the morning, and he was free to sit down to a book, he would never even touch one without first carefully washing his hands and face.

In the workshop Maggie's place was a leather-seated stool like her father's, a yard or so away from his, to leave room for his elbows in drawing out the rosined threads as he sewed his work. There every morning she would resume whatever work she had left unfinished the night before. It was a curious trait in the father, inherited at an early age by the daughter, that he would never rise from a finished job, however near it might be quitting time, without having begun another one to go on with in the morning. Thus he kept himself from wasting time as so many unproductive persons do "between jobs." Always moving directly from one to another, he found himself ready each morning to take right up where he left off with no loss of momentum. It was wonderful how much cleaner Maggie managed to keep her hands. But then to her naturally fell the lighter work. She declared herself ambitious, however, of one day making a perfect pair of top boots with her own hands, from top to bottom.

The advantages she gained from this constant interaction with her father were incalculable. To the great benefit and rapid development of her freedom of thought, the soutar would avoid no subject as unsuitable for the girl's consideration, insisting only on its being regarded from the highest attainable point of view. Matters of little or no significance they seldom, if ever, discussed. Though she was full of an honest hilarity that was ever ready to break out when occasion occurred, she was at the same time incapable of a light word upon a sacred subject. Very early in life she became aware of the kind of joke her father would take or refuse. The light use especially of any word of the Lord would sink him in a profound silence. If it were an ordinary man who had said it, he might rebuke him by asking if he remembered who said those words. But if it was a clergyman who thus spoke lightly, MacLear was likely to respond more strongly.

Indeed the most powerful force in Maggie's education was the evident attitude of her father toward the Son of Man. Around the name of Jesus gathered his whole consciousness and hope of well-being. And it was hardly surprising that certain of his ways of thinking should pass into the mind of his child, and there show themselves as original and necessary truths. Mingling with her delight in the inanimate powers of nature, in the sun and the wind, in the rain and the growth, in the running waters and the darkness sown with stars, was such a sense of the presence of God that she felt he might appear at any moment to her or her father.

Two or three miles away, in the heart of the hills, on the outskirts of the farm of Stonecross, lived an old cottar and his wife, who paid a few shillings of rent to Mr. Blatherwick for the acre or two their ancestors had redeemed from the heather and bog. Their one son remained at home with them, and they gave occasional service on the farm when needed. They were much respected by both Peter and Marion Blatherwick, as well as by the small circle to which they were known in the neighboring village of Tiltowie—better known and more respected still in that region called the kingdom of heaven. For they were such as he to whom the promise was given that he should see the angels ascending and descending on the Son of Man. They had been close to the cobbler for many years and had long heartily loved and respected him, since even before the death of his wife. They could not exactly pity the motherless Maggie, seeing she had such a father, yet they lost no opportunity to befriend her. For old Eppie Cormack especially had occasional moments of anxiety as to how the soutar's bairn would grow up without a mother's care. No sooner, however, did the character of the little one begin to show itself, than Eppie's worries began to lessen; and long before the present time the child and the childlike old woman were fast friends. For this reason Maggie was often invited to spend a day at their home at Bogsheuch—oftener in fact than she felt a liberty to leave her father and their work in the shop, though not oftener than she would have liked to go.

One morning early in the summer, when first the hillsides had begun to look attractive, a small wooden agricultural cart, such as is now but seldom seen, with little paint left except on its two red wheels, and drawn by a thin, long-haired horse, stopped at the door of the soutar's house—clay-floored and straw-thatched, in a back lane of the village. It was a cart Mr. Cormack used in the cultivation of his little holding, and his son who was now driving it—now nearly middle-aged himself—was likely to succeed to the hut and acres of Bogsheuch and continue the little farming they were able to do long after his father had laid his tools down in exchange for his rest. Man and cart and horse were all well known to the soutar and Maggie, and on this particular day they had come with an invitation, more pressing than usual, to pay them a visit.

Father and daughter consulted together and arrived at the conclusion that she should go with Andrew; work was more slack than usual, and nobody was in need of a promised job that the cobbler could not finish by himself in good time. Despite a slight pang at the thought of leaving her father alone, Maggie jumped up joyfully and set about preparing their dinner. In the meantime, Andrew went to carry out a few items of business that the mistress at Stonecross and his mother at Bogsheuch had given him. By the time he returned, MacLear and his daughter were just finishing their humble dinner, and Maggie was in her Sunday dress, with her weekday things and a petticoat in a bundle, for she hoped to be of some use to Eppie with the work during her visit.

Andrew brought the cart to the door, and Maggie scrambled into it.

"Take a piece wi' ye," said her father, following her to the cart. "Ye hadna muckle dinner, an' ye may be hungry again afore ye hae the long road ahind ye!"

He put several pieces of oatcake in her hand, which she took with a loving smile. They set out at a walking pace, which Andrew made no attempt to quicken.

It was far from a comfortable carriage, and there was not so much as a wisp of straw in the bottom of it for her to sit on. But the change to the out-of-doors from the close attention to her work—the open air on her face and the free rush of the thoughts that came crowding into her brain—at once put her in a blissful mood. Even the few dull remarks that the slow-thinking Andrew made at intervals from his perch on the front of the cart seemed to come to her from the mysterious world that lay in the fairy-like folds of the huddled hills about them. Everything Maggie saw or heard that afternoon seemed to wear the glamour of God's imagination, which is at once the birth and the very truth of everything. Selfishness alone can rub away that divine gilding, without which gold itself is poor indeed.

Suddenly the little horse came to a stop and stood still. Waking up from a snooze, Andrew at once jumped to the ground, and still half asleep began to search about for the cause of the sudden stop. Jess, the old horse, though she could not make haste, never had been known to stand still while still able to walk. On her part, however, Maggie had for sometime noted that they were making very slow progress.

"She's a dead cripple!" said Andrew at length, straightening his long back after an examination of Jess's forefeet. He came to Maggie's side of the cart with a serious face. "I dinna believe the creature can gae one step further. Yet I canna see what's happened t' her!"

Maggie jumped out of the cart, and again Andrew attempted to lead the horse by the rein. But it was immediately clear the animal was in pain.

"It would be cruelty!" he said. "We must jist loose her, an' take her if we can t' the How o' the Mains. They'll gie her a nicht's quarters there, poor thing! An' we'll see if they can tak ye in as weel, Maggie. The maister'll len' me a horse t' come fer ye in the mornin'."

"I winna hear o' it!" answered Maggie. "I can tramp the rest o' the way as weel's you, Andrew!"

"But I hae the things t' carry, an' that'll lea' me no han' t' help ye o'er the burn!" he objected.

"What!" she returned. "I was sae tired o' sittin' that my legs are jist like t' rin awa' wi' me. Here, gie me that loaf. I'll carry that, an' my ain bit bundle as weel; then, I fancy, ye can manage the rest yersel'!"

Andrew never had a great deal to say, and against such a determined and quick thinking young lass as Maggie, by now he had nothing. But her readiness relieved him of some anxiety, for he knew his mother would be very uncomfortable if he went home without her.

The darkness gradually came on, and as it deepened Maggie's spirits rose. And the wind became to her a live shadow, in which—with no eye-boundaries to the space enclosing her—she could go on imagining according to the freedom of her own wild will. As the world and everything in it disappeared, it grew easier to imagine Jesus making the darkness light about him, and then stepping from it plain before her sight. That could be no trouble to him, she told herself. Since he was everywhere, he must be there. If she were but fit to see him, then surely he would come to her.

Her father had several times spoken in such a manner to her, talking about the various appearances of the Lord after his resurrection, and his promise that he would be with his disciples always to the end of the world. Even after he had gone back to his Father, had he not appeared to the Apostle Paul? Might it not be that he had shown himself to many another through the long ages?

In any case, he was everywhere, she thought, and always about them, although now, perhaps from lack of faith in the earth, he had not been seen for a long time. And she remembered her father once saying that nobody could even *think* a thing if there was no possible truth in it. The Lord went away that they might believe in him when they could not see him, and so they would be in him, and he in them!

"I dinna think," said Maggie to herself, as she trudged along beside the delight-fully silent Andrew, "that my father would be the least astonished—only filled wi' an awful gladness—if at some moment, walkin' by his side, the Lord was to call him by his name and appear t' him. He would but think he had jist stepped oot upon him frae some secret door, an' would say, 'I thoucht I would see ye someday, Lord! I was aye longin' efter a sicht o' ye, Lord, an' here ye are!'"

5

· · · · · · · · · · · · · · · ·

The Baby

*A*s they walked silently along, Maggie's thoughts still on the Lord, all at once the cry of an infant came through the dark. Maggie's first thought was of the Lord when he first appeared on earth as a baby.

She stopped in the dusky starlight, and listened with her very soul.

"Andrew!" she said, for she heard the sound of his steps continuing on in front of her, though she could but vaguely see him, "Andrew, what was yon cry?"

"I heard nothin'," answered Andrew, stopping and listening.

Then came a second cry, a feeble, sad wail, and this time both of them heard it.

Maggie darted off in the direction where it seemed to come from, and she did not have far to run, for the tiny voice could hardly have reached any great distance.

They had been climbing a dreary, desolate ridge where the road was a mere stony hollow, in winter a path for the rain rather than the feet of men. On each side of it lay a wild moor covered with heather and low berry-bearing shrubs. Under a big bush Maggie saw something glimmer. She flew toward it, and found a child. It might have been a year old, but was so small and poorly nourished that its age was hard to guess.

With the instinct of a mother, she caught it up and clasped it close to her panting chest. She was delighted to find its crying cease the moment it felt her arms about it. Andrew had dropped the things he had been carrying, and had started after her, and now met her halfway back to the road, so absorbed in her newfound treasure that she scarcely noticed him. He turned and followed, but, to his amazement, the moment she reached the road she turned back down the hill the way they had come. Clearly she could think of nothing but carrying the infant home to her father, and here even the slow perception of her companion understood her actions.

"Maggie, Maggie," he cried after her, "ye'll both be dead afore ye get home! Come on t' my mither. There never was a wuman like her for bairns! She'll ken better than any father what t' do wi't!"

Maggie at once recovered her senses, and knew he was right—but not before she had received an insight that was never afterward to leave her: now she understood the heart of the Son of Man, come to find and carry back the stray children to their Father and his. When afterward she told her father what she had then felt, he answered her with just the four words and no more.

"Lassie, ye hae it!"

Happily by now the moon had begun to inch its way up, so that Andrew was soon able to find the things they had dropped. Maggie wrapped the baby up in the winsey petticoat she had been carrying, for the night air was growing colder. Andrew picked up his loaf and other packages, and they set out again for Bogsheuch, Maggie's heart overwhelmed with gladness. She had not yet come to the point of asking what an infant could be doing alone on the moor; she was only exultant she had found it. Had the precious little thing been twice the weight, so exuberant were her feelings of wealth and delight that she could easily have carried it twice the distance, although the road was so rough that she was in constant terror of stumbling as she walked along.

Every now and then Andrew gave a little chuckle at the ludicrousness of their homecoming, and every so often had to stop and pick up one or another of his many parcels. But Maggie strode on in front, full of a sense of possession, and with the feeling of having at last entered into her heavenly inheritance. As a result she was almost startled when suddenly they came in sight of the turf cottage, in whose window a small oil lamp was burning. Before they even reached the door, Eppie appeared, welcoming them with an overflow of questions.

"What on earth—" she began.

" 'Tis a bonny wee bairnie, whose mither has left it!" interrupted Maggie, running up to her and laying the child in her arms.

Mrs. Cormack stood and stared—first at Maggie, then at the bundle that now lay in her own arms. Tenderly searching the petticoat, at last the old mother found the little one's face, and uncovered the sleeping child.

"Eh, the poor mither!" she said, and hurriedly recovered it.

"It's mine!" cried Maggie. "I found it honest!"

"It's mither may hae lost it honest, Maggie!" said Eppie.

"Weel, its mither can come for it, if she wants it. It's mine till she does anyway!" rejoined the girl.

"Nae doobt o' that!" replied the old woman, scarcely questioning that the infant had been left to perish by some worthless tramp. "Ye'll maybe hae it longer than ye'll care to keep it!"

"That's nae very likely," answered Maggie with a smile as she stood in the doorway: "it's one o' the Lord's own lammies that he came to the hills to seek. He's found this one!"

"Weel, weel, my bonnie doo, it canna be for me to contradick ye!—But woe is me, for a foolish auld wife! Come in, come in, the more welcome that ye're so long expected!—But bless me, Andrew, what hae ye done wi' the cart, an' the beastie?"

In a few words, for brevity was easy to him, Andrew told the story of what had happened.

"It must hae been the Lord's mercy! The poor beastie has to suffer for the sake o' the bairnie!"

She got them their supper, which was keeping hot by the fire, and then sent

Maggie to her bed in the *ben-end,* or inside the best room, where she laid the baby after washing him and wrapping him in a soft, well-worn shirt of her own. But Maggie could scarcely sleep for listening to the baby's breathing lest it should stop. Eppie sat in the kitchen with Andrew until the light, slowly traveling round the north, deepened in the east and at last climbed the sky, leading up to the sun himself. Andrew then rose and set off toward Stonecross, which he reached before the house was yet astir, and then set about to feed and groom his horse.

All the next day Maggie was ill at ease, anticipating the appearance of the mother. The baby seemed nothing the worse for his exposure, and although thin and pale, appeared in other respects to be a healthy child, and took heartily the food offered him. He was decently though poorly clad, and very clean. The Cormacks made inquiry at every farmhouse and cottage within range of the moor, and the tale of the child's finding was quickly known throughout the entire neighborhood. But to Maggie's satisfaction nothing about the mother was discovered. By the time her visit came to an end, she was feeling tolerably secure in her new possession, and was anxious to return with it in triumph to her father.

The long-haired horse was not yet equal to the journey after its injury, and thus Maggie had to walk home. But Eppie accompanied her, bent on taking her share in the burden of the child, although it was with difficulty she persuaded Maggie to yield it even for a time. When they arrived and Maggie laid the child in her father's arms, the soutar rose from his stool and received him like Simeon taking the infant Jesus from the arms of his mother. For a moment he held him in silence, then restored him again to his daughter, sat down on his stool, and picked up his tool and a shoe. Then suddenly becoming aware of a breach in his manners, he rose again at once.

"I beg yer pardon, Mistress Cormack," he said. "I was clean forgettin' any breedin' I ever had!—Maggie, take oor frien' into the hoose, an' make her rest while ye get something for her after her long walk. I'll be in mysel' in a minute or two to hae a talk wi' her. I hae but a few mair stitches to put into this sole! The three o' us must take some serious coonsel t'gither aboot this God-sent bairn! I doobtna that he's come wi' a blessing to this hoose, but we must pray aboot what we're to do. An' we must pray for the mither o' him! Eh, but it was a merciful fittin' o' things t'gither that the poor bairn an' Maggie should that night come t'gither. The angels must hae been aboot the moor that day—even as they must hae been aboot the field an' the flock an' the shepherds an' the inn-stable on that gran' night!"

That same moment a neighbor entered, who had previously heard and misinterpreted the story, and now had caught sight of their arrival and had come to gather what gossip she could under the pretense of concern.

"Eh, soutar, but ye're a man sorely oppressed by Providence!" she said. "Who do ye think's been at fault there wi' yer daughter?"

The anger of the cobbler sprang up.

"Get oot o' my hoose ye ill-thinkin' woman!" he said, "an' comena here again except it be to beg my pardon an' that o' this good woman an' my bonny lass here! The Lord keep her frae ill-tongues!"

The outraged father, whom all the town knew for a man of the gentlest temper and great courtesy, stood towering. The woman stood one moment dazed and uncertain, then turned and fled. Maggie went into the house with Mrs. Cormack; and when the soutar joined them after completing his job, he never said a word about her. After Eppie had had some tea with them, she rose, bade them a good-day, and without visiting another house in the village, made her way back to her own cottage.

As soon as the baby was asleep, Maggie went back to the kitchen where her father still sat working.

"Ye're late tonight, Father," she said.

"I am that, lassie. But ye see I canna look for help frae you for some time noo. Ye'll hae enough to do wi' that bairn, an' we hae him to feed noo as well as oorsel's."

"It's little he'll want for a while at least, Father," answered Maggie. "But," she went on in a serious tone, "what kin' o' mither could leave her bairn oot there in the eerie night?—an' why?"

"She must hae been some poor lassie that hadna yet learned to think o' God's will first. Nae doobt she believed in some man, an' perhaps he promised to marry her, an' she didna ken he was a liar an' wasna strong enough to heed the voice inside her saying *ye mustna do it.* An' sae she let him do what he like wi' her, an' made himsel' the father o' a bairnie that wasna meant for him. She should never hae permitted such liberties to make a mither o' her afore she was married. Such fools hae an awful time o' it. For fowk is always lookin' doon on them. Doubtless, if it was like this, the rascal ran away and left her to fend for hersel'. An' naebody would help her, an' she had to beg bread for hersel' and a drop o' milk here an' there for the bairnie. Sae that at last she lost heart an' left it, jist as Hagar left hers beneath the bush in the wilderness afore God showed her the bonny well o' water."

"Do ye really think it happened sae, Father?" asked Maggie.

"Who kens, lassie? But 'tis not so unusual a story."

"I hardly ken which o' them was the worst—father or mither!"

"Nor do I!" said the soutar, "but if there were lies told, it must be the one that lied to the other who's counted the worse."

"There canna be many such men."

" 'Deed there's a heap o' them," rejoined her father; "but woe for the poor lassie that believes them."

"She kenned what was right all the time, Father! She canna be blameless."

"That's true, my dautie. But to know is no aye to un'erstand. An' even to un'erstand is no aye to see right into a truth. No woman's safe—or man either—that hasna the love o' God, the great Love, in her heart all the time! What's best in her may turn to be her greatest danger. An' the higher ye rise ye come into the worst danger, till once ye're fairly in the one safe place, the heart o' the Father. There an' only there are ye safe—safe frae earth, frae hell, an' frae yer own heart!

All the temptations, even such as made the heavenly hosts themselves fall frae heaven to hell, canna touch ye there! But when man or woman repents, an' humbles himsel', there he is to lift them up—an' higher than they ever stood afore!"

"Then they're no to be despised for their fall into sin?"

"None despises them, lassie, but them that haena yet learned the danger they're in o' that same fall themsel's. Many a one, I'm thinkin', is kept frae fallin' jist because she's no far enough on to get the good o' the shame, but would jist sink farther an' farther."

"But Eppie tells me that most o' them that trips goes on fallin' an' never gets up again."

"Ow, ay—that's as true perhaps as far as we short-lived an' shortsighted creatures see o' them! But this world's but the beginnin', an' the glory o' Christ, who's the very Love o' the Father, spreads a heap further than that. It's not for naething we're told hoo the sinner women came to him frae all sides. They needed him badly, an' came. Never one o' them was too bad to be let come up close to him, an' some o' such women un'erstood things he said that many respectable women couldna get a glimpse o'. There's aye rain enough in the sweet heavens, as Maister Shakespeare says, to wash the very hand o' murder white as snow. The creatin' heart is full o' such rain. Love him, lassie, an' ye'll never dirty the bonny white gown ye brought frae his heart!"

The soutar's face was solemn and white, and traces of tears were running down the furrows of his cheeks. At length Maggie spoke.

"Supposin' the mither o' my bairnie is a woman like that, do ye think that *her* disgrace will stick to *him*?"

"Only in such minds as never saw the lovely greatness o' God."

"But such bairns comena int' the world as God would hae them come!"

"But your bairnie is come, and that he couldna do withoot the creatin' will o' the Father! Doobtless such bairnies hae to suffer frae the prood judgment o' their fellow men an' women. But they may get much good an' little ill frae that—a good nobody can take frae them. Eh, the poor bairnie that has a father that would leave him an' his mither helpless. Such must someday be sore affronted wi' themsel's, that disgrace both the wife that should hae been, an' the bairn that shouldna. But he has another as weel—a right gran' lovin' Father to run to! The one thing, Maggie, that you an' me has to do, if the Lord sees fit for him to bide wi' us a spell, is never to let the bairn ken the missin' o' father or mither, an' sae lead him to the one Father, the only real an' true one.—There, he's wailin', the bonny wee man! "

Maggie ran to quiet the little one, but soon returned, and sitting down again beside her father, asked him for a piece of work.

And all this time, through his own indifference, the would-be-grand preacher knew nothing of the fact that somewhere in the world, without father or mother, lived and breathed a silent witness against him.

6

· · · · · · · · · · · · · · · · ·

The Vagrant

*I*sy managed to lengthen her visit to her grandmother, and thus postponed her return to her aunt's until James was gone, for she dreaded being in the house with him. She did return, however, and by and by the time came when she had to face the appalling fact that the dreaded moment was quickly approaching when she would no longer be able to conceal the change in her position.

Her first thought was how she could protect the good name of her lover from scandal, and avoid involving him in the coming ruin of her reputation. With this intent, she vowed, both to God and to herself, absolute silence concerning the past. Even James's name should never pass her lips!

And it was not that hard to keep the vow, even when her aunt took measures to draw her secret from her. Eventually her hour came, and she passed through it and found herself still alive, with her lips locked tight on her secret. In vain did her aunt ply her with questions, but she felt that to answer a single one of them would be to wrong him who had wronged her, and to lose her last righteous hold upon the man who had at least once loved her a little. He had most likely, she thought, all but forgotten her very existence by now, for he had never written to her, or made any effort to discover what had become of her. She clung to the conviction that he must never have heard that she had become pregnant.

At length she realized that to remain where she was would be the ruin of her aunt, for who would lodge in the same house with *her*! She must leave at once, yet she had not the least idea where she should go. Her exhausted physical condition, her longing to go, yet the impossibility of going at once, brought such despair to her mind, already weakened by the demands of the baby, that more than once she was on the point of taking poison. But the thought of her child gave her strength to live on. To add to her misery came the idea that—as fixed had been her resolve to silence—she had in some way been false to James, that she had betrayed him, brought him to shame, and forever ruined his prospects for advancement in the church. That must be why she never heard another word from him! She would never see him again!

All of these notions and convictions grew so steadily within her consciousness that one morning when her infant was not yet a month old, she crept out of the house and wandered out into the world, with just one shilling in the pocket of her dress.

Where she went and how she and the baby survived even she did not know. For a time her memory seemed to lose all hold upon her and everything about that time remained a blank. When she began to come to herself, it seemed that some weeks had passed, but she had no knowledge of where she had been or for how long her mind had been astray. Across the blank spaces of her brain were cloud-like trails of blotted dreams, and vague survivals of gratitude for bread and pieces of money. From what she could gather she had been heading north, first more-or-less along the eastern seaboard, then gradually inland. Everything she became aware of surprised her, except the child in her arms—already she could never forget him. Her sad story had been plain to everyone she met, and she had received thousands of kindnesses that her memory could not hold. At length, whether intentionally or not she did not know, she found herself on the road toward Banchory and Alford, and eventually in a neighborhood to which she had heard James Blatherwick refer.

Here again a blank came over her memory—till suddenly once more she came to herself and became conscious of being. She was alone on a wide moor in a dim night, with her hungry child. She had just given him the last drop of nourishment he could draw from her, and was now wailing in her arms. A great despair came over her, and unable to carry him another step farther, she laid him down from her helpless hands into a bush. He was starving and she must get him some milk! She went staggering about, looking under the great stones and into the clumps of heather for something he could drink, hardly knowing what she was doing. At last she sank onto the ground, herself weak from hunger, and fell into a kind of faint. When she came to herself, she searched all about for the child in vain, not even remembering the exact place where she had left him. This was the same evening when Maggie came along with Andrew and found the baby. All that night, and a great part of the next day, Isy went searching all about the moor, but without finding the baby. Finally she discovered what she thought was the spot where she had left him, and not finding him there came to the conclusion that some wild beast had carried him off. A little ways off was a small peat-pond, and she immediately ran toward it with the thought of drowning herself. A man happened to be cutting peats nearby, saw her, threw down his spade and ran to stop her. He thought she was out of her mind, and tried to console her. He gave her a few halfpence and directed her to the next town. For a long time thereafter she wandered about, asking everyone she saw about the child, with alternating disappointment and expectation. Every day something happened that served to keep the life in her, and at last she reached the county-town, where she was taken to a place of shelter.

7

•••••••••••••••••••

The Preacher

*J*ames Blatherwick was proving himself not unacceptable to his native parish. He was thought to be a rising man, inasmuch as his fluency in the pulpit was far ahead of his insight. He soon came to take an interest in the soutar, noting him a man far in advance of the rest of his parishioners in certain spiritual matters, but at the same time he knew that he was regarded by many as a wild fanatic, if not a dangerous heretic. Because of this he perceived that for him to be accepted by the majority of his people, he would be on far safer ground to differ with the soutar rather than to agree with him, at least until his influence was more firmly established.

In Tiltowie he followed the same course as he had in the south, using the doctrinal phrases he had always been accustomed to, and that he knew his parishioners would be comfortable with. His chief goal was always toward eloquence. Yet not eloquence alone, but eloquence acknowledged as such by those who heard him. And this he had indeed largely already achieved—eloquence, that is, such as ignorant and wordy people value. But insight into truth as even his father and a few other plain people in the neighborhood possessed, he showed little sign of ever attaining.

He had noted that the soutar used almost none of the set religious phrases of the good people of the village, who devoutly followed the traditions of the elders. But he knew little as to what the cobbler did not believe, and still less of what he did believe. John MacLear could not even speak the name of God without a confession of faith immeasurably beyond anything inhabiting the consciousness of the parson. And on his part, the cobbler soon began to notice in young James a total absence of enthusiasm with regard to the things of the spiritual realm. Never did his face light up when he spoke of the Son of God, of his death, or of his resurrection. Never did he make mention of the kingdom of heaven as if it were anything more venerable than the kingdom of Great Britain and Ireland.

What exactly interested the young preacher in the old soutar it would be difficult to say. But the soutar's interest in James was a prayerful one; here was a young man, he could see, who needed more of the Son of Man than he presently had. Thus, toward that end he would be faithful to lift him up into the mind of his Father in heaven. Hence it was that the two began to have more and more to do with each other.

On one occasion the parson took upon himself to remonstrate with what seemed to him the audacity of his most unusual parishioner.

"Don't you think you are going just a little too far there, Mr. MacLear?" he said.

"Ye mean too far into the dark, Mr. Blatherwick?"

"Yes, that is what I mean. You speculate too boldly where there is no light to show what might be and what might not."

"But dinna ye think, sir, that that's the very direction where the dark grows a wee bit thinner, though I grant ye there's nothing yet to call light?"

"But the human soul is just as apt to deceive itself as the human eye. It is always ready to take a flash inside itself for something real," said Blatherwick.

"Nae doobt, nae doobt! But when the true light comes, ye aye ken the difference! A man may take the dark for light, but he canna take the light for darkness!"

"And there must always be something for the light to shine upon, otherwise the man sees nothing," said the parson.

"There's thought an' possible insight in the man!" said the soutar to himself. Then to Blatherwick, he replied, "Maybe, like the Ephesians, ye haena yet found oot aboot the Holy Spirit, sir?"

"No man dares deny that!"

"But a man might not *know* it, though he dares not deny it. None but them that follows where he leads can ken truthfully that he is."

"We must beware of private interpretation!" suggested James.

"If a man doesna hear the word spoken to his ain sel', he has nae word to trust in. The Scripture is to him but a sealed book; he walks in the dark. If a man has light, he has none the less that another's present. If there be two or three prayin' together, the fourth may hae none o' it, an' each one o' the three has what he's able to receive, an' what he kens in himsel' as light. Each one must hae the revelation into his ain sel'. An' if it be so, hoo are we to get any truth not yet revealed, 'cep' we go oot into the dark t' meet it? Ye must walk carefully, I admit, in the mirk, but ye must go ahead if ye would win at anythin'."

"But suppose you know enough to keep going, and do not care to venture into the dark and ask so many questions about things you don't know."

"If a man holds on practicin' what he does ken, the hunger'll wake in him after more. I'm thinkin' the angels desired long afore they could see into certain things they wanted t' ken aboot. But ye may be sure they werena left withoot as much light as would lead honest fowk safely on."

"But suppose they couldn't tell whether what they thought they saw was true light or not?"

"Then they would have to fall back upon the will o' the great Light. We ken weel enough that he wants us all t' see as he himsel' sees. If we seek that Light, we'll reach it; if we carena for it, we're gaein' nowhere, an' may come in sore need o' some sharp discipline."

"I'm afraid I can't quite follow you. The fact is, I have been so long occupied with the Bible history, and the new discoveries that bear upon it, that I have had but little time for such spiritual metaphysics."

"An' what is the good o' history, or such metaphysics as ye call it as is the very soul o' history, but to help ye see Christ? An' what's the good o' Christ but see to see God wi' yer heart an' yer un'erstandin' both as t' ken that ye're seein' him, an' see to receive him into yer very nature? Ye mind hoo the Lord said that none could ken his Father but him to whom the Son would reveal him? Sir, 'tis time ye had a glimpse o' that! Ye ken naethin' till ye ken God—an' he's the only person a man truly can ken in his heart."

"Well, you must be a long way ahead of me, and for the present I'm afraid there's nothing for it but to say good-night to you."

And with the words the minister departed.

"Lord," said the soutar, as he sat guiding his awl through the sole and welt of the shoe he was working on, "there's surely somethin' at work in the yoong man! Surely he canna be that far from wakin' up to see and ken that he sees and kens nothin'. Lord, put down the dyke o' learnin' an' self-righteousness that he canna see over the top o', an' let him see thee on the other side o' it. Lord, send him the grace o' open eyes, to see where an' what he is, that he may cry oot wi' the rest o' us, poor blind bodies, to them that won't see, 'Wake, thou that sleepest, an' come oot o' thy grave, an' see the light o' thy grave, an' see the light o' the Father in the face o' the Son.'"

As the minister went away he was trying to classify the cobbler, whom he thought to place in some sect of the Middle-Age mystics. At the same time something strange seemed to hover about the man, refusing to be handled in that way. And from that day onward, the minister could not quite get the little man out of his mind. Something in his own heart, what he would have called his religious sense, could almost grasp a hint of what the soutar must mean, though he could neither isolate nor define it.

Faithless as he had behaved to Isy, James Blatherwick was not consciously—that is, with purpose or intent—a deceitful man. On the contrary, he had always cherished a strong faith in his own honor. But faith in a thing, in an idea, in a notion, is no proof or sign that the thing actually exists. And in the present case it had no root except in the man's thought of himself. The man who thought so much of his honor was in truth a moral unreality, a cowardly fellow who, in the hope of escaping the consequences of his actions, carried himself as one beyond reproof.

The question must be asked how such a one would ever have the power of spiritual vision developed in him. How should such a one ever see God—ever exist in the same region as that in which the soutar had long lived? To be sure, such spiritual vision would never come without trials of some kind to open the doors of his heart. And James's had already begun, though he did not yet recognize them as such. But his hour was drawing closer.

Still there was this much reality in him, and he had made this much progress that, holding fast to his resolve never to slide again into sin, he was also aware of a dim suspicion of something he had not seen, but which he might become able to see. And a small part of him was half resolved to think and read with the intent to find out what this strange man seemed to know, or thought he knew.

8

· · · · · · · · · · · · · · · · · · ·

The Visit

*J*ames had of course seen Maggie on numerous occasions, whenever in fact he came to call on the soutar. Usually she sat silently beside her father, both working away while the young parson conversed with the cobbler. However, he had not yet beheld the changes readily evident in her since the days of their childhood. And neither had he taken sufficient interest in the little household to ask who the child was whom he had once or twice seen her ministering to with such a tender show of devotion.

One day he went to call and knocked on the soutar's door. Maggie opened it with the baby in her arms, with whom she had just been having a game. Her face was in a glow, her hair tossed about, and her dark eyes were flashing with excitement.

To Blatherwick, without any particularly great interest in life, and in the net of a vaguely haunting trouble that was causing him no immediate concern, the poor girl, below him in station, as he took for granted, somehow struck him at the moment as beautiful. And indeed she was far more beautiful than he was able to appreciate. Besides, it had not been long since he had been refused by another, and at such a time a man is all the readier to fall in love afresh. All these factors had laid James's heart, such as it was, open to assault from a new quarter from which he foresaw no danger. "That's a very fine baby you have," he said. "Whose is he?"

"Mine, sir," answered Maggie with some triumph.

"Oh, indeed; I did not know," answered the parson, a little bewildered.

"At least," Maggie resumed a little hurriedly, "I have the best right to him at the moment."

She cannot possibly be his mother, thought the minister, and resolved in his mind to question his housekeeper about the child when he returned home.

"Is your father in the house?" he asked, but without waiting for an answer, went on, "But such a big child is too heavy for you to carry about."

"No one bit!" rejoined Maggie. "An' who's to carry him but me? Would ye hae my pet go travelin' the world upon his two bonny wee legs, wi'oot the wings he left ahind him? Na, na! they must grow a heap stronger first. His ain mamma would carry him if he were twice the size! Noo, come an' we'll go ben the hoose an' see Daddy."

They entered the kitchen, where Maggie sat down with the baby on her own stool beside her father, who looked up from his labor.

"Weel, Minister, hoo are ye today? Is the grave any lighter upon that top o' ye?" he said with a smile that looked almost cunning.

"I do not understand you, Mr. MacLear," answered James.

"Na, ye canna. If ye could, ye wouldna be sae comfortable as ye seem."

"I can't think why you should be rude to me, Mr. MacLear!"

"If ye saw the hoose on fire all aboot a man in a dead drunken sleep, maybe ye might not be in too great a hurry to be polite to him," remarked the soutar.

"Dare you suggest that I have been drinking?" cried the parson.

"Not for a single moment, sir. An' I beg yer pardon for causin' ye to think so. I don't believe ye were ever overtaken wi' drink in all yer life. An' perhaps I shouldna be sae ready to speak in parables, for it's not everybody that can or will un'erstand them. But ye canna hae forgotten that cry o' the Apostle o' the Gentiles—'Wake up, thou that sleepest!' For even the dead wake when the trumpet blast batters at their ears! What's impossible, ye ken, is possible, an' *very* possible, wi' God."

"It seems to me that the Apostle makes allusion in that passage to the condition of the Gentile nations. But may undoubtedly apply also to the conversion of any unbelieving man from the error of his ways."

"Weel," said the cobbler, turning half round, and looking the minister full in the face, "are *ye* converted, sir? Or are ye but turnin' frae side to side in yer coffin—seekin' a sleepin' assurance that ye're awake?"

"You are plain spoken anyway!" said the minister, rising.

"Maybe I am at last, sir. An' maybe I hae been too long comin' to the point o' bein' so plain. Perhaps I've been too afraid that ye would count me ill-fashioned—or what ye call rude."

The parson was already halfway to the door, for he was quite angry—which was hardly surprising. But with the latch still in his hand, he turned, and there was Maggie, standing in the middle of the floor with the child in her arms, looking as if she meant to follow him.

"Don't anger him, Father," said Maggie; "he disna ken better."

"Weel I ken that, my dautie. But I canna help thinkin' he's maybe no that far frae the wakin'. God grant I be right aboot that! Eh, if he would but wake up, what a man he would make! He knows a heap o' things—only what's that where a man has nae light!"

"I certainly do not see things as you would have me believe you see them," said Blatherwick, with the angry flush on his face intensified all the more at hearing the two speak thus about him. "And I fear you are hardly capable of persuading me that you do!"

The baby seemed to sense the anger in the room, for here it sent forth a potent cry. Clasping him close, Maggie ran from the room, jostling James in the doorway as he stood aside to let her pass.

"I am afraid I frightened the little man!" he said.

"'Deed, sir, it may have been you, or it may hae been me that frightened him," rejoined the soutar. " 'Tis a thing I'm sore to blame in—that when I'm right in earnest, I'm aye too ready to speak almost as if I was angry. Sir, I humbly beg yer pardon."

"I too beg yours," said the parson. "I was in the wrong."

The heart of the old man was again drawn to the youth. He laid aside his shoe, turned on his stool, and said solemnly. "At this moment, sir, I would willingly die if by doin' so the light o' that uprisin' we spoke o' might break through upon ye."

"I believe you," said James, "but," he went on, with an attempt at humor, "it wouldn't be so much for you to do after all, seeing as how you would immediately find yourself in a better place!"

"Maybe where the penitent thief sat, some eighteen hunner years ago, waitin' t' be called up higher," rejoined the soutar with a watery smile.

The parson opened the door and went home—where his knees found their way to the carpet, a place they had been none too familiar with till now.

From that day Blatherwick began to go more often to the soutar's, and before long went almost every other day, at least for a few minutes. And on such occasions generally had a short interview with Maggie and the baby as well, in both of whom, having heard the story of the child from the soutar, he took a growing interest.

"You seem to love him as if he were your own, Maggie!" he said one morning to the girl.

"An' isna he my ain? Didna God himsel' give me the bairn into my very arms—or all but?" she rejoined.

"Suppose he were to die," suggested the minister. "Such children often do."

"I needna think aboot that," she answered. "I would just hae t' say, as many a one has said afore me: 'The Lord gave'—ye ken the rest, sir."

Day by day Maggie grew more beautiful in the minister's eyes, until at last he was not only ready to say that he loved her, but to disregard any further worldy ambitions for her sake.

9

· · · · · · · · · · · · · · · · ·

The Proposal

*O*n the morning of a certain Saturday—a day of the week he always made a holiday—Blatherwick resolved to let Maggie know without further delay that he loved her. His confession was made all the more imperative in that he was scheduled to preach for a brother clergyman at Deemouth in Aberdeen, and he felt that if he left his fate with Maggie unknown, his mind would not be cool enough for him to do well in the pulpit. But neither disappointment from a previous experience nor new love had yet served to free him from his vanity and arrogance: he regarded his approaching declaration as about to confer a great honor and favor upon the young woman of low background.

In his previous disappointment in the south he had asked a lady to descend a little from her social pedestal, in the belief that he offered her a greater than proportionate counter-elevation. And thus now, in his suit to Maggie where the situation was so greatly reversed, he was almost unable to conceive the possibility of her turning him down.

When he called, she would have shown him into the kitchen, but he took her by the arm, and leading her to the *ben-end* of the house, at once began his concocted speech. Scarcely had she gathered his meaning, however, when he was stopped by the startled look on her face.

"An' what would ye hae me do wi' the bairn?" she asked.

But the minister was sufficiently in love to disregard the unexpected interruption. His pride was indeed a little hurt that she should show more concern for a child than himself, but he resisted any show of it, reflecting that her maternal anxiety was not an altogether unnatural one.

"Oh, we shall easily find some experienced mother," he answered, "who will understand better than you how to take care of him."

"Na, na!" she rejoined. "I hae both a father an' a bairn t' look after. An' that's aboot as much as I'll ever be up to."

So saying, she rose and carried the little one up to the room her father now occupied, without casting a single glance of farewell in the direction of her would-be lover.

Blatherwick stood there astonished. Could it be that she had not understood him? It could hardly be that she did not appreciate his offer! Her devotion to the child was indeed absurdly engrossing, but that would be put right very soon. He need not fear such a rivalry as that, however unpleasant at the moment. The very idea of that little vagrant, from no one could tell where, coming between him and the girl he would make his wife—why the thing was preposterous!

He glanced around him. The room looked very empty! He heard her step above him through the thin floor; she was obviously walking back and forth with the senseless little animal. He caught up his hat, and with a flushed face of annoyance went straight out to the room where the soutar sat at his work.

"Mr. MacLear," he said, "I have come to ask you if you will give me your daughter to be my wife."

"Ow, so that's it!" returned the soutar without raising his eyes.

"You have no objection, I hope?" continued the minister, finding him silent.

"What does the lass say hersel'? Ye didna come to me first, I reckon."

"She said that she could not leave the child. But she cannot mean that."

"An' what for no? If that's her answer, then there's nae need for me to voice objections."

"But I shall soon persuade her to withdraw hers."

"Then I should have objections—more than one—to put t' the fore."

"You surprise me. Is not a woman to leave father and mother and cleave to her husband?"

"Ow, ay—if the woman is his wife. Then let none separate them! But there's anither sayin', sir, that may hae somethin' to do wi' Maggie's answer."

"And what is that?"

"That man or woman must leave father and mother, wife and child, for the sake o' the Son o' Man."

"You surely aren't papist enough to think that means a minister is not to marry?"

"Not at all, sir. But I hae nae doobt that's what it'll come to atween you an' Maggie."

"You mean that she will not marry?"

"I mean that she winna marry you, sir."

"But just think how much more she could do for Christ as a minister's wife."

"But what if she considered marryin' you as the same as refusing to leave all for the Son o' Man?"

"Why should she think that?"

"Because see far as I see, she canna think that ye hae left all for him."

"Ah, so that is what you have been teaching her! She does not say that of herself! You have not left her free to choose!"

"The question never came up atween us. She's perfectly free t' take her ain way—an' she kens she is. Ye dinna seem to think it possible she should take *his* will rather than yours—that the love o' Christ should mean more to her than the love offered her by James Blatherwick."

"But allowing that you and I have different opinions on some points, must that be a reason why she and I should not love each other?"

"No reason whatever, sir—if ye can an' do. An' that may be a bigger if than ye realize. But beyond that, ye winna get Maggie to marry ye see long as she doesna believe ye love her Lord as weel as she loves him hersel'. It's no a common love that Maggie bears to her Lord, an' if ye loved her wi' a love worthy o' her, ye would see that."

"Then you will promise me not to interfere."

"I'll promise ye nothin', sir, 'cep to do my duty by her—sae far as I un'erstand what that duty is. If I thought that Maggie didna love him as weel at least as I do, I would go upon my auld knees to her, an' entreat her to love him wi' all her heart an' soul an' stren'th an' mind. An' when I had done that, she might marry who she would—hangman or minister: no a word would I say. For trouble she must hae, an' trouble she will get—I thank my God, who giveth to all men liberally and upbraideth not."

"Then I am free to do my best to win her?"

"Ye are, sir, an' afore tomorrow I winna pass a word wi' her upon the subject."

"Thank you, sir," returned the minister, and took his leave.

"The makin's of a fine lad!" said the soutar aloud to himself as he resumed his work; "but his heart is no yet clear—no crystal clear—no clear like the Son o' Man."

He looked up and saw his daughter in the doorway.

"No a word, lassie," he said. "I'm unable t' talk wi' ye this minute. No a word to me aboot anythin' or anybody today, but what's absolute necessary."

"As ye wish, Father," rejoined Maggie. "I'm gaein oot t' see auld Eppie; I saw her in the baker's shop a minute ago—the bairnie's asleep."

"Very weel. If I hear him, I'll atten' t' him."

"Thank ye, Father," returned Maggie, and left the house.

Having to start that same afternoon for Deemouth, and still feeling it impossible to preach at his ease as long as things remained the way they were, the minister had hung about and was watching the soutar's door. When he saw it open and Maggie walk out, for a moment he flattered himself that she was sorry for her behavior to him and had come to look for him. But her start when she saw him satisfied him that such was not her intent. He quickly began to explain his presence.

"I've been waiting to see you, Margaret," he said. "I'm starting in an hour or so for Aberdeen, but I could not bear to go without telling you that your father has no objection to my saying to you what I please. He says he will not talk with you about me before tomorrow morning, and as I cannot possibly get back before Monday, I have no choice but to now express to you how real is my love. I admire your father, but he seems to hold the affections God has given us of small account compared with his judgment of the strength and reality of them."

"Did he no tell ye I was free to do or say what I liked?" rejoined Maggie rather sharply.

"Yes, he did say something to that effect."

"Then for mysel', I tell ye, Mister Blatherwick, I dinna care to see ye again, unless it be ye're callin' on my father, for I ken he's taken a great anxiety aboot ye."

"Do you mean what you say, Margaret?" said the minister, in a voice that betrayed not a little genuine emotion.

"I do mean it," she answered.

"Not even if I tell you that I am both ready and willing to take the child with you, and bring him up as if he was my own?"

"He wouldna *be* yer ain!"

"Quite as much as yours!"

"Hardly," she returned with a curious little laugh. "But I simply cannot believe ye love God wi' all yer heart. An' that is what matters most o' all in this."

"But dare you say that for yorself, Margaret?"

"No. But I do *want* to love God wi' my whole heart. An' God takes that almost as good as doin' it, leastways so my father always says. Mr. Blatherwick, are ye a real Christian? Or are ye sure ye're no a hypocrite? Ye have made it yer business to teach people man's chief end in life, which is to love God like that. But do ye yersel'? I would like t' ken. But I hae nae right t' question ye, for I dinna believe ye ken yersel'."

"Well, perhaps I do not. But I see there is no occasion to say more!"

"No, none," answered Maggie.

He lifted his hat and turned away to the coach office.

10

....

The Realization

*I*t would be difficult to represent the condition of mind in which James Blatherwick sat on the box-seat of the Defiance coach that evening behind four gray thoroughbreds, carrying him at the rate of ten miles an hour toward the coast. Hurt pride, indignation, and a certain mild revenge in contemplating Maggie's disappointment when at length she should become aware of the distinction he had gained and she had lost were its main components. He never noted a feature of the scenery that went hurrying past him, and yet the time did not seem to go slowly, for he was astonished when the coach stopped at Deemouth, and he found his journey at an end.

He got down rather cramped and stiff, and started out on a stroll about the streets to stretch his legs and see what was going on. He was glad he did not have to preach in the morning, and would have all afternoon to go over his sermon.

The streets were lit with gas, for Saturday was always a sort of market night, and at that moment they were crowded with girls going merrily home from the paper mill at the close of the week's labor. To his eyes, which had very little sympathy with gladness of any kind, the sight only called up by contrast the very different scene upon which his eyes would look down the next evening from the vantage point of the pulpit. The church would be filled with an eminently respectable congregation—to which he would be setting forth the results of certain recent geographical discoveries and local identifications, not knowing that already even later discoveries had rendered all he was about to say more than doubtful.

While sunk in a not very profound reverie, he was turning the corner of a narrow street when he was all but knocked down by a girl whom someone else in the crowd had pushed violently against him. Recoiling from the impact and unable to recover her balance, she fell on the granite pavement. Annoyed and half-angry, he began to walk on, paying no attention to the accident, when something in the pale face of the girl lying there motionless suddenly stopped him with the strong suggestion of someone he had once known. But almost the same instant the crowd gathered around and hid her from his view.

Shocked to find himself so unexpectedly reminded of Isy, he turned away and walked on, saying to himself that it couldn't possibly have been her. When he looked round again before crossing the street, the crowd had vanished, and the sidewalk was nearly empty. He spoke to a policeman who just then came up, but he had seen nothing of the occurrence, and remarked only that the girls at the paper mills were a rough lot.

In another moment his mind was busy with a passage in his sermon that seemed about to escape his memory. It was still impossible for him to talk freely and extemporaneously, and he memorized all his sermons. It was not out of the fullness of the heart that his mouth had yet spoken as a minister.

He went to the house of his friend Mr. Robertson, whom he had come to assist, had supper with him and his wife, and retired early. In the morning he went to his friend's church, in the afternoon rehearsed his sermon, and when the evening came, climbed the pulpitstair, and was soon engrossed in the rites of his delivery.

But as he seemed to be pouring out his soul in the long extempore prayer, he suddenly opened his eyes as if unconsciously compelled, and that same moment saw, in the front of the gallery before him, a face he could not doubt to be that of Isy.

Her gaze was fixed upon him; he saw her shiver, and knew that she saw and recognized him. He felt himself grow blind. His head swam, and he felt as if some material force was bending down his body.

Such was his self-possession, however, that he reclosed his eyes and went on with his prayer—if that could in any sense be called a prayer that he uttered without any feeling or true knowing behind the words themselves.

For the rest of the hour, through a mighty effort of the will, he maintained command of his thoughts and words and speech. He held his eyes fast that he might not see her again, but was constantly aware of the figure of Isy before him, with its gaze fixed motionless upon him. He began at last to wonder vaguely whether she might not be dead and had come back from the grave to haunt him as a mysterious thought-spectre.

But at the close of the sermon, when the people stood up to sing, she rose with them, and the half-dazed preacher sat down, exhausted with emotion, conflict, and effort at self-command. When he rose once more for the benediction, she was gone, and again he took refuge in the doubt whether she had indeed ever been present at all.

Later, after Mrs. Robertson had retired and James was sitting with his host over their tumbler of toddy, a knock came to the door. Mr. Robertson went to open it, and in a moment returned, saying it was a policeman to let him know that a woman was lying drunk at the bottom of his doorsteps, and to inquire what he wished done with her.

"I told him," said Mr. Robertson, "to take the poor creature to the station, and in the morning I would come and see if I could do anything for her. When they're ill the next day, sometimes you have half a chance with them; but it's seldom any use."

A horrible suspicion that it was Isy herself laid hold of James. For a moment he was almost inclined to follow the men to the station, but his friend would be sure to go with him, and then what might come of it! She had kept silent so long, however, it was probably that she had lost all care about him, and if left alone would no doubt say nothing. Thus he reasoned with himself against doing anything, lost in considerations of his own position and reputation, shrinking from the very thought of looking the disreputable creature in the eyes. Yet the awful consciousness haunted him that, if she had fallen into drunken habits and possibly worse, it was his fault, and the ruin of the once lovely creature lay at his door and his alone.

He went quickly to his room and to bed, where for a long while he lay, unable even to think.

Then all at once, with gathered force, the frightful reality, the keen bare truth broke upon him like a huge, cold wave. Suddenly he had a clear vision of his guilt, and the vision was conscious of itself as *his* guilt. He saw it rounded in a gray fog of life-chilling dismay. What was he but a truth-breaker and a liar! *What am I*, said his conscience, *but a cruel, self-seeking, contemptible sneak who, afraid of losing the praises of men, crept away unseen, and left the woman to bear alone our common sin?* What was he but a whited sepulchre, full of dead men's bones?—a fellow posing in the pulpit as an example to the faithful, but knowing all the time that somewhere in the land lived a woman—once a loving, trusting woman—who with a single word could hold him up to the world as a hypocrite?

He sprang to the floor; the cold hand of an invisible ghost seemed clutching at his throat. But what could he do? He felt utterly helpless, but in truth, though the realization of his guilt had at last dawned on him, he still did not dare look the question in the face as to what he could do. He crept ignominiously into his bed, and, gradually growing a little less uncomfortable, began to reason with himself that things were not so bad as they had seemed for a moment. He said to himself that many another had fallen in like fashion with him, but the fault was forgotten, and had never reappeared against him. No culprit was ever required to bear witness against himself! He must learn to discipline and repress his over-sensitivity, otherwise it would one day seize him at a disadvantage, and betray him into self-exposure.

Thus he reasoned, and he sank back into his former condition as one of the all but dead. The loud alarm of his rousing conscience ceased, and he fell asleep with the decision to get away from Deemouth the first thing in the morning before Mr. Robertson awoke and before anything about the girl should be done that might somehow involve him.

How much better it would have been for him to hold on to his repentant mood and awake to tell everything! But very few of his practical ideas, however much brooded over at night, lived to become live fruit in the morning; not once had he ever embodied in action an impulse toward atonement. He could welcome the thought of a final release from sin and suffering at the end of the world, but he always did his best to forget that at the very moment he was suffering because of wrong he had done for which he was taking not the least trouble to make the amends that were possible to him. He had lived for himself, to the destruction of one whom he had once loved, and to the denial of his Lord and Master!

More than twice on his way home in the early morning, he all but turned to go back to the police station. But it was, as usual, only *all* but, and he kept walking on to the coach-office.

11

••••••••••••••••••••

The Two Ministers

*E*ven before James's flight was discovered in the morning, Mr. Robertson was on his way to do what he could for one of whom he knew nothing. The policemen returning from night duty found him already at the door of the office. He was at once admitted, for he was well known to most of them.

He found the poor woman miserably recovered from the effects of the night before. She looked so woeful that the heart of the good man immediately filled with profound pity. He recognized before him a creature whose hope was at its very end, to the verge of despair. She neither looked up nor spoke, but what he could see of her face appeared only ashamed, not sullen nor vengeful. When he spoke to her, she lifted her head a little, but not her eyes to his face. Tenderly, as if to the little one he had left behind in bed at his own house, he spoke to her child-soothing words of sympathy, which his tone carried to her heart, though she could hardly pay attention to the words. She lifted her lost eyes at length, saw his face, and burst into tears.

"Na, na," she cried, "ye canna help me, sir! There's naething that you or any-body can do for me! For God's sake, gie me a drink—a drink o' anything!"

"The thing to do you good is a cup of hot tea. You can't have had a thing to eat this morning. I have a cab waiting me at the door. Come home with me, my poor bairn. My wife'll have a cup of tea ready for you in a moment. You and me'll have our breakfast together."

"Ken ye what ye're sayin', sir? I darena look an honest woman in the face."

"I know a lot about folk of all kinds—more than you probably know yourself. I know more about you, too, than you think, for I've seen you in my own kirk more than once or twice. The Sunday night before last I was preaching straight into your bonny face, and saw you crying, and almost crying myself. Come away home with me, my dear. My wife's another just like myself, and'll turn nothing to you but the smiling side of her face. She's a fine, hardy, good woman, my wife. Come and meet her!"

Isy rose to her feet.

"Eh, but I would like t' look once more into the face o' a bonny, clean woman!" she said. "I'll go, sir—only, I pray ye, sir, hurry an' take me oot o' the sight o' other folk."

"Ay, ay; we'll have you out of here in a moment," answered Mr. Robertson. "Put the fine down to me," he whispered to the inspector as they passed him on their way out.

The man returned his nod and took no further notice.

"I thought that was what would come o' it," he murmured to himself, watching them leave with a smile. But indeed, he little knew what was going to come of it in the end!

The good minister, whose heart was the teacher of his head, and who was not ashamed either of himself or his companion, showed Isy into their little breakfast-parlor and then ran up the stair to his wife. He told her he had brought the young woman home, and wanted her to come down at once. Mrs. Robertson was in the middle of dressing their only child. She left the little one in the care of their one servant, and hurried downstairs to welcome the poor shivering bird of the night. She opened the door, stood silently for a brief moment, then opened her arms wide, and the girl fled to their shelter. But her strength failed her on the way, and she fell to the floor. Instantly the other was down by her side. Mr. Robertson hastened to her, and between them they got her on the couch.

"Shall I get the brandy?" said Mrs. Robertson.

"Try a cup of tea," he answered.

His wife hurried to the kitchen and soon had the tea poured out and cooling. But Isy still lay motionless. Then the minister's wife raised the helpless head on her arm, put a spoonful of the tea to her lips, and was delighted when the girl opened her mouth to swallow it. The next minute she opened her eyes, and would have risen, but the hand of the older woman held her down.

"I want t' tell ye," moaned Isy feebly, "that ye dinna ken who ye hae taken into yer hoose. Let me get up to get my breath, or I'll no be able t' tell ye."

"Drink the tea, and then say what you like. There's no hurry. You'll have time enough."

The poor girl opened her eyes wide and gazed for a moment at Mrs. Robertson. Then she took the cup and drank the tea. Her new friend went on: "You must just be content to bide where you are for a day or two. I have clothes enough to give you all the change you want."

"Eh, mem! Fowk'll speak ill o' ye if they see me in yer hoose!"

"Let them say what they please! What's folk but muckle geese!"

"But there's the minister, an' what people'll think o' him!"

"Hoots! What will he care?" said his wife. "Ask him yerself what he thinks of gossip!"

"Indeed," answered her husband, "I never heeded it enough to tell. There's but one word I heed, and that's my Master's."

"Eh, but ye canna lift me oot o' the pit!" groaned the poor girl.

"God helping, we can," returned the minister. "But you're not in the pit yet by a long road."

"I dinna ken what's to come o' me," she groaned.

"That we'll soon see! Breakfast's to come of you first, and then my wife and me will have a talk and see what's to be done. You can say what you please, and no ill folk will come near you."

A pitiful smile flashed across Isy's face, and with it returned the almost babyish look that used to form part of her charm. Like an obedient child she set herself to eat and drink what she could, and when she had evidently done her best, the minister took her cup and plate.

"Now, put your feet up on the sofa," said the minister, "and tell us everything."

"No," returned Isy. "I cannot tell you *everything*."

"Then tell us what you please—so long as it's true, and that I'm sure it will be," he replied.

"I will, sir," she answered.

For several minutes she was silent, as if thinking how to begin, then after a sigh or two, she spoke.

"I'm not a good woman," she began. "Perhaps I am worse than you think me.—Oh, my baby! my baby!" she cried, and burst into tears.

"We will not think badly of you," the minister's wife reassured. "But tell me just one thing: what made you go straight from the church to the public house last night? The two don't go so well together."

"It was this, ma'am," she replied, attempting to resume the more refined speech of the south. "I had a dreadful shock that night from seeing someone in the church whom I had thought never to see again. And when I got out into the street, I turned so sick that somebody gave me a drink of whiskey, and, not having been used to it for some time, I disgraced myself. But indeed, I have a much worse trouble and shame upon me than that—one you would hardly believe, ma'am."

"I understand," said Mrs. Robertson, "and you saw him in church—the man that got you into trouble. I thought that must be it—won't you tell me all about it?"

"I will not name his name. I was the most to blame, for I knew better. And I would rather die than do him any more harm."

"Then don't say another word. I only thought it might be a relief to you. But I have no right to try to draw it out of you, and I wouldn't, except you want to tell me. I will never again ask you anything about him. There! You have my promise. Now, tell us what you please, and not a word more. The minister is sure to find something to comfort you."

"What can anybody say or do to comfort such as me, ma'am? I am lost—lost out of sight! Nothing can save me! The Savior himself wouldn't open the door to a woman that left her infant child out in the dark night! That's what I did!" she cried, and ended with a pitiful wail.

After a few moments she grew a little calmer, and then resumed.

"I would not have you think I wanted to get rid of the little darling. But my wits went all of a sudden, and a terror came upon me. Could it have been the hunger, do you think? I became frantic to find some milk for him, though what I was thinking of out on that barren moor I have not an idea. I laid him down in the heather, and ran from him. How far I went, I do not know. But whether I lost my way back, or what I did, or how it was, I cannot tell, only I could not find him. Then for a while I must have been clean out of my mind, and was haunted with visions of him being pulled at by the wild foxes. Even now, at night, every now and then it comes back, and I cannot get the sight out of my head. For a while it drove me to drink, but I got rid of that until just last night, when again I was overcome. Oh, if I could only keep from seeing them when I'm falling asleep!"

She gave a smothered scream and hid her face in her hands. Mrs. Robertson, weeping herself by now, tried to comfort her, but it seemed in vain.

"The worst of it is," Isy resumed, "—for I must confess everything, ma'am— is that I cannot tell what I may have done when the drink was on me. I may have even told his name, though I remember nothing about it. It must be months since I tasted a drop till last night. And now I've done it again, and I'm not fit for him even to cast a look at me. My heart's just like to break when I think I may have been false to him, as well as false to my bairn. If the devils would just come and take me I'd be grateful!"

"My dear," came the voice of the minister where he sat listening to every word she uttered, "nothing but the hand of the Son of Man will come near you out of the dark, soft-stroking your heart, and closing up the terrible gash in it. In the name of God, the Savior of men, I tell you, dautie, the day will come when you'll smile in the very face of the Lord himself at the thought of what he has brought you through—Lord Jesus, hold tightly to your poor bairn and to hers, and give her back her own. Thy will be done!—Go on with your tale, lassie."

" 'Deed, sir, I can say no more. I fear I'm still some sick."

She fell back on the sofa, her face very pale.

The minister was a big man. He took her in his arms and carried her to a room they always kept ready on the chance of a visit from "one of the least of these."

At the top of the stair stood their little daughter, a child of five or six.

"Who is it, mother?" she whispered as Mrs. Robertson passed, following her husband and Isy. "Is she very dead?"

"No, darling," answered her mother; "it is an angel that has lost her way, and is tired—so tired! You must be very quiet and not disturb her. Her head is going to ache very much."

The child turned and went down the stair, step by step, softly saying, "I will tell my rabbit not to make any noise—and to be as white as he can."

Once more they succeeded in bringing back the light of consciousness to Isy's clouded spirit. She woke in a soft white bed, with two faces of compassion bending over her, closed her eyes again with a smile of sweet contentment, and was soon wrapped in a wholesome slumber.

In the meantime the minister enslaved to himself rather than liberated from it as was his friend, had reached home and found a ghastly loneliness awaiting him at the manse. How much deeper it was even than that surrounding the woman he had forsaken! She had lost her repute and her baby; he had lost his God.

He had never seen the Almighty's shape, and did not have his Word abiding in him. And now the vision of him was closed in an unfathomable abyss of darkness. The signs of God were around him in the Book, around him in the work, around him in his fellow humanity, and around him in his own existence—but the external signs only! God himself did not speak to him, did not manifest himself to him.

God was not where James Blatherwick had ever sought him. He was not in any place where there was the least likelihood of his ever looking for or finding him.

12

The Question

*B*latherwick still knew nothing about the existence of his child. If he had, the knowledge might have altered the thoughts going through his mind on his way home to Tiltowie from the city, namely a half-conscious satisfaction he felt at having been preserved from marrying a woman who had now proved capable of disgracing him in the very streets. But at the same time he passed through many alternations of thought and feeling. Up and down, this way and that, went the changing currents of self-judgment or self-consolation, and of new dread of discovery. Never for two moments following one another was his mind clear, his purpose determined, his line set straight for honesty.

But in the end he sank again to that lowest of paths toward which his mind was ever bent: He must live up—not to the law of righteousness, but to the outward show of what a minister ought to be like. He must watch his appearance before men! He must keep up the deception he had begun in childhood, and had, until lately, practiced unknowingly.

Now that he knew what he was doing, he went on, not knowing how to get rid of it, shrinking in what must be regarded as cowardice from the confession that would have been the only thing able to set him free. Now he sought only how to conceal his deception. He was miserable in knowing himself to be not what he seemed—to be compelled to look like one that had not sinned. He grumbled in his heart that God should have forsaken him so far as to allow him to disgrace himself before his own conscience.

He did not yet see that his foulness, the sin that was part of his nature, was ingrained, that a man might change the color of his skin or a leopard his spots as soon as he would rid himself of that which was an intrinsic part of his being. He did not see that he had never yet looked purity in the face, that the fall which disgraced him in his own eyes was but the necessary outcome of his character— that it was no accident but an unavoidable result.

Even to begin the purification, without which his moral and spiritual being must perish eternally, he would have to look on himself as he was. Yet he shrank from recognizing himself, and thought his true self lay hidden from all. It is strange to say, but many a man will never yield to see himself as he truly is until he becomes aware of the eyes of other men fixed upon him. Then first, ever to himself, will he be driven to confess what he has long all but known.

Blatherwick's hour was on its way, slow in coming, but no longer to be avoided. His soul was ripening to self-declaration. The ugly flower of self must blossom to show its nature for what it is. What a hold God has upon us in this inevitable ripening of the unseen into the invisible and present. The flower is there and must appear.

In the meantime he suffered, and walked on in silence, walking like a servant of the Ancient of Days, but knowing himself a whited sepulchre. Within him he felt the dead body that could not rest until it was laid bare to the sun; but all the time he comforted himself that he kept himself from falling a second time, and hoping that the *once* would not be remembered against him. Did not the fact that it was apparently forgotten, most likely never even known, indicate that he was forgiven of God? And so, unrepentant, he remained unforgiven, and continued a hypocrite and slave of sin.

But the hideous thing was not altogether concealed. Something was showing under the covering whiteness. His mother saw that something shapeless haunted him, and often asked herself what it could be, but always shrank even from con-jecturing. His father, too, felt that he was removed a great distance from him, and that his son's supposed feeding of the flock had done nothing to bring him and his parents nearer to each other. What could be hidden, he wondered, beneath the mask of that unsmiling face?

But there was one humble observer who saw deeper than either of the par-ents—John MacLear, the village soutar.

One day, after about two weeks, the minister walked into the cobbler's work-shop and found him there as usual. His hands were working away diligently, but his thoughts had for some time been brooding over the fact that God is not the God of the perfect only, but of the growing as well; not the God only of the righteous, but of such as hunger and thirst after righteousness.

"God, blow in the smoking flax, an' tie up the bruised reed!" he was saying to himself aloud when the minister walked in.

Now, as is the case in some other mystical natures, a certain something had been developed in the soutar very much like a spirit of prophecy. It took the form of an insight that occasionally laid bare to him in a measure the thoughts and intents of the heart of others, without the exercise of his will to that end. Perhaps it was rather merely the reasoning faculty of his mind working unconsciously, of putting together outward signs, and drawing from them the conclusion of the facts at which they pointed. In any case, he often found himself in the unusual position of seeing more deeply into another's heart than the other was aware of.

Upon this occasion, after their greeting, the soutar suddenly looked up at his visitor with a certain fixed expression. The first glance he had cast that day on the minister's face had shown him that he looked ill, and he now saw that something in the man's heart was eating away at it like a cancer.

Almost immediately the question arose in his brain: Could he be the father of the little one in the next room? But almost the same instant he shut it into the darkest closet of his mind, shrinking from the secret of another soul, as from lifting a corner of the veil that hid the Holy of Holies! The next moment, however, came the thought: What if it *was* true, and what if as a result the man stood in need of the offices of a true friend? It was one thing to pry into a man's secret; it was another to help him escape from it!

The soutar sat looking at him for a moment, as if out of this very thought, and as a result the minister felt the hot blood rush to his cheeks.

"Ye dinna look too weel, Minister," said the soutar. "Is there anythin' the matter wi' ye, sir?"

"Nothing worth mentioning," answered the parson. "I sometimes have a touch of headache in the early morning, especially when I have been up later than usual over my books the night before. But it always goes away during the day."

"Ow weel, that's no, as ye say, a very serious thing. I couldna help fanceyin' ye had somethin' out of the ordinary on your mind."

"Nothing, nothing," rejoined the minister, with a feeble laugh. "—But," he went on—and something seemed to send the words to his lips without giving him time to think—"it is curious you should say that, for I was just thinking what was the real intent of the Apostle in his injunction to confess our faults one to another."

The moment he had spoken the words he felt almost as if he had proclaimed his very secret from the housetop. He would have begun the sentence afresh, with some notion of correcting it, but again he felt the hot blood shoot to his face. *I must go on with something!* he thought to himself, *or those sharp eyes of the old man's will see right through me!*

"It came into my mind," he went on, "that I should like to know what you thought about the passage. It surely cannot give the least ground for directly spoken confession. I understand perfectly how a man may want to consult a friend in any difficulty—and that friend is naturally the minister, but—"

This was by no means a thing he had meant to say, but he seemed carried on to say he knew not what. It was as if the will of God was driving the man to the brink of a pure confession—to the cleansing of his bosom "of that perilous stuff that weighs upon the heart."

"Do you think, for instance," he continued, thus driven, "that a man is bound to tell *everything*—even to the friend he loves best?"

"I think," answered the soutar, making what effort he could to speak plainly so he would not be misunderstood, so important did he consider his words, "that we must answer the *what* before we enter upon the *how much*. An' I think, first o' all, that we must ask, To *whom* are we bound to confess?—an' there surely is the answer, to him to whom we hae done the wrong. If we hae been grumbling in our hearts, it is to God we must confess: who else has to do wi' the matter? To *him* we must flee the moment oor eyes are opened to what we've been aboot. But if we hae wronged one o' oor fellow creatures, who are we to go to wi' oor confession but that same fellow creature? It seems to me we must go to that man first—even afore we go to God himsel'. Not one moment must we indulge procrastination on the plea o' prayin' instead o' confessin'. From oor very knees we must rise in haste, an' say to brother or sister, 'I've done ye this or that wrong: forgive me.' God can wait for yer prayer better than ye, or him ye've wronged, can wait for yer confession! After that ye must make yer best attempt to make up for the wrong. 'Confess yer sins,' I think it means, 'each o' ye to the other against whom ye hae done the offense.'—Don't ye think that's the common sense o' the matter?"

"Indeed, I think you must be right," replied the minister, who was thinking of no such thing, but rather how he might recover his retreat. "I will go home at once and think it all over. Indeed, I am now all but convinced that what you say must be what the Apostle intended!"

With a great sigh of relief of which he was not aware, Blatherwick rose and walked from the kitchen, hoping he looked—not guilty, but sunk in thought. In truth he was unable to think. Oppressed and burdened down with the sense of a duty too unpleasant to even think about, he went home to his cheerless manse, where his housekeeper was the only person he had to speak to, a woman incapable of comforting anybody.

He went straight to his study, knelt down, but found he could not pray the simplest prayer. Not a word would come, and he could not pray without words. For the moment he was dead, and in hell—so far perished that he felt nothing.

He rose and sought the open air, but it brought him no restoration. He had not heeded his friend's advice. He was not even able to contemplate the thought of the one thing possible to him—had not moved even in spirit a step closer to Isy. The only comfort he could now find for his guilty soul was the thought that he could do nothing, for he did not even know where Isy was to be found. When he remembered the next moment that his friend Robertson must be able to find her—for if it was not her at his doorstep, she *did* at least occasionally attend his church. He soothed his conscience with the reflection that there was no coach till the next morning, and in the meantime he could write a letter. A letter would reach the minister almost as soon as he could himself.

But what would Robertson think? He might give the letter to his wife to read. They concealed nothing from each other. That would never do. So he only walked the faster, tired himself out, and earned an appetite as the result of his day's work. He ate a good dinner, although with little enjoyment, and fell asleep in his chair. No letter was written to Robertson that day. No letter of such sort was ever written. The spirit was not willing, and the flesh was weakness itself.

In the evening he took up a learned commentary on the Book of Job. But he never even approached the discovery of what Job wanted, received, and was satisfied with in the end. He never saw that what he himself needed, but did not desire, was the same thing—a sight of God! He never discovered that, when God came to Job, Job forgot all he had intended to say to him—did not ask him a single question—because he suddenly knew that all was well. The student of Scripture remained blind to the fact that the very presence of the Loving One, the Father of men, proved sufficient in itself to answer every question, to still every doubt. But then James's heart was not pure like Job's, and therefore he could never have seen God. He did not even desire to see him, and so could see nothing as it was. He read with the blindness of the devil of self in his heart.

In Marlowe's *Faust,* Mephistopheles says to the student:

Where we are is hell;
And where hell is there must we ever be:
. . . . when all the world dissolves,
And every creature shall be purified,
All places shall be hell that are not heaven;

and it was thus that James fared; and thus he went to bed.

And while he lay there sleepless, his father and mother, some three miles away, were talking about him in bed.

13

· · · · · · · · · · · · · · · · · ·

The Parents

*M*arion and Peter Blatherwick had lain silent for some time, thinking about their son. They had been reflecting how little satisfaction his being a minister had brought them. And in so thinking they had gone back in their minds to a certain time, long before, when they had had a talk together about him as a schoolboy.

Even then the heart of the mother had been aware of his coldness, his seeming unconsciousness of his parents as having any share in his life. Scotch parents are seldom outwardly affectionate to their children. But not the less in them, possibly all the hotter because of their outward coldness, burns the deep and central fire—

that eternal fire without which the world would turn to a frozen mass, the love of parent for the child. That fire must burn while the Father of all men lives! That fire must burn until the universe is the Father and his children, and none beside. That fire, however long held down and crushed by the weight of unkindled fuel, must go on to gather heat, and, gathering, it must glow, and at last break forth in the scorching, yea, devouring flames of a righteous indignation: the Father must and *will* be supreme that his children perish not.

But as yet *the Father* endured and was silent, so too the child-parents must endure and be still. In the meantime their son remained hidden from them as by a thick moral hedge. He never came out from behind it, never stood clear before them, and they were unable to break through to him. There was no angelic traitor within his citadel of indifference to draw back the bolts of its iron gates and let them in. They had gone on hoping, and hoping in vain, for some change in him, but at last had to confess it a relief when he left the house and went to Edinburgh.

But the occasion of their talk about the lad was long before that.

The two children were in bed and asleep, and the parents were lying then, as they lay now, sleepless.

"Hoo's Jamie been gettin' on today?" said his father.

"Weel enough, I suppose," answered his mother, who did not then speak Scotch quite so broad as her husband's, although a good deal broader than her mother, the wife of a country doctor, would have permitted when she was a child. "He's always busy at his books. He's a diligent boy, but as to hoo he's gettin' on, I can't say. He never lets a word go from him as to what he's doin' one way or another. 'What *can* he be thinkin' aboot?' I sometimes say to mysel'—sometimes over and over. When I go into the parlor, where he always sits till he has done his lessons, he never lifts his head to show that he hears me, or cares who's there or who isn't. And as soon as he's done, he takes a book and goes up to his room, or oot aboot the house, or into the field or the barn, and never comes near me! I sometimes wonder if he would ever miss me dead!" she ended with a great sigh.

"Hoot awa', woman! dinna go on like that," returned her husband. "The laddie's like the rest o' laddies. They're jist like pup doggies till their eyes come open, an' they ken them that brought them here. He's bound to make a good man, an' he canna do that without learnin' to be a good son to her that bore him! Ye canna say he ever disobeyed ye. Ye hae told me that a hunner times!"

"I have that! But I would hae had no occasion to dwell upon the fact if he had ever given me, jist noo an' then, a wee sign o' any affection."

"Ay, doobtless, but signs are nae proofs. The affection o' the lad may be there, but the signs o' it missin'.—But I ken weel hoo the heart o' ye's workin', my ain auld dautie," he added, anxious to comfort her who was nearer to him than son or daughter.

He paused a moment, then resumed. "I dinna think it would be weel for me to say anything to him aboot his behavior to ye. It might only make things worse, for he wouldna ken what I was aimin' at. I dinna believe he has a notion of anythin' amiss in himsel', an' I fear he would only think I was hard upon him for nae reason. Ye see, if a thing doesna come o' itsel', no cryin' upon it will make it lift its head—see long at least as a man himsel' kens naethin' aboot it."

"I'm sure ye're right, Peter," answered his wife. "I ken weel that scolding'll never make love spread oot its wings—except it be to flee away. Naethin' but fleein' can come o' scoldin'."

"It may do even worse than makin' him run," rejoined Peter. "Scoldin' may drive love clean oot o' sight. But we better go to oor ain sleep, lass!—We hae one anither, come what may."

"That's true, Peter. But aye the more I hae you, the more I want my Jamie!" cried the poor mother.

The father said no more. But after a while he rose, stole softly to his son's room. His wife heard him, and followed him, and found him on his knees by the bedside, his face buried in the blankets where his boy lay asleep with calm, dreamless countenance.

At length she took her husband's hand and led him back to bed.

"To think," she said as they went, "that he's the same bairnie I gazed at till my soul ran oot my eyes! I well remember hoo I laughed and cried both at once to think that I was the mother o' the manchild. An' I thought I then kenned what was in the heart o' Mary when she clasped the blessed one to her bosom!"

"May that same bairnie, born t' be oor remedy for sins, bring oor child to his right mind afore he's too auld to repent!" responded the father in a broken voice.

"Why was the heart o' a mither put into me?" groaned Marion. "Why was I made a woman, whose life is for the bearin' o' bairns to the great Father o' all, if this was to be my reward?—Na, na, Lord," she went on, interrupting and checking herself, "I want nothin' but thy will, an' weel I ken that ye wouldna hae me think such was thy will."

The memory of that earlier conversation took both the parents for a time into the silence of their own hearts. It would not be altogether truthful to say that they had taken no pleasure in the advancement of their son in the years since then. The mother was glad to be proud of his position, such as it was, in place of the happiness she could not find—proud with the love for him that lay incorruptible in her being. But the love that is all on one side, though it be stronger than death, can hardly be so strong as life! A poor, maimed, one-winged thing, such love cannot soar into any region of conscious bliss. Even when it soars into the region where God himself dwells, it is but to partake there of the divine sorrow that his heartless children cause him. But this poor pride notwithstanding, neither father nor mother dwelt much upon what their neighbors called James's success, or cared to talk about it. To do so they would have felt genuine hypocrisy so long as their relationship with him was so far from perfect. Never to anyone but each other did they allude to the bitterness of their own hearts. And now the daughter was also gone to whom the mother had at one time been able to unburden herself, because she understood and was able to share in her parents' misery over her brother.

So in silence the parents grieved, and the lad grew, and when James Blatherwick left Stonecross for the university, it was with scarce a backward look, with nothing in his heart but eagerness for the status that awaited him. He gained one of the highest bursaries, and never gave so much as a thought to the son of the poor widow who had competed with him, and who, because of his failure, had been forced to leave his ambition for an education behind him and go to work in a shop. This same young man, however, soon became able to keep his mother in what was to her nothing less than happy luxury, which is far more than can be said about the successful James.

As often as James returned home for the vacations, things between him and his parents were unchanged. By his third return, the heart of his sister had stopped beating any the faster at the thought of his arrival home: she knew that he would but shake hands limply, let hers drop, and a moment later be sat down to read. Before the time for him to take his degree came four years after he had begun, she had passed out of this life and to the great Father. James never missed her, and neither wished nor was asked to go home to her funeral. To his mother he was never anything more or less than quite civil, and on her part she never asked him to do anything for her. He came and went as he pleased, cared for nothing done on the farm or about the house, and seemed in his own thoughts and studies to have more than enough to occupy him. He had grown up to be a strong as well as a handsome youth, and had dropped almost every sign of his country breeding. He never spoke a word in his mother dialect, but spoke good English with a Scotch accent.

His father had to sadly realize that his son was far too fine a gentleman to show any interest in agriculture, or to put his hand to the least share in that oldest and most dignified of callings. His mother continued to look forward, although with fading interest, to the time when he should be the messenger of a gospel that he in no way understood. But his father did not at all share her anticipation.

He was an intelligent youth, and by the time he went to Edinburgh to learn theology he was relatively accomplished in mathematics, chemistry, and the classics. His first aspiration was to show himself a gentleman in the eyes of the bubble-head calling itself Society—of which in fact he knew nothing. After that his goal was to have his eloquence, at present existent only in his ambitious imagination, recognized by the public. These were the two devils, or rather the two forms of the one devil Vanity, that possessed him. He looked down on his parents, and on the whole circumstance of their ordered existence, as unworthy of him because it was old-fashioned and rural, concerned only with God's earth and God's animals, and having nothing to do with the shows of life. And yet to many the ways of life in the house of his parents, in contrast with the son's views of life, would have seemed altogether admirable. To such, the homely and simple ways of the unassuming homestead would have appeared very warm and attractive.

But James took little interest in any of this, and none at all in the ways of the humble people, tradesmen and craftsmen of the neighboring village. He never felt the common humanity that made him one with them. Had he turned his feelings into thoughts and words, he would have said, "I cannot help being the son of a farmer, but at least my mother's father was a doctor; and had I been consulted, my father should have been at least an officer in one of His Majesty's services, not a treader of dung or artificial manure!"

The root of his folly lay in his groundless self-esteem, fed by a certain literature that fed the notion that rising in the world and gaining the praise of men was the highest of callings. But the man whom we call *the Savior*, and who knew the secret of Life, warned his followers that they must not seek that sort of distinction if they would be the children of the Father who claimed them.

After both parents had lain silent for a good many moments, they began again to speak of their son.

"I was jist thinkin', Peter," said Marion, "o' the last time we spoke together aboot the laddie—it must be nigh six years since then, I'm thinkin'."

"'Deed, I canna say. Ye may be right," replied her husband.

"It's no such a pleasant subject that we should hae much to say aboot it. He's a man noo, an' weel looked upon, but it makes little difference to his parents. He's jist as hard as ever, an' as far as man could weel be frae them he came frae—never a word to the one or the other o' us! If we were two dogs he couldna hae less to say to us. I'll bet Frostie says more in one half hoor to his tyke than Jamie has said to you or me since he first gaed away to college!"

"Bairns is a queer kind o' blessin'!" continued the mother. "But, eh! it's what may lie behind the silence that frightens me!"

"What do ye mean, lass!"

"Ow, nothin' maybe," returned Marion, bursting into tears. "But all at once it was borne in upon me that there must be somethin' to account for the thing. At the same time I dare not ask God. For there's somethin' worse noo than was even there when he was a boy. He has such a look, as if he couldna see nor hear anythin' but what's inside him. It's an awful thing for a mither to say o' her own laddie, an' it makes my heart like to break!—as if I had ben false to my ain flesh an' blood!—Eh, Peter, what can it be?"

"Maybe it's nothin' at a'. Maybe he's in love."

"Nae, Peter. Love makes a man look up, not doon at his ain feet! It makes him hold his head back an' look oot in front o' him—no at his ain inside! It makes a man straight in the back, strong in the arm, an' bold in the heart. Didna it you, Peter?"

"Maybe it did; I dinna weel remember. But I see it can hardly be love wi' the lad. Still, even his parents mustna judge him, 'specially as he's one o' the Lord's ministers—maybe one o' the Lord's elect."

"It's awful to think—I hardly dare say it, Peter! But was nae minister o' the gospel ever a heepocreete?—like one o' the auld scribes an' Pharisees? Oh, Peter, wouldna it be terrible if oor only ain son was—"

But here she broke down and could not finish the frightful sentence. The farmer left his bed and dropped into a chair beside it. The next moment he sank on his knees, and hiding his face in his hand, groaned, as from a thicket of torture.

"God in heaven, hae mercy upon the whole lot o' us!"

Then, apparently unconscious of what he did, he went wandering from the room, down the kitchen, and out to the barn on his bare feet, closing the door of the house behind him. In the barn he threw himself face downward on a heap of loose straw and lay there motionless. His wife wept alone in her bed, and hardly missed him. It required little reflection on her part to understand where he had gone or what he was doing. He was crying from the bitterness of a wounded father's heart, to the Father of fathers.

"God, ye're a father yersel'," he groaned, "an' sae ye ken hoo it's tearin' at my heart! I'm no accusin' Jamie, Lord, for ye ken weel hoo little I ken aboot him. He never opened the book o' his heart to *me*! Oh, God, grant that he has nothin' to hide; but if he has, Lord, pluck it oot o' him, an' *him* oot o' the mud! I dinna ken hoo to pray for him, Lord, for I'm in the dark. But deliver him some way, Lord, I pray thee, for his mither's sake!—Lord, deliver the heart o' her frae the awfulest o' all her fears—that her ain son's a heepocreete, a Judas-man!"

He remained there praying upon the straw while hour after hour passed, pleading with the great Father for his son; his soul now lost in dull fatigue, until at length the dawn looked in on the night-weary earth, and into the two sorrow-laden hearts, bringing with it a comfort they did not seek to understand.

14

The Fire

But the prayers of his parents brought no solace to the mind of the weak, hard-hearted, and guilty son. He continued to succeed in temporarily soothing his conscience with some narcotic of false comfort, and even as his father prayed, he himself slept the sleep of the houseless, who look up to no watchful eye over them, and whose covering is narrower than they can wrap themselves in.

Ah, those nights! Alas for the sleepless human soul out in the eternal cold! But such was James's heartless state at present that if his mother had come to him in the morning with her tear-dimmed eyes, he would never have asked himself what could be troubling her, would not have had sympathy enough even to see that she was unhappy, would never have suspected himself as the cause of her red eyes and aching head. The only good thing in him was the uneasiness of his heart and the trouble of his mind, of which he was constantly aware.

Thank God, there was no way around the purifying fire! He could not escape it; he must pass through it!

15

....

The Proposition

*T*he world little knows what a power among men is he who simply and thoroughly believes in him who is Lord of the world to save men from their sins! He may be neither wise nor prudent in the world's eyes. He may be clothed in no attractive colors or in any word of power. And yet if he has but that love for his neighbor that is rooted in and springs from love to his God, he is always a redeeming, reconciling influence among his fellows. The Robertsons were genial of heart, loving and tender toward man or woman in need of them, and their door was always open for such to enter and find help. If the parson insisted on the wrath of God against sin, he did not fail to give assurance of the Lord's tenderness toward such that had fallen.

Together the godly pair at length persuaded Isobel of the eager forgiveness of the Son of Man. They assured her that he could not drive from him the very worst of sinners, but loved—nothing less than tenderly loved—anyone who turned his face to the Father. She would no doubt, they said, have to bear her trespass in the eyes of the unforgiving who looked upon her, but the Lord would lift her high and welcome her to the home of the glad-hearted.

But poor Isy, who regarded her fault as both against God and the man who had misled her, was sick at heart. She insisted that nothing God himself could do could ever restore her, for nothing could erase the fact that she had fallen. God might be ready to forgive her, but could not love her! Jesus might have made satisfaction for her sin, but how could that make any difference in or to her? She was troubled that Jesus should have so suffered, but that could not give her back her purity, or the peace of mind she once possessed. That was gone forever! Never to all eternity could she be innocent again. Life had lost all interest for her.

And yet, strange to say, along with this suffering of mind came a requickening of her long dormant imagination. Sometimes she would wake from a dream where she stood in blessed nakedness with a deluge of cool, comforting rain pouring upon her from the sweetness of heaven. And every night to her sinful bosom came back the soft innocent hands of the child she had lost. But then she would always dream that she was Hagar, casting her child away, and fleeing from the sight of his death. More than once she dreamed that an angel came to her, and went out to look for her boy—only to return and lay him in her arms, dead from some wild beast.

When the first few days of her sojourn with the Good Samaritans were over, and she had gathered enough strength to feel she ought not to burden them any longer, they positively refused to let her leave. They began to try to revive her spirits by reawakening in her the hope of finding her lost child. They set inquiry on foot in every direction, and promised to let her know the moment they began to feel inconvenienced by her presence.

"Inasmuch as ye did it to one of the least of these, ye did it to me!" insisted Mrs. Robertson upon one of the poor girl's outbursts of self-pity. "Was the Lord a burden to Mary and Lazarus?"

"But that doesn't apply to me, ma'am," objected Isy. "I'm none of his!"

"Who is then? Whom did he come to save? Are you not one of his lost sheep? Are you not weary and heavy-laden? Will you never let him feel at home with you? Are you to say who he is to love and who he isn't? Are you to tell him who are fit to be counted his, and who are not good enough?" Isy was silent for a long time. The foundations of her coming peace were being dug deeper and laid wider.

Isy still found it impossible, from the disordered state of her mind, to give any careful thought to where she had laid her child down. And Maggie, who loved him passionately, and believed him willfully abandoned, had no desire to discover one who could claim him, but was unworthy of him. Therefore, for a long time neither she nor her father ever talked, or encouraged talk, about him. Nevertheless, certain questioning busybodies began to sniff about and give tongue. It was all very well, they said, for the cobbler and his Maggie to pose as rescuers and benefactors; but whose was the child? His growth nevertheless went on all the same, and however such hints might seem to concern him, happily they never reached him. And yet all the time, in the not so distant city, a loving woman was weeping and pining for lack of him, whose conduct, in the eyes of the Robertsons, was blameless. But although mentally and spiritually she was growing rapidly, she seemed to have lost all hope. For deeper in her soul, and nearer the root of her misery than even the loss of her child, lay the character and conduct of the man whom she had loved. His neglect of her burned at the bands of her life; and her friends soon began to fear that she was on the verge of a slow downward slide upon which there is seldom any turning.

Mr. and Mrs. Robertson had long been on very friendly terms with the farmer of Stonecross and his wife. And thinking about the condition of their guest, it was natural that the thought of Mrs. Blatherwick should occur to them as one who might be able to give the kind of help the poor girl needed. Since the death of their own daughter, the Blatherwicks had not even had a servant with them at the farm, and the parson thought that the potential relationship could not help but be beneficial to both sides. He decided, therefore, to pay their friends at Stonecross a visit and tell them all they knew about Isy.

It was a lovely morning in the decline of summer when the minister mounted the top of the coach to wait, silent and a little anxious, for the appearance of the coachman from the office, after which he thrust the waybill into the pocket of his huge greatcoat, to gather his reins and climb heavily to his perch. A journey of four hours, through a not very interesting country, but along a splendid road in the direction of Inverness, would carry him to the village where the soutar lived and where James Blatherwick was parson. Passing through gentle rolling farm-land, the corn was nearly full grown, but still green, without sign of the coming gold of perfection that was still some weeks away. After his arrival in Tiltowie, a walk of about three miles awaited him—a long and somewhat weary way for the townminister—accustomed indeed to tramping the hard pavements, but not to long walks unbroken by calls.

Climbing at last the hill on which the farmhouse stood, he caught sight of Peter Blatherwick in a nearby field of barley stubble, with the reins of a pair of powerful Clydesdales in his hands, wrestling with the earth as it strove to wrench from his hold the stilts of the plough whose share and courter he was guiding through it. Peter's delight was in the open air, and hard work in it. He was far above the vulgar idea that a man rises in the social scale to the degree he ceases to labor with his hands. No more could he have imagined that a man advances in the kingdom of heaven by being made an elder.

As to his higher nature, the farmer believed in God—that is, he tried to do what God required of him, and thus was on the straight road to know him. He talked little about religion, and was not one to take sides on doctrinal issues. When he heard people advocating or opposing the claims of this or that party in the church, he would turn away with a smile such as men yield to the talk of children. He had no time, he would say, for that kind of thing. He had enough to do in trying to faithfully practice what was beyond dispute.

He was a reading man, one who not merely drank at every open source he came across, but thought over what he read, and was therefore a man of true intelligence, who was regarded by his neighbors with more than ordinary respect. He had been the first in the district to apply certain discoveries in chemistry to agriculture, and had made use of them with notable results on his own farm, and setting an example which his neighbors were so ready to follow that the region, nowise remarkable for its soil, soon became rather remarkably known for its crops.

The noteworthiest thing in him, however, was his *humanity*, shown first and chiefly in the width and strength of his family affections. He had a strong drawing, not only to his immediate relations, but to all of his blood, and they were many, for he came of an old family that had been long settled in the neighborhood. In worldly affairs, he was better than most of the region, having added not a little to the small amount of land his father had left him. But he was by no means a lover of money, being open-handed to his wife, upon whom a miser is usually the first to exercise his parsimony. There was, however, at Stonecross little call for the spending of money, and still less temptation from without, for the simple life of the Blatherwicks was supplied in most of its necessities from the farm itself. In disposition Peter was a good-humored, even merry, man, with a playful answer almost always ready for a greeting neighbor.

The minister waved a greeting to the farmer from a distance and went first to the house, which stood close at hand, with its low gable toward him.

Mr. Robertson passed a low window, through which he had a glimpse of the pretty old-fashioned parlor within, as he went round to the front to knock at the nearer of two green-painted doors.

Mrs. Blatherwick came to open it, and finding who it was that knocked—of all the men the most welcome in her present mood of disconsolation over her son—received him with the hearty simplicity of an evident welcome. Though she was not yet prepared to open her heart and let him see into its sorrow, the appearance of the minister brought her, nevertheless, as it were the dawn of a winter morning after a long night of pain.

She led him into the low-ceiled parlor and into the green gloom of the big hydrangea that filled the front window, and the ancient scent of the withered rose-leaves in the gorgeous china on the goldbordered table-cover. There the minister sat, and after a few commonplaces silently pondered how to make the proposition he had in his mind.

Marion Blatherwick was a good-looking woman, with a quiet strong expression, and sweet gray eyes. The daughter of a country surgeon, she had been left an orphan without means, but was so generally respected that everyone said Mr. Blatherwick had never done better than when he married her. There had very early grown up a sense of distance between her and her son, and now her heart would sometimes go longing after him as if he were one of those who died in their infancy. But her dead daughter, gone beyond range of eye and ear, seemed never to have left them: there was no separation, only distance between them.

"I have taken the liberty, Mrs. Blatherwick, of coming to ask your help in a great perplexity," began Mr. Robertson, with a hesitancy she had never seen in him before.

"Weel, sir, 'tis an honor to me, I'm sure!" she answered.

"Wait until you hear what it is," rejoined the minister. "We, that is, my wife and I, have a poor lass at home with us. We've taken a great interest in her for some weeks past, but now we're almost at our wits' end about what to do with her next. She's sad in heart and not in the best of health and altogether without hope. And she stands in a desperate need of a change."

"Weel, that ouchtna be much o' a difficulty atween auld frien's like oorsel's, Mr. Robertson! Ye would hae us take her in for a while, till she begins to look up a bit, poor thing? Hoo auld is she?"

"She can hardly be more than twenty, or about that—near what your own lassie would have been by this time, if she had ripened here instead of going away to the grand finishing school of the just made perfect. And, indeed, she's not altogether unlike your own lass."

"Eh, sir, bring her to me! My heart's waitin' for her. But what aboot her ain mither? She maunna lose her!"

"She has no mother! But I don't want you to do anything hastily. I must tell you about her first."

"I'm content that she's a friend o' yers. I weel ken ye would never hae me take into my hoose one what wasna fit."

"The fact is, she's had a terrible misfortune."

The good woman drew back slightly, then asked hurriedly.

"There's no bairn, is there?"

"Indeed there is—but part of the misery is that the child's disappeared, and she's breaking her heart over him. She's almost out of her mind, ma'am! Not that she's anything but perfectly reasonable, and she never gives us a grain of trouble. And I can't doubt but that she'd be a great help to you for however long you would let her stay. But she's just haunted with the idea that she put the baby down and left him, and she doesn't know where. Truly ma'am, I think she's one of the lambs of the Lord's own flock!"

"That's no the way the lambs o' *his* flock are in the way o' behavin' themsel's! I fear, sir, that ye may be lettin' yer heart run away wi' yer judgment."

"I have always considered Mary Magdalene one of the Lord's own lambs, that he left the rest to look for, and this is such another. If you help him to come upon her, you'll carry her home between you rejoicing. And you'll remember how he stood between one far worse than her and the men that fain would have shamed her, and then he sent them away like so many dogs—those great Pharisees—with their tails between their legs."

"Ay, ye're right, sir!" cried his hostess. "To think that my heart should hae made me doobt yer word as one o' the Lord's servants, I beg yer pardon. Will ye no bide the night wi' us an' go back by the mornin' coach?"

"I will that, ma'am—and I thank you kindly! I am a bit fatigued with the hill road, and the walk was a bit longer than I'm used to."

"Then I must go an' see aboot dinner," said Marion, rising. "I winna be long."

Later, after the farmer had anticipated the hour for unyoking and had hurried home, they enjoyed their dinner together, and then sat in the cool of a sweet summer evening in the garden in front of the house, among roses and lilies and poppy heads and long pink-striped grasses. The minister opened wide his heart and told them all he knew and thought about Isy. And so prejudiced were they in her favor by what he said of her that whatever anxieties might have yet remained about the new relation into which they were about to enter were soon absorbed in the hopeful expectation of her arrival. Indeed, the prospect of aiding one in the effort to rise to a new life was the best comfort he could have brought them in their own miseries about James.

When he reached home, the minister was startled, even dismayed by the pallor that came over Isy's face when she heard the name and abode of the friends that he assured her would welcome her warmly.

"They'll be wanting to know everything!" she sobbed.

"You tell them everything they have a right to know," returned the minister. "They are good people, and will not ask more. Beyond that, they will respect your silence."

"There's one thing, as you know, that I can't and won't tell. To hold my tongue about that is the one particle of honesty left possible to me. It's enough that I should have been the cause of the poor man's sin, and I'm not going to bring upon him any of the consequences of it as well."

"We will not go into the question of whether you or he was the more to blame," returned the parson, "but I heartily approve of your resolve, and admire your firmness in holding to it. The time may come when you *ought* to tell; but until then, I shall not even allow myself to wonder who the faithless man may be."

Isy burst into tears.

"Don't call him that, sir! Don't drive me to doubt him. I deserve nothing! And for my bonny bairn, he must by this time be back home to the Lord that sent him!"

Thus assured that her secret would be respected by those to whom she was going, Isy ceased to show further reluctance to accept the shelter offered her. And in truth, underneath the dread of encountering James Blatherwick's parents, lay hidden in her mind the fearful joy of catching a chance glimpse of the man whom she still loved with the forgiving tenderness of a true, and therefore strong, heart.

With a trembling, fluttering bosom therefore, she took her place not many days thereafter on the coach beside Mr. Robertson, to go with him to the refuge he had found for her.

16

The Refuge

*O*nce more out in the country, the beauties of the world began to work the will of its Maker upon Isy's poor lacerated soul. And afar in its hidden deeps the process of healing was already begun. Sorrow would often return unbidden, would at times even rise like a crested wave and threaten despair, but the Real and the True, long hidden from her by false treatment and by the lying judgments of men and women, was now at length beginning to reveal itself to her tear-blinded vision. Hope was lifting a feeble head above the tangled weeds of the subsiding deluge, and before long the girl would be able to see and understand how little the Father, whose judgment in the truth of things, cares what at any time his child may have been or done the moment that child gives herself up to be made what he would have her! Looking down into the hearts of men, he sees differences there of which the self-important world takes no heed. For indeed, many that count themselves of the first, he sees the last—and what he sees, alone *is*. Kings and emperors may be utterly forgotten, while a gutter-child, a thief, a girl who in this world never had even a notion of purity, may lie smiling in the arms of the Eternal, even as the head of a lordly house that still flourishes like a green baytree may be wandering about with the dogs beyond the walls of the city.

In the open world, the power of the present God began at once to influence

Isobel, for there, although dimly, she yet looked into his open face, sketched vaguely in the mighty something we call nature—chiefly on the great vault we call heaven. Shapely but undefined; perfect in form, yet limitless in depth; blue and persistent, yet ever evading capture by human heart in human eye; this sphere of fashioned boundlessness, of definite shapelessness, called up in her heart the formless children of upheavedness—grandeur, namely, and awe, hope and desire: all rushed together toward the dawn of the unspeakable One who, dwelling in that heaven, is above all heavens; mighty and unchangeable, yet childlike; inexorable, yet tender as never was mother; devoted as never yet was any child except one. Isy, indeed, understood little of all this; yet she wept, she knew not why; and it was not for sorrow.

When the coach journey was over, and she turned her back upon the house where her child lay and entered the desolate hill-country, a strange feeling began to invade her counsciousness. It seemed at first but an old mood, worn shadowy; then it seemed like the return of an old dream, then a painful, confused, half-forgotten memory. But at length it cleared and settled into a conviction that she had been in the same region before, and had had, although a passing, yet a painful acquaintance with it. And finally she concluded that she must be near the spot where she had left and lost her baby.

Suddenly everything that had befallen her became fused in her mind into a troubled conglomerate of hunger and cold and weariness, of help and hurt, of deliverance and returning pain. They all mingled with the scene around her, and there condensed into the memory of that one event—of which this must assuredly be the actual place! She looked upon the widespread wastes of heather and peat, great stones here and there, half buried in it, half sticking out of it. Surely she was waiting there for something to come to pass! Surely behind this veil of the seen, a child must be standing with outstretched arms, hungering after his mother!

But just as suddenly, alas!—her certainty of recollection faded from her, and of the memory itself remained nothing but a ruin. And all the time it took to dawn into brilliance and fade back out into darkness had measured but a few weary steps by the side of her companion, who was himself lost in the glad meditation of a glad sermon for the next Sunday about the lost sheep carried home with jubilance, forgetting all the while how unfit was the poor sheep beside him for such a fatiguing tramp up hill and down, along what was little more than the stony bed of a winter's torrent of a stream.

All at once Isy darted aside from the rough track, scrambled up the steep ban, and ran like one demented into a great clump of heather, through which she began to search with frantic hands. The minister stopped, bewildered, and stood to watch her, almost fearing for a moment that she had again lost her wits. She got on top of a stone in the middle of the slump, turned several times around, gazed in every direction over the moor, then descended with a hopeless look, and came slowly back to him.

"I beg your pardon," she said. "I thought I had a glimpse of my infant through the heather. I am sure this is the very spot where I left him!"

Then the next moment she faltered and said, "Have we far to go yet, sir?" and before he could even give her an answer, she staggered to the bank at the side of the road and fell upon it.

The minister saw at once that he had been pushing her too hard. He stooped down and tried to help her to lie comfortably on the short grass, and then waited anxiously for her to recover. He could see no water nearby, but at least she had plenty of air!

In a little while she came to herself, sat up, and would have risen to resume the journey except that the minister, filled with compassion for her, picked her up in his arms and carried her to the top of the hill. She argued, but was unable to resist. Light as she was, however, he found it no easy task to bear her up the last part of the steep rise, and was glad to set her down at the top—where a fresh breeze was waiting to revive them both. She thanked him like a child whose father had come to her help, and they seated themselves together on the highest point of the moor, with a large, desolate stretch of land on every side of them.

"Oh, but you are good to me!" she said. "That just reminded me of the Hill of Difficulty in the *Pilgrim's Progress*."

"Oh, you know the story?" said the minister.

"My old grannie used to make me read it to her when she lay dying. I thought it long and tiresome then, but since you took me to your house, sir, I have remembered many things in it. I knew then that I was come to the house of the Interpreter. You've made me understand."

"I am glad of that, Isy! You see, I know some things that make me very glad, and so I want them to make you glad too. And the thing that makes me gladdest of all is just that God is what he is. To know that such a one is God over us and in us makes our very being a most precious delight. His children, those of them that know him, are all glad just because he is and because they are his children. Do you think a strong man like me would read sermons and say prayers and talk to people, doing nothing but shamefully easy work if he did not believe what he said?"

"I'm sure you have had hard enough work with me! I am a hard one to teach. I was in such a bog of ignorance and misery, but I think I am now getting my head up out of it. But please, let me ask you one thing: How is it that when the thought of God comes to me, I draw back as if I were afraid of him? If he be the kind of person you say he is, why can't I go close up to him?"

"I confess the same foolishness, my child, at times," answered the minister. "It can only be because we do not yet see God as he is—and that must be because we do not yet really understand Jesus—do not see the glory of God in his face. God is just like Jesus—exactly like him!"

The parson fell to wondering, as he had many times in the past, how it could be that so many, gentle and guiltless as this womanchild, recoiled from the thought of the Perfect One. Why should they not be always and irresistibly drawn toward the very idea of God, instead of afraid of him? Why, at least, should they not run to see and make sure whether God was indeed such a one or not? whether he was really Love itself?

They sat thinking and talking, with silences between. And while they thought and talked, the daystar was all the time rising unnoticed in their hearts. At length, finding herself much stronger, Isy rose, and they resumed their journey.

The door of the farmhouse stood open to receive them. But even before they reached it, a bright-looking little woman, with delicate lines of ingrained red in a sorrowful face, appeared in it, looking out with questioning eyes—like a mother bird just loosening her feet from the threshold of her nest to fly and meet them. Through the film that blinded those expectant eyes, Marion saw what manner of woman she was that drew nigh, and her motherhood went out to her. For in the love of Isy's yearning look, humbly seeking acceptance, and in her hesitating approach half-checked by gentle apology, Marion imagined she saw her own daughter coming back from the gates of death and sprang to meet her.

The meditating love of the minister obliterated itself, making him linger a step or two behind, waiting to see what would follow. When he saw the two folded each in the other's arms, and the fountain of love thus break forth from their encountering hearts, his soul leaped for joy of the new-created love—new, but not the less surely eternal. For God is love, and love is that which is, and was, and shall be for evermore—boundless, unconditional, self-existent, creative! "Truly," he said to himself, "God is love, and God is all in all! In him love evermore breaks forth anew into fresh personality—in every new consciousness, in every new child of the one creating Father. In every burning heart, in everything that hopes and fears and is, love is the creative presence, the center, the source of life, yea, life itself; yea, God himself!"

The elder woman drew herself a little back, held the poor white-faced thing at arms' length, and looked her through the face into the heart.

"My bonny lamb," she said, and hugged her close, "come home and be a good bairn, and no ill man shall touch ye again. There's my man waitin' for ye, to keep ye safe!"

Isy looked up, and over the shoulder of her hostess saw the strong paternal face of the farmer, full of silent welcome. He did not try to account for the strange emotion that filled him.

"Come in, lassie," he said, and led the way through the parlor, where the red sunset was shining through the low gable window, filling the place with the glamour of departing glory. "Sit ye doon on the sofa there; ye must be tired. Surely ye haena come all the long road frae Tiltowie upon yer ain two wee feet?"

"'Deed she has," answered the minister, who had followed them into the room.

Marion lingered outside, wiping away the tears that insisted on continuing to flow. For the one question, "What can be amiss wi' Jamie?" had returned upon her, haunting her heart. And with it had come the idea, though vague and formless, that their goodwill to the wandering outcast might perhaps do something to make up for whatever ill thing their James might have done. At last, instead of entering the parlor, she turned away into the kitchen to make their supper.

Isy sank back in the wide sofa, lost in refuge, and when he saw the look on her face, the minister said to himself, "She is feeling just as we shall all feel when first we know that nothing is near us but the Love itself that was before all worlds, and there is no doubt more, and no questioning more." Yet even as he thought it, the heart of the farmer, too, was full of the same longing after the heart of his boy who had never learned to cry *"Father!"*

Soon they sat down to their meal, the pleasantest of all meals, a farmhouse tea. Hardly anyone spoke, and no one missed the speech or was aware of the silence, until all at once Isy thought of her child and burst into tears. Then the mother, who sorrowed with such a different and so much more bitter sorrow, knowing what she was thinking, rose from the table, came up behind her, and said, "Noo ye must jist come awa' wi' me, and I'll show ye yer bed, and leave ye there! Ye need no even say good-night to naebody—ye'll see the minister again in the mornin'."

She took Isy away, half-carrying her and half-leading her; for Marion, although no bigger than Isy, was much stronger and could have carried her easily.

That night both of the mothers slept well, and both dreamed of their mothers and of their children. But in the morning nothing remained of their two dreams except two hopes in the one Father.

When Isy entered the little parlor the next morning, she found that she had slept so long that breakfast was over, and the minister was sitting in the garden and the farmer was already busy in his field. Marion heard her come in and brought her breakfast, beaming with the ministering spirit of service. Thinking that she would eat it better if left to herself, she then went back to her work. In a few minutes, however, Isy joined her, and began at once to lend a helping hand.

"Hoot, hoot! my dear!" cried her hostess, "ye haena taken time enough to make a proper breakfast oot o' it! If ye dinna learn to eat, we'll never get any good o' ye!"

"I can't eat—for gladness," returned Isy. "You're so good to me that I hardly dare think about it; it'll make me cry! Let me help you, ma'am, and I'll grow hungry enough by dinnertime."

Mrs. Blatherwick understood and said no more. She showed her what to do, and, happy as a child, Isy came and went at her pleasant orders rejoicing. Had she started in life with less devotion, she might have fared better; but the end was not yet, and the end must be known before we dare judge: result explains history. For the present it is enough to say that, with the comparative repose of mind she now enjoyed, with the good food she had, and the wholesome exercise, for Mrs. Blatherwick took care she should not work too hard, with the steady kindness shown her, and the consequent growth of her faith and hope, Isy's light-heartedness and good looks soon began to return, so that the dainty little creature was soon both prettier and lovelier than before. At the same time her face and figure, her ways and motions, continued to mingle themselves so inextricably in Marion's mind with those of her departed daughter that before long she began to feel as if she would never be able to part with her. And it was not long either before she told herself that the remarkable girl was equal to anything that had to be done in the house, and that the experience of a day or two would make her capable of the work of the dairy as well. Thus, Isy and her mistress, for so Isy insisted on calling her, speedily settled into their new relationship as if the situation had been made for it.

It did sometimes cross the girl's mind, with a sting of doubt, whether it was fair to hide from her new friends the full facts of her past, and the true relation in which she stood to them. But to quiet her conscience she had only to reflect that it was solely for the sake of the son they loved that she kept her silence. Further than James's protection she had no design, and cherished no scheme in her heart. The idea of influencing him in any way never once crossed the horizon of her thoughts. On the contrary, she was possessed by the notion that it was she who had done him a great wrong, and she shrank in horror from the danger of rendering it irretrievable. She had never thought the thing out as between her and him, never even said to herself that he too had been to blame. Her exaggerated notion of her own share of the fault had become so fixed in her mind that all she was capable of seeing was the possible injury she had done his prospects as a minister, which seemed to her a far greater wrong than any suffering of loss he might have brought upon her. For what was *she* beside *him*! What was the ruin of her life alongside the frustration of such magnificent prospects as his?

The sole alleviation of her misery in her mind was the comfort that thus far she seemed successfully to have avoided involving him in the results of her lack of self-restraint, results which she was sure had remained concealed from him to that day. In truth, never was a hidden wrong to a woman turned more eagerly and devotedly into loving service to the man's own parents. Many a time did the heart of James's mother, as she watched Isy's deft and dainty motions, regret that such a capable and love-inspiring girl should have made herself unworthy of her son. For despite what she regarded as the disparity of their social positions, she would gladly have welcomed Isy as a daughter had she, in Marion's mind, but been spotless and fit to be loved by him.

In the evenings, when the work of the day was done, Isy would ramble about the moor in the lingering rays of the last of the sunset and in the now quickly shortening twilight which followed. In those lazy, gentle hours, so spiritual in their tone that they seemed to come straight from the eternal spaces where there is no remembering and no forgetting, where time and space are motionless, and the spirit is at rest, Isy first began to read with conscious understanding. For now for the first time she fell into the company of books—old-fashioned ones, no doubt, but perhaps therefore all the more fit for her in that she was an old-fashioned, gentle, naive, and thoughtful child. With one or two volumes in her hand, she would steal out of sight of the farm, and wrapped in the solitude of the moor would sit and read until at last the light could reveal not a single word more. She read some geometry, enjoyed rhetoric and poetry more, but liked natural history best of all, with its engravings of birds and animals, poor as they were.

In a garret over the kitchen, she also found an English translation of Klopstock's *Messiah*, a poem which, in the middle of the last and present century, caused a great excitement in Germany, and contributed much to the development of religious feeling in that country, where the slow-subsiding ripple of its commotion is possibly not altogether unfelt even at the present day. She read the volume through as she strolled in those twilights, not without risking falling over a bush or stone before practice taught her to see at once both the way for her feet over the moor and the way for her eyes over the printed page. The book both pleased and suited her, the parts that interested her most being those about the repentant angel, Abaddon, who haunted the steps of the Savior and hovered about the cross while he was crucified.

The great question with her for a long time was whether the Savior must not have forgiven him. By slow degrees it became at last clear to her that he who came but to seek and to save the lost could not have closed the door against one that sought to return to his faithfulness. It would not be until she later came to know the soutar, however, that at length she understood the tireless redeeming attribute of the love of the Father, who had sent men blind and stupid and ill-conditioned into a world where they had to learn almost everything.

There were some few books of a more theological sort, which happily she neither could understand nor was able to imagine she understood, and which therefore she instinctively refused as affording her no potential nourishment either for thought or feeling. There was, besides, Dr. Johnson's *Rasselas*, which mildly interested her, and a book called *Dialogues of Devils*, which she read eagerly. And thus, if indeed her ignorance did not grow much less as a result of these books, at least her knowledge of it grew a little greater, and that is certainly a great step in the direction of the truest kind of knowledge.

And all the time the conviction continued to grow upon her that she had been in that region before, and that in truth she could not be far from the spot where she had laid her child down and lost him.

17

The Wisdom of the Wise Man

In the meantime the child was growing into a splendid boy, and was the delight of the humble dwelling to which Maggie had triumphantly borne him. But the mind of the soutar was busy in thought about how far their right in the boy approached the paternal. Were they justified in regarding him as their love-property before having made exhaustive inquiry as to who could possibly claim him? For nothing could liberate the finder of such a thing from the duty of restoring it upon demand, seeing that there as yet could be no certainty that the child had been deliberately and finally abandoned.

Maggie, indeed, regarded the baby as hers absolutely by right of rescue. But her father asked himself whether they might not be depriving his mother of the one remaining link between her and humanity, and so abandoning her helpless to the Enemy. Surely to take and withhold from any woman her child must be to do what was possible toward dividing her from the unseen and eternal! And he saw that for the sake of the truth in Maggie, both she and he must make every possible attempt to restore the child to his mother.

So the next time his daughter brought the infant to the kitchen, her father, who sat as usual under the small window to gather upon his work all the light to be had, turned his eyes with one quick glance at the child, and said, "Eh, the bonny, glad creature! Who can say that such as he, that haena his ain father and mither, mightna get frae the Lord himsel' a more particular and careful ootlook on life, if that be possible, than other bairns! I would like to believe that!"

"Eh, but ye think bonny, Father!" exclaimed Maggie. "Some say that such as he must turn oot anythin' but weel when they step oot into the world. Eh, but we must take care o' him, Father! But where *would* I be wi'oot you at my back?"

"And God at the back o' both!" rejoined the soutar. "I think the Almighty may hae a special diffeeculty wi' such as he, but none can judge anything or anybody till they see the final end o' it all. But I'm thinkin' it must aye be harder for one that hasna his ain mither to look to. Any other body, be she good as she may, must still be a makeshift mither. For one thing, he winna get the same natural discipline that every mither cat gives its kittens!"

"Maybe, maybe! I ken I couldna ever lay a finger upon the bonny creature mysel'!" said Maggie.

"There it is!" returned the father. "And we canna ken," he went on, "if we could expect much frae the wisdom o' the mither o' him if she had him. I doobt she might turn oot to be but a makeshift hersel'! There's many aboot him that'll be hard enough upon him, but none the wiser for that. Many a one'll look upon him as a bairn in whose existence God has had nae share. There's a heap o' mystery aboot all things, Maggie, from the very beginnin' to the very end. It may be that yon bairnie's in the worse danger just frae you and me, Maggie! We canna tell. Eh, but I wish his ain mither were gien back t' him! And who can tell but that she's needin' him worse than he's needin' her. 'Cause ye're no his ain mither, Maggie, an' I'm no his ain gran'father."

With his words the adoptive mother broke into a howl. "Father, Father, ye'll break my heart by sayin' that!" she all but yelled.

She laid the child on the top of her father's hands as they were in the very act of drawing his waxed ends through a piece of leather, and thus changing him in an instant from cobbler to nurse, she bolted from the kitchen and up the little stair. There she threw herself on her knees by the bedside, seeking instinctively and unconsciously the presence of him who sees in secret. But for a time she had nothing to say even to him and could only moan in the darkness that lay beneath her closed eyelids.

Suddenly she came to herself, and remembered that she too had abandoned the child and must go back to him.

But as she ran she heard loud noises of infantile jubilation. Reentering the kitchen she was at first amazed to see the soutar's hands moving persistently, if not quite so rapidly, as before with his work. The child hung at the back of her father's head, in the bend of the long jack-towel he had taken from behind the door, holding on by the gray hair of the back part of his head. There he tugged and crowed, while his caretaker bent over his labor, circumspect in every moment, never once forgetting the precious thing on his back, who was evidently delighted with his new style of being nursed, and only now and then made a wry face as some movement of the human machine too abrupt for his comfort. Evidently he took it all as intended solely for his pleasure.

Maggie burst out laughing through the tears that still filled her eyes, and the child, who could hear but not see her, began to cry a little. This roused the mother in her to a sense that he was being treated a bit too unceremoniously. She bound forward to liberate him, undid the towel, and seated herself with him in her lap. The grandfather, not sorry to be released, gave his shoulders a little relaxing shake, laughed an amused laugh, and set off boring and stitching and drawing at re-doubled speed.

"Weel, Maggie," he said interrogatively, without looking up.

"I saw that ye was right, Father, and it set me cryin', sae that I forgot the bairn, and you too. Go on and say what ye think fit. It's all true."

"There's little left for me to say noo, lassie. Ye hae begun to say it yersel'. But believe me, though ye can never be the bairn's ain mither, *she* can never be to him the same as ye hae been already, whatever more or better may follow. The part ye hae chosen is good enough never to be taken frae ye—in this world or the next."

"Thank ye, Father, for that. I'll do for the bairn what I can without forgettin' he's no mine but anither's. I mustna take frae her what's her ain."

Whenever he was at his work, the soutar constantly tried to "get into his Lord's company," as he said—endeavoring to understand some saying of his, or to discover his reason for saying it when he did. Often he would ponder why God would allow this or that to take place in the world, for it was his house, where he was always present and always at work. He never doubted that when once a thing had taken place, that it was by his will it came to pass, but he saw that evil itself, originating with man or his deceiver, was often made to subserve the final will of the All-in-All. And he knew that much must first be set right before the will of the Father could be done in earth as it was in heaven.

Therefore, in any new development of feeling in his child, he could recognize the pressure of a guiding hand in the formation of her life's history, revealing what was in her, and making room for what was as yet undeveloped. Hence, he could love what his child was *becoming*, even without being able to see it in advance. Thus was he able to understand St. John's words: "Beloved, now are we the sons of God, and it doth not yet appear what we shall be, but we know that, when he shall appear, we shall be like him, for we shall see him as he is." For first and foremost, and deepest of all, he positively and absolutely believed in the man whose history is found in St. John's Gospel—that is, he believed not only that such a man once was, and that every word he spoke was true, but he believed that the man was still in the world, and that every word he then spoke had always been, still was, and would always be true. Therefore, he also believed—which was the most important thing of all to both the Master and John MacLear, his disciple—that the chief end of his conscious life must be to live in the Lord's presence, and keep his affections ever afresh and constantly turning toward him, appealing to him for strength to believe and understand and then obey. Hence, every day he felt anew that he too was living in the house of God, among the things of the Father of Jesus.

The life influence of the soutar had already for some time been felt at Tiltowie. In a certain far-off way, men seemed to surmise what he was about, although they were incapable of estimating the nature or value of his pursuit of spiritual things. What their idea of him was may in a measure be gathered from the answer of the village fool when a passerby asked him, "Well, what's the soutar up to now?"

"Ow, as usual," answered the simpleton, "turnin' up ilka muckle stone to look for his Master beneath it!"

For in truth the cobbler did believe that the Lord of men was often walking to and fro in the earthly kingdom of his Father, watching what was going on there, and doing his best to bring it to its true and ideal condition. Never did John MacLear lift his eyes heavenward without a vague feeling that he might that very moment catch a sight of the glory of his coming Lord. If ever he fixed his eyes on the far horizon, it was never without receiving a shadowy suggestion that, like a sail towering over the edge of the world, the first great flag of the Lord's hitherward march might that moment be rising between earth and heaven. For certainly he would come unawares, and who then could tell what moment he might set his foot on the edge of the visible, and come out of the dark in which he had till that moment clothed himself as with a garment—to appear in the ancient glory of his transfiguration! Thus, the soutar was ever on the watch. And yet even when most deeply lost in such watching for his Savior, the lowest whisper of humanity was always loud enough to recall him to his "live work"—to wake him, that is to those around him, lest he should be found asleep to the needs of others at the moment of his Lord's coming. His was the same live readiness that had opened the ear of Maggie to the cry of the little one on the hillside. As his daily work was ministration to the weary feet of his Master's men, so was his soul ever awake to their sorrows and spiritual necessities.

"There's a whole world o' bonny work aboot me!" he would say. "I hae but to lay my hand to what's next me, and it's sure to be somethin' that wants doin'! I'm clean ashamed sometimes, when I wake up in the mornin', to find myself' doin' naething!"

Every evening while the summer lasted, he would go out alone for a walk, generally toward a certain wood near the town. For although it was of no great size and its trees were small, there lay the probability of escaping for a few moments from the eyes of men, and the chance of certain of another breed showing themselves.

"But I never cared that much aboot the angels," he once said to Maggie. "It's the perfect man, who was there wi' the Father afore ever an angel was heard tell o', that sends me upon my knees! When I see a man that but remin's me o' him, my heart rises up as if t' would almost leave my body ahind it! Love's the law o' the universe, and it jist works amazin'!"

One day a man saw him approaching in the distance, and knowing he had not yet perceived his presence, lay down behind a great stone to watch "the mad soutar" go by in the hope of hearing him say something insane. As John came nearer, the silent observer saw his lips moving and heard sounds coming from them. But as he passed, nothing was audible but the same words repeated over several times, with the same expression of surprise and joy as if they were in response to something discovered for the first time:—"Eh, Lord! Eh, Lord, I see! I un'erstand!—Lord, I'm yer ain—to the very death!—all yer ain!—Thy Father bless thee, Lord!—I ken ye care for naethin' else!—Eh, but my heart's glad, Lord!"

Ever afterward the man spoke about the soutar with a respect that resembled awe.

After that talk with her father about the child and his mother, a certain silent change appeared in Maggie. People saw in her face an expression which they took to resemble that of one whose child was ill and was expected to die. But what Maggie was feeling was only resignation to the will of her Lord; the child was not hers but the Lord's, lent to her for a season. She must walk softly, doing everything for him as under the eye of her Master, who might at any moment call to her, "Bring the child; I want him now!"

And before long she became as cheerful as before, although she never quite lost the still, solemn look as of one in the eternal spaces who was able to see beyond this world's horizon. She talked less with her father, but at the same time she seemed to live closer to him. Occasionally she would ask him to help her to understand something he had said, but even then he would not always try to make it plain.

"I see, lassie," he might answer, "that ye're no jist ready for it. It's true enough, though, and the day must come when ye'll see the thing itsel', and ken what it is, and that's the only way to get at the truth o' it. In fact, to see a thing, and know the thing, and be sure it's true, is all one and the same thing!" Such a word from her father was always enough to still and content the girl.

Her delight in the child, instead of growing less, went on increasing because of the awe rather than the dread of having at last to give him up.

18

· · · · · · · · · · · · · · · · · · ·

The Boots

*A*ll this time young James Blatherwick remained moody, apparently sunk in contemplation, but in fact mostly brooding, and meditating on himself rather than on the truth. Sometimes he felt as if he were losing his power of thinking altogether—especially in the middle of the week when he sat down to try to find something to say on the next Sunday. He had completely lost interest in the questions that had occupied him while he was a student and had imagined himself in preparation for what he called the ministry—never thinking how one was to minister who had not yet learned to obey, and had never sought anything but his own glorification. It was indeed little wonder he should lose interest in a profession his heart took so little interest in. What pleasure could a man find in holy labor who did not indeed offer his pay to purchase the Holy Ghost, but instead offered all he knew of the Holy Ghost to purchase popularity? No wonder he should find himself at length in lack of talk to pay for his one most needful thing. He had always been more or less dependent on commentaries for the minimal food he provided: was it any wonder that his guests should show less and less appetite for the dinners that came from his hand.

The hungry sheep looked up and were not fed!

To have food to give them, he must think! To think, he must have peace! To have peace, he must forget himself! To forget himself, he must repent and walk in the truth! To walk in the truth, he must love God and his neighbor!

Even to have an interest in the dry bone of religious criticism and doctrinal discussion, which was all he could find in his larder, he must broil it—and so burn away every scrap of meat left on it in the slow fire of his intellect, now dull and damp enough from lack of noble purpose. His last relation to his work, his fondly cherished intellect, was departing from him to leave him nothing more than lord of a dustheap. In the unsavory mound he grubbed and nosed and scraped about, but could not uncover a single fragment that smelt of true provender.

The morning of Saturday came, and he recognized with a burst of agonizing sweat that he dared not even face his congregation. He had not written one word to read to them, and extemporaneous utterance, from the vacancy of his mind and experience, was an impossibility to him. He could not even call up one meaningless phrase to articulate! He flung his concordance sprawling upon the floor, snatched up his hat and clerical cane, and hardly knowing what he was doing, presently found himself standing in front of the cobbler's door, where he had already knocked without the least idea of what he had come there seeking. The old parson, Mr. Pethrie, generally in a mood to quarrel with the soutar, had always walked straight into his workshop. But the new parson always waited on the doorstep for Maggie, whom he did not particularly want to see now, to admit him.

She opened the door wide before the minister had gathered his wits enough to know why he had come, or could think of anything to say. And the thought of the cobbler's deep-set black eyes about to fix themselves upon him put him in even greater uneasiness than usual.

"Do you think your father would have time," he asked, "to measure me for a pair of boots?"

Blatherwick was very particular about his footgear, and before this had always fitted himself in Aberdeen. But he had finally learned that nothing he could buy there approached in quality, either of material or workmanship, what the soutar supplied to his poorest customer. For, while he would mend anything worth mending, he would never *make* anything inferior.

" 'Deed, sir, he'll be glad an' prood to make ye as good a pair o' boots as he can make," answered Maggie. "Jist come in, an' let him ken what ye want. My bairn's cryin' and I must go to him; it's seldom he cries out."

The minister walked in at the open door of the kitchen and met the eyes of the cobbler.

"Welcome, sir!" said MacLear, and returned his eyes to his work.

"I would like you to make me a nice pair of boots," said the parson in as cheery a voice as he could muster. "Though I am afraid I am rather particular about the fit."

"And why shouldn't you be?" answered the soutar. "I'll do what I can anyway, I promise ye—but wi' more readiness than confidence as to the fit, for I canna profess a perfect fit the first time I make ye a pair o' the boots."

"Of course I should like to have them both neat and comfortable," said the parson.

"And sae would I. And when the time for a second pair comes, I'm sure I'd be closer to the ideal. But hoo will ye hae them made, sir?—I mean what sort o' boots would ye hae me make?"

"Oh, I leave that to you, Mr. MacLear!—a sort of half Wellington, I suppose—a neat pair of short boots."

"I un'erstand."

All of a sudden, moved by a sudden impulse that came from he knew not where, the minister began making conversation in an altogether new direction. "But tell me," he asked the cobbler, "what do you think of all this talk of the necessity of confessing one's sins to the priest; you must have read of it in the papers? I see they have actually gotten the miserable creature to confess to the murder of her little brother! Do you think they had any right to pressure her into such a confession? Remember the jury had already acquitted her."

"Has she really confessed? I hadn't read of it. I am glad o' it! Eh, the state o' that poor girl's conscience! It almost makes me cry to think o' it. With confession hope springs to life in the sin-oppressed soul. Eh, but it must be a gran' lightenin' thing to that poor girl! I'm right glad to hear o' it."

"I didn't know you favored the power and influence of the priesthood to such an extent, Mr. MacLear! We Presbyterian clergy are not in the habit of acting as detectives, taking it upon ourselves to act as agents of human justice. There is no one, whether he be guilty or not, who is not safe in what they tell us."

"As wi' any confessor, Catholic or Protestant," rejoined the soutar. "If I un'er-stand what ye told me, it means that they persuaded the poor soul to confess her guilt, and so put hersel' safe in the hands o' God."

"And is that not to come between God and the sinner?"

"Perhaps—in order to bring them together; to persuade the sinner to the first step toward reconceeliation wi' God, and peace in his ain mind."

"That he could take without the intervention of the priest."

"Ay, but not wi'oot his ain consenting will. And in this case, she wouldna and didna confess wi'oot bein' persuaded by the priest to do it."

"They had no right to threaten her."

"I agree wi' ye there. If they did they were wrong. But in any case, they did the very best thing for her that could be done. For they did get her to confess—and sae cast frae her the horror o' carrin' aboot in her secret heart the knowledge o' an unforgiven crime. All Christians agree, dinna ye think, that to be forgiven, a sin must be confessed?"

"Yes, to God—that is enough. No mere man has a right to know the sins of his neighbor."

"No even the man against whom the sin was committed?"

"Suppose the sin has never come to light, but remained hidden in the heart; is a man bound to confess it? For instance, is he bound to tell his neighbor that he used to hate him in his heart?"

"The time might come when to confess even that would ease a man's heart. But in such a case, the man's first duty, it seems to me, would be to watch for an opportunity o' doin' that neighbor a kin'ness. That would be the death blow to the hatred in his heart. But where a man has done an act o' injustice, some wrong to his neighbor, he has no choice, it seems to me, but confess it; that neighbor is the one frae whom first he has to ask an' receive forgiveness. He alone can lift the burden o' guilt off the man. An' we mustna forget," ended the soutar, "hoo the Lord said that there's naethin' hidden but must come to the licht one day!"

Now what could have led the minister so near the truth of his own story, like the murdered who haunts the proximity of the loudest witness against his crime, except the will of God working in him to set him free, I do not know. But he went on, driven by an impulse he neither understood nor suspected.

"Suppose the thing wasn't known, and wasn't in the least likely to be known, and that the man's confession, instead of serving any good end, would only de-stroy his reputation and usefulness, bring bitter grief upon those who loved him, and nothing but shame to the one he had wronged—what would you say then? I am putting out an entirely imaginary case for the sake of argument only."

Eh, but I'm beginnin' to doobt yer imaginary case, thought the soutar to himself, hardly even daring to think his thought clearly. But to James he replied, "Even so, it seems to me the offender would hae to look aboot him for one to trust to whom he could reveal the whole affair, to get his help to see and do what's right. It makes a great difference to look at a thing through anither man's eyes, in the supposed light o' anither man's conscience. The wrong done may hae caused more evil or injustice than the man himsel' kens. And what's the reputation ye speak o', or the usefulness o' sich a man? Hoo can it be worth anythin'? Isna it all a lie? The only way for sich a man to destroy the heepocrisy is for him to cry oot to the world and his Maker, 'I'm a heepocreete! I'm no man, but, Lord, make a man oot o'me!' "

As the soutar spoke, overcome by sympathy with the sinner, whom he could not help suspecting was in bodily presence before him, the minister stood listening with a face pale as death.

Witnessing this change coming over his young friend, and moved powerfully by the compassion for him rising within him, the cobbler went on in an outburst of feeling:

"For God's sake, minister, if ye hae any such thing on ye mind, hurry an' be oot wi' it! I dinna say *to me,* but to somebody—to anybody! Make a clean breast o' it, afore the Adversary has ye by the throat!"

But with his words the pride of superiority in station and learning came again awake in the minister. How could a mere shoemaker, from whom he had just ordered a pair of shoes, take such a liberty! He drew himself up to his full lanky height, and replied—"I am not aware, Mr. MacLear, that I have given you any pretext for addressing me in such terms! I told you that I was merely asking about an imaginary case. You have shown me how unsafe it is to enter into a discussion with one of a limited education. It is my own fault, however, and I beg your pardon for having thoughtlessly led you into such a pitfall! Good morning to you!"

As he closed the door he congratulated himself on having so fortunately turned aside the course of a conversation whose dangerous drift he seemed now finally to recognize. But he little realized how much he had already conveyed to the wide-eyed observation of one well-schooled in the symptoms of human unrest.

"I must watch my thoughts and words," he reflected, "lest they betray me!" And as he continued on his way he resolved to conceal himself yet more carefully from the one man in the place who could have helped cut for him the snare of the fowler.

"I was too hasty wi' him!" concluded the soutar to himself after his visitor had left. "But I think the truth has taken some grip o' him. His conscience is wakin' up, I fancy, and growlin' a bit. And where that tyke has once taken hold, he's no ready to loosen or let gae! We must jist lie quiet a bit and see. His hoor will come!"

The minister was one who turned pale when angry, and thus walked home with such a white face that a woman who met him said to herself, "I wonder what can ail the minister, bonny lad! He's lookin' as scared as a corpse! I doobt that fule body the soutar's been angerin' him wi' his talk!"

Despite his anger, the first thing he did when he reached the manse was to turn to one of the chapters he thought the soutar had vaguely quoted from, and which, through all his irritation, had strangely enough remained vaguely in his memory. But the passage suggested nothing out of which he could fabricate a sermon, and he was left no nearer that end than before.

How could it be otherwise with a heart that was quite content to have God no nearer than a merely adoptive Father? His interview with the cobbler had rendered the machinery of his thought factory no fitter than before for weaving a tangled wisp of loose ends into the homogeneous web of a sermon. And at last he was driven to his old stock of carefully preserved preordination sermons, where he was unfortunate enough to make choice of the one least of all fitted to awake comprehension of interest in his audience.

His selection made, and the rest of the day thus cleared for inaction, he sat down and wrote a letter. Ever since his fall he had been successfully practicing the art of throwing occasional morsels toward his conscience, which was more clever in catching them than they were in quieting the said howler's restiveness. This letter was the sole result of his talk with John MacLear. It was addressed to one of his divinity classmates, and in it he asked incidentally whether his old friend had ever heard anything of the little girl—he could just remember her name and the pretty face of her—Isy, general helper to her aunt's lodgers in the Canongate, of whom he had been one. He had often wondered, he said, what had become of her, for he had been almost in love with her for a time. I don't doubt that the inquiry was the merest pretense with the sole object of deceiving himself into the notion of his having at least made one attempt to discover Isy's whereabouts.

His friend forgot to answer the question, and James Blatherwick never alluded to his having put it to him.

19

The Sermon

Never did a Sunday dawn more wretched upon a human soul. At least James did not have to climb into his watchman's tower, the pulpit, without some pretense of a proclamation to give. But on that very morning, his father had put the mare between the shafts of the gig to drive his wife to Tiltowie and their son's church, instead of the nearer and more accessible one in the next parish, where they usually went.

It was hardly surprising that they should find themselves so dissatisfied with the spiritual food set before them that they wished they had remained at home. The moment the service was over, Mr. Blatherwick felt inclined to climb back into the gig and return at once without even waiting to speak with his son. He had nothing to say about the sermon that would be pleasant either for his son or his wife to hear. But Marion argued with him, almost to the point of anger, and Peter was compelled to yield. Thus they waited, Peter almost sullenly, in the churchyard for the minister's appearance.

"Weel, Jamie," said his father, shaking hands with him, "yon was some hardened porridge ye gave us this mornin'!—an' the meal itsel' was both auld an' sour."

The mother gave her son a pitiful smile, as if to soften her husband's severity, but she said no word. Haunted by the taste of failure the sermon had left in his own mouth, and troubled as well by the self-conscious waking of self-recognition, James could hardly look his father in the face. He felt as if he had been rebuked by him, as though he were still a child, in front of his whole congregation.

"Father," he replied in a tone of some injury, "you do not know how difficult it is to preach a fresh sermon every Sunday!"

"Call ye that fresh, Jamie? To me it was like the moldy husks o' the half-famished swine! Man, I wish such provender would drive ye where there's better food, an' to spare! Yon was lumps o' brose in a pig-wash o' stourum! I'd think ye'd ken the differ' atween sich like an' true food!"

James made a wry face, and the sight of his annoyance broke the ice gathering over the well-spring in his mother's heart. Tears rose in her eyes, and for one brief moment she saw the minister again as her own tiny bairn. But he gave her no filial response. His own ambition, and his desire for the praise of men, had blocked in him the movements of the divine and corrupted the most wholesome of his feelings. This combined with his father's comments caused him to welcome freely the false conviction that his parents had never had any sympathy with him or cared the least about his preaching. All reacted together in a sudden flow of resentment and a thickening of the ice between them. Some fundamental shock would be necessary to unsettle and dislodge that deeply rooted, overmastering ice over his innermost being, if ever his wintered heart was to feel the power of a reviving spring!

The threesome family stood in helpless silence for a few moments, and then the father said to the mother, "Weel, I doobt we must be settin' oot for home, Marion."

"Will you not come to the manse and have something to eat before you go?" asked James, not without anxiety that his housekeeper should be taken by surprise, and their acceptance of his invitation annoy her. He lived in constant dread of offending his housekeeper.

"Nae, thank ye," returned his father, "it would likely taste o' blown dust."

It was a rude remark. But Peter was not in a kind mood, and when love itself is unkind, it is apt to be burning and bitter and merciless.

Marion burst into tears. James turned away, and walked home with a gait of wounded dignity. Peter went hastily toward the churchyard gate, to interrupt with the bit his mare's leisurely feed of oats. Marion saw his hands tremble pitifully as he put the headstall over the creature's ears, and reproached herself that she had given him such a cold-hearted son. In a helpless way, she climbed into the gig and sat waiting for her husband.

They drove away from the tombs of the church graveyard, but they carried the feeling of death with them. Neither spoke a word all the way. Not until she was dismounting at their own door did the mother venture her sole remark, "Eh, sirs!" It meant a world of unexpressed and inexpressible misery. She went straight up to the little garret where she kept her Sunday bonnet, and where she said her prayers when she was in special misery. After a while she came down to her bedroom, there washed her face, and sadly prepared for a hungerless encounter with the dinner Isy had been getting ready for them—hoping to hear something about the sermon, perhaps even some little word about the minister himself.

But Isy, too, had to share in the disappointment of that glorious Sunday morning. Not a word passed between her master and mistress. Their son was called pastor of the flock, but he was rather the porter of the sheepfold than the shepherd of the sheep. He was very careful that the church should be clean and properly swept, and sometimes even painted, but about the temple of the Holy Spirit, the hearts of his sheep, he knew nothing.

The gloom of his parents, their sense of failure and loss, grew and deepened all the dull hot afternoon, until it seemed almost to pass their power of endurance. At last, however, it abated, as does every pain, for life is at its root: thereto ordained, it slew itself by exhaustion. But even though she felt better by degrees, the mother could only think of the coming of another new day that would bring the old trouble back upon her—the gnawing, sickening pain that she was childless—her daughter gone and no son left. Nonetheless, however, when the new day came, it brought with it its own new possibility of living yet one day more.

But their son the minister was far more to be pitied than those whom he gave misery. All night long he slept with a sense of ill-usage sublying his consciousness and dominating his dreams. But when the morning broke there came the thought into his brain that possibly he had not acted in the most seemly fashion when he turned and left his father and mother in the churchyard. Of course they had not treated him well. But what would his congregation have thought to see him leave them as he did—and some of them might have been lingering in the churchyard? His only thought, however, was not toward repentance, but to take precautions against their natural judgment of his behavior.

After breakfast, as custom was every Monday morning, he set out for what he called a quiet stroll. But his thoughts kept returning, ever with fresh resentment, to the soutar's insinuation two days before.

Suddenly the face of Maggie arose before him, quickly displacing the phantasm of her father. His thoughts came before he could stop them, and suddenly he was asking himself the question, "What was the *real* history of the baby on whom she spent such an irrational amount of devotion?" The soutar's tale of her finding him was too apocryphal! Might not Maggie have made a moral slip? Or why should the pretensions of the soutar be absolutely trusted? With the idea arose in him a certain satisfaction in the possible prospect of learning that this man, so ready to believe evil of his neighbor, had not succeeded in keeping his own house undefiled. He tried to rebuke himself the next moment, it is true, for having harbored even a moment's satisfaction in the wrongdoing of another: it was unbefitting the pastor of a Christian flock. But the thought came and went, and he took no conscious trouble to try to cast it out. When he returned from his walk, he put a question or two to his housekeeper about the child, but she only smiled faintly and shook her head knowingly, as if she knew more than she chose to tell.

After his two o'clock dinner, he thought it would be Christian-like to forgive his parents and call at Stonecross: the action would tend to wipe out any undesirable offense on the minds of his parents, and also to prevent any gossip that might injure him in his sacred profession. He had not been to see them for a long time, and though such visits gave him no satisfaction, he never dreamed of attributing it to his own lack of cordiality. But he judged it prudent to avoid any appearance of neglect, and therefore thought that in the future it might be his duty to attempt a hurried call about once a month. He excused himself for his infrequency in the past because of the distance and his not being a good walker. And even after he had made up his mind, he was in no haste to set out, but had a long snooze in his armchair first. So it was almost evening before he climbed the hill and came in sight of the low gable behind which he was born.

Isy was in the garden gathering up the linen she had spread out to dry on the gooseberry bushes. The moment his head came in sight at the top of the brae, she knew him at once, and stooping behind the gooseberries, she fled to the back of the house, and then away to the moor on the other side. James saw the white flutter of the sheet, but nothing of the hands that took it. He had heard that his mother had a nice young woman to help her in the house, but he had so little interest in home affairs that the news had waked no curiosity in him.

Ever since she came to Stonecross, Isy had been on the lookout lest James should unexpectedly come upon her, and be surprised into an involuntary disclosure of his relation to her. Despite her long hope of seeing him again, she remained vigilant, for the longer he delayed, the more certain it became that he must soon appear. She did not intend to avoid him altogether, only to take heed not to startle him into any recognition of her in the presence of his mother. But when she saw him approaching the house, her courage failed her, and she fled to the fields to avoid the danger of betraying both herself and him. In truth, she was ashamed of meeting him, in her imagination feeling guilty and exposed to his just reproaches. All the time he remained with his mother, she kept watching the house, not once showing herself until he was gone. Then she would reappear as if just returned from the moor, where Mrs. Blatherwick imagined her still indulging the hope of finding her baby. Her mistress had come more and more to doubt the existence of the child, taking the supposed fancy for nothing but a half-crazy survival from the time of her insanity before the Robertsons found her.

The minister made a comforting peace with his mother, telling her a part of the truth, namely that he had been much out of sorts during the week and quite unable to write a new sermon. At the last he had been driven to take an old one, and so hurriedly that he had failed to recall correctly the subject and nature of it. He had actually begun to read it, he said, before discovering that it was altogether unsuitable—at which very moment, fatally for his equanimity, he saw his parents in the congregation. He was so dismayed that he could not recover his self-possession, and from all this had come his apparent lack of cordiality. It was a lame yet somewhat plausible excuse, and served to silence for the moment, if not to satisfy, his mother's heart. His father was out-of-doors, and James did not see him.

20

The Passing

As time went on, the terror of discovery grew rather than abated in the mind of the minister. He could not tell why it should be so, for no news of Isy had reached him. In his quieter moments, he felt almost certain that she could not have passed so completely out of his horizon if she were still in the world. It was when he was most persuaded of this that he was able to live most comfortably and forget the past, of which he was unable to recall any portion with satisfaction. The darkness and silence left over it by his unrepented offense, gave it, in the retrospect of his thoughts, a threatening aspect—out of which any moment might burst the hidden enemy, the thing that might be known, and more not be known! He managed to derive a feeble cowardly comfort in the reflection that he had done nothing to hide the miserable fact. He even persuaded himself that if he could he *would* not now do anything further to keep it secret. He would leave all that to Providence, which seemed till now to have wrought on his behalf. He would but keep a silence that no gentleman must break! Besides, who had any claim to know a mere passing fault? Why should there be any call for a confession, about which the soutar had carried on so foolishly?

If the secret should threaten to creep out, he would not, he flattered himself, move a finger to keep it hidden. On the contrary, that moment he would disappear in some trackless solitude, rejoicing that he had nothing left to wish hidden. As to the charge of hypocrisy that was sure to follow, he was innocent. He had never said anything he did not believe! He had never once posed as a man of Christian experience—like the cobbler, for instance! He had simply been overtaken in a fault, which he had never repeated, never would repeat, and which he was willing, he believed, to atone for in any way he could.

On the following Saturday, the soutar was hard at work all day long on the new boots the minister had ordered, which indeed he had almost forgotten in his anxiety for the young man. For MacLear was now thoroughly convinced that some hidden offense lay deep within the minister's mind. He was anxious to finish the boots so that he might take them to him that same night, and possibily find an opportunity to say something further in the way of helping point the man toward returning health. For nothing attracted the soutar more than an opportunity of doing anything to lift from a human soul, even but a single fold of the darkness that covered it, and so let the light nearer to the troubled heart.

As to what it might be that was harassing the minister's soul, he sternly repressed in himself all curiosity. He had no particular desire that James should unburden himself to him, but hoped what he said would send him seeking counsel from someone who could help him, and that in time they would gradually be able to resume their friendly relationship with each other. For somehow there was that in the gloomy parson which attracted the cheery and hopeful cobbler, and he hoped the young man's trouble might yet prove to be the hunger of his heart after a spiritual food he had not yet begun to find. He might not yet have understood, the soutar thought, the good news about God—that he was just what Jesus was to those who saw the glory of God in his face. The minister could not, he thought, have learned much about the truth concerning his heavenly Father, for it seemed to wake in him no gladness, no power of life, no strength to *be*. For him Christ had not risen, but lay wrapped in his death clothes. So far as James's experience was concerned, the larks and the angels must all be mistaken in singing as they did! For there was no power of the resurrection in his life!

Late that night, so late in fact that the cobbler worried that the housekeeper had probably retired for the night, he rang the bell of the manse door. And indeed it was the minister himself who answered the door to see MacLear on the other side of the threshold with the new boots in his hand.

Since their last encounter, the minister had come to feel that the soutar must suspect him of something; otherwise, why would he have said what he did? He was now bent on removing any negative impression his words might have had. Therefore he wanted to appear to be harboring no offense over his parishioner's last words, and so obliterate any suggestion of needed confession on his own part. Thus he now addressed him almost lightly, with a tone very different from his usually gloomy spirit.

"Oh, MacLear," he said, "I am glad to see you have just managed to escape breaking the Sabbath! You have had a close shave! There are only ten minutes more to the awful midnight hour!"

"I doobt, sir, it would hae broken the Sabbath worse than to fail in my word wi' my work on yer boots," returned the soutar.

"Ah well, we won't argue about it. But if we were inclined to be strict, the Sabbath began some"—here he looked at his watch—"some five and three-quarters hours ago; that is, at six of the clock, the evening of Saturday."

"Hoot, minister, ye ken ye're wrong there! for Jew-wise, it began at six o'clock on the Friday night! But ye hae made it plain frae the pulpit that ye hae no superstition aboot the first day o' the week, which alone has anythin' to do wi' us Christians. I for one confess nae obligation but to drop workin', and sit doon wi' clean hands, or as clean as I can weel make them, to the spiritual table o' my Lord, where I aye try as well to wear a clean and cheerful face—that is, sae far as the sermon will permit. For isna it the bonny day when the Lord would hae us sit doon and eat wi' himsel', who made the heavens and the earth, and the waters under the earth that hold it up. And will he, upon this day, at the last gran' marriage feast, poor oot the bonny red wine, and say, 'Sit ye doon, bairns, and take o' my best!'"

"Ay, ay, MacLear, that's a fine way to think of the Sabbath!" rejoined the minister, "and the very way I am in the habit of thinking of it myself! I'm greatly obliged to you for bringing home my boots. Come in and put them there on that bench in the window. It's about time we were all going to bed, I think—especially myself, tomorrow being sermon-day."

The soutar went home and to his bed, sorry that he had said nothing.

The next evening he listened to the best sermon he had yet heard from that pulpit—a summary of the facts bearing on the resurrection of our Lord. A large part of the congregation, however, was anything but pleased, for the minister had admitted the impossibility of reconciling, in every particular detail, the differing account of the doings and seeings of those who witnessed it.

"—As if," said the soutar, "the Lord wasna to show himsel' openly till all that saw the thing were agreed to their recollection o' what fowk had reported!"

He went home edified and uplifted by his fresh contemplation of the story of his Master's victory. Thank God, he thought, his pains were over at last, and through death he was Lord forever over death and evil, over pain and loss and fear. He was Lord also of all thinking and feeling and judgment, able to give repentance and restoration, and to set right all that self-will had set wrong.

So greatly did the heart of his humble disciple rejoice him that he scandalized the reposing Sabbath-street by breaking out, as he went home, into a somewhat unmelodious song, "They are all gaene down to hell wi' the weapons of their war!" to a tune nobody knew but himself, and which he could never have sung again. "O Faithful an' True," he broke out again as he reached his own house; but stopped suddenly, saying, "Tut, tut, the fowk'll think I hae been drinkin'!—Eh," he continued to himself as he went in, "if I might but once hear the name that no man kens but himsel'!"

The next day he was very tired and could get through but little work. So on the next he decided to take a little holiday. Therefore he put a large piece of oatcake in his pocket, told Maggie he was going for a walk in the hills, and then disappeared with a single backward look and lingering smile.

After walking some distance in quiet peace, and having for a long while met no one—by which he meant that no special thought had arisen in his mind—he turned and headed toward Stonecross. He had known Peter Blatherwick for many years, and honored him as one in whom there was no guile, and now suddenly the desire came upon him to visit him.

He knocked on the door, and to his surprise the farmer himself came to answer it, and stood there in silence with a look that seemed to say, "I know you, but what can you be wanting with me?" His face was troubled, and looked not only sorrowful, but scared as well. Usually ruddy with health, and calm with contentment, it was now very pale and white, and seemed, as he held the door-handle without a word of welcome, that of one aware of something unseen behind him.

"What ails ye, Mr. Blatherwick?" asked the soutar in a voice of sympathetic anxiety. "I hope there's naething come o'er the mistress."

"Nae, thank ye; she's very weel. But a dreadful thing has jist befallen us. Only an hour ago oor Isy—the girl we brought into oor home not so long ago—jist dropped doon dead. Ye would hae thought she was shot wi' a gun. The one moment she was standin' talkie' wi' her mistress in the kitchen, and the next she was in a heap on the floor!—But come in, come in!"

"Eh, the bonnie lassie!" cried the shoemaker, making no move to enter. "I remember her weel, though I saw her only once—a fine delicate picture o' a lassie, that looked up at ye as if she made ye kin'ly welcome to anything she could give or get for ye! Was she ailin'?"

"No so bad! Though she was weak all along, at death's very door when Mister Robertson found her in Aberdeen. But I had thought she was comin' back to her health right weel. Yet we'll see her no more till the earth gives up her dead. The wife's in there wi' what's left o' her, cryin' as if she would cry her eyes oot. Eh, but she loved her!—Doon she dropped, and never a moment to say her prayers!"

"That matters no much—not a hair, in fact!" returned the soutar. "It was the Father o' her that took her, and none other. He wanted her home; and he's no one to do anything ill, or at the wrong moment! If a minute more had been any good to her, don't ye think she would hae had that minute?"

"Willna ye come in and see her? Some fowk canna bide to look upon the dead, but ye're no one o' such."

"No, I darena be such a one. I'll willin'ly go wi' ye to look upon the face o' one that's won through."

"Come then, and maybe the Lord'll give ye a word o' comfort for the mistress, for she's takin' on terrible aboot her. It breaks my heart to see her."

"The heart o' both king and cobbler's in the hand o' the Lord," answered the soutar solemnly, "and if my heart hears anything, my tongue'll be ready to speak the same."

He followed the farmer—who walked softly, as if he feared disturbing the sleeper upon whom even the sudden silences of the world would break no more.

Mr. Blatherwick led the way to the parlor, and through it to a little room behind which they used as the guest chamber. There, on a little white bed with white curtains drawn all the way back, lay the form of Isobel. The eyes of the soutar, in whom had lingered yet still a small hope, at once revealed that he saw she was indeed gone to return no more. Her lovely little face, although its eyes were closed, was even lovelier than before. But her arms and hands lay straight by her sides; their work was gone from them and nothing was left them to do. No voice would call her anymore; she might sleep on and take her rest.

"I had but to lay them straight," sobbed her mistress. "Her eyes she had closed herself. Eh, but she *was* a bonny lassie—and a good one!—hardly less than a bairn to me!"

"And to me as weel!" added Peter, with a choked sob.

"And no once had I paid her a penny in wages!" cried Marion, with sudden remorseful memory, as if she had done the girl a great wrong.

"She never wanted it—and never will noo," said her husband.

"Eh, she was a decent, right lovable creature!" cried Marion. "She never *said* anythin' to judge by, but I had a hope that she may hae been one o' the Lord's ain."

"Is that all ye can say, mem?" interposed the soutar. "Surely ye wouldna dare imagine that she dropped oot o' *his* hands!"

"Nae," returned Marion. "But I would right fain ken her fair into them! For who is there to assure us o' her faith in the atonement?"

" 'Deed, I kenna, and I carena, mem! I hope she had faith in naething but the Lord himsel'! Alive or dead, we're in *his* hands who died for us, revealin' his Father to us," said the soutar. "And if she didna ken him afore, she will noo! The holy one will be wi' her in the dark, or whatever comes!—O God, hold up her head, and let not the waters go ower her!"

So-called theology tried to rise, dull and rampant and indignant, in the minds of both Peter and Marion. But the solemn face of the dead kept them from dispute, and Love was ready to hope, if not quite to believe. Nevertheless, to those guileless souls, the words of the soutar sounded like blasphemy: was not her fate already settled—to the one side of eternity or the other—and forever to remain the same? Had not death in a moment turned her into an immortal angel, or an equally immortal devil? Yet how could they argue the possibility, with the peaceful face before them, that as loving and gentle as she was, she could not be as utterly indifferent to the heart of the living God as if he had never created her—nay, even had become hateful to him!

No one spoke, and after gazing on the dead for a while, prayer overflowing his heart but never reaching his lips, the soutar placed in her hands a rose that he had picked on his walk, turned slowly, and departed without a word.

Just about the time he reached his own door, he met the minister, and told him of the sorrow that had befallen his parents, adding that it was plain they were sorely in need of his sympathy. Although James thought it unusual that they would be so troubled by the death of a mere servant, he was yet roused by the tale to do the duty of his profession. Though his heart had never yet drawn him either to the house of mourning or the house of joy, he judged that it would be becoming of him to pay another visit to Stonecross, though he did think it unfortunate that he should have to go again so soon. It pleased the soutar, however, to see him turn about and start for the farm with a quicker stride than he had used since his return to Tiltowie.

James had not the slightest forboding of whom he was about to see in the arms of death. But even had he had some feeling of what was awaiting him, I dare not even conjecture the mood with which he would have approached the house—whether one of conscience or of relief. But utterly unconscious of the discovery toward which he was rushing, he hurried on, with almost a faint sense of pleasure at the thought of having to expostulate with his mother upon the waste of such an unnecessary expenditure of feeling. Toward his father, he was aware of a more active feeling of disapproval, not an altogether unusual thing. There are many in the world who have not yet learned to love; still less to trust their parents. James Blatherwick was one of those whose sluggish natures require, for the melting of their stubbornness and their remolding into forms of strength and beauty, such a concentration of the love of God that it becomes a consuming fire.

21

The Vigil

Night had fallen by the time James reached the farm. The place was silent, its doors were all shut, and when he went inside not a soul was to be seen. No one came to meet him, for no one had even thought of him, and certainly no one, except it were the dead, desired his coming.

He went into the parlor, and there, from the dim chamber beyond whose door stood open, appeared his mother. Her heart big with grief, she clasped him in her arms and laid her face against his chest. Higher than that she could not reach, and nearer than his breastbone she could not get to him. No endearment had ever been natural to James. He had never encouraged or missed any, and did not know how to receive it when it was offered.

"I am distressed, Mother," he began, "to see you so upset. I cannot help thinking such a display of feeling to be unnecessary. If I may say so, it seems unreasonable. You cannot, in such a brief period as this new maid of yours has spent with you, have developed such an affection for her. The young woman can hardly be a relative. The suddenness of the occurrence, of which I only heard from my shoemaker, MacLear, must have played terribly upon your nerves! Come, come, dear Mother, you must compose yourself! It is quite unworthy of you to yield to such an unnatural and uncalled-for grief. Surely a Christian like you should meet such a thing with calmness. Was it not Schiller who said, 'Death cannot be an evil, for it is universal'?"

During this foolish speech, the gentle woman had been restraining her sobs behind her handkerchief. But as she heard her son's cold commonplaces, it was perhaps a little wholesome anger that roused her and made her able to speak.

"Ye didna ken her, laddie," she cried, "or ye would never say such a thing! But I doobt if ever ye could hae come to ken her as she was—such a bonny, hearty soul as once dwelt in yon white-faced, patient thing lying in the room there— with the sting oot o' her heart at last, and left the sharper in mine! But me and yer father, we loved her. She was more a daughter than a servant to us, wi' a lovin' kindness no to be looked for frae any son!—Jist gae into the room there, if ye will, and ye'll see what'll maybe soften yer heart a bit, and let ye understand the heartache that's come to the two old fowk ye never cared much aboot!"

James was bitterly aggrieved by this personal remark by his mother. What had *he* ever done to offend her? Had he not always behaved himself properly toward them? What right had she to say such things to him! Had he not fulfilled the expectation with which his father sent him to college? Had he not gained a position whose reflected splendor crowned them the parents of James Blatherwick? She showed him none of the consideration or respect he had so justly earned but never demanded!

He rose suddenly, and with never a thought other than to get out of his mother's presence for a moment so as to make his displeasure clear, stalked heedlessly into the presence of the more heedless dead.

The night had fallen, but the small window of the room looked westward and a bar of golden light yet lay like a resurrection stone over the spot where the sun was buried. A pale, sad gleam, softly vanishing, hovered, hardly rested, upon the lovely, still, unlooking face that lay white on the scarcely whiter pillow. For an instant, the sharp, low light blinded him a little, yet he seemed to have something before him not altogether unfamiliar, giving him a suggestion as of something he had once known, perhaps ought now to recognize, but had forgotten. The reality of it seemed to be obscured by the strange autumnal light entering almost horizontally.

Concluding himself oddly affected by the sight of the room he had always regarded with some awe in his childhood, and had not set foot in for a long time, he drew a little nearer to the bed in order to look closer at the face of this servant whose loss was causing his mother such an unreasonably poignant sorrow.

The sense of something known grew stronger. Yet still he did not fully recognize the death-changed countenance, although he was sure that he *had* seen that still and quiet face before. If she would but open those eyes for a moment, he was certain he should know at once who it was.

Then the true suspicion flashed upon him: Good God! *could it be* the dead Isy?

Of course not! It was the merest illusion! a nonsensical fancy caused by the irregular mingling of the light and darkness. In the daytime he would never have been so fooled by his imagination! Yet even as he said this to himself, he stood as one transfixed, with his face leaning close down staring upon the face of the dead. It was only like her; it could not be the same face! Still he could not turn and go from it! And as he stared, the dead face seemed to come nearer him through the darkness, growing more and more like the only girl he had ever, though then only in fancy, loved. If it was not she, how could the dead look so like the living he had once known? At length what doubt was left changed suddenly to an assurance that it must be she. And with the realization, he breathed a sigh of such false relief as he had not known since his sin, and with that sigh he left the room. He passed his mother, who still wept in the now deeper dusk of the parlor, made the observation that there was no moon and that it would be quite dark before he reached home, and with that bade her good-night and went out.

Peter had been unable to sit any longer inactive and had some time before gone out to the stable. However, when he had been foiled in the attempt to occupy himself, he came back into the house and sat down by his wife. She began to talk about the funeral preparations and the people they should invite. But such sorrow overtook him afresh, that even his wife, inconsolable as she was herself, was surprised at the depth of his grief for one who was no relative. To him it seemed indelicate, almost heartless that she should talk so soon of burying the dear one but just gone from their sight.

"What's the hurry?" he expostulated. "Isna there time enough to think aboot all that in the morn? Let my soul rest a moment wi' death, and dinna talk more aboot yer funeral. 'Sufficient to the day,' ye ken."

"Eh, Peter, I'm no like you. When the soul's gone, I can take no contentment in the presence o' the poor worthless body, lookin' what it never more can be. But be it as ye will, my man. It's a sore heart ye hae as well as mine, and we must bear one anither's burdens. The dear girl may lie as we hae laid her the night through. There's little enough to be done for her anyway; she's a bonny clean corpse as ever was, and may weel lie a few days afore we put her away. I dinna think there's need to watch her; no dogs or cats'll come near her. I hae aye wondered what for fowk would sit up wi' the dead, yet I remember weel that they did it in the old times."

In this alone she showed that the girl she lamented was not her own, for when her daughter died, her body was never for a moment left with the eternal spaces, as if she might wake and be terrified to find herself alone. Then, as if God had forgotten them, they went to bed without saying their usual prayers together. I fancy the visit of her son had been to Marion like the chill of a wandering iceberg.

In the morning the farmer was up first as usual, and went into the death-chamber and down by the side of the bed. And as he sat looking at the white face, he became aware of the faintest possible tinge of color on the lips. Were his eyes deceiving him? It must be his fancy, or at best an accident without significance— for he had heard of such a thing. Still, even if his *eyes* were deceiving him, he could not think of hiding away such death out of sight. The merest counterfeit of life was too sacred for burial. This might have been just how the little daughter of Jairus looked when the Lord took her by the hand before she arose! It was no wonder Peter could not entertain the thought of her immediate burial. They must at least wait some sign, some unmistakable proof of change begun.

Therefore, instead of going outside into the yard to set in motion the preparations necessary for the coming harvest, Peter sat on with the dead: He could not leave her until his wife should come to take his place and keep her company. He brought a Bible from the next room, sat down again and waited beside her. In doubtful, timid, tremulous hope—a mere sense of scarcely possible possibility, he waited for what he could not consent to believe he waited for. He would not deceive himself nor raise his wife's hopes. He would say nothing, but wait to see how it appeared to her. He would ask her no leading question, but merely watch for any look of surprise she might betray.

By and by his wife appeared, gazed a moment on the dead, looked pitifully in her husband's face, and went out again.

"She sees naething!" said Peter to himself. "I'll go to my work. But I winna hae her laid aside afore I'm a good bit surer o' what she is—a livin' soul or a dead body."

With a sad sense of vanished self-delusion, he rose and went out. As he passed through the kitchen, his wife followed him to the door.

"Ye'll send a message to the carpenter aboot a coffin today?" she whispered.

"I'm not likely to forget," he answered; "but there's nae hurry, seein' there's no life concerned."

"Nae, none; the more's the pity," she answered; and Peter knew, with a glad relief, that his wife was coming to herself from the terrible blow.

She sent their hired man to the Cormack's cottage to tell Eppie to come to her.

The old woman came, heard what details there were to the sad story, shook her head mournfully, and found nothing to say. But together they set about preparing the body for burial. That done, the mind of Mrs. Blatherwick was at ease, and she sat down expecting the visit of the carpenter. But he did not come.

On the Thursday morning the soutar came to inquire about his friends at Stonecross, and Mrs. Blatherwick gave him a message to Willie Webster, the carpenter, to see about the coffin.

But catching sight of the farmer in the yard, the soutar went and had a talk with him. The result was that he took no message to Willie Webster, and when Peter went in to his midday dinner, he still said there was no hurry. Why should she be so anxious to heap earth over the dead? In his heart of hearts he still fancied he saw the same possible color in Isy's cheek, the same that is in the heart of the palest blush-rose, which is either glow or pallor as you choose to think it. So the first days of Isy's death passed, and still she lay in state, ready for the grave, but unburied.

A good many of the neighbors came to see her, and were admitted where she lay. Some of them warned Marion that when the change came, it would come suddenly. But still Peter would not hear of her being buried. By this time Marion had come to see, or to imagine with her husband, that she saw the color. So each in turn, they kept watching her. Who could tell but that the Lord might be going to work a miracle for them, and was not in the meantime only trying them, to see how long their patience and hope would endure.

22

•••••••••••••••••••

The Waking

The report spread through the neighborhood and reached Tiltowie, where it speedily pervaded street and lane: "The lass at Stonecross is lying dead, and looking as alive as ever!" From all quarters the people went crowding to see the strange sight, and would have overrun the house had they not been met with less than a cordial reception: the farmer set men at every door and would admit no one. Angry and ashamed, they all turned and went—except for a few of the more inquisitive, who continued lurking about in the hope of hearing something to carry home and enlarge upon their gossip.

The minister insisted on disbelieving the whole thing, and yet he could not help being very uncomfortable by the report. Always a foe to the supernatural, in his own mind silently questioning the truth of the biblical record of miracles in general, he still found himself haunted by a fear which he dared not formulate. Of course, whatever might be taking place, it could be no miracle, but the mere natural effect of natural causes! Nonetheless, however, did he dread what might happen. He feared Isy and what she might say.

For a time, therefore, he dared not go near the place. The girl might be in a trance. She might suddenly revive and call out his name! She might even reveal all! What if, indeed, she were being even now kept alive to tell the truth and disgrace him before the whole world! Horrible as was the thought, might it not be a good idea, in view of the possibility of her revival, for him to be present to hear anything she might say, so he could take precaution against it? He decided, therefore, to go to Stonecross and ask about her, heartily hoping to find her undoubtedly and irrecoverably dead.

In the meantime, Peter had been growing more and more expectant, and had nearly forgotten all about the coffin, when a fresh rumor came to the ears of William Webster that the young woman at Stonecross was indeed and unmistakably gone. Having already lost patience over the uncertainty of the thing, this builder of houses for the dead questioned no longer what was to be done. He immediately set himself to his supposed task.

That same night, as the minister was making plans to go to the farm, he passed Webster and his man in town, carrying the coffin through the darkness in the direction of Stonecross. He saw what it was, and his heart gave a throb of satisfaction. When the two men reached Stonecross in the pitch-blackness of a gathering storm, they stupidly set up their burden on end by the first door, then went to the other, where they made a vain effort to convey to the deaf Eppie a knowledge of what they had done. She made them no intelligible reply, so there they left the coffin, leaning up against the wall, and, eager to get back to their homes before the storm broke upon them, they set off at what speed was possible on the rough and dark road to Tiltowie, now in their turn passing the minister on his way.

By the time James arrived at the farm, it was too dark for him to see the ghastly sentinel standing at the nearest door. He walked into the parlor, and there met his father coming from the little room where his wife was seated.

To James's astonishment his father greeted him more cheerfully than usual. James cast a hurried, perplexed look on the face of the unburied dead, saw that it seemed in no way changed, and kept a bewildered silence.

"Isna this a most amazin' and hopeful thing?" cried his father. "What *can* there be to come oot o' it! Eh, but the ways o' the Almighty are truly no to be understood by mortal man! The lass must surely be intended for marvelous things to be dealt wi' after such an extra-ordnar' fashion! Night after night the bonny creature lies here, as quiet as if she had never seen trouble, for five days, and no change past upon her, no more than the three holy bairns in the fiery furnace! I'm jist in a tremble to think what's to come oot o' it all. God only kens! What do ye think, Jamie?—When the Lord was dead upon the cross, they waited but two nights, and there he was up and afore them! Here we hae waited these days—and naething even to prove that she's dead! still less any sign that she'll ever speak again!—What do ye think o' it, man?"

"If ever she returns to life, I greatly doobt she'll bring back her senses wi' her!" said the mother, joining them from the inner chamber.

"I can think o' naething but that bonny lassie lyin' there neither dead nor alive! I jist wonder, James, that ye're no concerned and filled wi' doobt and even dread."

"We're all in the hands of the God who created life and death," returned James in a pious tone.

The father held his peace.

"And he'll bring light oot o' the very dark o' the grave!" said the mother.

Her faith, or at least her hope, once set going, went further than her husband's, and she had a greater power of waiting than he. James had sorely tried both her patience and her hope, and not even now had she given up on him.

"Ye'll bide and share oor watch this one night, Jamie?" said Peter. "It's a ghostly kind o' thing to wake up in the dark wi' a dead corpse aside ye!—No that even yet I give her up for dead! but I canna help feelin' some eerie like—no to say afraid. Bide, man, and see the night oot wi' us."

James had little inclination to add another to the party, and began to murmur something about his housekeeper. But his mother cut him short with an indignant remark.

"Hoot! what's a housekeeper aside o' kin?"

James had not a word to answer. Greatly as he shrank from the ordeal, he must encounter it without show of reluctance. He dared not even propose to sit in the kitchen instead. With better courage than will, he consented to share their vigil.

His mother went to prepare supper for them. His father rose, and saying he would have a look at the night, went toward the door; for nothing could quite smother the anxiety of the husbandman. But determined not to be left alone with that thing in the chamber, James glided past him and to the door.

In the meantime the wind had been rising, and the coffin had been tilting and resettling on its narrower end. When James opened the door, the gruesome thing fell forward just as he crossed the threshold, knocked him down, and fell over on top of him. His father, close behind, tumbled over the obstruction. "Curse the fule, Willie Webster!" he cried. "Had he naethin' better to do than send coffins aboot that naebody wanted—and then set them doon like rat traps to fall over poor Jamie!"

He lifted the thing off his son, who rose unhurt, but both amazed and offended at the mishap, and went back inside to join his mother in the kitchen.

"Dinna tell yer mither aboot the ill-fared thing, Jamie," said Peter, who then picked up the offensive vehicle, awkward burden as it was, and carried it to the back of the cornyard. There he shoved it over the low wall into the dry ditch at its foot, where he heaped dirty straw from the stable over it.

"It'll be long," he vowed to himself, "before Willie hears the last o' this!— and longer yet before he sees the glint o' the money he thought he was earnin' by it! the muckle idiot! He may turn it into a bread-kist, or whatever he likes, the gomf!"

Before he reentered the house, he walked a little way up the hill to cast over the land a farmer's look of inquiry as to the coming night, and then went in, shaking his head at what the clouds boded.

Marion had brought their simple supper into the parlor, and was sitting there along with James waiting for him. When they had ended their meal and Eppie had removed the remnants, the husband and wife went into the adjoining room and sat down by the bedside, where James presently joined them with a book in his hand. When she had cleaned up and *rested* the fire in the kitchen, Eppie came into the parlor and sat on the edge of a chair just inside the door.

Peter had said nothing about the night, and indeed, in his anger at the carpenter, had hardly paid much attention to how imminent the storm actually was. But the air had grown very sultry, and the night was black as pitch. It was plain that long before morning, a terrible storm must break. But midnight came and went, and all was very still.

Suddenly the storm broke upon them with a vibrating flash of angry lightning that seemed to sting their eyeballs, and was replaced the next instant by a darkness that seemed to crush them like a ponderous weight. Then all at once the weight itself seemed torn and shattered into sound—into heaps of bursting, roaring, tumultuous billows. Another flash, yet another and another followed, each with its crashing uproar of celestial avalanches.

At the first flash Peter had risen and gone to the large window of the parlor to discover, if possible, in what direction the storm was traveling. Marion followed him, and James was left alone with the dead. He sat, not daring to move. But when the third flash came, it flickered and played so long about the dead face that it seemed for minutes vividly visible, and his gaze remained fixed upon it, fascinated by what he saw.

The same moment, without a single preparatory movement, Isy was on her feet on top of the bed.

A great cry reached the ears of the father and mother. They hurried into the chamber. James lay motionless and senseless on the floor: a man's nerve is not necessarily proportioned to the hardness of his heart! The awful reality of the thing had overwhelmed him.

Isy had by now fallen, and lay gasping and sighing on the bed. She knew nothing of what had happened to her; she did not yet even know herself—and especially did not know that her faithless lover lay on the floor by her bedside.

When the mother entered, she saw nothing—only heard Isy's breathing. But when her husband came with a candle, and she saw her son on the floor, she forgot all about Isy. She dropped on her knees beside him and lamented over him as if he were dead.

But very different was the effect upon Peter when he saw Isy coming to herself. It was a miracle indeed! It could be nothing less! White as her face was, there was in it an unmistakable look of reviving life. When she opened her eyes and saw her master bending over her, she greeted him with a faint smile, closed her eyes again, and lay still. James soon also began to show signs of recovery, and his father turned to him.

With the old sullen look of his boyhood, he glanced up at his mother, still overwhelming him with caresses and tears.

"Let me up," he said in a complaining voice, wiping his face. "I feel so strange! What can have made me turn so sick all at once?"

"Isy's come to life again!" said his mother.

"Oh!" he returned.

"Ye're surely no sorry for that!" rejoined his mother, with a reaction of disappointment at his lack of sympathy. As she spoke she rose again to her feet.

"I'm pleased enough to hear it—why shouldn't I be?" he answered. "But she gave me a terrible start! You see, I never expected it as you did."

"Weel, ye *are* heartless!" exclaimed his father. "Hae ye nae spark o' fellow-feelin' wi' yer ain mither, when the lass comes to life that she's been mournin' these five days? But losh! she's off again—dead or in a dream, I kenna!—Is it possible she's aboot to slip frae oor hands again?"

James turned away and murmured something inaudible.

But Isy had only fainted, and after some eager ministrations on the part of Peter, she came to herself once more and lay breathing hard, her forehead wet as with the dew of death.

The farmer ran out to the loft in the yard, called the herd-boy, a clever lad, and told him to get up and ride for the doctor as fast as the mare could lay her feet to the road.

"Tell him Isy has come to life," he said, "and he must get oot here quick or she'll be dead again afore he gets to her. If ye canna get the one doctor, away wi' ye to the other, and dinna leave him till ye see him in the saddle and started. Then ye can ease up on the mare, and come home at yer leisure. He'll be here long afore ye! Tell him I'll pay him any fee he likes! Now away wi' ye like the very devil!"

When the boy returned on the mare's back a few minutes later, the farmer was waiting for him with a bottle of whiskey in his hand.

"Na, na!" he said, seeing the lad eye the bottle, "it's no for you! Ye need the small wit ye ever had. It's no you that has to gallop; ye hae but to stay on her back.—Here, Susy!"

He poured half a tumblerful into a soup-plate, then held it out to the mare who licked it up greedily, and immediately started off at a good pace.

Peter carried the bottle to the chamber and got Isy to swallow a little, after which she began to recover again. Nor did Marion forget to administer a share to James, who was not only a little in need of it.

When the doctor arrived within an hour, full of amazed incredulity, he found Isy in a troubled sleep and James gone to bed.

23

· · · · · · · · · · · · · · · · · ·

The Meeting

*T*he next day, though very weak, Isy was much better. But she was too ill to get up, and Marion seemed now in her element, with two invalids to look after, both of whom were dear to her. She hardly knew for which to be more grateful—her son, given helpless into her hands, unable to repel the love she lavished upon him; or the girl whom God had taken from the very throat of the swallowing grave.

Her heart, at first bubbling over with gladness, eventually grew calmer when she came to realize how very ill James was, although she could not imagine the cause of his seeming collapse.

James was indeed not only very ill, but grew slowly worse, for he lay struggling at last in the Backbite of Conscience, who had him fixed in its hold and was giving him grave concern. From whence the holy dog came we know, but how he got hold of him to begin its saving torment, who can understand but God the maker of men. The beginnings of conscience, as all beginnings, are infinitesimal and wrapt in the mystery of creation.

I may venture to convey its results only, not its modes of operation or their stages. It was the wind blowing where it listed, doing everything and explaining nothing. The wind from the timeless and spaceless and formless region of God's feeling and God's thought blew open the eyes of this man's mind so that he saw and became aware that he saw. It blew away the long-gathered vapors of his self-satisfaction and conceit; it blew wide the windows of his soul that the sweet odor of his father's and mother's thoughts concerning him might enter. And when it entered he knew it for what it was; it blew back to him his own judgments of them and their doings, and he saw those judgments side by side with his new insights into their real thoughts and feelings. It blew away the desert of his own moral dullness, indifference, and selfishness that had so long hidden beneath them the watersprings of his own heart. It cleared all his conscious being and made him understand that he had never before loved his mother or his father, or anyone in fact; that he had never loved the Lord Christ, his Master, or cared in the least that he had died for him. He saw that he had never loved Isy—least of all when to himself he pleaded in his own excuse that he had loved her. That blowing wind, which he could not see nor could tell where it came from—still less where it was going—began to blow together his soul and those of his parents.

For the first time the love in his father and in his mother drew him, and the memories of his childhood drew him, for the heart of God himself was drawing him. And as he yielded to that drawing, God continued to draw ever more and more strongly, until at last—I know not how God did it or what he did to the soul of James Blatherwick to make it different from what it was—it grew capable of loving. First he yielded to his mother's love, because he could not help it; then he began to do something he had never done before in his life—he began to will to love others because he *could* love. With this start, he became conscious of the power to love and gradually grew to love still more. And thus did James at last start on the road toward becoming what he had to become or perish.

But before he reached this point, he had to pass through wild regions of torment and horror. He had to know himself all but mad. Both his body and soul had to be parched with fever, thirst, and fear. He had to sleep and dream lovely dreams of coolness and peace and courage, then wake and know that all his life he had been dead, and now first was coming to life. He saw for the first time that indeed it was good to be alive. He saw that now life was possible, because life was to love, and love was to live. What love was, or how he might lay hold of it, he still could not tell—he only knew that it came from and was the will and joy of the Father and the Son.

Even before his spiritual vision arrived at this point, the falseness and meanness of his behavior to Isy had become plain to him. The realization of what he had done brought with it such an overpowering self-contempt that he was tempted to destroy himself to escape the knowledge that he was himself the very man who had been such a creature who could do such things. But by and by he grew reconciled to the fact that he must live on; for otherwise, how could he do anything to make atonement for his actions? And with the thought of reparation, and with it possible forgiveness and reconcilement, his old love for Isy rushed in like a flood, at last grown into something more noble and more worthy of the word *love*. But until this final change arrived, his occasional bouts of remorse touched almost on madness, and for some time it seemed doubtful whether his mind might not retain a permanent tinge of insanity. During the time of his recovery, as he was ministered to by his mother, and his mental and spiritual journey, he came to feel a huge disgust for his position as parish minister. Occasionally he found himself bitterly blaming his parents for not interfering with his choice of a profession that had been his ruin and which he now detested.

One day he suddenly called out as they stood by his bed.

"Oh, Mother! Oh, Father! *Why* did you allow me such hypocrisy? *Why* did you not bring me up as a farmer, to walk at the plough-tail? It was the pulpit that ruined me—the notion that I had to live up to the pattern of the minister even before recognizing anything real in myself! What a royal road to hypocrisy! Now I am lost. I shall never get back to bare honesty, not to say innocence! They are both gone forever!"

The poor mother could only imagine it his humility that made him accuse himself of hypocrisy because he had not fulfilled all the smallest details of his great office.

"Jamie, dear," she cried, "ye must cast yer care upon him that careth for ye! He kens ye hae done yer best, though not yer very best, for who could dare say that. Ye hae at least done what ye could!"

"Na, na," he answered, resuming the speech of his boyhood—a far better sign of him than his mother understood. "I ken too muckle, and that muckle too weel, to lay such flattering words to my soul! It's jist as black as the night!"

"Hoots! ye're dreaming, laddie! The Lord kens his own. He'll see that they come through unburnt."

"The Lord doesna make any a hypocrite on purpose, doobtless. But if a man sin after he has once come to the knowledge o' the truth, there remaineth for him—ye ken the rest o' it as weel as I do mysel', Mither! My only hope lies in the doobt o' whether I *had* ever come to a knowledge o' the truth—or hae yet!—Maybe no!"

"Laddie, ye're no in yer right mind! It's fearsome to listen to ye!"

"It'll be worse to hear me roarin' wi' the rich man in the flames o' hell!"

"Peter! Peter!" cried Marion, driven almost to distraction, "here's yer own son, poor fellow, blasphemin' like one o' the condemned! He jist makes me shiver!"

But she received no answer, for at the moment her husband was nowhere near. In her despair she called out, "Isy! Isy! come and see if ye can do anything to quiet this sick bairn."

It was the third day of his fever, and by this time Isy was much better—able to eat and go about the house. She sprang from her bed, where at the moment she lay resting.

"Coming, mistress!" she answered.

She and James had not met since her resurrection, as Peter always called it.

"Isy! Isy!" cried James the moment he heard her approaching, "come in and hold the devil off me!"

He had risen to his elbow and was looking eagerly toward the door.

Isy entered. James threw his arms wide open, and with glowing eyes clasped her to him. She made no resistance. His mother would think it was all because of his fever. He immediately broke into wild words of love, repentance, and devotion.

"Don't heed him a hair, mem—he's clean out of his head!" Isy said in a low voice, making no attempt to free herself from his embrace, but treating him like a delirious child. "There must be something about me, mem, that quiets him a bit. It's in the brain, you know; the feverish brain! We mustn't contradict him; he must have his own way for a while."

But such was James's behavior to Isy that it was impossible for the mother not to suspect at least that this must not be the first time they had met. And presently she began to think to herself, as she examined her memory, that she must have seen Isy someplace before she ever came to Stonecross. But she could recall nothing.

By and by her husband came in to have his dinner. She sent Eppie up to take Isy's place, with the message that she was to come down at once. Isy obeyed, entered the kitchen a few moments later, where she dropped trembling into the first chair she came to. The farmer, already seated at the table, looked up anxiously.

"Bairn," he said, "ye're so pale! Ye're no fit to be aboot! Ye must be cautious, or ye'll be over the burn yet before ye're safe upon this side o' it! Preserve us all! We canna lose ye twice in one month!"

"Jist answer me one question, Isy, and I'll ask ye nae mair," said Marion.

"Na, na, never a question!" interrupted Peter; "no afore the shadow o' death has left the hoose! Draw ye up to the table, my bonny bairn."

But still Isy sat motionless, looking even more deathlike than while in her trance. Peter got up and made her swallow a little whiskey. When she revived, glad to put herself under his protection, she took the chair he had placed for her beside him and made a futile attempt at eating.

"It's small wonder the poor thing hasna muckle appetite," remarked Mrs. Blatherwick, "considerin' the way yon ravin' laddie up the stairs has been carryin' on to her!"

"What's that?" asked her husband.

"But ye're no to make anythin' o' that, Isy!" added her mistress.

"Not a bit, mem," returned Isy. "I know well it means nothing but the heat of the burning brain! I'm right glad, though, that the sight of me did seem to comfort him some."

"Weel, I'm no sae sure!" answered Marion. "But we'll say nae more aboot that noo. My husband says nae; and his word's law in this hoose."

Isy resumed her presence of dining. Presently Eppie came down, went to her master, and said, "Andrew's come, sir, to ask after the yoong minister and Isy. Am I to ask him in?"

"Ay, and give him some dinner," answered the farmer.

The old woman set a chair for her son by the door, and proceeded to attend to him. James was thus left alone upstairs.

Silence again fell, and the appearance of eating was resumed, Peter and Andrew being the only ones who made a reality of it. Marion was occupied in her mind with many things, especially a growing doubt about Isy. The girl must have some secret, something having to do with their James. She had known something all the time; had she been taking advantage of their lack of suspicions? Thus she sat thinking and glooming.

All at once a cry of misery came from the room above. Isy started to her feet. But Marion was up before her.

"Sit doon this minute," she said in a commanding voice. "I'll gae to him mysel'!" And with the words she left the room.

Peter laid down his knife and fork, then half rose, staring bewildered by his wife's sharp speech, and finally followed her from the room.

"Oh, my baby! my baby!" cried Isy. "If only I still had you. It was God who gave you to me, or how could I love you so? And the mistress winna believe that I even had a bairnie! Noo she'll be sayin' that I killed my bonny wee man! And yet, even for *his* sake, I never once wished ye hadna been born! And noo, when the father o' him's ill, and cryin' oot for me, they winna let me near him!"

The last words left her lips in a wailing shriek.

Then first she saw that her master had reentered. Wiping her eyes hurriedly, she turned to him with a pitiful, apologetic smile.

"Dinna be sore angered wi' me, sir. I canna help bein' glad that I had him, though to lose him has given me such a sore heart."

Suddenly she stopped, terrified: how much had he heard? She did not even know what she might have said. But the farmer resumed his dinner and went on eating as if she had not spoken at all. But he had heard well enough nearly everything she said, and now sat inwardly digesting her words.

Isy was silent, saying to herself, "If only he loved me, I should be content and want nothing more. I would never even care if he said it. I would be so good to him that he could not help loving me a little!"

I wonder whether she would have been so hopeful had she known how his own mother had loved him, and how long she had looked in vain for any love from him in return. And when Isy vowed in her heart never to let James know that she had borne him a son, she never saw that in so doing she would be withholding from him the most potent of influences for his repentance and restoration to God and his parents.

She did not see James again that night. And before she fell asleep at last in the small hours of the morning, she had made up her mind that before the dawn had fully broken upon the moor, she would—as the best and only thing left her to do for him—be as far away from Stonecross as she could get.

She would go back to Deemouth, and again seek work in the paper mills.

24

· · · · · · · · · · · · · · · · ·

The Reunion

$\mathcal{I}$sy awoke with the first of the gray dawn. The house was utterly still. She rose and dressed herself in soundless haste.

It was hard to leave, knowing James was still ill, but she had no choice. She held her breath and listened, but all was still. She opened her door softly; not a sound reached her ear as she crept down the stair. She did not have to unlock nor unbolt the door to leave the house, for it was never locked up.

A dreadful sense of the old wandering desolation came back upon her as she stepped across the threshold, and now she had no baby to comfort her! She was leaving a moldy peace and a withered love behind her, and had once more to encounter the rough, coarse world. It was with sadness that she left the place where she had found welcome, and where she had been loved, and where she had learned so much. She feared the moor she had to cross and the old dreams she must there encounter. But even in the midst of her loneliness in the growing light of dawn, she suddenly remembered that she had not left God, and that her Maker was with her and would not forsake her. In that knowledge she walked on, although she soon became very tired.

Of the several roads that led from the farm, the only one she knew was the one by which Mr. Robertson had first brought her to Stonecross. She would take it back to the village where they had left the coach, and surely there she would be able to find some way to return to Aberdeen.

The walk was very tiring, for she was weak from her prolonged inactivity as well as from the crowd of emotions that had accompanied her recovery. Long before she reached Tiltowie, she was all but worn out. She stopped at the only house she had come to on the way and asked for a drink of water. The woman, the only person she had seen, for it was still early morning and the road was a rather deserted one, gave her milk instead. It strengthened her sufficiently for her to reach the end of her first day's journey; and for many days thereafter she did not have to make a second.

Isy had seen the cobbler once at the farm. And going about her work she had heard scraps of his conversations with the mistress. She had been greatly struck by certain of the things he said, and had often wished for the opportunity of a talk with him. As she reached the village on that same morning, walking along a narrow lane and hearing a cobbler's hammer at work, she glanced through a window of the house she was passing and at once recognized the soutar, John MacLear. He looked up as she obscured his light, and could scarcely believe his eyes to see before him so early in the day Mrs. Blatherwick's maid, concerning whom there had been such a marveling talk for days. She did not look well, and he wondered what she was doing up and so far from home.

She smiled to him and passed from the window with a respectful nod. He sprang to his feet, ran to the door, and overtook her at once.

"I'm jist aboot to drop my work, mem, and hae my breakfast. Will ye no come in and share wi' an auld man and a young lass? Ye hae come a right long way and look some tired."

"Thank you kindly, sir," returned Isy. "I am a bit tired! But how did you know who I was?"

"Weel, I canna jist say I ken ye by the name fowk call ye, and still less do I ken ye by the name the Lord calls ye. But none o' that matters so much to her that knows *he* has a name growin' for her—or rather, a name she's growin' to. Eh, what a day that will be when every habitant o' the holy city will walk the streets well kenned and weel kennin'!"

"Ay, sir, I understand you. For I heard you once say something like that to the mistress, the night you brought home the master's shoes to Stonecross. And I'm right glad to see you again."

They were already in the house, for she had followed him almost mechanically. The soutar was setting for her the only chair there was in the room when the cry of a child reached their ears.

The girl started to her feet. A rosy flush of delight overspread her countenance. She began to tremble from head to foot, and seemed almost on the point of either running toward the cry or fainting on the floor.

"Ay," exclaimed the soutar, with one of his sudden flashes of unquestioning insight, "by the look o' ye, ye ken that for the cry o' yer ain bairn, my bonny lass! Ye'll hae been missin' him sorely, I don't doobt!—There! sit ye doon and I'll hae him in yer arms afore anither minute's past!"

She obeyed him and sat down, her eyes fixed wildly on the door. The soutar made haste and ran to fetch the child. When he returned with him in his arms, he found her sitting bolt upright with her hands already apart to receive him, and her eyes alive as he had never seen them before.

"My Jamie! My own bairn!" she cried, seizing him and drawing him to her with a grasp that, trembling, yet seemed to cling to him desperately, and a look almost of defiance, as if she dared the world to take him from her again.

"Oh, my God!" she cried in an agony of thankfulness. "I know you now! I know you now! Never more will I doubt you, my God!—Lost and found!—Lost for a wee, and found again forever!"

Then she caught sight of Maggie, who had entered the room behind her father, and now stood staring at her motionless—with a look of gladness indeed, yet not entirely of gladness.

"I know," Isy broke out, "that you're grudging me looking at him so. It's true that it's you that's been mothering him since I lost my wits. It's true that I ran away and left him. But ever since, I have sought him with my tears! You mustn't bear me any ill-will—There!" she added, holding him out to Maggie, "I haven't even kissed him yet! But you will let me kiss him before you take him away again?—my own bairnie, whose very coming I had to be ashamed of! Oh my God! But he knows nothing about it, and won't for years to come! I thank God that I haven't had to shoo the birds and the beasts off his bonny wee body! It might have been, but for you, my bonny lass!—and for you, sir!" she went on, turning to the cobbler.

Maggie took the child from her arms, then held up his little face for his mother to kiss, until he began to whimper a little. Then Maggie sat down with him in her lap, and Isy stood absorbed, looking at him.

At last she said with a deep sigh, "And now I must be gone, and I don't know how I'm to go! I have found him and I must leave him, but I hope not for very long! Maybe you'll keep him yet a while—say for a week or more. He's been so long unused to a vagrant life that I doubt it would well agree with him. And I must be away back to Aberdeen if I can get anybody to give me a lift."

"Na, na, that'll never do," returned Maggie, beginning to cry. "My father'll be glad enough to keep him. Only we hae no right over him, and ye must have him again when ye will."

"But you see, I have no place to take him to," said Isy.

All this time the soutar had been watching the two girls with a divine look in his black eyes and rugged face. Now at last he opened his mouth and spoke.

"Ye need no ither place but right here," he said. "Go inside the hoose wi' Maggie, my dear. Lay ye doon on her bed, and she'll lay the bairnie beside ye, and bring yer breakfast there to ye.—Leave them there tigether, Maggie, my doo," he went on with infinite tenderness, "and come and give me a hand as soon as ye hae brewed the tea and gotten a loaf o' white bread. I'll hae my porridge a bit later."

Maggie obeyed at once, and took Isy to the other end of the house, where the soutar had long ago given up his bed to her and the baby.

When all had their breakfast, she sat down in her old place beside her father, and for a long time they worked together without a word spoken.

"I don't think, Father," said Maggie at length, "that I hae been attendin' to ye properly! I'm afraid the bairnie's been makin' me forget."

"No a hair, dautie!' returned the old soutar. "The needs o' the little one stood far afore mine; he *had* to be seen to first. And noo that we hae the mither o' him, we'll get on famously! Isna she a fine creature, and right mitherlike wi' the bairn? That was all I was concerned aboot. We'll get her story frae her before long, and then we'll ken better hoo to help her on wi' her life. And there can be nae fear but, atween you and me, and the Almighty at the back o' us, we'll hae bread enough for the quaternion o' us!"

He laughed at the odd word as it fell from his mouth and the Acts of the Apostles. Maggie laughed too, and wiped her eyes.

Before long Maggie realized that she had never been so happy in her life. Not only did she not have to give up the baby she had grown to love almost as much as if it had been her own; she gained a sister as well. Isy told them as much as she could without breaking her resolve to keep secret a certain name. She wrote to Mr. Robertson, telling him where she was and that she had found her baby. He came with his wife to see her, and thus began a friendship between the soutar and him which Mr. Robertson always declared one of the most fortunate things that had ever befallen him.

"That soutar-body," he would say, "knows more about God and his kingdom, the heart of it and the ways of it, than any man I ever heard of—and so humble!— just like the Son of God himself!"

Before many days passed, however, a great anxiety laid hold of the little household, for wee Jamie was taken so ill that the doctor had to be sent for. For some days the child had a high fever and looked pitifully white. When first the illness came upon him and he ceased being so active, no one could please him but the soutar himself, and he, discarding his work at once, gave himself up to the child's service. Before long, however, he required more skillful handling, and then no one would do but Maggie, to whom he had been more accustomed. Isy could get no share in the labor of love except when he was asleep.

But Maggie was always very careful over the feelings of the poor mother, and though the child had to be in her own arms when awake, she would always, the minute he was securely asleep, lay him softly upon Isy's lap.

Maggie soon got high above her initial twinges of jealousy that one of the happiest moments in her life was when first the child consented to leave her arms for those of his mother. And when he was once more able to scurry about, Isy took her part with Maggie in putting hand and needle to the lining of the more delicate of the soutar's shoes.

25

·················

The Repentance

There was great concern, and not a little alarm, at Stonecross because of the disappearance of Isy. But James continued so ill that his parents were hardly able to take much thought about anybody else.

At last the fever left him, and he began to recover, but he lay still and silent, seeming to take no interest in anything, and remembering nothing he had said. He hardly even remembered that he had seen Isy. And all the while his parents did not stop to wonder what could have caused such a sudden and inexplicable illness.

His weakened conscience was still at work in him, and had more to do with his feeble condition than the prolonged fever. At length his parents began to question his slow recovery and became convinced that he had something on his mind that was interfering with it. Both of them, in their own way, were confident it had to do with Isy. But whereas Marion had grown suspicious of the girl, her husband, having overheard certain of the words that fell from Isy when she thought herself alone, was intently though quietly waiting for what must follow.

"I don't doobt, Peter," began Marion one morning, after a long talk with the cottar's wife, who had been telling her of Isy's having taken up temporary lodgings with the soutar, "that the girl Isy had more to do wi' Jamie's attack than we ken. It seems to me he's long been broodin' over something we ken naethin' aboot."

"That would hardly be strange. When was it that we ever kent anything gaein' on in that mysterious laddie? Na, but he needs a good conscience of his own, for did anybody ever ken enough aboot it or him to say right or wrong to him? But if ye hae a thought he's ever wronged that lassie, I'll say he'll never come to health o' body or mind till he's confessed, and God has forgiven him. He must confess!"

"Hoot, Peter, dinna be sae suspicious o' yer own son. It's no like ye. I wouldna let one ill thought o' poor Jamie inside this auld head o' mine! It's the lassie, I'll take my oath; it's that Isy that's at the bottom o' whate'er it is."

"Ye're too ready wi' yer oath, Marion, to what ye ken naethin' aboot! I say again, if he's done any wrong to that bonny creature—and it wouldna take ower muckle to convince me o' it—he'll hae to take his stand, minister or no minister, upon his repentance."

"Dare ye speak that way aboot yer ain son—ay, and mine, Peter Blatherwick! And the Lord's ordained minister besides!" cried Marion, driven almost to her wits' ends, but more by the persistent haunting of her own suspicion, which she could not repress, than the terror of her husband's words. "Besides," she added, "dinna ye see that nae doobt *he* wouldna be the first to fall into the snare o' a designin' woman, and would it be for his ain father to expose him to public contempt? Ye part should be to cover up whatever little sin he may be wreslin' wi'."

"Dare *ye* speak o' a thing like that as a little sin? Do ye call lyin' and heepocrisy a little sin? I allow the sin itsel' may not be damnable alone, but hoo big might it not grow wi' other and worse sins upon the back o' it? Startin' wi' lyin' and little sins, a man may in the end grow to be a creature not fit to be pulled up wi' the weeds. Eh me, but my pride in the laddie! It'll be small pride for me if this fearsome thing turn oot to be true!"

"What could be such a fearsome thing? He's done nae ill thing, I tell ye."

Peter remained silent.

"And who would dare say it's true?" added Marion, almost fiercely.

"Nae one but himself. And if it be sae, and he doesna confess, the rod laid upon him'll be the rod o' iron that smashes a man like a crock o' clay.—I must take Jamie to task."

"Noo jist take ye care, Peter, that ye dinna quench the smokin' flax."

"I'm more likely to get the bruised reed into my naked palm," returned Peter. "But I'll say naethin, till he's a wee better, for we mustna drive him to despair!— Eh, if he would only repent! What I wouldna do to clear him—that is, to ken him innocent o' any wrong. I would die o' thanksgiving!"

"Well, we're no called upon sae far as that," said Marion. "A lass is aye able to take care o' hersel'."

"God hae mercy upon the two o' them!" said Peter, and after that both parents were silent.

In the afternoon James was a good deal better, and when his father went in to see him, his first words were—"I doubt, Father, that I'm likely to preach again. I've come to see that I was never fit for the work, or had any call to it."

"It may be sae, Jamie," answered his father. "But we'll keep frae conclusions till ye're better and able to judge wi'oot the bias o' illness or distemper."

"But, Father," James went on, and for the first time since he was the merest child, Peter saw tears running down his cheeks. "I have been a terrible hypocrite! Yet my eyes are open at last. I see myself as I am."

"Weel, there's the Lord close by to take ye by the hand like Enoch. Tell me, laddie, hae ye anythin' on yer mind that ye would like to confess and be eased o' the burden frae it?"

James lay still for a few moments; then he said, almost inaudibly, "I think I could tell my mother better than you, Father."

"It'll all be one which one o' us ye tell. The forgivin' and the forgettin' will be one deed—by the two o' us at once! I'll go and cry doon the stair to yer mither to come up and hear ye." For Peter knew by experience that good notions must be taken advantage of in their first ripeness. "We mustna try the Spirit wi' any delays!" he added, as he went to the head of the stair, where he called aloud to his wife. Then returning to the bedside he resumed his seat, saying, "I'll jist bide a minute till she comes."

He did not want to let in any risk between his going and her coming, for he knew how quickly minds may change. But the moment she appeared, he left the room, gently closing the door behind him.

Then the trembling, convicted soul plucked up what courage his so long stubborn and yet cringing heart was capable of, and began.

"Mother, there was a lass I came to know in Edinburgh, when I was a divinity student there, and—"

"Ay, ay, I ken all aboot it!" interrupted his mother, eager to spare him; "—an ill-fared, designin' limmer that might hae kent better than to make advances to the son o' a respectable woman that way!—such, I doubtna, as would deceive the very elect!"

"No, no, Mother. She was none of that sort. She was both bonny and good, and pleasant to the heart as to the sight. She would have saved me if I had been true to her. She was one of the Lord's making, as he has made but a few."

"What for didna she keep away frae ye until ye had married her then? Dinna tell me she didna lay hersel' oot to make a prey o' ye?"

"Mother, you're slandering yourself!—I'll say not a word more."

"I'm sure neither yer father nor myself would hae stood in yer way frae marryin' her!" said Marion, retreating from the false position she had taken.

She did not know herself, or how bitter would have been her opposition to a marriage with one like Isy; for she had set her mind on a distinguished match for her Jamie.

"God knows how I wished I had kept a hold on myself! Then I might have stepped out of the dirt of my hypocrisy instead of falling head over heels into it. I was aye a hypocrite, but she would maybe have found me out and made me look at myself."

He did not know the probability that, if he had not fallen, he would have but sunk all the deeper in the worst bog of all, self-satisfaction, and nonetheless have played her false, and left her with a broken heart.

If anyone would argue that it would thus be better to do wrong and repent than to resist the devil in the first place, I warn him that in such a case he will not repent until the sorrows of death and the pains of hell itself lay hold upon him. An overtaking fault may be beaten out with a few stripes on the back. But a willful wrong shall not come out but by many stripes and a far deeper repentance. The doer of the latter must share, not with Judas, for he did repent, although too late, but with such as have taken from themselves the power of repentance.

"Was there no mark left o' her disgrace?" asked his mother, at last admitting to the dread possibility in full of what her son had done. "Wasna there a bairn to make it manifest?"

"None I ever heard tell of."

"In that case, she's no muckle the worse, and ye needna go on lamentin'," said Marion, the justifying spirit now full at work in her. "*She'll* no be the one to tell! And ye mustna, for her sake! Sae take comfort over what's gone and done wi', and canna come back again, and mustna happen again.—Eh, but it's God mercy there was nae bairn!"

Thus had the mother herself become an evil counselor, crying, "Peace! peace!" when there was no peace, and tempting her son to continue on in his falsehood and become a devil. But one thing yet rose up for the truth in his miserable heart—his reviving and growing love for Isy. It had seemed smothered in selfishness, but was alive and operative, God only knows how—perhaps through feverish, incoherent, forgotten dreams.

He had expected his mother to help him in his repentance, even should the path before him be one of social disgrace. He knew that repentance and reparation must go hand in hand. He had been the cowering slave of a false reputation, but his illness had roused him, set repentance before him, brought confession within sight, and placed purity within the reach of prayer. But he was surprised at her resistance in his attempt to do what he now knew to be right.

"I must go to her," he cried, "the minute I'm able to be up!—Where is she, Mother?"

"Upon nae account see her, Jamie! It would be but to fall again into her snare!" answered his mother, with decision in her look and tone. "We're to abstain frae all appearance o' evil—as ye ken better than I can tell ye."

"But Isy's not an appearance of evil, Mother."

"Ye say weel there, I confess. Na, she's no an appearance; she's the very thing! Keep frae her, as ye would frae the ill one himsel'!"

"Did she ever let on what there had been between us?"

"Na, never. She kenned well what would come o' that!"

"What, Mother?"

"The ootside o' the door!"

"Do you think she told anybody?"

"Many a one, I don't doobt."

"Well, I don't believe it. I am sure she's been as silent as death."

"Hoo ken ye that?—Why didna she say a word to yer ain mither?"

"Because she was set on holding her tongue. Was she to bring such a tale of me to the very house I was born in? As long as I hold my tongue, she'll never wag hers.—Eh, but she's a true one! *She's* one you can trust!"

"Weel, I allow she's done as a woman should—the fault bein' her ain."

"The fault being mine, Mother; she wouldn't tell what would disgrace me."

"She might hae kenned her secret would be safe wi' me."

"I might have said the same but for the way you are speaking of her this very minute! Where is she, Mother? Where's Isy?"

"'Deed, she's made a moonlight flight o' it."

"I told you she would never tell on me! Did she have any money?"

"Hoo can I tell?"

"Did you pay her any wages?"

"She gae me no time! But she's no likely to tell noo, for hearin' her tale, who would take her in?"

"Eh, Mother, but you are hardhearted."

"I ken a harder, Jamie!"

"That's me! And you're right, Mother! But if you would have me love you from this minute to the end of my days, be a little fair to Isy. I have been a damned scoundrel to her!"

"Jamie, Jamie! Ye're provokin' the Lord to anger—swearin' like that in his very face—and you a minister."

" 'Tis hardly swearing, Mother, when I speak only the truth. I provoked him a heap worse when I left Isy to suffer her shame. Don't you remember how the Apostle Peter cursed when he said to Simon Magus, 'Go to hell with your money'?"

"She's told the soutar anyway."

"What! Has *he* gotten a hold of her?"

"Ay, he has! And dinna ye think it'll be all over the toon long afore this?"

"And how will you face the truth, Mother?"

"We must tell yer father and get him to quiet the soutar! For *her*, we must jist stop her mouth with a bunch o' bank notes."

"That would make it almost impossible for even her to forgive you or me either any longer."

"And who's she to speak o' forgivin'?"

The door opened and Peter entered. He strode up to his wife and stood over her like an angel of vengeance. His very lips were white with wrath.

"After thirty years o' married life, noo first to ken my wife as a messenger o' Satan!" he panted.

She fell on her knees before him.

"But think o' Jamie, Peter!" she pleaded. "I would lose my soul for Jamie."

"Ay, and lose his as weel!" he returned. "Lose what's yer own to lose—and that's no yer soul, nor yet Jamie's! He's no yours to save, but ye're doing all ye can to destroy him—and perhaps ye'll succeed! Would ye send him straight away to hell for the sake o' a good name—a lie! a hypocrisy! Call ye that bein' a Christian mither, Marion?—But, Jamie, I'm off to the toon, on me two feet, for the mare's crippled—the very devil's in the hoose and the stable and all it would seem! I'm away to fetch Isy home! And, Jamie, ye'll jist tell her afore me and yer mither that as soon as ye're able to crawl to the kirk wi' her, ye'll marry her afore the world and take her home to the manse wi' ye."

"Hoot, Peter! Would ye disgrace him afore all the beggars o' Tiltowie?"

"Ay, and afore God, that kens all things wi'oot anybody tellin' him! My hand and heart shall be clear o' this abomination!"

"Marry a maiden that never said *nae?*—a lass that's nae a maiden, nor ever will be!—Hoots!"

"And who's to blame for that?"

"She is hersel'!"

"Nae, Marion, 'tis Jamie and nae other! I'm surprised at ye! Oot o' my sight I tell ye! Lord, I kenna hoo I'm to win over this!"

He turned from her with a groan and went toward the open door, almost like one struck blind.

"Oh, Father!" cried James, "forgive my mother before you go or my heart will break. It's the awfulest thing to see the two of you arguing this way."

"She's no sorry one bit for what she's said," replied Peter.

"I am, I am, Peter!" cried Marion, breaking down at once. "Do what ye will, and I'll follow ye—only let it be done quietly, wi'oot din or proclamation. Why should everybody ken everythin'? Who has the right to see into other folk's hearts and lives? The world could hardly go on if that was the way o' it."

"Father," said James, "I thank God that now you know all. Such a weight it takes off me! I'll be well now in no time! I think I'll go to Isy myself. But I wish you hadn't come in quite so soon. For I wasn't giving in to my mother. I was but thinking how to say what was in me to say without making her more upset than could be helped. Believe me, Father, if you can, that I was determined to confess all, no matter what she may have said to me."

"I believe ye, my bairn, and I thank God I hae that muckle power o' belief left in me. I confess I was in too great a hurry, and I'm sure ye were takin' the right way wi' yer poor mither. Ye see, she loved ye see weel that she could think o' naething or naebody but yersel'. That's the way wi' mithers, Jamie, if ye only kenned it! She was close to sinnin' an awful sin for yer sake, man!"

He turned again to his wife.

"That's what comes o' lovin' the praise o' men, Marion. Easy it passes into the fear o' men and disregard o' the Holy—But I'm away down to the soutar, and tell him the change that's come over us. He'll nae doobt be a hair surprised!"

"I'm ready to go with you, Father—or will be in a minute!" said James, getting ready to spring out of bed.

"Na, na; ye're no fit!" interposed his father. "I would hae to be takin' ye on my back afore we was at the foot o' the brae! Stay at home and keep yer mither company."

"Ay, bide, Jamie, and I winna come near ye," sobbed his mother.

"Anything to please you, Mother—but I'm more fit than my father thinks," said James as he settled down again in bed.

So Peter went, leaving mother and son silent together.

At last the mother spoke.

"It's the shame o' it, Jamie," she said.

"The shame was in what I did, Mother, and in hiding from that shame," he answered. "Now I have but the dregs to drink, and them I must endure with patience, for I have well deserved to drink them! But poor Isy, she must have sorely suffered! I hardly dare think what she must have come through."

"Her mither couldna hae brought her up right. The first o' the fault lay in the upbringin'."

"There's another whose upbringing wasn't to blame. My upbringing was all it ought to have been—and see how bad I turned out!"

"It wasna what it ought to hae been. I see it all plain noo! I was aye too afraid o' makin' ye hate me, and see I didna train ye like I should.—Oh, Isy, Isy, I hae done ye wrong. I ken ye could never hae laid yersel' oot to snare him—it wasna in ye to do it."

"Thank you, Mother! It was truly all my fault. And now my life shall go to make it up to her."

"And I must see to the manse," rejoined his mother, "to put all in order for ye."

"As you like, Mother. But for the manse, I will have to clear out of that. I can speak no more from that pulpit! I've been a hypocrite in it too long already. The thought of it makes me shudder!"

"Speak no like that o' the pulpit, Jamie, where so many holy men hae stood up and spoken the Word o' God. Ye'll be a burnin and shinin' light in that pulpit before many a long day after we're dead and home."

"The more holy men that have there borne witness, the less dares any living lie stand there bragging and blazing in the face of God and man. It's shame of myself that makes me hate the place, Mother. Once and no more will I stand there, making of it my stool of repentance, and then down the steps and away, like Adam from the garden."

"And what's to come o' Eve? Are ye goin', like him, to say, 'The woman thou gavest to me—it was all her fault'?"

"You know I'm takin the blame upon myself."

"But hoo can ye take it upon yersel' if ye stand up there an' confess? Fowk'll aye give her a full share in the blame at least. Ye must hae some care o' the lass— that is, if after all ye're goin' to make her yer wife, as ye profess. And what are ye goin' to turn yer hand to next, seein' ye hae already laid it to the plough and turned back?"

"To the plough again, Mother—the real plough this time! From the kirk door I'll come home like the prodigal to my father's house and say to him, 'Set me to the plough, Father. See if I can't be something like a son to you after all'!"

26

. . . .

The Forgiveness

Thus wrought in young James Blatherwick—pastor, sinner, and soon-to-be child of God—that mighty power, mysterious in his origin as marvelous in its result, which had been at work in him all the time he lay sick and overwhelmed with feverish phantasms. But the result was certainly no phantasm. His repentance was true. He had been dead, and was now alive! God and the man met at last! As to *how* God turned the man's heart, that shall remain the eternal mystery. We can only say, "Thou, God, knowest." To understand that we should have to go down below the foundation of the universe itself, underneath creation, and there see God send out from himself man, the spirit, forever distinguished yet never divided from the Lord, forever dependent upon and growing in him, never complete outside of him because his origin, his very life, is founded in the Infinite; never outside of God, because in him only he lives and moves and breathes and grows, and *has* his being.

Brothers and sisters, let us not linger to ask how these things can be. Let us turn at once to this Being in whom the I and me are created and have meaning, and let us make haste to obey him. Only in obeying shall we become all we are capable of being; thus only shall we learn and understand all we are capable of learning and understanding. The pure in heart shall see God; and to see him is to know all things.

Thoughts similar to these were in the meditations of the soutar as he watched the farmer stride away into the dusk of the gathering twilight, going home with a light heart to his wife and repentant son. Peter had told the cobbler that James's sickness had brought to light a sin of his youth whose concealment had been long troubling him, and that he was now bent on making all the reparation he could.

"Mr. Robertson," said Peter, "brought the lass to oor hoose, never sayin' a word aboot Jamie, for he didna ken they were anythin' to one anither. And the girl never said one word aboot him to us."

The soutar went to the door and called Isy. She came and stood humbly before her old master.

"Weel, Isy," said the farmer kindly, "ye gave us a clever slip yon mornin', and a bit of a fright besides! What possessed ye to do such a thing, lass?"

She stood, in obvious distress, and made no answer.

"Hoot, lassie, tell me," insisted Peter. "I haena been an ill master to ye, have I?"

"Sir, you have been like the master of us all to me. But I can't—that is, I mustn't—or rather, I'm determined not to say a word of the thing to anybody."

"Did ye think my wife was afraid the minister might fall in love wi' ye?"

"Well, sir, there might have been something like that in it. But I so wanted to find my bairn again, for in that trance I lay so long, I saw or heard something I took for a sign that he was still alive, and not that far away.—And—would you believe it, sir?—in this very house I found him, and here I have him, and I'm just as happy now as I was miserable before. Is it wrong of me that I can't be sorry anymore?"

"And noo," said Mr. Blatherwick, "ye hae but one thing left to confess—and that's who's the father o' him."

"No, that I can't do, sir. It's enough that I've disgraced *myself*! You wouldn't have me disgrace another as well! What good would that be?"

"It would help ye bear the disgrace."

"No, not a hair, sir. *He* couldn't stand the disgrace half so well as me. I reckon the man's the weaker vessel; the woman has her bairn to fend for, and that takes her thoughts off the shame."

"Ye dinna tell me he gives ye naethin' to help ye maintain the child?"

"I tell you nothing, sir. He never even knew there was a child!"

"Hoot, toot! ye canna be sae simple. It's no possible ye never told him and that he didna ken!"

"I was too ashamed. Ye see, it was all my fault—and it was naebody's business. I wasn't going to have *his* name mixed up with a lass like myself. So I went away, and he never saw me again, and he never heard nothing of the child. And you mustn't try to make me tell you, for I have no right to, and surely you can't have the heart to make me!—But that you shall not anyway! For I won't tell!"

"I dinna blame ye, Isy. But there's jist one thing I'm determined aboot—and that is that the rascal shall marry ye."

Isy's face flushed. She had been taken too much by surprise to hide her pleasure at such a thought. But the flush faded, and presently Mr. Blatherwick saw that she was fighting within herself. Then the shadow of a crafty smile flitted across her face.

"Surely you wouldn't marry me to a rascal, sir," she answered. "Ill as I behaved to you, I can hardly have deserved that at your hand."

"That's what he'll hae to do, though—jist marry ye! I'll make him!"

"I won't have him forced! It's me that has the right over him, and no other man or woman. He shall not be made to act against his will. What would you have me—thinking I would take a man that was forced to marry me. No, no, there can't be none of that! And you can't make him marry me if I won't marry him!—No, thank you."

"Weel, my bonny lady," said Peter, "ye're some yoong lassie. If I had a prince for a son, I would tell ye that ye could hae him—provided he was worth the takin'."

"And I would say to you, sir, 'No—not if he wasn't willing,'" answered Isy, and ran from the room.

"Weel, what do ye think o' the lass by this time, Mr. Blatherwick?" said the soutar, with a flash in his eye.

"I think jist what I thought afore," answered Peter; "she's one in a million. If Jamie isna ready to leave father and mother and kirk and steeple, and cleave to that young woman and her only, he's no a mere fool, he's a miserable wicked fool, and I'll never speak a word to him again, wi' my will, if I live to the age o' auld Methuselah!"

"Take care what ye say to him, though—Isy'll be upon ye! Ye mustn't try to persuade him," said the soutar, laughing. "But listen to me, Mr. Blatherwick, and don't say a word to the minister aboot the bairnie."

"Na, na. It'll be best to let him find that oot for himsel'.—And noo I must be gaein."

He strode to the door, holding his head high, and left without another word. The soutar closed the door and returned to his work, saying aloud as he went, "Lord, let me ever and aye see thy face and desire nothing more—except that the whole world, O Lord, may behold it likewise!"

Peter Blatherwick went home joyous at heart. His son was his son again—and no villain!—only a poor creature, as is every man until he turns to the Lord and leaves behind him every ambition and care for the judgment of men. He rejoiced that the girl he and Marion had befriended would be a strength to his son, that she had proved herself to be a right noble young woman. And he praised the Father of men that the very wanderings and backslidings of those he loved had brought about their repentance and restoration.

"Here I am!" he cried as he entered the house. "I hae seen the lass once more, and she's better and bonnier than ever!"

"Ow, ay! Ye're jist like all the men I ever kenned," said Marion with a smile; "—easily taken in wi' the skin-side!"

"Doobtless! For the Maker has taken a heap o' pains wi' the skin! Anyway, yon lassie's a special one, I can tell ye that. Jamie should be on his knees to her this very moment—no sittin' there gazin' as if his two eyes were two bullets, fired off but never got oot o' their barrels!"

"Hoot, would ye hae him go on his knees to any but the one?"

"Ay, would I—to one that's nearer God's likeness than he has been to her—

and that's oor Isy.—I think, Jamie, that ye might be fit for a drive in the mornin'. I'll take ye to the toon if ye be ready, and let ye say whate'er ye hae to say to her."

James agreed. He did not sleep much that night, yet nevertheless was greatly improved by the next day and well able to get out of bed. Before noon they were at the soutar's door. MacLear opened it himself and took the minister straight to the *ben-end* of the house, where Isy sat alone. She rose, and with downcast eyes went to meet him.

"Isy," he faltered, "can you forgive me? And will you marry me as soon as we're able? I'm ashamed of myself as I can be!"

"You don't have so much to be ashamed of as I do. It was my fault."

"But to not hold my face to it! Isy, I have been a scoundrel to you! I'm so disgusted with myself I can hardly look myself in the face."

"You didn't know where I was! I ran away so nobody would know."

"What reason was there for anybody to know? I'm sure you never told."

Isy went to the door and called Maggie. James stared after her, bewildered.

"This was the reason," she said, reentering with the child and laying him in James's arms.

He gasped with astonishment.

"Is this mine?" he stammered.

"Yours and mine," she replied. "Wasn't God a heap better than I deserved? Such a bonny bairn! Not a mark, not a spot on him from head to foot to tell that he had no business to be here!—Give the bonny wee man a kiss. Hold him close to you, and he'll take the pain out of your heart. He's your own son! He came to me bringing the Lord's forgiveness long before I had the heart to ask for it. Eh, but we must do our best to make it up to God's bairn for the wrong we did him before he was born! But he'll be like his great Father, and forgive us both."

As soon as Maggie had given the child to his mother, she went to her father and sat down beside him, crying softly. He turned on his leather stool and looked at her.

"Rejoice wi' them, Maggie, my doo," he said. "Ye haena lost the one; ye hae gained the two! God himsel' is glad, and the Shepherd's glad, and the angels are all makin' such a flut-flutter wi' their muckle wings, that I can almost hear them!"

Maggie turned to him, wiped her eyes, and smiled. Thereafter her tears were ones of unrestrained joy.

I will not dwell on the delight of James and Isobel, thus restored to each other, the one from a sea of sadness, the other from a gulf of perdition. The one had deserved many stripes, the other but a few. Needful measure had been measured to each, and repentance had brought them together. Our sins and our iniquities shall be no more remembered against us when we take refuge with the Father of Jesus and of us. Nothing we have done can separate us from Him—nothing except our abiding in the darkness and refusing to come to the light.

Before James left the house, the soutar took him aside and said, "Dare I offer ye a word o' advice'?"

"Indeed you may!'" answered the young man with humility. "How would it be possible for me to keep from doing anything you might tell me; for you and my father and Isy between you have saved my very soul!"

"Weel, I would jist ask that ye take no further step o' consequence afore ye see Mister Robertson. Ye see, I would like to see ye put yersel's in the hands o' a man that kens ye both, and the half o' yer story already. Then take his advice what ye ought to do next."

"I will—and thank you, Mr. MacLear! One thing only I hope—that neither you nor he will seek to persuade me to go on preaching. One thing I'm set on, and that is to deliver my soul from hypocrisy, and to walk softly all the rest of my days. Happy man would I have been had they set me from the first to follow the plough and cut the grain and gather the stooks into the barn—instead of creeping into a leaky boat to fish for men with a foul and tangled net! I'm affronted and ashamed of myself!—Eh, the presumption of the thing! But I have been well and righteously punished! The Father drew his hand out of mine and let me try to go on alone. And down I came! For I was fit for nothing but to fall. Nothing less could have brought me to myself—and it took a long time. I hope Mr. Robertson will see the thing as I do myself."

The very next day Peter and James set out together for Aberdeen, and the news which father and son carried them filled the Robertsons with more than pleasure. And if their reception of him made James feel like the repentant prodigal he was, it was by its heartiness and their jubilation over Isy.

The next Sunday Mr. Robertson preached in James's pulpit, announcing the engagement between James Blatherwick and Isobel Rose. The two following Sundays he repeated his visit to Tiltowie, and on the third Monday married them at Stonecross. Then also was the little one baptized, by the name of Peter, in his father's arms—amid much gladness, not unmingled with a humble and righteous shame. The soutar and Maggie were the only friends present besides the Robertsons.

Before the gathering broke up, the farmer put his big Bible into the hands of the soutar, with the request that he would lead their prayers. This was very nearly what he said:

"O God, to whom we belong heart and soul, body and blood and bones, hoo great thou art, and hoo close to us. You only, Lord, hold true ownership ower us! We bless thee heartily, rejoicin' in what thou hast made us, and still more in what thou art thysel'. Take to thy heart and hold them there, these thy two repentant sinners, and thy own little one and theirs, who's innocent as thou hast made him. Give them such grace to bring him up that he be none the worse for the wrong they did him afore he was born. And let the knowledge o' his parents' fault hold him safe frae anything suchlike in his own life. And may they both be the better for their fall, and live a heap more to the glory o' their Father because o' that slip! And if ever again the minister should preach thy Word, may it be wi' the better un'erstandin', and the more fervor. And to that end give him the height and depth and breadth and length o' thy forgivin' love. Thy name be glorified! Amen!"

"I'll never preach again!" whispered James to the soutar as they rose from their knees.

"I winna be altogether sure o' that!" returned the soutar. "Doobtless, ye'll do as the Spirit shows ye."

James made no answer. The nèxt morning, James sent to the clerk of the synod his resignation of his parish and office.

No sooner had Marion, repentant under her husband's terrible rebuke, set herself to resist her rampant pride than the indwelling goodness swelled up in her like a reviving spring, and she began to be her old and lovely self again. Little Peter, whom they had renamed after his grandfather, with his beauty and winsome ways, melted and scattered the last lingering rack of her fog-like ambition for her son. Twenty times in a morning would she drop her work to catch up and caress her grandson, overwhelming him with endearments, while over the return of his mother, now her second daughter indeed, she was jubilant.

From the first announcement of the proposed marriage, she had begun cleaning and setting to rights the parlor, making it over entirely for Isy and James's use. But the moment Isy discovered her intent, she protested obstinately. The very morning after the wedding she was down in the kitchen, and had put the water on the fire for the porridge before her husband was awake. Before her new mother was down or her father-in-law came in from his last preparations for the harvest, it was already boiling, and the table laid for breakfast.

"I know well," she said to her mother, "that I have no right to counter you. But you were glad enough of my help when I first came to be your servant-lass, and why shouldn't things be just the same now? I know all the ways of the place and that they'll leave me plenty of time for the bairnie. You must just let me step again into my own old place. And if anybody comes, it won't take me a minute to make myself tidy as becomes a minister's wife.—Only he says that's to be all over now, and there'll be no need."

With that she broke into a little song, and went on with her work, singing.

At breakfast, James made a request of his father that he might turn a certain unused loft into a room for himself and Isy and little Peter. His father made no objection, and thus he set about the scheme at once, but was interrupted in his work by the speedy beginning of an exceptionally plentiful harvest.

The very day the cutting of the oats began, James appeared on the field with the other scythe-men, prepared to do his best. What delighted his father even more than his work—which began slowly as he learned the way, but soon made rapid progress—was the way he talked with the men and women in the field. Every show of superiority had vanished from his bearing and speech, and he was simply himself, behaving like the others, only with greater courtesy.

When the hour for the noonday meal arrived, Isy appeared with her mother-in-law and old Eppie, carrying the food for the laborers and leading little Peter in her hand. For a while the company was enlivened by the child's merriment, after which he was laid with his bottle in the shadow of an overarching stook of grain, and went to sleep, his mother watching him while she took her first lesson in gathering and binding the sheaves. When he awoke, his grandfather sent the whole family home for the rest of the day.

"Hoots, Isy, my dautie," he said when she protested that she could well finish her work, "would ye make a slave driver o' me, and bring disgrace upon the name o' yer father?"

Then she smiled and obeyed, and went at once with her husband, both of them tired indeed, but happier than they had ever before been in their lives.

27

The Healing

The next morning James was in the field with the rest long before the sun was up. Day by day he grew stronger in mind and in body, until at length he was not only quite equal to the harvest work, but capable of anything required of a farm servant.

His deliverance from the slavery of Sunday prayers and sermons, and his consequent sense of freedom and its delight, greatly favored his growth in health and strength. Before the winter came, however, he had begun to find his heart turning toward the pulpit with a waking desire to again expound God's truths, this time with reality. For almost as soon as his day's work ceased to exhaust him, he had begun to take up the study of the sayings and doings of the Lord of men, eager to verify the relation in which he stood toward him, and through him, toward that eternal atmosphere in which he lived and moved and had his being, God himself.

One day, with a sudden questioning hunger, he rose in haste from his knees and turned, almost trembling, to his Greek New Testament to find whether the words of the Master, "If any man will do the will of the Father," meant "If any man *is willing* to do the will of the Father." Finding that to be just exactly what they did mean, he was able to be at rest sufficiently to go on asking and hoping. And it was not long thereafter before he began to feel he had something worth telling, and must tell it to anyone that would hear. Heartily he set himself to pray for that Spirit of truth, which the Lord had promised to them that asked it of their Father in heaven.

He talked with his wife about what he had found. Then he talked with his father and later the soutar.

The cobbler had for many years made a certain use of his Sundays by which he now saw he might be of service to James: He went four miles into the country to a farm on the other side of Stonecross to hold a Sunday school. It was the last farm for a long way in that direction. Beyond it lay an unproductive region, consisting mostly of peat moss and lone, barren hills—where the waters above the firmament were but imperfectly divided from the waters below the firmament. There roots of the hills came rather close together and the waters gathered, making many marshy places, with only very occasionally here and there a patch of ground on which crops could be raised.

There were, however, many more houses, such as they were, than could have been expected from the appearance of the district. In one spot, indeed, not far from this farm, there was even a small, thin hamlet. It was a long way from church or parish-school, so without anyone to minister to the spiritual needs of the people, it had become a rather rough and ignorant place, with a good many superstitions—none of them in their nature especially mischievous, except indeed as they blurred the idea of divine care and government. It was just the sort of place for bogill-baes and brownie-baes, boodies, goblins, and water-kelpies to linger and disport themselves, long after they had disappeared elsewhere.

Therefore, when the late minister came seeking his counsel, the cobbler proposed, without giving any special reason for it, that he should accompany him the next Sunday afternoon to his school at Bogiescratt. James consented, and the soutar called for him at Stonecross on his way.

"Mr. MacLear," said James as they walked along the rough parish road together, "I have but just arrived at a point I ought to have reached before I ever entertained a thought of addressing anyone about religion. Perhaps I knew some little things *about* religion, but certainly I knew nothing *of* it, least of all had I made any discoveries for myself in spiritual matters. And before that, how can a man possibly understand or know anything whatever about it? Even now I may be presuming to dare to say so, but at least I seem to have begun to recognize a little of the relation between a man and the God who made him. And with the sense of that, as I was saying to you last Friday, there has risen in my mind a new desire to communicate to my fellow-men something of what I have seen and learned. One thing I hope at least, that I shall henceforth be free from any temptation to show off or elevate myself above anyone, and I pray that at first hint of such I shall be immediately made aware of my danger and be given the grace to pull myself out of that pit. And one thing I have resolved upon—that if ever I preach again, I will never again write a sermon. I know I shall make many blunders, and do the thing very badly. But failure itself will keep me from conceit—will keep me, I hope, from thinking of myself at all, enabling me to leave myself in God's hands, and willing to fail if he please. Don't you think that we ought to be able to place ourselves as confidently in God's hands as did the early Christians?"

"I do that, Master James!" answered the soutar. "Hide yersel' in God, and when ye rise before men, speak oot o' that secret place—and fear naethin'. Look yer congregation straight in the eye and say what at the moment ye think and feel, and dinna hesitate to give them the best ye hae."

"Do you really think the Lord might be able to use me again? I mean to speak to his people?"

"Who can tell? We must wait on his guidance. But to answer yer question—ay, do I think he can! If he pleases, which I hope he will!"

"Thank you, thank you, sir! I think I understand," replied James. "If ever I do speak again, I should like it to begin in your school."

"Ye shall then—this very day, if ye like, if ye feel the Lord callin' ye to do so," rejoined the soutar. "I think ye hae somethin', even noo, upon yer mind that ye would like to say to them—but we'll see hoo ye feel aboot it after I hae said a word to them first."

"When you have said what you want to say, Mr. MacLear, give me a look. If I have anything to say, I will respond to your sign. Then you can introduce me, saying what you will."

The cobbler held out his hand to his new disciple, and they continued their journey mostly in silence.

When they reached the farmhouse, the small gathering was nearly complete. It was comprised mostly of farm laborers, but a few of the group worked in a quarry where serpentine lay under the peat. In this serpentine there occasionally occurred veins of soapstone of such thickness as to be itself the object of the quarrier. It was used in the making of porcelain, and small quantities were needed for other purposes.

When the soutar began, James was a little shocked at first to hear him use his mother-tongue as if in ordinary conversation. He put on no preachy tone or airs, and it was completely different from anything James had ever heard from any pulpit. But any sense of its unsuitableness soon vanished, and James began to feel that the vernacular gave his friend additional power of expression.

"My frien's," he began, "I was jist thinkin' as I came ower the hill, hoo we were all made wi' different powers—some o' us able to do one thing best, and some anither. And that led me to remark that it was the same wi' the world we live in—some parts o' it fit for growin' oats, and some barley, and some wheat, or potatoes, and hoo every varyin' piece has to be turned to its own best use. We all ken what a lot o' uses the bonny green-and-red mottlet marble can be put to. But it wouldna do weel for buildin' hooses, specially if there were many streaks o' soapstone in it. Still it's not that the soapstone itsel's o' nae use, for ye ken there are a heap o' uses it can be put to. For one thing, the tailor takes a bait o' it to mark where he's to send the shears along the cloth when he's cuttin' oot a pair o' breeches. And again they mix it up wi' the clay they take for the finer kind o' crockery. But upon the ither hand, there's one thing it's used for by some that canna be considert a right use to make o' it. There's one wild tribe in America they tell me that eat a heap o' it—and that's a thing I canna un'erstan.

"But ye see what I'm drivin' at? It's this—that things hae aye to be put to their right uses. There are good uses, and there are better uses, and then there are aye the *best* uses. And where a thing can be put to its best use, it's a shame to put them to any ither use but that.

"Noo, what's the best use o' a man—what's a man made for? The catechism says, *to glorify God*. And hoo is he to do that? Jist by doin' the will o' God. For the one perfect man said he was born into the world for that one special purpose—to do the will o' him that sent him. A man's for a heap o' uses, but that one use covers them all. When he's doin' the will o' God, he's doin' all things. Still there are various ways in which a man can be doin' the will o' his Father in heaven, and the great thing for each one is to find oot the best way *he* can set aboot doin' that will.

"Noo, here's a man sittin' aside me that I must help set to the best use he's fit for—and that is, telling ither fowk what he kens aboot the God that made him and them, and stirrin' them up to do what the Lord would hae them do. The fact is, that the young man was once a minister o' the Kirk o' Scotland, but when he was a yoong man, he fell into a great fault—a yoong man's fault—I'm no gaein to excuse it—dinna think that. Only I charge ye to remember hoo many things ye hae done yersel's that ye hae to be ashamed o', though some o' them may never seem to come to the light. And be sure o' this—my friend has repented right sorely. Like the prodigal, he grew ashamed o' what he had done, and he gave up his kirk and went home to work on his father's farm. And that's what he's at noo, even though he be a scholar, and a right good one. And by his repentance, he's learnt a heap that he didna ken afore, and that he couldna hae learnt any ither way than by turnin' wi' shame frae the path o' the transgressor. I hae brought him wi' me this day, to tell ye somethin'—he hasna said to me what—that the Lord in his mercy has telled him. I'll say nae more. Mr. Blatherwick, will ye please tell us what the Lord has put in yer mind to say'?"

The soutar sat down and James got up, white and trembling a little. For a moment or two he was unable to speak, but at last he overcame his emotion, and falling at once into the old Scots tongue, he began.

"My frien's, I hae little right to stand up afore ye and say anything. For as some oo ye ken, if no afore, then at least noo frae what my frien' the soutar hae jist be tellin' ye. I was once a minister o' the kirk, but upon a time I behaved mysel' sae ill that, when I came to my senses, I saw it my duty to withdraw frae it. But noo I seem to hae gotten some more light upon spiritual matters that I didna hae afore, and to ken some things I didna ken afore. Sae turnin' my back upon my past sin, and believin' God has forgiven me, and is willin' I should set my hand to his plough once more, I hae thought to make a new beginnin' here in a quiet humble fashion, tellin' ye somethin' o' what I hae begun, in the mercy o' God, to un'erstand a wee for mysel'. Sae noo, if ye'll turn, them o' ye that has brought yer books wi' ye, to the seventh chapter o' John's gospel, and the seventeenth verse, ye'll read wi' me what the Lord says there to the fowk o' Jerusalem: *If any man be willin' to do his will, he'll ken whether what I tell him comes frae God, or whether I say it only oot o' my ain head.* Look at it for yersel's, for that's what it says in the Greek, which is plainer than the English to them that un'erstand the auld Greek tongue. If anybody *be willin'* to do the will o' God, he'll ken whether my teachin' comes frae God, or I say it o' mysel'."

From there he went on to tell them that, if they kept trusting in God, and doing what Jesus told them, any mistake they made would but help them the better to understand what God and his Son would have them do. The Lord gave them no promise, he said, of knowing what this or that man ought to do, but only of knowing what the man himself ought to do. He illustrated this by the rebuke the Lord gave Peter when he inquired into the will of God concerning his friend rather than himself.

The little congregation seemed to hang upon his words, and as they were going away thanked him heartily for thus talking to them.

28

·····················

The Restoration

All through the winter James accompanied the soutar to his Sunday school, sometimes on his father's old gig-horse, but oftener on foot. His father would occasionally go also, and then the men of Stonecross began to go with the cottar and his wife; so that the little company of them gradually increased to about thirty men and women and about half as many children.

In general, the soutar gave a short opening address, but he always had "the minister" speak, and thus James Blatherwick, while encountering many hidden experiences, went through his apprenticeship in extemporary preaching. Hardly knowing how, he grew capable at length of following out a train of thought in his own mind even while he spoke, made all the more real and living and powerful by the sight of the eager faces of his humble friends fixed upon him, sometimes ever seeming to anticipate the things he was saying. He felt at times that he was almost able to see their thoughts taking reality and form to accompany him where he led them as he spoke; while the stream of his thought, as it disappeared from his consciousness and memory, seemed to settle in the minds of those who heard him, like seed cast on open soil—some of it, at least, to grow up in resolves and bring forth fruit.

And all along the road as the friends returned to their homes, now in darkness and rain, sometimes in wind and snow, they had such things to think of and talk about that the way never seemed long. Thus dwindled by degrees Blatherwick's self-reflection and self-seeking, and growing conscious of the divine life both in him and around him, he grew at the same time altogether less conscious of himself.

On one such homecoming, as his wife was helping him off with his wet boots, he looked up in her face and said, "To think, Isy, that here I am, a dull, selfish creature, so long striving for knowledge and influence only for myself, now at last grown able to feel in my heart all the way home that I took every step, one after the other, only by the strength of God in me, caring for me as my own making

Father!—Do you know what I'm trying to say, Isy, my dear?"

"I can't be altogether certain I understand," she answered, "but I'll keep thinking about it, and maybe I'll come to it."

"I can ask no more," said James, "for until the Lord lets you see a thing, how can you or I or anybody see the thing that he must see first? And what is there for us to desire but to see things as God sees them and would have us see them? I used to think the soutar such a simpleton when he was saying the very things that I'm trying to say now. I saw no more what he was after than that poor collie there at my feet—maybe not half so much, for who can tell what he might not be thinking with that faraway look of his!"

"Do you think, James, that we'll ever be able to see inside the doggies, and know what they're thinking?"

"I wouldn't wonder what we might not come to. For you know Paul says, 'All things are yours, and you are Christ's, and Christ is God's!' Who can tell but that the very hearts of the doggies may one day lie bare and open to our hearts as to the heart of him with whom they and we have to do. Eh, but the thoughts of a doggie must be a wonderful sight. And then to think of the thoughts of Christ about that doggie! We'll know them, I don't doubt, someday. I'm surer about that than about knowing the thoughts of the doggie himself!"

Another Sunday night, having come home through a terrible storm of thunder and lightning, he said to Isy, "I have been feeling, all the way home, as if before long I might have to give a wider testimony. The apostles and the first Christians, you see, had to bear testimony to the fact that the man that was hanged and died upon the cross, the same was up again and out of the grave and going about the world. Now I can't bear testimony to that, for I wasn't at that time aware of anything. But I might be called upon to bear testimony to the fact that, where once he lay dead and buried, there he's come alive at last—that is, in the sepulchre of my heart! For I have seen him now, and know him now—the hope of glory in my heart and life. Whatever he said once, that I now believe forever!"

The talks James Blatherwick and the soutar had together were wonderful. Occasionally Mr. Robertson joined them, for he still came weekly to conduct services in the parish church. Whether it was the two or the three of them gathered together, it was chiefly the cobbler that spoke, while James in particular sat and listened in silence. On one occasion, however, James had spoken out freely, and indeed eloquently, and Mr. Robertson, whom the cobbler accompanied to his inn that night, spoke to him about James before they parted.

"Do you see any good reason, Mr. MacLear, why this man should not resume his pastoral office?"

"One thing at least I am sure of," answered the soutar, "—that he is far fitter for it than ever he was in his life before."

Mr. Robertson repeated this to James the next day, adding, "And I am certain everyone who knows you will vote for the restoration of your license."

"I must speak both to Isy and to the Lord about it," answered James with simplicity.

"That is quite right, of course," rejoined Mr. Robertson. "I tell my wife everything that I am at liberty to tell."

"Will not some public recognition of my reinstatement be necessary?" suggested James.

"I will have a talk with the leaders of the synod, and let you know what they say," answered Mr. Robertson.

"Of course I am ready," returned Blatherwick, "to make any public confession judged necessary or desirable; but that would involve my wife. And although I know perfectly well that she will be ready for anything required of her, it remains not the less my part to do my best to shield her. I do know, however, that restoration in the biblical sense goes in two directions. And it is not until I have made what restoration lies within my grasp to account for my sins that I can in any sense be publicly restored."

"You are quite right. The two go hand in hand, just as forgiveness must be born in God's heart and then bear fruit between fellow men and women. Of one thing I think you may be sure—that with our present moderator, your case will be handled with more than delicacy—with tenderness!"

"I do not doubt it! I appreciate your generosity. But make sure he knows that I am willing, not only to be restored, but also to make restoration to any others I may have hurt. I have tried to do so already, but he may request something public. But I must have a talk with my wife about it. She is sure to know what will be best."

"My advice is to leave it in the hands of the moderator. We have no right to choose, appoint, or apportion our own penalties. I will share your heart with him, and I know we can trust him to speak on behalf of the Lord."

James went home and laid the whole matter before his wife.

Instead of looking frightened, or even anxious, Isy laid little Peter softly in his crib, threw her arms round James's neck, and cried, "Thank God, my husband, that you have come to this! Don't leave me out of whatever confessions must be made, I beg of you. I am more than ready to accept my shame. I have always said I was to blame. It was I who should have known better!"

"You trusted me, and I proved quite unworthy of your confidence! But did ever a man have a wife to be so proud of as you!"

Mr. Robertson brought the matter carefully before the synod. But neither James nor Isy ever heard anything more of it—except the announcement of the cordial renewal of James's license. This was soon followed by the offer of a church in the poorest and most populous parish north of the Tweed.

"See the loving power at the heart of things, Isy!" said James to his wife. "Out of evil God has brought good, the best good, and nothing but the good!—a good ripened through my sin and selfishness and ambition, bringing upon you as well as me disgrace and suffering. The evil in me had to come out and show itself before it could be cleared away! Some people nothing but an earthquake will rouse from their dead sleep. I was one of such! God in his mercy brought on the earthquake to wake me and save me from death.

"Ignorant people go about always asking why God permits evil. *We* know why! So that we might come to know—really know!—what good is like, and therefore what God himself is like. It may be that he could with a word eliminate evil altogether and cause it to cease. But what would that teach us about good? The word might make us good like oxen or harmless sheep, but would that be a worthy image of him who was made in the image of God? For a man to cease to be *capable* of evil, he must cease to be man! What would the goodness be that could not help being good—that had no choice in the matter, but must be such because it was so made? God chooses to be good, otherwise he would not be God: Man must choose to be good, otherwise he cannot be the son of God."

"God is good, isn't he, James!"

"And so good to us! Just think where we each might be if he *hadn't* shown us ourselves, even in our sin. We might never have known his goodness had it not been for the evil in us."

"Oh, but that was such a hard time! To think that he was with us every step."

"That is how grand the love of the Father of men is, Isy—that he gives them a share, and that share as necessary as his own, in the making of themselves. Thus, and only thus, by willing—by choosing—the good, can they become partakers of the divine nature. All the discipline, all the pain of the world exists for the sake of this—that we may come to choose the good. God is teaching us to know good and evil in some real degree *as they are* and not as they *seem* to the incomplete. So shall we learn to choose the good and refuse the evil. He would make his children see the two things, good and evil, in some measure as they are, and then say whether they will be good children or not. If they fail and choose the evil, he will take yet harder measures with them, salting them with continually deeper pains and cleansing of the refiner's fire.

"If at last it should prove possible for a created being to see good and evil as they are, and choose the evil, then, and only then, there would, I presume, be nothing left for God but to set his foot upon him and crush him as we might a noxious insect.

"But God is deeper in us than our own life. Yea, God's life is the very center and creative cause of that life which we call *ours*. Therefore is the Life in us stronger than the Death, inasmuch as the creating Good is stronger than the created Evil."

The
Laird's
Inheritance

To my sons:
Robin Mark, Patrick Jeremy, and Gregory Erich.

To them I offer myself, with the prayer and hope that both their mother Judy and I might give to them in some small measure what Cosmo's father passed along to him—the exhortation to do justly, to love mercy, and to walk humbly with our God.

This inheritance I as a father would pass along to you, my sons, with all the fullness of God's blessings, in the inheritance he gives us when we lay everything on the altar for him—an inheritance not made with hands, nor an inheritance of houses, lands or possessions—but an inheritance of God's spirit dwelling within us.

And to all fathers everywhere who love their sons and daughters and desire for them the *true* inheritance of God's children as inheritors of the earth, I would also dedicate my part in this present volume.

Michael Phillips

Contents

Introduction

George MacDonald (1824–1905)—Scottish novelist, poet, preacher, essayist, and literary figure of the late 19th century—was a household name in Britain and many parts of the United States between 1870 and 1910. His more than fifty books sold in the multiple millions, and he was widely recognized in the first rank among an impressive roster of English-speaking authors.

However, in the seventy years following his death, MacDonald's fame, like that of many of his Victorian colleagues, diminished; one by one his books went out of print. By the latter half of the 20th century his name as a literary force had vanished from sight, with the exception here and there of pockets of interest in his fantasy and fairy stories. But in the genre for which he was most widely known in his own time—the adult Victorian novel, of which he wrote approximately thirty—not a single book remained in print.

One of his own books, however, proved prophetic concerning the spiritual truths which MacDonald planted in his lifetime but which seemingly had been forgotten. In *Paul Faber, Surgeon*, reissued in this series as *The Lady's Confession*, his memorable character Joseph Polwarth says, "Perhaps you are not aware that many of the seeds which fall to the ground, and do not grow, yet, strange to tell . . . retain the power of growth. . . . It is well enough known that if you dig deep in any old garden, such as this one, ancient—perhaps forgotten—flowers will appear. The fashion has changed, they have been neglected or uprooted, but all the time their life is hid below."

Indeed, through the years there were those who continued to spade the ground and upturn the soil where the long-buried seeds of George MacDonald's imaginative work had been concealed, each playing a unique part in bringing the forgotten novels back into public attention.

The first new shoots began to break through in earnest in the 1970's with increased reisssuings of MacDonald's works by a variety of publishers. These publications ushered in the full flowering of MacDonald's reputation for a whole new generation in the 1980's, with the republication of his adult fiction in a widespread way for the first time since his own lifetime.

As part of this resurgence of interest, it has been my privilege to edit the Classic Reprint Series of George MacDonald's novels issued since 1982 by Bethany House Publishers, in which MacDonald's original books of 400 to 600 pages—often heavily infused with old Scots dialect—have been pared down and translated, making them accessible to today's readers.

Those who have read other of his novels, or are familiar with his life through his biography, are well acquainted with MacDonald's passionate love for his Scottish homeland. Most of the novels considered by critics as his strongest achieve their excellence because they capture what must be regarded as the essential flavor of this land as viewed through MacDonald's eyes.

Certainly high in this rank must be included this book, originally published in 1881 under the title *Warlock o' Glenwarlock*, which was changed the following year to *Castle Warlock*, and is here republished as *The Laird's Inheritance*. It came at the very height of MacDonald's career, in the midst of a period of phenomenal output. *Warlock o' Glenwarlock*, one of MacDonald's longest books (714 pages), was full of Scottish brogue, and presented a memorable and vivid picture of the Highlands southwest of MacDonald's hometown of Huntly. The setting is the remote valley known as "The Cabrach," situated some twelve to fifteen miles from MacDonald's birthplace, between Rhynie and Dufftown, in what could be considered the foothills of the Grampian Mountains, the most expansive region of Scotland's central Highlands. The area is barren and solitary, beautiful only to one who loves the Highlands as MacDonald did. It made an impression on the young boy who vacationed there with his family, and he returned to it several times later in life in preparation for this book. His opening sketch of the region must stand as one of the most graphic descriptions ever to flow from his pen, and paints a true portrait of the essential mystique of the area.

There are those who voice concern about the spiritual implications of fiction, thinking that the novel is somehow less "real" than a more didactic book. The reality of fiction, however, lies on a deeper plane than mere "factness." Reality is a function of truth. And truth—however conveyed—*is* real. There is, therefore, a reality pervading the novels of George MacDonald, because the situations and characters point toward truth, and toward the One in whom is contained all truth.

By communicating his message in such a fashion, George MacDonald was following the example of his Lord. For fiction was frequently the vehicle the Lord used in order to best convey principles of life in God's kingdom. As he spoke to ordinary people, he found that telling them stories through nonfactual characters was the *best* means to express realities and truths they might not have grasped so deeply in any other way. "Do good to your neighbor" was not a teaching which originated with Jesus but had been set forth by hundreds of great men before. But it was Jesus who penetrated clearly and incisively to the very heart of the matter with his parable of the Good Samaritan, immortalizing the truth as no one before or after has ever done. In fictional format, the truth came alive for all time. Through the nonfactual, but highly *real* genre of the parable, Jesus brought spiritual principles to life.

Similarly, George MacDonald employed fiction to achieve precisely the same goal. *The Laird's Inheritance* illustrates in story form many abiding truths of the Kingdom. When the disciples asked Jesus about giving up all for him, his reply was, "No one who has left home, or land, or family for the sake of the kingdom will fail to receive many times as much in this age, and in the age to come." George MacDonald used a plot revolving around the loss of an earthly inheritance of land to tell of the deeper inheritance of God's kingdom. Whether the earthly inheritance is won or lost is beside the point; the riches of the Kingdom outshine all earthly gain. In the old castle, so insignificant in the world's eyes, good only as a ruin to him who would buy it from Cosmo's father, lies a secret—what Jesus calls "the mystery of the kingdom"—found in the heart of Cosmo's father, a secret that illuminates the riches of God's life within us. The true inheritance was there all along—but only for those with eyes to see it. The value in the eternal realm is not on the surface, but in the heart.

Yet such an inheritance is not won without sacrifice. As Jesus said, the inheritance of houses and lands and riches, in this age and in the age to come, does not come to everyone—it comes to those who have left everything for the sake of the Kingdom. Thus, the inheritance which comes to Cosmo in the end comes as a direct result of his sacrificial laying down of everything he holds dear on a worldly plane. He has to lay down his ancient family home, the land, the inheritance that in the world should rightfully be his, and lay them all on the altar. Cosmo's true and lasting inheritance comes only after he is stripped of every last vestige of self, and is ready to go out into the world as a beggar with only the shirt on his back. At that point God can step in and give him fully of Himself. For though our earthly inheritance may be lost, Jesus has said that his people will inherit the whole earth.

It is precisely the legacy of *this* inheritance—an inheritance not passed down by the hands of men, but by the hand of God into men's hearts—that Cosmo's father gives to him. Cosmo then passes it into future generations in the flow of his descendants and God's people. As has been the case since Old Testament times, the heritage of God is passed from fathers to sons, from mothers to daughters, from parents to children.

Warlock o' Glenwarlock is, like several other of MacDonald's novels, highly autobiographical. We instantly recognize in young Cosmo Warlock the thoughtful Robert Falconer, and indeed the boy George MacDonald himself. Cosmo's grandmother is reminiscent of George's own. The boy has grown up without his mother, reminding us of the death of George MacDonald's mother when he was eight. As Cosmo matures, he goes to college, turns to writing poems, and takes a job as a tutor—all of which parallels MacDonald's experience. The description of the tutorship is almost purely autobiographical, revealing almost exact insight into what we know of MacDonald's assignment in London between 1845 and 1847. And like MacDonald's, Cosmo's father managed a rather large estate of land whose fortunes were on the decline.

Most striking of all, however, is the love which exists between Cosmo and his aging father—in the heart of which pulsated the earliest attraction of the boy toward the heartbeat of God himself. Through this relationship the inheritance of God is passed, hand to hand, from father to son, just as—though Jesus performed the miracle—it was in the hands of the disciples that the loaves and fishes actually multiplied. MacDonald unquestionably draws upon the memory of his own long relationship with his father when he says: "Nobody knows what the relation of father and son may yet come to. Those who accept the relationship in Christian terms are bound to recognize that there must be in it depths more infinite than our eyes can behold, ages away from being fathomed yet. For is it not a small and finite reproduction of the loftiest mystery in human ken—that of the infinite Father and infinite Son? If man be made in the image of God, then must not human fatherhood and sonship be the earthly image of the eternal relation between God and Jesus?"

Through the mouth of Cosmo's father, the essence of what makes up the godly life is articulated. What matters, he says to his son, is not the accumulation of wealth, not the inheritance, not the land, not the castle; what matters—what comprises the life, the inheritance I give you—is to do justly, to love mercy, and to walk humbly with your God.

The desire of his father's heart is particularly moving: "But gien I've ever had onything to ca' an ambition, Cosmo, it has been that my son should be ane o' the wise, wi' faith to believe what his father had learned afore him, an' sae start farther on upo' the narrow way than his father had startit."

As reflected in Warlock's words, the Scots dialect is an intrinsic part of this book's unique Highland flavor. People often ask about the nature of the dialect, but the study of the origins of languages is a complex field, and being no linguistic historian, I can only offer some rudimentary observations. It seems there are essentially four major language groups identifiable in the Scots dialect called "doric." George MacDonald grew up with this dialect, and it found its way into at least ten of his books; MacDonald himself once referred to it as "the broad Saxon of Aberdeen." Those elements are Gaelic (an ancient Celtic language, now almost dead except for remote Highland and island regions of western Scotland and Ireland), Scandinavian, German, and English.

The Scots dialect, at first glance can be difficult to decipher, though with practice and familiarity it becomes easier. The Scots tend to drop certain consonants, and differences in pronunciation make Scots distinct from common English. Thus, "of" in a MacDonald original or a Robert Burns poem becomes *o'*, "have" becomes *hae*, "all" becomes *a'*, "so" becomes *sae*, "with" becomes *wi'*, "you" becomes *ye*, "and" becomes *an'*, "own" becomes *ain*, "young" becomes *yoong*, "how" becomes *hoo*, "about" becomes *aboot*, "well" becomes *weel*, "our" becomes *oor*, "old" becomes *auld*, and so on.

A number of words and phrases, though still English, take on a peculiarly Scottish tone or flavor when spoken—still recognizable, but altered to fit the rough, rhythmic, and rapid Scottish tongue. Thus, "where" becomes *whaur*, "from" becomes *frae*, "don't" becomes *dinna*, "can't" becomes *canna*.

Any language has colloquialisms, and Scottish has more than its share—words such as *gloamin'* (dusk), *mind* (remember), *gowk* (fool or lout), *burn* (stream), *laird* (landowner), and *bairn* (child).

And finally, many thousands of Scottish words are simply foreign to contemporary English, such as: *ken* ("know" from German), *ilk* (every), *lauchen* ("laugh" from German), *gar* (make), *lippen* (trust), *lave* (rest or remainder), *speir* (ask), *ohn* ("without" from German), *gien* (if), *gaein* ("go" or "going" from German), and *siller* (money).

Most of the dialect has been removed from the other MacDonald reprints, but in this particular book the dialect seems fundamentally linked to the Highlands and the struggle of the people who lived there in the 19th century. Thus, in *The Laird's Inheritance* most of the foreign words, phrases, and expressions have been translated, but a healthy portion of Scottish spellings of words remain, sometimes altered a bit to make them look more familiar.

Both the publisher and I encourage your response to this, and to any of George MacDonald's books. I have prepared a small pamphlet on George Mac-Donald, his life, and his work, which is available upon request at the address below. And for those of you interested further in the life of George MacDonald, I would point you in the direction of the Bethany House publication *George Mac-Donald: Scotland's Beloved Storyteller.*

God bless you!

An' noo I wiss ye a' a guid readin'!

Michael Phillips
One Way Book Shop
1707 E Street
Eureka, California 95501

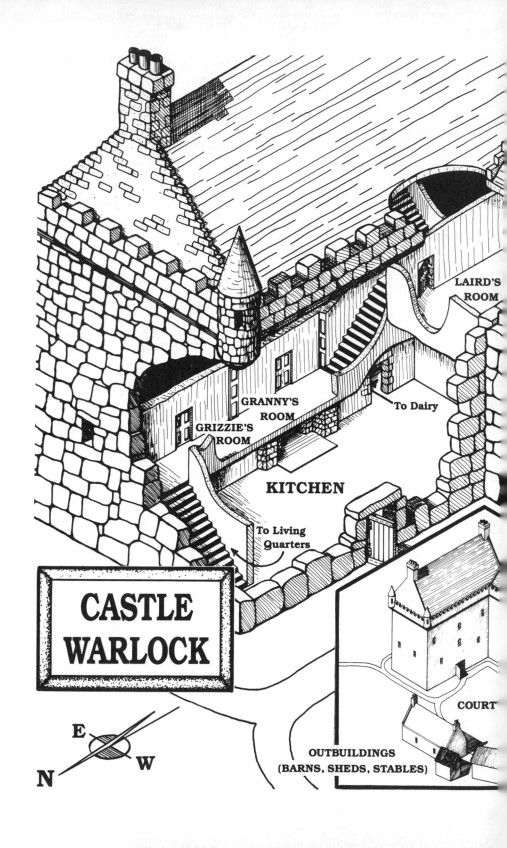

LAIRD'S ROOM

GRANNY'S ROOM

GRIZZIE'S ROOM

To Dairy

KITCHEN

To Living Quarters

CASTLE WARLOCK

E

W

N

COURT

OUTBUILDINGS
(BARNS, SHEDS, STABLES)

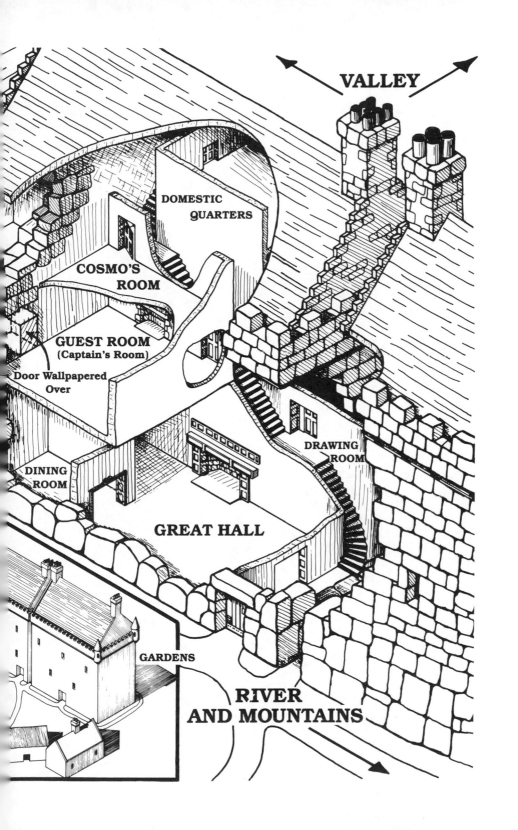

VALLEY

DOMESTIC
QUARTERS

COSMO'S
ROOM

GUEST ROOM
(Captain's Room)

Door Wallpapered
Over

DINING
ROOM

DRAWING
ROOM

GREAT HALL

GARDENS

RIVER
AND MOUNTAINS

1

· · · · · · · · · · · · · · · · · · ·

Castle Warlock

$\mathcal{I}$t was a rough, wild glen to which the family had given its name far back in times unknown, lying in the debatable land between Highlands and Lowlands. Most of its inhabitants spoke both Scots and Gaelic, and there was often to be found in them a notable mingling of the characteristics of the otherwise widely differing Celt and Teuton. The country produced more barley than wheat, more oats than barley, more heather than oats, more boulders than trees, and more snow than anything.

It was a solitary, thinly populated region on the eastern edge of the central Scottish Highlands, mostly made up of bare hills and partially cultivated glens. Each of these valleys had its own small stream, on the banks of which grew here and there a silver birch, a mountain ash, or an alder, but with nothing capable of giving much shade or shelter, except for cliffy banks and big stones. From many a spot you might look in all directions and see not a sign of habitation of either man or beast. But even then you might smell the perfume of a peat fire, although you might be long in finding out where it came from. For the houses of that region, if indeed the dwellings could be called houses, were often so hard to distinguish from the ground on which they were built that except for the smoke of fresh peats coming freely out of their wide-mouthed chimneys, it required an experienced eye to discover the human nest.

The valleys that opened northward produced little. There the snow might occasionally be seen lying on patches of still-green oats, destined now only for fodder. But where the valley ran east and west, and any tolerable ground looked to the south, there things were altogether different. There the graceful oats would wave and rustle in the ripening wind, and in the small gardens would lurk a few cherished strawberries, while potatoes and peas would be plentiful in their season.

Upon a natural terrace in such a slope to the south stood Castle Warlock.

But it turned no smiling face to the region from which came the warmth and the growth. A more grim, repellant, uninviting building would be hard to find. And yet from its extreme simplicity, its utter indifference to its own looks, its repose, its weight, and its gray historical consciousness, no one who loved old houses would have thought of calling it ugly.

The castle, like the hard-featured face of a Scottish matron, suggested no end of story and character. She might turn a defensive if not defiant face to the world, but inside where she carefully tended the fires of life, it was warm. Summer and winter the chimneys of that desolate-looking house smoked. For though the country was inclement, and the people who lived in it poor, the great sullen hills surrounding it for miles in all directions held clasped to their bare cold bosoms, exposed to all the bitterness of freezing winds and summer hail, the warmth of centuries. The peat bogs of those hills were the store closets and wine cellars of the sun, hoarding the elixir of physical life. And although the walls of the castle were so thick that in winter they kept the warmth generated within them from wandering out and being lost on the awful wastes of homeless hillside and moor, they also prevented the brief summer heat of the wayfaring sun from entering with freedom, and hence the fires were needed in the summer as well.

The house was very old, and built for more kinds of shelter than are thought of in our days. For the enemies of our ancestors were not only the cold, and the fierce wind, and the rain, and the snow, but men as well—enemies harder to keep out than the raging storm or the creeping frost. Hence, the more hospitable a house could be, the less must it look what it was: it must wear its face haughty, and turn its smiles inward.

The House of Glenwarlock, as it was sometimes called, consisted of three massive, narrow, tall blocks of building. Two of them stood end to end with but a few feet of space between, and the third stood at right angles to the two. The two which stood end to end were originally the principal parts. Hardly any windows were to be seen on the side that looked out into the valley, but in the third, of more recent construction, though it looked much the same age, there were more windows, but none in the lowest story. Narrow as these buildings were, and four stories high, they had a solid, ponderous look, suggesting such a thickness of the walls as to leave very little hollow inside for the indwellers. On the side away from the valley was a kind of court, completed by the stables and cowhouses, and toward this court were most of the windows—many of them so small that they seemed to belong more to the cottages round about the area than to a house built by the lords of the soil. The courtyard was now merely a farmyard.

At one time there must have been outer defenses to the castle, but they were no longer distinguishable to the inexperienced eye. Indeed, the windowless walls of the house itself seemed strong enough to repel any attack without artillery—unless the assailants got into the court. Even there, however, the windows evidenced signs of having been enlarged, if not increased in number, at a later period.

In that block of the house which stood at right angles to the rest was the kitchen, whose door opened immediately onto the court. Behind the kitchen, in that part which had no windows to the valley, was the milk cellar, as they called the dairy, and places for household storage. A rough pathway ran along the foot of the walls, connecting the doors in the three different buildings. Of these, the kitchen door usually stood open. Sometimes the snow would be coming down the wide chimney, with little soft hisses in the fire, and the business of the house going on without a thought of closing it to the cold of winter, though from the open door you could not have even seen across the courtyard for the thick-falling white flakes.

At the time this narrative begins, however, summer held the old house and the older hills in its embrace. The sun poured torrents of light and heat into the valley, and the slopes of it were covered with green. The bees contented themselves with the flowers, while the heather was getting its bloom ready, and a boy of fourteen sat in a little garden. Dropped like a belt of beauty about the feet of the grim old walls, the garden lay on the south side between the house and the slope where the grain began—now with the ear half formed.

The boy sat on a big stone, which once must have had something to do with the house itself or its defenses, but which he had never known as anything except a seat for him to sit upon. His back was leaning against the old stone wall, and he was in truth meditating, although he did not look as if he were. He was already more than a budding philosopher, though he could not yet have put into recognizable shape the thought that was now passing through his mind. In brief it was this: he was thinking about how glad the bees would be when their crop of heather was ripe; then he thought how they preferred the heather to the flowers; then, that the one must taste the nicer to them than the other. This last thought awoke the question whether their taste of sweet was the same as his. If it was, he thought to himself, then there was something in the makeup of the bee that was the same with the makeup of the boy. And if that was true, then perhaps someday a boy might, if he wanted, try out the taste of being a bee for a little while.

But to look at him as he sat there, nobody would have thought he was doing anything but basking in the sun. The scents of the flowers all about his feet came and went on the eddies of the air, while the windy noises of the insects, the watery noises of the pigeons, the noises from the poultry yard, and the song of the mountain river all visited his brain as well through the portal of his ears. But at the moment the boy seemed lost in the mere fundamental satisfaction of existence.

Broad summer was indeed on the earth and the whole land was for a time bathed in sunlight. Yet although the country was his native land, and he loved it with the love of his country's poets, the consciousness of the boy could not break free from a certain strange kind of trouble—connected with, if not resulting from, the landscape before him. He was a Celt through many of his ancestors, and his mother in particular, and his soul was thus full of undefined emotion and an ever-recurring impulse to break out in song.

There were a few books in the house, among them certain of his countrymen's best volumes of verse. From the reading of these had arisen this result—that, in the midst of his enjoyment of the world around him, he found himself every now and then sighing after a lovelier nature than that before his eyes. In the books he read of mountains, if not wilder, yet loftier and more savage than his own; of skies more glorious; of forests such as he knew only from one or two old engravings in the house, upon which he looked with a strange, inexplicable reverence. He would sometimes wake weeping from a dream of mountains or of tossing waters.

Once with his waking eyes he saw a mist afar off, between the hills that began the horizon. It grew rosy after the sun was down and his heart filled as with the joy of a new discovery. Around him, it is true, the waters rushed down from their hills, but their banks had little beauty. Not merely did the lack of trees distress him, but the channels of the streams and rivers near his home cut their way only through beds of rough gravel, and their bare surroundings were desolate without grandeur—at least to eyes that had not yet pierced to the soul of them. He had not yet learned to admire the lucent brown of the bog waters. There seemed to be in the boy a strain of some race used to a richer home. And yet all the time the frozen regions of the north drew his fancy ten times more than Italy or Egypt.

His name was Cosmo, a name brought from Italy by one of the line who had sold his sword and fought for strangers. Some of the younger branches of the family had followed the same evil profession—chiefly from poverty, but also in some cases from the inborn love of fighting that seems to characterize the Celt. The last soldier of them had served the East India Company both by sea and land: tradition more than hinted that he had chiefly served himself. But since then the heads of the family had been peaceful farmers of their own land, managing to draw a scanty subsistence from an estate that had dwindled to but a twentieth of what it had been a few centuries earlier. Even then, however, it could never have made its proprietor rich in anything but the devotion of his tenants. Both the land and its people were poor of body, but wealthy in what you must look beyond the surface to find.

Growing too hot as he sat between the sun and the wall, Cosmo rose and walked to the other side of the house beyond the courtyard, and crossing a small patch of grass he came upon one unfailing delight in his life—a preacher whose inarticulate voice had been at times louder in his ear than any other since he was born. It was a mountain stream which went through a channel of rock—almost satisfying his fastidious fancy for grandeur—roaring, rushing, and sometimes thundering, with an arrow-like foamy swiftness, down to the river in the glen below. The rocks were very dark and the foam stood out brilliant against them. From the hilltop above it came, sloping steep and far. When you looked up it seemed to come flowing from the horizon itself, and when you looked down, it seemed to have suddenly found it could no more return to the upper regions it had left high behind it, and in disgust had accepted its lot to shoot headlong into the abyss below. There was not much water in it now, but enough to make a joyous white rush through the deep-worn brown of the rock. In the autumn and spring it came down gloriously, dark and fierce, as if it sought the very center of the earth, wild with greed for an absolute rest at the end of its journey.

The boy stood and gazed into the water, as he had done hundreds of times on hundreds of days before. Whenever he grew weary he would seek this endless water, when the things about him put on their too-ordinary look. Let the hillsides around and the gravel-lined bed of the stream higher up be as dull as they might, at this particular spot it seemed inspired and sent forth by some essence of mystery and endless possibility.

There was in him an unusual combination of the power to read both the hidden internal significance of things and the scientific nature that simply obeys the laws upon it. He knew that the stream was in its second stage when it rose from the earth and rushed past the house, that it was gathered first from the great ocean, through millions of smallest ducts, up to the reservoirs of the sky, thence to descend in snows and rains, and wander down and up through the veins of the earth. But even knowing these facts, the sense of the stream's mystery had not begun to lessen in his spirit.

Happily for him, the poetic nature was not merely predominant in him, but dominant, sending itself as a pervading spirit through the scientific knowledge that otherwise would have meant little. His poetic nature illuminated the outward facts which his eyes saw with a polarized ray, revealing life's meaning at a deeper level than the physical senses could comprehend alone. All this, however, was as yet as indefinite as it was operative in him, and I am telling of him what he could not have told of himself. His poetic bent, which always sought meaning beyond facts, had not yet been turned inward upon himself.

He stood gazing, on this particular day, in a different mood than any that had come to him before. He had, as he stood, begun to see something new about this same stream. He recognized that what in the stream had drawn him from earliest childhood, with an indefinite pleasure, was the vague sense of its *mystery*—which is the form the infinite always takes first to the simplest and liveliest hearts. It was because it was *always* flowing that he loved it, because it could not stop. Where it came from was completely unknown to him, and he did not even care to know. When he later learned that it came flowing out of the dark hard earth, the mystery only grew. He imagined a wondrous cavity below in black rock, where the water gathered and gathered—nobody could think how.

And when still later he had to shift its source to the sky, it was no less marvelous, and more lovely. It was a closer binding together of the gentle earth and the awful heavens. These were a region of endless hopes and ever recurrent despairs, and that his beloved finite stream should rise there was an added joy, and gave a mighty hope with respect to the unknown. But from the sky he was sent back to the earth in further pursuit. For where did the rain come from, his books told him, but from the sea? He had read of the sea, though he had never yet seen it, and he knew it was magnificent and mighty. How was the sky fed but from the sea? How was the dark fountain fed but from the sky? How was the torrent fed but from the fountain?

As he stood thus, near the old gray walls, the nest of his family for countless generations, with the scent of the flowers in his nostrils, and the sound of the bees in his ears, it slowly began to dawn on him that he was losing something which had been a precious part of his childhood—the mysterious, infinite idea of endless, inexplicable, original birth, of outflowing because of essential existence within! For years he had thought the stream began in the black earth—there and nowhere beyond. Now he saw that there was no original production or creation anymore. The stream was simply part of a great scientific process. There was no mystery as he had always thought. Like a great dish, the mighty ocean was skimmed of invisible particles, which were gathered aloft into sponges, all water and no sponge. And from this, through many an airy, many an earthly channel, his ancient, self-creating fountain was fed only by what had to be, and thus it was deflowered of its mystery.

He grew very sad, and well he might. Moved by the spring eternal in himself, of which the love in his heart was but a river-shape, he turned away from the now-commonplace stream and, without knowing why, sought another of the human element about the place.

2

The Kitchen

*C*osmo entered the wide kitchen, paved with large slabs of slate. One brilliant gray-blue spot of sunlight lay on the floor, entering through a small window to the east and making the peat fire glow a deep red by contrast. Over the fire a three-legged pot hung from a great chain, with something slowly cooking in it. On the floor between the fire and sun spot lay a cat, content with fate and the world. At the corner of the fire sat an old lady in a high-backed padded chair. She had her back to the door as the boy entered, and was knitting without regarding her needles.

This was his grandmother. The daughter of a small laird in the next parish, she had started life with rather a too-large sense of her own importance by virtue of that of her family, and she had still not lived long enough to get rid of it. She had clung to it all the more since the time of her marriage because nothing had seemed to go well with the family into which she had married. She and her husband had struggled and worked hard, but to no seeming purpose; poverty had drawn its meshes closer and closer around them. They had but one son, the present laird, and when he had come of age, he succeeded to an estate yet smaller and more heavily in debt. To all appearance he would ultimately leave it to Cosmo in no better condition, if he had it to leave at all by then. From the growing fear of its final loss, he loved the place more than any of his ancestors had loved it, and his attachment to the property had descended yet stronger to his son.

But although the elder Warlock wrestled and fought against encroaching poverty, with little success, he never forgot small rights in his anxiety to be rid of large claims against him. What was possible for man to do he did to keep poverty from bearing hard on the people who were his dependents, and never master or landlord was more beloved. Such being his character and the condition of his affairs, it is not very surprising that he should have passed middle age before thinking seriously of marriage. And even then he did not fall in love in the ordinary sense of the phrase. Rather, he reasoned that it would be cowardice to fear poverty so greatly as to run the boat of the Warlocks aground, and leave the scrag end of a property and a history without a man to take them up, and possibly bear them on to redemption; for who could tell what life might be in the stock yet? Anyhow, it would be better to leave an heir to take the remnant in charge, and at least carry the name a generation further, even if it should be into yet deeper poverty. A Warlock could face his fate.

Thereupon he began to visit a woman of thirty-five, the daughter of the last clergyman of the parish, and he had been accepted by her with little hesitation. She was a brave capable woman, fully informed of the state of his affairs, and she married him in the hope of doing something to help him out of his difficulties. She had saved up a few pounds and a trifle her mother had left her, and these she placed unreservedly at his disposal. In his abounding honesty, he spent it on his creditors, bettering things for a time, and greatly relieving his mind and giving the life in him a fresh start. His marriage set the laird growing again—and that is the only final path out of oppression.

Whatever were their feelings for one another on their wedding day, those of the laird were at least those of a gentleman. But it would be a good thing indeed, if, at the end of five years, the love of most pairs who marry for love were equal to that of Warlock and his middle-aged wife. And now that she was gone, his reverence for her memory was stronger yet. Almost from the day of his marriage the miseries of life had lost half their bitterness, and had not returned even at her death.

Many outsiders, however, even those who respected him as an honest man, believed that somehow or other he must be to blame for the circumstances he was in. Either this, or God did not take care of the just man. Such was the unspoken conclusion of many who imagined that they understood the Book of Job, and who took Warlock's rare honesty to be pride or unjustifiable free-handedness instead. Hence, they came to think and speak of him as a poor creature, and soon the man, through the keen sensitivity of his nature, became aware of the fact.

He was a far finer nature than those who thus judged him, of whom some would no doubt have gotten out of their difficulties sooner than he—only he was more honorable in debt than they were out of it. His wife, a woman of strong sense with an undeveloped stratum of poetry in her heart, was able to appreciate the finer elements of his nature; and she let him see very plainly that she did. This proved a great strength and a lifting up of the head to the husband, who most of his life had been oppressed by the opposition of his mother, whom the neighbors regarded as a woman of strength and good sense. And though he now had to fight the wolf of poverty as constantly as before, things after his wife's death looked much more acceptable to him as he viewed them through the love of his wife rather than through the eyes of his neighbors.

They had been married five years before she brought him an heir to the property, and she lived five years more to train him. Then, after a short illness, she departed, and left the now aging man virtually alone with his little child, a vibrant spark of vitality amidst the ancient surroundings. This was little Cosmo who now, somewhat sore at heart from the result of his meditations, entered the kitchen.

Another woman was sitting on a three-legged stool just inside the door, paring potatoes. Cutting off parings that the watching old lady by the fire judged far too thick, she threw each potato into a bowl of water. She looked nearly as old as her mistress, though she was really ten years younger. She had come with the late mistress from her father's house, and had always taken, and still took her part against the opposing faction of the place—namely the grandmother.

A second seat—comfortable enough, but not particularly soft—stood at the opposite corner of the fire. It was a simple wide armchair of elm with a cushion covered in horsehair. This was the laird's seat, generally empty all morning until dinnertime. Not once looking up, Cosmo walked straight to it, diagonally across the floor, and seated himself like one lost in thought.

Now and then as she peeled, Grizzie would cast a keen glance at him out of her bright blue eyes, round whose fire the wrinkles had gathered like ashes. Her eyes were sweet and pleasant, and the expression of her face was one of lovely devotion. But otherwise she was far from beautiful. She gave a grim smile to herself every time she glanced up at him from her potatoes, as much as to say she knew well enough what he was thinking, though no one else did. *He'll be a man yet!* she said to herself.

The old lady also now and then looked over her stocking at the boy, where he sat with his back to the white pine dresser, ornate with the homeliest dishes.

"It'll be lang afore ye fill that chair, Cossie, my man!" she said at length—but not with the smile of play, rather with the look of admonition, as if it was the boy's first duty to grow wide enough to fill the chair and thus restore the symmetry of the world.

Cosmo glanced up but did not speak, and presently was lost again in the thoughts from which his grandmother had roused him as with a jolt.

"What are ye dreamin' aboot, Cossie?" she said again, in a tone wavering but imperative.

Her speech was that of a gentlewoman of the old time, when the highest born in Scotland spoke in the old Scots tongue.

Still Cosmo did not reply.

Reverie does not always agree well with manners. But it would have been hard for him to answer the old lady's question besides—not that he did not know something at least of what was going on in his mind, but at the same time he instinctively knew that it would have sounded like nothing but jabber in her ears.

"Mph!" she said, offended at his silence. "Ye'll hae t' learn manners afore ye're laird o' Glenwarlock, young Cosmo!"

A shadow of indignation passed over Grizzie's rippled face, but she said nothing. There was a time to speak and a time to be silent. It was not that Grizzie was altogether indebted to Solomon for this wisdom, but also to her own experience and practice. The pared potatoes only splashed the louder in the water as they fell. And the old lady knew as well what that meant, as surely as if the splashes had been articulate sounds from the mouth of the old maid.

The boy rose, and coming forward rather like one walking in his sleep, stood before his grandmother, and said, "What was ye saying, Gran'mamma?"

"I was sayin' what ye wadna hearken to, an' that's enough," she answered, perfectly willing to show her offense.

"Say it again, Gran'mamma, please. I wasna listening."

"Na! Ye'll come t' nothin' but trouble followin' yer own fule fancies. Cosmo, if ye give ower muckle tether t' yer thoughts, someday ye'll fall right in the muddy pool, followin' what has neither sense in it nor this warl's gude. What was ye thinkin' aboot now? Tell me that, an' I'll let ye be."

"I was thinkin' about the burnie, Gran'mamma."

"It would be tellin' ye to let the burnie run, an' stick to yer book, laddie!"

"The burnie will run, Gran'mamma, and the book will wait," said Cosmo, perhaps not understanding his own words very clearly himself.

"Ye're gettin' on t' be a man, now," said his grandmother, heedless of his words, "an' ye must learn t' put away bairnly things. There's a heap dependin' on ye, Cosmo. Ye'll be the fifth o' the name in the family, an' I'm feart ye may be the last. It's but small honor to any man, laddie, to be the last, an' if ye dinna gather the wit ye hae an' do the best ye can, ye winna be the laird o' Glenwarlock for lang. If it wasna for Grizzie there, who has no right t' o'erhear the affairs o' the family, I might think the time had come for enlightenin' ye upo' things it's no suitable ye should go ignorant o'. But we'll put it aff till a mair convenient sizzon, atween oor ain two selves."

"An' a mair convenient spokesman, I hope, my leddy," said Grizzie, deeply offended.

"An' who should that be?" rejoined her mistress.

"Ow, who but the laird himsel'?" answered Grizzie. "Who's t' come atween father an' son wi' light upo' family affairs? Not even the mistress hersel' would hae presumed upo' that."

"Keep yer ain place, Grizzie," said the old lady with dignity.

And Grizzie, who had gone further than propriety could justify, held her peace. Only the potatoes splashed yet louder in the bowl. Her mistress sat grimly silent, for though she had had the last word and had been obeyed, she was rebuked in herself. Judging the interview over, Cosmo turned and went back to his father's chair, but just as he was seating himself in it, his father appeared in the doorway.

The form was that of a tall, thin man, a little bent at the knees and bowed in the back, who yet carried himself with no small dignity, cloaked in an air of general apology. He wore large strong shoes fit for boggy land; blue, ribbed, woolen stockings; knee breeches of homemade cloth—coarse cloth, shorn from their own sheep, and spun, woven, and made at home; an old blue dress coat with bright buttons, and a drab waistcoat which had once been yellow.

"Weel, Grizzie!" he said in a gentle, rather sad voice, "I'm too early today."

He never passed Grizzie without greeting her, and Grizzie's devotion to him was like that of a slave and sister mingled.

"Na, laird," she answered, "ye can never be too soon for yer ain folk, though ye may be for yer ain stomach. The taties winna be lang boilin' today. They're some small."

"That's because ye pare them o'er much, Grizzie," said the grandmother.

Grizzie made no reply.

The moment young Cosmo saw whose shadow darkened the doorway, he rose quickly and, standing with his hand upon the arm of the chair, waited for his father to seat himself in it. The laird acknowledged his attention with a smile, sat down, and looked suddenly even older still. He put his hand out to the boy across the low arm of the chair, and the boy laid his hand in his father's. Thus they remained, without saying a word. The laird leaned back and sat resting. All were silent.

Despite the oddity of his dress, no one who had any knowledge of humanity could have failed to see in the laird of Glenwarlock a high-bred gentleman. His face was small and its skin had long since begun to wrinkle. His mouth was sweet, but he had lost several of his teeth and the lips had mostly fallen in. His chin, however, was large and strong, while his blue eyes looked out from under his narrow, high forehead with a softly piercing glance of great gentleness. A little gray hair clustered about his temples and the back of his head. Three days' growth of gray beard protruded from his chin, for now that he had nobody, he would say he had not the heart to shave every morning.

For some time he sat looking straight in front of him, smiling at his mother's hands as they knitted, she casting on him now and then a look that seemed to express the consciousness of blame for not having made a better job of him, or for having given him too much to do in the care of himself. For even his mother did not believe in him further than that he had the best of possible intentions in what he did. At the same time, she never doubted that he was more of a man than his son would ever be, seeing as how they had such different mothers.

"Grizzie," said the laird, "do ye hae a drop o' sour milk? I'm some thirsty."

"Ay, that I hae, sir!" answered Grizzie quickly. She rose and went into the darker region behind the kitchen, from where she presently emerged with a white basin full of rich milk—indeed, it was half cream. Without explanation or apology she handed it to her master, who took it and drank it all down.

"Hoots, woman!" he said, "would ye make me a skin and bone calf! That's no sour milk!"

"I'm sorry it's no to yer taste, laird," returned Grizzie, "but I hae none better."

"Ye told me ye had sour milk," said the laird—without a hint of offense, but rather in the tone of apology for having by mistake made away with something too good for him.

"Weel, laird," replied Grizzie, "it's nothin' but the laird's own milk, an' if ye dinna ken what's good for ye at your time o' life, it's weel there should be another that does. What has a man o' your years t' do with drinkin' sour milk—enough t' turn everythin' inside ye sour besides!"

"Hoots, Grizzie," said the laird, in the gentlest tone, and the contest went no further. In a minute or two the laird rose and went out, and Cosmo went with him.

Before Cosmo's mother died, old Mrs. Warlock would have been indignant at the idea of sitting in the kitchen in the midst of the common goings and comings of the house. But things had combined to bring her to it. She found herself very lonely seated in state in the drawing room. As there was no longer a daughter-in-law to go and come, she learned little or nothing of what was doing about the place. Also, as time went on, and the sight of money grew rarer and rarer, it became more desirable to economize light in the winter. Peats were always to be had of course, so the drawing room could be made nearly as warm as the kitchen. But for the oil to be burned in the simplest of lamps, money had to be paid—and of all ordinary things, money was the seldomest seen at Castle Warlock.

Thus one winter, for the sake of company, of warmth, and of economy, Mistress Warlock had her chair carried to the kitchen. Once it was done, her presence there grew into a custom and lasted into the summer as well. To the laird it was a matter of no consequence where he sat, ate, or slept. When his wife was alive, wherever she was, that was the place for him; when she was gone, all places were the same to him. Hence it came that the other rooms of the house were by degrees almost neglected. Both the dining room and the drawing room grew very cold, cold as with the coldness of what is dead. Though he slept in the same part of the house by choice, the young laird Cosmo did not often enter either room. But he had a notion of vastness and grandeur concerning them in his mind, and along with that a vague sense of sanctity, springing no doubt from the same root as all veneration for place that men seem so naturally inclined to. And at length will we not come to feel all places and all times and all spaces sanctified, because they are the outcome of the eternal nature and the eternal thought?

When we have God, all is holy, and we are at home.

3

·················

Between Father and Son

As soon as they were out of the kitchen door, the boy put his hand into his father's. The father grasped it, and without a word spoken, they walked on together. They would often be half a day together without a word passing between them. To be near one another seemed enough for each.

Cosmo had thought his father was going somewhere about the farm to see how things were getting on. But instead of crossing to the other side of the court or leaving through the gate toward the fields, the laird turned to the left and led the way to the adjacent building, where he stopped at a door at the farther end of the front of it. It was a heavy oak door, studded with great broad iron knobs arranged in angular patterns. It was set deep in the thick wall and the key was in the lock, for it was seldom anybody but Cosmo entered the place, except to open the windows and do other necessary pieces of occasional maintenance. In this building were the dining and drawing rooms, and immediately above the latter a state bedroom in which nobody had slept for many years.

The door led into a narrow passage, and from this passage a good-sized hall opened to the left—barely furnished, but with a huge fireplace, and a great old table that had often feasted jubilant companies. The walls were plastered, now stained with the dampness that had come through the stone walls. Against them were mounted a few molding heads of wild animals—the stag and the fox and the otter, and also one ancient wolf's head—wherever that had been killed.

But it was not into this room that the laird led his son. The passage ended in a stone stair that went up between the two walls. The steps were much worn, and there was so little headroom that the laird could not ascend all the way without stooping. Cosmo was short enough yet to stand up all the way, but it always gave him a feeling of imprisonment to pass through the narrow curve, though he did so at least twice every day. That staircase was the oldest-looking thing about the place.

At the top of it the laird turned to the right and lifted the latch of a dark-looking door. It screaked horribly as it opened. He entered and undid a shutter, letting in a flash of young summer light into the ancient room. It was a long time since Cosmo had been in the drawing room, and the look of it affected him like a withered flower.

It was a well-furnished room. A lady with taste must have at one time presided over it. The furniture in it was very modern compared with the house, but not much of it was younger than the last James or Queen Anne, and it all had a stately old-maidish look. On the floor was an old, old carpet, wondrously darned and skillfully patched, with all its colors faded into a sweet faint ghost-like harmony. Several spider-legged, inlaid tables stood about the room, but most of the chairs were of a sturdier make, one or two of rich carved work of India, no doubt a great rarity when first brought to Glenwarlock. The walls had once had color, now faint and indistinct in the little light that came through the one small deep-set window. There were three of four cabinets, one of them Japanese; and on a table a case of gorgeous hummingbird figurines. A variety of knickknacks and ornaments crowded the chimneypiece, which stood over an iron grate with bulging bars, and a tall brass fender.

How still and solemnly quiet it all was in the middle of the great triumphant sunny day—like some far-down hollow in a rock where a beautiful gem was hiding away from the sight of human eye! The room looked as if it was all done with life—as if it were a room in an Egyptian tomb—yet it was full of the memories of keenest life. Cosmo knew there was treasure upon treasure of wonder and curiosity hidden in those cabinets, some of which he had seen, and more he would like to see. But it was not to show him any of these that his father had now brought him to the room.

Not once letting go of the right hand of the boy, still clasped in his own, the laird closed the door, advanced the whole length of the room, stopped at a sofa covered with a rich brocade, seated himself upon it, drew his son gently between his knees, and began to talk to him.

There was this difference between the relation of these two and that of most fathers and sons, that, taken in this way into solemn solitude by his old father, the boy felt no dismay, no sense of fault, no troubled expectation of discipline or admonition. Reverence and love held equal sway in his feeling toward his father. While the grandmother looked down on Cosmo as the son of his mother, for that very reason his father, in a strange and lovely way, reverenced the boy. And the reaction in the son was utter devotion.

Cosmo stood and looked into his father's eyes—the eyes of the two of them were of the same color, that bright sweet soft Norwegian blue—his right hand still clasped in his father's left, and his left hand leaning gently on his father's knee. A silent man ordinarily, Cosmo's father suffered from no lack of the power of speech, for he had a Celtic gift of simple eloquence.

"This is your birthday, my son," he began.

"Yes, Papa."

"You are now fourteen."

"Yes, Papa."

"You are growing into quite a man."

"I don't know, Papa."

"So much of a man, at least, my Cosmo, that I am going to treat you like a man on this day and tell you some things that I have never talked about to anyone since your mother's death. You remember your mother, Cosmo?"

He was hardly ever alone with the boy without asking this question—not from forgetfulness, but from the desire to keep his son's remembrance of her fresh.

"Yes, Papa, I do."

The laird always spoke Scotch to his mother and to Grizzie, both of whom would have been offended had he addressed them in book-English. But to his Marion's son he always spoke in the best English he had, and Cosmo did his best in return.

"Tell me what you remember about her," said the old man.

He had heard the same thing again and again from the boy, yet every time it was as if he hoped and watched for some fresh revelation from the lips of the lad.

"I remember," said the boy, "a tall beautiful woman, with long hair, which she brushed in front of a big, big mirror."

The love of the son, kept alive by the love of her husband, glorified through the mists of memory, gave to the mother a form greater than that in which he had actually beheld her. Tall to the boy of five, she was little above average height, yet the husband too saw her stately in his dreams. There was nothing remarkable about her face, except her tender expression, which had continually gathered grace after her marriage, but the husband as well as the child called her absolutely beautiful.

"What color were her eyes, Cosmo?"

"I don't know. I never saw the color of them. But I remember they looked at me as if I could run right into them."

"We must be very good that we may see her again someday, my boy."

"I will try. I do try, Papa."

"You see, Cosmo, when a woman like that is taken from us, the least we can do is to give her the same love and the same obedience after she is gone as when she was with us. It may be that God lets her look down and watch us—who can tell? She can't be very anxious about me now, for I am getting old and my warfare is nearly over. She knows I have been trying to keep the straight path, as far as I could see it, though sometimes the grass and heather has got the better of it, so that it was hard to find. But *you* must remember, Cosmo, that it is not enough to be a good boy, as I shall tell her you have always been: you've got to be a good man, and that is a different and sometimes a harder thing. For as soon as a man has to do with other men, he finds they expect him to do things they ought to be ashamed of, and then he has to stand on his own honest legs, and not move an inch for all their pushing and pulling. And when a man loves his fellowman and tries to do good for him and be on good terms with him, that is not easy. The thing is just this, Cosmo—when you are a full-grown man, you must still be a boy. That's the difficulty. For man to be a boy, and still a good boy, he must be a thorough man. And you can't keep true to your mother, or be a thorough man, except you remember him who is father and mother both to all of us.

"I wish my Marion were here to teach you as she taught me. She taught me to pray, Cosmo, as I have tried to teach you—when I was in any trouble, just to go into my closet, and shut the door, and pray to my Father who is in secret. But I am getting old and tired, and shall soon go where I hope to learn faster. Oh, my boy, listen to your father who loves you! Never do anything you would be ashamed for your mother or me to know. Remember, nothing drops out; everything hid shall be revealed. But of all things, if ever you should fail or fall, don't lie still because you are down. Get up again—for God's sake, for your mother's sake, for my sake—get up and try again.

"And now it is time you should know a little about the family of which you come. I don't doubt there have been some in it who would consider me a foolish man for bringing you up as I have done, but those of them who are up there with your mother don't. They see that the business of life is not to get as much as you can, but to do justly, and love mercy, and walk humbly with your God. They may say I have made a poor thing of it, but I shall not hang my head before the public of that country because I've let the land slip from me. Some would tell me I ought to shudder at the thought of leaving you to such poverty, but I am too concerned about you yourself, my boy, to think about the hardships that may be awaiting you. The inheritance of your earthly father may be this land about us here, an inheritance that is dwindling, and which we may lose someday. But the inheritance of your Father in heaven, a Father who owns the cattle on a thousand hills, and all the hills of the earth, is an inheritance no one can take from you. And that is the legacy I want to leave you, my son, a heritage of righteousness, of truth, of love for God, and of service to your kind. That is a more lasting inheritance than any earthly fortune that I could pass on to you.

"So, Cosmo, I do not care what people may think. I should be far more afraid about you if I were leaving you rich. I have seen rich people do things I never knew a poor man to do. I don't mean to say anything against the rich—there's good and bad of all sorts. But I just can't be so very sorry that I am leaving you to poverty, though if I might have had my way, it wouldn't have been so bad. But he knows best who loves best. I have struggled hard to keep the old place for you, but there's hardly an acre outside the garden and close by that wasn't mortgaged before I even came into the property. I've been all my life trying to pay it off but have made little progress. The house is free, however, and the garden. And don't you part with the old place, my boy, except you see that you genuinely *ought* to and that God is leading you to. But rather than anything not out-and-out honest, anything the least doubtful, sell every stone. Let it all go rather than sacrificing an inch of honesty, even if it means you should have to beg your way home to us. Stay clean, my son, as the day you were born."

Here Cosmo interrupted his father to ask what *mortgaged* meant. This led to an attempt on the part of the laird to instruct him in the whole state of the affairs of the property. He showed him where all the papers were kept and directed him to whom to go for any legal advice. At last, weary of business, of which he had all his life had more than enough, he turned to more pleasant matters and began to tell him stories of the family.

By this time dinner was nearly ready downstairs.

"What in mercy can hae come o' the laird, do ye think, my leddy?" said Grizzie to her mistress. "It's the yoong laird's birthday, but I dinna ken where t' go t' call them t' their dinner."

"Run an' ring the great bell," said the grandmother, mindful of old glories.

"Deed, I'll do nothin' o' the kind," said Grizzie to herself. "It's eneuch t' raise a whole regiment—if it didna fall doon upon my heid."

But she had her own ideas, and looking about she found the great door open, and ascended the stairs.

The two were sitting at a table, with the genealogical tree of the family spread out before them, the father telling story after story and the son listening in delight. They were so absorbed that Grizzie's knock startled them.

"Yer dinner is ready, Laird," she said, standing erect in the doorway.

"Very weel, thank ye, Grizzie," returned the laird. "Cosmo, we'll take a walk this evening, and then I'll tell you more about that brother of my grandfather's. Come along to dinner now. I hope ye hae somethin' in honor o' the occasion, Grizzie," he added in a whisper when he reached the door, where the old woman waited to follow them.

"I put a cock an' a leek together," answered Grizzie, "an' they'll be none the worse that ye hae kept them in the pot a while longer. Cosmo," she went on when they had descended and overtaken the boy, who was waiting for them at the foot of the stairs, "the Lord bless ye upon this bonnie day!"

The table in the kitchen was covered with a clean cloth of the finest of home-spun linen, and everything set out just as nicely as if the meal had been spread in the dining room. The old lady was already sitting at the head of the table awaiting their arrival. She made a kind speech to the boy, hoping he would be master of the place for many years after his father and she had left him.

Then the meal began. It did not last long. They had the soup first, and then the fowl that had been boiled in it, with a small second dish of potatoes. Delicate pancakes followed, and dinner was over—except for the laird, who had a little toddy after.

Leaving the table, Cosmo wandered out, pondering some of the things his father had been telling him.

4

· · · · · · · · · · · · · · · · ·

An Afternoon Sleep

Without having any definite thought where he meant to go, Cosmo soon found himself out of sight of the house, in a favorite haunt, but one in which he always had a peculiar feeling of strangeness—even, to a degree, exile. He had descended the stream that rushed past the end of the house till it joined the valley river. He then followed the river up to where it took a sudden sharp turn, and a little far-ther. Crossing it, he found himself in a lonely nook of the glen with steep slopes about him on all sides, some of them covered with grass, others rugged and un-productive. He threw himself down in the clover a short distance from the small river, and immediately felt as if he were miles from home. No shadow of life was to be seen—no cottage chimney, no smoke, no human being, no work of human hands, no sign of cultivation except the grass and clover.

Now whether it was that in childhood he had learned that here he was beyond his father's land, or that some early sense of loneliness in the place had been de-veloped by his imagination into a fixed feeling, I cannot well say. But certainly as often as he came, sometimes to spend hours in the spot, he felt like a hermit of the wilderness cut off from human society, and was haunted with a vague sense of nearby hostility. Probably it came of a historical fancy that the little valley ought to be theirs, or once had been, and now was not, even though there had been no injury done through whatever geographical changes had come about through the years.

This sense of *away-from-homeness*, however, was not strong enough to keep

Cosmo from falling into a dreamy reverie that by degrees naturally ended in slumber. Seldom is sleep far from one who lies on his back in the grass, with the sound of water in his ears. Indeed, a nap in the open air was almost an essential ingredient to a holiday such as Cosmo had been accustomed to make of his birthday. As constantly active as his mind was—perhaps in part because of that activity—he was ready to fall asleep at any moment when warm and lying flat on his back.

When he woke from a dreamless sleep, his half-roused senses could not lay hold of the extraordinary sight before them. Though the sun was yet some distance above the horizon, it was at his back and behind one of the hills as he lay with his head low in the grass. And what could be the strange thing which he saw on the crest of the hill before him? Was it a fire in a grate, thinned away by the sunlight? Even in heraldry the combination he beheld would have been a strange one. There stood a frightful-looking creature half-consumed in light—yet a pale light, not nearly so strong as the sun. And he thought he saw four legs. Suddenly he burst out laughing, and laughed so hard the hills echoed. His sleep-blinded eyes had at last found their focus and clarity.

"I see!" he said, "I see what it is! It's James Gracie's coo 'at's been jumpin' ower the mune, an' is stuck upo' 't!"

In very truth, there was the moon between the legs of the cow! She did not remain there long, however, but was soon on the cow's back, as she crept up and up in the face of the sun. It made him think of a couplet that Grizzie had taught him when he was a child:

Whan the coo loups ower the mune,
The reid gowd rains intil men's shune.

Grizzie, who was out looking for him, heard the roar of his laughter, and thus found him where he lay.

"Eh, Cosmo, laddie, ye'll get yer death o' cauld!" she cried. "An' preserve us! what set ye laughin' in such a fearsome fashion!"

"Ye would hae laughed yersel' t' see James Gracie's coo wi' the mune atween the hin' an' the fore legs o' her."

"Hoots! I see naethin' t' laugh at in that. The poor coo couldna help where the mune would go."

Again Cosmo burst into a great laugh, and this time Grizzie, both alarmed and angry, seized hold of him by the arm and tried to pull him up. "Get up, I tell ye!" she cried. "The laird's askin' what's come o' ye, that ye're nae come home t' yer tea."

But instead of rising Cosmo only laughed all the more, and went on until at length Grizzie made use of a terrible threat.

"If ye dinna hold yer tongue wi' that fool laughin', I'll not tell ye another tale afore Martinmas."

"Will ye tell me one tonight if I hold my tongue an' go home wi' ye?"

"Ay, that I will—that is, if I can remember one."

He rose at once and laughed no more, and they walked home together in complete peace.

After tea his father went out with him for a stroll, and to call on James Gracie, the owner of the cow whose sight on the hill had so much amused him. He was an old man, with an elderly wife and a granddaughter—a weaver by trade, whose father and grandfather before him had for years done the weaving work, both in linen and wool, required by "them at the castle." His ancestors had been on the land from time immemorial, it seemed, though he had only a small cottage and a little bit of land, barely enough to feed the translunar cow.

But poor place as James's was, if the laird would have sold it, the price would have gone a long way toward clearing the rest of his property of its debts. For the location of the small parcel was such as to make it especially desirable in the eyes of the neighbor on the border of whose land it lay. The man was a lord of session and had taken his title from the place, which he inherited from his father; who, although a laird, had been so little of a gentleman that the lordship had not been enough to make one of his son. He was one of those trim, orderly men who above all desire tidiness: tidiness in law, in divinity, in morals, in estate, in garden, in house, in person. Naturally the dwelling of James Gracie was an eyesore to this man, visible as it was from several of his windows, and from almost anywhere on the private road to his house. For it was certainly not a tidy place. It was not dirty, and to any life-loving nature it was as pleasant to know as it was picturesque to look at. But some of the rich seem to recoil at the very sight of poverty, and this Lord Lickmyloof—that was not his real title, but he was better known by it than by the name of his land—could not bear the sight of the cottage that no painter would have omitted from the landscape. It haunted him as if it were an evil thing.

5

School

The next morning, on his way to school with his books hung over his shoulder in a green bag, Cosmo took the steep farm road to the parish road that ran along the border of the river, and followed it downward until it came out from among the hills in a comparative plain. But there were still hills around him on all sides—not very high, few of them more than a couple thousand feet, but bleak and bare, even under the glow of the summer sun. For the time of heather was not yet come, when they would look warm and rich to the eye of the poet and painter. Most of the farmers there, however, would have laughed at the thought of being asked to admire these hills. Whatever their color or shape, they were incapable of producing crops or yielding money. In truth, many who now admire the landscape

from a distance would be unable to do so if, like those farmers, they had to struggle with nature for a bare living. And the struggle in that region, with its early,
long-lasting, bitter winters, and the barrenness of the soil in many parts, was a
severe one.

Leaving the river, the road ascended a little and joined the main road, which
went on a level track along land redeemed in recent years from the vast expanse
of peat moss. It went straight for two miles, fenced from the fields in many parts
by low stone walls without mortar, and in other parts by dykes of earth. These
were covered with grass for the vagrant cow, sprinkled with the loveliest little wild
flowers for the poet-peasant, burrowed in by wild bees for the adventurous delight
of the honey-drawn schoolboy. How glad I am that such earthen dykes had not
quite vanished from Scotland before my own time! Some of the fields had only
a small ditch between them and the road, and some of them had no kind of fence
at all. It was a dreary road even in summer, though not necessarily without its
lovable features—especially the dykes. Wherever there is anything to love, there
is beauty in some form.

A short way past the second milestone he came to the first straggling houses
of the village. It was called Muir of Warlock, named after the moor on which it
stood, as the moor was called after the river that ran through it, and the river
named after the glen, which took its name from the family—so that the Warlocks
had scattered their name all around them.

It was a somewhat dismal-looking village—except to those who knew its people. To some it was beautiful—as the plainest face is beautiful to him who knows
a sweet soul inside it. The highway ran through it—a broad, fine road. Some of
the cottages stood immediately on the path next to the road, others receded a
little. They were almost all of one story, built of stone and rough-cast with a coat
of plaster, with roofs of thick thatch. As Cosmo walked along he saw all the trades
at work; from blacksmith to tailor, everyone was busy. Now and then he was met
by a strong scent as of burning leather—the smell of the oak bark that some of
the housewives used for fuel after the dye had been extracted from it in the tan-
ning-pit. But mostly the air was filled with the smell of burning peat.

Cosmo knew almost everybody and was kindly greeted as he went along—
particularly that some of them had heard from their children that he had not been
to school the day before because it was his birthday. Many of those who greeted
him, however, remarked after he was past that his birthday hardly brought him
enough to keep it with. The worship of Mammon is by no means a vulgarity
confined to the rich. Many of these same people, having next to nothing themselves, still thought of money, houses, and lands as the only inheritances worth
having. They were living examples that Mammon can be worshiped equally by
those who do not have it as by those who do.

Was it nothing to Cosmo to inherit a long line of ancestors whose story he
knew—their virtues, their faults, their wickedness, their humiliation? Was it nothing to inherit the nobility of a father such as his, the graciousness of a mother
such as that father helped him to remember? Was there no occasion for the laird

to rejoice in the birth of a boy whom he believed to have inherited all the virtues of his race, and left all their vices behind?

But however they might regard the holiday, none of the villagers forgot that Cosmo was the "yoong laird," despite the poverty of his house. They all knew that in past times the birthday of the heir had been a holiday for the whole school as well as to himself, and remembered that the introduction of the change had been brought about by the present schoolmaster. Indeed, though there were in the neighborhood several landed proprietors—all of them *lairds*—whose lands came nearer, and although the village itself had ceased to belong to the family, nevertheless throughout the village Warlock was always called *the* laird. And the better parts of even the money-loving and money-trusting among its inhabitants honored him as the best man in the country, though "he had so little skeel at haudin' his ain nest t'gither." But even so, there is scarce a money-making man who does not believe poverty the cousin, if not the child, of fault. Few who are themselves permitted to be financially successful realize that it may be the will of God that other men should be, in that way, unsuccessful, so that better men can be made of them in the end.

All the inhabitants of Muir of Warlock liked the young laird, and those who knew him best loved him. For if he had no lands, neither had he any pride, they said, and was as happy sitting with any old woman and sharing her tea as at a lord's table. And he was no less a favorite at school, even though he was not capable of asserting himself and some of the bigger boys were less than friendly with him. One point in his conduct was particularly distasteful to them: he had a passion for fair play, and could never bring himself to be in a position of the least advantage over another. He shrank from being above another, and thus gave the appearance of one withdrawn, a seeming weakness for the more aggressive to exploit.

The boy walked steadily on, greeting the tailor through his open window, the shoemaker on his stool at the door of his cottage this lovely summer morning, and the smith in his nimbus of sparks through the half door of his smithy. Receiving from each a kindly reply, he came to the school. There, on the heels of the master, the boys and girls were already crowding through the door, and he entered along with them. The religious preliminaries came first, which consisted of a dry and apparently grudging recognition of a sovereignty that required homage, and the reading of a chapter of the Bible in class. The *secular* business was then proceeding, and Cosmo was sitting with his books in front of him, occupied with a hard passage in *Caesar*, when the master left his desk and came up to him.

"You'll have to make up for lost time today, Cosmo," he said.

"The time wasn't lost, sir."

His answer made the master angry, but he restrained himself.

"I'm glad of that. I may then expect to find you prepared with your lessons for today."

"I learned my lessons for yesterday," Cosmo answered, "from my father. And my father says it's not play to learn lessons, in or out of school."

"Your father's not master of this school."

"He's maister o' me," returned the boy, relapsing into his mother-tongue from the anger springing up in him at the appearance of the man's disapproval of his father.

The master took the youth's devotion to his father for insolence to himself.

"I shall say no more," he rejoined, "till I find how you do in your class. Even if you are the best scholar here, that is no reason why you should be allowed to idle away the hours. But perhaps your father does not mean to send you to college?"

"My father hasna said, an' I haena asked," answered Cosmo, with his eyes down on his book.

Still misinterpreting the boy, the conceit and ill-temper of the master now overcame him, and he forgot both his proprieties and his English tongue altogether.

"Haud on that way, laddie, an' ye'll be as great a fule as yer father himsel'!" he said.

Cosmo rose from his seat, white as the wall behind him, looked in his master's eyes, picked up his *Caesar*, and threw the book in his face. Most boys would have then bolted for the door, but that was not Cosmo's idea of bearing witness to his father. He stood still as a statue and waited.

He did not have to wait long. A corner of the book had struck the man's eye. He clapped his hand to it and for a moment seemed lost in suffering. The next he clenched his hand into a man's fist and sent it straight into Cosmo's face with the full force of which he was capable in his somewhat weakened condition. Cosmo fell backward, struck his head on the foot of the next desk, and lay where he fell.

A shriek arose, and a girl of almost sixteen came rushing up. She was the granddaughter of James Gracie, friend and tenant of the laird.

"Go to your seat, Agnes!" shouted the master, who turned from her and stood, with his handkerchief to one eye, looking down on the boy. So little did he really know Cosmo that he suspected him of pretending to be more hurt than he was.

"Touch me if ye dare!" cried Agnes, stooping down.

"Leave him alone!" shouted the master, and seizing her, pulled her away, and threw her back so that she almost fell as well.

But by this time the pain in his eye had subsided a little, and he began to doubt whether indeed the boy was pretending as he had first imagined. He also began to feel a little uneasy as to the possible consequences of his hasty act—not half so uneasy, however, as he would have felt had the laird been as well-to-do as his neighbor, Lord Lickmyloof, who would be rather pleased should he hear that some grief had befallen either Cosmo or the lass Agnes Gracie. Therefore, although he would have been ready to shrink with shame had the door at that moment opened and the laird entered, he did not much fear any serious consequences from the unexpected failure of his self-command.

He dragged the boy up by the arm and tried to set him on his seat, but he fell forward with his face on the desk. With a second cry, Agnes sprang forward. She was a strong girl, accustomed to all kinds of work both indoors and out. She took hold of Cosmo round the waist from behind, pulled him from the seat, and drew him to the door. The master had had enough of it and did not try to stop her. At the door she took him in her arms, and literally ran with him along the street.

She did not have to pass many houses before she came to that of her grandfather's mother—a very old woman, I need hardly say, but in tolerable health and still strong nevertheless. She sat at her spinning wheel with her door wide open. Suddenly, and to her dulled sense of hearing, almost noiselessly, Aggie came staggering in with her burden. She dropped him on the old woman's bed and herself on the floor, both her heart and lungs going wildly.

"In the name o' all!" cried her great-grandmother, stopping her wheel, breaking her thread, and letting the end twist madly up among the revolving iron teeth, emerging from the mist of their own speed, in which a moment before they had looked ethereal as the vibration film of an insect's wings.

She rose with a haste marvelous for her years, and looked down on the form of the girl.

"It cud ne'er be my ain Aggie," she said, "to rush into my quaiet hoose that way, fling a man upo' my bed, an' fall her whole len'th upo' my flure!"

But Agnes was not yet able to reply. She could only make signs with her hand to the bed, which she did with such energy that her great-grandmother—she called her *Grannie*, as did the entire village—turned toward it at once. She could not see well, and the box bed was dark, so she did not recognize Cosmo at first. But the moment she suspected who it was, she too gave a cry.

"What's come o' the bairn?" she said.

"The maister knockit him doon," gasped Agnes.

"Eh, lassie! Run for the doctor."

"No," came a feeble voice from the bed. "I dinna want nothin' said o' the business."

"Are ye sore hurt, my bairn?" asked the old woman, approaching Cosmo.

"My heid's some painful, but I'll just lie still a wee an' then I'll be able t' go hame. I'm some sick. I winna go back t' the school today."

"Na, my bonnie man, that he shallna!" cried Grannie in a tone mingled of pity and indignation.

A moment more and Agnes rose from the earth, for indeed the floor was earth, quite fresh, and the two did all they could to make him comfortable. Aggie would have gone at once to let his father know; once her breath came back she was none the worse for her fierce exertion. But Cosmo said, "Bide a wee, Aggie, an' we'll go hame t'gether. I'll be better in two or three minutes."

But he did not get better as fast as he expected, and the only condition on which Grannie would comply with his request not to send for the doctor was that Agnes should go and tell his father.

"But, Aggie!" said Cosmo, "dinna let him think there's anythin' t' be frightened aboot. 'Tis nothin' but a wee knap o' the heid. I'm sure the maister dinna mean me any serious hurt. But my father's sure t' give him fair play!"

Agnes set out and Cosmo fell asleep.

He slept a long time and woke feeling better. Agnes hurried to Glenwarlock, and found the laird in the yard.

"Weel, lassie!" he said, "what brings you here this time of day? Why aren't you in school?"

"It's the yoong laird!" said Aggie.

"What's happened to him?" asked the laird in an anxious tone.

"It's not so much, he says himsel'. But his heid's still some sore."

"What makes his head sore? He was well enough when he left this morning."

"The maister knockit him doon."

The laird looked as if someone had struck him in the face. The blood reddened in his forehead, and his old eyes flashed like two stars. All the battle-fury of the old fighting race seemed to swell up from ancient fountains among the unnumbered roots of his being. He clenched his withered fist, drew himself up straight, and straightened his knees. For a moment he felt as in the prime of life and its pride.

Then his fist relaxed, his hand fell by his side, and he bowed his head.

"The Lord have mercy on me!" he murmured. "I was almost to take the affairs of one of his own into *my* hands!"

He covered his face with his wrinkled hands, and the girl stood beside him in awe-filled silence. But she did not quite comprehend what was going on inside his heart, and was thus troubled at seeing him stand so still. In the trembling voice of one who would comfort her superior, she said, "Dinna cry, laird. He'll be better, I'm thinkin', afore ye even see him. It was Grannie made me come—no him."

Speechless, the laird turned, and without even going back inside the house, walked away toward the village. He had reached the valley road before he discovered that Agnes was behind him.

"Don't you come, Aggie," he said, "you may be wanted at home."

"Ye dinna think I would leave ye, laird—'cep' ye was t' send me away! I'm most as good as a man t' go wi' ye—wi' the advantage o' bein' a wuman, as my mither tells me." She called her grandmother *mother*. "She says we're more darin' than any man—but, God forgie me!—not more darin' than the yoong laird when he flang his *Caesar* straight int' the maister's face."

The laird stopped, turned sharply around, and looked at her.

"What did he do that for?" he said.

" 'Cause he called ye a fule," answered the girl with the utmost simplicity, and no less reverence.

The laird drew himself up once more, and looked twenty years younger. But it was not pride that inspired him, nor indignation, but the father's joy at finding in his son his champion.

"Many have called me that, lassie, though not to my face nor to that of my bairn. Whether I deserve it or not, only One knows. It's not by the word of man that I stand or fall, but it's how my master looks upon my poor attempts to go by the things he says. Remember this, lassie—let folk say as they like, but do as *he* likes, and before all is done they'll be on their knees to you. And so they'll be yet to my son—though I'm troubled that he hurt the master—even if he deserved it."

"What else cud he do, sir? It wasna for himsel' he struck him. An' then he ne'er moved an inch, but stud there like a rock, an' liftit no han' t' defen' himsel', but jist let the maister hit him."

The pair walked hurriedly on. Before they reached the village, the midday recess had come and everybody knew what had happened. Most were loudly praising of the boy's behavior, and many eyes watched from window and door as the laird tramped swiftly down the street to Grannie's, where all had learned the young laird was lying. But no one spoke, or showed that he was looking, and the laird walked straight on, with his eyes to the ground. And as did the laird, so did Aggie.

The door of the cottage stood open. There was a step down, but the laird knew it well. Turning to the left through a short passage, he lifted the latch of the inner door, bowed his tall head, and entered the room. With a bow to Grannie, he went straight up to the bed, discovered that Cosmo slept, and stood looking at him with a full heart. Who can tell but him who knows it how much more it is to be understood by one's own than by all the world! By one's own one learns to love all God's creatures, and from one's own one gets strength to meet the injustices of the world.

The room was dark, though it was summer. It had two windows—one to the street and one to the garden behind. Both ceiling and floor were of a dark brown, for the beams and boards of the one were old and penetrated with smoke, and the other was of hard-beaten clay, into which also had been worked much smoke and an undefinable blackness. The windows were occupied with different of Grannie's favored plants, so that little light could get in, and that little was half swallowed by the general brownness. A tall eight-day clock stood in one corner, up to which whoever would learn from it the time had to advance confidentially, and consult its face on tiptoe, with peering eyes. Beside it was a beautifully polished chest of drawers; a nice tea table stood in the center, and some dark shiny wooden chairs against the walls. A closet opened at the head of the bed, and at the foot of it was the door of the room and the passage, so that it stood in a recess, to which were wooden doors, seldom closed. A fire, partly of peat, partly of tan, burned on the little hearth.

Cosmo opened his eyes and saw those of his father looking down upon him. He stretched out his arms and drew the aged head upon his chest. His heart was too full of love to speak.

"How are you, my boy?" said the father, gently releasing himself. "I know all about it; you don't need to trouble yourself to tell me more than just how you are."

"Better, Father, much better," answered Cosmo. "But there is one thing I must tell you. Just before it happened we were reading in the Bible class about Samson—how the Spirit of the Lord came upon him, and with the jawbone of an ass he slew so many of the Philistines. And when the master said that bad word about you, it seemed as if the Spirit of the Lord came upon me; for I was not in a rage, but filled with what seemed a holy indignation. And as I had no ass's jawbone handy, I took my *Caesar*, and threw it as straight as I could in the master's face. But I am not so sure about it now."

"Take ye nae thoucht aboot it, Cosmo, my bairn," said the old woman; "it's not a hair beyond what he deserved 'at dared put such a word t' the best man in a' the country. By the han' o' a babe, as he did Goliath, hath the Lord rebuked the enemy. The Lord himsel's on yer side, laird, t' give ye sich a brave son."

"I never knew him to lift his hand before," said the laird, "except it was to the Kirkmalloch bull, when he ran at him and me."

"All the more likely it *was* the Speerit o' the Lord, as the bairn himsel' was sayin'," remarked Grannie in a tone of confidence; "an' where the Speerit o' the Lord is, there's liberty," she added, thinking less of the suitableness of the quotation than of the aptness of the words in it to excuse Cosmo's action. Warlock stooped and kissed the face of his son, and went to fetch the doctor. Before he returned, Cosmo was asleep again. The doctor would not have him waked. From his pulse and the nature of his sleep, he judged he was doing well. He had heard all about the affair, assured the laird there was no danger, said he would call again, and recommended him to go home. The boy must remain where he was for the night, he said, and if the least ground for uneasiness should show itself, he would ride over and tell him.

"I don't know what to think," returned the laird; "it would be a trouble and inconvenience to Grannie."

"Deed, Laird, ye should be ashamed t' say sich a thing; it'll be naethin' o' the kind!" cried the old woman. "Here he's t' stay. There's anither bed in the closet there. But truth, what wi' the rheumatics an' the din o' the rats, many's the night I canna sleep onyway. An' t' hae the yoong laird sleepin' in my bed an' me keepin' watch ower him, it'll be jist like haein' an angel in the hoose t' look after. I'll be somebody again for one night, I can tell ye! An' it's a lang time, sir, since I was onybody in the warl'! I so hope they'll hae somethin' for old folk t' do in the next!"

"Hoots, Mistress Forsyth," returned the laird, "there'll be nobody old there!"

"How am I t' get in then, sir? I'm old, if onybody ever was old! An' how's ye t' get in yersel'—for ye must be some old yersel' by this time, though I remember weel yer father a bit loonie in a tartan kilt."

"What would you say to be made young again, old friend?" suggested the laird with a sweet smile.

"Eh, sir! There's naethin' t' that effect in the word."

"Hoots!" rejoined the laird. "There's room for young and old alike, Grannie, though we'll be neither young nor old there, I don't doubt. But here, it's by being young and then growing old that we learn how to live there."

"Ay, yoong like the bonnie man there on the bed."

"Young, Grannie, but growing to a man faster than the eyes of the old like us can see. Sometimes I want to tell the laddie there all the things I would do for him if I could, forgetting that he has a growing heart of his own to tell him a score of things—ay, hundreds of things! Don't you know that the spirit of man is the candle of the Lord?"

"But so many follows their own fancies—that ye must allow, Laird! An' what comes o' yer can'le then?"

"The fact that such men never look where the light falls, but always in some other direction, doesn't mean the light's not there just the same. They just don't care to walk by it. But them that order their ways by what light they have, there's no fear of them. Even should they stumble, they shall not fall."

"Deed, Laird, I'm thinkin' ye may be right. I hae stumblet many's the time, but I'm no doon yet. An' I hae a good hope that maybe, poor disciple as I am, the Maister may let on that he knows me when that great an' terrible day o' the Lord comes."

Cosmo began to stir. His father went to the bedside and saw at a glance that the boy was better. He told him what the doctor had said. Cosmo said he was quite able to get up and go home. But his father would not hear of it.

"I can't think of you walking all that way back alone, Papa," objected Cosmo.

"Ye dinna think, Cosmo," interposed Aggie, "that I'm goin' t' let the laird go home himsel', an' me here t' be his bodyguard! I know my duty better than that."

But the laird did not go till they had all had tea together, and the doctor had again come and gone, and given his decided opinion that all Cosmo needed was a little rest and that he would be quite well in a day or two.

Then at length his father left him, and set out with Aggie for Glenwarlock.

6

. . . .

Dreams

The gloamin' came down much sooner in Grannie's cottage than on the sides of the eastward hills, but the old woman made up her little fire, and it glowed as a bright heart in the shadowy place. Though the room was always dusky, it was never at this season quite dark at any time of the night. The fire was not absolutely necessary, except for the little cooking required by the invalid, but she welcomed the excuse for a little extra warmth to her old limbs during the night watches. Then she sat down in her great chair and all was still.

"Why aren't ye spinnin', Grannie?" said Cosmo. "I like t' hear the wheel singin' like a little flea on the window. It spins in my head long threads o' thoughts an' dreams and would-be's. Next t' hearin' ye tell a tale, I like t' hear yer wheel goin'. It has a way o' its own wi' me!"

"I was feart it might vex ye," answered Grannie, and as she spoke she rose, and lit her lamp, though she scarcely needed light for her spinning, and sat down to her wheel.

For a long time Cosmo lay and listened, building castles in the air to the music, which, like the drone of the bagpipes, was so monotonous that he could use it to accompany any dream-time of his own.

When a man comes to trust in God thoroughly, he shrinks from castle-building, lest his faintest fancy should run counter to that loveliest will. But a boy's dreams are nevertheless part of his education. And the true heart will not leave the blessed conscience out, even in its dreams.

Cosmo's dreams were mostly of a lovely woman, much older than himself, who was kind to him, and whom he obeyed and was ready to serve like a slave. They came, of course, from the heart that needed and delighted in the thought of a mother, but they also had in them the memory—faint, far-off, and dim—of his own mother, and the imaginations of her roused by his father's many talks with him about her. He dreamed now of one, now of another loving power, of the fire, the air, the earth, or the water—each of them a gracious woman, who favored, helped, and protected him through innumerable dangers and trials. To those who labor in the direction of their own ideal, dreams will do no hurt, but rather foster the ideal.

When at length the spinning wheel ceased its hum, the silence was to Cosmo like the silence after a song, and his thoughts refused to do their humming alone. He had been in a wondrous region where he dwelt with sylphs in a great palace, built on the treetops of a forest of ages old; where the air was so full of life that it bathed every limb of the tree and was to his ethereal body as water. Every room of the palace in the tree rocked like the baby's cradle. The birds nestled in its cellars, and the squirrels ran up and down its stairs, and the woodpeckers pulled themselves along its columns and rails by their beaks. The wind swung the whole city with a rhythmic roll, and the sway as of tempest waves was like a great symphony of movement. Far below, lower than the cellars, the deer and the mice and dormice and the foxes and all the wild things of the forest ran in its caves.

From this high city of the sylphs, watched and loved and taught by the most gracious and graceful and tender and powerful of beings, he fell suddenly into Grannie's box bed with the departed hum of her wheel spinning out its last thread of sound in his disappointed brain.

In after years, when he remembered the enchanting dreams of his boyhood, instead of sighing after them as something gone forever, he would say to himself, "What does it matter that they are gone? In the heavenly kingdom my own mother is waiting for me, fairer and stronger, and more real than the dreams. I imagined the elves; God imagined my mother."

The unconscious magician of the whole mystery, who had seemed to the boy to be spinning his very brain into dreams, rose, drew near the bed as if to finish the ruthless destruction, and with her long broom swept down the very cobwebs of his airy fantasy, saying, "Is ye wakin', Cosmo, my bairn?"

"Ay, am I," answered Cosmo, with a strange sense of loss: when would he ever have another dream like that again?

"Weel, ye must hae yer supper, an' then ye must say yer prayers, an' hae done wi' Tuesday an' go on t' Wednesday."

"I want no supper, thank ye," said the boy.

"Ye must hae somethin', my bonny man, for 'tis nae good for them 'at eats ower little, as weel's them 'at eats ower much. So we'll hae a bit o' parritch an' cream. Or would ye prefer a sup o' fine gruel, sich as yer mither used t' like weel from my hand, when it so happent I was in the hoose?" The offer seemed to the boy to bring a little nearer the mother whose memory he worshiped, and so he chose the gruel.

He watched from his nest the whole process of its making. It took a time of its own, for one of the secrets of good gruel is a long acquaintance with the fire. Many a time the picture of that room returned to him in far different circumstances, like a dream of quiet and self-sustained delight—though his own companion was an aged woman.

When he had eaten, he fell asleep once more, and when he awoke again it was in the middle of the night. The lamp was nearly burned out; it had a long, red, disreputable nose that spoke of midnight hours and exhausted oil. The old lady was dozing in her chair. The clock had just struck something, for the sound of its bell was still faintly pulsing in the air. He sat up and looked out into the room. He felt as if something—he could not tell what—had been going on besides the striking of the clock, and was not yet over, as if something were now being done in the room. But there the old woman slept, motionless, and apparently perfectly calm. It could not, however, have been as perfect a sleep as it seemed, for presently she began to talk. At first came only broken sentences, occasionally with a long pause, and just as Cosmo thought she had finished, she would begin again.

There was something awful to the imagination of the boy in the coming of words from the lips of one apparently so unconscious. Her voice was like the voice of one speaking from another world. Cosmo was a brave boy where obedience and duty were concerned, but conscience and imagination were each enough to make him tremble. To tremble and to turn one's back in cowardice, however, are very different things, and of the latter Cosmo knew nothing. His hair began to rise on his head, but that head he never hid beneath the covers. He sat and stared into the gloom, where the old woman lay in her huge chair, muttering at irregular intervals.

Presently she began to talk a little more continuously. And gradually Cosmo's heart got a little quieter, no longer making such a noise in his ears, and he was able to hear better. After a few seemingly unconnected words, she began to murmur something that sounded like verses. Cosmo soon realized that she was saying the same thing over and over, and at length he was able to remember every word of the few lines. This was what he recalled afterwards—but by that time he was uncertain whether the whole thing had not been but a dream:

Catch her naig an' pu' his tail:
In his hin' heel ca' a nail;
Rug his lugs frae one anither—
Stan' up, an' ca' the king yer brither.

When he first repeated the words to himself, the old woman continued to mutter them, and he could not help laughing; and though the noise was repressed, it yet roused her. She woke, not like most young people, with slow gradation of consciousness, but all at once was wide awake. She sat up in her chair.

"Was I snorin', laddie, that ye laughed?" she asked in a tone of slight offense.

"No," replied Cosmo. "It was only that ye was saying something funny—in your sleep, ye know—a funny jingle o' poetry it was."

He repeated the rhyme, and Grannie burst into a merry laugh—which however lasted but an instant, after which she sobered suddenly.

"I dinna wonder I was sayin' ower the fule words," she said, "for I was dreamin' o' the only one I ever heard say them, an' that was when I was a lass— maybe aboot thirty. Anybody might hae heard him sayin' them—ower an' ower t' himsel', as if he cudna weary o' them. But naebody but mysel' seemed t' take ony notice o' them. I used t' wonder whether he fully un'erstude what he was sayin'—but truth! how cud there be ony sense in such carryin' on?"

"Was there more t' the ballad?" asked Cosmo.

"If there was, I heard none o' it," replied Grannie. "He wasna one t' sing, the auld captain.—Did ye never hear tell o' him, laddie?"

"If ye mean the old brother o' the laird o' that time, him that came home from his seafaring t' the East Indies—"

"Ay, ay, that's him! Ye heard o' him! He had a ship o' his own, an' made many a voyage afore any o' us was born, an' was an auld man when at length he came home, as the sang says—too old t' go t' sea anymore. I'll ne'er forget the look o' the man when I first saw him, nor the hurry an' the scurry when his face came in at the gate. Ye see, nobody knew where he was. Eh, but he was not a bonny man, an' folk say he didna die a natural death. Hoo that may be I dinna weel know; there *were* strange things aboot the affair—things that won't like t' be speaked aboot. One thing's for certain, an' that is that the place has never thrived since then. But for that matter, it hadn't thrived for many a long time afore. An' there was sich a gaggle o' awful stories rangin' the country, like ghosts nobody cud get a grip o'—as t' how he had gotten the money, the money that nobody e'er saw, for on that money, as I told ye, nobody ever cast an eye. Some said he had been a pirate on the high seas, an' had taken the money in lumps o' gold from poor ships that hadna men enough to hold on t' it. Some said he had been a privateer, an' others said there was small difference atween the twa. An' some would hae it that he was one o' them that took an' sold the poor black folk that couldna help bein' black. But nobody knew hoo he had gathered his money;

maybe there was none, for nobody, as I was tellin' ye, ever had the smallest glimpse o' money aboot him. For a close-handed kind o' man he was if e'er there was one! Aye ready was he t' borrow a shillin' from any fule that would give him one, an' long had him that lent it forgotten to look for it before he thought o' payin' it back.

"It was only a year or twa that he lived aboot the place, an' nobody cared much for his company, though e'eryone was afraid t' let him know that he wasna welcome here or there, for who could tell but he might pull oot the sword he carried an' make an' end o' him! For indeed, he feared na God nor man nor the judgment o' Scripture. He drank a heap, for anybody he called upon aye pulled oot the whisky bottle, wantin' t' please the man they were feared at."

The voice of the old woman went sounding in the ears of the boy, on and on in the gloom, and through it, possibly from the still confused condition of his head, he constantly kept hearing the rhymes she had repeated to him. They seemed to have laid hold on him, perhaps from their very foolishness, in an odd, inexplicable way—

Catch yer naig an' pu' his tail:
In his hin' heel ca' a nail;
Rug his lugs frae one anither—
Stan' up, an' ca' the king yer brither.

On and on went the rhyme, and on and on went the old woman's voice.

"Weel, there came a time when an English lord began t' be seen aboot the place, an' that was not a common sight in oor poor country. He was a frien', folk said, o' the young Marquis o' Lossie. He went all aboot, lookin' at this an' lookin' at that, an' where or hoo he fell in wi' *him*, I dinna ken, but before long the twa o' them was a heap together. They played cards together, they drank together, they drove out together, an' what made sich frien's o' them nobody could imagine. For the one was a rough sailor, an' the other was a yoong lad, little more, an' a fine gentleman as weel's a bonny man. But the upshot o' it was an ill one, for maybe aboot a month after there came a night when the captain didna come home. For ye must un'erstan', wi' all his rough ways an' his drinkin' an' his card-playin', he was aye home at night, an' safe in his bed, where he slept in the best room in the castle. Ay, he would come home, often as drunk as man could be, but home he came. Sleep int' the afternoon o' the next day he would, but ne'er oot o' his own bed—or if no in his own bed, for I foun' him once mysel' lyin' snorin' upon the floor, it was aye int' his own room, as I say, an' no in any strange place drunk or sober.

"So there was some surprise at his no appearin' an' folk spoke o' it, but not that much, for nobody cared in their heart what came o' the man. Still when the men went oot t' their work, they were bound t' give a look if there was any sign o' him. It was easy t' think that he might hae been at last too owertaken wi' drink t' be able t' get home. But that wasna it, though when they came upon him lyin' on his back in the hollow yonder that looks up t' my daughter's wee meadow o' grass for her cow, they thought he had slept there all night. An' so he had, but it was the sleep that knows no wakin'—at least no the kin' o' wakin' that comes wi' the mornin'!"

Cosmo recognized with a shudder his favorite spot, where on his birthday, as on many a day before, he had fallen asleep. But the old woman went on with her story.

"Dead was the auld captain—as dead as ever was a man that had none left t' cry for him. But though there was nae cryin', there was sich a hullabaloo raised upon the discovery! They were all frightened, an' they ran; the doctor came, an' the minister, an' the lawyer, an' the gravedigger. But when a man's dead, what can all the world do for him but bury him? There was many a conjecture as t' hoo he came by his death, an' many a doobt it wasna by fair play. Some said he died by his ain hand, driven t' it by the enemy. An' it was true the blade he carried was lyin' on the grass beside him. But some that examined him said the hole in the side o' him wasna made wi' that. But o' all that came t' ask aboot him, the English lord was none. He had vanished the country. The general opinion settled doon t' this, that they twa must hae fallen oot at cards, an' fought it oot, an' the auld captain for all his skill an' experience had had the worst o' it, an' so there they foun' him. But I reckon, Cosmo, yer father'll hae telled ye aboot the thing many a time afore noo, an' I'm jist borin' ye by carryin' on, an' keepin' ye from sleepin'."

"Na, Grannie," answered Cosmo, "he never told me what ye're tellin' me noo. He did tell me that there was sich a man, and the ill end he came to. And I think he was goin' t' tell me more when Grizzie came t' say the dinner was ready. That was only yesterday—or the day before, I'm thinking, by this time. But what do ye think could have been in his head wi' the jingle aboot the horse?"

"Ow! what would be in it but jist foolish nonsense? Ye know some folk has a funny trick o' sayin' the same thing ower and ower t' themsel's wi' oot any sense t' it. There was the auld laird himsel'; he was one such. Aye an' ower and ower again he would be sayin' t' himsel', 'A hun'er poun'! Ay, a hun'er poun'!' It mattered na what he would be speakin' aboot, or who to, in it would come!—in the middle o' anythin', ye couldna tell when or where,—'A hun'er poun'!' says he; 'Ay, a hun'er poun'!' Folk laughed at first, but soon got used t' it, an' came hardly t' know that he said it, for what hasna sense has little hearin'. An' I don't doobt those rhymes wasna even a verse o' an auld ballad, but jist a cletter o' clinkin' nonsense that he had learned from some bairn maybe, an' couldna get oot o' his head any other way but jist t' say it—jist like a cat when it goes scratchin' at the door, ye hae t' get up, whether ye will or not, an' let the creature oot."

Cosmo did not feel quite satisfied with the explanation, but he made no objection to it.

"I must allow, hooever," the old woman went on, "that once ye get a hold o' *them*, they take a grip o' you, an' hae a way o' hauntin' ye like, as they did the man himsel', so that ye canna get rid o' them. It comes only noo an' then, but when the fit's upon me, I canna get them oot o' my head. The verse goes on tumblin' ower an' ower till I'm jist disgusted wi' it. Away it wanna go, maybe for a whole day, an' then it mayna come again for months."

True enough, the rhyme was already running about in Cosmo's head like a mouse, and he fell asleep with it ringing in the ears of his mind.

Before he woke again, which was in the broad daylight, he had a curious dream.

He dreamed that he was out in the moonlight. It was a summer night—late. But there was something very strange about the night. Right up in the top of it was the moon, looking down as if she knew all about it, and something was going to happen. He did not like the look of her—he had never seen her look like that before, and he went home just to get away from her.

As he was going up the stairs to his room, something—he could not tell what—moved him to stop at the door of the drawing room and go in. It was flooded with moonlight, but he did not mind that, so long as he could keep out of sight of the moon herself. Still, it had a strange, eerie look, with its various pieces of furniture casting different shadows from those that by rights belonged to them. He gazed at this thing and that thing, as if he had never seen them before. The place seemed to have cast a spell over him so that he could not leave it. He sat down on the ancient brocaded couch, and sat staring with a sense—which by degrees grew dreadful—that he was where he should not be, and that if he did not get up and go, something would happen. But he could not rise. Not that he felt any physical impediment, but he could not make a resolve strong enough— like one in boring company who wants to leave but keeps waiting in vain for a fit opportunity to stand up and go. Delay grew to agony, but still he sat.

Gradually he became aware that he was not alone. His whole skin seemed to shudder with a sense of presence. As he gazed straight in front of him, very slowly the form of a man grew visible, until he saw it quite plainly in the chair on the opposite side of the fireplace—a seafaring man in a blue coat, with a red sash round his waist, in which two pistols and a dagger were kept. He too sat motionless, fixing on Cosmo the stare of fierce eyes, black yet glowing, as if set on fire of hell. They filled him with fear, but something seemed to sustain him under it. When he thought about it upon waking, he almost fancied that a third presence must have been in the room for his protection. The face that stared at him was brown and red and weatherbeaten, cut across with a great scar, and wearing an expression of horror trying not to look horrible. Cosmo's fear threatened to turn him into clay, but he met it bravely, fought against it, and did not yield. Still the figure stared, as if it would fascinate him into submission. At length it slowly rose, and with a look of mingled pain and fierceness, turned, and led the way from the room. The spell was immediately either broken or changed enough that Cosmo was able to rise and follow him: even in his dreams he was a boy of courage, and feared nothing so much as yielding to fear.

The figure went on, without turning its head, up the stair to the best bedroom, the guestroom of the house, which was seldom visited. Still following, Cosmo entered the room after it. The figure walked across the middle of the room, as if making for the bed, but in the middle of the floor suddenly turned, and went round by the foot of the bed to the other side of it and behind the curtains. Cosmo followed, but when he reached the other side, the man was nowhere to be seen and he woke, his heart beating terribly.

By this time Grannie was snoring in her chair. Otherwise he would have told her his dream in his desire to shake himself loose from its atmosphere. For a while he lay looking at the dying fire and the streak of pale light from the setting moon that stole in at the window. Slowly he fell fast asleep, and slept far into the morning, long after lessons were begun in the school, and village affairs were in the full swing of their daily routine. He had not yet finished his breakfast when his father entered.

"I'm quite well, Papa," answered the boy to his father's gentle yet eager inquiry. "I'm perfectly able to go to school in the afternoon."

"I don't want you to go again, Cosmo," his father replied seriously. "It could not be pleasant for yourself or for the master. The proper relation between you is destroyed."

"If you think I was wrong, Papa, I will make an apology."

"If you had done it for yourself, I would say you must. But as it was, I am not prepared to say so."

"What am I to do, then? How am I to get ready for college?"

The laird gave a sigh and made no answer. Alas, there were more difficulties than that in the path to college.

He turned away and went to call on the minister while Cosmo got up and dressed. Except a little singing in his head when he bent down, he could feel no consequences of the double blow.

Grannie was by this time again at her wheel, and Cosmo sat down in her chair to await his father's return.

"Where did you say the captain slept when he was at the castle?" he asked across the buzz and whiz and hum of the wheel. Through the low window, between the leaves of the many plants that shaded it, he could see the sun shining hot upon the bare street, but inside it was softly gloomy filled with the murmuring sound of the wheel.

"Whaur but in the best bedroom?" answered Grannie. "Nothin' less would please *him*, I can assure ye. For once the Marquis came t' the hoose, an' there came wi' him a fearsome storm, sich as comes but seldom in a life as lang as mine. Thereupon, yer father, that is, yer gran'father—or would it be yer grit-gran'father—I'm turnin' some confused wi' ye all—anyhoo, he said t' the captain that he would do weel t' offer his room t' his guest. But would he, do ye think? Na, no him! He grew reid in the face, an' then white as a sheet, an' looked t' be in the awfulest inside rage. So yer gran'father, no that he was feart at him, for I'll be boun' he never was feart afore the face o' man, but jist no willin' t' anger his ain kin, held his tongue an' said no more, an' the Marquis had the second best bed, for he slept in Glenwarlock's own."

Cosmo then told her the dream he had had in the night, describing the person he had seen in it as closely as he could. All the time Grannie had been speaking it was to the accompaniment of her wheel, but Cosmo had not got far with his narrative when she ceased spinning, and sat absorbed—listening as to a real occurrence rather than the feverish dream of a boy.

When he ended, "It must hae been the auld captain himsel'!" she said under her breath, and with a sigh she then shut her mouth and remained silent, leaving Cosmo to wonder about her statement. But he could not help noting that there seemed a strangeness about her silence. Indeed, she said nothing until his father returned.

7

• • • • • • • • • • • • • • • • • •

Home

*C*osmo was not particularly fond of school, and he was particularly fond of holidays. Hence, his father's decision that he should go to school no more after the unpleasant incident seemed to him the promise of an endless joy. The very sun seemed swelling in his heart as he walked home with his father. A whole day of home and its pleasures was before him. Every shadow about the old place was a delight to him. No one ever loved the things into which he had been born more than Cosmo. There was hardly anything that could be called beauty about Castle Warlock—strength and gloom were its main characteristics—but its very stones were dear to the boy. There never were such bees, there never were such thick walls, there never were such storms, never such a rushing river, as those about his beloved home! He felt this way even though, as I have said, he longed for more beauty of mountain and wood than the country around could afford him.

And the books belonging to the house! Could there possibly be any such collection in the world to match it? In truth, they were very few—all contained in a closet opening out of his father's bedroom. But Cosmo had a feeling of inexhaustible wealth in them—partly because his father had not yet allowed him to read everything there, but restricted him to certain of the shelves—as much to cultivate self-restraint in him as to keep one or two of the books from him—and partly because he read books in such a way that he believed in them after he had read them, never imagining himself capable of exhausting them. And the range of his taste was certainly not limited. While he revelled in *The Arabian Nights*, he also read other books considerably different in both scope and style.

Yet as much as Cosmo was fond of reading, to enjoy life it was enough for him simply to lie in the grass. In certain moods the smell of the commonest flower would drive him half crazy with delight. On a holiday his head would be haunted with old ballads like a sunflower with bees; on other days they would only come and go. He even loved nursery rhymes—only in his mind somehow or other they became glorified. The swing and hum and sound of a line, even if the words themselves had little discovered meaning, would play its tune to him as well as any mountain stream. One of those that on this day kept coming and coming—not coming and going—just as Grannie said the foolish rhyme haunted the old captain, was that which two days before had come into his head when he first caught sight of the moon playing bo-peep with him between the cow's legs:

Whan the coo loups ower the mune,
The reid gowd rains intil men's shune.

There was no doubt at one time a poet in the Glenwarlock nursery, for there were rhymes and modifications of rhymes floating about the family, but nobody could quite account for them. Cosmo's mother had been fond of verse, and although he could not remember many of her favorite rhymes, his father did; he delighted in saying them over and over to her child, even before the boy was capable of understanding them. One of them was:

Make not of thy heart a casket,
    Opening seldom, quick to close;
But of bread a wide-mouthed basket,
    And a cup that overflows.

And another:

The gadfly makes the horse run swift:
"Speed," quoth the gadfly, "is my gift."

These served as dim lights on the all-but-vanished mother, of whom the boy himself knew so little.

In God alone, the perfect end,
Wilt thou find thyself or friend.

The dream of Cosmo's life was to live all his days in the house of his forefathers, or—if he was compelled to be away from it—at least to return to it before the end of his life. Next to that of the fairy-mother-lady, his fondest fancy in his castle-building was not to make a fortune, but to return home with one in order to make the house of his fathers beautiful and the heart of his father glad. He did not think so much about the land yet: the country was open to him as if it had been all his own. Still, he had quite a different feeling for that portion which lay within the sorely neglected borders; to have seen the smallest nook of that sold would have been likely to break his heart.

In him the love of the place was in danger of becoming almost like a disease. There was in it something, if not of the avarice that grasps, yet of the avarice that clings. In the matter of money itself, he was very generous. But then he had had so little of that—not yet enough to learn to love it! And he had as yet not the slightest idea of any way, other than manual labor, in which to make money. The only way in which he ever dreamed of coming into possession of a fortune—it was another of his favorite daydreams—was finding a room he had never seen or heard of before in the old house, and in it a hoard of incredible riches. Such things had been—why might it not happen again?

As they walked, Cosmo's father told him he had been thinking all night what the best thing would be to do with him, and that he had come to the conclusion to ask his friend Peter Simon—the wits of the neighborhood called him Simon Peter—to take charge of his education.

"He is a man of peculiar opinions," he said, "as I daresay you may have heard. But everything in him is on a scale so grand that to fear harm from him would be to sin against the truth. A man must learn to judge for himself, and he will teach you that. I have seen in him so much that I recognize as good and great that I am compelled to believe in him, even where the things he believes appear to me to be out of line, or even extravagant. A man's character must sometimes go a long way to cause you to believe in him, even where in matters of mere opinion—not nearly so important a thing as character—you find that you differ."

"I have heard that he believes in ghosts, Papa," said Cosmo.

His father smiled and made no answer. He had been born into an age whose incredulity was fast approaching the extreme of superstition; and the denial of many things that had long been believed in the country had become widespread, even in the remote region where his property lay. Like his land, the laird's mind lay in a sort of borderland because of the age. An active believer in the care and providence of God, with no difficulty in accepting any miracle recorded in the Bible, he was nevertheless inclined to skepticism where the record was silent.

"Do *you* believe in ghosts, Papa?" said Cosmo, noting his father's silence. "The schoolmaster says none but fools believe in ghosts or angels or that sort of thing now. He calls it all nothing but superstition."

"Mr. Simon said the other day," answered his father, "that the fear of super-stition might amount to a different kind of superstition itself, and become the most dangerous kind of all."

"Do you think so, Papa?"

"I could well believe it. Besides, I have always found Mr. Simon so reasonable, even where his opinion differed from mine, that I cannot help leaning toward anything he thinks."

The boy rejoiced to hear his father talk like this, for he had a strong leaning toward the imaginative and the supernatural. Up to now, from the schoolmaster's assertions and his father's silence, he had supposed that nothing could be believed but what was scientifically provable or specifically told in the Bible. It began to dawn on him that we live in a universe of marvels of which we know only the outsides. We turn our world into the unbelievable by taking the mere outsides for all, even while we know the roots of the seen remain unseen. Cosmo was therefore delighted at the thought of making closer acquaintance with a man like

Mr. Simon. All day long he thought about the prospect, and in the twilight went out wandering over the hills.

At this season, there was no night there any more than there is all through the year in heaven. Indeed, we have seldom any real positive night in this world—so many provisions have been made against it. Every time we say, "What a lovely night!" we speak of a breach, a rift in the old night. There is light more or less at all times; otherwise there could be no beauty. Many a night is but a low starry day, a day with a softened background against which the far-off suns of millions of other days show themselves: when the near vision vanishes, the farther hope awakens. It is nowhere said of heaven, "There shall be no twilight there."

8

·················

Cosmo the Student

The twilight had not yet reached the depth of its mysteriousness when Cosmo, returning home from a large, leisurely loop of wandering over several hills, finishing by walking up to James Gracie's cottage. As he passed the window he saw a little light and went to the door and knocked. Had it been daytime, he would have gone straight in. Agnes came and opened it cautiously, for there were occasionally tramps about.

"Eh! it's you!" she cried with a glad voice when she saw the shape of Cosmo in the dimness. "There's naethin' wrong I hope," she added, changing her tone.

"No, nothing," answered Cosmo. "I only wanted t' let ye know that I wasn't going back t' the school anymore."

"Weel, I dinna wonder at that!" returned Agnes with a little sigh. "After the way the maister behaved t' ye, the laird could ill let ye go there again. "But what's he goin' t' do wi' ye, Master Cosmo, if a body might ask that has nae right t' be curious?"

"He's sending me t' Mister Simon," answered Cosmo.

"I wish I was goin' too," sighed Aggie. "I'm jist feart that I'll come t' hate the maister after ye're no t' be seen there, Cosmo. An' we mustn't hate. But it would be a heap easier no t' hate him if I had naethin' t' do with him."

"But the harvest holiday will be here soon," answered Cosmo, "and then the harvest itself. And when ye go back, by then ye'll have gotten over it."

"Na, I doobt it, Cosmo. For ye see, as I hae heard my father say, the Gracies are terrible for rememberin'. Na, there's no forgettin' o' naethin'. Why should anythin' be forgotten? It's a cowardly kind o' thing t' forget."

"Some things, I don't doobt, have t' be forgotten," returned Cosmo thoughtfully. "If ye forgive a body, for instance, ye must forget too—not so much, I'm thinking, for the sake o' them that did ye the wrong, for who would pick up a foul thing once it was dropped?—but for yer own sake. For what have ye done right, my father says, must be forgotten out o' sight for fear o' corruption, for nothing comes t' stink worse than a good deed hung up in the moonlight o' the memory."

"Eh!" exclaimed Aggie, "but ye're fearsome wise fer a lad o' yer years."

"I would be a gowk," remarked Cosmo, "if I knew nothing, with such a father as yon o' mine. What would ye think o' yersel' if the daughter o' James Gracie were no more wise than Meg Scroggie?"

Agnes laughed, but made no reply, for the voice of her grandmother came out of the dark.

"Who's that, Aggie, that ye're holdin' sich a confab wi' in the middle o' the night? Ye told me ye had t' stay up fer yer lessons!"

"I was busy at them, Mither, when Master Cosmo knocked at the door."

"Weel, what for are ye lettin' him stan' there? Ye may hae yer talk wi' *him* as long as ye like—within reason, that is. Tell him t' come in."

"No, no, Mistress Gracie," answered Cosmo. "I must be goin' back home. I've had a nice long walk. It's not that I'm tired, but I am sleepy. Only I was so pleased that I was goin' t' learn my lessons wi' Mister Simon that I had t' tell Aggie. She might hae been wonderin' and thinkin' I wasn't better if she hadna seen me at school in the mornin'."

"I'd hae her go t' the castle the first thing in the mornin' t' see if the laird had any erran' in the toon afore the school. We don't care so much for the maister if anybody at the hoose be in want o' us."

"Is there nothing I could help ye wi' Aggie, afore I go?" asked Cosmo. "Somebody told me ye were trying your hand at algebra."

"Nobody had any business t' tell ye any sich thing," returned Aggie rather angrily. "It's not that I would think o' sich a thing at the school. They would laugh at me! But I jist want t' un'erstan' the thing. I canna un'erstan' hoo folk can count wi' letters an' crosses an' strokes in place o' figures. I been at it a whole week noo—by mysel', ye know—an' I'm none nearer it yet. I'm thinkin' it's somethin' as if *x* was a horse an' *y* was a coo, an' *z* was a cart, or anythin' other ye might hae t' call it. An' ye bargain away aboot the *x* and the *y* an' the *z*, an' leave the horse in the stable an' the coo in the byre, an' the cart in the shed, till ye hae settled it all. But *ye* know aboot algebra, dinna ye, Master Cosmo?"

"Not the half, not even the hundredth part. I only know enough t' hold me goin' on a little further. A body must hae learned a heap o' anything afore the light breaks oot upon it. Ye have t' struggle through in the darkness first. I doobt if anybody understands anythin' altogether until he's able at a moment's notice t' explain it sae clearly as t' make anither see right into the heart o' it. And I couldna make ye see what's at the bottom o' what ye asked me."

"I'm thinkin', hooever, Cosmo, a body must be near seein' it himsel' afore another can shed light on it for him."

"Ye may be right there," yielded Cosmo. "Jist let me see where ye are," he went on. "I may be able to help ye, though I couldna explain everythin' all at once. It would be a hard thing for those that need help if nobody could help them but someone who knew everything there was t' know aboot a thing."

Without a word Aggie turned and led the way to the other end of the room. An iron lamp, burning the coarsest of train oil, hung against the wall, and under that she had placed the one movable table in the kitchen, which was white as scouring could make it. Upon it lay a slate and book of algebra.

"My cousin Willie lent me the book," said Aggie.

"Why didn't ye come t' me for one? I could have given ye a better one than that," expostulated Cosmo.

Aggie hesitated, but, as the daylight, she did not hesitate long. She turned her face from him, then answered.

"I wanted t' give ye a surprise, Master Cosmo. Dinna ye remember tellin' me once that ye saw no reason why a lassie shouldna un'erstan' jist as weel as a laddie? I wanted t' see whether ye was right or wrong. An' as algebra looked the most oonlikely thing, I thought I would tackle that, an' settle the question at once. But, eh! I'm sore feart ye was wrong, Cosmo!"

"Then I must do my best t' prove myself in the right," returned Cosmo. "I never said anybody could learn everythin' by themselves, when they needed help, ye know. There's not many laddies that could do that, and fewer still that would try."

They sat down together at the table, and in half an hour or so Aggie had begun to see the faint light of at least the false dawn through the thickets of algebra. It was nearly midnight when Cosmo rose, and then Aggie would not let him go alone, but insisted on accompanying him to the gate of the court.

It was a curious relation between the two. While Agnes looked up to Cosmo, about two years younger than herself, as immeasurably her superior in all that pertained to the intellect, she assumed over him a sort of general human superiority, something like that which a mother will assert over the most gifted of sons. One has seen, with a kind of sacred amusement, the high priest of many literary and artistic circles set down with rebuke by his mother as if he had still been a boy. That Agnes never treated Cosmo with this degree of protective condescension came from the fact that she was very nearly as much a child of the light as he was. Being a woman, and being older, she felt more of the mother that every woman feels, and made the most of it. It was to her a merely natural thing to act as his protector. Indeed, with respect to the Warlock family in general, she counted herself possessed of the right to serve any one of them to the last drop of her blood. From infancy she had heard the laird spoken of—without any distinction made between the present laird and the last—as the noblest, best, and kindest of men, as the power which had been for generations over the family of the Gracies, and for their help and healing. And hence it was impressed upon her deepest consciousness that one of the main reasons for her existence was her relation to the family of Glenwarlock.

Despite the familiarity there was between them—Agnes had only recently begun to put the *Master* before Cosmo's name, and forgot it as often as she remembered it—as they went toward the castle, although they were entirely alone in the deep dusk, the girl kept a little behind the boy—not behind his back, but on his left hand in the next rank. Their talk, in the still, dark air, sounded loud all the way as they went. Strange talk it would have been counted by many, and indeed unintelligible, for it ranged over a vast surface of their sea of thoughts and was the talk of two wise children, wise not only above their own years, but above those of the prudent and successful in the world's eyes. Riches no doubt favor stupidity. Poverty, where the heart is right, favors mental and moral development. They parted at the gate and Cosmo went to his room and to bed.

But although his father allowed him such liberty, and was glad the boy felt the night as holy as the day—so that no one ever asked where he had been or what hour he had come home—not an eye was closed in the house until his entering footsteps were heard. The grandmother lay angry at the unheard-of freedom her son gave his son; it was neither decent nor in order; it was against all ancient rule of family life; she must speak about it! But she never did speak about it, for she was now in her turn afraid of the son who, without a particle of obstinacy in his makeup, yet took what she called his own way. Grizzie kept grumbling to herself that the laddie was sure to come to "mischief." The laird for his part spent most of the time of his son's absence awake praying for him—not that he might be the restorer of the family, but that he might be able to accept the will of God as the best thing for family as for individual. If his boy might but reach the spirit-land unsoiled and noble, his prayers would be answered.

But Cosmo went up to bed without a suspicion that the air around him was full of such holy messengers heavenward for his sake. He imagined none anxious about him—either with the anxiety of grandmother or of servant-friend or of great-hearted father.

As he passed the door of the spare room, immediately below his own, his dream, preceded by a cold shiver, came to his memory. But he refused to quicken his pace or to glance over his shoulder as he went up the second flight of stairs. Without any need of a candle, in the still faint twilight which is the ghosts' day, he threw off his clothes, and was presently buried in the grave of his bed, under the sod of the blankets and covered over with the death of sleep.

The moment he woke in the morning he jumped out of bed. A new era in his life was at hand, the thought of which had been subconsciously present in his dreams, and was operative the instant he became aware of waking life. He put on his clothes in a hurry, without any care, for this was but a temporary dressing anyway. He shot down the stairs and outside, then in like manner down the hill, reaching the spot where, with a final dart, the torrent flowed into the quiet stream of the valley. In the channel of rock and gravel the stream had hollowed a deep basin. This was Cosmo's bath—and a splendid one. His clothes were off again more quickly than he had put them on, and headfirst he shot like the torrent into the boiling mass, where for a few moments he yielded himself to the sport of the frothy water, and was tossed and tumbled about. Soon, however, down in the heart of the boil, he struck out, and shooting from under the fall, rose to the surface beyond it, panting and blowing. To get out on the bank was then the work of one moment, and to plunge in again that of the next. Half a dozen times, with scarcely a pause between them, he plunged in, was tossed and overwhelmed, struggled, escaped, and plunged in again. Then he ran for a few moments up and down the bank to dry himself, and dressing again, ran home to finish getting dressed. He read a chapter of his Bible, no more than was required by many a parent of many a boy who got little good of the task. But Cosmo's father had never made a requirement of it, and when next he knelt down at his bedside, he did not merely "say his prayers." But before long certain sensations began to warn him that there was an invention in the world called breakfast, and rising he went to the kitchen, where he found Grizzie making the porridge.

"Be sure ye put enough salt in it today, Grizzie," he said. "It was too bland yesterday."

"An' what was it like yesterday evenin', Cosmo?" asked the old woman, irritated at being found fault with in a matter she counted herself as near perfection in as ever mortal could.

"I had none last night, ye remember," answered Cosmo. "I was oot all the evening."

"An' where got ye yer supper?"

"Oh, I didn't want any. Hoot! I'm forgettin'. Aggie gave me a quarter o' bread as I came by, or rather as I left, after givin' her a hand with her algebra."

"What's that for a lass t' be takin' up her time wi'? I never heard o' sich a thing! What's the nature o' it, Cosmo?"

He tried to give her some far-off idea of the sort of thing algebra was, but apparently without success, for at length she cried, "Na, sirs! I hae heard o' cairts, an' bogles, an' witchcraft, an' astronomy, but sich a thing as this ye bring me noo, I never did hear tell o'! What can the world be comin' t'—an' does yer father know what ye spen' yer midnight hours doin', laddie, gain' teachin' the lass-bairns o' the country?"

She was interrupted by the entrance of the laird, and they sat down to breakfast. For about the last year the grandmother had begun to take hers in her own room.

Grizzie was full of anxiety to know what the laird would say to the discovery she had just made, but she dared not make an allusion to the conduct of his son. She would have to be content to lead the conversation in the direction of it, hoping it might naturally appear. So about the middle of Cosmo's breakfast, that is about two minutes after he had attacked his porridge, she approached her design, if not exactly the object she desired, with the remark, "Did ye never hear the auld sayin', sir—

"Whaur's neither sun nor mune,
Evil things come abune—?"

"I almost think I have, Grizzie," answered the laird. "But what makes ye think o' it noo?"

"I canna but think, sir," returned Grizzie, "as I lie in the dark, o' the heap o' things that dinna belong in the kirk, oot an' aboot as sharp as a hawk, when the yoong laird is no in his bed—oot wi' his algibbry an' astronomy, an' all that kin' o' thing! 'Deed, sir, it wouldna be canny if they came t' know o' it."

"Who came t' know o' what, Grizzie?" asked the laird with a twinkle in his eye and a glance at Cosmo, who sat gazing curiously at the old woman.

"Them that the sayin' speaks o', sir," said Grizzie, answering the first part of the double question, as she placed two boiled eggs before her master.

The laird smiled; he was too kind to laugh. There were many that did laugh at old Grizzie, but never the laird.

"Did *ye* never hear the old sayin', Grizzie," he said:

"Throu the heather an' how gaed the creepin' thing,
But abune was the waught o' an angel's wing—?"

"Ay, I hae heard it—nowhere 'cept here in this hoose," answered Grizzie; she would disparage the authority of the saying by a doubt as to its genuineness. "But, sir, ye should never temp' providence. Who knows what may be oot in the night?"

"To *him*, Grizzie, the night shineth as the day."

"Weel, sir," cried Grizzie, "is it possible ye had forgotten what's so weel known t' all the country roon'? The auld captain, that canna lie still in his grave, because o'—because o' whatever the rizzon may be? Anyway he's not still yet; an' some thinks he's doomed t' haunt the hoose till the day o' jeedgment."

"I suspect there winna be much o' the hoose left for him t' haunt by that time, Grizzie," said the laird. "But what for should ye put such fule things int' the bairn's head? An' if the ghost haunts the hoose, isn't he better oot o' it? Would ye hae him come home t' sich company?"

This question posed, Grizzie held her peace for the time.

"Come, Cosmo," said the laird, rising from his chair; and they set out together for Mr. Simon's cottage.

9

• • • • • • • • • • • • • •

Peter Simon

The man with the inverted biblical name was not a native of the district, but had been living in it for some two years now. Reports said that he was the son of a small tradesman in a city not too far distant. But to those who knew him he made no secret of the fact that he had been found by such a man, when only a child of a few months, lying on a sidewalk of that city one stormy, desolate Christmas Eve. It was a dark night, with the wind blowing bitterly from the north, and the tradesman seemed to be the only inhabitant of the coldest city in Scotland who dared face it. He had just closed his shop, had taken home to one of his customers a forgotten order, and was returning to his childless wife when he all but stumbled over the infant. Before stooping down to lift him, he looked all about to see if there was nobody around. But there was not a human being in sight, and the wind was blowing like a blast from a frozen hell. There was nothing else to be done but to pick up the child. He did so, and carried it home, grumbling to himself all the way. What right had the morsel to be lying there in the dark and cold? What would his wife say? What would the neighbors think? He grumbled all the way home.

His wife was no more happy than he at first, but it required but one day—Christmas Day, in which nothing could well be done—to reconcile them to the gift. And from that day onward, as they brought him up, they blessed the day when they found him. It was a story fit to make the truehearted reader both laugh and cry; but there is no room or time for it.

As they were poor—hardly able, not merely to make both ends meet, but to bring them far enough round the parcel of their necessities to let them see each other—their friends called their behavior in declining to hand the child over to the parish authorities utter folly. How could they expect to prosper when they acted with so little foresight, making the struggle for existence all the more severe? These neighbors did not reckon what strength the additional motive, what heart the new love, what uplifting the hope of help from on high, kindled by their righteous deed, might give them—for God likes far better to help people from the inside than from the outside. They did not think that this might be just the fresh sting of life that the fainting pair required.

In fact, from that time on the couple began to get on a little better. And as the boy grew and needed more, they seemed always to have what was necessary. For it so happened that the boy turned out to be one of God's creatures, and it looked as if his Maker, who happened also to be the Ruler of the world, was not altogether displeased with those who had taken him to their hearts instead of leaving him to the parish. The child was the light of the house and of the shop, a beauty to the eyes, and a joy in the heart of both. But perhaps the best proof that they had done right lay in the fact that they began to love each other better from the very day after they had taken him in.

As the foundling grew they sent him to the grammar school and then to college—not a very difficult affair in that city. At college he did not greatly distinguish himself, for his special gifts were not of a kind to distinguish a man much, either in that city or anywhere in this world. But he grew and prospered nevertheless, and became a schoolmaster in one of the schools. His father and mother, as he called them, would gladly have made a minister of him, but he would never hear of that. He lived with them till they died, always bringing home his salary to them, minus the little he spent on books. His life, his devotion, and his loving gratitude so worked upon them that the kingdom of heaven opened its doors to them and they were the happiest old couple in that city. They looked upon their foundling as a divine messenger, an angel entertained not for long unawares. They never spent a penny of his salary, but added to it, and saved it up, and when they went, very strangely left all they had to this same angel of a beggar instead of to their own blood relations, who would have been very glad of it, for they had a good deal more of their own.

After his parents' deaths he did not care to live longer in any city, but sought a place as a librarian. He lived for many years in the family of an English lord, and when time's changes made it necessary that he should depart, he retired to the cottage on the Warlock. There he was now living the quietest of quiet lives, cultivating the acquaintance of but a few—chiefly that of the laird, James Gracie, and the minister of the parish. Among the people of the neighborhood he was regarded as "no a'together there." This judgment possibly arose in part from the fact that he often wandered about the fields from morning to night, and sometimes from night to morning. And he never drank anything worthy of the name of drink—seldom anything but water or milk! That he never ate animal flesh was not so notable in that region, where many others did the same. As he was no propagandist, few had any true notion of his opinions, beyond a general impression that they were unsound.

Cosmo had heard some of the peculiarities attributed to him, and was filled with curious expectation about the man he was about to meet. For oddly enough he had never yet seen him except at a distance. But anxiety, not untinged with awe, was mingled with his curiosity.

Mr. Simon's cottage was some distance up the valley, at an angle where it turned westward. It stood on the left bank of the Warlock, at the foot of a small cliff that sheltered it from the north, while in front the stream came galloping down to it from the sunset. The immediate bank between the cottage and the water was rocky and dry, but the ground on which the cottage stood was soil washed from the hills. There Mr. Simon had a little garden for flowers and vegetables, with a summer seat in which he smoked his pipe in the evening—for however inconsistent the habit may seem with the rest of the man, smoke he did. Slowly and gently and broodingly did the man smoke, thinking a great deal more than he smoked, and making one pipe last a long time. His garden was full of flowers, but of the most ordinary kinds; rarity was no recommendation to him. Some may think that in this he was unlike himself, seeing that his opinions were of the rarest. But in truth, Peter Simon never once in all his life adopted an opinion because of its strangeness. He never *adopted* an opinion at all. He believed— he loved what seemed to him true. How it looked to others concerned him very little.

The cottage was of stone and lime, nonetheless so thoroughly built that the stones were unhewn and were the very shapes that nature had made them. It was *harled*—that is, rough-cast or plastered—and shone very white both in sun and moon. It contained but two rooms and a closet between, with one under the thatch for the old woman who kept house for him. Altogether it was a very ordinary, and not very promising abode.

But when they were shown inside to the best room of the place, the parlor,

Cosmo was struck with astonishment: the walls from floor to ceiling were covered with books. Not a square foot all over was vacant. Even the chimneypiece was absorbed, assimilated, turned into a bookshelf, and so obliterated. Mr. Simon's pipe lay on the hob, and there was not another place it could have lain. There was not a shelf, a cupboard to be seen. Books, books everywhere, and nothing but books! Even the door that led to the closet where he slept was covered over, and like the mantleshelf, obliterated with books. There were about twelve hundred in all; to the eyes of Cosmo it seemed a mighty library—a treasurehouse for a royal sage.

There was no one in the room when they entered, and Cosmo was still staring in silent astonishment when suddenly Mr. Simon was talking to his father. The door had not opened and Cosmo could not tell how he had come in. To the eyes of the boy the small man before him assumed gigantic proportions.

But he was in truth below middle height, somewhat round-shouldered, with long arms and small, well-shaped hands. His hair was plentiful, grizzled, and cut short. His head was large and his forehead wide, with overhanging brows. His eyes were small, dark, and brilliant; his nose had a certain look of decision; his mouth was large, and his chin strong; his complexion dark, and his skin rugged. His face was not at first sight particularly attractive; indeed it was rather gloomy—till he smiled. For that smile was the interpreter of the mouth, and, through the mouth, of the face, which was never the same as before to one that had seen it.

After a word or two about the book he had borrowed, the laird took his departure, saying the sooner he left master and pupil to themselves the better. Mr. Simon gave him a smile, and presently Cosmo was facing his near future, not without some anxiety.

10

· · · · · · · · · · · · · · · · ·

The New Schooling

Without a word Mr. Simon opened a drawer, took from it about twenty sheets of paper, and handed one of them to Cosmo. Upon it was printed a stanza—one, and no more.

"Read that," he said, with a glance that showed through his eyes the light burning inside him, "and tell me if you understand it. I don't want you to ponder over it, but merely to say after one reading whether you know what it means."

Cosmo obeyed and read.

"I can't make heads or tails of it, sir," he answered, looking over the top of the paper like an imprisoned sheep.

Mr. Simon took it from him and handed him another.

"Try that," he said.

Cosmo read, put his hand to his head, and looked troubled.

"Don't distress yourself," said Mr. Simon. "It doesn't matter in the least; I am only trying to discover where to begin."

The remark conveyed but little consolation to the pupil who would gladly have stood well in his own eyes before his new master.

One after another Mr. Simon handed him the papers he held. About the fifth or sixth, Cosmo exclaimed, "I do understand that, sir."

"Very well," returned Mr. Simon, without showing any special satisfaction, and immediately handed him another.

This was again a mystery to Cosmo, and cast a shadow over the face of the embryo student. One by one, Mr. Simon handed him all he held. Out of the score there were three Cosmo said he understood, and four he thought he should understand if he were allowed to read them over two or three times. But Mr. Simon put them all together again and back into the drawer.

"Now I shall know what I am about," he said. "Tell me what you have been doing at school."

If this was a book on education it might be worthwhile to give some account of Peter Simon's ways of furthering human growth. But intellectual development is not my main business or interest, and I mean to say little more concerning Cosmo's than that, after about six weeks' work, the boy one day begged Mr. Simon to let him look at those papers again, and found to his delight that he understood all but three or four of them.

That first day, Mr. Simon gave him an ode of Horace and a poem by Wordsworth to copy—telling him to put in every point as it was in the book exactly, but to note any improvement he thought might be made. He told him also to look and see whether he could see any resemblance between the two poems.

As he sat surrounded by the many books, Cosmo felt as if he were in the heart of a cloud of witnesses.

That first day was sufficient to make the heart of the boy cleave to his new master. For one thing, Mr. Simon, in anything done, took note first of the things that pleased him, and only after that proceeded to remark on the faults—most of which he treated as imperfections, letting Cosmo see plainly that he understood how he had come to go wrong.

Such an education as Mr. Simon was thus attempting with Cosmo is hardly to be given to more than one at a time. And indeed, there are few boys on whom it would not be lost labor. Cosmo, however, was now almost as eager to go to his lessons as he would have been before to spend a holiday. Mr. Simon never gave him anything to do at home, believing it the imperative duty of a teacher to leave room for a youngster to grow on his own, and that what a boy does by himself is of greater importance than what he does with any teacher. Such leisure time may be of rather small consequence for the multitude of boys, but it is absolutely necessary wherever one is born with a creative individuality. Therefore, when Cosmo went home he read or wrote what he pleased, wandered about at his will, and dreamed to his heart's content. And it was not long before he discovered that his dreams themselves were becoming of greater importance to him—and that they also were being influenced by Mr. Simon.

One day Cosmo came late, his eyes red and swollen with weeping. His master looked at him almost wistfully, but said nothing until he had settled for a while into his work and was a little composed. He then asked him what was wrong, and the boy told him.

Among the horses on the farm was a certain small mare, which, although she worked as hard as any, was yet an excellent one to ride. As often as there was not much work doing, Cosmo rode her where he would, and the boy and mare were greatly attached to each other. Sometimes, in the prime of the summer weather, when the harvest was drawing nigh, and the school had its long yearly holiday, he would have her every day for several weeks. They would be out for hours together, perhaps not far from home all the time—on the top of a hill, whence Cosmo could see the castle below. There, the whole sleepy afternoon, he would lie in the heather, with Linty the mare feeding among it, ready to come at his call, receive him on her back, and carry him where he wished.

But alas! Though supple and active, Linty was old, and the day could not be distant when they must part company: she was then twenty-nine. And now—the night before, she had been taken ill: there was a disease among the horses. The men had been up with her all night, and Grizzie too: she had fetched her own pillow and put it under her head, then sat by for hours. When Cosmo left, she was a little better, but the fears were greatly against the possibility of her recovery.

"She's so terribly old, you see, sir," said Cosmo, as he ended his tale of woe and burst out crying again.

"Cosmo," said Mr. Simon, "your heart is faithful to your mare, but is it equally faithful to him that made your mare?"

"I know it's his will," answered Cosmo. "I know mares must die, but eh! she was such a good one! Sir, I can't stand it!"

"You know who sits by the dying sparrow?" said Mr. Simon. "Cosmo, there was a better one than Grizzie, and nearer to Linty all the long night. Things weren't going so ill with her as you thought. Life's an awful mystery, Cosmo, but it's just the one thing the Maker of it can keep nearest to, for it's nearest to himself. Folk may tell me," he went on, more now as if he were talking to himself than to the boy, "that I should content myself with what I see and hear, and leave all my speculations alone. But with dying men and mares all about, how can I? If I had nothing but what I see and hear, grand and bonny as a heap of it is, I would just smother for want of room."

"But what's the good of it all, when I'll never see her again?" sobbed Cosmo.

"Who says such a thing, laddie?"

"Everyone," answered Cosmo, astonished at the question.

"Master *Everybody* has a lot of the gowk in him still, Cosmo," replied his master. "In fact, he's no more than an infant yet, though he would speak as if the whole universe of wisdom and knowledge was open to him. There's not a word of the kind in the whole Bible, nor in the heart of man—nor in the heart of the Maker, I don't believe, Cosmo. Do *you* believe that the little foal of a donkey that carried the master of us all along the road from Bethany to Jerusalem came to such an ill end as to be forgotten by him he carried? No, no, my son! If I have any power to read the truth of things, the life that's given is not taken. That a thing can love and be loved—and that's your little mare, Cosmo—is just the same as to say it's immortal, for God is love, and whatever partakes of the essence of God can't die, but must go on living till it pleases him to say stop, which he'll never say. Whatever comes of the creature, the love it wakened in a human breast can no more be lost than the object of the same."

By this time the face of the man was glowing. His confidence entered Cosmo's heart, and when the master ceased, he turned with a sigh of gladness and relief to his work and wept no more. The possible entrance of Linty to an enlarged existence widened the whole heaven of his conscious being. The wellspring of life within him seemed to rush forth, and through his grief and its consolation, the boy made a great stride toward manhood.

One day in the first week of his new schooling, Cosmo happened to mention Aggie's difficulty with her algebra, and her anxiety about whether it was true that a girl could do as well as a boy. Mr. Simon was very interested, and with the instinct of the true hunter whose business it is to hunt death for the sake of life, he began to think whether here might not be another prepared to receive. He knew her father well, but had made no acquaintance with Agnes yet. Indeed, the girl was a little afraid of him, for he looked as if he were always thinking about things nobody else knew of, although like everyone else who saw it, she did find his smile reassuring. No doubt the peculiar feeling of the neighbors concerning him had caused her—without realizing it—to associate with him the idea of something not quite canny. However, when she heard from Cosmo what sort of man his new master was, she would have given anything to be able to learn from him. And before long she had her chance. Old Dorothy, Mr. Simon's servant and housekeeper, was one day taken ill. Cosmo mentioned the fact in Aggie's hearing, and after but a word to her mother she ran to offer her assistance until the old woman was better.

It turned out that "auld Dorty," as the neighbors called her, not without some doubtful hint as to the quality of her temper, was not very seriously ailing, yet sufficiently so to accept a little help for the rougher work of the house. Because of these circumstances, it happened one day that while Aggie was on her knees washing the slabs of the passage that led through to the back door, the master, as she always called him now that Cosmo was his pupil, came from his room and saw her there. She rose in haste, mechanically drying her hands in her apron.

"How's the algebra getting on, Agnes?" he said.

"Nothin's gettin' on very weel since Master Cosmo left the school, sir. I dinna seem t' hae the heart for the learnin' that I had when he was there."

"I understand, Agnes," returned the master. "Would you like to have some lessons with me? I don't say along with Cosmo; you would hardly be able for that at present, I fancy, but at such times as you could manage to come—odd times when you weren't needed."

"There's nothing I would like half so weel, sir," said Aggie. "There's jist a kind o' hunger in me for un'erstandin' things. It's from bein' so much wi' Master Cosmo, I'm thinkin'—ever since he was a bairn, ye know, sir. For being two years older, I was a kin' o' wee nurse t' him. An' ever since then we hae had no secrets from one anither. An' ye know what he's like—always wantin' t' get t' the bottom o' things, an' that's infected me, so that I canna rest when I see anybody un'erstandin' a thing, till I set aboot gettin' a grip o' it mysel'."

"A very good infection to take, Agnes," replied the master with a smile of pleasure, "and one that will do more for you than the chicken pox. Come to me as often as you can—and whenever you like. I think I shall be able to tell you some things to make you happier."

" 'Deed, sir, I'm in no need of happiness! O' that I hae more than I deserve. But I want more than that. I canna say what it is, for the hunger is for what I dinna have."

Another of God's children, said the master to himself, *and full of the groanings of the spirit! "The wilderness and the solitary place shall be glad for them."*

He often quoted scripture as the people of the New Testament did—not much minding the original application of the words. Those who are filled with the Spirit have always taken liberties with the letter.

That very evening before she went home, they had a talk about algebra, and several other things. Agnes went to school no more, but almost every day went to see the master, avoiding the hours when Cosmo would be there.

11
• • • • • • • • • • • • • • • • • •

Grannie's Ghost Story

Things went on very quietly. The glorious days of harvest came and went, and left the fields bare for the wintry revelling of great blasts. The potatoes were all dug up, then buried again—deeper than before, in pits, with sheets of straw and blankets of earth to protect them from the biting of the frost. Their stalks and many weeds with them were burned and their ashes scattered. Some of the land was plowed, and some left till the spring. Before the autumn rains the stock of peats was brought from the hill, where they had been drying through the hot weather, and a splendid stack they made. Coal was carted from the nearest seaport, though not in such quantity as the laird would have liked, for money was as scarce as ever. Everything available for firewood was collected, and, if of any size, put under the saw and axe, then stored in the house. Good preparations were thus made for the siege of the winter.

In their poverty, partly no doubt from consideration and to keep them from the added expense of guests, they seemed to be mostly forgotten by neighbors, friends, or relatives. The family was like an old thistle head, withering on its wintry stalk, alone in a windswept field. All the summer through not a single visitor, friend or stranger, had visited or slept in the house. A fresh face was unseen by young Cosmo. The human heart, like the human body, can live without much variety to feed on, but its house is built on a lordly scale for hospitality, and is capable of welcoming every new face as a new revelation.

Steadily Cosmo went to his day's work with the master, steadily returned to his home. He saw nothing new, yet learned day by day, as he went and came, to love still more, not only the faces of the men and women, but the aspects of the country in which he was born, to read the lines and shades of its varying beauty. If the land was not luxuriant enough to satisfy his ideal, it had yet endless loveliness to disclose to one whose love made him seek to understand it. Autumn made him sad, for it was not in harmony with the forward look of his young life, which, though not ambitious, was vaguely expectant. But when the hoarfrosts appeared, when the clouds gathered, when the winds began to wail, and the snows to fall, then his spirits rose to meet the invading death. The old castle grew grayer and grayer outside, but ruddier and merrier within. (Oh, that awful gray and white Scottish winter—dear to my heart as I sit and write with window wide open to the blue skies of Italy's December!)

Cosmo kept up his morning bath in "the pot" as long as he could. But when sleet and rain came, he could no longer dry himself by running about. He did not care for it longer, but waited for the snow to come in plenty, which was a sure thing, for then he had a substitute. In the depth of winter, when the cold was at its strongest and the snow lay deep, he would jump from his warm bed with the first glimmer of morning and run out, in a light gray with the grayness of what is frozen, to a hollow on the hillside a few yards from the house. There he would pull off his night clothes and roll in the snow, kneading handfuls of it, and rubbing himself with it all over.

Thus he believed he strengthened himself to stand the cool of the day; happily he was strong enough to stand the strengthening, and so increase his hardihood. What would have been death to many was to him invigoration. He knew nothing of boxing, or rowing, or billiards, but he could run and jump well, and ride fairly, and above all he could endure. In the last harvest for the first time he had wielded a scythe, and had held his own with the rest, though with a fierce struggle. And the following spring he not only held the plow, but by patient persistence and fearlessness trained two young bulls to go in it, saving many weeks labor of a pair of horses. It filled his father with pride and hope for the boy's coming fight with the world. Even the eyes of his grandmother would brighten after that at mention of him. She began to feel proud that she had a share in the existence of the lad; might he not be something by the time he was a man?

But one thing troubled her—he was no sportsman. He never went out to hunt the otter, or to shoot rabbits or hares or grouse or partridges. And that was unnatural! The fact was, ever since that talk with master about Linty, he could not bear to kill anything, and was now and then haunted by the dying eyes of the pigeon he shot the first time he had handled a gun. The grandmother thought it a defect in his manhood that he did not like shooting, when in fact it revealed his true manhood all the more—for no man whose heart is growing after the image of Christ's can take lightly killing of any kind for any reason. Cosmo's heart was larger and tenderer then the woman's, and got in the way of what was necessary to be a hunter.

His father had never troubled his young life with details concerning the family affairs. He had only let him know that, for many years, through extravagance and carelessness in those who had preceded him, things had been going from bad to worse. But this was enough to wake in the boy the desire, which grew in him as he grew, to rescue what was left of the estate from its burdens, and restore it to independence and so to honor. He said nothing of it to his father, however, feeling the presumption of thinking he would be able to do something his father had been unable to do himself.

He went to the village this winter more often than before, and seldom without going to see Mistress Forsyth, whom he, like the rest, always called Grannie. She suffered a great deal from rheumatism, which she described as a sorrow in her bones. But she never lost her patience, and so got the good of a trouble that would seem specially sent as the concluding discipline of old people for this world, that they may start well in the next. Before the winter set in, the laird had seen that she was well provided with peats—that much he could do, because it cost him nothing but labor. Cosmo himself had taken each of the several cart loads, with the mare Linty between the shafts. But no amount of fire could keep the frost out of the old woman's body, or the sorrow out of her bones. She had to be in bed a good deal and needed her great-granddaughter Agnes to help her. When the bitter weather came, soon after Christmas, Agnes had to be with her almost constantly. She had grown a little graver, but was always cheerful; except for anxiety that her mother would be overworked, or her father catch a cold, she seemed as happy with her grandmother as at home.

One afternoon when the clouds were rising and the wind blew keen from the north, Cosmo left Glenwarlock to go to the village—mainly to see Grannie. He tramped the two and a half miles all in the joy of youthful conflict with the wind and weather, and reached the old woman's cottage radiant. The snow lay deep and powdery with frost, and the struggle with space from a bad footing on the world had brought the blood to his cheeks and the sparkle to his eyes. He found Grannie sitting up in bed, and Aggie getting her tea—to which Cosmo contributed a bottle of milk he had brought her, an article rare enough in the winter when there was so little grass for the cows. Aggie drew the old woman's chair to the fire for him, and he sat down and ate barley-meal scones and drank tea with them. Grannie was a little better than usual, for every disease has its inconsistencies, and pain will abate before an access. And so, with storm at hand, threaded with fiery serpents for her bones, she was talking more than for days previously. Her voice came feebly from the bed to Cosmo's ears, while he leaned back in her great chair and Aggie removed the tea things.

"Did ye ever dream any mair aboot the auld captain, Cosmo?" she asked. From her tone he could not tell whether she spoke seriously or was amusing herself with the idea.

"Not once," he answered. "What makes ye ask, Grannie?"

She said nothing for a few minutes and Cosmo thought she had let the subject drop. Aggie had returned to her seat and he was talking to her about Euclid when Grannie began again, and this time her voice revealed that she was quite in earnest.

"Ye're weel nigh a man noo, Cosmo," she said. "A body may dare speak t' ye aboot things a body wouldna be willin' to' say t' a bairn for fear o' frightenin' him more than his wee heart could stan'. When a lad can wrestle wi' a pair o' bulls, an' get the upper hand o' them an' make them do his biddin', he wouldna need t' take fright at—" There she paused.

This preamble was enough in itself—not exactly to bring Cosmo's heart into his mouth, but to send a little more of his blood from his brain to his heart than was altogether welcome there. His imagination, however, was more eager than apprehensive, and his desire to hear was greater than his dread of what he might hear about. He would not have turned his back on any terror, though he knew well enough what fear was. He looked at Aggie as much as to say, "What can be coming?" and she stared at him in turn with dilated pupils, as if something dreadful were about to be evoked by the threatened narrative. Neither spoke a word, but their souls got into their ears, and there sat listening. The hearing was all the more likely to be frightening when so prefaced by Grannie.

"There's no guid ever came o' not callin' things by their ain names," she began, "an' it's my mind that if ever a man was a villain, an' if ever a man had reason not t' lie quiet when he was doon, that man was yer father's uncle—his gran'uncle, that is, the auld captain, as we called him. Fowk said he sol' his soul t' the Ill One: hoo that may be, I wouldna care' t' be able t' tell, but I am sure that his was a soul ill at ease—both here an' hereafter. Them that slept beneath me, for there was two menservants aboot the hoose at the time—an' truth, there was need o' them an' more, sich were the goin's on! An' they slept where I'm told ye sleep noo, Cosmo—them that slept there told me that never a night passed that they didna hear soun's beneath them that there was no manner o' accountin' for nor explainin', as fowks be so set upon doin' nooadays wi' everythin'. Them that heard it tellt me there was no accountin', as I told ye, for what sounded like the beggin' an' groanin' o' a man as if the enemy were bodily present t' the poor sinner."

"He might have been but jabberin' in his sleep," ventured Cosmo, but Aggie gave him a nudge of warning.

"Ay, might it," returned the old woman with calm scorn. "An' it might nae doobt hae been snorin' or a cat speakin' wi' a man's tongue, or any o' many things, 'cept the truth that ye're not willin' t' hear."

"I *am* willin' t' hear the worst truth ye dare tell me, Grannie!" cried Cosmo, terrified lest he had choked off the fountain. He was more afraid of losing the story than of hearing the worst tale that could be told, even about the room he slept in last night, and must go back to sleep in again tonight.

Grannie was mollified, and went on.

"As I was sayin', he might weel be ill at ease, the auld captain, if half was true that was said o' him. But I almost think yer father counted it proven that he had led a deevilich life among the pirates. Only, if he did, where was the wages o' his ineequity? Nae doobt he got the wages that the apostles speaks o', which is, as ye well ken, death—'the wages o' sin is death.' But mostly sich sinners get first wages o' another kin' from the master o' them. For truth! he has no need to be near in his dealin's wi' them, seein' there's nae buyin' nor sellin' where he is, an' all the gold he has doon yonder in the bowels o' the earth would jist lie there doin' nothin' if he sent none o' it up above, where fer the most part it works his will. No, he seldom scrimps t' them that follows his biddin'. But in this case, where, I say, was the wages? Nonetheless, he aye carried himsel' like one that could lay doon the law o' this world, an' claimed no small consideration. Yet there was never sign or mark o' the proper foundation for sich assumption o' the right t' respect.

"It turned oot, or came t' be said, that the Englishman that fowk believed t' hae killed him was some far-off kin t' the family, an' the two had come t'gether before, somewhere in foreign parts. But that's neither here nor there, nor why he killed him, or whose fault it was: aboot all that, nothing was ever known for certain.

"Weel, it was an awful thing, ye may be sure, t' quiet fowk, sich as we was—'cept for the drinkin' an' sich like, since ever the auld captain came wi' his reprobate ways. 'Twas a sad thing, I'm saying', t' hae a dead man all at once on oor hands, for, let the men do what they like, the worst o' it comes upon the women. Let a bairn come t' mischance, or the man turn over the kettle, an' it's aye, 'Run for Jean this, or Bauby that,' t' set right what they hae set wrong. Even when a man kills a body, it's the women hae t' make the best o' it, an' make the corpse look decent. An' there's some o' them not that easy t' make look decent! Truth, there's many a one that looks bonnier dead than alive, but that wasna the case wi' the auld captain, for he looked as if he had died cursin', as he was bound t' do, if he died as he lived. His mouth was drawn fearful, as if his last oath had choked him. Whether he had fair play or not, the death he died was a just one; for them that draws the sword must perish by the sword. When they foun' him, the right hand o' the corpse was stretchin' oot, as if he was cryin' t' somebody runnin' away t' bide an' take him wi' him. Only, if he took him that same night, he couldna hae carried him far. 'Deed, maybe the auld sinner was ower much, even for *him*.

"They brought him home, an' laid the corpse o' him upon his ain bed, where, I reckon, up till this night, he had tried t' sleep more than he had slept. An' that very night, who should I see—but I'm jist goin' t' tell ye all aboot it, an' hoo it was, an' then ye can say yersel's. Since my ain auld mither died, I haena opened my mooth t' mortal man upon the subject."

The eyes of the two listeners were fixed upon the narrator in the very height of expectation. A real ghost story from the lips of one they knew, and must believe in, was a thing of dread delight. Like ghosts themselves, they were altogether unconscious of body, rapt in listening.

"Ye may weel believe," resumed the old woman after a short pause, "that none o' us was ower willin' t' sit wi' the corpse for long, for, as I say, he wasna a comely corpse t' be alone wi'. Sae auld Auntie Jean an' mysel', we agreed that we would take the thing upon oorsel's, for as two, we could trust t' one anither no t' be ower feart. There hadna been time yet for the corpse t' be laid int' the coffin, though in the quiet o' the dark, as we sat we thought we could hear the tap-tappin' as they hammered the brass nails int' it away ower in Geordie Lumsden's shop, at the Muir o' Warlock. We were sittin', Auntie Jean an' mysel', in the middle o' the room—no wi' oor backs t' the bed, nor yet wi' oor faces, for we dared not turn either o' them t' it. In the one case, who could tell what we might see, an' in the other, who could tell what might be lookin' at us! We were sittin', I say, wi' oor faces t' the door o' the room, an' Auntie was noddin' a wee, for she was turnin' auld by that time, but I was as wide awake as any kitty by a mouse hole, when suddenly there came a kind o' scraping sound at the door latch that sent the very sowl o' me up int' the attic o' my head. An' afore I had time t' ken hoo sore afraid I was, the door began t' open; an' stare as I would, not believin' my ain eyes, open that door did, slowly, slowly, quiet, quiet, jist as my auld Grannie used t' tell o' the dead man comin' doon the chimney, a piece at a time, an' joinin' t'gether upon the floor. I was turned t' stone, like, that I didna believe I could hae fallen from the chair if I had fainted clean away. An' eh but it took a time t' open that door! But at last, as sure as ye sit there, ye two, an' no another—"

At the word, Cosmo's heart came swelling up into his throat, but he dared not look round to assure himself that they were indeed two sitting there and not another—

"—in came the auld captain, one foot after another! Ask if I was sure o' him! Didna I ken him as well as my ain father—as weel as my ain minister—as weel as my ain man? He came in, I say, the auld captain himsel'—an' ey, such an evil look!—the very look o' death—frozen upon the face o' the corpse! The live blood turned stagnant in my inside. He came on an' on, but not straight for where we sat, or I dinna think the small reason I had left would had stayed wi' me, but as if he were headin' for his bed. T' tell God's truth, for I darena lie, for fear o' haein' t' look upon the like o' it again, my auld auntie declared afterward that she saw nothin'. She must hae been asleep, an' a merciful thing it was for her, poor body! but she didn't live long after that. He made straight for the bed, as I thought. *The Lord preserve us!* I thought. *Is he gaen t' lie doon wi' his own corpse?* But he turned away, an' roun' t' the foot o' the bed t' the other side o' it, an' I saw no more; an' for a while Auntie Jean sat by herself with the dead, for I lay upon the floor, an' neither saw nor heard. But when I came t' mysel', wasna I thankful that I wasna dead, for he might hae gotten me then, an' there was no sayin' what he might hae done t' me! But, think ye, would Auntie Jean believe that I had seen him, or that it was anythin' but a dream that had come ower me atween wakin' an' sleepin'! Na, no she! for she had slept through it hersel'!"

For some time the room was silent, as was fitting for the close of such a story. Nothing but the solemn tick of the tall clock was to be heard. On and on it went, as steady as before. Ghosts were nothing special to the clock; it had to measure out the time both for ghosts and unghosts.

"But what could the ghost hae been wantin'? Not the corpse, for he turned away, ye said," Cosmo ventured to remark after a few moments.

"Who can say what ghosts may be after, laddie? But, truth t' tell, when ye see live fowk so given ower t' the body that they're never happy but when they're eatin' or drinkin'—an' the auld captain was seldom through wi' his glass that he wasn't cryin' for the whiskey or the hot water for the next—when the body's the best half o' them, like, an' they must aye be doin' somethin' wi' it, ye needna wonder that the ghost o' one sich like should fin' himsel' feelin' eerie an' lonesome like, wantin' his empty sack t' fill, an' so tryin' t' get back t' hae a look at the body t' see what he might be able t' fin'."

"But he didna go t' the corpse," said Cosmo.

" 'Cause he wasna allowed," said Grannie. "He would hae been int' his auld body again in a moment, ye may be certain, if it had been in his power. But the deevils couldna go int' the swine wi'oot permission."

"Ay, I see," said Cosmo.

"But jist ye ask yer new master," Grannie went on, "what he thinks aboot it, for I once heard him speak right wise words t' my son, James Gracie, aboot sich things. I weel remember him talkin' aboot the ghost o' an alderman, who they say was some great Lon'on man, an' the fillin' o' his sack—but I made nae mention o' this particular occasion I'm tellin' ye o' noo."

12

· · · · · · · · · · · · · · · · ·

The Storm Guest

Again a deep silence descended on the room. The twilight had long fallen and settled down into the dark. The only thing that acknowledged and answered the clock was the red glow of the peats on the hearth. To Cosmo, as he sat sunk in thought, the clock and the fire seemed to be holding a silent talk. Presently there came a great and sudden blast of wind, which roused Cosmo and made him think to himself that it was time to be going home. And there was another reason besides the threatening storm: he had the night before begun to read aloud one of Sir

Walter Scott's novels to the assembled family, and Grizzie would be getting anxious for another portion of it before she went to bed.

"I'm glad t' see ye so much better, Grannie," he said. "I'll say good night noo, an' look in again in the mornin'."

"Weel, I'm obliged t' ye," replied the old woman. "There's been but few o' yer kin, be their faults what they might, who would forget any who needed a kind deed! Aggie, lass, ye'll go wi' him a ways, willna ye?"

All those in whom yet lingered any shadow of honor toward the fast-fading chieftainship of Glenwarlock seemed to cherish the notion that the heir of the house had to be tended and cared for like a child—that was what they were in the world for. Doubtless a pitying sense of the misfortunes of the family had much to do with the feeling.

"There's no occasion," and "I'll do that," came from the two young people in one breath.

Cosmo rose, and began to put on his plaid blanket, crossing it over back and chest to leave his arms free: that way the wind would get the least hold on him. Agnes went to the closet for her plaid also—of the same tartan, and drawing it over her head and pinning it under her chin was presently ready for the stormy way. Then she turned to Cosmo, who was pinning his plaid together at the throat, when the wind came with a sudden howl, rushed down the chimney, and drove the level smoke into the middle of the room. It could not shake the cottage—it lay too low: neither could it rattle its windows—they were not made to open; but it bellowed over it like a wave over a rock, and as if in contempt, blew its smoke back into its throat.

"It'll be an evil night, I don't doobt, Cosmo," said Agnes, "an' I wish ye safe int' the castle wi' yer fowk."

Cosmo laughed. "The wind knows me," he said.

"God forbid!" cried the old woman from the bed. "Dinna ye ken who's the Prince o' it, laddie? Makena jest o' the powers that be."

"If they be not ordained o' God, what are they but a jest?" returned Cosmo. "Eh, but ye would make a bonny fool o' me, Grannie, t' hae me feart at the de'il an' all! I canna alt'gether help it wi' the ghosts, an' I'm ashamed o' myself for that. But I *am not* gaein t' heed the de'il. I defy him an' all his works. He's but a coward, ye know, Grannie, for when ye resist him, he runs away."

She made no answer. Cosmo shook hands with her and went, followed by Agnes, who locked the door behind her and put the key in her pocket.

It was indeed a wild night. The wind was rushing from the north, full of sharp stinging particles, something between snowflakes and hailstones. Down the wide village street it came right in their faces. Through it, as through a thin shifting sheet, they saw on both sides the flickering lights of the many homes, but before them lay darkness and the moor, a chaos of wind and snow. Worst of all, the snow on the road was not sticking, and their feet felt as if they were walking on sand. As long as the footing is good, one can get on even in the face of a northerly storm. But to heave with a shifting fulcrum is hard. Nevertheless, Cosmo rejoiced;

invisible though the wild waste was to him through the snow, it was nevertheless a presence, and his young heart rushed to the contest. There was no fear of ghosts in such a storm! The ghosts might be there, but there was no time to heed them, and that was as good as them not being there—perhaps better, if we knew all.

"Bide a wee, Cosmo!" cried Agnes and, leaving him in the middle of the street where they were walking, ran across to one of the houses and entered—lifting the latch without knocking. No neighbor troubled another to come and open the door; if there was no one at home, the key in the lock outside showed it.

Cosmo turned his back to the wind and stood waiting. From the door that Aggie opened came through the wind and snow the sound of the shoemaker's hammer on his lapstone.

"Could ye spare the mistress for an hour, or maybe twa, t' keep Grannie company, John Nauchty?" said Agnes.

"Weel that," answered the soutar, hammering away.

"I dinna see her," said Aggie.

"She'll be in in a minute. She's run over the road t' get a dip o' a can'le," returned the man.

"If she isn't speedy she'll hae t' light it t' fin' her ain door," said Agnes merrily, to whom the approaching fight with the elements was as welcome as to Cosmo. She had made up her mind to go with him all the way, let him protest as he might.

"Ow na! She'll listen, an' hear the hammer," replied the shoemaker.

"Weel, take the key, an' ye winna forget, John?" said Aggie, laying the key among his tools. "Grannie's lyin' there hersel', an' if the hoose was t' take fire, what could come o' her?"

"God forbid anybody should forget Grannie!" rejoined the man heartily; "but fire would hae a small chance t'night."

Agnes thanked him and left. All the time he had not missed a single stroke of his hammer on the leather between it and his lapstone.

When she rejoined Cosmo where he stood leaning his back against the wind in the middle of the road, he said, "Come nae farther, Aggie. It's an ill night and it grows worse. There's nae good in it, neither, for we winna hear one anither speak wi'oot stoppin' an' turnin' oor backs t' it. Go t' yer Grannie; she'll be feart aboot ye."

"Nae a bit. I must see ye oot o' the toon."

They fought their way along the street, and out onto the open moor, the greater part of which was still heather and swamp. Peat bog and plowed land was all one waste of snow. Creation seemed nothing but the snow that had fallen, the snow that was falling, and the snow that had yet to fall.

"Go back noo, Aggie," said Cosmo again. "What's the good o' two where only one needs be, an' both hae t' fight for themsel's?"

"I'm no gaein' back yet," persisted Aggie. "Two's better in anythin' than one alone. The soutar's wife's gaein in t' see Grannie, an' Grannie'll like her talk a heap better than mine. She thinks I had nae mair brains than a hen, 'cause I canna remember things that were nearly forgotten before I was born."

Cosmo let go any further attempts at useless persuasion, and they struggled on together, through the snow above and the snow beneath. At this Aggie was more than a match for Cosmo. Lighter and smaller, and perhaps with larger lungs in proportion, she bored her way through the blast better than he, and the moment he began again to try to tell her to go home, she would increase the distance between them, and go on in front where he knew she could not hear a word he said.

At last, being then a little ahead, she turned her back to the wind, and waited for him to catch up.

"Noo, ye've had enough o' it!" he said. "An' I must turn an' go back wi' you, or ye'll never get home."

Aggie broke into a loud laugh that rang like music through the storm.

"A likely thing!" she cried. "Go back yersel', Cosmo, an' sit by Grannie's fire, an' I'll go on t' the castle an' let them ken where ye are. If ye dinna do that, I'll tell ye once for all, I'm no gaein' t' leave ye till I see ye safe inside yer ain walls."

"But, Aggie," pleaded Cosmo, "what'll ye make folk think o' me that would hae a lassie go home wi' me for fear the wind might blow me into the sea? Ye'll bring me t' shame, Aggie."

"A lassie, do ye say!" cried Aggie. "An' me auld enough t' be yer mither! But I'll take good care there shall be nae affront in it."

As she spoke the wind pounced upon them with a fiercer gust than any that had preceded. Instinctively they grasped each other, as if from the wish, if they should be blown away, to be blown away together.

"Eh, that's a rough one!" said Cosmo, and again Aggie laughed merrily.

While they were standing there, the moon rose. Far indeed from being visible, she yet shed a little glimmer of light over the plain, revealing a world as wild as ever the frozen north could be—as wild as any poet's despairing vision of desolation. It was ghastly. The only similarity to life was the perplexed and multitudinous motion of the drifting, falling flakes. No shape was to be seen, no sound but that of the wind to be heard.

The moment the fury of the blast abated, Agnes turned and, without a word, began again her boring march, forcing her way through the obstructions of wind and snow. Unable to prevent her, Cosmo followed. But he comforted himself with the thought that, if the storm continued, he would get his father to use his authority against her attempting a return before the morning. The soutar's wife was one of Grannie's best cronies, and there was no fear of her being deserted through the night.

Aggie kept the lead she had taken, till there could be no more question of her not going on, and they were now drawing near the road that struck off to the left, along the bank of the Warlock River, leading up among the valleys and low hills, most of which had once been the property of the house of Warlock. All at once she stopped suddenly, this time without turning her back to the wind, and Cosmo was immediately beside her.

"What's that, Cosmo?" she said, and Cosmo thought he detected anxiety in her tone. He looked forward and saw what seemed a glimmer of light, but might only be something whiter in the whiteness. No! it was certainly a light of some kind—but whether on the road he could not tell. There was no house in that direction! It moved! Now it was gone! There it was again! There were two of them—two huge pale eyes, rolling from side to side. Grannie's warning about the Prince of the power of the air darted into Cosmo's mind. It was awful!

But anyhow, the devil was not to be run from. And now it was becoming all the more plain that the something was not off on the moor, but right on the road in front of them and coming toward them. It came nearer and nearer, and grew vaguely visible—a huge blundering mass—animal or what, they could not tell. But in the wind came sounds that might be human—the sounds of encouragement and incitation to horses. And now it approached no more but seemed to have stopped. With common impulse they ran toward it.

It was a traveling carriage—a rare sight in those parts at any time, and rarer still in winter. Both of them had certainly seen one before, but never one bearing a pair of lighted carriage lamps, with reflectors to make of them fiendish eyes. There were two horses, and the driver could do nothing to make them take a single step farther. Indeed, they could not. They had tried and tried and done their best, but were unable to move the carriage an inch.

Cosmo looked up on top of the carriage. The driver was little more than a boy, nearly dead with cold. Already Aggie had a forefoot of the near horse in her hand. Cosmo ran to the other.

"Their feet's full o' snow," said Aggie.

"Ay, it's bad hard," said Cosmo. "They must hae come ower a soft place; they can't do anythin' but slip aroun' like this."

"Hae ye yer knife, Cosmo?" asked Aggie.

Just then a young lady in a swansdown traveling hood put her head out of the carriage window. She had heard an unintelligible conversation—and but one word she could understand. They must be robbers! Why else would they want a knife in a snowstorm? Why else would they have stopped the carriage? She gave a little cry of alarm. Aggie dropped the hoof and went to the window.

"What do you want, mem?" she asked.

"What's the matter?" the lady returned in a shaky voice, but reassured to see a young girl before her. "Why doesn't the coachman go on?"

"He canna, mem. The horse canna get through the snow, no more'n ye could yersel', mem, if the soles o' yer shune were made o' ice. But we'll soon set that right. Hoo far hae ye come, mem, if I may ask? Aigh, mem, it's a miserable night!"

The lady did not understand much of what Aggie said, for she was English, returning from her first visit to Scotland, but, half guessing her question, she replied that they had come from Cairntod and were going on to Howglen. She said they had been much longer on the road than they expected, and were now getting worried.

"I sorely doobt ye'll get t' Howglen t'night," said Aggie. "But surely ye're not alone?" she added.

"My father is with me," said the lady, looking back into the dark carriage, "but I think he is asleep, and I don't want to wake him while we are standing still."

Peeping in, Aggie caught sight of somebody muffled, leaning back in the other corner of the carriage, and breathing heavily. To her not altogether unaccustomed eye, it seemed he might have had more than was good for him in the way of refreshment.

Cosmo was busy clearing the snow from the horses' hoofs. The driver, stupid or dazed, sat on the box, helpless as a parrot on a swinging perch.

"You'll never get t' Howglen t'night, mem," said Aggie.

"We must put up where we can, then," answered the lady.

"I dinna know of a place nearer, fit for gentlefolk, mem."

"What are we to do, then?" asked the lady anxiously.

"Wait a minute, mem, till we hear what Cosmo has t' say."

"That is a peculiar name!" remarked the lady.

"It's the name lairds o' Glenwarlock hae borne for generations," answered Aggie, "though the name itsel' is not from this country, but from Italy."

"And who is this Cosmo whose advice you would have me ask?"

"He's the yoong laird himsel', mem. Eh! but ye must be a stranger not t' ken the name o' Warlock."

"Indeed, I am a stranger—and I can't help wishing, if there is much more of this weather between us and England, that I had been more of a stranger still."

"Deed, mem, we hae a heap o' weather up here, as like this as one snowflake is t' anither. But we take what's sent."

"And where is this Cosmo? How are we to find him?"

"He's right here, mem. Only he's busy cleanin' oot yer poor horses' hoofs."

"I thought you said he was a lord!"

"Na, I didna say that, mem. He's nae lord. But he's laird, an' some lairds is better than most any lords—an' he's Warlock o' Glenwarlock—at least he will be someday."

By now all the eight hoofs were cleared of the hard-packed snow. The next moment Cosmo's head appeared, a little behind that of Aggie, and in the light of the lamp the lady saw the handsome face of a lad who seemed to be about sixteen.

"Here he is, mem! This is the yoong laird. Ye ask *him* what ye're t' do, an' do as he tells ye," said Aggie, and drew back.

"Is that girl your sister?" asked the lady with a little abruptness, for the best bred are not always the most polite. In reality she was about the same age as Aggie, but her breeding made her seem two or three years older.

"No, my lady," answered Cosmo, who had learned from the lad on the box her name and rank. "She is the daughter of one of my father's tenants."

Lady Joan Scudamore thought it very odd that the youth should be on such familiar terms with the daughter of a tenant crofter—out alone with her in the middle of a hideous storm. No doubt the girl looked up to him, but apparently from the same level, as one sharing in the pride of the family. Should she take the girl's advice, and seek his, or press on for Howglen? There was no counsel to be had from her father just at present.

"We want very much to reach Howglen—I think that is what you call the place," she said.

"You can't get there tonight, I'm afraid," returned Cosmo. "The road is, as you see, no road at all. The horses would have their shoes filled again with snow before you were the tenth way there, and would be able to walk not another step."

The lady glanced round at her sleeping companion with a look of perplexity.

"My father will make you welcome, my lady," continued Cosmo, "if you will come with us. We can give you only what English people must think poor fare, for we're not—"

"I should be glad to sit anywhere all night where there is a fire," she interrupted. "I am nearly frozen."

"We can do a little better for you than that, though not so well as we should like. Perhaps, as we can't make any show, we are the more likely to do our best for your comfort."

"You are very kind. I will promise to be comfortable," said the lady. She found herself becoming a trifle interested in this odd Scotch calf.

"Welcome then, to Glenwarlock!" said Cosmo. "Come, Aggie, take one o' them by the head: they're gaein' wi' us. We must turn the horses' heads, my lady. I fear they won't like facing the wind. I can't make out whether your driver is half dead or half drunk or more than half frozen; but Aggie and I will take care of the horses."

"What a terrible country!" said the lady to herself. "The coachmen get drunk! The boys are prigs! There is no distinction between the owners of the soil and the tenants who farm it! And it snows from morning to night, and from one week's end to another!"

Aggie had taken the head of the near horse, and Cosmo took that of the other. The driver said nothing, letting them do as they pleased. With some difficulty, for the road was by now indistinguishable from the ditches that bounded it on both sides, they got the carriage turned around. But when the weary animals received the storm in their faces, Agnes and Cosmo had to employ all their powers of persuasion, first to get them to stand still, and then to advance a little. Gradually, by leading, and patting, and encouraging them in a language they understood, they were coaxed as far as the parish road, and there turning their sides to the wind, and no longer their eyes and noses, they began to move with a little will of their own. For horses have so much hope that the mere fact of having made a turn is enough to revive them with the expectation of cover and food and repose. They presently reached a more sheltered part of the road, and if now and then they had to drag the carriage through deeper snow, they were at least no longer buffeted by the cruel wind or stung by its frosty arrows.

All this time the gentleman inside slept—and it was hardly surprising. For, lunching in the last town and not finding the wine suitable, he had fallen back upon an accomplishment of his youth, and taken himself to toddy. That he had found that at least fit to drink was proved by the state in which he was now carried along.

They reached at last the steep ascent from the parish road to Castle Warlock. The two conductors were worried about whether the horses would face it; but the moment their heads came round, whether it was only that another turn brought fresh hope, or that the wind sent some stray odor of hay or oats to their wide nostrils, I cannot tell. But finding the ground tolerably clear, they took to it with a will, and tore up with the last efforts of all but exhausted strength, Cosmo and Aggie running along beside them all the way.

13

The Castle Inn

The noise of their approach, heard within the lonely winter castle, awoke profound conjecture, and Grizzie proceeded to light the lantern so that she might learn what catastrophe could possibly have caused such a phenomenon: something awful must have taken place! Perhaps they had cut off the king's head as they did in France! But such was the rapidity of the horses' approach in the hope of rest and warmth and supper that the carriage was in front of the very door before she had gotten the long wick of the tallow candle to acknowledge the dominion of fire. The laird rose in haste from his armchair and went to the door. There stood the carriage, in the cloud of steam that rose from the heaving sides of the horses. And there were Cosmo and Agnes at the door of it, assisting somebody to descent. The laird was never in a hurry. He was too thorough a gentleman to trouble approach by uneasy advance, and he had no fear of anything Cosmo had done. Therefore he stood in the kitchen door, calmly expectant.

A long-cloaked young lady got down and came toward him—a handsome girl of what looked to be eighteen, tall and somewhat stately, but clearly tired and probably in need of food as well as rest. He bowed in an old-fashioned manner, and held out his hand to welcome her. She gave him hers graciously and thanked him for the hospitality his son had offered them.

"Come in, come in, miss," said the old man. "The fireside is the best place for explanations. Welcome to a poor house but a warm hearth! So much we can yet offer to stranger-friends."

He led the way and she followed him into the kitchen. On a small piece of carpet before the fire stood the two chairs of state, each protected by a large antique screen. The grandmother rose from hers with dignified difficulty when she perceived the quality of the entering stranger.

"Mother," said the laird, "it is not often we have the pleasure of visitors at this time of year!"

"The more is the rare foot welcome," she answered, making Lady Joan as low a curtsey as she dared. She could not quite reckon on her power of recovery.

Lady Joan returned the gesture, little impressed with the honor done her, but recognizing that she was in the presence of a gentlewoman. She took the laird's seat at his invitation and gazed wearily at the fire.

The next moment a not very pleasant-looking old man entered, supported on one side by Cosmo and on the other by Agnes. They had had no little difficulty in waking him up, and he entered, vaguely supposing that they had arrived at the inn where they had been supposed to spend the night. If his grumbling and swearing as he advanced was subdued, it was only because he was not sufficiently awake to use more vigor. The laird left the lady and came to meet him, but the man took no notice of him, regarding his welcome as the mere obligation of a landlord. Instead, he turned shivering toward the fire where Grizzie was in the process of setting him a chair.

As soon as Lord Mergwain was seated, Cosmo drew his father aside, told him the names of their guests, and in what straits he had found them, adding that the lady and the horses were sober enough, but that he could not answer for the other two.

"We have been spending some weeks at Canmore Castle in Ross-shire, and are now on our way home," said Lady Joan to Mistress Warlock.

"You have come a long way around," remarked the old lady, not so pleased with the manners of her male visitor, on whom she kept casting a full glance every now and then.

"We have," replied Lady Joan. "We turned out of our way to visit an old friend of Papa's, and have found ourselves stormbound ever since. We sent our servants on this morning. They are, I hope, by this time, waiting for us at Howglen."

The fire had been thawing the sleep out of Lord Mergwain, and now at length he was sufficiently awake to be annoyed that his daughter should hold so much conversation with the folk of the poor inn.

"Can't you show us a room?" he said gruffly. "And get us something to eat!"

"We are doing the best we can for your lordship," replied the laird. "But we were not expecting visitors, and one of the rooms you will have to occupy has not been used for some time. In such weather as this, it will take two or three hours of a good fire to make it warm enough to sleep in. But I will go myself and see that the servant is making what haste she can."

He put on his hat over his nightcap and made for the door.

"That's right, landlord!" cried his lordship. "Always see to the comfort of your guests yourself. But bless me! You don't mean we have to go out of doors to reach our bedrooms?"

"I am afraid we can't help it," returned the laird. "There used to be a passage connecting the two houses, but for some reason or other—I never heard what— it was closed in my father's time."

"He must have been an old fool!" remarked the visitor.

"My lord!"

"I said your father must have been an old fool," repeated his lordship testily.

"You are speaking of my husband!" said Mistress Warlock, drawing herself up with dignity.

"I can't help that. I didn't give you away. Let's have some supper, will you? I want a tumbler of toddy, and without something to eat it might make me drunk."

Lady Joan sat silent, with a look half of contempt, half of mischievous enjoyment on her handsome face. She had to suffer from her father's rudeness too often not to enjoy when it brought him into an embarrassing scrape. But the laird was sharper than she thought, and seeing both the old man's condition and his mistake in the nature of the place where they were, he humored the joke along. His mother rose, trembling with indignation. He gave her his arm and conducted her to a stair which ascended immediately from the kitchen, whispering to her on the way that the man was the worse for having drunk too much, and they must not quarrel with him. She retired without another word to their guests. He then called Cosmo and Agnes, who were talking together in low voices at the other end of the kitchen, and taking them to Grizzie in the spare room, told them to help her that she might sooner be able to come back and get the supper ready.

"I am afraid, my lord," he said when he returned, "that we are but poorly provided for such guests as your lordship, but we will do what we can."

"A horrible country!" growled his lordship. "Now look, I don't want jaw—I want drink!"

"What drink would your lordship have? If it be in my power—"

"I doubt, for all your talk, if you've got anything but your miserable whiskey!" interrupted Lord Mergwain.

Now the laird had some remnants of old wine in the once well-stocked cellar, and, thankless as his visitor seemed likely to turn out, his hospitality would not allow him to withhold what he had.

"I have a few bottles of claret," he said, "—if it is not too old—I do not understand much about wine myself."

"Let's have it up!" cried his lordship. "We'll see. If you don't know good wine, I do. I'm old enough for any wine."

The laird went to the wine cellar, which had once been the dungeon of the castle, and brought up a most respectable looking magnum, dirty as a burrowing terrier, and to the eye of the imagination hoary with age. The eyes of the lord glistened at the sight. Eagerly he stretched out both hands toward it. They actually trembled with desire. Hardly could he endure the delay of its uncorking.

"Decant it. Leave the last glassful in the bottom."

The laird filled a decanter and set it before him.

"Haven't you a larger jug?"

"No, my lord."

"Then fill another decanter, and remember the last glass."

"I have not got another decanter, my lord."

"Not got two decanters, you fool?" sneered his lordship, enraged at not having the whole bottle set down to him at once. "But after all," he resumed, "it might not even be worth a glass, not to say a decanter. Bring the bottle. Set it down—carefully! Bring a glass. You should have brought the glasses first. Bring three . . . I like to change my glass. Hurry, will you!"

The laird made haste, smiling at the urgency of his visitor. Lord Mergwain listened to the glug-glug in the long neck of the decanter as if it had been a song of love, and the moment it was over, was holding the glass to his nose.

"Humph! Not much aroma here!" he growled. "I ought to have made the old fool"—the laird must have been some fifteen years younger than he—"set it down in front of the fire—only what would have become of me while it had been thawing? It's no wonder, though. By the time I've been buried as long, I shall need thawing too!"

The wine, however, turned out more satisfactory to the palate of the toper than to his nostrils. In truth, he had drunk so much that day as to be incapable of doing it justice, yet he set himself to enjoy it. How that should be possible to a man for whom the accompanying dried olives of memory could do so little, I find it difficult to understand. One would think, to enjoy his wine alone, a man must have either good memories or good hopes. Lord Mergwain had forgotten the taste of hope, and most men would shrink from the least scene of the panorama that made up his past. However, there he sat, and there he drank, and now and then even smiled grimly.

The laird set a pair of brass candlesticks on the table—there had long since ceased to be any silver utensils anymore in the house of Glenwarlock—and then retired to a wooden chair at the end of the hearth. On his way he took from a shelf an old much-thumbed book which Mr. Simon had lent him—the *Journal of George Fox*, and the panorama which then for a while kept passing before his mind's eye was very much different than that passing before Lord Mergwain's.

In a few minutes Grizzie entered, carrying a newly killed fowl, its head almost touching the ground at the end of its long, limp neck. She seated herself on a stool about the middle of the large room, and proceeded to pluck and otherwise prepare it for the fire. Last of all, she split it open from end to end, turning it into something like an illegible heraldic crest, and then approached the fire, the fowl in one hand and the cast-iron in the other.

"I doobt I must get his lordship t' sit back a wee from the fire," she said. "I must jist bran'er this chickie for his supper."

Lady Joan had taken Mrs. Warlock's chair, and her father had taken the laird's, and pulled it right in front of the fire, where a small pine table supported his bottle, his decanter, and his three glasses.

"What does the woman mean?" said his lordship. "Is my room not ready yet? Or haven't you a parlor to sit in? I don't relish feasting my nose so much in advance of my other senses."

"Ow! nae fear o' yer lordship's nose, 'cept it be from yer lordship's own stockings, my lord!" said Grizzie. "But I'll take the creatur oot t' the shed an' singe it there first. But 'deed, I wouldna advise ye t' go t' yer room a minute afore ye need, for it winna be that warm t'night. I had made a fire that's both big and bright an' fit t' roast Beelzebub—an' it's some days, I should say weeks, since there was a fire in't, an' the place needs time t' take the heat int' its auld nooks."

She might have said years, and not a few of those, instead of weeks, but her truthfulness did not drive her that far. She turned and left the house, carrying with her the bird to singe.

"Here," said his lordship to his host, "move back this table and chair a bit, will you? I don't relish having the old witch fussing about my knees being in her way. What a mistake it is not to have rooms ready for whoever may come!"

The laird rose, laid his book down, and moved the table, then helped his guest to rise, moved his chair, and placed the screen again between him and the door. Lord Mergwain resettled himself to his bottle.

In the meantime, in the guest chamber, which had for so long entertained neither friend nor stranger, Cosmo and Aggie were busy—too busy to talk much—airing the linen, dusting the furniture, setting things tidy, and keeping up a roaring fire. For this purpose the remnants of an old broken-down cart, of which the axle had not been greased for years, had been fetched from the winter-store, and the wood and peats, together with a shovelful of coal to give the composition a little body, had made a glorious glow. But the heat had hardly yet begun to affect sensibly the general atmosphere of the place. It was a large room, the same size as the drawing room, and even less familiar to Cosmo. For if the latter filled him with a kind of loving awe, the room they were now in caused him a kind of faint terror, so that even in broad daylight he was not willing to enter it. Now and then he would open the door in passing and stand looking into it. But to go in was too much, and he could not even endure the looking in for more than a few seconds. At the same time it gave him a certain kind of pleasure to know that there was such a room in the house—almost as if the room gave the castle a mysterious window that looked out upon the infinite. These feelings associated with the room had been part of him since even before old Grannie's story, and were as much a mystery as the room itself. He never remembered hearing other tales concerning it. He may have heard hints—a word dropped may have made its impression and roused fancies outlasting the memory of their origin. For feelings, like memories of scents and sounds, remain even after the related facts have vanished.

What it was about the room that scared him he could not tell, but the scare was there. With a companion like Aggie, however, even after hearing Grannie's terrible reminiscence, he was able to be in the room with only a mild, almost pleasant, degree of dread. Although this was true only with regard to the part of the room on the side of the bed next to the fire. The bed itself—not to mention the shadowy region beyond it—on which the pirate had lain, he could not regard without a sense of awful terror.

In the strength of Aggie's presence he was now able to take a survey of the room such as never before. His eyes wandered over walls, floor, and ceiling, when suddenly a question arose in his mind: *Is there,* he asked himself, *a door on the other side of the bed? Did Grannie mention such a door?* he wondered next, though he could not be sure of the answer. He looked all about him, but saw no door other than that by which they had entered, but at the head of the bed, on the other side, was a space hidden by the curtain of the bed: it might be there! He would find out when they went to put the sheets on the bed! He dared not go until then. But even as he thought it, he went—at once.

He walked behind the bed and trembled. It was the strangest feeling. If it was not fear exactly, it was something very much like it, but with a mixture of wondrous pleasure at the same time. For there he saw a door! The curtains hid Aggie from his view, and for a moment he felt as if he were miles alone and the urge was strong to rush back to the refuge of her presence. But he would not yield to the folly, and compelled himself instead to walk to the door.

Whether he was more disappointed or relieved he could not at first tell; instead of a door, leaning against the wall, was nothing but an old dark screen, in stamped leather, from which the gilding was long faded. He found himself disappointed.

"Aggie," he called, still on the farther side of the bed—he called out gently, but trembled at the sound of his own voice—"did ye ever hear—did Grannie ever make mention o' a door that the auld captain gaed oot at?"

"Shh, shh!" cried Aggie in a loud hissing whisper that seemed to pierce the marrow of Cosmo's bones. "Ye must say nothin' aboot that in this room. Wait till we're oot. Then we'll close the door an' let the fire work. It'll hae enough t' do afore it can make this place warm: the cold in this room's not an ordinary one. Somethin's strange aboot it."

Cosmo could no longer endure having the great, old, hearse-like bed between him and Aggie. With a shiver in the very middle of his body, he hastened to the other side. There lay the country of air and fire and safe earthly homeliness: the side he left was the dank region of the unknown.

They hurried on with the rest of their work. Aggie insisted on being at the farther side of the bed when they made it. Not another word was spoken between them till they were safe from the room and had closed its door behind them.

They went up to Cosmo's room, to make it fit for the lady. They opened a chest and took from it another set of curtains, clean blankets, fine sheets, and a counterpane of silk patchwork—all stored there by his mother, Cosmo loved to think—and put them all on the bed. After a chair or two from the drawing room had been moved in, the room was so changed that Cosmo said he would hardly have known it. They then filled the grate with as much fuel as it would hold, and ran down the two flights of stairs and back to the kitchen. At the kitchen door, however, Aggie gave her companion the slip, and set out to return to Grannie at Muir o' Warlock.

Cosmo found the table spread for supper, the English lord sitting with his wine before him, and the lady in his grandmother's chair, leaning back and yawning wearily. Lord Mergwain was not now a very pleasant lord to look at, whatever he might once have been. He was red-faced and bleary-eyed, and his nose was too big and too red. His eyes had once been blue, but tobacco and liquor—everything but tears—had washed from them almost all the color. It added to the strangeness of his appearance that he wore a dark black wig, so that to the unnatural came the untimely, and enhanced the withered. His mouth, full of very white and poorly fitting false teeth, had a cruel expression, and death seemed to look out every time he grinned.

As soon as he and Lady Joan were seated at the supper table with Grizzie to wait upon them, the laird and Cosmo left the kitchen and went to the spare room, for the laird judged that, considering the temper and mistake her father was in, the lady would be more comfortable in their absence.

"Cosmo," he said, standing with his back to the fire once he had made it up again, "I cannot help feeling as if I had known that man before. But I can recall no circumstances for it. You have never seen him, my boy, have you?"

"I don't think so, Papa; and I don't care if I never see him again," answered Cosmo. "The lady is pretty, but not particularly pleasant, I think, though she is a lord's daughter."

"Ah, but such a lord, Cosmo!" returned his father. "When a man goes on drinking like that, he is little better than a cheese under the spigot of a wine cask; he lives to keep his body well-soaked that it may be all the nicer for worms. Cosmo, my son, the material part of us ought to keep growing gradually thinner, to let the soul out when its time comes, and the soul ought to keep growing bigger and stronger every day until it finally bursts the body as a growing nut does its shell. If instead the body grows thicker and thicker, lessening the room within, it squeezes the life out of the soul, and when such a man's body dies, his soul is found a shrivelled thing, too poor to be a comfort to itself or to anybody else. Cosmo, to see that man drink makes me ashamed of my tumbler of toddy. And now that I think of it, I don't believe it does me any good, and just to make sure I am in earnest, from this hour I am going to determine to take no more."

From that day, the laird drank nothing but water, much to the pleasure of Peter Simon, who was by choice a water drinker.

"What a howling night it is, Cosmo!" the laird resumed. "If that poor old drinker had tried to get on to Howglen, he would have been frozen to death. When the drink is out of the drunkard, he has nothing to resist with."

By this time Lord Mergwain had had his supper and had begun to drink again. Grizzie wanted to get rid of him that she might clean up her kitchen. But he would not move. He was quite comfortable where he was, he said, and he didn't care if it was in the kitchen. His daughter might go when she pleased; the bottle was better company than the whole houseful!

Grizzie was on the point of losing her temper with him altogether when the laird returned to the kitchen. He found her standing before him with her two hands on her two hips. He lingered a moment at the door to hear what she was saying.

"Na, na, my lord!" expostulated Grizzie, "I canna leave ye here. Yer lordship'll soon be past takin' care o' yersel'. I canna leave ye alone, my lord; ye might set the hoose on fire an' burn both stable an' byre, an' horses an' carts, an' sheds an' all o' us t' white ashes in oor beds!"

"Hold your outlandish gibberish," returned his lordship. "Go and fetch me some whiskey. This stuff is too cold to go to sleep on in such weather."

"De'il a drap or drap o' whuskey, or anythin' else yer lordship'll hae from my han' this night! Ye hae had ower much already, if ye were but capable o' un'erstan'in what state ye are in. A bonny lordship!" she muttered to herself as she turned from him.

The laird thought it time to show himself, and went forward. Lord Mergwain had not understood half of what Grizzie said, but had found sufficient provocation in the tone, and was much too angry for any articulate attempt at speech beyond swearing.

"My lord," said the laird, "I think you will find your room tolerably comfortable now. Shall I show you the way?"

"No, indeed! I'm not going to stir. Fetch me a bottle of your whiskey—that's pretty safe to be good."

"Indeed, my lord, you shall take no more drink tonight," said the laird. He took the bottle, which was nearly empty, and carried it from the table.

Though nearly past everything else, his guest was not yet too far gone to swear with vigor, and the volley that now came pouring from his outraged heart was such that, for the sake of Grizzie and Cosmo, the laird took the bottle, and said that if his lordship would drink it in his own room, he could have what was left of it.

Not too drunk to see where his advantage lay, Lord Mergwain yielded. The thundering imprecation sank from bellowing to growling, then to muttering, and the storm gradually subsided. The laird gave him one arm, Cosmo another, and Grizzie came behind, ready to support or push, and so in procession they moved from the kitchen along the pathway outside, his lordship grumbling and slipping, hauled, carried, and shoved—through the great door, as they called it, up the stairs, past the drawing room, and into the chamber that Cosmo and Aggie had prepared for him. There he was deposited in an easy chair before the huge fire, and was fast asleep in a moment. Lady Joan had followed them, and while they were in her father's room, had passed up to her own, so that when they reentered the kitchen there was nobody there. With a sigh of relief the laird sank into his mother's chair. After a little while he sent Cosmo to bed, and rejoicing in the quiet, again got the *Journal of George Fox* and began to read. When Grizzie had puttered about for a while, she too went to bed, and the laird was alone.

When he had read about an hour, he thought it time to see after his guest. He rose and went to his room. He found him still asleep in his chair in front of the fire. But he could not be left there through such a night, for the fire would go out, and then a pack of wolves would hardly be worse than the invading cold. It was by no means an easy task to rouse him, and after much labor and contrivance all he was able to do was relieve him of his coat and boots. At length the laird had to satisfy his hospitality with getting him into bed in the remainder of his clothes.

He then heaped fresh fuel on the fire, put out the candles, and left him to what repose there might be for him. Returning to his chair in the kitchen and his book, the laird read for another hour and then went to bed. His room was in the same block, above that of his mother.

14

· · · · · · · · · · · · · · · · ·

That Night

*C*osmo's temporary quarters were in one of several rooms on the floor above his own, which had formerly been occupied by domestics when there were many more about the place. He went to bed, but after about three hours woke very cold—so cold that he could not go to sleep again. He got up, piled on his bed everything protective he could find and tried again. But it was no use. Cosmo could keep himself warm enough in the open air, or if he couldn't he didn't mind. But to be cold in bed was more than he could endure. He got up again. Why shouldn't he find something to do instead of lying shivering on an inhospitable couch? When anything disturbed his sleep on a summer night, he got up and went outside. And though he was naturally less inclined to do so on such a night as this, he would still rather do so than lie sleepless with cold.

On the opposite side of the court, in a gap between the stable and the byre, the men had heaped up the snow from the rest of the yard and Cosmo had been excavating a tunnel in it. He had little interest in throwing snowballs, but as a plastic substance, as a thing that could be made into shapes, the snow was an endless delight to him. In connection with this mound he had conceived an idea in his imagination; except for the interruption of their visitors he would already have put it to the test.

Into the middle of the mound he had bored a tunnel, and then hollowed out what might be called a negative human shape, the mold, as it were, of a life-sized man with his arms and legs stretched out. His object was to try to illuminate it with a lantern to see if the image would shine through the snow. That very night, on his return from Muir of Warlock he had intended to light him up, and now that he was driven out by the cold, he would brave the enemy and make his experiment.

He dressed himself, crept softly out, and for preparation, would have a good run. He trotted down the hill, beating his feet hard, until he reached the more level road where he set out at full speed and was soon warm as any boy would care to be.

About three o'clock in the morning, the laird woke suddenly without knowing why. But it did not take him long to know why he should not go back to sleep again. From a distance, as it seemed, through the stillness of the night, in rapid succession, came three distant shrieks, as from the throat of a human being in mortal terror. He had never heard such shrieks. He could not tell if they came from some part of his own house. He sprang out of bed, thinking first of his boy and next of the old man whom he had left drunk in his bed, and dressed as fast as he could, expecting every moment a renewed assault of the horrible sound. But all he heard was the hasty running of far-off feet.

He hurried down, carefully passing his mother's door. Listening as he passed, he heard nothing, and went on. But in truth the old lady lay in her bed trembling, too terrified to move or utter a sound. In the next room he heard Grizzie moving about, as if like himself getting up and dressing as quickly as she could. Down to the kitchen he ran, hurrying to get outside and to the great door. But when he opened the kitchen door, a strange sight met his eyes and stopped him immediately.

The night was dark as pitch, for, though the snow had ceased to fall, great clouds of it yet filled the vault of the sky, and behind them was no moon from which any glimmer might come soaking through. But on the opposite side of the court, the heap of snow was shining with an unknown, faint phosphorescent radiance. The whole heap was illuminated and was plainly visible. But the strangest thing was that the core of the light had a vague shadowy resemblance to the form of a man. There were the body and outstretched limbs of one who had cast himself on the ground in weariness, ready for the grave which had found him. The vision flickered and faded, revived, and then faded again. In his wonder, the laird forgot the cries that had roused him and stood and gazed. It was the strangest, ghostliest thing he had ever seen! Surely he was on the verge of discovering some phenomenon unknown before this very moment!

What Grizzie would have taken it for, unhappily we do not know, for just as the laird heard her footsteps on the stair, and was himself starting to cross the frozen space toward the strange mound of snow, the light, which had been gradually growing more and more pale, suddenly went out. With its disappearance, the laird remembered the errand which had called him out at this hour, and hurried toward the great door, with Grizzie now at his heels.

He opened it.

All was still. Feeling his way in the thick darkness, he went softly up the stairs.

Cosmo had but just left the last remnants of his candle-ends burning, and climbed back up to his room, delighted with the success of his experiment, when those hideous screams rent the night. His heart stood still. Without knowing why, involuntarily he associated them with what he had just been about, and for a moment felt like a murderer. The next instant he caught up his light and rushed from the room, like his father, to see if there was anything amiss with their guest.

As he reached the bottom of the first stair, the door of his own room opened, and out came Lady Joan, with a cloak thrown over her nightgown, and looking like marble with wide eyes. Yet somehow Cosmo felt it was not she who had shrieked, and passing her without a second look, led the way farther down, and she followed.

When the laird opened the door of the guest chamber, there was his boy in his clothes, with a candle in his hand, and the lady in her nightgown, standing in the middle of the floor, and looking down with dread on their faces. There lay Lord Mergwain—or was it but the deserted house of a living soul? The face was drawn a little to one side, and had a mingled expression of horror and ludicrousness. Upon a closer investigation, the laird almost concluded he was dead. But on the merest chance there was still life within him, they must do something— and quickly. Cosmo seemed dazed, and Lady Joan stood staring with a lost look, more of fright than of sorrow. And there was Grizzie, peeping through between them with bright, searching eyes. On her countenance was neither dismay, anxiety, nor distraction. She nodded her head now and then as she gazed, looking as if she had expected it all, and here it was.

"Run an' fetch hot water as fast as ye can, Grizzie," said the laird. "My dear lady Joan, go and dress, or you will freeze to death. We will do all we can. Cosmo, get the fire up as quickly as possible—it is not quite out. But first you and I must get him into bed and cover him up warm, and I will rub his hands and feet till the hot water comes."

Everyone did as the laird said. A pail of hot water was soon brought, the fire was soon lighted, and the lady soon returned more warmly clad. He made Grizzie put the pail on a chair by the bedside, and they got his feet in without raising him or taking him out of the blankets. Before long he gave a deep sigh, and presently showed other signs of revival. When at length he opened his eyes, he stared around him wildly, and for a moment it seemed he had lost his senses. But the laird said he might not yet have got over the drink he had taken, and if he could be got to sleep, he would wake better in the morning. They removed some more of his clothes, laid him down again, and made him as comfortable as they could, with hot bottles about him. The laird said he would sit with him and would call Lady Joan if it seemed necessary. To judge by her behavior, he gathered that such an occurrence was not altogether strange to her. She went away readily, more like one relieved than anxious.

But there had arisen in the mind of the laird the question of whether Cosmo might without knowing it have had something to do with the frightful event. When first he entered the room, there was Cosmo, dressed and with a light in his hand: the seeming phosphorescence in the snow must have been one of his ploys. Could that have been the source of the shock to the dazed brain of the drinker?

His lordship was breathing more softly and regularly by this time, though every now and then would half wake with a cry—a dreadful thing to hear from a sleeping old man. Father and son drew their chairs close to the fire and to each other.

"Did you see that peculiar appearance in the pile of snow on the other side of the court, Cosmo?" asked the laird.

"Yes, Papa," replied the boy. "I made it myself." He then told him all about his experiment. "You're not upset with me, are you, Papa?" he added, seeing the laird look rather grave.

"No, my son," answered his father. "I am only uneasy about whether that should have had anything to do with this sad affair concerning our guest."

"How could that be, Papa?" asked Cosmo.

"He may have looked out of the window and seen it, and, in the half-foolish stupor he was in, taken it for something supernatural."

"But why should that have done him any harm?"

"It may have terrified him."

"Why should it terrify him?"

"There may be things we don't know about," replied his father. "But I cannot help feeling rather uneasy about it."

"Do *you* see anything frightful about my man of light, Papa?" asked Cosmo.

"No," answered his father thoughtfully. "But the thing was in the shape of a man—a man lying at full length as if he were dead, and indeed in his grave. The poor lord might have taken it for his spirit—an omen of his coming end."

"But he is an Englishman, Papa, and the English don't believe in the second sight."

"That does make it less likely. Few Lowlanders do, be they English or Scotch."

"Do you believe in it, Papa?"

"Well, you see," returned the laird with a slight smile, "like yourself, I am neither pure Highlander nor pure Lowlander, and the natural consequence is that I am not very sure whether I believe in it or not. But I have heard many stories difficult to explain on other terms."

"Still," said Cosmo, "Lord Mergwain would be more to blame himself if the thing caused him a fright, for no man with a good conscience would have been so frightened as that, even at his own wraith."

"That may be true; still I cannot help being sorry anything should happen to a stranger in our house. You and I, Cosmo, would have our house be a place of refuge. Be that as it may, you had better go to bed now. There is no reason in tiring two people when one is enough."

"But, Papa, I got up because I was so cold I couldn't sleep. If you will let me, I would much rather sit with you."

That his son should have been cold in the night distressed the laird. He felt as if he had neglected his own for the sake of strangers. Therefore, he yielded and allowed the boy to remain.

They had talked in low voices for fear of disturbing the sleeper, and now were silent. Cosmo rolled himself in his plaid, lay down at his father's feet on the floor, and was soon fast asleep: with his father there, the room had lost all its terrors. Many a time in after years did that night, that room, that fire, and the feeling of his father over his head, while the bad lord lay snoring within the dark curtains, come back to his mind. And from the memory he would try to remind himself that, if he were toward his great Father in his house as he was then toward his earthly father in his, he would never fear anything.

To know oneself safe amid storm and darkness, amid fire and water, amid disease and pain, even during the approach of death, is to be a Christian, for that is how the Master felt in the hour of darkness, because he knew it as fact.

All night long, at intervals, the old man moaned, and every now and then he would mutter unintelligible sentences, sown with ugly, sometimes fearful words. In the gray of morning he woke.

"Bring me a brandy!" he cried in a voice of discontent.

The laird rose and went to him. When he saw the face above him, a horror came upon him—a look like that they had found frozen on his face in the middle of the night.

"Who are you?" he gasped. "Where am I?"

"You came here in the storm last night, my lord," said the laird.

"Cursed place! I never had such horrible dreams in my life. Where am I—do you hear? Why don't you answer me?"

"You are at Castle Warlock, my lord," replied the laird.

He shrieked at the words, and threw off the covers and sprang from the bed.

"I beg of you, my lord, to lie down again. You were very ill in the night."

"I won't stay another hour in this blasted hole!" roared his guest. "Out of my way, you fool! Where's Joan? Tell her to get up and come directly. Tell her I'm off. I'd as soon go to bed in the snowdrifts than stay another hour in this abominable old lime kiln."

The laird let him rave on: it was useless to oppose him. He grabbed at his clothes to dress himself, but his poor old hands trembled with rage, fear, drink, and eagerness. The laird did his best to help him, but he seemed not even to notice.

"I will get you some hot water, my lord," he said at length, moving toward the door.

"No!" shrieked the old man. "If you go out of that door, I will throw myself out of this window."

The laird turned at once, and in silence waited on him like a servant. He poured him out some cold water, but the man would not use it. He would neither eat nor drink nor wash till he was out of the horrible dungeon, he said. The next moment he cried for water, drank three mouthfuls eagerly, threw the glass from him, and broke it on the hearth.

The instant he was dressed, he dropped into the great chair and closed his eyes.

"Your lordship must allow me to fetch some fuel," said the laird; "the room is growing cold."

"No, I tell you!" cried Lord Mergwain, opening his eyes and sitting up. "If you attempt to leave the room I'll send a bullet after you. God have mercy! what's that at my feet?"

"It's only my son," replied the laird gently. "We have been with you all night—since you were taken ill, that is."

"When was that? What do you mean by that?" he said, looking up sharply, with a face of more intelligence than he had yet shown.

"Your lordship had some sort of fit in the night, and if you do not compose yourself, I fear a return of it."

"You well may, if I stay here," he returned—then, after a pause, "Did I talk?" he asked.

"Yes, my lord—a good deal."

"What did I say?"

"Nothing I could understand, my lord."

"And you did your best, I don't doubt!" rejoined his lordship with a sneer.

"I told your lordship I heard nothing."

"No matter. I don't intend to sleep another night under your roof."

"That will be as it may, my lord."

"What do you mean?"

"Look at the weather, my lord. Cosmo!"

The boy was still asleep, oblivious to the turmoil around him, but at the sound of his name from his father's lips, he started at once to his feet.

"Go and wake Grizzie," said the laird, "and tell her to get breakfast ready as fast as she can. Then bring some peat for the fire and some hot water for his lordship."

Cosmo ran to obey. Grizzie had been up for more than an hour, and was going about with the look of one absorbed in a tale of magic and devilry. Her mouth was closed up tightly as if nothing could make her speak, but her eyes were wide and flashing, and now and then she would nod her head knowingly. Whatever Cosmo required, she attended to at once, but not one solitary word did she utter.

He went back with the fuel and they made up the fire. Lord Mergwain was again lying back exhausted in his chair with his eyes closed.

"Why won't you give me my brandy—do you hear?" he cried all at once. "—Oh, I thought it was my own rascal! Get me some brandy, will you?"

"There is none in the house, my lord," said his host.

"What a miserable sort of inn to keep! No brandy!"

"My lord, you are at Castle Warlock."

"Oh, that's it . . . yes! I remember. I knew your father, or your grandfather, or your grandson, or somebody! I must be gone out of here at once! Tell them to hitch the horses. Little I thought when I left Cairntod where I was going to find myself! I would rather be in hell and have done with it. Lord! Lord! to think of a trifle like that not being forgotten yet! Give me brandy, I tell you. There's some in my coat somewhere. Look, will you! I don't even know where it is!"

He threw himself back in his chair. The laird set about looking for the coat and brandy. Perhaps it would be well to let him have some. But he could find nothing, and made to leave the room to look elsewhere. But his lordship burst out afresh, "I tell you—and confound you for having to be told twice—I will not

be left alone with that child! He's as good as nobody! What could *he* do if—"
Here he left the sentence unfinished.

"Very well, my lord," responded the laird, "I will not leave you. Cosmo shall
go and look for the brandy flask in your lordship's overcoat."

"Yes, yes, good boy! You go and look for it. You're all Cosmos, are you? Will
the line never come to an end? A cursed line for me—if it shouldn't be a rope-
line to hang me with! But I had the best of the grave after all!—though I did lose
my two rings. Confounded old cheating son! It was doing the world a good turn,
and Glenwarlock a better one—Look! what are you listening there for? Would
you hang a man, laird—I mean when you could get no good out of it?"

"I never had occasion to consider the question," answered the laird.

"Ho! ho! haven't you? Let me tell you it's quite time you did consider it. It's
no joke when a man has to decide without time to think. He's pretty sure to decide
wrong."

"That depends, I should think, my lord, on the way in which he has been in
the habit of deciding."

"Come now! none of your Scotch sermons to me! You Scotch always were a
set of hypocrites! Confound the whole nation!"

"To judge by your last speech, my lord—"

"Oh, by my last speech, eh? By my dying declaration? I tell you, it's fairer to
judge a man by anything rather than by his speech. That only serves to hide what
he's thinking. I wish I might be judged by mine, though, and not by my deeds.
I've done a good many things in my time I would rather forget, now that age has
clawed me in his clutches. So have you. So has everybody. I don't see why I should
fare worse than the rest."

At this point Cosmo returned with the brandy flask, which he had found in
the old man's overcoat. His lordship stretched out both hands to it, more eagerly
even than when he had reached for the claret the night before—hands trembling
with feebleness and hunger for strength. Paying no attention to his host's offer
of water and a glass, he put it to his mouth and swallowed three great gulps hurriedly. Then he breathed deeply, drew himself up in the chair, and glanced around
him with a look of gathering arrogance. A kind of fierce question was in his eyes—
as much as to say, *Now, then, what do you make of it all—what do you think of me
and my extraordinary behavior?* After a moment's silence, he said, "What puzzles
me is how the deuce I came, of all places, to this place! I don't believe, in all my
wicked life, I ever made such a fool of myself before—and I've made many a fool
of myself, too!"

Receiving no answer, he took another pull at his flask. The laird stood a little
behind and watched him, harking back upon old stories, putting this and that
together, and resolving to have a talk with old Grannie.

A minute or two more and his lordship got up and proceeded to wash his face
and hands, ordering Cosmo about as if he had been his valet.

"Richard's himself again!" he said in a would-be jaunty voice the moment he had finished, and looked in a cocky sort of way at the laird. But the latter thought he still saw trouble underneath the look.

"Now then, Mr. Warlock, where's this breakfast of yours?" he said.

"For that, my lord," replied the laird, "you must come to the kitchen. The dining room in this weather would freeze the very marrow of your bones."

"I don't want it freezing!" said his lordship with a shudder. "The kitchen, to be sure! I couldn't ask for a better place. I'll be hanged if I enter this room again!" he muttered to himself. "My tastes are quite as simple as yours, Mr. Warlock, though I have not had the same opportunity of indulging them."

He seemed rapidly returning to the semblance of what he would have called a gentleman.

He rose, and the laird led the way. Lord Mergwain followed, and Cosmo, coming immediately behind him, heard him muttering to himself all the way down the stairs: "Mere confounded nonsense! Nothing whatever but the drink!— I must say I prefer the daylight after all. Yes! that's the drawing room. What's done's done—and more than done, for it can't be done again!"

They stepped into a nipping and eager air from the great door. The storm had ceased but the snow lay much deeper, and all the world seemed folded in a shiny death, of which the white mounds were the graves. All the morning it had been snowing busily, for no footsteps were between the two doors but those of Cosmo.

When they reached the kitchen there was a grand fire on the hearth and a great pot on the fire, in which the porridge was swelling in huge bubbles that burst in sighs. Old Grizzie was bustling about; her sense of the awful in no way was to be measured by the degree of her fear: she believed and did not fear— much. She had an instinctive consciousness that a woman was a match for the devil any day.

"I am sorry we have no coffee for your lordship," said the laird. "To tell you the truth, we seldom have anything more for breakfast than our country's porridge. I hope you can take tea? Our Grizzie's scones are good, with plenty of butter."

His lordship had in the meantime taken another pull at his brandy flask, and was growing more and more polite.

"The man would be hard to please," he said, "who would not be enticed to eat by such a display of food. Tea for me, before everything!—How am I to pretend to swallow the stuff?" he murmured to himself.—"But," he went on aloud, "didn't that cheating rascal leave you—"

He stopped abruptly, and the laird saw his eyes fix upon something on the table. Following the look, he saw that it was a certain pepper pot—a piece of old china in the shape of a clumsily made horse, with holes between the ears for the pepper to pour out of.

"I see, my lord," he said, "that you are interested in the pepper pot. It is curious, is it not? It has been in the house a long time—longer than anybody knows. Which of my great-grandmothers let it take her fancy, it is impossible to say. But I suppose the reason it was purchased in the first place is that a horse such as this has been the crest of our family from time immemorial."

"Curse the crest, and the horse too!" said his lordship.

The laird was taken aback by the words. For the last few minutes his guest had been behaving so much like a civilized being that he was not prepared for such a sudden relapse. But the entrance of Lady Joan, looking radiant, diverted the current of things for the moment.

The fact was, that, like many old people, Lord Mergwain had fallen into a habit of speaking in his worse moods without the least restraint. In his better moods, which were indeed only good by comparison, he usually spoke in the same way without even being aware of it.

The rest of the breakfast passed in peace. The visitors had tea, oatcakes, and scones, with fresh butter and jam. Lady Joan, despite all the frost and snow, had a newly laid egg—the only one, while the laird and Cosmo ate their porridge and milk—the latter very scanty at this season of the year, and tasting not a little of turnip—and Grizzie, seated on a stool at some distance from the table, had her porridge with jam. Mrs. Warlock had not yet come out of her room.

When the meal was over, Lord Mergwain turned to his host and said, "Will you oblige me, Mr. Warlock, by sending orders to my coachman to have the horses hitched as soon as possible? We must not infringe anymore on your hospitality. Confound me if I will stay an hour longer in this hole of a place, even though it be daylight!"

"Papa!" cried Lady Joan.

His lordship looked a little confused, and then sought to put the best face on his blunder.

"Pardon me, Mr. Warlock," he said. "I have always had a bad habit of speech, and now that I am an old man I am not improving on it."

"Don't mention it, my lord," returned the laird. "I will go and see about the carriage; but I am more than doubtful."

He left the kitchen and Cosmo followed him. Lord Mergwain turned to his daughter.

"What does the man mean? Doubtful indeed! I tell you, Joan, I am going at once. So don't you side with him if he wants us to stay. He may have his reasons. I knew this confounded place before you were born, and I hate it."

"Very good, Papa!" replied Lady Joan with a slight curl of her lip. "I don't see why you should think I would want to stay."

They had spoken aloud, regardless of Grizzie's presence.

"May it be lang afore ye're in a worse an' a warmer place, my lord, an' my lady," said the old woman, with the greatest politeness of false manner she knew how to assume. When people were rude, she thought she had a right to be rude in return. But they took no more notice than if they had not heard.

15

....

The Next Day

It was a glorious morning. The wind had fallen and the sun was shining as if he would say, *Keep up your hearts; I am up here still. I have not forgotten you.*

But the rest of nature lay dead, with a great white sheet spread over it all. Not dead, for the inner life of the earth can never be killed any more than can the inner life of man. It is only to the eyes of his neighbors that the just man dies. To himself, and to those on the other side, he does not die, but is born instead: "He that liveth and believeth in me shall never die." But the poor old lord felt the approaching dank and cold of the sepulchre as the end of all things to him— if indeed he would be permitted to lie there, and not have to get up and go to worse quarters still.

"I am sorry to have to tell you this, my lord," said the laird when he reentered the kitchen, "that both our roads and your horses are in such a state that it would be impossible for you to proceed today."

His guest turned white through all the discoloration years of drink had brought to his countenance. His very soul grew too white to swear. He stood silent, his thick bottom lip trembling.

"Though the wind fell last night," resumed the laird, "the snow came on again before the morning, and it appears impossible that you could get through. To attempt it would be to run no small risk of your lives."

"Joan," said Lord Mergwain, "go and tell the rascal to hitch the horses."

Lady Joan rose at once, took her shawl, put it over her head, and went. Cosmo ran to open the door for her. The laird looked on and said not a word: the headstrong old man would have to find out for himself that the thing could not be done!

"Will you come and find the coachman for me, Cosmo?" said Lady Joan, reaching the door and turning with a flash of her white teeth and dark eyes that bewitched the boy. For the first time, in the morning light and the brilliance of the snow, he saw that she was beautiful. When the shadows were dark about her, the darkness of her complexion obscured itself. But against the white sheen she stood out darkly radiant. He especially noted the long eyelashes that made a softening twilight round the low horizon-like luminousness of her eyes.

Through the deep snow between the kitchen and the stable were none but his father's footsteps. He cast a glance at her small feet, daintily shod in little more than sandals; she would not be able to put one of them anywhere without sinking beyond her ankle in the snow.

"My lady," he said, "you'll get your feet soaking wet! Please ask your papa if I could go and give his message. It will do just as well."

"I must go myself," she answered. "Sometimes he will trust no one but me."

"Then wait just a moment," said Cosmo. "Come to the drawing room. I won't delay you more than two minutes. The path there, you see, is pretty well trodden."

He led the way, and she followed.

The fire was lit and burning well; for Grizzie had seen what would be the outcome of the affair and determined that she would not have strangers in the kitchen all day. She had therefore lit the fire early. Lady Joan walked straight to it and dropped with a little shiver into a chair in front of the hearth.

Cosmo left her and ran to his own room. He presently returned with a pair of thick woolen stockings, knitted in green and red by his grandmother, and took them to Lady Joan. Within another two or three minutes they were again on their way to the stable. Cosmo heard the coachman, as she called him, whistling at the far end of the room. The lad was not much more than a stableboy. Lady Joan gave him her father's orders.

He stared at her with an open mouth, and then pointed to one of the stalls. There stood an utterly wretched horse, his head hanging down listlessly, not even interested in the food in front of him. It was clear there was no hope there. She turned and looked at Cosmo.

"All the better for us, my lady!" replied Cosmo. "Now we will have your beautiful eyes with us all the longer! They were lost in the dark last night, because they are made of it, but now that we see them, we don't want to part with them."

She looked at him and smiled, thinking to herself that the boy would be dangerous before long. Together they went back to the kitchen, where not a word had been spoken since they had left. Grizzie was removing the breakfast things; Lord Mergwain was seated by the fire, staring into it; and the laird had got his *Journal of George Fox* and was reading diligently: when nothing was to be done, the deeper mind of the laird grew immediately active.

When Lady Joan entered, her father sat up straight in his chair, looking as though he was anticipating opposition.

"One of the horses is quite unfit, my lord," she said.

"Then by my soul, we'll start with the other!" he replied, in a tone that sounded as if it were defying heaven or earth or whatever else said no to him.

"As your lordship pleases," returned Joan.

"My lord," said the laird, lowering his book to his knee, "if I thought four cart horses would pull you through to Howglen before tonight, I would give them to you at once. But you would simply stick, horses and all, in the banks of snow."

The old man uttered an exclamation with an awful solemnity and said no more. He collapsed and sat huddled up, staring into the fire.

"You must just make the best of your quarters here; they are entirely at your service, my lord," said the laird. "We shall not starve. There are sheep on the place, pigs and poultry, and plenty of oatmeal, though very little flour. There is milk, too—and a little wine, and I think we shall do well enough."

Lord Mergwain made no answer, but in his silence seemed to make up his mind to the inevitable.

"Have you any more of that claret?" he asked.

"Not much, I'm sorry to say," answered the laird, "but it is your lordship's while it lasts."

"If it lasts, I shall drink your cellar dry," rejoined his lordship with a feeble grin. "I may as well make a clean breast of it. From my childhood I have never known what it was not to be thirsty. I believe thirst to be the one unfailing birthmark of the family. I was what the Methodists call a drunkard before I was born. My father died of drink. So did my grandfather. You must have some pity on me if I should want more than what seems reasonable. The only faculty ever cultivated in our family was drinking, and I am sorry to say it has not been brought to perfection yet. Perfection is to get drunk and never know it. But I have bad dreams, sir! I have bad dreams! And the worst of it is, if once I have a bad dream, I am sure to have it again, and if it comes first in a strange place, it will come every night until I leave that place. I had a very bad one last night, as you know. I grant it came because I drank too much yesterday, but that won't keep it from coming again tonight."

He jumped to his feet, the muscles of his face working frightfully.

"Send for your horses, Mr. Warlock!" he cried. "Have them hitched at once. Four of them, you said. At once—at once! I must leave. If it be to hell itself, go I must, and will!"

"My lord," said the laird, "I cannot send you from my house in this weather. As your host I am bound to do my best for you, especially as I understand the country and you do not. I said you should have my horses if I thought they could take you through, but I do not think so. Besides, the change in the weather is, in my judgment, a deceitful one. Tonight may be worse than the last. Poor as your accommodation here is, it is better than the open road between here and Howglen, though undoubtedly if you tried it, before tomorrow morning you would be snug in the heart of some pile of snow."

"Look here, sir," said Lord Mergwain, and rising he went up to the laird and laid his hand on his shoulder, "if I stay, will you give me another room, and promise to share it with me tonight? I am aware it is an odd request to make, but, as I tell you, we have been drinking for generations, and my nerves are the worse for it. It's rather hard that the sins of the fathers should be visited on the children. I have enough to mind with my own, let alone my father's! Everyone should bear his own burden. I can't bear mine. If I could, it's not much my father's would trouble me!"

"My lord, I will do anything I can for you—anything but consent to your leaving Castle Warlock today."

"You will spend the night with me then?"

"I will."

"But not in that room, you know."

"Anywhere you please in the house, my lord, except my mother's room."

"Then I'll stay.—Joan, we will not go till tomorrow."

The laird smiled; he doubted the hope of so speedy a departure. Joan turned to Cosmo.

"Will you take me about the place?" she said.

"If you mean indoors," interposed the laird. "It is a curious old house, and might be of some interest to you."

"I should like nothing better. May I go with Cosmo?"

"Certainly. He will be delighted to attend to you. Here are the keys of the cabinets in the drawing room, Cosmo."

"Is the place very old, Cosmo?" asked Lady Joan as they left and went on their way.

"Nobody knows how old the oldest part of it is," answered Cosmo. "But you must ask my father. I don't know much of the history of it, though I know the place itself as well as he does."

"You are very fond of it, then?"

"There could never be any place like it to me, my lady. I know it is not very beautiful, but I love it nonetheless for that. I sometimes think I love it all the more for its ruggedness—even ugliness, if you want to call it that. If my mother had not been beautiful, I should love her all the same."

They arrived in the drawing room and Lady Joan took her former place by the fire. She did not know what to make of all this. How *could* people be happy, she thought, in such a dreary, cold, wretched country, with such poverty-stricken home and surroundings, and nothing to amuse them from one week to another? Yet they seemed happy to a degree completely foreign to her. For alas, her home was far from a blessed one. As she had no fountain of contentment open inside herself, she had to look entirely to foreign supply for her life necessities. And as life's *true* necessities can never be supplied from without, her life was not a flourishing one.

Cosmo proceeded to take some of the family treasures from their shelves, but Lady Joan regarded them listlessly, with her thoughts far away. Now and then she turned a weary gaze toward the window, but all she saw out of it was a great hilly country, dreary as sunshine and white cold could make it. It was a picture of her own life. Evil greater than she knew had spread a winter around her. If her father suffered for the sins of his fathers, she suffered for his, and because of them had to dwell in desolation and loneliness.

"This is said to be solid silver," Cosmo remarked as he showed her a curious little statuette of a horse, decorated with Indian engraving. Its eyes seemed to be rubies, and saddle and bridle and housing were studded with small gems. It was of no particular artistic value, but Cosmo saw the eyes of the lady fixed upon it with a strange look.

"That is the only thing they say the old captain ever gave his brother, my great-grandfather," said Cosmo. "But I'm sorry," he added, "I haven't told you the story of the old captain."

The boy already felt as if he had known their guest for years; the hearts of the young are divinely hospitable. Perhaps that is why the Master said concerning children, "Of such is the kingdom of heaven."

Lady Joan took the horse in her hand and looked at it more closely.

"It is very heavy," she remarked.

"It is said to be solid silver," repeated Cosmo.

She laid it down, and put her hand to her forehead, but said nothing.

They heard the steps and voices of the two gentlemen ascending the stairs. Lady Joan grabbed the horse, rose hastily, held it out to Cosmo, and said, "Quick! quick! put it away. Don't let my father see it!"

Cosmo looked surprised, but obeyed at once, put it back, and had just closed the doors of the cabinet when Lord Mergwain and his father entered the room.

They were a peculiar-looking pair—Lord Mergwain in antiquated dress, quite worn, and not very clean nor in very good condition. He gave the appearance of being a dilapidated, miserable, feeble old man, with a carriage that seemed apprehensive of everything, every other moment casting about him a glance of question, as if an evil spirit came running to the entrance of his eye-caves, looked out, and retreated. Then the laird came behind him, a head higher, looking older than his years, but bearing on his face a look of peace, his keen eyes clear, and, when turned on his guest, filled with compassion rather than hospitality.

"Now, my lord," he said as they advanced from the door, "we will set you in a warm corner by the fire and you must make the best of it. We can't have everything as we would like it. That is not what the world was made for."

His lordship returned him no answer, but threw a look from under his black wig—a look of superior knowledge—of the wisdom of the world.

You are an old fool, it said, *but you are master here. Ah! how little you know!*

He tottered to the fire where Cosmo had already set a chair for him. Something in the look of it displeased him. He glanced round the room.

"Fetch me that chair, my boy," he said, and Cosmo hastened to substitute the one he had indicated. His lordship dropped into the chair and began to rub his knees with his hands and gaze into the fire. Cosmo drew a chair as near Lady Joan as he thought polite. The laird made up the fire and turned away, saying he must go and see the sick horse.

"Mr. Warlock!" said Lord Mergwain, almost with a snarl, "you are not going to deprive us of the only pleasure we have—that of your company?"

"I shall be back in a few minutes, my lord," replied his host, adding, "I must see about lunch, too."

"That was wonderful claret!" said his lordship thoughtfully.

"I shall see to the claret, my lord."

"If I *might* suggest, let it be brought here. A gentle airing under my own eye, just an introduction to the fire, would improve what is otherwise perfect. And," he added as the laird was going, "you haven't got a pack of cards, have you?"

"I believe there is a pack somewhere in the house," replied the laird, "but it is very old, and I fear too much soiled for your lordship's hands."

"Oh, confound the dirt!" said his lordship. "Let us have them. They're the only thing to make the time pass."

"Do you have a library?" asked Lady Joan—mainly to say something, for she was not particularly fond of books; like most people she had not yet really learned to read.

"What do you want with a library?" growled her father. "Books are nothing but a pack of lies, not half so good for killing time as a pack of cards. You're going to play with me, not read books!"

"With pleasure, Papa," responded Lady Joan.

"I don't want to kill the time. I should like to keep it alive forever," said Cosmo with a peaceful look at the beautiful lady.

"Hold your tongue! You are an idiot!" said his lordship angrily. "Old and young," he went on, unaware of what he said, "the breed is idiotic. 'Tis time it were played out."

Cosmo's eyes flashed. But the rude old man was too old to be served as he had served the schoolmaster. He was their guest, too, and the father of the lady by his side.

The hand of the lady stole to his, and patting it gently seemed to say as plainly as if she had spoken, *Don't mind him: he is an old man and does not know what he is saying.* He looked up in her face, and his anger was gone.

"Come with me," he said, rising. "I will show you what books we do have. There may be one you would like another time. We shall be back before the cards come."

"Joan!" cried her father, "sit still."

She glanced an appeal for consideration to Cosmo, and did not move. Cosmo sat down again. A few minutes passed in silence. Father and daughter stared into the fire. So did Cosmo. But into what different three worlds did the fire stare! The old man rose and went to the window.

"I *must* get away from this abominable place," he said, "if it costs me my life."

He looked out and shuddered. The world seemed impassable, a dead world on which the foot of the living could take no hold, could measure no distance, make no progress. Not a print of man or of beast was visible. It was like a world not yet discovered.

"I am as good as tied to the stake . . . I hear the fire roaring already!" he muttered. "My fate has found me, caught me like a rat, and is going to make an end of me! In my time nobody believed such things! Now they seem to be coming into fashion again!"

Just then the laird reentered.

"Well, have you brought the cards?" said Lord Mergwain, turning from the window.

"I have, my lord. I am sorry it is such a poor pack, but we never play.— Cosmo, I think you had better come with me."

"Hold on, laird, we're going to have a game."

"Cosmo does not understand cards."

"I will teach him," said Lady Joan. "He shall be a live dummy for a few rounds; that will be enough for him to learn."

"I doubt you will want to play for mere counters, my lord," persisted the laird, "and we cannot play for money."

"I don't care what the stakes are," said Lord Mergwain, "—sixpence, if you like—so long as it is money. No one but a fool cares for victory where nothing tangible is won by it."

"I am sorry to disappoint your lordship," returned the laird, "but neither my son nor I will play for money. Perhaps you would like a game of backgammon?"

"Will you bet on the game?"

"On nothing, my lord."

"Oh, confound you!"

He turned again and went to the window.

"This is frightful!" he muttered to himself. "Nothing whatever to help one forget. If the day goes on like this I am liable to spill everything. Maybe I should. But I believe I would laugh right in the middle of the telling. And that fellow lurking somewhere all the time about the place, watching his chance when the night comes! It's horrible. I shall go mad!"

He was like a bird in a cage that knows he cannot get out and yet keeps trying. Twenty times that morning he went to the window, saying, "I must get out of here!" and then returned again to his seat by the fire. Lady Joan tried to talk and Cosmo did his best to amuse her. The laird endeavored to entertain his lordship, but with small success. And so the morning crept away. At last Grizzie came with the oddly poetic news, "Sir an' my lord," she said, "come ye doon the stair. The kettle's hot, an' the chairs is set, an' yer dinner's waitin' ye there."

The laird rose and offered his arm to Lady Joan. Lord Mergwain gave a grunt and looked a little pleased at the news; no discomfort or suffering of any kind made him indifferent to luncheon or dinner, for after each came the bottle.

When they reached the kitchen, he looked first eagerly, then uneasily around the room; no bottle or decanter was to be seen! A cloud gathered, lowering and heavy, on his face. The laird saw it, and remembered that he had forgotten his dearest delight, and immediately vanished in the region behind.

As was her custom, Mrs. Warlock was already seated at the head of the table. She bowed her head slightly to his lordship, and motioned him to a chair on her right hand. He took it with a courteous acknowledgment, of which he would hardly have been capable had he not guessed on what errand his host was gone.

"I hope your ladyship is well this morning?" he said.

"Ye revive an auld custom, my lord," returned his hostess, "—clean oot o' fashion noo-a-days. A laird's wife has no right t' be called *my leddy*, 'cept by ancient custom."

"Oh well, if you look at it like that," returned his lordship, "three-fourths of the titles in use today are merely of courtesy. Joan there has no more right than yourself to be called *my lady*. Neither has my son Borland the smallest right to the title *lord*; it is mine, and mine only, as much as Mergwain."

The old lady turned her head sharply and fixed a stolen but searching gaze on her guest, and to the end of the meal took every opportunity to regard him unobserved. From the other end of the table her son saw her looks and guessed her suspicions.

Mrs. Warlock, always ready to welcome anything mysterious, had already discussed at length what had passed in the night with Grizzie—the accidental result of which was the temporary disappearance of all their little rivalries in the common interest of an awful and impending uncertainty. She had never before heard the title to which Lord Borland of the old time was heir. But now that all doubt as to the identity of the man was over, let her strain her vision as she might, she still could not see the youthful visage of the guest of long ago in the face before her, now deformed by the years. *More will surely be heard before next dawn,* she said to herself. *Who can tell what might come as a result of the presence of one in the house who had evidently long waited his arrival? Who can tell, in fact, how much a certain inmate of the house*—she hesitated to call him a member of the family—*and, in all probability, of a worse place as well, had to do with the storm that drove Borland here, and the storms that might detain him there?* Already there were signs of a fresh onset of the elements! The wind was rising; it had begun to moan in the chimney, and from the direction from which it now blew it was certain to bring more snow.

The dinner went on. The great decanter before the fire was gathering genial might from the soft insinuation of limpid warmth, renewing as much of its youth as was to be desired in wine. But there was not a drop to drink on the table except water, and the old lord found it hard not to grumble inwardly. The sight of the bottle before the fire, however, did much to enable him, not to be patient, but he kept eyeing the bottle, and gathering comfort.

Grizzie eyed him from behind, almost as he eyed the bottle. She eyed him as she might the devil caught in the toils of the archangel; and if she did not bring against him a railing accusation, it was more from cunning than politeness. *Ah, my fine fellow!* her eyes said, *He is after you! He will be here presently!*

Grizzie afforded a perfect example of a relation that is one of the loveliest in humanity—absolute service without a shade of servility. She would have died for her master, but even to him she must speak her mind. She worshiped one living man, and that is the first step toward the love of all men. Some will talk glowingly about humanity, and be scornful as a dog to the next needy embodiment of it that comes their way. She would have wept bitter tears had the privilege of washing the laird's feet been taken from her. With the tenderness of a ministering angel and mother combined, her eyes waited upon her master. And in return she took comfort in the assurance that the laird would follow her to the grave, would miss her, and at times think that nobody could do something or other so much to his liking as old Grizzie. And if, like the old captain, she might be permitted to creep about the place after nightfall, she desired nothing better than the chance of serving him still, if but by rolling a stone out of his way.

16

•••••••••••••••••

Grizzie's Tale

*W*hen dinner was over the laird asked his guest whether he would take his wine where he was or in the drawing room. He declined the proposal, on the ground of respect for her ladyship's apartment. So the old lord sat in the kitchen and drank his wine; and the old lady sat by the fire and knitted her stocking, went to sleep, and woke up, and went to sleep again a score of times, and enjoyed her afternoon. Not a word passed between the two: now, in his old age, Lord Mergwain never talked over his bottle; he gave his mind to it.

The laird went and came, unconsciously anxious to be out of the way of his guest, and consciously anxious not to neglect him, but nothing was said on either side. The old lady knitted and dozed, and his lordship sat and drank. And as he drank, the braver he grew, and the more confident that the events of the past night were but the foolish consequences of having mingled so many liquors, which, from the state of the thermometer, had grown cold in his stomach and bred wierd fancies. *With two bottles like this under my belt,* he said to himself, *I would defy them all, but this stupid curmudgeon of a host will never fetch me a second! If he had not been so stingy last night, I should have got through it well enough!*

Lady Joan and Cosmo had been all over the house, and were now sitting in the drawing room, silent in the firelight. Lady Joan did not yet find Cosmo much of a companion, though she liked to have him beside her, and would have felt the dreariness more penetrating without him. But to Cosmo her presence was an experience as marvelous and lovely as it was new and strange.

"Shall I tell you a story, my lady?" he said.

"Yes, if you please," she answered, finding herself caught in a shoal of sad thoughts, and willing to let them drift.

"Then I will try. But I doubt I can tell it as well as Grizzie told it to me. Her old-fashioned way suits the story. And then I must make English of the Scots so that your ladyship will understand it, and that goes still worse with it."

"Do try, anyway," she said.

"There was once a girl in the Highlands," began Cosmo, "—not very far from here it was, who was so beautiful that every young man in the neighborhood fell in love with her. She was the daughter of a sheep farmer who had a great many sheep that fed about over the hills, and she helped her father to look after them, and was as good and obedient as any lamb of his flock. Her name was Mary.

"Her father had a young shepherd a year or two older than Mary, and of course he was in love with her, too. He was very strong and very handsome, and a good shepherd. He was out on the hills all day, from morning to night, seeing that the sheep did their duty and ate plenty of grass, so as to give plenty of good wool and good mutton when it was wanted.—That's the way Grizzie tells the story, my lady, though not so you would understand her.—And it came to pass that the young shepherd and Mary grew fond of each other. But Mary's father was too well off to show favor to a poor shepherd lad. He told Alister that he would never let his daughter marry him, and he told Mary that she must have nothing more to do with or say to Alister. Mary felt obliged to do what her father told her, but in her heart she did not give up Alister, and felt sure that Alister did not give her up, for he was a brave and honest youth.

"Of course, Alister was always wanting to see Mary, and did see her many times when nobody, not even Mary herself, knew it. One day she was out on the hill rather late, and when the gloaming came down, she sat on a stone wishing in her heart that she might see Alister. Suddenly from out of the descending darkness someone came running toward her. But it was not Alister, but a local farmer, a man who was also in love with Mary, though people said he was a coward.

"Now just at that time a terrible story was going about the glen of a beast in the hills that went about biting every living thing he could get at. And whatever he bit went raving mad and eventually died. He just came up with a rush, bit whatever creature he was attacking, and was out of sight in a moment. He appeared—nobody ever saw from where—and was gone. There was great terror wherever the story was heard, so that people would hardly go out of doors after sundown. Some said it was a sheepdog, but some who thought they had seen it said it was too large for any collie, and was, they believed, a mad wolf; for though there are no wolves in Scotland now, my lady, there were at one time, and this is a very old story."

Lady Joan yawned audibly.

"I am wearing you, my lady," said Cosmo.

"No, no, dear boy!" answered Lady Joan, a little ashamed of herself. "It is only that I am very tired. I think the cold does that to one."

"I will tell you the rest another time," said Cosmo.

"No, no; please go on. I want to hear the rest of it."

"Well," resumed Cosmo, "the news of this wolf, or whatever it was, had come to this farmer that very day for the first time, and he was hurrying home with his head and his heart and his heels full of it. And when he saw Mary sitting on the white stone by the path, feeling as safe as she could be, instead of stopping and taking her and her sheep home, he hurried past her, crying out, 'Gae hame, Mary. There's a mad beast on the hill. Rin, rin—as fast as ye can. Never min' yer sheep.' His last words came from a good distance away, for he never even slowed his step while he spoke to her.

"Mary got up at once. But you may be sure, my lady, that a girl like that was not going to leave her sheep alone on the hill. She began to gather them together, and was just setting out with them for home when a creature like a huge dog came bounding upon her out of the edge of the night. The same instant, up from behind a rock a few yards away, jumped Alister, and made straight for the beast with his staff. He was not near enough to get between Mary and the beast, but just as the wolf was upon Mary he got close enough, and heaved a great blow at him, which would have knocked him down anyway. But at that very instant Mary threw herself toward Alister, and his terrible blow came down upon her—that's what Grizzie says—and away went the wolf, leaping and bounding, and never uttering a cry.

"What Alister did next, Grizzie never says—only that he came staggering up to her father's door with dead Mary in his arms, carried her in, laid her on the bed, and left again. They found the blow on her head, and when they undressed her they also found the bite of the wolf. And they soon guessed how it had been, and said it was well she had died so, for it was much better than going mad first. But the farmer, because he already hated Alister, and knew that Alister must have seen him running away, told everyone that he himself was rushing to defend Mary and that the blow that killed her from Alister's hand was meant for him. But very few people believed him.

"From that day Alister left his shepherding and gave himself to the hunting of the mad wolf: such a creature should not be allowed to live, and he must do some good thing for Mary's sake. So he followed and followed, hunting the horrible creature to destroy him. Some said he lived on his hate of the wolf, never eating anything at all. But some of the people of the hills, when they heard he had been seen, set out in front of their doors at night milk and oatcakes. And in the morning, sometimes, they would be gone, taken as if by a human being and not an animal.

"By and by a strange story came to be told. For a certain old woman, whom everyone said had the second sight, said that one night late, as she was coming home from her daughter's house, she saw Alister lying in the heather, and another sitting with him. She saw Alister plain enough with her first or bodily eyes. But with her second eyes, in which lay the second sight, she saw his head lying on a woman's lap—and that woman was Mary, whom he had killed. He was fast asleep, and whether he knew what pillow his head was lying on, she could not tell. But she saw the woman as plainly as if with her bodily eyes—only with the difference which there always was, she said, and which she did not know how to describe, between the things seen by the one pair of eyes and the things seen by the other.

"She stood and looked at them for some time, but neither moved. It was in the twilight, and as it grew darker she could see Alister less and less clearly, but always Mary better and better—till at last the moon rose, and then she saw Alister again, and Mary no more. But, through the moonlight, three times she heard a little moan, half very glad, and half a little sad.

"When they heard the wise woman's story, the people—who had something of a horror of Alister because of his having killed a human being—began to feel differently toward him, and to look rather disapprovingly upon Mary's father, whose unkindness had kept them apart. They now began to say that God had sent the wolf to fetch Mary that he might give her and Alister to each other in spite of Mary's father—for God had many a way of doing a thing, every one better than another.

"But that did not help Alister find the wolf. The winter came, however, and that did help him, for the snow let him see the trail and follow it faster. The wonder was that the animal, being mad, lived so long; but some said that although the wolf was mad, he was not mad in the ordinary way.

"At last, one morning in the month of December, when the snow lay heavy on the ground, some men came upon a track which they all agreed must be that of the wolf. They went and got their weapons and set out after it. They followed and followed, and the trail led them high into the hills. They came at length to a point where a human track joined that of the wolf, and they concluded that Alister was after him. Up and up the mountain they went—sometimes losing the track from the great springs the wolf took—now across a great chasm which they had to go around, now up the face of a rock too steep for the snow to lie upon. The human track sometimes followed it, sometimes disappeared for long spaces at a time.

"But at last, almost at the top of the mountain, they saw before them two dark spots in a little hollow, and when they reached it, there was the wolf, dead in a mass of frozen blood and trampled snow. It was a huge, gaunt, gray carcass, with the foam frozen about its jaws and stabbed in many places, which showed the fight had been a close one. All the snow was beaten about, as if with many feet, which showed still more plainly what a tussle it had been. A little farther on lay Alister, as if asleep, stretched at full length, with his face to the sky. He had been dead for many hours, they thought, but the smile had not faded, which his spirit left behind as it went. All about his body were the marks of the brute's teeth—everywhere except on his face. That had been splattered with blood, but it had been wiped away. His dirk was lying not far off, and his skean dhu close by his hand.

"There is but one thing more—and I think that is just the thing that made me want to tell you the story. The men who found Alister declared when they came home, and ever after when they told the story—Grizzie says her grand-mother used always to say so—that when they lifted him to bring him away, they saw in the snow the mark of his body, deep-pressed into the snow, but only as far as his shoulders. There was no mark of the head whatever. And when they told this to the wise woman, she answered only, 'Of coorse! of coorse! if I had been wi' ye, lads, I would hae seen more!' When they pressed her to speak more plainly, she only shook her head and muttered, 'Dull-witted gowks!' That's all, my lady."

In the kitchen things were going on even more quietly than in the drawing room. The English lord sat in front of the fire with his wine. Mistress Warlock sat in her armchair, knitting and dozing. The laird had taken his place at the other corner and was again reading the *Journal of George Fox*. And Grizzie was bustling about with less noise than she liked and wishing heartily she were free of his lord-ship that she might get on with her work. Scarcely a word was spoken.

It began to grow dark; the lid of the night was closing upon them before half a summer's day would have been over. But it mattered little; the snow had put a stop to the work of the world. Grizzie put on the kettle for her mistress's tea. The old lady turned her forty winks into four hundred and slept outright. All at once his lordship came alive to the fact that the day was gone, shifted uneasily in his chair, poured out a bumper of claret, drank it quickly, and pulled his chair a little nearer to the fire.

His hostess saw these movements with satisfaction: her soul was not hospitable toward him, and the devil in her was gratified with the sight of his discomposure. Her eyes sought those of Grizzie.

"Go t' the door, Grizzie," she said, "an' see what the night's like. I'm thinkin' by the cry o' the win', it'll be a wull mirk again.—What think ye, laird?"

Her son looked up from his book, where he had been beholding a large breadth of light on the spiritual sky, and answered, somewhat abstractedly, but with the gentle politeness he always showed her, "I should not wonder if it came on to snow again."

Lord Mergwain shifted uneasily. Grizzie returned from her inspection of the weather.

"It's black oot, wi' great thuds o' win'," she said.

"Had we better not go to the drawing room, my lord?" said the laird. "I think, Grizzie," he went on, "you must get supper early."

His lordship sat as if he did not mean to move.

"Will you not come, Lord Mergwain?" said the laird. "We had better go before the night gets worse."

"I will stay where I am."

"Come, my lord, I will carry your wine."

"The bottle is empty," replied his lordship gruffly, as if reproaching his host for not being aware of the fact and having another at hand to follow.

"Then—" said the laird, and hesitated.

"Then you'll fetch me another!" put in his lordship, as if answering an unposed question that ought not even be asked. "I won't stir a peg without it. Get me another large bottle at once!"

The laird reflected another moment, then turned and disappeared into the milk cellar, from which a steep stone stairway led down to the ancient dungeon.

"The master's gone wi'oot a light," muttered Grizzie. "I hope he winna see anythin'."

It was an enigmatical utterance, and it angered Lord Mergwain.

"What the deuce should he see when he has to feel his way with his hands?" he snarled.

"There's some things, my lord, that can better afford t' come oot in the dark than in the light," replied Grizzie.

His lordship said nothing in rejoinder, but kept looking every now and then toward the door of the milk cellar—whether solely in anxiety for the appearance of the wine may be doubtful. The moment the laird emerged from his dive into the darkness, bearing with him the pearl-oyster of its deep, his lordship rose, proud that for an old man he could stand so steady, and straightened himself up to his full height, which was not so great. He made to follow the laird, catching up the first bottle before they left the room in which, notwithstanding his assertion, he knew there was yet a glass or two. The laird gave his guest an arm, and Grizzie, leaving the door open to cast a little light on their way, followed close behind.

When they reached the drawing room, his lordship, out of breath from the long flight of stairs, they found Lady Joan teaching Cosmo backgammon. They got his lordship into his chair by the fire, with a small table by him with the first bottle on it, and the fresh one at his feet in front of the fire: with the contents of one such inside him, and another coming on, he looked more cheerful than since first he entered the house. But a look of trouble was nevertheless visible in his countenance.

A few poverty-stricken attempts at conversation followed, to which Lord Mergwain contributed nothing. Lost in himself, he kept his eyes fixed on the ripening bottle, waiting with heroic self-denial.

Presently Grizzie came with the tea things, and as she set them down, remarked with cunningly devised look of unconsciousness: " 'Tis a gurly night; no a pinch o' light. An' the win' blawin' like deevils; the Power o' the air, he's oot wi' a rair, an' the snow rins roon' upon sweevils."

"What do you mean, woman? Would you drive me mad with your gibberish?" cried his lordship, getting up and going to the window.

"Ow, na, my lord!" returned Grizzie quietly. "Mad's mad, but there's worse than mad."

"Grizzie!" said the laird, and she did not speak again.

Lurking in Grizzie was the suspicion, less than latent in the minds of the few who had any memory of the old captain, that he had been robbed as well as murdered—though nothing had ever been missed that was known to belong to him, except indeed an odd walking stick he used to carry. And if this was so, then the property, whatever it was, had belonged to his rightful heir, Warlock of Glenwarlock. Hence mainly arose Grizzie's desire to play upon the fears of the English lord; for might he not be driven by sheer terror to make restitution?

The laird fetched a book of old ballads and offered to read one or two to make the time pass. Lord Mergwain gave a scornful grunt, but Lady Joan welcomed the proposal. For more than an hour the laird read ballad after ballad, but nobody, not even himself, paid very close attention. But the time passed. His lordship grew sleepy, began to nod, and seemed to forget his wine. At length he fell asleep. But when the laird would have made him more comfortable, with a yell of defiance he started to his feet wide awake. Coming to himself at once, he tried to laugh, and said from his childhood he had been furious when waked suddenly. Then he settled himself in the chair and fell fast asleep again.

Still the evening wore on. Suppertime came. His lordship woke, but would have no supper and took to his bottle again. Lady Joan and Cosmo went to the kitchen, and the laird had his porridge brought up to the drawing room.

Finally it was time to go to bed. Lady Joan retired. The laird would not allow Cosmo to sit up another night, and he went also. The lord and the laird were left together, the one again asleep and dreaming who knows what, the other wide awake, but absorbed in the story of a man whose thoughts, fresh from above, were life to himself and a mockery to his generation.

17

....

The Captain's Revenge

The wind had now risen to blizzard force.

The house was like a rock assaulted by the waves of an ocean tempest. The laird had closed all the shutters and drawn the old curtains across them. The sturdy old house did not shake, for nothing other than an earthquake could have made it tremble. The snow was fast gathering in heaps on the windowsills, on the frames, and every smallest ledge where it could lie. In the midst of the blackness and the roaring wind, the house was being covered with spots of silent whiteness, resting on every projection, every rough edge of the building. In his own house as he was, a sense of fierce desolation and foreign invasion took possession of the soul of the laird. He had made a huge fire and heaped up beside it great stores of fuel, but, though his body was warm, his soul inside it felt the ravaging cold outside.

By the fire he had placed for his lordship the antique brocade-covered sofa that he might lie down when he pleased, and himself occupied the great chair on the other side. From the center of this fire-defended heart, even the rest of the room outside it looked cold and waste. And all around them the wind and snow raved; the clouds that garnered the snow, shaken by mad winds, whirled and tossed and buffeted to make them yield their treasures. Lord Mergwain heard it, and drank. The laird listened, and lifted up his heart. Not much passed between them. The memories of the English lord were not such as he felt it fit to share with the dull old Scotsman beside him who knew nothing of the world. Men who salute a neighbor as a man of the world, paying him the greatest compliment they know in acknowledging him of their kind, recoil with a sort of fear from the man who is alien to them. Lord Mergwain regarded the odd-looking laird as a fool; the laird looked on him with something of the pity an angel must feel for the wretch to whom he is sent to give his last chance before the sorer and more painful measures be taken in which angels are not the ministers.

But the wine was at last beginning to work its too-oft repeated influence on the sagging and much-frayed nerves of the old man. A yellowish remnant of withered pink began to smear his far-off west: he dared not look to the east; that lay terribly cold and gray.

He smiled with a little curl of his lip now and then, as he thought of the advantages he had had in the game of life. For alas! it had never with him risen to the dignity of a battle. He was as proud of a successful ruse as a hero of a well-fought and well-won battle on the field. "I had him there!" stood with him for the joy of a job well done.

Seeming to himself as he drank to gradually be recovering the common sense of his self-vaunted nature, he assured himself that he now saw plainly the true facts of things—that his present outlook and vision were correct, and the horrors of the previous night were nothing more than the result of an upset stomach. He was a man once more.

Alas for the man who draws his courage from drink! Alas, too, for the man who draws his courage from his health, or any other passing strength. The touch of a pin on this or that spot of his mortal house will change him from a leader of armies or a hunter of tigers in the jungle to one who shudders at a centipede!

A glass or two more, and his lordship found himself laughing at the terror of the night. He had been a thorough fool not to go to bed like other people, instead of sitting by the fire with a porridge-eating Scotsman, who regarded him as one of the wicked, afraid of the darkness. The thought may have passed from his mind to that of his host, for almost the same moment the laird spoke.

"Don't you think you had better go to bed when you have finished your bottle, my lord?"

With the words a cold swell, as from the returning tide of some dead sea, stole in, swift and black, filling every cranny of the old man's conscious being.

"I thought better of you than that, laird!" he cried. "I took you for a man of your word. You promised to sit up with me!"

"I did, my lord, and I am ready to keep my promise. I only thought you looked as if you might have changed your mind. And in such a night as this, bed is the best place for everybody."

"That depends," answered his lordship, and took a drink.

"Would your lordship think me rude if I were to take a book?"

"I don't want a noise. It doesn't go well with old wine like this. It would only spoil it. No, thank you."

"I did not propose to read aloud, my lord—only to myself."

"Oh, that changes the matter. I wouldn't object to that."

The laird got his Journal and was soon lost in the communion of a kindred soul.

By and by the boat of his lordship's brain was again drifting toward the side of such imagination as was in him, as intoxication began to set in. He began to cast uneasy glances toward the book the laird was holding.

"What's that you are reading?" he said at length. "It looks like a book of magic."

"On the contrary," replied the laird, "it is a religious book of the very best sort."

"Oh, indeed! Well, I have no objection to a little religion—in its own place. There it is all right."

"Would your lordship like to hear a little of the book, then?"

"No, no! by no means! Things sacred ought not to be mixed up with the everyday. I keep my religion for church. That is the proper place for it, and there you are in the mood for it. Do not mistake me; it is out of respect that I decline."

He drank, and the laird dropped back into the depths of his volume. The night wore on. His lordship did not drink fast. There was no hope of another bottle, and the wine must cover the entire period of his necessity: he dared not encounter the night without the sustaining knowledge of its presence. At last he began to nod, and by slow degrees sank on the sofa. Very softly the laird covered him and went back to his book.

The storm went raging on as if it would never stop. The minutes crawled slowly along. The laird, giving all his attention to George Fox, lost all measure of time, because he read with delight. At last he found himself invaded by that soft physical peace which heralds the approach of sleep. He tried to rouse himself. He wanted to read, for he was in one of the most interesting passages he had yet come to. But he could not fend off the sweet enemy, and soon fell into a soundless and dreamless sleep.

He woke so suddenly that for a moment he hardly knew even himself. There lay upon him the weight of an indefinable oppression—the horror of a darkness too vague to be combated. The fire had burned low and his very bones seemed to shiver. The candle flames were down in the sockets of the candlesticks, and the voice of the storm outside was like a scream of victory.

He cast his eyes on his guest. Sleeping still, he half lay, half leaned in the corner of the sofa, breathing heavily. He could not see his face clearly because of the flapping and flickering of the candle flames and the shadows they sent waving all over. Suddenly, without opening his eyes, the old man raised himself to a sitting posture. For the first time the laird then saw his face more clearly, and upon it the expression as of one suffering from some horrible nightmare—terrified, wrathful, and disgusted, all in one. He rose quickly to rouse him from his drunken dream. But before he reached him, the old man's eyes opened, and his expression changed—not to one of relief, but to utter collapse, as if the sleep-dulled horrors of the dream had now grown all the more real to him as he woke. His lips trembled, his right arm rose slowly from the shoulder and stuck straight out in the direction of his host, while his hand hung from the wrist, and he stared as if he was gazing upon the tormenting horrors of hell that had come to lay their claim upon him.

But it did not seem to the laird that, even though he was looking straight toward him, his eyes were resting on him. They appeared to be focused instead on something beyond him. It was like the stare of one demented, and it invaded—possessed the laird. A physical terror seized him. He felt the skin of his head contracting; his hair was about to stand on end! He forced himself forward a step to lay his hand on Lord Mergwain and bring him to himself. But his lordship uttered a terrible cry, between a scream and a yell, and sank back on the sofa. The same instant the spell was broken and the laird was himself again, and he sprang forward to his guest.

Lord Mergwain lay with his mouth wide open and the same look with which they had found him the night before in the guest room. His arm stuck straight out from his body. The laird pressed it down, but it rose again as soon as he let go. He could not for a moment doubt that the man was dead. There was that about him which assured him of it; what it was he could not have told.

The first thought that came to him was that his daughter must not see him so. He tied up his jaw, laid him on the sofa, lighted fresh candles, and went to call Grizzie.

He felt his way down the dark stair, fought his way through the wind to the kitchen, from which he climbed to Grizzie's room. He found she was already out of bed and putting on her clothes. She had not been asleep, she said, and added something obscure which the laird took to mean that she had been expecting a summons.

"He's gone t' his account, Grizzie," said the laird in a trembling voice.

"Ye winna wake the hoose, will ye?" she said. "I dinna think it would be any service t' deid or livin'."

"I'll not do that, Grizzie. But come ye an' look at him," said the laird, "an' tell what ye think. I haena doobt he's deid, but if ye hae any, we'll do what we can. Then we'll sit up wi' the corpse t'gether, an' let yoong an' auld take the rest they hae more need o' than the likes o' you an' me."

It was a proud moment in Grizzie's life, one she never forgot, when the laird addressed her thus. She was ready in a moment and they went together.

"The Prince is haein' his way t'night!" she murmured to herself as they bored their way through the wind to the great door.

When she came to where the corpse lay, she stood for some moments looking down upon it without uttering a sound. There was no emotion in the fixed gaze of her eye. She had been brought up in a stern school. She made neither solemn reflection, nor uttered hope which her theology forbade her to cherish.

"Ye think wi' me that he's deid—dinna ye, Grizzie?" said the laird, in a voice that seemed to himself to intrude on the solemn silence.

She removed the handkerchief and the jaw fell.

"He's gone t' his accoont," she said. "It's a great amoont, an' more on the ill side than he'll weel be able t' stan'. 'Tis sad enough, Laird, when we hae t' go at the Lord's call, but when the messenger comes from the low gate, we must jist let go an' forget. But so long as he's a man, we must do what we can—an' that's what we did last night; so I'll run an' get hot water."

She did so, and they used every means they could think of for his recovery, but at length gave it up, heaped him over with blankets, for the last chance of spontaneous revival, and then sat down together and awaited the slow-traveling, feeble dawn.

After they had sat in silence for nearly an hour, the laird spoke.

"We'll read a Psalm together, Grizzie," he said.

"Ay, do that, Laird. It'll keep them away for the time bein', though it can profit but little in the end."

The laird drew from his pocket a small, much-worn Bible that had been his Marion's, and by the body of the dead sinner, in the heart of the howling storm and the waste of the night, he read the words of the ninety-first Psalm.

When he ended, they were aware that the storm had begun to yield, and by slow degrees it sank as the morning came on. Nothing more was said between them until the first faintest glimmer of dawn began to appear. Then Grizzie rose, like one who had overstepped her work, and said: "I must t' my work, Laird—what think ye?"

The laird rose also, and by a common impulse they went and looked at the corpse—for corpse it now was, beyond all question, cold as the snow outside. After a brief, low-voiced conference, they proceeded to carry it to the guest room, where they laid it upon the bed and covered it with a sheet, dead in the room where it dared not sleep, a mound of cold and white as any snow-wreath outside. It looked as if Winter had forced his way into the house, and left this one snow-drift. Grizzie went about her duties, and the laird back to his book.

A great awe fell upon Cosmo when he heard what visit and what departure had taken place in the midst of the storm and darkness. Lady Joan turned white as the dead and spoke not a word. A few tears rolled from the luminous dark of her eyes, like the dew slow gathering in a night of stars, but she was very still. The bond between her and her father had not been a pleasant one. The laird persuaded her not to see the body.

All that day things went on in the house much as usual, with a little more silence perhaps. The wind unmoving on the frozen earth; the sun shone cold as a diamond; and the fresh snow glittered and gleamed and sparkled like a dead sea of lightning.

The laird was just thinking which of his men to send to the village when the door opened and in came Agnes. Grannie had sent her, she said, to inquire after them. Grannie had had a troubled night, and the moment she awoke began to talk about the laird, his visitors, and what the storm must have been like round lonely Castle Warlock. The drifts were tremendous, she said, but she had made her way without too much difficulty. So the laird, partly to send Cosmo from the house of death into the world of life, told him to go with Aggie, and give directions to the carpenter for the making of a coffin.

How long the body might have to lie with them, no one could tell, for the storm had stopped in a hard frost, and there could be no postal communication for many days. The laird judged it better, therefore, as soon as the coffin arrived, to place the body in a death-chapel prepared for it by nature herself. With their shovels he and Cosmo fashioned the mound, already hollowed by the boy in play, into the shape of a large rectangle, then opened wide the side of it, to receive the coffin as into a sepulchre in a rock. The men brought it, laid it in, and closed the entrance again with snow. Where Cosmo's hollow man of light had shone, lay the body of the wicked old nobleman.

18

....

Lady Joan

The same day Lady Joan wrote to her brother Borland, now Lord Mergwain, telling him what had taken place. But it would be quite some time before she received his answer, for the mail from England reached the neighboring city but intermittently, and was there stopped altogether, so far as Howglen and Muir of Warlock were concerned. The laird told her she must have patience, and assured her that her continuing presence was welcome to them.

The following weeks were for Cosmo ones of enchantment, as wondrous as any dream, for it had at the heart of it the deeper marvel of a live and beautiful lady.

Lady Joan looked older than she was, but she would be eighteen and a woman before long. Both her life consciousness and her spirits—only in a few do they mean the same—had been kept down by her family relations. Her father, since his health had begun to decline, would go nowhere without her, though he spoke seldom a pleasant, and often a very unpleasant, word to her. He never praised her to her face. When at home she always had to be within his reach. There he lived much as we have seen him in the laird's house, caring for nobody's comfort but his own and difficult to keep in good humor. He paid no attention to business: his estates had long been under trustees. He lolled about in his room, diverting himself with a horrible monkey he taught ugly tricks, drank almost constantly, and threw dice by himself for hours on end—doing what he could, which was little, toward the poor object of killing time.

Joan's brother Borland was of the respectably selfish class. He knew his presence was a certain protection to her, yet he gave himself no trouble to look after her; he was not his sister's keeper. Therefore, at home Joan led a lonely life where everything around her was left to run wild. The lawn had become a meadow, and the park a mere pasture for cattle. The shrubbery was an impassable tangle, and the flower garden a wilderness. She could do nothing to set things right, and lived about the place like a poor relation. At school, which she left at fifteen, she had learned nothing to be of any vital use to her. Without a mother, without a companion, she had to find what solace and pastime she could. In the huge house there was not a piano fit to play on, and her only source of indoor amusement was a library containing a large disproportion of books in old French bindings, with much tarnished gilding on the backs, having been imported to decorate the walls with the illusion of knowledge rather than because anyone in the family possessed any love for the insides, or souls, of books. Still, a native purity of soul kept her lovely, and capable of becoming lovelier.

The mystery of all mysteries is the upward tendency of so many souls through so much that would defile their wings, while so many others, perhaps with great outward advantages, seem never to look up at all. But the keenest of moral philosophers are but poor mole-eyed creatures! One day, I trust, we shall laugh at many a difficulty that now seems insurmountable.

Lady Joan did not like ugly things, and so shrank from evil things. She was the less in danger from liberty because of the disgust in her of the tones and words of her father. She had learned self-defense early.

The day after her father died, Cosmo proposed to Lady Joan a walk in the snow. He saw her properly provided for with ample clothing, and they set out together in the brilliant light of a rapidly declining western sun, even though it had but just passed the low noon. The moment she stepped from the threshold, Joan was invaded by an almost giddy sense of freedom. The keen air and the impeding snow sent the warm blood to her cheeks, and her heart beat as if newborn into a better world. She was annoyed with herself. But it was in vain that she called herself heartless and indifferent to the loss of her father. How could she feel so terrible? There was the sun in the sky—not warm, but dazzling bright and shining straight into her very being! The air, instinct with life, was filling her lungs like water drunk by a thirsty soul. Life, for the first time in years, seemed good! It was a blessed thing for the eyes to behold the wonders of nature. Let death do what it can, there is just one thing it cannot destroy, and that is life!

Over the stream's torrent they walked on a bridge of snow, and listening could hear, far down, hidden below the thick white blanket, the noise of its hidden rushing. Away and up the hill they went; the hidden torrent of Joan's blood flowed clearer, and her heart sang to her soul. Everything began to look to her like something in a story—herself a princess, and her attendant a younger brother, traveling with her to meet the tide of adventure. Such a brother was a luxury she had never had—very different from an older one. He talked so strangely too—at one moment like a child, at the next like an old man! She felt a charm in both, but understood neither. Through confidence in his father, he was capable of receiving wisdom far beyond what he could have thought out for himself, and he sometimes said things that seemed to most who heard them far beyond his years. Some people only understand enough of a truth to reject it, but Cosmo's reception by faith turned to sight, as all true faith does at last, and formed a soil for thought more immediately than his own.

They had been climbing a steep hill, very difficult in the snow, and had finally reached the top, where they stood for a moment panting, with another ascent beyond them.

"Don't you find yourself always wanting to climb and climb, Lady Joan?" said the boy.

"Call me Joan, and I will answer you."

"Then, Joan—don't you always want to be getting up higher than you are?"

"No, I don't think I do."

"I believe you do, only you don't know it. When I get on the top of that hill there, it always seems to me such a little way up! And Mr. Simon tells me I should feel much the same, even if it were the top of the highest peak in the Himalayas."

Lady Joan did not reply, and Cosmo too was silent for a time.

"Don't you think," he began again, "though life is so very good, that you would get very tired if you thought you had to live in this world always—for ever and ever, and never, never get out of it?"

"No, I don't," said Joan. "I can't say I find life so nice as you think it, but one keeps hoping it may turn to something better."

She was amused with his talk—so manly and beyond his years!

"There must be more out there," he said. "Otherwise there would be no promise in the stars. They look like promises now, don't they? I do not believe God would ever show us a thing he did not mean to give us."

"You are a very odd boy, Cosmo. I am almost afraid to listen to you. You say such presumptuous things!"

Cosmo laughed a little gentle laugh.

"How can you love God, Joan, and be afraid to speak before him? I should no more dream of his being angry with me for thinking he made me for great and glad things, and was altogether generous toward me, than I could imagine my father angry with me for wishing to be as wise and as good as he is, when I know it is wise and good he most wants me to be."

"Ah, but he is your father, you know, and that is very different!"

"I know it is very different—God is so much, much more my Father than is the laird of Glenwarlock! He is even nearer to me, though my father is the best father that ever lived. God, you know, Joan, is more than anybody knows what to say about. Sometimes, when I am lying in bed at night, my heart swells to think of it. You think it strange that I talk so?"

"Rather, yes—I must confess so. Is it a good thing to think so much about religion at your age? There is a time for everything. You talk like one of those good little children in books that always die—at least I have heard of such books; I never read any of them."

Cosmo laughed again.

"Which of us is happier—you or me? The moment I saw you, I thought you looked like one that hadn't enough of something; but if you knew that the great beautiful person we call God was always near you, it would be impossible for you to go on being sad."

Joan gave a great sigh. "You must surely understand, Cosmo," she said, "that while we are in this world, we must live as people of this world, not of another."

"But you can't mean that the people of this world should live apart from him who put them in it. He is all the same, in this world, and in every other. The thought of God fills me so full of life that I want to go and do something for everybody. I don't think I shall be miserable when my father dies."

"Oh, Cosmo! And with such a good father as yours! I am shocked!"

Cosmo turned and looked at her.

"Lady Joan," he said slowly, "if my father were taken from me, I should be so proud of him, I should have no room to be miserable. I cannot see him now, and yet I am glad because my father *is*—way down there in the old castle. And when he is gone from me, I shall be glad still, for he will be somewhere all the same—with God as he is now. We shall meet again one day, after all."

The sun was down, and the cold, blue-gray twilight came creeping from the east. They turned and walked home through a luminous dusk. It would not be dark all night, though the moon did not rise till late, for the snow gave out a ghostly radiance. Far below were the lights of the castle, and across an unbroken waste of whiteness, the gleams of the village. The air was as keen as an essence of points and edges, and the thought of the kitchen fire grew pleasant. Cosmo took Joan's hand, and down the hill they ran, swiftly descending what they had climbed with such toil.

As they ran, Joan looked again at Cosmo. An attendant boy-angel he seemed, whose business it was to console her. If he were her brother, she would be well content never to leave the harsh place. For the strange old laird was such a gentleman, and this odd boy, absolutely unnatural in his goodness, was nevertheless charming! She did not yet know that goodness is the only nature. She regarded it as a noble sort of disease—as something at least that was possible to have too much of. She had not a suspicion that goodness and nothing else is life and health—and what the universe demands of us is to be good boys and girls.

When she reached the door, she felt as if she were waking out of a dream, in which she had been led along strange paths by a curious angel. For indeed, Cosmo was a strong, vigorous, hopeful, trusting boy of God's in this world, and would be just such a boy in the next—namely, one who did his work and was ready for whatever was meant to come.

When Joan entered the kitchen from all that world of snow outside, she knew for a moment how a little bird feels when creeping under the wing of his mother. Those old Hebrews—what poets they were! Holy and homely and daring, they delighted in the wings of the Almighty. Then first Joan was aware of simple confidence, of safety and satisfaction and loss of care; for the old laird in the red nightcap would see to everything! Nothing could go wrong when he was in charge! And hardly was she seated when she felt a new fold of his protection about her: he told her he had had her room changed that she might be near his mother and Grizzie, and would not have to go outside to reach it.

Cosmo heard with delight that his father had given up his room to Lady Joan, and would thus share his. To sleep with his father was one of the greatest joys the world held for him. Such a sense of safety and comfort—of hen's wings—was nowhere else to be had on the face of the great world. It was the full type of conscious well-being, of softness and warmth and peace in the heart of strength.

They all sat together round the kitchen fire. The laird fell into a gentle monologue, in which, to Joan's thinking, he talked even more strangely than Cosmo. Things born in the fire and the smoke, like the song of the three holy children, issued from the furnace clothed in softest moonlight. Joan said to herself it was plain where the boy got his oddity; but what she called oddity was but sense from a deeper source than she knew the existence of. He read them also passages of the book then occupying him so much: Joan wondered what attraction such a jumble of good words and no sense could have for a man so capable in ordinary affairs.

Then came supper; and after that, for the first time in her life, Joan was present when a man had the presumption to speak directly to his Maker from his own heart without the help of a book. This she found odder than all the rest; she had never heard of such a thing! So peculiar were his utterances that it never occurred to her that the man might be meaning something. Further from her still was the thought that perhaps God liked to hear him, was listening to him and understanding him, and would give him the things he asked. She heard only an extraordinary gibberish, supposedly suitable for a religious observance—family prayers, perhaps. She felt confused, troubled, ashamed—so entirely out of her element that she never knew until they rose that the rest were kneeling while she sat staring into the fire. Then she felt guilty and shy, but nobody seemed to take the least notice. The unpleasantness of it all, however, did not keep her from thinking, *Oh, how delightful it would be to live in a house where everybody understood, and loved, and thought about everybody else!*

She did not know that she was wishing for nothing more, and something a little less, than the kingdom of heaven—the very thing she thought the laird and Cosmo so strange for troubling their heads about. If men's wishes are not always for what the kingdom of heaven would bring them, their miseries at least are all for the lack of that kingdom.

That night Joan dreamed herself on a desert island, where she had to go through great hardships, but where everybody was good to everybody, and never thought of taking care except of each other; and that, when a beautiful ship came to carry her away, she cried and would not go.

Three weeks of all kinds of weather—except warm—followed, ending with torrents of rain and a rapid thaw. But before that time Joan had got as mindless of the weather as Cosmo. Nothing kept her indoors, and as she always attended to Grizzie's injunctions the moment she returned, no harm came from it, and she grew much stronger. It is not encountering the weather that is dangerous, but encountering it when the strength is not up to the encounter. Cosmo and Joan would come in wet from head to foot, change their clothes, have a good meal, sleep well, and wake in the morning without the least cold. They would spend the hours between breakfast and dinner climbing the bank of a hill-stream dammed by the snow, swollen by the thaw, and now rushing with a roar to the valley; or fighting their way through wind and sleet to the top of some wild expanse of hill-moorland—waste bog and dry, stony soil as far as the eye could see, a hopeless region, except that it made the hope in their hearts glow the brighter. Or they might climb a gully, deep-worn by the centuries and the torrents that rushed down its trench when it rained heavily—hearing the wind sweep across it above their heads but feeling no breath of its presence, till emerging suddenly upon its plane, they had to struggle with it for a very foothold upon the round earth.

In such contests with nature Lady Joan delighted. It was so nice, she said, to have a downright good fight, and with nobody in a bad temper! She would come home from the windy war with her face glowing, her eyes flashing, her hair challenging storm from every point of the compass, and her heart merry with very peacefulness. Her only thoughts of trouble were that her father's body lay unburied, and that Borland would come and take her away.

When the thaw came at last, the laird had the coffin brought again into the guest room, and there placed on trestles, to wait the coming of the new Lord Mergwain.

Passing the letter announcing his departure, he arrived at length, and with him an assistant, a man of business. Lady Joan's heart gave a small beat of pleasure at the sight of him, and then lay quiet, sad, and apprehensive. The cold, proper salute he gave her seemed to belong to some sunless world, after the life of true humanity she had been living lately.

He uttered one commonplace statement concerning his father's death, and never alluded to it again; behaved in a dignified manner to the laird, as to an inferior to whom he was under an unpleasant obligation. And after the snub with which he met the boy's friendly approach, he took no further notice of Cosmo.

He was seated but three minutes when he began to ask for the laird's assistance in the removal of the body; could not be prevailed upon to accept any refreshment; had a messenger sent instantly to procure the nearest hearse and four horses; and that same afternoon started for England, following the body, and taking his sister with him.

19

······················

Catch Yer Naig

And so the moon died out of Cosmo's heaven. But it was only the moon. The sun remained to him—his father—visible type of the great sun, whose light is too keen for souls, and heart and spirit only can bear. It was a hard time for young Cosmo, for suddenly she had come, suddenly entered his heart, and suddenly departed. But there was this difference in Cosmo, that after the first of the seemingly unendurable, he did not wander moodily about and make everybody uncomfortable because he was uncomfortable. Instead, he sought more of the company of his father, and of Mr. Simon, from whom he had been separated while Lady Joan was with them.

Such a visit as they had had was seen as an opportunity most precious in the eyes of the laird. With the sacred instinct of a father, he could see what society of a lady would do for his boy. Not two days had passed before he began to be aware of a clearing of his speech, of greater directness in his replies, of a deepening of the atmosphere of his reverence. And when now the time of angelic visitation was over, with his usual wisdom the laird understood the heartache her abrupt departure must cause his son, and he allowed him plenty of time to recover himself from it. Once he came upon him weeping. But not in the least way did he rebuke him or suggest weakness in his tears. He went up to him, laid his hand gently on his head, stood thus for a moment, then turned without a word, and left him. And in no way did he regret the freedom he had given him. He knew what the sharp things of life are to the human plant, that its frosts are as necessary as sunshine, its great passion-winds as its gentle rains. Toward the end of his son's being molded by the hand of God, he knew that the hand of man must humbly follow the great lines of nature, ready to withhold itself, anxious not to interfere. Most people resist this marvelous process. But there is no escaping the mill that grinds slowly and grinds small, and those who refuse to be living stones in the living temple must be ground into mortar for it.

The next day, of his own choice, Cosmo went to Mr. Simon, who also knew how to treat the growing plant. He set him to such work as should harmonize with his recent experience, and so drew him gently from his past. Thus things slid gently back into their old grooves. An era of blessedness had vanished, but it was not lost; it was added to his life, gathered up into his being. From this time on, he grew faster, and from the days of his mourning emerged more of a man and more able to look the world in the face.

From that time also he learned more rapidly and understood things more clearly. He never came to show any great superiority in the knowledge or faculties prized of this world, whose judgment differs from that of God's kingdom in regard to the relative value of the moral and the intellectual. Nevertheless, both his father and his tutor saw the desirability, if it could somehow be managed, of his going to college the following winter. As to how it could be managed financially, the laird thought long and hard, but saw at this point no glimmer of light in the darkness of apparent impossibility.

Old servants of the true sort have a kind of family instinct. From the atmosphere about them, from words dropped that were never meant for them, and from thoughtful or troubled looks, they manage to come by a notion of how the wind is blowing. Thus Grizzie was capable of drawing accurate conclusions from what she saw. She marked the increased anxiety on the face of her master, noted his frequent talks with Mr. Simon, noted too how fervently at prayers the laird entreated guidance to do the right thing, and from all this put together that the laird's trouble had to do with Cosmo's future. As a result she came to the resolution of offering—not advice, that she would never have presumed upon—but a suggestion.

One night the laird sat in the kitchen revolving in his mind the whole question again: Was it right to spend money on his son's education that might go instead to the creditors? Yet even if it was so, where was the money to come from?

He sat in his chair, with his book open on his knees. His mother and Cosmo had already gone to bed, and Grizzie was preparing to follow them. The laird was generally the last to go. Grizzie had been eying him at intervals for the last half hour, and now drew near and stood before him. Her master took no notice of her, and she stood thus in silence for a moment and then began.

"Laird," she said, " 'tis plain ye're in trouble, an' if ye would let a body speak that kens nothin'—"

She paused a moment.

"Speak away, Grizzie," the laird answered. "I'm hearin' ye. There's none has a better right t' her say in this hoose."

"I hae nae right," replied Grizzie, "but what ye alloo me, Laird. An' I wouldna wish the Lord t' gie me any mair. But when I see ye in trouble, many's the time I hold my tongue, for I hae naethin' t' say an' nae help t' give. But last night there came a thought int' my heid, an' it might hae come t' a far wiser heid than mine, but seein' it did come t' mine, it would look as if the Lord might hae put it there. So, I said t' mysel', I'll jist submit the thing t' the laird, an' he'll soon discern whether it be from the Lord or no."

"Say on, Grizzie," returned the laird. "It should surprise no one t' get a message from the Lord by the mouth o' one o' his handmaidens."

"Weel, it's this, Laird. I hae often been in the grand drawin' room, when ye would be lettin' the yoong laird or somebody see the bonny things in the cabinets. And I had aye heard ye say o' one o' them—yon bonny little horsie, ye ken, that they say the auld captain gave t' yer gran'father—I hae aye heard ye say hoo it was solid silver—'said t' be' ye would aye always add."

"True! true!" said the laird.

"Weel, ye see, Laird," Grizzie went on, "I'm no sich a born idiot as t' think ye would value the possession o' sich a plaything above the yoong laird's education; so ye must hae some reason for no meltin' it doon—seein' siller must aye be worth plenty—if there be enough o' it. So, like the minister, I come t' the conclusion. But hae I yer leave, Laird, t' speak?"

"Go on, go on, Grizzie," said the laird almost eagerly.

"Weel, Laird—I winna say *feart*, for I never saw yer lairdship afraid afore bull or bully, but I could well believe ye wouldna willingly anger one that the Lord lets go up an' doon on the earth, when he would be far better in it, restin' in his grave till the resurrection—only he was ne'er one o' the saints! But I would jist remin' ye, Laird, that all gifts are yer own, t' do wi' what ye like; an' I would not heed a man, no t' say creature that belongs rightly t' no world at all, that would act like a bairn an' want back what he had given. For him, he's nothin' but a dead man that winna lie still. Many a bairn canna sleep 'cause he's behaved ill the day afore! An I hae heard auld Grannie talk aboot the expense he caused, what wi' his drink an' the gran' ootlandish dishes he had t' hae! Sae, as I say, it would be but fair for the auld captain t' contreebute somethin' t' the current necessities o' the hoose."

"Weel reasoned, Grizzie!" cried the laird. "An' I thank ye more for yer thought than for yer reasons. The thing shall be looked into first thing in the mornin'! The little horse ne'er came into my head. I must be growin' auld, Grizzie, no t' hae thought o' a thing sae plain! But 'tis the way wi' all the best things. They're sae good when ye get a hold o' them that ye canna un'erstan' hoo ye never thought o' them afore."

"I'm aulder than you, sir. Sae it must hae been the Lord himsel' that put it int' me."

"We'll see in the mornin, Grizzie. For all I ken, the thing may be nae better than a bit o' brass. I hae thought many a time that it looked in places a lot like brass. But I'll take it in the mornin' t' Jaimie Merson. We'll see what he say's t' it. If anybody in these parts has any authority in sich matters, it's Jamie. An' I thank ye heartily, Grizzie."

But Grizzie was not well pleased that her master should so lightly pass the reasoned portion of her utterance; like many a prophet, she prized more the part of her prophecy that came from herself than the part that came from the Lord.

The moment Grizzie was gone to her room, the laird fell on his knees and gave God thanks for the word he had received by his messenger—if indeed it pleased him that such Grizzie should prove to be.

"O Lord," he said, "with you the future is as the present, and the past as the future. In the long past it may be that you provided this supply for my present need—did even then prepare the answer to the prayers with which you knew I would assail your ear. Never in all my need have I so much desired money as now for the good of my boy. But if this be but one of my hopes, not one of your intents, give me the patience of a son, O Father."

With these words he rose from his knees, and taking his book, read and enjoyed into the dead of night.

That same night, Cosmo, who was again in his own room, dreamed a very odd, confused dream, of which he could give but little account in the morning—something about horses shod with shoes of gold, which they cast from their heels in a shoe-storm as they ran, and which anybody might have for the picking up. And throughout the dream was diffused an unaccountable flavor of the old villain, the sea captain, although nowhere did he come into the story.

When he came down to breakfast, his father told him, to his delight, that he was going to Muir of Warlock and would like him to go with him. He ran like a hare up the waterside to let Mr. Simon know, and was back by the time his father was ready.

20

•••••••••••••••••••

The Watchmaker

It was a lovely day. There would be plenty of cold and rough weather yet, but the winter was over and gone, and even to that late region of the north, the time of the singing of birds was come. The air was soft, with streaks of cold in it. The fields lay about all wet, but there was the sun above whose business it was to dry them. There were no leaves yet on the few trees and hedges, but preparations had long been made, and the sap was now rising in their many stems, like the mercury in all the thermometers.

Up also rose the larks, joy fluttering in their wings and quivering in their throats. They always know when the time to praise God is come, for it is when they begin to feel happy: more cannot be expected of them. And are they not therein already on the level of most of us Christians who in this mood and that praise God? And indeed are not the birds and the rest of the creatures Christians in the sense of belonging to the creation groaning after a redemption they do not know, in the same way that men and women groan in misery from not being yet the sons and daughters of God they will one day become?

As they went, the laird told Cosmo what errand was taking him to the village. The boy walked by his father's side as if in a fairy tale, for did they not have with them a strange thing that might prove the talisman to open doors of many treasure caves?

They went straight to the shop, if shop it could be called, of James Merson, the watchmaker of the village. There all its little ornamental business was done—a silver spoon might be engraved, a new clasp put to a brooch, a wedding ring of sterling or gold purchased. There a secondhand watch might be had, taken in exchange from plowman or croftsman. James was poor, for there was not much trade in his line, and so was never able to have much of a stock; but he was an excellent watchmaker—so at least his town folk believed. And in a small village it soon appears whether a watchmaker, or any other tradesman, has got it in him.

He was a thin, pale man, with a mixed look of rabbit and ferret, a high narrow forehead, and keen gray eyes. His workshop and showroom was the kitchen, partly for the sake of his wife's company, partly because there was the largest window the cottage had to offer. In this window was hung almost his whole stock, and a table in front of it was covered with his work and tools. He was stooping over it, his lens in his eye, busy with a watch of which several portions lay beside him, protected from the dust by an inverted and footless wineglass, when the laird and Cosmo entered. He put down his pinion and file, pushed back his chair, and rose to receive them.

"A fine morning, James!" said the laird. "I hope you're well."

"Much the same as usual, Laird, and I thank ye," answered James with a large smile. "I'm not on the road to be what they call a millionaire, and I'm not yet on the welfare of the parish—something between the two, I'm thinking."

"There's many of us in like condition, James," responded the laird; "otherwise we wouldn't be coming to tax your skill today."

"I'm your humble servant, Laird. It wouldn't be a watch for the young laird?"

"No, no," said the laird quickly, sorry to have raised even so much of a vain hope in the mind of the man. "I'm as far from a watch as you are from the bank. But I have here in my pouch a little statue that's been in the house for many years. And just this last night it was put into my head that there might be some good in it, seeing as the tradition of the family has been that it's silver. For my own part, I have my doubts. But if anybody hereabout can tell the truth of it, you must be the man. And so I've brought it, to find out what you would say about it."

"I'll do my best, Laird," returned James. "Let's have a look at the article."

The laird took the horse from his pocket and handed it to him. James regarded it for some time with interest, examining it with care.

"It's a bonny fine bit of carved work," he said. "The ornamentation has taken a heap of time and labor—more than some would think it worth, no doubt. It's the way of the heathens with their graven images, but why with a horsie like this, I don't know. However, that's neither here nor there. Ye didn't come to me to ask how or why it was made. It's what it's made of that's the question. It's some too yellow for silver, and it's black in spots, which is more like it—but that may be from dirt. Without testing it, I wouldn't want to say what it is. But it's mighty heavy!"

So saying he carried it to his table, put it down, and went to a corner cupboard. From it he brought out a stoppered vial. He gave it a little shake and took out the stopper. It was followed by a dense white fume. With the stopper he touched the horse underneath, then looked closely at the spot. He then replaced the stopper and the bottle, and stood by the cupboard, gazing at nothing for a moment. Then he turned to the laird, with a peculiar look and a hesitating expression.

"No, Laird," he said, "it's not silver. Aquafortis won't bite on it. I would mix it with muriatic and try that, but I have none handy, and besides it would take time to tell. Do you know where it came from? One thing I'm sure of—it's not silver!"

"I'm sorry to hear it," rejoined the laird, with a faint smile and a little sigh. "Well, we're no worse off than we were before, Cosmo! But poor Grizzie! She'll be dreadfully disappointed.—Give me the little horsie, James. We'll take him home again. It's not his fault, poor thing, that he's not better made."

"Would ye not tell me where the little thing came from, or is supposed to have come from, sir? Have ye ever heard it said, for instance, that the old captain they tell of had brought it?"

"That's what I've heard said," answered the laird.

"Well, sir," returned James, "if ye have no objection, I would like to find out what the thing *is* made of."

"It matters little," said the laird, "seeing we now know what it's *not* made of. But do what you want with it, James."

"Sit ye down then, laird, if ye have nothing more pressing, and see what I make of it," said the watchmaker, setting him a chair.

"But I don't like to take up your time," replied the laird.

"Oh, my time's not so precious! I can get through my work without sweating," said James with a smile in which was mingled a half-comical sadness. "And I could not spend it better to my own mind than by serving yerself, sir."

The laird thanked him and sat down. Cosmo placed himself on a stool beside his father.

"I have nothing on hand today," James Merson went on, "but a watch of James Gracie's—one of yer own folk, laird. He tells me it was yer grandfather that gave it to his grandfather. It's a queer, old-fashioned kind of thing—almost too complicated for me. Ye see, old age is about the worst disease horses and watches can get: there's so little left to come and go upon!"

While the homely assayer spoke to his guests, he was making his preparations.

"I won't meddle with men. I leave them to the doctors and ministers," replied James, with another wide, silent laugh.

By this time he had got a pair of scales carefully adjusted, a small tin vessel in one of them and balancing weights in the other. Then he went to the rack over the dresser, and mildly lamenting his wife's absence and his own inability to lay his hand on the precise things he wanted, he brought out a dish and a bowl. The dish he placed on the table with the bowl on it, which he then filled with water to the very brim. He then took the horse, placed it gently in the bowl, which was large enough to receive it entirely. Setting the bowl and horse aside, and then taking the dish into which the water had overflowed from the bowl, he poured this water into the tin vessel on the scale, and added weights to the opposite until they balanced each other. He noted the weight with a piece of chalk on the table. Next he removed everything from the scales, took the horse, wiped it dry in his apron, and weighed it carefully. That done, he sat down, and leaning back in his chair, seemed to his visitors to be making a calculation; only the conjecture did not quite fit the strange, inscrutable expression on his face. The laird began to think he must be one of those who delight to cover up knowledge with mystery.

"Well, Laird," said James at length, "the weight of what ye have given me makes me doubtful where no doubt should be at all. But I'm bound to say, outside the risk of making some mistake, of the grounds of which I know knowing, for else I wouldn't have made it, that this little horsie of yours, by all that my knowledge or skill can tell me—this little horsie—and if it be not what I say, I *cannot* see why it shouldn't be so—only, ye see, Laird, when we think we know a thing, there's a heap more we don't know. Few know better, at least few have a right to know better than I do myself, what a poor creature man is, and how liable he is to make mistakes, even when he's doing his best to be in the right, and for anything I know, there may have been great discoveries made without ever coming to my hearing. And yet I dare not withhold the conclusion I'm driven to, and so I'm bound to tell ye, Laird, that yer expectations from this knot of metal—for metal we must allow it to be, whatever else it isn't—yer expectations, I say, are altogether wrong, for it's no more silver than my wife's kitchen poker!"

"Well, man," said the laird with a laugh, "if the thing be so plain, what makes you go so far around the bush to say it? Do you take Cosmo and me here for bairns that would fall down crying if you told them their lamb wasn't a living one but only a bit of cotton stuck on a stick? Come, Cosmo. I'm none the less obliged to you, James," he added as he rose, "though I could well wish your opinion had been such as would have put it in my power to offer you a fee for it."

"The less said about that the better, Laird!" replied James with imperturbability and his large silent smile. "The truth's the truth, whether it's paid for or not. But before ye go it's but fair to tell ye—only I wouldn't like to be held strictly accountable for the opinion, seeing it's not my profession, as they call it, but I've done my best, and if I be wrong, I had no ill design in it."

"Bless my soul!" cried the laird with more impatience than Cosmo had ever seen him show, "is the man mad, or does he take me for a fool?"

"There's some things, Laird," resumed James, "that have to be approached with circumspection and a proper regard to the impression they may make. Now, disclaiming any desire to look like a scoundrel, which I would rather look like to anybody than yerself, Laird."

The laird turned hastily. "Come, Cosmo," he said again.

Cosmo went to the door, troubled to see his father annoyed with the unintelligibility of the man.

"Well, if you *will* go," said James, "I must just take my life in my hand, and—"

"Hoot, man! take your tongue in your teeth; it'll be more to the purpose!" cried the laird, laughing, for he was getting over his impatience in the ridiculousness of the situation. "My life in my hand, he says! Man, I haven't carried a longknife for years! I set it aside with the kilt!"

"Well, it might be the better that ye hadn't. Once more, if ye would but listen to one that confesses he ought to know, even should he be in the wrong, I tell ye that horsie is *not* silver—no, nor anything like it."

"Plague take the man! What is it, then?" cried the laird.

"Why didn't you ask me that before?" rejoined James. "It would have given me the ability to tell ye—to the best of my ability, that is. When I'm not sure, I wouldn't volunteer anything. I wouldn't say nothing till I was adjured like an evil spirit."

"Well," said the laird seriously, at last entering into the humor of the thing, "herewith I adjure thee, thou contrary and inarticulate spirit, that thou tell me whereof and of what substance this same toy horse is composed, manufactured, or made of."

"Toy here, toy there!" returned James. "So far as any capability of mine, or any pure skill I have, will allow testimony—though mind ye, Laird, I won't take the consequences of being in the wrong—though I would rather take them than be in the wrong—"

The laird turned abruptly and left the shop, followed by Cosmo. He began to think that the man must have lost his senses. But when the watchmaker saw them walking steadily along the street in the direction of home, he darted out of the door and ran after them.

"If ye *will* go, Laird," he said in an injured tone, "ye might have just let me end the sentence I had begun!"

"There's no end to your sentences, man!" said the laird. "That's the only thing in them that was forgotten, unless it was the sense."

"Well, good day to ye, Laird!" returned James. "Only," he added, drawing a step nearer and speaking in a subdued confidential voice, "don't let yer horsie run away on the road home, for I swear to ye, if there be any truth in the laws of nature, he's not silver, nor anything like it—"

"Hoots!" said the laird, and turned and began walking away with great strides.

"But," the watchmaker continued, almost running to keep up with him, and speaking in a low, harsh, hurried voice, as if thrusting the words into his ears, "neither more nor less than solid gold—pure gold, not a grain of alloy!"

That said, he turned, went back at the same speed, shot himself into his cottage, and closed the door.

The father and son stopped and looked at each other for a moment. Then the laird walked slowly on. After a minute or two, Cosmo glanced up in his face, but his father did not return the glance, and the boy saw that he was talking to another. By and by he heard him murmur to himself, "The gifts of God are without repentance."

Not a word passed between them as they went home, though all the time it seemed to both father and son that they were holding the closest conversation. The moment they reached the castle the laird went to his room—to where his few books lay, and got out a volume of an old encyclopedia, where he read all he could find about gold. Then he descended to the kitchen, rummaged out a rusty old pair of scales, and with their help arrived at the conclusion that the horse weighed about three pounds avoirdupois. It might be worth about a hundred and fifty pounds. Ready money, this was a treasure in the eyes of one whose hand had seldom indeed closed upon more than ten pounds at once. Here was ample provision for the four years of his boy's college life, and more! It would leave some for his creditors besides. It is true that the golden horse, hoofs, and skin, and hair of jewels, could do but little toward the carting away of the huge debts that crushed Glenwarlock. But not the less was it a heavenly messenger of goodwill to the laird.

Many think it of no use to help the poor man because they cannot lift him beyond the reach of the providence which intends there shall always be poor on the earth. But is the only worthwhile help necessarily permanent? Even temporary relief gives a glad rebound of the heart to the poor man. For a man like the laird of Glenwarlock, capable of a large outlook, an inburst of light, however temporary, is to him a foretaste of the final deliverance. While the rich giver is saying, "Poor fellow, he will be just as bad next month!" the poor fellow is breathing the airs of paradise, reaping more joy of life in half a day than his benefactor in half a year, for help is a quick seed and of rapid growth.

Everything in this world is but temporary. Why should temporary help be undervalued? Would you not pull out a drowning swimmer because he will swim again tomorrow? The only question is, *Does it help?* Jonah might grumble at the withering of his gourd, but if it had not grown at all, would he ever have preached to Nineveh? The news of the watchmaker set the laird on a high mountain, from which he gazed into the promised land.

The rich, so far as money needs are concerned, live under a cloudless sky of summer—rather dreary and shallow, however lovely its blue light. When a breach is made through a darkened sky, the poor man sees deeper into the blue because of the framing clouds—sees up to worlds invisible in the broad glare. I know not how those born rich, still less those who have given themselves with success to the making of money, can learn that God is the all in all of men, for this world's needs as well as for the eternal needs. I know they may learn it, for the Lord has said that God can even teach the rich, and I have known wealthy men who seemed to know that truth as well as any poor man. But generally, the rich do not have the same opportunity of knowing God—nor the same conscious need of him— that the poor man has.

And when, so far as things to have and to hold are concerned, everyone is poor alike, and so far as any need of them is concerned, all are rich alike, the advantage will be all on the side of such as, neither having nor needing, do not desire them. In the meantime, the rich man who, without pitying his friend that he is not rich also, cheerfully helps him over a stone where he cannot carry him up the hill of his difficulty, rejoicing to do for him what God allows, is like God himself. The great Lover of his children gives infinitely, though he will not take from man his suffering until strength is perfected in his weakness.

Later that evening the laird called Cosmo, and they went out together for a walk in the fields, where they might commune in quiet. There they talked over the calculation the laird had made of the probable worth of the horse. He did not, unlike most prudent men, think it necessary to warn his son against too sure an expectation. In matters of hope as well as fear, he judged the morrow must look after itself.

Let us hold by our hopes; all colors are shreds of the rainbow. There is the rainbow of the waterfall, of the paddle wheel, of the falling wave: none of them is the rainbow, yet they are all of it. But even should they vanish, and even should the rainbow in the sky vanish, that hope which set it there, and will set it there again, will never vanish. By our hopes are we saved. There is many a thing we could do better without than hope, for our hopes ever point beyond the thing hoped for. The bow is the damask flower on the woven teardrops of the world; hope is the shimmer on the dingy warp of trouble shot with the golden woof of God's intent.

Cosmo never forgot that walk in the fields with his father. When the money was long gone after the melted horse, that hour spent among the great *horse-daisies* that adorned the thin soil of one of the few fields yet their own remained with him—to be his for ever—a portion of the inheritance of the meek. The joy had brought their hearts yet closer to each other, for one of the lovelinesses of true love is that it may and must always be more. In a little hollow they knelt together on the thin grass and gave God thanks for the golden horse on which Cosmo was to ride to the temple of knowledge.

Afterward they had a long talk over the strange thing. All these years had the lump of gold been lying in the house, ready for their time of need. For to the laird, what were land or family or ancient name compared with the learning that opens doors? It is the handmaiden of the understanding, which is the servant of wisdom, who reads in the heart of him who made the heaven and the earth and the sea and the fountains of water and the conscience of man!

They began to imagine together how the thing had come to pass. It could hardly be that the old captain did not know what a priceless thing he gave. No doubt he had intended sometime, perhaps in the knowledge of approaching death, to say something about it, and in the meantime, probably with cunning for its better safety, had treated it as a thing of comparatively slight value. They next each asked each other how it had come into existence. Either it had belonged to some wealthy prince, they concluded, or the old captain had had it made for himself as a convenient shape in which to carry with him, if not exactly ready money, certainly available wealth. Cosmo suggested that possibly, for better concealment, it had been silvered; and the laird afterward learned from the jeweller to whom he sold it that such was indeed the case. And its worth exceeded the laird's calculation, chiefly because of the tiny jewels with which it was studded.

Cosmo repeated to his father the rhyme he had learned from dreaming Grannie, and what Grannie herself had said about it. Now the laird smiled, and now he looked grave, but neither of them saw the connection between the rhyme and the horse of gold. For one thing, great as was the wealth it brought them, the old captain could hardly have expected it to give anyone boldness to the degree of arrogance specified. What man would call the king his brother on the strength of a little statue worth a hundred and fifty pounds?

When Grizzie learned the result of her advice, she said, "Praise be thankit!" and turned away. The next moment Cosmo heard her murmuring to herself:

"Whan the coo loups ower the mune,
The reid gowd rains intil men's shune."

21

Cosmo's High Calling

That night Cosmo could not sleep. It was a warm summer night, though not yet summer—a soft dewy night, full of genial magic and growth. He dressed himself and went out. It was deliciously cool and damp, but with no shiver. The stars were bright. There was no moon, but the night was yet so far from dark that it seemed conscious throughout of some distant light that illumined it without shine. And his heart felt like the night, as if it held a deeper life than he could ever know.

He wandered about till he came to the field where he had been with his father the day before. He was not thinking actively; any effort would break the spell in which he moved! For the moment he would be but a human plant, gathering comfort from the soft coolness and the dew when the sun had ceased his demands. The coolness and the dew sank into him and made his soul long for the thing that waits the asking.

He came to the spot where his father and he had prayed together, and there he knelt and lifted up his face to the stars. Oh, mighty, true church of all churches—where the Son of Man prayed! In the temple made by man's hands he taught, but here, under the starry roof, was his house of prayer, church where not a mark is to be seen of human hand! This was the church of God's building, the only fitting type of a yet greater, a yet holier church, whose stars are the burning eyes of self-forgetting love, whose worship is a ceaseless ministration of self-forgetting deeds—the one real ideal church, the body of the living Christ, built of the hearts and souls of men and women out of every nation and every creed, through all time and over all the world, redeemed alike from Judaism, paganism, and all the false Christianities that darken and dishonor the true.

Cosmo knelt and looked up. Something awoke within him, and he lifted up his heart, sending his soul aloft through the invisible.

Softly through the night came a gentle call: "Cosmo."

He started, looked around, but saw no one.

"Cosmo!" came the call again.

The sky was shining with the stars, but he saw nothing else. He looked all round his narrow horizon, the edge of the hollow between him and the sky, but nothing was there; its edge was unbroken by any other shape than the grass, the daisies, ox-eyes, and stars. A soft dreamy wind came over the edge of the bank and breathed on his cheek. The voice came again.

"Cosmo."

It seemed to come from far away, so soft and gentle was it, and yet it seemed near.

"It has called me three times," said Cosmo, rising to his feet.

As he stood, there was the head of Simon Peter, as some called him, rising like a dark sun over the top of the hollow. In the faint light Cosmo knew him at once, gave a cry of pleasure, and ran to meet him.

"You called so softly," said Cosmo, "I did not know your voice."

"And you are disappointed! You thought it was a voice from some region beyond this world! I am sorry. I called softly because I wanted to let you know I was approaching and was afraid of startling you."

"I admit," replied Cosmo, "that a little hope was beginning to flutter that perhaps I was called from somewhere in the unseen—like Samuel, you know; but I was too glad to see you to be much disappointed. I do sometimes wonder though, if there is a world beyond as we talk about, why there should be so little communication between it and us. Never in my life have I had one whisper from that world."

"You are saying a great deal more than you can possibly know, Cosmo," answered Mr. Simon. "You have had no communication you recognize, I grant. And I, who am so much older than you, must say the same. But the air around me may be full of angels and spirits—I do not know. I like to think they may somehow be with us no matter how unseen they are. But so long as I am able to believe and hope in the one great Spirit, the Holy Spirit that fills all, it really does not matter, for He is all in all and fills all things, and all is well."

"But why might not something show itself once—just for once, if only to give one a start in the right direction?" asked Cosmo.

"I will tell you one reason," returned Mr. Simon, "—the same reason everything is as it is, and neither this nor that nor any other way. Things are the way they are because it is best for us it should be so. Suppose you saw a strange sign or wonder—one of two things would likely follow: you would either come to doubt it after it had vanished, or it would grow common to you as you remembered it. No doubt, if visions would make us sure about God, he does not care about the kind of sureness they can give. Or he does not care about our being made sure in that way.

"A thing, Cosmo, might be of little value gained in one way; while gained in another might be a vital invaluable part of the process of life. God wants us to be sure of a thing by knowing the heart from which it comes. That is the only worthy assurance. To truly *know*, he will have us go in at the great door of obedient faith; and faith, as you know, has to do with things *not* seen. If anybody thinks he has found a back stair into the house of the knowledge of God, he will find it lands him at a doorless wall. It is the assurance that comes inside one's heart of beholding himself, of seeing what he is, that God wants to produce in us. And he would not have us think we know him before we do, for in that error many thousands walk in a vain show.

"And yet, if I do so humbly as his child, I am free to imagine, for God has given us our imaginations as well as our wills for his glory. And I imagine space full of life invisible. As I came just now through the fields, I lost myself for a time in the feeling that I was walking in the midst of lovely people of God that I have known, some in person, some by their books. Perhaps they were with me—are with me—now. For who can distinguish the many ways in which God speaks to us by his Spirit? The moment a thought is given me, whether directly from God, or through something I may have just read, or by a conversation with another, that same instant my own thought rushes to mingle with it, and I can no more tell them apart. Some stray hints from the world beyond may mingle even with the folly and stupidity of my dreams. The Bible speaks many times of God's guiding his people through them."

"But if you cannot distinguish, where is the good?" Cosmo asked.

"It is the quality of a thing, not how it arrived, that is the point. And for anything I know, true things may often be mingled with things not originating with God at all. God's spirit may be taking advantage of the door set ajar by sleep to whisper a message of love or repentance, and the troubled brain or heart or stomach may be sending forth fumes that cloud the vision, causing evil echoes to mingle with the hearing. When you look at any bright thing for a time and then close your eyes, you still see the shape of it, but in different colors. This figure has come to you from the outside world, but the brain has altered it. Even the shape itself is reproduced with but partial accuracy.

"But it is well I should remind you again that the things around us are just as full of marvel as those into which you are so anxious to look from the world beyond. The only thing worth a man's care is the will of God, and that will is the same whether in this world or in the next. That will has made this world ours, not the next. For nothing can be ours until God has given it to us. Curiosity is but the contemptible human shadow of the holy thing wonder. No, my son, let us make the best we can of this life that we may become able to make the best of the next also."

"And how do you make the best of this one?" asked Cosmo.

"Simply by falling in with God's design in the making of you, and allowing him to work out his plan in you. That design must be worked out—cannot be worked out without you. You must walk in the front of things with the will of God—not be dragged in the sweep of his garment that makes the storm behind him! To walk with God is to go hand in hand with him, like a boy with his father. Then, as to the other world, or any world, as to the past sorrow, the vanished joy, the coming fear—all is well! For the design of the making, the loving, the pitiful, the beautiful God is marching on toward divine completion. Let your prayer, my son, be like this: 'O Maker of me, go on making me, and let me help you. Come, O Father! Here I am. Let us go on. I know that my words are those of a child, but it is your own child who prays to you. It is your dark I walk in. It is your hand I hold.' "

The words of the teacher sank into the heart of Cosmo, for his spirit was already in the lofty condition of being capable of receiving wisdom directly from another. It is a lofty condition, indeed, and they who scorn it only show that they have not reached it—nor are likely to reach it soon. Those who will not be taught through eye or ear must be taught through the skin, and that is generally a long as well as a painful process. All Cosmo's maturity came from his having faith in those who were higher than he. His childlike faith had not yet been tried. But the trials of a pure, honest, teachable youth, however severe, must be very different from those of one who is unteachable. The former are for growth, the latter for change.

22

....

To College

The summer and autumn still had to pass before Cosmo would leave home for the university in the north. He spent the time in steady work with Mr. Simon. But the steadier his work, and the greater his enjoyment of it, the dearer was his liberty and the keener his delight in the world around him. He worked so well that he could afford to dream too, and his excursions and his imaginings alike took wider and wider sweeps—while for both, ever in the near or far distance, lay the harbor, the nest of his home. It drew him even when it lay behind him. But the godsend of the golden horse gave him such a wealth and freedom that he now began to dream in new directions, namely, of things he would do if he were rich. And his fancies in this direction turned chiefly on the enlarging and beautifying of the castle—but always with no slightest hint of destroying a single feature of its ancient dignity.

A portion of the early summer he spent in enlarging the garden on the south side of the house. He grew particularly fond of the spot, almost forsaking for it his formerly favored stone, and in the pauses of his gardening would sit with his back against a low wall of stone which protruded out of the ground, dreaming of the days to come. Here he would sometimes bring his book, and read or write for hours, perhaps drawing plans of the changes and additions he would make, of the passages and galleries that might be contrived to connect the various portions of the house, and of the restoration of old defenses. The whole thing may have been visionary and impractical, but it exercised his constructive faculty; exercise is growth, and growth in any direction, if the heart be true, is growth in all directions.

The days glided by. Fervid Summer slid away round the shoulder of the world and made room for her dignified matron sister. Lady Autumn swept her frayed and discolored train out of the great hall-door of the world, and old brother Winter, who so assiduously waits upon the house, and cleans its innermost recesses, was creeping around it, biding his time, but eager to get to his work. The day drew near when Cosmo would leave the house of his fathers, the walls that framed almost all his fancies, the home where it was his unchanging dream to spend his life until he went to his mother in heaven.

I will not follow his intellectual development—the things he studied, the data he acquired, the facts he assimilated. The *real* education of the youth is enough for this narrative. Suffice it to say that in Cosmo's case the former contributed to the latter, a result sadly lacking from most formal educational systems.

Cosmo's mind was too much filled with high hopes and lofty judgments to be tempted like a common nature in the new circumstances in which he found himself. He had few companions. Those whom he liked best could not give him much. They looked up to him far more than he knew, for they had a vague suspicion that he was a genius. But they ministered to his heart. The unworthy among his fellow students scorned him, and called him Baby Warlock—for more than once he had turned his back and walked away from them when their conversation had grown disrespectful toward something or someone whom Cosmo valued. None of them, however, cared to pick a quarrel with him. The devil finds it easier to persuade fools that there is dignity in the knowledge of evil than to give them courage.

The studious did not care about Cosmo, for neither was he of their sort. Now and then, however, one of them would be mildly startled by a request from him for assistance in some passage or problem, which, because he did not *go in for* what they counted scholarship, they could hardly believe him interested. Cosmo regarded everything from a vantagepoint of which they had no inkling. In his instinctive reach after life, he assimilated all food that came in his way. His growing life was his sole impulse after knowledge. And already he saw a glimmer here and there in regions of mathematics and science that had never occurred to the eyes of those other hard-studying youths. That was because he read books of poetry and philosophy of which they had never heard. As the years went by, he passed his examinations creditably, and in a few cases, with unexpected and unsought distinction.

Of city society, as such, he had no knowledge. He did, however, make several acquaintances among the tradespeople.

His father had been so pleased with the jeweler to whom he sold the golden horse that he requested Cosmo to call on him in the city. Cosmo found him a dignified old gentleman—nonetheless of a gentleman, and all the more of a man, that he had in his youth worked with his own hands. He took a liking to Cosmo, and was much pleased with his ready interest in whatever he told him. For Cosmo was never tired of listening to anyone who talked of what he knew. Nobody ever listened better than Cosmo to any story of human life, however humble. Everybody seemed to him of his own family. This made him, however, all the more disgusted when he came upon anything false in character or low in behavior. Incapable of excusing himself, he was incapable of excusing others also. But though gentleness toward the faults of others is an indispensable fruit of life, it is perhaps well it should be a comparatively late one. There is danger of foreign excuse re-acting on home conduct. Excuse ought to be rooted in profoundest obedience and outgoing love. To say that *anything* is too small to matter is of the devil; to say anything is too great to forgive is not of God.

Cosmo liked best to hear Mr. Burns talk about precious stones. There he was great, for he had a passion for them, and Cosmo was more than ready to be in-fected by it. They would spend hours talking about the different and comparative merits of individual stones that had at one time or another passed through his hands, and on the way they were cut, or ought to have been cut, about the con-ditions of size, shape, and water as indicating the special best way of cutting them, and about the various settings as bringing out the qualities of different kinds of stones.

One day he came upon the subject of the weather in relation to stones. On such a sort of day you ought to buy this or that kind of stone; on such another you must avoid buying this or that kind and seek rather to sell.

It was at this moment that the human gem was turned at that angle to the light which revealed to Cosmo—who had till now believed him an immaculate tradesman—the flaw in it.

"If I could but buy plenty of such sapphires," said Mr. Burns, "on a foggy afternoon like this, when the air is as yellow as a cairngorm, and sell them the first summer-like day of spring, I should make a fortune in a very few years."

"But you wouldn't do it, Mr. Burns?" Cosmo ventured to suggest, his tone revealing some foreboding anxiety.

"Why not?" rejoined Mr. Burns, lifting his gray eyes, with some wonder in them, and looking Cosmo in the face. His mind also was crossed by a painful doubt: was the young man a mere innocent? Was he *not all there?*

"Because it is not honest," replied Cosmo.

"Not honest!" exclaimed the jeweler, with a sense of injury. "I present the thing as it is and leave the customer to make his decision according to his knowl-edge. There is no deception in the affair. The stone is as God made it, and the day is as God made it; only my knowledge enables me to use both to better pur-pose than my neighbor can."

"Then a man's knowledge is for himself alone?" said Cosmo.

"How can you make such bones about it. The first acknowledged principle in business is to buy in the cheapest market and sell in the best."

"Where does the love of your neighbor come in, then?"

"That has nothing to do with business; it belongs to the relations of social life. No command must be interpreted so as to make it impossible to obey it. Business would come to a standstill—no man could make money that way."

"And that is what you think we are sent here for, to make money?"

"Most people do. I don't know about being *sent for.* But I don't know what else I'm behind this counter for but to make money. The world would hardly go on upon any other supposition."

Cosmo left the shop that day bewildered and unhappy, and from that time on made far fewer visits to see Mr. Burns. In after years he repented of having dropped the old gentleman's friendship, for he was forever under obligation to him. And if a man will have to do only with those who are perfect, he would have to cut himself off first of all. Yet Cosmo had learned a good deal from the man, even though his settings were more common than artistic. He had come to enjoy a stone, its color and light and quality, like a poet. The very rainbow was lovelier to Cosmo after learning some of the secrets of precious stones. Their study served also his spiritually poetic nature, by rousing questions of the relations between beauty fixed and beauty evanescent; between the beauty of stones and the beauty of flowers; between the beauty of art and the beauty of sunsets and faces. He saw that where life entered, it brought the greatest kind of beauty of all. Many were the strange, gladsome, hopeful, corrective thoughts born in him as a result of his inquiries about the gems in Mr. Burns's shop. For every question is a door handle.

At college Cosmo lived as simply as at home. The education he received, if consisting in the amount and accuracy of facts learned, was no doubt not on a par with the great universities of the south. But if education is the supply of material to a growing manhood, the education provided there was all a man needed who was man enough to aid his own growth. And for those who have not already reached that point, it is a matter of infinite inconsequence what material things they may be given to study.

Hoping to ease his father's finances somewhat, in his second year Cosmo sought engagements in teaching and soon had two hours every day occupied— one with a private pupil, and the other in a public school. The master of that school used afterward to say that the laird of Glenwarlock had in him elements of the real teacher. He had not in vain been the pupil of Peter Simon—whose greatest gift lay in this, that he not only taught, but taught to teach. Life is propagation. The Spirit of God always sends its life downward and onward. For making a man accurate, there is nothing like having to impart what he possesses. Cosmo learned more by trying to teach what he thought he knew than by trying to learn what he did not know.

In his third year it was necessary for him to earn even more of his own way. For the laird found that his neighbor, Lord Lickmyloff, had been straining every means in his power to get what remained of the Warlock estate into his hands. The discovery sent a pang to the heart of the laird, for he could hardly doubt that his lordship's desire was to obtain and then foreclose upon every mortgage to every part of the property. He had refused James Gracie's cottage, and now he would have his castle! But the day had not come yet, and as no one could tell what was best for his boy, no one could say what would come to pass, or foretell what deliverance might be in store for them! The clouds must break somehow, and the sun is always behind them! So, as a hundred times before, he gathered heart and went on doing his best and trusting his hardest.

The summers at home between the sessions were times of paradise to Cosmo. For the first time he himself now seemed to begin to understand the simple greatness of his father and appreciate the teaching of Mr. Simon.

And now the question arose: What was Cosmo to do after he had earned his degree? He could not remain at home. There was nothing for him to do there except the work of a farm laborer. He would have undertaken that gladly if the property had been secure, if only for the opportunity to be with his father. But the only chance of relieving the land of the debts against it was for him to take up some other profession. The only thing he had a leaning to was that of chemistry. This science was at the time beginning to receive a great deal of attention in view of agricultural and manufacturing purposes and promised a sure source of income to the man who was borne well in front upon its rising tide. But alas, even more money would be required if such a hope was to be realized. Additional education would still be necessary, costing a large sum, before his knowledge would be of money-value, fit for offer in the scientific market. He would have to go to Germany to study under Liebig, or to Edinburgh to study under Gregory. But there was no money to do so; the plan for the present at least could not be seriously entertained.

There was nothing left but to go on teaching.

23

A Tutorship

It can hardly be anything but unpleasant in certain ways for a youth to move from a house and lands where he is a son and take a subordinate position in another. But the discipline is invaluable. To meet what but for dignity would sometimes be humiliation, to do one's work in spite of misunderstanding, and accept one's duty completely, is no easy matter. There are certainly as many happy teaching situations as unhappy, and surely for such as find them the experience is a great joy. Suffice it to say that in Cosmo's first tutorship such was not the case—severe, unreasonable, and uncaring were the demands and expectations placed on him. As to how Cosmo stood up under this ordeal, I will only say that he never gave up trying to do better.

His great delight and consolation were his father's letters, which he treasured as if they had been a lover's, as indeed they were in a much deeper and truer sense than most love letters. The two wrote regularly, sharing their best and deepest with each other. The letters also of Mr. Simon did much to uplift him.

Nobody knows what the relation of father and son may yet come to. Those who accept the relationship in Christian terms are bound to recognize that there must be in it depths more infinite than our eyes can behold, ages away from being fathomed yet. For is it not a small and finite reproduction of the loftiest mystery in human ken—that of the infinite Father and infinite Son? If man be made in the image of God, then must not human fatherhood and sonship be the earthly image of the eternal relation between God and Jesus?

One happy thing was that he had a good deal of time to himself. The job his friends of the university had found for him was in the south of Scotland, almost on the borders. His employers were neither pleasant nor interesting. Had they taken it upon themselves to learn anything of Cosmo's history, they would have made more of an effort to be agreeable with him, for they were the sort of people who made much of birth and family. But Cosmo had no particular desire to make great efforts to come near where it was impossible to be near, and was content with what they accorded him as a poor student and careful teacher.

Cosmo remained with them two years, and during that time did not go home, for by living simply he had more money to send, but as he entered his third year he began to feel life growing heavy upon him, and longed to see his father.

Before the end of the next quarter, Mr. Baird sent him a message, informing him that because of certain unfortunate financial reversals he was compelled to dispense with his services. He regretted the necessity, he said, for the children were doing well, but the situation had grown so bad so suddenly that he had no choice, not only to let him go, but to beg him to excuse some delay in the payment of his quarter's salary now due.

Hearing this, Cosmo was sorry, and somewhat upset—for his father's sake more than his own—to have been denied the customary quarter's notice. However, he said what he could to make light of the trouble to his employer. Of the money that he had already earned during the previous three months, he never did receive so much as a farthing. The worst of it was that he had almost come to the bottom of his resources—and had not nearly enough to get him home.

He went to his room in great perplexity. He would not trouble his father about his finances; money for the estate was more vital than his luxury in travel. But before he had the chance to decide what he would do, a servant knocked at the door and, true to the day, handed Cosmo the expected letter from his father— this time enclosing one from Lady Joan.

Though they had not seen her since her departure, they had not lost hearing of her. Lady Joan retained a lively remembrance of her visit, and to both father and son the occasional letter from her was a rare pleasure. But from her letters seemed to issue to the inner ear of the laird a tone of oppression. Yet she said so little about her outward circumstances, hardly even alluding to her brother, that he could not account for her apparent mood except to conclude that things did not go well with her at home. The one he had now sent was particularly sad, and had so touched his heart that he suggested the idea of Cosmo's paying her a visit during his coming holidays. It might comfort her a little, he said, to see him.

Cosmo jumped up from reading the letter, excited with the possibilities. What better idea than to go as soon as possible? He was much more likely to find a new job in England than in Scotland. And as for his traveling expenses, he knew very well how to make a little go a long way. He sat down and wrote immediately to his father, telling him what had happened and what he planned to do. The moment the letter was off he set about making his preparations. He would not have time to write to Lady Joan and wait for a reply, nor would he have any other option but to travel by foot. It would take him days to reach Yorkshire, where she lived on the northern border. But the idea of such a journey, with the goal of seeing the beautiful lady again before him, was entrancing. To set out free, to walk on and on for days, not knowing what would appear next at any turn of the road—it was like reading a story that came to life in the reading!

That very night he said his farewells to the family, so he would be able to start very early the next morning. The father and mother were plainly sorry; the children looked serious, and one of them cried.

When the morning came, it was a lovely spring one, and he set out with his stick and his knapsack and his heart as light as that of the skylark that seemed to accompany him for a long way. He walked twenty miles that day for a beginning, and slept in a little village, whose roosters awakened him even before the dawn. He increased his distance every day, and felt as if he could go on this way for years.

But before he reached his destination, what people call a misfortune came upon him. I do not myself believe there is any such thing; what men call misfortune is merely the shadow side of a good.

One day he had passed through a lovely country and in the evening found himself on a dreary moorland. As night overtook him it grew very cold and began to rain. He decided to make an attempt to seek shelter at the first house he came to, and just before it had grown completely dark he came to some not very inviting places on the brow of the descent from the moor, the first of which was an inn. The landlady received him, and made him as comfortable as she could, but as the quarters were not particularly homey, he rose even earlier than he had intended and started out again in a pouring rain. He had paid his bill the night before, intending to stop at the first shop where he could buy a loaf of bread for breakfast.

The clouds were sweeping along in great gray masses, with yellow lights between them, and every now and then they would let the sun look out for a moment, and the valley would send up the loveliest smile from the sweet grass or growing grain, all wet with the rain that made it strong for the sun. He saw a river, and bridges, and houses, and in the distance the ugly smokestacks of a manufacturing town. Still it rained and the sun would not shine out. He had grown very hungry, and at length reached a tiny village, and in it he came to a cottage with a window that displayed loaves. He went in, took the largest he saw, and was about to tear a great piece off it when he thought it would be more polite to pay for it first. He put his hand into his pocket. It was well he did so, for in his pocket was no pocketbook! Either it had been stolen at the inn, or he had lost it on the way. He put down the loaf.

"I am very sorry," he said, "but I have just discovered that I have lost my money."

The woman looked him in the face with keen inquiring eyes; then, apparently satisfied with her scrutiny, smiled and said, "Don't trouble yourself, sir. You can pay me as you come back. I hope you lost none too much?"

"Not much, but all I had," answered Cosmo. "I am much obliged to you, but I'm not likely to be this way again, so I can't accept your kindness. I am sorry to have troubled you."

As he spoke he turned away and had laid his hand on the latch of the door when the woman spoke again.

"Take the loaf," she said; "it'll all be the same in less than a hundred years."

Had she looked well-to-do, he would have taken the loaf and promised to send the money. But he could not bring himself to do so with a poor woman, possibly with a large family, to whom the price of such a loaf might be no small matter. He thanked her again, but shook his head, and with a "Good morning," turned and left the shop.

He had hardly gone more than a step or two when he heard the woman running after him. Her eyes were full of tears. What fountain had been opened, I cannot tell; perhaps only that of sympathy with the hungry youth.

"Take the loaf," she said again. "Don't be vexed with an old woman. I'm not so pinched at present. Take the loaf and be welcome to it, and pay me when you can."

Cosmo put down her name and address, and as he took the loaf, kissed the hard-working hand that gave it to him. She uttered a little cry of reproach at the action, threw her apron over her head, and went back into her house.

The tide rose in Cosmo's heart and he left the hamlet eating almost ravenously. He ate his loaf with as hearty a relish as ever he took Grizzie's porridge, and that is saying as much for his appetite, if not necessarily for the bread, as words can. He had swallowed it almost before he knew it, and felt at first as if he could eat another. But after a drink of water from a well by the roadside, he found that he had had enough, and went walking on his way as strong and able as if he had had coffee and eggs and a steak, and a dozen things besides. Had the opportunity arisen he could have given half his loaf to any hungry man he met, but he would not have saved half of it for a need that might never come. Today's obedience is the only true provision for tomorrow, and those who are anxious about the morrow are all the more likely to bring its troubles upon them by the neglect of duty which care brings. Some say that care for the morrow is what distinguishes the man from the beast; certainly it is one of the many things that distinguish the slave of nature from the child of God.

He was passing the outskirts of the large town he had seen when he became again aware of the approach of hunger. One of the distinguishing features of Cosmo's character was a sort of childlike boldness toward his fellowmen. Coming presently to a villa with a smooth-shaven lawn, and seeing a man leaning over the gate that opened from the road, he went up to him and said, "Do you happen to have anything you want done about the place, sir? I do not have even money enough for my dinner."

The man, one with whom the world seemed to have gone to his very wish at every turn, looked him all over.

"A fellow like you ought to be ashamed to beg," he said.

"I made a particular point of *not* begging," returned Cosmo. "It is one thing to beg for work and another to beg for food. I didn't ask you to make a job for me; I asked if there was any work about the place you wanted done. I'm sorry to have troubled you. Good morning, sir."

He turned, and for the second time that day was stopped short as he went.

"I say! If you can be as sharp with your work as you are with your tongue, I just may have a job for you. My coachman left me this morning, and I now find the stable is in a terrible mess. If you clean it out and set things to rights—which I have my doubts you can do—I will give you your dinner."

"Very well," returned Cosmo. "But I give you fair warning that I'm very hungry. Only on the other hand, I don't care what I have to eat."

"Look here," said the man, "your hands look more like they're used to loafing than work! I'm not sure your work will be worth your dinner."

"Then don't give me any," rejoined Cosmo, laughing. "If the proof of the pudding be in the eating, the proof of the stable must be in the cleaning. Let me see the place."

Much wondering what a fellow walking through the country with a good-looking coat and no money could be about, the man led the way to his stable.

In a mess the stable certainly was.

"The new man is coming this evening," he said, "and I would rather he didn't see things in such a state. After this, he might think anything good enough! My former coachman took to drink, the rascal—and that, young man, is the end of all things."

"I'll soon set the place to rights," said Cosmo. "Let's see—where shall I find a graip?"

"A grape? What the deuce do you want with grapes in a stable?"

"I forgot where I was, sir," answered Cosmo, laughing. "I am a Scotsman, and so I am in the habit of calling things by old-fashioned names. That is what we call a three- or four-pronged fork in my country. The word comes from the same root as the German *greifen*, and our own *grip*, and *grope*, and *grab*—and *grub* too!" he added, "which in the present case is significant."

"Oh, you are a scholar, are you? Then you are either a Scotch gardener on the tramp after a job, or a young gentleman who has made bad use of his privileges. But it puzzles me that a principled young fellow like you should be going about the country as you are. Come now, there must be some reason for your being adrift like this!"

"Of course there is, sir; and if I were sure you would believe me, I would tell you enough to make you understand it."

"A cautious Scotsman!"

"Yes, for whatever I told you, you would probably doubt."

"You have done something wrong!"

"Were *you* never in any difficulty?" asked Cosmo, who by now had found a tool to serve his purposes and was already at work. "Have you always had your pockets full when you were doing right? It is not just to suspect a man because he is poor. The best men have rarely been rich."

Receiving no reply, Cosmo raised his head. The man was gone.

Cosmo finished his job, set everything right as far as he could, and then went to the kitchen door and requested the master to come and inspect his work. But the master only sent orders to the cook to give the young man his dinner and let him go about his business.

Cosmo ate heartily, and cook and maid were more polite than their master. He thanked them and went his way, and in the strength of the food walked many miles into the night—for now he had no daily goals before him, only the final one which would end his journey.

It was a clear, moonless, starry night, cold after the rain but the easier to walk in. The wind now and then breathed a single breath and ceased; but that breath was piercing. He buttoned his coat and trudged on. The hours went and went. He could not be far from Cairncarque, and hoped to be nearly within sight of it by break of day.

Midnight was not long past when a pale old moon came up and looked drearily at him. For some time he had been walking as if in a dream, and now the moon mingled with the dream in a strange fashion. She was hardly above the hill when an odd-shaped cloud crossed her path, and Cosmo's sleep-bewildered eyes saw in the cloud the body and legs of James Gracie's cow, straddling across the poor, withered heel-rind of the moon. Then another cloud, high among the stars, began to drop large drops of rain upon his head. "That's the reid gowd rainin'," he said to himself. He was gradually sinking under the power of invading sleep. He kept saying to himself that he must seek some shelter. But then he would find the next instant that he had dozed off even as he walked. The wind rose and blew sharp stings of rain in his face, which woke him a little. He looked about him, everything looking like a dream. He could remember feeling overwhelmed with sleep in a dream. Still he did not think he was dreaming: for one thing, he had never been so tired in a dream!

The road at last opened on a triangular piece of grass, looking like a village green. In the middle of it stood a great old tree, with a bench around it. He dropped on the bench and was asleep in a moment.

The wind blew and the rain fell. Cold and discomfort ruled his dim consciousness, but he slept like one of the dead. When the sun rose, it found him lying full length on the bare-worn wet earth at the foot of the tree. When he at last came to himself he could hardly drag himself to his feet. His body ached all over and it was with the greatest of difficulty that he forced his limbs to raise him. But he was then too sick to govern them properly, and he staggered about like a drunken man, hardly able to keep himself from collapsing again.

He saw a pond in the green, made for it, washed his face, and felt a little revived. On the other side of the green he saw a little shop. Without thinking he put his hand in his pocket and discovered there sixpence: the maid must have dropped it in when she waited for him at dinner. Rejoiced by the gift, he tried to run, to get some warmth into his arms and legs, but with no success. The moment the shop was opened, he spent his sixpence and learned that he was only about three miles from the end of his journey. He set out again, therefore, with good courage, but the moment he tried to eat, mouth and throat refused to do their work—he was indeed more ill than he ever remembered being. As he walked he got a little better, however, and trudged manfully on. By and by he was able to eat a bit of bread and felt better for it. But as he recovered, he suddenly became aware of what a disreputable appearance he must have from the dirt and his fatigue. How could he possibly approach Lady Joan in such a condition! He would rather lie down and die on the roadside than present himself dirty and sick at Cairncarque!

Coming to a watering place for horses on the roadside, he sat down beside it, opened his bag, and tried to make himself as presentable as possible. He washed again, changed his shirt, and continued on.

At the turn of the road, all at once rose the towers of Cairncarque. There was a castle indeed, with its large square towers at every corner, and its still larger two towers in the middle of its front, its moat and the causeway where there had once been a drawbridge! That was a real castle—such as he had read of in books, such as he had seen in pictures! Castle Warlock would fit bodily into half a quarter of it—would be swallowed up like a mouthful and never seen again! Castle Warlock was twice as old—that was something. But why had not Lady Joan told him hundreds of stories about Cairncarque, instead of letting him gabble on about their little place? Perhaps she did not love her castle as he did his, for she had no such father in it. That must be what made the difference.

Was he actually going to see her again? Would she be the same as before? For him the years between had vanished, and he was no more a man, but the boy who had climbed the wintry hills with her.

But as he drew near, Cosmo's heart began to sink and a strange reluctance seized him. He could not go up to the door. What servant in England would admit a fellow like him to the presence of a grand lady? How could he walk up to the great door looking like one who had slept the night in his lodging on the cold ground! He would look around a little first, and find some quiet way of approaching the house. Therefore he turned away from the front of the castle and followed the road that skirted the dilapidated fortification which surrounded it, arriving at length at a door in a brick wall, apparently that of a garden—ancient, and green, and gray with lichens. With the eyes of his imagination he thought that the other side must be the loveliest picture of warmth, order, and care—with stately yews and cedars, fruit trees and fountains, clean-swept walks and shady paths. Ah, what it would be like to have such a garden at Glenwarlock!

He turned to the door, tried it, and with a little difficulty succeeded in opening it. The vision in his mind immediately vanished.

24

······················

In the Garden of Cairncarque

What met Cosmo's eye was a garden indeed, but a garden whose ragged desolation looked as if the devil had taken to gardening in it. It was almost a pain to see. The fruit trees were running wild with endless shoots. Everything all about grew in disorder. The walks were covered with weeds, and almost impassable in many places with unpruned branches, while here lay a heap of rubbish, there a smashed flower pot, here a crushed water bucket, there a broken dinner plate. He followed a path that led away from the wall and came upon a fountain with no water in it, in a cracked basin dry as a lizard-haunted wall, near a marble statue without a nose and streaked about with green. Like an army of desolation in single file, they revealed to Cosmo the age-long neglect of the place.

Then he came to a great hedge of yew, very high, but very thin, like a fence of old wire that had caught cart loads of withered rubbish in its meshes. He heard the sounds of a shovel, and by the accompanying sounds judged the tool was being handled by an old man. He looked through the hedge and caught sight of him. He was old—bent with years, but tough and wiry, and it seemed to Cosmo that the sounds he uttered—grunts more than groans—were more the result of impatience than physical weakness. As Cosmo stood looking at him, wondering what sort of man this was he was going to have to deal with, the man began to mutter. After another moment ot two he ceased digging, drew himself up as straight as he could, and, leaning on his spade, went on as if addressing his congregation of cabbages.

"Who cares for an auld man like me?" Cosmo heard him say. "I kenna what for there should be auld men made! The bones o' me might melt inside o' me, an' never a sowl alive do mair for me nor bury me t' get rid o' the stink! No 'at I'm sae auld mysel' 'at them would hae my place would hae me!"

What could be more perfect? Cosmo thought. *Here is a fellow countryman!* He therefore made his way along the hedge until he found a place where he could get through and then approached the man who had by this time resumed his work, though in a listless fashion. As he came nearer, Cosmo read an ill temper in every line of his countryman's face, yet he approached him with confidence, for Scotsman out of their own country are noted for their hospitality to each other.

"Hoo's a' wi' ye?" he cried, sending his mother tongue in advance of his presence.

"Wha's speirin? an' what richt hae ye t' speir?" returned the old man in an angry voice, and lifting himself quickly, though with an aching sigh, looked at him with hard blue eyes.

"A countryman o' ye ain," answered Cosmo.

"Many a one is that, wha's none the more welcome. Give an accoont o' yersel' or the dogs'll be loosed upon ye in a jiffy. Haith, this is no place for lan'loupers!"

"Hae ye been long aboot the place?" asked Cosmo.

"Longer nor ye're likely t' be, I'm thinkin'. Whaur come ye frae?"

The old man had dropped his spade. Cosmo took it up and began to dig.

"Lay doon that spade!" cried its owner, and would have taken it from him, but Cosmo delayed giving it back.

"Hoot, man!" he said. "I would but let ye see I'm no lan'louper an' can weel handle a spade. Stand a bit an' rest yer bones."

"An' what do ye expect t' come o' it? Ye're after somethin', as sure as the de'il."

"What I expect it would be hard to say. But what I don't expect is to be treated like a vagabond. Come, I'll give you a good hour's work for a place to wash myself and change my clothes."

"Hae ye the clathes?"

"Here in my bag."

"An' what for du ye want new clathes on? What'll ye du then?"

"Give ye anither hour's work for the heel o' a loaf o' bread an' a drink o' water."

"Ye'll be wantin' me t' gie ye a job, I'll wager!"

"If ye had a day's work, or maybe two—" began Cosmo, thinking how much rather he would fall in with Lady Joan about the garden than to go up to the house unannounced.

"I weel thought there was more in't than ye was sayin'! 'Tis jist like the likes o' ye! Go away wi ye, an' dinna let me see yer face again, or I'll call t' them who'll take accoont o' ye."

"Hoot, man!" returned Cosmo, continuing to turn the ground over with the shovel, "ye're some hard upon a neighbor!"

"Neebor! Ye're no neebor o' mine! Go away wi' ye, I tell ye!"

"Did nobody never gie you a helpin' hand that ye're so hard on another who needs one?"

"If onybody ever did, it wasna you."

"But don't ye think ye're bound to do the same again?"

"Ay, t' him 'at did it—but I tell ye ye're no the man. Sae go aboot yer business."

"Someday you may want somebody else to do ye a good turn."

"I've done plenty t' give me a claim on consideration. I hae grown auld upon this place. What hae *ye* done, my man?"

"I wouldna hae the chance of doing anything if everyone was like you. But did ye never hear tell o' one that said: 'Ye would do nothing for none o' mine, so ye refused me as well'?"

"Deed, an' I will refuse yersel'," returned the old man. "Sich a child for jaw an' cheek—I never saw one—as the auld song says! Whaur on this earth did ye come frae?"

He was a small, withered man, with a thin wizened face, crowned by a much-worn fur cap. His mouth had been so long drawn down at each corner as by weights of discontent that it formed nearly a half-circle. His eyebrows were lifted as far as they would go above his red-lidded blue eyes, and there was a succession of ripply wrinkles over each of them, which met in the middle of his forehead, so that he was all over arches. Under his cap stuck out enormous ears, much too large for his face. Huge veiny hands hung trembling by his sides, but they trembled more from anger than from age.

"I told ye that already," answered Cosmo. "I come frae the auld country."

"De'il tak the auld country! What care I for the auld country! 'Tis a broad place, an' longer than it is broad, an' there's many a one in it an' oot o' it that's no worth the parritch his mither put int' him. Eh, the beggars I hae seen come t' me like yersel'! Ow ay! it was aye work they would hae! What coonty are ye frae, wi' the lang legs an' the lang backbone o' ye?"

Cosmo told him.

The hands of the old man rose from his sides and made right angles of his elbows.

"Weel," he said slowly, "that's no an ill coonty t' come frae. I may say *that*, for I belang t' it mysel'. But what part o't ran ye frae when ye came away?"

"I ran from no part, but I came from home in the north part o' it," answered Cosmo and bent again to his work with the spade.

The man came a step nearer, and without looking up Cosmo was aware that he was regarding him intently.

"Ay! ay!" he said at last, in a tone of reflection mingled with dawning interest. "I once kent a terrible rascal that came frae over by that way: what did they call the parish ye're frae?"

Cosmo told him.

"Lord bless me!" cried the old man and came close up to him. "But na!" he resumed, and stepped back a pace, "somebody's been tellin' ye what t' say t' win my good graces!"

Cosmo gave him no answer. The man stood a moment expecting some reply, then broke out angrily all over again.

"Why do ye make no answer when a body speirs ye a question?"

"I would answer no man who was not prepared to believe me," said Cosmo quietly, in his best English.

The dignity of his tone had far more effect on the man than the friendliness of their mother tongue.

"Maybe ye wouldna object t' tell me the name o' the toon nearest t' ye when ye was at home?" said the old man, his tone altered somewhat.

"It was called Muir o' Warlock," Cosmo answered.

"Lord, man! come int' the hoose. Ye must be sore in need o' somethin' t' put int' ye! All the way frae Muir o' Warlock! A toonsman o' my own! Scotland's a muckle place—but Muir o' Warlock! Come in, man, come in!"

He took the spade from Cosmo's hands, threw it down, and led the way toward the house.

The old man had a heart after all! How strange is the power of that comparatively poor thing, local association! This man's heart was not yet big enough to love a Scotsman, but it was big enough to love a man from Muir o' Warlock. And was that not a beginning as good as any? It does not matter where or how one begins if only one does begin! There are no doubt many who have not got further in love than their own family. There are others who have learned that for the true heart there is neither Frenchman nor Englishman, neither Jew nor Greek, neither white nor black—only the sons and daughters of God. There may be some who have learned to love all the people of their own planet, but have not yet learned to look with patience upon those of Saturn or Venus. Others there must be, who, wherever there is a creature of God's making, love each in its capacity for love, from the angel before God's throne to the animal of the earth, from the man of this world of ours to the man of some system of worlds which no human telescope has yet brought within the ken of earthly astronomer. And to that it must come with every one of us, for not until then are we true men and true women—the children, that is, of him in whose image we are made.

Cosmo followed very willingly, longing for water and a clothes brush rather than for food. The cold and damp, fatigue and exposure of the night were telling upon him more than he knew, and all the time he was at work in the garden, he had been experiencing previously unknown pains in his limbs.

The gardener brought him to a half-ruinous wing of the house that extended into what had possibly once been a very lovely and extensive garden but which was now as I have described it. They came to a small kitchen, opening under a great sloping buttress, and there he presented him to his wife, an English woman some ten years younger than himself. She received him cautiously, but soon had made him some breakfast. He sat down by her little fire and drank some tea, but felt shivery and could not eat. In dread lest the invading sickness should overpower him if he yielded to it for even a moment, he hurried to get out again into the sun and rejoin the old man who had gone back to his cabbage patch. There he pulled off his coat and once more grabbed the spade, for work seemed the only way of meeting his enemy hand to hand. But the moment he began he was hot all over, and the moment he stopped to take a breath he began to shiver. As long as he could stand, however, he would not give in.

"How many years have you been gardener here?" he asked, forcing himself to talk.

"Forty-five year, an' I'm nearhan' tired o't."

"The present lord is a young man, is he not?"

"Ay; he canna be muckle beyon' thirty-five."

"What sort of man is he?"

"Weel, it's hard t' say. He's one o' them that naebody says weel o', an' naebody wants t' say ill o'—yet."

"Surely there can't be much amiss with him then?"

"Weel, I wouldna go freely sae far as t' say that. You that's a man o' sense, ye must weel un'erstan', if it was only frae yer catechism, that there's both sins o' o-mission, an' sins o' co-mission. Noo, what sins o' co-mission may lie at my lord's door, I dinna ken, an' few can say, an' we're no t' judge. But for the o-mission, ye hae but t' see hoo he neglects that bonny sister o' his, t' be far enough frae thinkin' a saint o' him."

Silence followed. Cosmo would go no further in that direction: it would be fair to neither Lady Joan nor the gardener, who spoke as to one who knew nothing of the family.

"Noo the father," resumed his new friend, "—poor man, he's deid an' damned this many a day!—an' eh, but he was an ill one!—but as to Leddy Joan, he would hardly bide her oot o' his sight. He couldn't be that agreeable company t' the likes o' her, poor leddy, for he was a rough-spoken, swearin' auld sinner as ever lived, but sich as he had he gave t' her, an' was said t' hae been a fine gentleman in his yoong days. Some would hae it that he changed alt'gether all o' a sudden. An' they would hae it that it came o' blood-guiltiness—for they say he had lifted his hand again' his neebor. An' they warned me, long as it was since I left it, never t' let him ken I came frae yon part o' the country, or he would be rid o' me like that, one way or anither. Ay, it was a gran' name that o' Warlock in those parts. Though they tell me it goes nae for sae much noo. I hae heard said that ever since the auld lord here made away wi' the laird o' Glenwarlock, the family there ne'er had any luck. I would like t' ken what ye, as a yoong man o' sense, think o' that. It appears t' me some queer kind o' justice! There's jist some things 'at naebody can un'erstan'—an' that's one o' them—what for, cause oor graceless auld lord—he was yoong then—took the life o' the laird o' Glenwarlock, the family o' Warlock should ne'er thrive frae that day t' this! Answer me that riddle, yoong man, if ye can."

"Maybe it was to keep them that came after from any more keeping of such ill company," Cosmo ventured to suggest, recalling to mind what his father was, and at the same time what most of those who preceded him were.

"That's still some hard though," insisted the gardener.

"But," said Cosmo, "they say there that it was a brother o' the laird, not the laird himsel', that the English lord killed."

"Na, na; they're wrang there. For auld Jean, whom I remember a weel fared woman, though no sae bonny as when he brought her wi' him as a yoong lass— auld Jean said it was the laird. But that was long after the thing was ower an' little more taken notice o'. Na, na, it was the laird himsel' that the master killed—the father o' the present laird, I'm thinkin'. What aged man might he be—did ye ever hear tell?"

"He's a man well on toward seventy," answered Cosmo, with a pang at the thought.

"Ay; that'll be aboot it! There can be no doobt it was his father oor lord killed—an' as little that after he did it he gaed doon the broad road t' the de'il as fast as ever he could run. It was just like as wi' Judas. Some said he had sold himsel' t' the de'il, but I'm thinkin' that wasna necessary. He was t' get him anyway. An' would ye believe it, it's both said an' believed—that he came by his deith in some extraordinary way, no accoontable for, but plainly uncanny. One thing's sure as deith itsel', he was taken sudden, an' in the very hoose where, many a long year afore, he committed the deed o' darkness."

A pause followed, and then the narrator resumed.

"I'm thinkin' that when he began t' know himsel' growin' auld, his deed came back t' him, and that would be why he couldna stand t' hae my leddy oot o' his sight, or at least beyond the cry o' his tongue. Troth! he would sometimes come aboot the place, where I would be at my work, cursin' an' swearin' as if he had sold his soul t' all the de'ils t'gether, an' sae might take his will o' anything' he could get his tongue round! But I never heeded him that much, for ye see it wasna him that paid me; but the trustees paid me, an' so I was independent like, an' let him say his say. But it was aye an oonsatisfactory kin' o' thing, for the trustees caredna a bit aboot keepin' the place decent, an' they jist allowed the auld lord an' me, an' no a man more nor less—for the garden, that is. That's hoo the place comes t' be in sich a disgraceful condeetion. If it hadna been for reasons o' my own, I would hae gone many's the time, for the sight o' the ruin o' things was beyon' bearin'. But I had t' bear it, sae I bore't an' looked upon the things as the will o' a Providence that shouldna be meddled wi'. I brought mysel' in fact t' that degree o' submission an' I gae mysel' no trouble more, but jist confined my energies t' the raisin' o' the kale an' cabbage, the onions an' the potatoes wanted aboot the place."

"And are things no better since the present lord succeeded?" asked Cosmo.

"No a hair—'cep' it be that there's no sae many ill words flyin' aboot the place. But the lord never sets his nose int' the garden, or asks hoo things are goin' on. He does nothin' but root aboot in his boratory, as he calls it—bore-a-whig, or bore-a-tory, it's little t' me—makin' concoctions an' smells there fit t' scomfish a whale an' make him stick his nose beneath the water for a breath o' fresh air. He's so hard hearted that he never sae much as eats his dinner alongside his own sister, 'cep' it be when he has company an' wants t' look like other folk. If it didna go sae well wi' her in the auld man's time, it goes worst wi' her noo. For sae long as he was aboot the yard there was aye somebody t' ken whether she was livin' or deid. T' see a bonnie lass like her strayin' aboot the place wi' only an auld book, day after day, 'tis enough t' break a man's heart."

"Do the neighbors take no notice of her?"

"None o' her own dignity, like. Ye see she's nothin' but bonny. She *has* nothin'. The title an' the wealth all went t' her brither. An' though she's as good a creature as ever lived, the cold ground o' her poverty gathers the fog o' an ill report. But I'm thinkin' maybe she's the prooder for her poverty, an' winna go t' her inferiors sae long as her equals dinna invite her. She goes sometimes t' the doctor's—but he's a kin' o' frien' o' the earls, 'cause he likes the chemistry-stuff—but that's the yoong doctor."

"Does her brother never go out to dinner anywhere and take her with him?"

"Nobody cares aboot his lordship in the whole countryside, sae far as I can learn. There's one or twa great men from Lon'on that comes sometimes, t' smell hoo he's gettin on wi' his stinks, but de'il a neebor comes nigh the hoose. Ow, he's a great man, I make nae doobt, away frae home! He's aye writin' letters t' the newspapers an' they print them—aboot this an' that—aboot beasties in the water an' lectreesity, an' I kenna what all. An' some says that he'll be a rich man someday, the moment he's done findin' oot somethin' or other he's been wrestlin' wi' for ten year or sae. But the gentry never thinks nothin' o' a man sae long as he's only doin' his best—or his worst, as the case may be—t' lay his hand upon the money that's flyin' aboot him like a snowdrift. *When* he's gotten it, it's doon they're all upon their knees t' him."

"Then his sister has no companions at all?"

"She goes sometimes t' see the doctor's lass, an' sometimes she comes here an' has her dinner wi' her, themsel's two. Never another comes near the place."

All this time Cosmo had been turning over the cabbage ground, working all the harder that he still hoped to work off the sickness that yet kept growing upon him. The sun was hot, and his head, which had been aching more or less all day, now began to throb violently.

The spade suddenly dropped from his hands and he fell on his face in the soft dirt.

"What's this!" cried the old man, running up to him in a fright.

He caught hold of him by an arm and turned him on his back. His face was white as a sheet, and the very life seemed to have gone out of him.

25

A Sickbed Reunion

When Cosmo came to himself he had not a notion where he was. His chief awareness was of what seemed a great weight on him. He would have turned on his side, but a ponderous heap of blankets prevented him from even raising an arm—and yet he was cold. He tried to think back to what he could last remember of himself, but for a long time he could only recall a confused dream of discomfort and painful effort. At last, however, the garden came to his mind, then the work with the shovel, and the old man's talk.

"I've been sick!" he said to himself. "I fell down . . . I hope they haven't buried me."

With an agony of will he got an arm in motion and felt feebly about him. His hand struck against something solid, and what seemed like a handful of earth fell with a hollow rumble. Alas, this seemed ominous! Where could he be but in his coffin! The thought was hardly a pleasant one, but he was too weak, and had been wandering too long in the limbo of peculiar fancies, to be much dismayed. He said to himself he would not have to suffer long—he must soon go to sleep, and then would die in peace.

Fatigued, he lay for some time motionless. It was very dark, and by and by he became aware of a thin, dim, darkly gray light growing about him. If this was a coffin, it was a large one: there was a wall—miles away! Still the light grew, and with it the assurance that this could be no coffin or sepulchre, but a room of some kind. But there was little consolation in that, for there was no sign of comfort. Above him was a bare, dirty, stained ceiling, with a hole in the plaster. Around him were bare, dirty-white walls. There were no curtains or other signs of life. The plaster was falling in great patches from the ill-kept walls. He tried again and this time succeeded in turning on his side. A wooden chair stood a little beyond his reach, and upon it a bottle and a teacup. Not another article of furniture could he see. Right under the hole in the ceiling a board was partly rotted away in the floor and a cold, damp air, smelling of earth and decaying wood, seemed to be steaming up through it. In a few minutes, he said to himself, he would get up and get out of the hideous place. But he must lie a little longer and come to himself. But what had become of his strength? Could one night's illness have reduced him to this!

He could hardly even think properly, but he continued to go on thinking of where his strength might be. If it appeared to be lost for a season, as he lay here, was it in reality still there, hid in God? If so, then all was well. For if God chose that his child should lie there, today, and tomorrow, or till next year, how could he be troubled? He turned his back on the ugly room and was presently fast asleep again.

Many who from Sunday to Sunday, read the poems of a certain king brought up a shepherd lad, never stop to bring the truths of those poems into their daily lives. They read, "I will both lay me down in peace and sleep, for thou, Lord, only makest me to dwell in safety." Yet these readers never think that such a feeling ought to rule in their own hearts in consequence. Therefore, such might consider it preposterous that Cosmo should have such a feeling of absolute trust in God as he did. Such men and women build stone houses, but never a spiritual nest. They cannot believe such a *practical* faith possible. And they may never believe it before they begin to do it.

I can hardly wonder that so many reject Christianity when they see so many would-be champions of it holding their beliefs at arm's length—in their Bibles, in their theories, in their churches, in their clergymen, in their prayerbooks, in the last devotional page they have read—all things separate from their real selves—rather than in their hearts on their beds in the stillness. God is nearer to me than the air I breathe, nearer to me than the heart of wife or child, nearer to me than my own consciousness of myself, nearer to me than the words in which I speak to him, nearer than the thought roused in me by the story of his perfect son. The unbelievers might well rejoice in the loss of such a God as many Christians would make of him. But if he be indeed the Father of our Lord Jesus Christ, then to all eternity let me say only, "Amen, Lord, your will be done!"

Cosmo had been ill a whole week—in fever and pain, and was now almost as weak as a baby. The old man had gone for his wife, and between them they had got him to the house. They took him directly to the room where he now lay, for they themselves had but one room. They spared some of their own poor comforts to furnish the bare bed for him, and there he lay, like one adrift in a rotten boat on the ebbing ocean of life, while the old woman trudged away to the village to tell the doctor that there was a young Scots gardener taken suddenly ill at their quarters in the castle.

The doctor sent his son, a man about thirty, who after traveling some years as a medical attendant to a nobleman had settled in his native village as his father's partner. He prescribed some medicine for Cosmo, hoping there was nothing infectious about the sickness. He had come every day during the week, and the night before had been with him from dark to dawn.

The gardener's wife had informed Lady Joan that a young Scotsman who had come to her husband seeking employment had been suddenly taken ill and was now lying in a room in the old wing. Lady Joan had said that she would speak to the housekeeper to let her have whatever she wanted for him. The doctor saw Lady Joan almost every time he came to see Cosmo, and she would inquire how his patient was getting on. She would also hear the housekeeper's complaints of the difficulty she had in getting wine from the butler—of which there was no lack, only he begrudged giving any of it up, for he was doing his best to drink up the stock the old lord had left behind him, intending to take his leave of the place with the last bottle. The castle was like a small deserted village, and there was no necessity for a person in one part of it knowing what was taking place in another. Thus Lady Joan had never troubled herself about such disputes.

But that same morning she had received a letter from the laird of Glenwarlock, saying that he was uneasy about his son. He had been so inconsiderate, he informed her, as to set out to visit her without asking her first, or even warning her. And since the letter announcing his departure, received two weeks before, he had not heard of or from him.

This set Lady Joan immediately to thinking. And the result was that she went to the gardener's wife and asked her about the appearance of her patient. In the old woman's answers she certainly could not recognize any particular likeness to Cosmo. But he had no doubt changed a great deal in seven years, and she could not satisfy herself without seeing the young man.

Cosmo lay fast asleep and dreaming—pleasant dreams now, for with the fever gone life was free to build its own castles. He was dreaming of Lady Joan, when he felt as if a warm sunny cloud came over him, which made him open his eyes. They gradually cleared, and above him he saw the face of his many dreams—a little sadder than it was in them, but more beautiful.

Cosmo had so much of the childlike in him that illness made him almost a very child again. When he saw Joan's face bending over him, he put his arm round her neck and drew her face down to his. Hearts get uppermost in illness, and people behave as they would not when healthy.

Lady Joan had not been able to decide whether the pale, worn youth could indeed be the lad Cosmo. And when he opened his eyes she was not at all prepared for such an outburst of familiarity. The moment he released her she drew quickly back. But such a smile flooded Cosmo's face, mingled with such a look of apology that seemed to say, "How could I help it?" that she was ashamed of herself. It was the same true face as the boy's, with its old look of devotion. To make it right again, she stooped and kissed his forehead.

"Thank you," murmured Cosmo, his voice sounding to him like that of another. "Don't be angry with me. I am but a baby, and have no mother. When I saw you, it was as if heaven had come down to me and I hardly realized what I was doing. How beautiful you are, and how good of you to come to me!"

"Oh, Cosmo!" cried Lady Joan—and now large and silent tears were running down her cheeks—"to think of the way you and your father took me and my father in, and here you have been lying ill—I don't even know for how long—in a place not fit for a beggar!"

"That's just what I am," returned Cosmo with a smile, quickly feeling much better. "I have such a long story to tell you, Joan! I remember all about it now."

"Why didn't you write?" said Joan, but even as she said it, she realized it would have done no good if he had, for what she would have been compelled to do because of her brother. "Or why didn't you send for me at once when you came? They told me there was a young gardener lying ill, and I never dreamed it could be you. But I know if you had heard at Castle Warlock that a stranger was lying ill somewhere about the place, you would have gone to him at once."

"Never mind," said Cosmo. "It's all right now. I have you and it makes me well again all at once. Now that I see you standing there, all the time is vanished between when I last saw you and now. The present joins right on to the past. But you look sad, Joan!—I *may* call you Joan still, mayn't I?"

"Surely, Cosmo. What else would you call me? I haven't many who call me Joan."

"But what makes you look sad?"

"Isn't it enough that I am sad for how I have treated you?"

"You didn't know it was me," said Cosmo. "And besides, you'll do differently another time."

"How can I be sure of that? My very heart grows stupid living here all alone."

"Well, you will have trouble enough with me for a while," said Cosmo.

Lady Joan's face flushed with pleasure. "The first thing," she said, "is to write to your father. When he knows I have got you, he won't be uneasy. I will go and do it at once."

Almost the moment she left him, Cosmo fell fast asleep again.

But now it was Lady Joan who was in perplexity. She was miserable to think of Cosmo in such a place, yet she could not help thinking to herself that it was probably good he hadn't written, for she would surely have had to ask him not to come. Now that he was in the house, she dared not tell her brother, and if she tried to move him to any comfortable room in the castle, he would be sure to hear of it from the butler, for the less faith carried, the more favor curried.

Only one thing was in her power to do: she could make the room he was in comparatively comfortable. Therefore, as soon as she had written a hurried letter to the laird, she quickly went through some of the rooms nearest the part where Cosmo lay, taking this and that for her purpose. In the huge and all but uninhabited place there were naturally many available pieces of furniture. With the assistance of the gardener and his wife, she carried these to his room. When she found he was fast asleep she worked with as much energy as possible to try to make the place look as different as she could before he woke. With noiseless steps she entered and left the room fifty times. And by making use of a door which had not been opened for perhaps a hundred years, she avoided attracting the least attention.

26

Recuperation

*W*hen Cosmo next opened his eyes he was bewildered all over again. Which was the dream—that poor, shabby room or this vision of luxury? Could it possibly be the same room? Nothing seemed the same, but he doubted having been moved. Yes, the ceiling was the same—the power of the good fairy had not reached to the transformation of that! But instead of the hole in the plaster on the wall, his eyes fell on a piece of rich old tapestry. Curtains of silk damask hung round his bed. A quilt of red satin lay over him. Everything had been changed. He felt like a tended child in absolute peace. Cosmo had nothing on his mind to trouble it. His consciousness was stored with lovely images because in temperament and faith, he was a poet. The evil vapors of fever had just lifted from his brain, and were floating away, and he felt the pressure of no duty, but was like the bird of the air lying under its mother's wing, dreaming of flight. The soul of Cosmo floated in rapturous quiet, like the evening star in a rosy cloud.

The old-fashioned little grate had a small, keen fire burning in it, attempting to bring what summer was possible into the musty atmosphere of the room. The hole in the floor had vanished under a richly faded Turkish carpet, and a luxurious sofa, in blue damask, faded almost to yellow, stood before the fire. And there in an easy chair by the corner of the hearth sat the fairy godmother herself, as if she had but waved her wand and everything had come to her will! The fact was, however, that the poor fairy was not a little tired in legs and arms and feet and hands and head, and for the moment preferred to sit thinking about what she had done rather than do anything else.

Cosmo lay watching her. He dared not move a hand lest she should move. She turned her eyes and saw those of the youth fixed upon her, smiled as she had not smiled before, for a great weight was off her heart now that the room gave him a little welcome. True, it was after all but a hypocrite of a room—a hypocrite, however, whose meaning was better than its looks.

He put out his hand and she rose and came and laid hers in it. Suddenly he let it go.

"I'm sorry," he said. "I don't know when my hands were washed! The last I remember is digging with them in the garden. I would so like to wash."

"You can't even sit up yet," said Lady Joan. "But if you like I will bring you a wet towel. I daresay it will make you feel good."

She poured water into a basin from a kettle on the hob, dipped part of a towel into it, and brought it to him. He tried to use it, but his hands could hardly obey him so that she took it from him, and she wiped his face and hands and then dried them—so gently, so softly, he thought that must be how his mother did with him when he was a baby. All the time he lay looking up at her with a grateful smile. She then set about preparing him some tea and toast, during which he watched her every motion. When he had had the tea, he fell asleep, and when he woke next he was alone.

An hour or so later the gardener's wife brought him a bowl of soup, and when he had taken it, she told him she would leave him for the night. If he wanted anything he must pull the string she had tied to the bedpost. He was very weary, but so comfortable and so happy, his brain full of bright yet soft-colored things, that he felt he would not mind being left alone for ages. He was but twenty-two, with a pure conscience—so might he not well lie quiet in his bed?

By the middle of the night, however, the tide of returning health stopped briefly. He became delirious again, his pulse very high, and terrible images tormented him, through which persistently passed over and over the figure of the old captain, always swinging a stick about his head, and crooning to himself the foolish rhyme:

"Catch yer naig an' pu' his tail;
In his hin' heel caw a nail;
Rug his lugs frae ane' anither;
Stan' up, an' ca' the king yer brither."

At last he felt as if, from the top of a mountain a hundred miles away, a cold cloud came journeying through the sky and descended upon him. He opened his eyes; there was Joan, and the cold cloud was her soft cool hand on his forehead. The next thing he knew was that she was feeding him like a child. But he did not know that she never left him again till the morning, when, seeing him gently asleep, she stole away like a ghost in the gray dawn.

The next day he was better, but for several nights the fever returned, and always in his dreams he was haunted by variations on the theme of the old captain. And for several days he felt as if he did not want to get better, but would lie forever a dreamer in the enchanted palace of the old ruin. But that was only his weakness, and gradually he gained strength.

Every morning and every afternoon Lady Joan visited him, waited on him, talked to him, read to him; and seldom would be absent for a whole evening— then only on the rare occasion when Lord Mergwain, having someone to dine with him of the more ordinary social stamp, desired her presence as lady of the house. Even then she would manage a quick look in on Cosmo now and then. She did not know much about books, but would take up this or that, almost as it chanced to fall into her hand in the library. And Cosmo cared little what she read, so long as he could hear her voice, which often beguiled him into the sweetest sleep with visions of home and his father. During this time he would often talk verse in his sleep, such as to Lady Joan seemed lovely, though she could never get hold of it, she said; for always, just as she seemed on the point of understanding it, he would cease, and her ears would ache with the silence.

One warm evening, when he was now a good deal better and able to sit up a part of the day, Cosmo was lying on the sofa watching Joan's face as she read. Through the age-dusted window came the glowing beams of the setting sun. They fell on her hands, and her hands reflected them, in a pale, rosy gleam, upon her face.

"How beautiful you are in the red light, Joan!" said Cosmo.

"You mustn't flatter me, Cosmo. You don't know what harm it may do me."

"I love you too much to flatter you," he said.

She raised the book and began to read again, thinking more about this strange youth than the words on the page before her. It is not surprising that although a little younger, Cosmo was a good way ahead of Joan both in knowledge and understanding. Hence the conversations they now had were to Joan like water to a thirsty soul. Years before she had thought Cosmo a wonderful boy who said the strangest things. Now he said even more wonderful things, she thought, but now he seemed to know they were strange, and so did his best to make it easier for her to receive them.

On Cosmo's side, like the gardener who awaits the blossoming of some strange plant, he waited patiently for something entrancing to issue from the sweet twilight sadnesses of Joan's being, the gleams that died into the dusk, the deep voiceless ponderings into which she would fall.

They talked about any book they were reading. But it mattered little what it was, for even a stupid book served as well as another to set their own fountains flowing. That afternoon Joan was reading from one written at the beginning of the century, a modern fairy tale of sorts. And this was what she read.

27
. . . .

The Knight Who Spoke the Truth

There was once a country in which lived a knight whom no lady of the land would love, because he spoke the truth. All the other knights of that land would say to the ladies they loved that they were the most beautiful and the most gracious and in every way the best of any women to be found anywhere. Thus the ladies of that land were taught to love their own praise best. And secondly they loved the knights who were the best praisers of each.

The knight who would not speak except truly, they mockingly named him Sir Verity, which some of them miscalled Severity—for the more he loved, the more it was impossible for him to tell a lie. And so it came about that eventually he was hated by all of them.

Greedy to gain his commendations, one lady after another would draw him on to speak of those things she judged her finest points. But never could any of them gain from him anything other than a true judgment. One day a certain lady said unto him, "Which of us, do you think, Sir Verity, has the darkest eyes of all the ladies here at the court of our lord the king?"

And he answered her, "Verily, I think the queen!"

Then she said unto him, "Who then has the bluest eyes of all the ladies at the court of our lord the king?"—for her own eyes were the color of the heavens when the year is young.

And he answered, "I think truly the lady Coryphane has the bluest of all their blue eyes."

Then she said, "And I think by your answer, Severity, that you do not love me, for otherwise you would have known that my eyes are as blue as Coryphane's."

"Nay, truly," he answered, "for my heart knows well that your eyes are blue, and that they are lovely, and are to me the dearest of all eyes, but to say they are the bluest of all eyes, that I may not, for if I did so I would be no true man."

At his words the lady was somewhat ashamed, and to cover her vanity, did answer, "You may well be right, Sir Knight, for I cannot see my own eyes, and men do say that you speak nothing but the truth. But be the truth as it may, every knight yet says to his own mistress that in all things she is the paragon of the world."

"Then," said the knight, "she that knows that every man speaks thus must also know that only one of them all can possibly speak the truth. And not willingly would I add to the multitude of lies that go about in the world."

"Now I am sure you do not love me!" cried the lady; "for all men do say of my eyes that they are the bluest of all the ladies at the court."

"Lady," said Sir Verity solemnly, "as I said before, in very truth, your eyes are to me the dearest of all eyes. But they might be the bluest or the blackest, the greenest or the grayest, yet would I love them all the same. For none of those colors would they be dear to me but because they were your eyes. For I love your eyes because they are yours, not you because your eyes are this or that."

Then the lady broke out into bitter weeping and would not be comforted. For in that country it was the pride of a lady's life to lie lapped in praises, and breathe the air of the flatteries blown into her ears by them who would be counted her lovers.

Then the knight said to himself, "It seems to me that the ladies in this land will never love man aright, for they do not want the truth from men's lips. Unless they may each think themselves better than all the rest, then life is not dear to them. I will leave this land and go where the truth may be spoken and the speaker of it not be hated."

He put on his armor, mounted his horse, and rode forth to leave the land. And it came to pass that on his way he entered a great wood. And as he went through the wood, he heard a sobbing and a crying in the wood. And he said to himself, "Verily, there is someone here who has been wronged. I will go and help!"

So he searched about until he came to the foot of a great oak, where he found an old woman in a gray cloak, with her face in her hands, weeping.

"What ails thee, good mother?" he said.

"I am not good, and I am not your mother," she answered, then began again to weep.

"Ah!" thought the knight, "here is a woman who loves the truth, for she speaks the truth, and would not that anything but the truth be spoken!—How can I help thee, woman?" he then said to her, "although you are right in saying you are not my mother, and I may not call you good."

"By leaving me," she answered.

"Then I will ride on my way," said the knight, and turning, rode on his way.

Then the woman rose to her feet and followed him.

"Why do you follow me," said the knight, "if I may do nothing to serve you?"

"I follow you," she answered him, "because you speak the truth, and yet because you yourself are not true."

"If you are speaking the truth in a mystery, speak it out plainly," he said.

"Why are you riding about the world?" she asked.

And he replied, "Verily to help those who are oppressed, for I have no mistress to whom I may do honor."

"Nay, Sir Knight," she said, "but to get a name for yourself and great glory is why you ride about the world. Verily you are not a man who loves the deepest essence of the truth."

At these words of the woman the knight clapped his spurs to his horse and would have ridden from her, for he did not like to be reviled, and so he told her. But she followed him and said to him as he rode, "Your own heart whispers to you that I speak the truth. It is only from yourself you are trying to flee."

Then the knight listened, and lo!, his own heart was telling him that what the woman said was indeed so. Then he drew in the reins of his bridle and looked down upon the woman and said to her, "Verily, you have spoken well. But if I be not true, yet would I be true. Come with me. I will take you upon my horse behind me, and together we will ride through the world. You shall speak to me the truth, and I will hear you. And with my sword I will plead whatever cause you have against any. So shall it go well with you and me, for I do not only want to love what is truly spoken, but be in myself true as well."

Then he reached down his hand, and she put her hand in his hand, and her foot upon his foot, and so sprang lightly up behind him, and they rode on together. And as they rode he said unto her, "Verily you are the first woman I have found who has spoken the truth to me, as I do to others. Only your truth is better than mine." But she returned him no answer. Then he said to her again, "Do you not love the truth?" And again she gave him no answer, and he marveled at her silence. Then he said unto her yet again, "Surely you are not one of those who speak the truth out of envy or ill *will, and yet do not love to hear it spoken to them. Woman, do you love the truth, or only to speak it sharply against others?"*

"If I do not love the truth," she answered, "I yet love them that love it. But tell me now, Sir Knight, what do you think of me?"

"I know not how to answer," said the knight, "for that is what I would fain know myself, namely what to think of you."

"Then I will now try you," she said, "to see whether you speak the truth or not. Tell me to my face, for I am a woman, what do you think of that face."

Then the knight said to himself, "Surely I could never, out of pity, of my own will say to a woman that she was ugly. But if she will have it, then she must hear the truth."

"Come, come!" said the woman, "will you not speak the truth?"

"Yea, I will," he answered.

"Then I ask you again," she said, "what do you think of me?"

And the knight replied, "Truly I do not think of you as one of the well-favored among women."

"Do you then think," she said, and her voice was full of anger, which it seemed she was trying to hide, "that I am not pleasant to look upon? No man has ever said so unto me, though many have turned away from me because I spoke the truth unto them."

"Now surely you are saying what is not so!" said the knight, for he was grieved to think she would speak out of anger and not love for the truth, inasmuch as she also sought that men should praise her.

"Truly I say that which is so," she answered.

Then the knight was angered and spoke roughly to her, "Therefore, woman, I will tell you that which you demanded of me: Verily I think of you as one, to my thinking, of the worst-looking and least to be desired among women whom I have seen."

Then she laughed aloud and said to him, "Nay, but did I not tell you that you dared not speak the thing to my face? For now you say it not to my face, but behind your own back!"

And in anger the knight turned in his saddle, crying, "I tell you, to your ill-shapen and ugly face, that—" And there he ceased and could speak not another word, but with open mouth sat silent. For behind him he saw a woman the glory of her kind, more beautiful than man ever hoped to see out of heaven.

"I told you," she said, "you could not say the thing to my face!"

"For that would be the greatest lie ever uttered," answered the knight, "seeing that verily I do believe you the loveliest among women, God be praised! Nevertheless, I will not go with you one step farther, so as to peril my soul's health, except, as you yourself have taught me to inquire, you tell me you love the truth in all ways—in great ways as well as small."

"This much I will tell you," she answered, "that I love you because you love the truth. If I say no more, it is because it seems to me a mortal must be humble when speaking of great things. Verily the truth is mighty, it comes on many levels, and will subdue my heart unto itself."

"And will you help me to do the truth?" asked the knight.

"So the great truth help me!" she answered.

And they rode on together, and thereafter parted no more. Here ends the story of the knight that spoke the truth.

Lady Joan ceased, and there was silence in the room. She looked back over the pages as if she had not quite understood, and Cosmo, who had understood entirely, watched the lovely, dark, anxious face. He saw she had not mastered the story, but, which was next best, knew she had not. He therefore began to help her to find the shapes of her difficulties, and then followed a conversation neither of them ever forgot concerning the degrees of truth: as Cosmo labeled them— the truth of fact, the truth of vital relationship, and the truth of action.

28

Cosmo and the Doctor

Soon Cosmo began to recover more rapidly—as well he might, he told Joan, with such a heavenly servant to wait on him. The very next day he was up almost the whole of it. But that very day Joan was with him less than before. She would bring him books and leave them, saying he did not require a nurse anymore now that he was able to feed himself. And Cosmo could not help sometimes thinking that her manner toward him was also a little changed. Twenty times a day he asked himself what could have come between them. Had he hurt her, presumed on her kindness, unconsciously played the role of the schoolmaster with her? Yet despite this, when they did meet and talk, they almost always seemed to get back to nearly the same place before they parted again, and Cosmo tried to persuade himself that any change there might be was only the result of growing familiarity. But nonetheless did he find himself mourning over something that was gone—a delicate color on the verge of the meeting sky and sea of their two natures.

But how differently the hours went when she was with him, and when he lay thinking whether she was coming! His heart swelled like a rosebud ready to burst into a flaming flower when she drew near, and folded itself together when she went, as if to save up all its perfume and strength for her return. Everything he read that pleased him must be shared with Joan. Everything beautiful he saw twice—with his own eyes and as he imagined it in the eyes of Joan. He was always trying to see things as he thought she would see them.

But soon he made a discovery about himself that troubled him. Not once since he was ill had he thought deeply about the story of Jesus or lost himself in prayer. Not once since finding Joan had he been flooded with the presence of God, or had any such vision of truth as every now and then used to fill him. Lady Joan saw that he was sad, and questioned him. But even to her he could not open his mind on such a matter; near as they were, they had not yet got near enough to each other for that.

In the growth of the individual man, epochs of truth and moods follow in succession, the one for the moment displacing the other, until the mind shall at length have gained power to blend the new at once with the preceding whole. But this can never be until our idea of God is large enough to fill and fit into every necessity of our nature. In most there are many empty cisterns and dried-up rivers hidden in parts of the being into which God has not yet come. There was not much of this kind of waste in Cosmo's world, but God was not yet inside his growing love for Joan.

So between these two an unrest had come, and they were no more sure of ease in each other's presence, although thought and word continued to go well between them, and usually all was nearly as simple and shining as ever.

The only house in the neighboring village where Lady Joan sometimes visited, as the gardener had told Cosmo, was that of the doctor, with whose daughter she had for some years, if not cultivated, yet admitted a sort of friendship. The two were very different, but Joan had no other acquaintances of her own age. In addition, Miss Jermyn had her own reasons for trying to please the lady of Cairncarque—namely, that her brother, a man about thirty, had a great admiration for Lady Joan, and to please him his sister would do almost anything. Their father also favored his son's ambition, for he hated the earl and knew what an annoyance it would be to him were his sister to fall in love with a mere doctor. And he liked Lady Joan and was far from blind to the consequence his family would gain by such an alliance. But he had no great hope that the relationship would go that far, for experience—of which few have more than a country doctor—had taught him that in every probability, his son's first advance would be for Lady Joan the signal to retire within the palisades of her rank. For there are those who will show any amount of friendliness with agreeable inferiors up to the moment when the least desire of a nearer approach manifests itself. That moment the old Adam is up in full pride like a spiritual turkey-cock, with swollen neck, roused feathers, and hideous gobble. The younger man, however, who also had his experiences, thought it possible that the utter isolation of Lady Joan, through the unpleasant reputation of her family, the disgraceful character of her father, the unfriendliness of her brother, and the poverty into which they had sunk, gave him incalculable advantages.

The father had been the medical advisor of the house for many years and, although Lord Mergwain accorded the medical practice of his day about the same relation to a science of therapeutics that old alchemy had to modern chemistry, yet the moment he felt ill he was sure to send for young Jermyn. Charles had also attended to Lady Joan in several illnesses. It is true she had on these occasions sent for the father, but for one reason and another, he had always, with many apologies, sent his son in his place. She was at first annoyed, but gradually got used to his attendance and to him as well. Thus he was able to gain the opportunity of tolerably free admission to the place, of which he made use of with increasing confidence, believing that he had no rival suitor for Joan's attentions.

And there was nothing so terribly unusual in such circumstances in his aspiring to win her. He was a man of good breeding and fine manners, with a wide
range of experiences, for he had traveled a great deal and been in the company of
persons of high position. And he was a man of some insight and versatility, and
was thus able to talk to Joan of the things he thought she would like. But though
he was not a rascal, who cares only to look like what will serve his purpose, he
was not yet an altogether true man, in the sense of wanting to appear on the
outside exactly as he was on the inside.

So far as Jermyn's attentions had gone, they were pleasant enough to Lady
Joan. They were at least a break in the boredom of her daily life. She was not one
of those who, unable to make the time alive, must kill it lest it kill them. But
neither was she of those who make their time so full that the day is too short for
them. Hence it came when he called that by and by she would offer him tea, and
when he went, would walk with him into the garden, and at length even accompanied him as far as the lodge on his way home.

Charles Jermyn was a tall, well-made man, with a clever and refined face,
which, if not much feeling, expressed great intelligence. He was admired a great
deal by the ladies of the neighborhood, considered by some of them to be quite
good–looking. A few said he was much too handsome for a doctor. He had a jolly
air about him, and a hearty way of shaking hands, which gave an impression of
honesty. And indeed, I think honesty would have been comparatively easy to him
had he set himself to cultivate it, but he had never given himself trouble about
anything except getting ahead in the world. You might rely on his word if he gave
it solemnly, but probably not otherwise. Absolute truth he would have felt a hin-
drance in the exercise of his profession.

Women, perhaps more than men, see in anyone who interests them not so
much what is actually there but rather a reflection of what they construct from
the hints that have pleased them. They build their imaginary shining knight out
of little more than bits of straw. Some of them it takes a miserable married lifetime
to undeceive. For some, not even that will suffice; they continue to see, if not an
angel, yet a very pardonable mortal and therefore an altogether lovable man, in
the husband in whom everybody else sees only a vile rascal. Whether sometimes
the wife or the world be nearer the truth will one day come out: the wife *may* be
a woman of insight, and see where no one else can.

In his youth the doctor had read a good deal of poetry, and enjoyed it in a
surface sort of way. And discovering that Lady Joan had fine taste in verse, he
made use of his knowledge there, always striving after the impression that he who
is able to quote has vital relation with the things he quotes. But it had never
entered the doctor's head that poetry could have anything to do with life—even
in the case of the poet himself, much less in that of his admirer! Never once had
it occurred to him to ask what kind of fool he must be to enjoy something if it
was false—nothing but fancies in the brain of the poet.

But not the less did Jermyn get down book after book, for many a year undusted
on his shelves, to try to find suitable verses that he might carry to the lady. But the

poetry had changed for him. Whereas he had once enjoyed it, or thought he had, it was to him now the ammunition of war, mere feathers for the darts of Cupid!

But Lady Joan saw no inconsistency in the result—it was hid in the man himself. To her he seemed a profound lover of poetry, who knew much she had never heard about. Once he contrived to spend a whole afternoon with her in the library, for he had a good deal of knowledge of the outsides of books and their title pages, and he had to find an opportunity to show it. One of his patients, with whom he had traveled, was a book collector, and he had learned much from him, chiefly from old book catalogues. With Lady Joan this learning, judiciously poured out, passed for a marvelous knowledge of books, and the country doctor began to assume in her eyes the proportions of a man of universal culture. He at least knew well how to use what he had, and succeeded in becoming something of seeming strength in the sweet lonely life. He could play the violin too, and tolerably well—with expression, though without much feeling from the heart. And he made sure Joan became acquainted, as if by accident, with this range of his accomplishments as well.

In the judgment of most who knew him, he was an excellent and indeed admirable man. "No nonsense about him," men would say, "A thorough family doctor, who knows how to humor patients," added certain mothers.

In that part of his professional duty which bordered on that of the nurse, the best in Jermyn came out. Few men could handle a patient so firmly and tenderly at the same time as he—an art hardly mastered by one in a thousand. Few were less sparing of self in the attempt to make patients comfortable. And from the moment when the simple-hearted Cosmo became aware of his attendance and ministration, something in him went out to the man. Cosmo was one in whom the gratitude was as enduring as ready. Next to the appearance of Lady Joan, all the time he was recovering he looked daily for the visit of the doctor. Nor did the doctor ever come without receiving his reward in an interview with the lady.

In this Jermyn gained another advantage. For Joan found herself compelled to take him into her confidence concerning her brother's ignorance of the presence of Cosmo in the house; and so he shared a secret with her. He did not, of course, altogether relish the idea of this Scotch lad being around, but plainly he was too young for Joan, and his presence had given him almost daily opportunity to call at the house, and he would soon find out whether there was any need to beware of him. By that time he would know what to do with him should any action prove necessary.

For the first week or so Joan did not mind how often the doctor found her with Cosmo, but after that she began to dislike it. She could scarcely have told why. But thereafter she began to manage to be elsewhere when he came. After the third time the doctor began to have a suspicion, and thus decided to use a little cunning to assist him. He had mentioned a time at which he would call the next day, but then he made his appearance an hour earlier, with an excuse ready on his lips for the change he had been "forced to make." He walked straight into the room without warning, as of course he might without giving any offense, his patient being a young man. There, as he had feared, he found Lady Joan. But she had heard, or possibly felt his coming, and as he entered she was handing Cosmo the newspaper with the words:

"There, you are quite able to read to yourself today. I will go and look again for the book you wanted." With that she turned, and gave a little start, for there stood the doctor.

"Oh, Doctor Jermyn!" she exclaimed, "I did not know you were there!" and held out her hand. "Our patient is getting on wonderfully now. You will let me see you before you leave the castle?"

She left the room, went quickly to her own, and saw in her mirror the red face of a lie, said to herself, "What will Cosmo think?" and burst into tears—the first she had shed since the day she found him.

The doctor was not taken in, but Cosmo was troubled and puzzled. In Jermyn's talk, however, and his own simplicity, he soon forgot the momentary strangeness of her behavior.

Because of his simplicity, Cosmo appeared to Jermyn younger than he was, while the doctor's manners and his knowledge of the world made Cosmo regard him as a much greater man than, in any sense or direction, he really was. His kindness having gained the youth's heart, he was ready to see in him everything that love was able to see.

"You are very good to me, Doctor Jermyn," he said one day, "so good I hardly know how to tell you what is weighing on my mind. But I do not know how or when I shall be able to pay you your fees. I hope you will not come to see me more than is necessary. And the first money I earn after I am on my feet, you shall be paid part at least of what I owe you."

The doctor laughed. It was such a schoolboy speech, he thought. It was a genuine relief to Cosmo to find him taking the thing so lightly.

"You were robbed on the way, Lady Joan tells me," Jermyn said.

"I am not sure I was robbed," returned Cosmo. "But in any case, even had I brought with me every penny I started with, I could not have paid you. My father and I are very poor, Mr. Jermyn."

"And my father and I are pretty well-to-do," said the doctor, laughing again.

"But," resumed Cosmo, "neither condition is a reason why you should not be paid."

"My dear fellow," said the doctor, laying his hand on the boy's, "I am not a very old man. It is not long ago that I was a student myself—in your country too—at Edinburgh. I have not forgotten what it is to be a student, or how often money is scarce."

"But I am not exactly a student now. I have been making a little money as a tutor, only—"

"Don't trouble your head about it," interrupted the doctor. "It is the merest trifle. Beside, I should never have thought of taking a fee from you! I am well paid in the pleasure of making your acquaintance. But there is one way," he added, "in which you could make me a return."

"What is that?" asked Cosmo eagerly.

"To borrow a little money from me for a few months? I am not at all hard up at present. I had to borrow many a time when I was in Edinburgh."

The boy-heart of Cosmo swelled at the man's generosity. But he felt it would be to do Joan a wrong to borrow money from the doctor and not from her. So with every possible word of appreciation, he declined the gracious offer.

Now the doctor was quite simple in behaving thus to Cosmo. Though a rather surface man, he was yet very friendly and a gentleman, and liked Cosmo as no respectable soul could help doing. It had not yet entered his mind to try to make him useful. But that same night he began to ask himself whether Cosmo might not somehow serve his hopes with regard to Joan. But first he must thoroughly understand the boy, and then make himself something in the eyes of the youth and raise himself in his estimation.

It was not long before the doctor imagined he did understand the boy, coming to believe him as innocent of evil as the day he was born. His eyes could not shine so, his mouth could not have that childlike—the doctor called it childish—smile otherwise. He also discovered that Cosmo had lofty ideas of duty in everything, that he was very trusting and slow to doubt another, and that with him poetry was not, as with Lady Joan, a mere delight, but an absolute passion. After such discoveries, he judged it would not be hard to make for himself, as for an idol, a high place in the imagination of the boy.

Therefore he began to bring to bear upon him his choicest fragments of knowledge, and all his power to talk of interesting things, and his familiarity with the world of imagination as embodied in books. He professed admiration for Milton's profoundest gems, and introduced Cosmo to Wordsworth's *Happy Warrior* and the best poems of Shelley.

Cosmo was so honest that he could not but regard the channel through which anything reached him as being one with the nature of that thing. How could a man transmit a truth who was not one in spirit with that truth? To his eyes, therefore, Jermyn sat in the reflex glory of Shelley and Wordsworth and every other radiant spirit through which he had widened his knowledge.

As he sat by his patient's bed, Jermyn would also tell him about his travels, and relate adventures in various parts of the world, and he began to come more often and stay longer, talking more and more freely, until at length in Cosmo's vision, the more impressionable perhaps from his weakness, the doctor came to assume the proportions almost of a hero, a paragon of doctors.

In all this, Jermyn, to use his own dignified imagery, was preparing an engine of assault against the heart of the lady. He had no very delicate feeling of the relation between man and woman, and felt no revulsion from the low custom of using whatever means might present itself to show himself to the best advantage—which he never doubted to be the truest presentation.

If he could send her a reflection of him in the mind of such an admirer as he was making of Cosmo, she would then see him more as he desired to be seen, and as he did not doubt he was.

29

·················

A Walk in the Garden

*A*t length Cosmo was able to go out, but Joan did not let him go out by himself. For several days he walked only a little, but sat a good deal in the sun, and rapidly recovered his strength. Finally, one glorious morning of summer, they went out together, intending to have a real little walk.

Lady Joan had first made sure that her brother was occupied in his laboratory, but she still dared not lead Cosmo to any part of the ground where he ever went. Therefore, she took him to the deserted portion he had seen his first day. It was long since the foot of a lady had pressed these ancient paths, longer since a merry speech had been heard in them.

Nothing is lovelier than the result of the half-neglect that often falls upon portions of great grounds when the owner's fancy has changed, and his care has turned to some newer and more favored spot; when there is moss on the walks but the weeds are few and fine; when the trees stand in their old honor, yet no branch is permitted to obstruct a path; when flowers have ceased to be sown or planted, but those that bloom are not disregarded; when only through some stately door is admission gained, and no chance foot is free to stray in.

But here it was altogether different. That stage of neglect was long past. The place was ragged, dirty, overgrown. There was between the picture I have drawn and this reality all the painful difference between stately and beautiful matron-hood, and the old age that, no longer capable of ministering to its own decencies, has grown careless of them.

"This garden is so ill-kept," said Joan in a tone almost of apology.

"The gardener told me some parts of the grounds were better kept than this," said Cosmo.

"Yes," answered Joan, "but none of them are anything like what they should be. My brother is so poor."

"I don't believe you know what it is to be really poor," said Cosmo.

"Oh, don't I!" returned Joan with a sigh. "My brother takes all the little money the trustees allow for his experiments."

"This part of the garden looks so melancholy! If I were here, I would never rest till I had got it into some sort of order with my own hands," said Cosmo. "Why don't you take me to a more cheerful part?"

She did not answer him. He looked in her face. It was very pale and there were tears in her eyes.

"Must I tell you, Cosmo?" she said.

"No, certainly, if you would rather not."

"But you might think it something wrong."

"I would never imagine you doing anything wrong, Joan."

"Then I must tell you, lest it should be wrong. My brother does not know you are here."

Now Cosmo had never imagined that Lord Mergwain did not know he was in the castle. It was true he had not come to see him, but that was a simple matter to explain if he desired to see Cosmo as little as Cosmo, from his recollection of him at Castle Warlock, desired to see Lord Mergwain. But it was no small shock to learn that he had all this time been in a man's house without his knowledge. No doubt, in good sense and justice, the house was Joan's too, however little the male aristocracy may be inclined to admit such a statement of rights. But there must be someone at the head of things, however ill he might occupy it; that place was naturally his lordship's, and he had at least a right to know who was in his house. Cosmo was very uncomfortable with the news. His silence frightened Joan.

"Are you angry with me, Cosmo?" she asked.

"Angry! No, Joan! How could I be angry with you? It only makes me feel rather like a thief where I have no business to be."

"I am sorry! But what could I do? You don't know my brother, or you would not wonder. He seems to have a kind of hatred of your family—I do not in the least know why. Could my father have said anything about you that he misunderstood? That could hardly be! And yet my father did say he knew your house many years before."

"I don't care about all that," said Cosmo, "but I cannot help feeling a little angered that he should behave so to you that you dare not tell him a thing. Now I *am* sorry I came without writing you first. But I can hardly say I am sorry I was taken ill, and for all the trouble I have been to you. For otherwise I would never have known how beautiful and good you are."

"I am not good! and I'm not beautiful!" cried Joan, bursting into tears. What a contrast was their house, and its hospitality, she thought, to that in which Cosmo lived one heart and one soul with his father!

"But," she resumed the next moment, wiping away her tears, "you must not think I have no right to do anything for you. My father left all his personal property to me, and I know there was money in his bureau, saved up for me—I *know* it; and I know too that my brother took it! I have never mentioned a word of it to anyone, but I can't have you feeling as if you had been taking what I had no right to give you."

They had come to the dried-up fountain, with its great cracked basin, in the center of which stood a parched naiad, pouring an endless nothing from her inverted vase, looking sad and forsaken. They sat down on the broad rim of the basin. Cosmo found himself thinking back to his youthful thoughts and imaginations concerning the hidden source of the stream that rushed forever along the base of Castle Warlock. The dry urn was a symbol to him of the end of all life that knows not its source.

They sat there silent, Joan thinking that Cosmo was brooding sadly on his newly discovered position concerning her brother. But yet a moment more and he began to tell her what was in his mind. He talked on until he had given her the whole metaphysical history of the development in him of the idea in connection with the torrent and its origin ever receding, like a decoy-hope that entices us to the truth, until at length he saw in God the one and only origin, the fountain of fountains, the Father of all lights and all true thoughts.

"If there were such an urn as that," he said, pointing to the naiad's, "ever renewing the water inside it without pipe or spring, it would be a true picture of the heart of God, ever sending forth life of itself, and of its own will, into the consciousness of us receiving the same."

He talked on, and talked as even Joan had never heard him before. And she understood him, for the lonely desire after life had done its work and had begun to open her inner eyes. More than ever she felt that he was a messenger to her from a higher region, that he had come to make it possible for her to enlarge her being.

Suddenly, with that inexplicable break in the chain of association over which thoughts seem to leap, Cosmo remembered that he had not yet sent the woman whose generous trust had saved him from long pangs of hunger, the price of her loaf. He quickly turned to Joan. Was not this a new chance of putting trust in her? Therefore he told her the whole story of his adventures on his way to her.

"Would you please lend me a half-sovereign—to send to the woman?" he added.

Joan burst into tears. It was some time before she could speak, but at last she told him plainly that she had no money, and dared not ask her brother, because he would want to know first what she meant to do with it. She did not tell him she gave her last penny to a beggar on the road the day he came, or that she often went for months without a coin in her pocket.

Cosmo was indignant at the mere thought. They sat silent—Cosmo wondering how he was ever to escape from this poverty-stricken grandeur to his own humble heaven at home—as poor, no doubt, but full of the dignity lacking here. He knew the state of things at home too well to imagine that his father could send him the sum necessary to travel north without borrowing it.

Joan's eyes were red with weeping when at length she looked pitifully up into Cosmo's face. Like a child he put both his arms around her, seeking to comfort her.

Suddenly there came a voice, calling her name in loud and angry tones. She turned white as the marble on which they sat, and threw a look of agonized terror to Cosmo.

"It's *him*!" said her lips, but hardly her voice.

The blood rushed from Cosmo's heart, as it had not for many days, and colored his thin face. He drew himself up, and rose with the look of one ready for love's sake to meet danger joyously. But Joan threw her arms round him now and held him.

"No, no!" she said, "We must go . . . this way! this way!" and letting him go, she darted into the shrubbery.

Cosmo hated turning his back on anyone, but the danger here was to Joan. Therefore he followed instantly.

She threaded her way swiftly through the thick-grown shrubs, hardly mindful of thorns and twigs. It was a wilderness for many yards, but suddenly the bushes parted, and Cosmo saw before him a neglected building, overgrown with ivy. The door of it stood half open, as if the last who left it had failed in a feeble attempt to shut it. Like a hunted animal Joan darted in, and up the creaking stair in front of her. Cosmo followed, every step threatening to give way under him.

The place was several degrees nearer ruin even than his room. Great green stains were on the walls, plaster was lying here and there, the floors, rotted everywhere with damp, were sinking in all directions. Yet there had been no wanton destruction, for the glass in the windows was very little broken. Merest neglect is all that is required to make of both man and his works a heap; for will is at the root of well-being, and nature speedily resumes what the will of man does not hold against her.

At the top of the stair, Joan turned into a room, and keeping along the wall, went cautiously to the window and listened.

"I don't think he will venture here," she panted. "The gardener tells me he seems as much afraid of the place as he and the rest of them. I don't mind it much—in the daytime. You are never frightened, Cosmo!"

As she spoke, she turned on him a face which, in spite of all the speed she had made, was yet pale as that of a ghost.

"I don't pretend never to be frightened," said Cosmo. "All I can say is I hope God will help me not to turn my back on anything, however frightened I may be."

But the room he was in seemed to him the most fearful place he had ever seen. His memory of the spare room at home with all the stories told of it seemed innocent beside this one. It was furnished like a little drawing room; everything in it was plainly as it had been left by the person who last occupied it. But the aspect of the whole was dreadful. The rottenness and dust were enough to scare even the ghosts, if they had any scare left in them. No doubt the rats had at one time had their share in the destruction, but it was long since they had forsaken the house. There was no disorder. The only thing that looked as if the room had been abandoned in haste was the door of a closet standing wide open. The house had a worse feel than a ghost could give it—worse than Joan knew, for no one had ever told her what would have added to her father's discredit.

Something in the corner of the closet just mentioned caught Cosmo's eye. He had a step toward it when a sharp moan from Joan's lips stopped him. He turned, saw her face full of new fear, and started back toward her, when she ran at him away from the window. She was trembling with fright. Cosmo held her to keep her from falling. They stood speechless, with faces like two moons in the daytime.

Presently Cosmo heard the rustling of twigs and the sounds of moving branches, noises which came nearer and nearer.

"Joan!" called out the same voice Cosmo had heard in the garden. She shook, and held so tightly to Cosmo's arm that she left marks of her fingers there. Cosmo would have gone to confront the enemy face to face, but she would not let him go. Then the shudder of a new resolve passed through her, and she began to pull him toward the closet. Involuntarily he resisted for a moment, but her action and look were imperative, and he yielded.

They entered the closet and he pulled the door to close it behind them. It resisted. He pulled harder. A rusted hinge gave way and the door dropped its front corner, so that he had partly to lift it to get it shut. Just as he succeeded, Joan's name on the voice of her fear echoed awfully through the moldy silences of the house. In the darkness of the closet, where there was barely room for two to stand, she clung like a child to Cosmo, trembling in his arms.

Hesitating steps were heard below. They went from one to another of the rooms, and then began to climb the stairs.

"Joan," whispered Cosmo, holding her to him, "whatever you do, keep quiet. Don't utter a sound. I will take care of you."

She pressed his shoulder, but did not speak.

The steps entered the room. Both Cosmo and Joan seemed to feel the eyes that looked all about it. Then the steps came toward the closet. It was the decisive moment! Cosmo was just on the point of bursting out with the cry of a wild animal when something checked him and he made up his mind to keep still to the very last moment possible. He put a hand on the lock and pressed the door down against the floor. In the faint light that came through the crack at the top of it, he could see the dark terror of Joan's eyes fixed on his face. A hand laid hold of the lock and pulled, and pulled but in vain. Probably then Mergwain saw that the door had fallen from its hinge. He turned the key, and the door had not altered its position too far for his locking them in. Then they heard him go down the stair and leave the house.

"He's not gone far!" said Cosmo. "He will come back and will have this closet open presently. You heard him lock it. We must get out at once. Please, let me go, Joan, dear. I must get the door open."

She drew back from him as far as the space would allow. He put his shoulder to the door and sent it into the middle of the room with a great crash, then ran and lifted it.

"Come, Joan! Quick!" he cried. "Help me to set it up again."

The moment something was to be done, Joan's heart returned to her. In an instant they had the door jammed into its place, with the bolt in the catch as Mergwain had left it.

"Now," said Cosmo, "we must get down the stair and hide somewhere below till he passes and comes up here again."

They ran to the kitchen and made for a small cellar opening off it. They were hardly in it when they heard him reenter and go up the stair. The moment he was safely beyond them, they crept out, and keeping close to the wall of the house, went round the back of it, and through the thicket to a footpath nearby, which led to the main road. It was a severe trial to Cosmo's strength, and now that the excitement of the adventure had relaxed he was all the weaker. As soon as Joan judged it safe, she made him sit down, and this time she supported him.

"I believe that wretched man of his put him up to it," she said. "He has found out something. You are far too good to think what he would do should he learn all. It was not an easy life with my father, Cosmo, but I would rather be living with him now, wherever he is, than go on living in that house with my brother."

"What should we do?" said Cosmo, trying to hide the exhaustion which was now sweeping over him in waves.

"I am going to take you to the Jermyns'. They are the only friends I have. Julia will be kind to you for my sake. I will tell them all about it. Young Dr. Jermyn knows already."

Alas, for Cosmo it was like being let down out of paradise into purgatory! But when we cannot stay longer in paradise, we must, like our first parents, make the best of our purgatory.

"You will be able to come and see me, will you not, Joan?"

"Yes, indeed!" she answered. "It will be easier in some ways than before. At home I never could get rid of the dread of being found out. As soon as I get you safely in, I must hurry home. Oh dear! How shall I keep clear of gossip? Only when you are safe I shall not care so much. But oh, for such days again as we used to have on the frozen hills by your home! There are the hills again every winter, but will the old days ever come again, Cosmo?"

"The old days never come again," answered Cosmo. "But do you know why, Joan?"

"No," murmured Joan sadly.

"Because they would be getting in the way of the new better days, whose turn it is now," replied Cosmo. "Tell God all about it, Joan, and he will give us better days than those. To some such a statement seems absurd. But it is just what we need—that kind of trust in him. Always before, when I have seemed to be just at the last gasp, things have taken a turn, and it has grown possible to go on again. And I have just such a hope for you."

"Ah, you are younger than I, Cosmo!" said Joan, more sadly than ever.

Cosmo laughed.

"Don't put on any airs to me on that ground," he said. "Leave that to Agnes. She is a year older than I, and always used to say when we were children that she was old enough to be my mother."

"But I am more than two years older than you, Cosmo," said Joan.

"How much, then—exactly?" asked Cosmo.

"Two years and a whole month," she answered.

"Then you must be old enough to be my grandmother! But I don't mean to be sat upon for that. Agnes gave me enough of that kind of thing!"

Whether Joan began to feel a little jealous of Agnes, or only more interested in her, it would be hard to say, but Cosmo now found he had to answer a good many questions concerning her. And when Joan learned what a capable girl Agnes was, understanding algebra and geometry, as Mr. Simon said, better than any boy he had taught, the earl's daughter did feel a little pain at the heart because of the cotter's.

At last they reached the village and the doctor's house. To Joan's relief, the first person they met was Charles. She at once told him the main part of their days' adventure. He proposed what Joan wished, and was by no means sorry at the turn things had taken—putting so much more of the game, as he called it, into his hands.

Things were speedily arranged, all that was necessary was told his father and sister, and Joan was invited to stay to lunch, which was just ready. She thought this would be best to do, especially as Jermyn and his sister would then walk home with her. What the doctor would say if he saw Mergwain, she did not venture to ask. She knew he would tell any number of stories to get her out of a scrape, while Cosmo would only do or endure anything, from thrashing her brother to being thrashed himself. But even for her, she knew he would never tell the whitest of lies.

A comfortable room was quickly prepared for Cosmo, and Jermyn made him go to bed at once. And he did not allow him to see Joan again, for he told her he was asleep, and she had better not disturb him—which was not true, but might have been, for all the doctor knew, for he had not been to see.

Joan did not fall in with her brother for a week, and when she saw him he did not allude to the affair. What was in his mind she did not know for months. Always, however, he was ready to believe that the mantle of the wickedness of his fathers, which he had so righteously refused to put on, had fallen upon his sister instead. Only he had no proof.

30

Catch Your Horse

When Cosmo was left alone in his room, with orders from the doctor to put himself to bed, he sank wearily on a chair that stood with its back to the light. Then first his eye fell upon the walking stick he carried. Joan had brought him a walking stick before they had gone into the garden together, but this was not the same one. This was a far fancier cane, one he had never seen before. He must have picked it up somewhere instead of his own! Where could it have been? He had no recollection either of laying down the other, or of picking one up.

After a time he began to recall that, in the room of the garden house, at the moment when Joan cried out because of the sound of her brother's approach, he was walking toward the closet to look at something that had attracted his attention just inside the door—seeming in the dim light, from its dull shine, to be the hilt of a sword. The handle of the walking stick he now held must be that very thing!

But he could not tell whether he had caught it up with any idea of defense, or simply because in the dark his hand had come into contact with it and instinctively closed upon it. And now that he had the chance to observe it, it was hardly any wonder that he should have been curious about it—the handle of the stick was an exact repetition of the form of the golden horse that had carried him to the university! Their common shape was so peculiar that not only was there no mistaking it, but no one who saw the two could have avoided the conviction that they were made by the same hand, probably at the same time, and whatever significance was connected to them was no doubt common to both as well. There was one important difference in the two, however: even if there were gold somewhere in this horse, it could be of small value. For the bamboo stick and horse handle and all were very light.

Proceeding to examine it, Cosmo found that every joint was double-mounted and could be unscrewed. There were three joints of the cane itself, each forming a small hollow cylinder. In the top one were a few grains of snuff, in the middle a little of something that looked like gold dust, and the third smelled of opium. The top of the cane had a cap of silver, with a screw that went into the lower part of the horse, which thus made a sort of crutch-handle to the stick. He had screwed off, and was proceeding to replace this handle, when his eye was arrested and his heart seemed to stand still.

The old captain's foolish rhyme came rushing back into his head. He jumped from his chair, took the thing to the window, and there in the light stood looking it over carefully. Beyond a doubt, this was his great grand-uncle's, the auld captain's stick, the only thing missing when his body was found!

He turned the handle upside down again. There could be no mistaking it! From one of the horse's delicately finished shoes, a tiny nail was missing, and its hole left empty. It was a hind shoe, too!

Caitch yer naig, an' pu' his tail;
In his hin' heel caw a nail!

"I do believe," he said to himself, "this is the horse that was in the old villain's head every time he uttered the rhyme!"

There must be a secret in the cane through which the old man had overreached himself! Had that secret, whatever it was, been discovered, or did it remain for him now to discover?

A passion of curiosity seized him. But the stick was not his property, and any discovery concerning it ought to be made with the consent and in the presence of its owner—her to whom the old lord had left his personal property.

And now Cosmo had to go through an experience as strange as it was new to him, for such a burning desire to conquer the secret of the stick came over him that he seemed almost possessed by it. It was so unlike himself that he was both ashamed and a little perturbed. He set it aside and went to bed.

But the haunting eagerness would not let him rest; it kept him tossing from side to side, and was mingled with strange fears that the stick should vanish as mysteriously as it had come—lest when he woke he should find it had been taken away.

He got out of bed, unscrewed the horse, and placed it under his pillow. But there it went on tormenting him. It went on drawing him, tempting him, mocking him. He could not keep his hands from it. A hundred times he resolved he would not touch it again, and he was able to keep his resolution so long as he thought of it. But the moment he forgot it, which he did repeatedly in wondering why Joan had not come to see him, the horse would be in his hand. Every time he woke from a moment's sleep, he found it in his hand.

After he had accompanied Lady Joan home, Jermyn came to him, found him feverish, and prescribed some medication for him. Disappointed that Joan was gone without seeing him, Cosmo's curiosity so entirely left him that he could not recall what it was like. And it did not reappear so long as he was awake. But all through his dreams the old captain kept reminding him that the stick was his own. "Do it; do it; don't put it off," he kept saying; but as often as Cosmo asked him what he meant, he could never hear his reply, and would wake yet again with the horse in his hand. In the morning he screwed it on the stick again and set it by his bedside.

31

· · · · · · · · · · · · · · · · · ·

Pull His Tail

About noon Joan came to see Cosmo. Both doctors happened to be out, and she was more like her former self than she had been for many days. She was hardly seated when he took the walking stick, and said, "Have you ever seen this before, Joan?"

"Do you remember showing me a horse just like that one, only larger?" she returned. "It was in the drawing room at your house."

"Quite well," he answered.

"It made me think of this," she continued, "which I had often seen in that same closet where I suppose you found it yesterday."

Cosmo unscrewed the joints and showed her the different containers.

"There's nothing in them," he said, "but I suspect there is something about this stick more than we can tell. Do you remember the silly Scotch rhyme I repeated the other day, when you told me I had been talking poetry in my sleep?"

"Yes," she answered.

"Those are words an uncle of my father, whom you may have heard of as the old captain, used to repeat very often." At this Joan's face blanched, but her back was to the light, and he did not see it. "I will tell you the words in English so you will be able to hear the sense in the foolishness of them. But now I must tell you that I am certain this walking stick once belonged to that same great uncle of mine. How it came into your father's possession I cannot say—and last night, as I was looking at it, I saw something that made me nearly sure this is the horse, insignificant as it looks, that was in my uncle's head when he repeated the verses. But I would do nothing to it without you."

"How kind of you, Cosmo!"

"Not kind. I would have no right. The stick is yours."

"How can that be if it belonged to your great uncle?" said Joan.

"Because it has been in your father's possession more than fifty years, and he left it to you. Besides, I cannot be absolutely certain it is the same."

"Then I will give it to you, Cosmo."

"I won't accept it, Joan—at least not before you know what it is you want to give me. And now for the rhyme—in English!

"Catch your horse and pull his tail;
In his hind heel drive a nail;
Pull his ears from one another:
Stand up and call the king your brother!

"What's to come of it, I know no more than you do, Joan," continued Cosmo, "but if you will allow me, I will do with this horse what the rhyme says, and if they belong to each other, we shall soon see."

"Do whatever you please, Cosmo," said Joan, with a slight tremble in her voice.

Cosmo began to screw off the top of the stick. Joan left her chair, drew nearer to the bed, and presently sat down on the edge of it, gazing with great wide eyes. She was even more moved than Cosmo. There was a shadow of horror in her look, as if she dreaded some frightful revelation. Her father's habit of muttering his thought aloud had given her many things to hear, although not many to understand. When the horse was free in Cosmo's hand, he set the stick aside, looked up, and said, "The first direction the rhyme gives is to pull his tail."

With that he pulled the horse's tail—of silver, apparently, like the rest of him—pulled it hard. But it seemed of the same piece as the rest of the body, and there was no visible result. With a hint of disappointment, he looked up at Joan, smiled, and said, "He doesn't seem to mind that! We'll try the next thing—which is to drive a nail in his hind heel. Now, look here, Joan. Here, in one of his hind shoes, is a hole that looks as if one of the nails had come out. That is what struck me, and brought the rhyme back into my head. But how to drive a nail into such a small hole as that?"

"Perhaps a tack would go in," said Joan, rising. "I'll pull one out of the carpet."

"I think a tack would be too large," said Cosmo. "Perhaps a brad out of the gimp of that chair would do. Or, I know! Have you got a hairpin?"

Joan sat down again on the bed, took off her bonnet, searched in her thick hair, and soon found one. Cosmo took it eagerly, and put it to the hole in the shoe. Nothing any larger would have gone in. He pushed it gently, then a little harder—felt as if something yielded a little, returning his pressure, and pushed a little harder still. Something gave way, and a low noise followed, as of a watch running down. The two faces looked at each other—one red, one pale. The sound ceased. They waited a little, in almost breathless silence. Nothing followed!

"Now," said Cosmo, "for the last thing!"

"Not quite the last," returned Joan, with what was nearly a hysterical laugh, trying to shake off the fear that grew upon her. "The last thing is to stand up and call the king your brother."

"That much, I daresay, we can omit," replied Cosmo. "The next thing then is to pull his ears from each other."

He took hold of one of the tiny ears between the finger and thumb of each hand and pulled. The body of the horse came apart, divided down the back, and showed inside of it a piece of paper. Cosmo took it out. It was crushed, rather than folded, around something soft. He handed it to Joan.

"It is your turn now, Joan," he said. "I have done my part. Now you open it."

Cosmo's eyes were fixed on the movements of Joan's fingers undoing the little parcel, as hers had been on his while he was finding it. Within the paper was a piece of cotton wool. Joan dropped the paper and unfolded the wool. Imbedded in the middle of it were two rings. The eyes of Cosmo fixed themselves on one of them—the eyes of Joan upon the other. In the one Cosmo recognized a large diamond; in the other Joan saw a dark stone engraved with the Mergwain arms.

"This is a very valuable diamond," said Cosmo, looking closely at it.

"Then that shall be your share, Cosmo," returned Joan. "I will keep this if you don't mind."

"What have you got?" asked Cosmo.

"My father's signet ring, I believe," she answered. "I have often heard him bemoan the loss of it."

Lord Mergwain's ring in the old captain's walking stick! Things began to put themselves together in Cosmo's mind. He sat thinking.

The old captain had won these rings from the young lord and put them for safety in the horse. Borland suspected, probably charged him with false play. They fought, and his lordship carried away the stick to recover his own; but he failed to find the rings, taking the compartments in the bamboo for all there was of stowage in it.

It was by degrees however, that this theory formed itself in Cosmo's mind. For the moment he saw only a glimmer of it.

In the meantime he was a little disappointed. Was this all there was to the great mystery of the captain's horse-rhyme? Joan sat silent, looking at the signet ring, and tears slowly came into her eyes.

"I *may* keep this ring, may I not, Cosmo?" she said.

"My dear Joan!" exclaimed Cosmo. "The ring is not mine to give anybody, but if you will give me the stick, I shall be greatly obliged to you."

"I will give it to you on one condition, Cosmo," answered Joan. "That you take the ring as well. I do not care about rings."

"I do," answered Cosmo. "But sooner than take this from you, Joan, I would part with the hope of ever seeing you again. Why, dear Joan, you don't know what this diamond is worth! And you have no money!"

"Neither have you! What is the thing worth?"

"I hate to say in case I am wrong. If I could weigh it, I would be able to tell better. But its worth must anyhow, I think, be somewhere toward two hundred pounds."

"Then take it, Cosmo. Or if you won't have it, give it to your father, with my dear love."

"My father would say to me, 'How could you bring it, Cosmo?' But I will not forget to give him the message. He will be delighted."

"But, Cosmo! It is of no use to me. How could I get the money you speak of for it? If I were to make an attempt of the kind, my brother would be sure to hear of it. I might just as well give it to him at once."

"That difficulty is easily overcome," answered Cosmo. "When I go I will take it with me. I know where to get a fair price for it—not always easy for anything. I will send you the money, and you will be quite rich for a little while."

"My brother opens all my letters," replied Joan. "I don't think he cares about reading them, but he sees who they are from."

"Do you have many letters, Joan?"

"Not many. Perhaps one a month."

"I could send it to Dr. Jermyn."

Joan hesitated a moment, but did not object. Almost the next instant they heard the doctor's step at the door and his hand on the lock. Joan rose hastily, picked up her hat, and sat down a little way off. Cosmo drew the ring and the pieces of the horse under the bedcovers.

Jermyn cast a keen glance on the two as he entered, took for confusion the remains of excitement, and said to himself he must make haste. He felt Cosmo's pulse, said he was feverish, then turned to Joan and said he must not talk, for he had not got over yesterday. Joan rose at once and took her leave, saying she would come and see the patient the next morning. Jermyn left the room with her, and sent Cosmo a drink to make him sleep.

When he had taken it, he soon began to get sleepy, and turned himself on the bed away from the light. But in doing so, the stick, which was leaning against the head of the bed, slipped and fell on the floor. The noise roused him, and he realized he should secure the ring—for which there could be no better place than the horse! It would no doubt rattle without the piece of cotton, so he put the ring into the cloth, replaced both in the horse, and set about trying to close it again.

But this was puzzling. There was neither spring nor notch, nor any other visible means of attachment between the two halves of the animal. But at length he noted that the tail had slipped a little way out, and was loose. Experimenting with it, he discovered that by holding the parts together, and winding the tail round and round, somehow the horse was restored to its former apparent solidity.

And now where would the horse be safest? Certainly on the walking stick where it belonged. He got out of bed to pick up the stick, and in so doing saw the piece of paper on the floor that had been around the cotton. He picked the paper up also, got into bed again, and began to screw the horse onto the bamboo, when his eyes focused for the first time on the paper and he caught sight of crossing lines on it. The appearance was like part of a diagram of some sort. He smoothed it out, and saw indeed a drawing, but one quite unintelligible to him. It must be a sketch of something—but of what? It might be of the fields constituting a property; it might be of the stones in a wall; it might be of an irregular mosaic; or perhaps it might be only a schoolboy's exercise in trigonometry for land-measuring.

It must mean something. But it could hardly be of consequence by now. But since it had been the old captain's—or perhaps the old lord's—he would replace it also where he had found it. Once more he unscrewed the horse from the stick, opened it with Joan's hairpin, placed the paper in it, closed it all up again, and lay down, glad that Joan had got such a ring, but thinking that the old captain had made a great deal of fuss about a small matter. He soon fell fast asleep, slept soundly, and woke feeling much better.

In the evening the doctor came and spent several hours with him, interesting and pleasing him more than ever.

Now that Joan had this ring, and his personal attachment to the doctor had so greatly increased, Cosmo found himself able to think again of the offer Jermyn had once made of lending him a little money, which at the time he had declined. He would take the ring to Mr. Burns on his way home, and then ask Joan to repay Dr. Jermyn out of what he sent her for it.

Therefore he told Jermyn as he sat by his bedside that he found himself obliged after all to accept his generous proposal of a loan, but would return the money even before he got home.

The doctor smiled, with reasons for satisfaction more than Cosmo knew, took his pocketbook out of his pocket, opened it, and said, "I have just cashed a check, fortunately, so you had better have the money at once. Don't bother yourself about it," he added, as he handed him the notes; "there is no hurry. I know it is safe."

"This is too much," said Cosmo.

"Never mind. It is better to have too much than too little. It will be just as easy to repay."

Cosmo thanked him and put the money under his pillow. The doctor bade him good night, and left him.

The moment Cosmo was alone a great longing arose in his heart to see his father. The first hour he was able to travel, he would set out for home! With his mind haunted with flashing water and speedwells and daisies and horse-gowans, he fell fast asleep and dreamed that his father and he were defending the castle from a great company of pirates, with the old captain at the head of them.

32

Northward

𝒯he next day Cosmo was better still, and he could not think why the doctor would not let him get up. And as the day went on he wondered all the more why Joan did not come to see him. The thought not once crossed his mind that it was all the doctor's doing. Jermyn wanted to prevent any interaction between them if he could till he should have sprung his spiritual mine, and that same night opened all his heart to Cosmo—that is, all he wanted to show.

In extravagant terms, he told his listener that his whole nature, heart and soul had for years been bound up in Lady Joan; that he had been tempted to deliver himself by death from despair; that if he had to live without her he would be of no use in the world, and would cease to care for anything. He begged his friend Cosmo Warlock, because he stood so well with the lady, to speak to her on his behalf. For if she would not favor him with her hand, he could no longer endure life.

Cosmo lay listening as one paralyzed. It was a silent yet mortal struggle. He held down his heart like a wild beast, which, if he let it up for one moment, would fly at his throat and strangle him. And the practiced eye of the doctor well perceived what was going on in him—the battle between loyalty to a new friend and the love of his heart. But he said to himself. *Better him than me! He is young and will get over it better than I should.* He read nobility and self-sacrifice in every shadow that crossed the youth's countenance, saying to himself that all was on his side, that he had not miscalculated a hairsbreadth—the boy would back down, for his sake, and Joan would be his! He saw at the same time Cosmo's heroic efforts to hide his sufferings. But inside, Cosmo longed for him to leave the room that he might enjoy his despair in the peace of solitude!

The night that followed was a terrible one for Cosmo. Before this moment he had hardly dared suspect the nature, and only now knew the force, and was about to prove the strength of the love with which he loved Joan. Great things may be foreseen, but they cannot be known until they arrive. His illness had been ripening him to this possibility of loss and suffering. His heart was now in blossom: for that some hearts must break. I may not say *full* blossom, for what the full blossom of the human heart is, even the holiest saint with the mightiest imagination cannot know—he can but see it shine from afar.

It was a severe duty that was now required of him—I do not mean the performance of the request the doctor had made. That Cosmo could never have even attempted with honesty. But it was enough that he must yield the lady of his dreams. Perhaps she did not love Jermyn—he could not tell. But Jermyn was his friend and had trusted in him, confessing that his soul was bound up in the lady. Therefore, one of them must go to the torture chamber, and when the question lay between him and another, Cosmo knew for which it must be. He himself was alone in Cosmo's hands; his own self was all he held and had power of; all he could offer and yield. Mr. Simon had taught him that, as a mother gives her children money to give, so God gives his children *selves*, with their wishes and choices, that they may have the true offering to lay upon the true altar; for on that altar nothing else will burn than *selves*.

A hard, tyrannical theory—and so it would appear to the man or woman who has neither the courage nor the sense of law to enable him to obey. Such have no awareness of the truth concerning that altar, that it is indeed the nest of God's heart, in which the poor, unsightly offering shall lie, until they come to shape and loveliness, and wings grow upon them to bear them back to us divinely precious. Cosmo *thought* none of all this now—it had vanished from his consciousness but was present in his life—that is, in his action. He did not feel, he *did* it.

Perhaps Joan might come one day to love me, Cosmo thought. *But in the meantime she is miserable with her brother, and when could I deliver her?* But here was one, and a far better and more experienced man than he, who could any moment take her to a house of her own where she would be a free woman. He could not come in the way. To do so would be to add to Joan's torment.

I do not mean that all this passed consciously through the mind of Cosmo that night. His suffering was too intense to allow anything that could be called rational thought. But such were the fundamental facts that lay below his unselfish resolve—such was the soil in which grew the fruits, that is, the deeds, the outcome of his nature.

Even God seemed to have left him. Alas for him who had so often lately offered to help another to pray, thinking the hour would never come to him when he could not pray! Now it had *come!* He did not even try to pray. For a season Cosmo had fallen in the eternal fight, and God seemed gone, and many things were rushing in upon him and overwhelming him. He did not yet know it, but it was not the loss of Joan but the seeming loss of his God that hollowed the last depth of his misery. Yet of all things that is the surest to pass. God never changes. Feelings are not scientific instruments for that which surrounds them. They speak only of themselves when they say, "I am cold; I am dark." They do not necessarily speak of truths. Perhaps the final victory of our Lord came when he followed the cry of *Why hast thou forsaken me?* with the words, *Father, into thy hands I commend my spirit.*

Shall we then bemoan any darkness? Shall we not rather gird up our strength to encounter it that we, too, from our side may break through the passage for the light beyond? He who fights with the dark shall know the gentleness that makes man great—the dawning countenance of the God of hope.

But that was not for Cosmo just yet. The night must fulfill its hours. Men are meant and sent to be troubled—that they may rise above the whole region of storm, above all possibility of being troubled.

Strange to say, there was no return of his fever, and as the darkness began to yield, he fell asleep.

Then came a curious dream. For ages it seemed Joan had been persuading him to go with her, and the old captain to go with him—the latter angry and pulling him, the former weeping and imploring. He would go with neither, and at last they both vanished. He sat alone on the side of a bare hill, and below him was all that remained of Castle Warlock. He had been dead so many years that it was now but a half-shapeless ruin of roofless walls, haggard and hollow and gray and desolate. It stood on its ridge like a solitary tooth in the jaw of some skeleton beast. But where was his father? How was it he had not yet found him, if he had been so long dead? He must rise and seek him! He must be somewhere in the universe!

Then a strain of music from the valley below came softly stealing up, at first barely audible. He listened. It grew as it rose, and held him bound. Like an upward river, it rose, and grew with a strong rushing, until it flooded all his heart and brain, working in him a marvelous good, which yet he did not understand. And all the time his eyes were upon the dead home of his fathers. Then, wonder of wonders, it began to change—to grow before his eyes! It was growing out of the earth like a plant! It grew and grew until it was as high as in the old days, and then it grew yet higher! A roof came upon it, and turrets and battlements—all to the sound of that creative music. And like fresh shoots from its stem, out from it went wings and walls. Like a great flower it was rushing visibly on to some mighty blossom of grandeur, when the dream suddenly left him, and he woke.

But instead of the enemy coming in upon him like a flood as his consciousness returned, to his astonishment he found his soul as calm as it was sad. God had returned to him while he slept, and he knew him as near as his own heart! The first thought that came was that God was Joan's God too, and therefore all was well. So long as God took care of her, and was with him, and his will was done in them both, all was on the way to be well so as nothing could be better. And with that he knew what he had to do—knew it without thinking—and he proceeded at once to do it. He rose and dressed himself.

It was still the gray of an early sunless morning. The dream had not crossed the shallows of the dawn. Quickly he gathered his few things into his knapsack, took his great-uncle's walking stick, saw that his money was safe, and stole quietly down the stair; softly he went out of the house, then left the village by the southward road so as not to encounter any inhabitants who might be astir at the early hour.

When he had walked about a mile, he turned into a road leading eastward, with the intention of going a few miles in that direction, and then turning to the north. But when he had traveled what to his weakness was a long distance, all at once, with the dismay of a perverse dream, above the trees rose the towers of Cairncarque. He turned back, and again southward.

But now, from tiredness, he had to sit down and rest as often as he was able to get up and walk. Coming to a village he learned that a coach for the north would pass within an hour. Therefore, he went to an inn, had some breakfast, and waited for it. Finding it would pass the village he had left, he took an inside place, and when it stopped for a moment in the one street of it, he saw Charles Jermyn cross it, evidently without a suspicion that his guest was not where he had left him.

When he had traveled some fifty miles, he left the coach and took himself once more to his feet—partly to save his money, partly because he felt the need of exercise to clear his thoughts. Alternately walking and riding, he found his strength increase as he went on, and his sorrow continued to be that of a cloudy summer day, but was never again, so long as the journey lasted, that of the fierce wintry tempest.

At length he drew nigh the city where he had spent his student years. On foot, weary and dusty, he entered it like a returning prodigal. Few Scotsmen would think he had made good use of his learning. But he had made the use of it God required; some Scotsmen, with and without other learning, have learned to think that a good use, in itself a sufficient success—for man came into the world not to make money, but to seek the kingdom and righteousness of God.

He walked straight into Mr. Burns' shop.

The jeweler did not know him at first, but the moment he spoke recognized him. Cosmo had been dubious what his reception might be, but Mr. Burns held out his hand as if they had parted only the day before, and said, "I thought I would see you again one day!"

"Mr. Burns," replied Cosmo, "I am very sorry I behaved to you as I did. I am no less sure about what I said than ever. But I am sorry I did not come to see you much after that. Perhaps we did not quite understand each other on either side."

"We shall understand each other better now, I fancy," said Mr. Burns. "I am glad you have not changed your opinion, for I have changed mine. If it weren't for you I would be retired by this time. But we'll have a talk about all that. Where are you bound?"

"I am on my way home," answered Cosmo. "I have not seen my father for more than two years."

"You'll do me the honor to put up at my house tonight, won't you? I am a bachelor, as you know, but will do my best to make you comfortable."

Cosmo gladly assented, and as it was now evening, Mr. Burns hastened the shutting of his shop, and in a few minutes they were seated at supper.

Their talk turned to divine righteousness in business, and thereafter Cosmo introduced the ring. He gave a short narrative of the finding of it, explaining the position of Lady Joan, and ended with telling him he had brought it to him, and with what object.

"I am extremely obliged to you, Mr. Warlock," replied the jeweler, "for placing such confidence in me, and that despite the mistaken principles I used to advocate. I have seen a little further since then, I am happy to say. The words you spoke, and I took so badly, would keep coming into my mind, and at the most inconvenient moments when I found myself in the middle of some transaction. At last I resolved to look the thing in the face and think it fairly out. The result is that, although I daresay nobody has recognized any difference in my way of doing business, there is one who must know a great difference: I now think of my neighbor's side of the bargain as well as my own. And I keep from doing anything that would anger me to find out I had not been sharp enough to prevent another from doing with me. The result is that I am not so rich this day as I might otherwise have been, but I enjoy life more, and hope God will forgive the days of my ignorance."

Cosmo could hardly reply for sheer pleasure. Mr. Burns saw his emotion and understood it. From that hour they were friends who respected and loved each other.

"And now for the ring!" said the jeweler.

Cosmo produced it.

Mr. Burns looked at it as if his keen eyes would pierce to the very heart of its mystery, turned it every way, examined it in every position relative to the light, removed it from its setting, went through the diamond catechism with it afresh, then weighed it, thought it over, and said, "What do you take the stone to be worth, Mr. Warlock?"

"Of course I can only guess," replied Cosmo. "But my impression is that it is worth more than a hundred and fifty, possibly two hundred pounds."

"You are right," answered Mr. Burns, "and you ought to have gone into my trade; you have a good eye for it. I could make a good jeweler of you. The ring is worth two hundred guineas, fair market value. But as I cannot ask from any customer more than it is absolutely worth, I must take my profit off your end: do you think that is fair?"

"Perfectly," answered Cosmo.

"Then I must give you only two hundred pounds for it, and take the extra ten pounds for myself. You see, it may be some time before I get my money again, so I think five percent on the amount is not more than the fair thing."

"It seems perfectly fair and moderate to me," replied Cosmo.

As soon as dinner was over, he sat down to write to Joan. While there was nothing that must be said, he had still feared writing. He wrote:

My dearest Joan,
As you have trusted me up till now, so trust me still, and wait for an expla-

nation of my peculiar behavior in going away without saying goodbye till the proper time comes—which must come one day, for our Master said more than once that there was nothing covered which should not be revealed, neither anything hid that should not be known. I feel sure, therefore, that I shall be allowed to tell you everything at some later time.

I am sending you a check. I borrowed fifteen pounds from Dr. Jermyn—a good deal more than I wanted. Therefore, I have got Mr. Burns, my friend and the jeweler in this city, to add five pounds to the two hundred which he gave me for the ring, and I beg you, Joan, for the sake of old times, and new also, to pay the fifteen pounds to Dr. Jermyn for me, which I would much rather owe to you than to him. The rest of it, the other ten pounds, I will pay you when I can—it may not be in this world. And in the next—what then, Joan? Why, then—but for that we will wait—who more earnestly than I?

To all the coming eternity, dear Joan, I shall never cease to love you—first for yourself, and then for your lovely goodness to me. May the only Perfection, whose only being is love, take you to his heart—as he is always trying to do with all of us! I mean to let him have all of me, if only I can get myself out of the way.

Dearest Joan, Your far-off but near friend,

COSMO WARLOCK

33

• • • • • • • • • • • • • • • •

Home Again

*E*arly the next day, while the sun was still casting huge diagonal shadows across the wide street, Cosmo climbed to the roof of the Defiance coach, his heart swelling at the thought of so soon seeing his father again. It was a lovely summer morning, cool and dewy, and from the champing clank of the bits, and the voices of the passengers, and guard, and coachman, Cosmo's mind sank into thoughts about the shadows all about him. Almost without realizing it, before long he was comparing the similarity between shadow and evil and law. He saw how the Jews came to attribute evil to the hand of God as well as good, and how Paul said that the law gave life to sin—in the same way as the sun, which is nothing but blinding light, causes shadows though there is no darkness in it at all. He saw too that in the spiritual world, we need a live sun strong enough to burn up all the shadows by shining through the things that cast them, and compelling their transparency—and that live sun is the God who is light, and in whom is no darkness at all. And where there is no longer anything covered or hid, could sin live at all? These and other similar thoughts held him until the noisy streets of the granite city of Aberdeen lay far behind him.

Swiftly the western road toward Inverurie and Rhynie flew from under the sixteen flashing shoes of the thoroughbreds that bore him along. The light and hope and strength of the newborn day were stirring, mounting, swelling—even in the heart of the sad lover. In every honest heart more or less, whether young or old, feeble or strong, the new summer day stirs, and will stir while the sun has heart enough for men to live on earth. Surely the live God is not absent from the symbol of his glory! The light and the hope are not there without him!

Cosmo had changed since first he sat behind such horses on his way to the university seven years earlier. It was the change of growth, but to him at this moment it felt like the growth of decay—as if he had been young then and was old now. Little could he yet imagine, at twenty-three, what age means! Devout youth as he was, he little understood how much more than he his father felt his dependence on God. Though his faith was real, many years had yet to pass before his faith knew the silent depths of his father's. It is the strength of God that gives life to every muscle and skill of the youth. But it looks so natural to him, seems so much his own, that in the glory of its possession, he does not feel it *as* the presence of the life-giving God. But when weakness begins to show itself—a shadow-background against which the strength is known and outlined—and the earthly begins to press against not only its own parts but also upon the spirit within, then indeed a man must believe in God with an entireness independent of feeling. In the growing feebleness of old age, weakness is the matrix of divine strength, from which a great gladness shall before long be born—the life which it is God's intent to share with his children.

Cosmo was on the way to know all this, but now his trouble sat heavy upon him. However, on this day the sun shone as if he knew nothing, or as if he knew all, and knew it to be well. Cosmo was going home, and the love of his father was a deep gladness in spite of another love's absence. Seldom is it so; but between the true father and the true son, it will always be so.

When he came within a mile of Muir o' Warlock, he left the coach to walk the rest of the way. He wanted to enjoy, in gentle, unruffled flow, the thoughts that kept coming and going like swallows between him and his nest as he approached it. Everything, even the most common things that met him as he went, had a strange beauty, as if—although he had known it so long—now for the first time was its innermost essence revealed by some polarized light from a source unseen. How small and poor the cottages looked—but how homelike! How sweet the smoke of their chimneys! How cold they must be in winter—but how warm were the hearts inside them! There was Jean Elder's Sunday linen spread like snow on her gooseberry bushes; there was the shoemaker's cow eating her hardest, as if she would devour the very turf that bordered the road—held from the grain on the other side of the low fence by a strong chain in the hand of a child of seven; and there was the first dahlia of the season in Jonathan Japp's garden!

As he entered the village, the road was empty of life except for a half-grown pig, a hen or two picking about, and several cats lying in the sun. He did not look about, for he was in no mood to delay his arrival with conversation, but he could not help wondering why he saw nobody about. Any passing stranger was usually enough to bring people to their doors. Sheltered behind rose trees or geraniums or hydrangeas behind their windows, however, not a few were peering at him as he passed.

The villagers had learned from someone on the coach that the young laird was coming. But a general feeling, strange to say, had got about which was subtly prejudiced against him. They had looked to hear great things of their favorite, and he had not made of himself the success they expected, and from their disappointment they imagined his blame. It troubled them to think of the old man, whom they all loved, sending his son to college on the golden horse, whose history had ever since been the cherished romance of the place, and after all that getting no tangible good of him. So when they saw him coming along, dusty and shabby—hardly well-dressed enough for a Sunday even in the country—they drew back from the peep-holes with a sigh, let him pass, and then looked again.

Cosmo suspected none of this, but kept on his way unconscious of the looks that watched him: the prodigal returning the less satisfactorily, guilty enough to repent.

After leaving the village, every step Cosmo took was like a revelation and a memory in one. When he turned off the main road, the hills came rushing to meet and welcome him. Yet it was only that they stood there changeless, eternally the same as they had always been: that was the welcome with which they met the heart that had always loved them. And the next turn was home itself, for that turn was at the base of the ridge on which the castle stood.

As he approached it a strange feeling of stillness came over him, which deepened as he drew nearer. It was as if his dream of lifelessness had returned! Was the place utterly empty? Was there no breathing soul in it? He heard no sound; there was no sign of life from cow-house or stable. A cart with one wheel stood in the cart shed; a harrow lay with spikes upward where he had hollowed the mound of snow so many years earlier. The fields themselves had a haggard sort of look. A crop of oats was ripening in that which stood nearest, but they covered only half of it; the rest was in potatoes. And among them the only show of life he saw was Aggie pulling weeds out from between the rows. All around the courtyard the doors were shut—all but the kitchen door; that stood wide open as usual.

A sickening fear came upon Cosmo. It was more than a week since he had heard from home. Could his father have died in that time, and therefore the place be desolate? He dared not enter the house. He would go to the garden first, and there pray and gather courage.

He went round the kitchen tower, as the nearest building was called, and made for his old seat, the big, smooth stone. But someone was sitting on it, with his head bent forward on his knees! It must be his father, but how changed he was! His look was that of a worn-out laborer—one who had borne the burden and heat of the day and is already half-asleep, waiting for the night. He sat as motionless as a statue; on the ground lay a spade which looked as if it had dropped from his hand as he sat upon the stone. Beside him lay Marion's Bible. For a moment Cosmo stood motionless.

But the first movement he made forward, the old man lifted his head with an expectant look, then rose quickly, and, unable to straighten himself completely, hurried stooping, with short steps, to meet him. He placed his hands on his son's shoulders, raised himself up, and for a few moments they were silent, each in the other's arms.

The laird drew back and looked his son in his face. A heavenly smile crossed the sadness of his countenance, and his wrinkled old hand closed tremblingly on Cosmo's shoulder.

"They canna take frae me my son!" he murmured, and from that time on rarely spoke to him except in the mother tongue.

He led him to the stone, where there was just room enough for two that loved each other, and they sat down together. The laird put his hand on his son's knee as Cosmo had done on his father's when a boy.

"Are ye the same, Cosmo?" he asked. "Are ye my ain bairn?"

"Father," returned Cosmo, "if it be possible, I love you more than ever. I'm come home to you, not to leave you again so long as I live. If you are in any need, I'll help in it if I can, or at least share it with you. Ay, I may well say I'm the same, only more of it!"

"The Lord's name be praised!" murmured the laird. "But do ye love *him* the same as ever, Cosmo?"

"Father, I don't love him the same—I hope I love him a heap better. He knows now that he may take his will with me. Nothing that I know of comes between him and me."

The old man raised his arm and put it round his boy's shoulders: he was not as so many fathers who make their children fear more than love them.

"Then, Lord, let me die in peace," he said, "for mine eyes hae seen thy salvation. But ye dinna look the same, Cosmo! Hoo is it?"

"I have come through much, lately," answered Cosmo. "I've been ailing in body and harassed in heart. I'll tell you all about it when we have time—and of that we'll have plenty, I'm sure, for I told you I won't leave you again. And if you had only let me know you were failing, I would have come home long ago. It was against the grain for me to stay away."

"The auld shouldn't lie upon the tap o' the yoong, Cosmo, my son."

"Father, I would willingly be a bed to you to lie upon if that would ease you. But I'm thinking we both may be able to lie softest in the will of the great Father, even when it's hardest."

"True as trowth!" returned the laird. "But ye're lookin' some tired-like, Cosmo!"

"I *am* tired, and awfully dry. I would so like a drink of milk."

The old man's head dropped, and he sat for the space of about a minute in silence. Then he lifted it up and said, looking with calm clear eyes into those of his son.

" 'Tis sore upon me, Cosmo, but I'll say yet the will o' the Lord be dune, when I haena a drop o' milk aboot the place t' set afore my only-begotten son when he comes home t' me frae a far country! Eh, Lord! when yer ain son came home frae his sore wrestle an' long sojourn among them that didna ken him nor thee, it wasna t' an auld shabby man he came home, but t' the Lord o' glory! Cosmo, the hand o' man's been so heavy upon me that coo after coo's gone frae me. Ye'll hae t' drink cauld water, my bairn!"

Again the old man's heart overcame him. His head sank and he murmured, "Lord, I haena a drop o' milk t' give my bairn—me that would gie him my hert's blood! But, Lord, who am I t' speak like that t' thee, who didst let thine own pour oot his very sowl's blood for him an me!"

"Father," said Cosmo, "I can do with water as well as anybody. Do you think I'm no more of a man than to care what I put into me? If you're poorer than ever, I'm prouder than ever to share it with you. Stay here, and I'll just run and get a drink and come right back."

"I'll go wi' ye, man," answered the laird, rising. "Grizzie's a heap occupied wi' yer gran'mither. She's been wearin' down for a fortnight. She's in no pain, the Lord be praised! an' she'll never ken the straits her hoose is come to. Cosmo, I hae been a terrible coward—dreadin' day an' night yer home-comin', not wantin' that ye should see such a broken man as yer father! But noo it's over, an' here ye are, an' my heart's lighter than it's been for many a year!"

Cosmo's own sorrow drew back into the distance from before the face of his father's. And with that it was as if a new well of life sprang up suddenly in his being.

"Father," he said, "we'll hold on to the straight road together. There's room for two abreast in it!"

"Ay! ay!" returned the laird with a smile; "that's the bonniest word ye could hae come home wi' t' me! We must jist perk up a bit, an' be patient, that patience may hae her perfect work. I'll hae another try—an' weel I may, for the light o' my auld eyes is this day restored t' me."

"And so grandmother's wearing away?"

"T' the land o' the leal, laddie."

"Will she know me?"

"No, she winna ken ye. She'll never ken anybody more in this warl'. But she'll ken plenty whaur she's goin'!"

He rose and they walked together toward the kitchen. There was nobody there, but they heard steps going to and fro in the room above. The laird made haste, but before he could lay his hand on a glass to get for Cosmo the water he wanted, Grizzie appeared on the stair, descending. She hurried down and across the floor to Cosmo, seized him by the hand, and looked him in the face with the anxiety of an angel-hen. Her look said what his father's voice had said just before: *Are ye all there—all that used t' be?*

"Hoo's gran'mamma?" asked Cosmo.

"Ow, doin' weel eneuch, sir. She has neither pain nor knowledge o' sorrow t' trouble her. The Lord grant the sowls o' us all such a dyin'!"

"Hae ye naethin' better than cauld water t' give him a drink o', Grizzie?" asked the laird in despair.

"Nae, 'cept he would condescen' t' a granie meal in't," returned Grizzie mournfully, looking at him with an anxious look, as if before the heir she was ashamed of the poverty of the house, and dreaded blame.

"Water, wi' meal please, Grizzie!" said Cosmo with a smile.

She brought it to him—cold water with a little meal sprinkled on the top of it—the same drink he used to give his old mare, now long departed to the place prepared for her.

"There's this to be said for the water, father," he remarked, as he set down the wooden bowl in which Grizzie had thought proper to supply it, "that it comes more direct from the hand of God himself—maybe than even the milk. But I don't know. For I don't doubt that organic chemistry may after all be nearer his hand than inorganic! Anyway, I never drank better drink. And if one day he but satisfies my soul's hunger after his righteousness as he has this minute satisfied my body's thirst for water, I'll be a happier man than any who ever danced or sang."

"It's an innocent creature that gives thanks for cauld water!" said Grizzie. "But I must get back t' my bairn up the stair. An' may it please the Lord t' lift her afore long, for they must be lookin' for her beyon' the burn by this time. When she wakes in the mornin', her tongue'll be no more scornin'!"

This was Grizzie's last comment against her mistress. The laird took no notice of it. He knew Grizzie's devotion, and, well as he loved his mother, could not but know also that there was some ground for the statement.

Scarcely a minute had passed when the voice of the old woman came from the top of the stair, calling aloud and excitedly, "Laird! Laird! come up directly. Come up, lairds both! She's comin' t' hersel'!"

They flew up the stairs, Cosmo helping his father, and they approached the bed together.

With smooth, colorless face, unearthly to look upon, the old lady lay motionless, her eyes wide open, looking up as if they saw something beyond the end of the bed, her lips moving but uttering no sound. At last came a murmur, in which Cosmo's ears alone were keen enough to discern the words.

"Marion, Marion," she said, "ye're in the lan' o' forgiveness! I hae done the lad no ill. He'll come home t' ye none the worse for any words o' mine. We're not all made sae good t' begin wi' as yersel', Marion!"

Here her voice became a mere murmur, so far as human ear could distinguish, and presently ceased. A minute or so more and her breathing grew intermittent. After a few deep respirations, at long intervals, it stopped.

"She'll be haein' it oot wi' my own mistress before lang!" remarked Grizzie to herself as she closed her eyes.

"Mother! Mother!" cried the laird, kneeling by the bedside. Cosmo knelt also, but no word of the prayers that ascended was audible. The laird was giving thanks that another was gone home, and Cosmo was praying for help to be to his father a true son, such as the Son of Man was to the Father of Man. They rose from their knees and went quietly down the stair; and as they went from the room, they heard Grizzie say to herself, "She's gone whaur there's mair—enough an' t' spare!"

The remains of lady Joan's ten pounds was enough to bury her.

They invited no one personally, but all the village came to her funeral.

34

The Laborer

$\mathcal{S}$uch power had been accumulated and brought to bear against Glenwarlock that at length he was reduced almost to the last extremity. He had had to part with all his horses even before his crops were all sown, and therefore had to dismiss his men, and try to sell some of the land as it stood, while getting some neighboring farmer to undertake the rest of the land for the one harvest left him. But those who might otherwise have bought and cultivated it were afraid of offending Lord Lickmyloof, whose hand was pretty generally seen in the turn of affairs.

So things had come to a bad pass with the laird and his household. A small crop of oats and one of potatoes were coming on, for which the laird did what little he could, assisted by Grizzie and Aggie at such times when they could leave their respective charges. But in the meantime the stock of meal was getting low, and the laird did not see where more was to come from. He and Grizzie had only porridge, with a little salt and butter, for two, and not unfrequently the third also of their daily meals. For a while Grizzie managed to keep alive a few fowls that picked about everywhere, finally making broth of them for her invalid, and persuading the laird to eat the little that was not boiled away. At length there was neither cackle nor crow about the place, so that to Cosmo it seemed dying out into absolute silence—after which would come the decay and crumbling he had looked down upon in his dream.

At once he began to do what he could for the ripening crops, resolving to hire himself out for the harvest to some place whose grain was later than Glenwarlock, so that he might be able to mow the oats at home first, and then when he had to leave, his father and Grizzie with the help of Aggie would be able to secure them.

Nothing could now prevent the closing of the net of the last mortgage about them. The only thing Cosmo could hope for after this was simply to keep his father and Grizzie alive to the end of their natural days. Shelter was secure, for they owned the castle free of any encumbrance. The winter would be drawing on, but there would be the oats and the potatoes, with what kale the garden would yield them, and he thought they had plenty of peats for fuel. Yet he would frequently find himself speculating, as he wandered aimlessly through the dreary silence of the buildings, how long he could keep his father warm by a judiciously ordered and gradual consumption of the place. The stables and cow-houses would afford a large quantity of fuel. The barn too had a great deal of heavy woodwork about it. And there was the third tower or block of the castle, for many years used for nothing but storage, whose whole thick floors he would thankfully honor, burning them to ashes in such a cause. In the spring there would be no land left them, but so long as he could save the house and garden, and find means of keeping his two alive in them, he would not grieve over its loss.

Agnes was a little shy of Cosmo—he had been away so long! But at intervals her shyness would yield and she would talk to him with much the same freedom as of old when they went to school together. In his rambles Cosmo would not pass her grandfather's cottage without going in to ask about him and his wife, and having a little chat with Aggie. Her truehearted ways made her, next to his father and Mr. Simon, the best comforter he had.

She was now a strong, well-grown, sunburnt woman, with rough hands and tender eyes. Occasionally she would yet give a sharp answer, but life and its needs and struggles had made her grave, and in general she would, like a soft cloud, brood a little before she gave a reply. She had by nature such a well-balanced mind, and had set herself so strenuously to do the right thing, that her cross seemed already her natural choice, as indeed it always is—of the deeper nature. In her Cosmo always found what strengthened him for the life he now had to lead, though, so long as at any moment he could have his father's company, he could not call or think his life hard, except insofar as he could not make his father's life as easy as he would like.

When the laird heard that his son, the heir of Glenwarlock, had hired himself for the harvest on a neighboring farm, he was silent. It weighed heavy both on the love and the pride of the father, which in this case were one, to think of his son as a hired servant of a rough, swearing man, who had made money as a butcher. The farm, too, was at such a distance that he would have to stay and sleep there. But the season of this silence, by the clock at least, was but of a few minutes duration. Presently the laird was on his knees thanking God that he had given him a son who would be an honor to any family out of heaven: there, he knew, every one was an honor to every other!

Before the harvest on the farm of Stanewhuns arrived, Cosmo had cut their own grain, with Grizzie to gather, Aggie to bind, and his father to stook, and so got himself into some measure of shape and training. It is true, he found it harder at Stanewhuns, where he had to keep up with more experienced scythe men. But within two days he was more than equal to it and able to set his father's heart at ease concerning his toil.

The time since his homecoming, despite all his troubles, had been blessed in his father's company. And not unfrequently would Mr. Simon come to visit, and the three, seated together in the old drawing room or on some hillside, would talk for hours about things both spiritual and practical—vastly different to those without eyes to see; one and the same to the truly wise. In the counsels they held, Cosmo represented the rising generation with its new thought, its new consciousness of need, and its new difficulties. He was delighted to find how readily his notions were received. For what all men need is the same—only the look of it changes as its nature expands before the growing soul or the growing generation, whose hunger and thirst at the same time grow with it. And coming from the higher to the lower, it must ever be in the shape of difficulty that the most precious revelations first appear. Even Mary, to whom first the highest revelation came—and came closer than to any other—had to sit and ponder over the great matter, and have the sword pass through her soul, before the thoughts of her heart could be revealed to her.

But Cosmo of the new time found himself at home with the men of the next older time, because both he and they were true; for in the truth there is neither old nor new. The well-instructed scribe of the kingdom is familiar with the new as well as old shapes of it, and can bring either kind from his treasury. There was not a question Cosmo could start but Mr. Simon had something at hand to contribute right to the point, and plenty more within the digging-scope of his thought-spade.

But now that he had to work all day, and at night saw no one with whom to take sweet counsel, Cosmo did feel lonely—even though it was a comfort to remember that his father was within his reach and he would see him the next Sunday. And at least he was spared having to share a room with several other men who might prove worse than undesirable company. For the farmer, whose rough speech and manners were a byword in the country, yet respected Cosmo's station sufficiently that he would not hear of his sleeping anywhere but in the best bedroom they had in the house. And from respect to the heir of a decayed family and valueless inheritance, he even modified his own habits so far as almost to cease swearing in his presence.

Appreciating this kindness, in his turn Cosmo tried to be agreeable to those around him, and in their short evenings—being weary, they retired early—would in his talk make such good use of his knowledge as to interest the whole family, so that afterward most of them declared it the most pleasant harvest time they had ever had.

Perhaps as a consequence the youngest daughter, who had been to a boarding school and had never before lifted a hand in the harvest field, appeared toward the end of the first week in the field where they were working, and took herself to gather behind Cosmo's scythe. But Cosmo was far too occupied with the rhythmic swing of his scythe to be aware of the honor done him by the admiring farmer's daughter. Still further was he from suspecting that it had anything to do with the appearance of Agnes one afternoon, who brought him a letter from his father, with which she had armed herself by telling him she was going there and could take a message to the young laird.

The harvest began on a Monday, and the week passed without Cosmo's once seeing his father. On the Sunday he rose early and set out for Castle Warlock. He would have gone the night before, but at the request of his master remained to witness the signing of his will. As he walked toward home he found that the week had given him such a consciousness of power as he had never had before. With the labor of his own hands he knew himself capable of earning bread for more than himself. And his limbs themselves seemed to know themselves stronger as a result of the work.

His way was mostly by footpaths, often up and down hill, now over a moor, now through a valley by a small stream. The freshness of the morning he found no less reviving than in the old boyish days, and he sang as he walked, taking huge breaths of the life that lay on the heathery hilltop. And as he sang the words came almost of themselves.

> Win' that blaws the simmer plaid,
> Ower the hie hill's shouthers laid,
> Green wi' gerse, an' reid wi' heather,
> Welcome wi' yer soul-like weather!
> Mony a win' there has been sent
> Oot 'aneth the firmament;
> Ilka ane its story has;
> Ilka ane began an' was;
> Ilka ane fell quaiet an' mute
> Whan its angel wark was oot.
> First gaed ane oot ower the mirk,
> Whan the maker gan to work;
> Ower it gaed and ower the sea,
> An' the warl' begud to be.
> Mony ane has come an' gane
> Sin' the time there was but ane:
> Ane was great an' strong, an' rent
> Rocks an' mountains as it went
> Afore the Lord, his trumpeter,
> Waukin' up the prophet's ear;
> Ane was like a steppin' soun'
> I' the mulberry taps abune;
> Then the Lord's ain steps did swing,
> Walkin' on afore his king;
> Ane lay doon like a scoldit pup
> At his feet an' gatna up,
> Whan the word the maister spak
> Drave the wull-cat billows back;
> And gaed frae his lips, an' dang
> To the earth the sodger thrang;
> Ane comes frae his hert to mine,
> Ilka day, to mak it fine.
> Breath o' God, eh! come an' blaw
> Frae my hert ilk fog awa';

Wauk me up, an' mak me strang,
Fill my hert wi' mony a sang,
Frae my lips again to stert,
Fillin' sails o' mony a hert,
Blawin' them ower seas dividin'
To the only place to bide in.

"Eh! Mr. Warlock! is that you singin' on the Sawbath day?" said the voice of a young woman behind him.

Cosmo turned and saw Elspeth, his master's daughter.

"Whaur's the wrang o' that, Miss Elsie?" he answered. "Arena we tellt t' sing an' mak melody t' the Lord?"

"Ay, but in yer hert, not oot loud—'cep' it be in the kirk. That's the place t' sing on Sundays. An' it wasna a psalm-tune ye was at."

"Maybe no. Maybe I was a bit ower happy for any tune in the tune books, an' had t' hae ane that came o' itsel'!"

"An' what would mak ye sae happy—if a body might speir?" asked Elspeth, peeping from under long lashes, with a shy, half-frightened, sidelong glance at the youth. She was a handsome girl of the milkmaid type, who wore a bonnet with pretty ribbons. She had many admirers and thought of herself as a young lady, and had therefore grown a little bold without knowing it. "Ye haena ower muckle at home t' make ye happy," she added sympathetically.

"I hae ilka thing to make me happy!" answered Cosmo, " 'cep' it be money. But maybe that'll come next—who kens? But where are ye boun' for, Miss Elsie?"

"For the Muir o' Warlock, t' see my sister, the schoolmaster's wife. Poor man! he's been ailin' ever sin' the spring. I little thought I was t' hae sich good company on the road! Ye hae made a great differen on my father, Mr. Warlock!"

"Your father is very kind t' me. So are ye all!" said Cosmo. "My father will be grateful to ye for bein' so friendly t' me."

"Was ye content wi' my gatherin' to ye—to yer scythe, I mean, Laird?" faltered Elspeth.

"Who could hae been better, Miss Elsie? Try as I wad, I couldna leave ye behind me."

"Did ye want t' leave me ahind ye?" rejoined Elsie, with a sidelong look and a blush, which Cosmo never saw. "I wouldn't seek a better t' gather from. But maybe ye dinna like my hands!"

The suggestion was, of course, entirely irrelevant to the gathering, for what could it matter to the mower what sort of hands the woman had who gathered his swath?

What Cosmo might have answered, or in what perplexity between truth and unwillingness to hurt the girl he might very soon have been landed, I need not speculate, seeing that all danger was suddenly swept away by a second voice which called out to Cosmo as unexpectedly as the first.

They had just passed a great stone on the roadside where Aggie was seated, and had been for some time, waiting for Cosmo. Recognizing the voices that approached her, she waited until the pair had passed her shelter, and then addressed Cosmo with a familiarity she had not used since his return—for which Aggie had her reasons.

"Cosmo!" she called, rising as she spoke, "winna ye wait for me? Ye hae words for two as weel as ane."

The moment Cosmo heard her voice he turned to meet her, glad enough.

"Eh! Aggie!" he said, "I'm pleased to see ye. It was right good o' ye t' come an' meet me! Hoo's yer father, an' hoo's mine?"

"They're both brawly," she answered, "an' happy enough at the thought o' seein' ye. If ye couldna look in upon mine t'day, he would walk doon t' the castle. Since yesterday mornin' the laird, Grizzie tells me, hasna rested a minute in one place, 'cep' in his bed. What for camna ye yesterday?"

As he was answering her question, Aggie cast a keen searching look at his companion. Elsie's face was as red as fire could have reddened it.

The two girls were hardly acquainted, nor would Elsie have dreamed of familiarity with the daughter of a poor cottar. Aggie seemed much further below her than she was below the young laird of Glenwarlock. Yet here was the rude girl addressing him as *Cosmo*—with the boldness of a sister! And he took it as a matter of course, and answered in similar style! It was unnatural! Indignation grew fierce within her. She might have been able to wake something in his heart toward her before they parted had it not been for this shameless cowgirl!

"Ye'll be gaein' t' see yer sister, Miss Elsie?" said Agnes, after a moment's pause.

Elspeth kept her head turned away and made her no answer. Reverting to Cosmo, Aggie asked him about a difficulty she had met with her studies, which she was still pursuing with Mr. Simon whenever spare moments could be had. So Elsie, who understood nothing of the subject, was thrown out of the conversation. She dropped a little behind, and took the role of the abandoned one. When Cosmo saw, he stopped, and they waited for her.

"Are we walkin' too fast for ye, Miss Elsie?" he said.

"Not at all," she answered, attempting her best English. "I can walk as fast as anyone."

Cosmo turned to Aggie and said, "Aggie, we had no right t' speak aboot things that only two kent when there was three walkin' t'gether. Ye see, Miss Elsie, Aggie an' me was at the school t'gether, an' we happened t' take up wi' the same kin' o' thing, particularly algebra an' geometry, an' sometimes we can hardly hold oor tongues frae talkin' o' the things we're learnin' when we get t'gether. Today it's made us overlook oor manners, an' I beg ye t' forgive us."

"I didna think it was a profitable conversation for the Sabbath day," said Elsie, with a smile meant to be chastening. It did not take but a few minutes more, however, for the two again to become absorbed together, and again Elsie was left out. Nor did this occur either through returning forgetfulness on the part of Aggie, or the naturally strong undertow of the tide of science in her brain, but rather from an undertow distinctly and cunningly more feminine. Once more

Elsie adopted the neglected role, dropped farther and farther behind, until the reality of the situation grew heavy on her soul, and she sat down by the roadside and wept. Finally she rose, in anger more than hurt, turned back, and took another way to the village.

Poor girl-heart! How many tears do fancies doomed to pass cost those who give them a night's lodging! But how is it that girls, ready to cry their eyes out for what they call love when the case is their own, can be so hardhearted in the case of another? Here was Agnes, not otherwise an ill-natured girl, positively exultant over Elsie's discomfort and disappearance. The girl had done her no wrong, yet this was how she talked to the inner ear of her conscience: *The impident limmer!—Makin' up t' a gentleman like oor laird 'at is t' be! Cudna he be doon a meenute but she must be upon 'im t' devoor him!—an' her father naethin' but the cursin' flesher o' Stanewhuns! Na, na! Cosmo's for Elsie's betters!* How difficult—yea, impossible!— it is for us to do as the Lord's life was spent to teach us, even when we try to convince ourselves we do so: that is, put others before ourselves. Impossible, perhaps, but nonetheless required!

Elsie appeared no more in any field that season.

What a day was that Sunday to Cosmo! Labor is the harbinger of joy, to prepare the way before him. His father received him home like a king come home with victory. And was he not a king? Did not the Lord say he was a king, because he came into the world to bear witness to the truth?

They walked together to church and home again, as happy as two boys let out of school—home to their poor dinner of new potatoes and a little milk, the latter brought by Aggie with her father's compliments "to his lairdship," as Grizzie gave the message. But how can such be called a poor dinner? Truth and Scotland forgive me, there is none so good!

Immediately after their dinner they went to the drawing room—an altogether pleasant place now in the summer, and full of the scent of the flowers Grizzie arranged in the old vases on the chimneypiece. The laird laid himself down on the brocade-covered sofa, and Cosmo sat close beside him on a low chair, and talked, and told him this and that, and read to him, till at last the old man fell asleep. Then Cosmo softly spread a covering upon him, and sat thinking over things sad and pleasant, until he too fell asleep, to be with Joan in his dreams. When he had dreamed of her in the old days, the two years she was older than him made of her almost a goddess, to revere but not approach. Now, however, the space between them had vanished in his mind—and especially in his heart.

At length the harvest was over, and Cosmo again went home. And in poverty-stricken Castle Warlock dwelt the most peaceful, contented household imaginable. But in it reigned a stillness almost awful. So great indeed was the silence that Grizzie said she had to make more noise than necessary in order that she would not hear the ghosts.

The poorer their fare, the more pains Grizzie took to make it palatable. The gruel the laird now always had for supper was cooked with love rather than fuel. With what a tender hand she washed his feet! What miracles of the laundress-art were the old shirts he wore! Now that he had no other woman to look after him, she was to him like a mother to a delicate child, in all but the mother's familiarity. But the cloud was cold to her also. She seldom said rhymes in her speech, which had long been a trademark of her broad Scotch tongue, especially when muttering to herself. And except when unusually excited, she never returned a sharp answer.

35

•••••••••••••••••••

The Schoolmaster

Within a week of returning home Cosmo received the following letter from Joan:

> My Dear Cosmo:
>
> Of course I cannot understand why you went away as you did. It makes me very unhappy, lest I was somehow to blame. But I trust you entirely. I too hope for the day when it will be impossible to hide anything. I will be more happy than you can imagine to pay Dr. Jermyn the money. I cannot do so just yet because the same day you left he was called to London on medical business, and has not yet returned.
>
> Give my love to your father. I hope you are safe and happy with him by this time. I wish I were with you! Will that day ever come again? I cannot tell you how I miss you. I only hope, dear Cosmo, it was not my fault you went away. I know my behavior was such as most people would have considered strange. But you are not most people, and I did and do think you understood it, and made all the allowance for me that could be made.
>
> I had almost forgot to thank you for the money. I do thank you, Cosmo, but I should have been much more grateful had you kept it. It is next to no use to me without you or your father! And to know I have such a large sum in the house that my brother knows nothing about quite frightens me sometimes. I wish you had left me the horse to hide it in. I feel like a thief, and I am sure my brother would think of me as one if he knew. Mind you do not make the slightest allusion to it in any of your letters, and ask your father not to do so either. It has just one comfort in it—that I could now, if driven to it, afford to run away. My love to your father.
>
> JOAN

Long before the letter had arrived, Cosmo had told his father everything and though he could not believe there was anything between Joan and the doctor, he quite approved of his son's conduct.

"Wait upon the Lord," he said, after listening to his son's narrative with the excitement of a young heart, the ache of an old one, and the hope of a strong one. "Wait patiently on him, and he will give you the desire of your heart."

They waited—and patiently.

Now that the harvest was past, the question again came—what could Cosmo do to make a little money? He had many an anxious talk on the matter with Mr. Simon but neither could think of anything. The weeks came and went, and the frosts came and went, and then came and stayed. And the snow fell and melted, and then fell and lay. Winter settled down with unmoving rigor upon Castle Warlock. And it had not lasted long before it became evident that the natural powers of the laird had begun to fail more rapidly. But sufficient unto the day is the evil thereof, and that truth applies in the matter of death as well as of life. If we are not to forestall the difficulties of living, surely we are not to forestall the sorrows of dying.

There was one thing, however, that troubled Cosmo. The good old man's appetite had begun to fail, and how was he to get for him what might tempt him to eat? But his father was always contented and never expressed a desire for anything that was not in the house.

He would have liked to have his father take his grandmother's room, warmer and nearer the kitchen. But he would not leave the one he had last occupied with his wife. He would go from that, he said, as she had gone. So Cosmo took his grandmother's, and there wrote and read—and when his father could not, in the very cold weather, leave his bed, Cosmo was within call of the slightest knock on his door. Every now and then, when the cold would abate a little, the laird would revive, and hope would grow strong in the mind of Cosmo that perhaps he might be intended to live many years. But it is hard to labor on without encouragement or any visible sign or hope of result.

Many a time did the Gracies go without milk that they might send for the laird the little their cow gave. But though Cosmo never refused their kindness, as indeed he had no right to, it went to his heart that the two old people should go without what they might need for his father. Mr. Simon, too, would now and then send something from his house or from the village—more often than Cosmo knew, for he had taken Grizzie into his confidence, and she was discreet. But in the middle of the winter a heavenly crumb fell to keep the human sparrows picking.

The schoolmaster at the Muir, who had nine or ten years earlier behaved so insolently to the Warlocks, had returned to his duties. But he was far from a young man now, had been getting worse for some time, and was at length unable to go on with his teaching duties. He must therefore provide a substitute, and Cosmo happened to hear that he was on the lookout for one.

Cosmo knew that if he had desired to be made parish schoolmaster, the influence of Lord Lickmyloof would have been too strong against him. But it seemed possible that his old master might have so far forgotten bygones as to be willing to employ him at least as a substitute. Therefore he went to him, was shown into the room where he sat wrapped in blankets, and laid before him his request.

Now the schoolmaster, although both worldly in his judgment and hasty in his temper, was not an altogether heartless man. Keen feelings are not always dissociated even from brutality. One thing will reach the heart that another will not; and much that looks like heartlessness may be mainly stupidity. After his first rush of passion, he had ever consciously regretted that he had used the word that incensed the boy. And although he had never to his own heart confessed himself in the wrong in knocking down the violator of the sacredness of the master's person, yet he had been unconsciously sorry for that also. Had he been sorrier, his pride would yet have come between him and confession, for it was as strong as his temper was quick.

So when the boy stood unexpectedly before him whom he had not set eyes on for years, a fine youth, down in the world, and come to beg a favor—it was a perfect opportunity for the old man, not only of making reparation without making a confession, but also of putting on the dignity of apparent forgiveness. Therefore he received Cosmo kindly, even with a slight stiffness at first, and having heard his request, immediately agreed to it graciously, which filled Cosmo with such gratitude that he could not help showing some emotion. The heart of the schoolmaster in its turn then asserted itself, and from that moment friendly relations were established between them.

Things were soon arranged. Cosmo was to be paid by the week and should begin his work the next morning. He returned to the castle in great happiness, taking with him one or two simple luxuries for his father from the village. That night he could hardly sleep.

He set about his duties with zeal. Teaching itself is a most difficult assignment to anyone desiring to make it genuine, and besides, Cosmo had to leave home early in all wintry weather and walk to the school through the bitterness of black frost, the shifting toil of deep snow, or the assault of fierce storm. But he thought nothing of his own labors; the only thing that was hard for him was having to leave his father all the winter day alone, for he generally did not get back till five o'clock.

But from this, in the heart of the laird there now arose a fresh gratitude for the son God had given him. Every time he received his son from the arms of the winter, it was like the welcoming of one lost and found again.

Into the stern weather of their need had stolen a summer day to keep hope alive. Cosmo spent all the time he had at home waiting with mind and body upon his father. He read to him, and sometimes played backgammon, and sometimes when he was more tired than usual would get Grizzie to come and tell again the stories she used to tell him when he was a child—some of which his father enjoyed all the more that he remembered having heard them when he was himself a child. Once after a particularly enjoyable tale that she had brought from her treasury— a story the laird remembered his grandmother saying she too had heard when she was a child, the laird said to her, "Eh! Grizzie! If ever one won a place in a family by her ain foreordeenment o' the Fatherly providence that looks after the families o' men, ye're that wuman! God bless ye, Grizzie!"

The laird could not have found a better word to please the old woman. It sunk in and in, for her pleasure could make no outward show, and there was no room for any growth in the devotion of her ministrations. Therefore she treasured it inside as one of her most priceless possessions.

And now Cosmo would take no more of the Gracies' milk, but gave Aggie a few coins every day to go to a farm nearby, and buy what was required for his father. And Aggie was regular as the clock, sunshine or storm.

There was another thing in which she was not quite so regular, but which she never missed when she could help it. As often as three and sometimes four times in the week, Cosmo would find her waiting for him somewhere on his way home, now just outside the village, now nearer Glenwarlock, depending on the hour when she had got through her work. The village talked, and Aggie knew it, but did not heed it. For she had now recovered her former position toward Cosmo in her own feeling. And it was one of the comforts of Cosmo's labor, when the contrariness or dullness of the human animal began to be too much for him, to think of the talk with Agnes he might hope was waiting for him when class was over. Under Mr. Simon she had made much progress, and was now a fit companion for any thinking man.

The road home was not half so long to Cosmo when Agnes walked it with him. Thinking inside, and laboring outside, she was, by virtue of the necessities of her life, such a woman as the most highly prized means of education, without the weight and seeming hindrances of struggle, cannot produce. One of the immortal women she was—for she had set out to grow forevermore. And of such no one can adequately predict the future, except him who knows what he is making of her.

Her behavior to Cosmo was that of a half sister who, born in a humbler position from which she could not rise, was nonetheless his sister and nonetheless loved him. Whether she had anything to struggle with inside in order to keep this position, I am not prepared to say. But I have a suspicion that the behavior of Elspeth, which so roused her scorn, had something to do with the restoring of the old relation, without thought of anything more, between them.

The most jealous of *reasonable* mothers could hardly have complained of her behavior in Cosmo's company, however much she might have disapproved of her seeking it as she did. But it is well that God, and not even reasonable mothers, has the ordering of those things in which they consider themselves most interested, and not unfrequently intrusive. In the meantime, God did order things between the two, and Agnes was not tempted to think of Cosmo as Elspeth had been wont to think of him.

Next to his father and Mr. Simon, Agnes Gracie was the most valued of Cosmo's friends. Mr. Burns came next. For Lady Joan, he never thought of her by the side of anybody else. If he had not learned to love her, I think he might now very well have loved Agnes. And if Cosmo had asked her now, when marriage was impossible, to marry him later when he could marry, I do not know what Agnes might have answered.

But he did not, and they remained the best of trusting friends.

36

• • • • • • • • • • • • • • • • • •

Grannie and the Stick

*T*his winter, the wind that drops the ripened fruit not plucked before, blew hard upon old Grannie, who had now passed her hundredth year. For some time Agnes had not been able to do much for her, but another great-grandchild, herself a widow and mother, was spending the winter with her. On his way to or from school, every day Cosmo looked in to see or ask about her. And when he heard she had had a bad night he would always think how a little of the earthly knowledge of the past of his family would fail with her. And upon one of these occasions he decided that he would at least find out whether she remembered the bamboo walking stick he had brought from Cairncarque.

He called when school was over and heard she was a little better, and the next morning brought the cane with him. That afternoon he called, learned that she had had a good night, and went in and found her in her chair by the fireside. He took his place by her so that the light from the window at her back would fall upon the stick.

He had not sat more than a minute when he saw her eyes fixed upon the horse.

"What's that ye hae there, Cosmo?" she asked.

"This?" returned Cosmo. "It's a cane I picked up upo' my travels. What think ye o' it?"

He held it out to her, but she did not move her hand toward it.

"Whaur got ye it?" she asked, her eyes growing larger as she looked.

"What makes ye ask, Grannie?" he returned, with assumed indifference.

"I dinna believe there was anither like the one that's like," she replied.

"In which case," rejoined Cosmo, "it must be the same. Ken ye anything aboot it?"

"Ay. An' sae do ye, or ye has less sense than I would hae thocht o' a Warlock. That stick's no a stick like other sticks, an' I wish I was nearer home."

"Ye dinna mean, Grannie, there's anything uncanny aboot the stick?" said Cosmo.

"I wouldna like t' think him near me that owned it," she replied.

"Who owned it, Grannie?"

"Smash it all to bits, laddie. There's somethin' by ordinar aboot it. The auld captain made o' it as if it had been his graven image. That was his stick ye hae in her han', whaurever ye got it. An' it was seldom oot o' his frae mornin' till nicht. Some said he took it t' bed wi' him. I kenna aboot that. But if by any accident he set it oot frae 'atween his knees, it was never oot o' the sicht o' his eyes. I hae seen him mysel', missin' it like, look up all o' a sudden as if his soul had been required o' him, an' grip it as if it had been his prodigal son come hame oonexpected."

Cosmo told her where he had found it.

"I tellt ye sae!" she cried. "The murderin' villain carried it wi' him, weel kennin' what was in it!"

Cosmo showed her the joints and their compartments, telling her he had searched them all, but had found nothing. She shook her head.

"Too late! too late!" she murmured. "The thievin' English lord was aforehan' wi' the heir!"

She seemed to fall into a kind of musing, and Cosmo bade her good night for the present. He had not yet made up his mind to show her the paper he had found in the top of the cane. He little thought that he was not to see her again in this world. For that same night she died.

Once his opportunity was over, and he could learn no more from her, Cosmo's mind turned again to the bamboo. According to Grannie, its owner habitually was anxious about its safety, and kept it continually under his eye. It did not seem likely that the rings had been in it long when it was taken from him; neither did it seem likely that he would have chosen to carry valuables about in such an instrument. It seemed unlikely therefore that he was so watchful over it because of valuable things concealed in it. What else could have made it so valuable? And as often as he turned the thing over in his mind, Cosmo's speculation inevitably settled on the unintelligible paper. It seemed that the paper had not been placed there for its own safety but rather to protect the jewels. But a man may crumple up his notes and thrust them in his pocket, yet care more about them than for whatever else might be there.

Thinking about the thing one night after he was in bed, he suddenly could not remember what he had done with the paper, for he had not seen it recently. He got up, took the stick, and opening the horse, which he could now do with his eyes closed, found it empty. He lay back down and tried to think what he could have done with it. It was a dark night, and his anxiety was not so great but that sleep presented its claim upon him. He resisted it however, not wanting to yield until he had remembered what had become of the paper.

But like a soundless tide, sleep kept creeping upon him, and he kept starting from it with successive spur-pricks of the will. In one of these revivals of wakefulness, he thought to himself that perhaps he had put it in his pocketbook; he stretched out his hand to the chair beside the bed where his clothes lay. Then came a gap in his consciousness, and the next thing he knew the pocketbook was in his hand, with the memory or the dream, he could not afterward tell which, of having searched it in vain.

He now felt so anxious he could rest no longer. He had to get up and look for the paper until he found it. He rose and lit his candle, went down the stair to the kitchen, and out of the house. Then first he began to doubt whether or not he was awake, but like one compelled he went on to the great door, and up to the drawing room. He became aware that the moon was shining and all at once remembered a former dream, and he knew it was coming to him again: there it was—the old captain, seated in his chair, with the moon on his face, and a ghastly look! He felt his hair about to stand on end with terror, but resisted with all his might. The rugged, scarred countenance gazed fixedly at him, and he did his best to return the gaze. The apparition rose and walked from the room, and Cosmo knew he had to follow it to the room above, which he had not once entered since his return. There, as before, it went to the other side of the bed, and disappeared. But this time the dream went a little farther. Despite his fear, Cosmo followed, and in the wall, by the head of the bed, he saw an open door. He hurried up to it, but seemed to strike against the wall, and woke.

He was in bed, but his heart was beating a quick march. His pocketbook was in his hand. He struck a match, and searching it, found the missing paper.

The next night, he told his dream to his father and Mr. Simon, and they had a talk about dreams and apparitions. Then all three pored over the paper. But far from arriving at any conclusion, they seemed hardly to get a glimpse of anything that could be called light upon its meaning.

All this time Cosmo had never written again to Joan. Both his father and he thought it better that only the laird should for the present keep up the correspondence; in matters of the heart, sometimes a withdrawal is the safest course of action. But months had passed without their hearing from her. The laird had by now written a third time and received no answer.

The day was now close upon them when the last of their land would be taken, leaving them nothing but the kitchen garden—a piece of ground of about half an acre, the little terraced flower-garden to the south of the castle, and the croft tenanted by James Gracie. They applied to Lord Lickmyloof to grant them a lease of the one field next to the castle, which the laird had been cultivating with the help of the two women, but he would not—his resentment was as strong as ever, and his design deeper than they saw.

The formal proceedings took their legal course. And after a certain day Lord Lickmyloof might have been seen from several of the windows of the castle walking the fields to the north and east, and giving orders about them to his bailiff. Within two weeks those to the north were no more to be entered from the precincts of the castle except by climbing over a *dry-stane dyke*; and before many more days had passed, they found him more determined than they could have imagined possible to give them annoyance.

He had obtained a copy of an old plan of the property, and from it had discovered, as he had expected and hoped, that the part of the road from the glen of the Warlock, which passed the gate of the castle, had been made by the present laird only about thirty years before. Now that the land no longer formed a continuous whole, the castle occupied an island in the midst of Lickmyloof's acquisitions—an island cut off from the main road except by that recent part just mentioned. Therefore the new owner—whether he was within his legal rights or not,

I do not know, but everybody knew the laird could not afford to go to the law to fight the action—gave orders that this road should be broken up from the point of departure, and a dry dyke built across the gate where stood the entrance to the castle.

However, the persons to whom the job was given, either ashamed or afraid, took advantage of an evening when they knew Cosmo would be away—he was, in fact, conducting a class for farm laborers—in order to do the work after dark. Thus it came about that, plodding homeward without so much of a suspicion what had taken place, Cosmo all at once found himself as he approached the gate, floundering among stones and broken ground, finally standing in front of a wall of stones blocking the entrance to his own house—an entrance which seemed to him as old as the hills around it, for it was older than his earthly life.

With a great leap he hurled himself over it, walked the rest of the way, and went to his father in such a rage as troubled the laird even more than any insolence of Lord Lickmyloof could have done.

"The scoundrel!" cried Cosmo. "I should like to give him a good drubbing—except that he's an old man! But I'll make him repent it!"

"Cosmo, my boy," said the old man, "you are meddling with what does not belong to you."

"I know it's your business, father, not mine, but—"

"It is no more my business than yours, my son! *Vengeance is mine, saith the Lord.*' An' the best o' it is," he went on, willing by a touch of humor in the truth he had to speak, to help turn the tide of Cosmo's wrath, "he'll take no more than's good for the sinner; whereas yersel', Cosmo, in the tune ye're in noo, would damn the poor auld Lickmyloof for ever an' ever! Man, he canna hurt me to the worth o' sich a heap o' firin'!" Then changing his tone to absolute seriousness, "Mind ye too, Cosmo," he went on, "that the Master never threatened, but always left the thing, whatever it was, to him that judges righteously. Ye want nothin' but fair play, my son, an' whether ye get it frae Lickmyloof or no, there's One that winna hold it frae ye. Ye'll get it, my son; ye'll get it! The Master'll hae all things set right in the end. An' if *he* binna in a hurry, we may weel bide. For mysel', the man has smitten me upon the one cheek, an' may hae the other to do on what he likes. It's no worth liftin' my auld arm to hold off the smack."

He laughed, and Cosmo laughed too—but grimly and out of tune. Then the laird told him that that very piece of the road was an improvement of his own that he had put in, and had cost him a good bit of blasting: it used to cross the stream twice before it got to the yard-gate. He hardly thought, he said, that Lickmyloof would like to have to restore it; for, besides the expense, it would cost him too much out of one of his best fields so to destroy it. In the meantime, they would have to contrive a way to connect themselves with that part of the road which his lordship would dare not touch. The worst of it was that there was no longer any direct way to get across the fields to James Gracie's cottage.

Already in bed when Cosmo returned home, Grizzie learned nothing that night of the evil news.

At the break of day Cosmo was up to see what could be done, and found that a few steps cut in the rocky terraces of the garden would bring one fairly easily to the road. He set about it immediately, and before breakfast time had finished the job.

The rage and indignation of Grizzie when she learned what had been done far surpassed Cosmo's, and served to secure him from any return of the attack. The flood of poetic abuse that she poured out seemed inexhaustible, sweeping along with it tale after tale against "that leein' Lickmyloof."

"Ay!" she concluded, and thereafter sank into a smoldering silence, "there was a footpath there afore ye was born, laird, blast or no blast! An' to that I can fetch them that can bear testimony, one o' them bein' none other than James Gracie himsel', who's ten long years ahead o' yer lairdship! An' let me see man or dog that'll keep me from havin' my say aboot it! They canna hang me, an' for less I carena."

37

· · · · · · · · · · · · · · · · · · ·

The Battle Over Grizzie's Path

The schoolmaster was at length over his illness and fit, for the time at least, to resume his labors. About a week after the breaking of the road, Cosmo ceased to attend the school for him.

Not long after, Mistress Gracie fell sick, and though for a while neither husband nor granddaughter thought seriously of her ailment, it proved more than her age, worn with hard work, could endure, and she began to sink. Then came time for Grizzie to go and help nurse her, for since Cosmo was home all day long, the laird could well spare her.

Father and son were now seldom out of each other's sight. Cosmo would often read beside him, and many times the two would talk about what the one had been reading. The capacity of the old man for taking in what was new was wonderful. Yet it was hardly to be wondered at, seeing it was the natural result of the constant practice of what he learned—for all truth understood becomes duty. To him that obeys well, the truth comes easy; to him who does not obey, it comes not at all, or comes in forms of fear and dismay. The true, that is the obedient man, cannot help seeing the truth, for it is the very business of his being—the natural concern of his soul. The religion of these two was obedience and prayer, their theories only the print of their spiritual feet as they walked homeward.

The road which Lord Lickmyloof had broken up went nearly straight from Castle Warlock to the cottage of the Gracies, where it joined the road that passed his lodge. The moment Grizzie's services were required for Mistress Gracie, she climbed the gate of the driveway, from the top of it stepped upon the new wall his lordship's men had put up, then let herself down onto the disfeatured road and set out to follow its track through the plowed land. In the evening she came back the same way, scrambled over the wall and the gate, and said never a word, nor was asked a question. To visit his tenants the laird himself went about a mile around, on a circuitous route not necessitating his setting a foot onto Lickmyloof's land. But he was not prepared to strain his authority with Grizzie, and therefore remained as one who knew nothing.

Before the week was out, her steps, and hers alone, had worn a visible and very practicable footpath across the enemy's field. And whether Lord Lickmyloof was away from home at the time, or that he wanted the trespassing violation to assume its most defined form before he moved in the matter, the week went by without notice taken.

On Sunday morning, however, as Grizzie was on her way to the cottage, she suddenly saw, over the edge of a hollow through which the path ran, the head of Lord Lickmyloof. He was following the track she had made from the other direction and would presently meet her. Her nostrils spread wide, like those of a war horse, for she too smelled the battle from afar.

"Here's auld Beelzebub at last! Walkin' to an' fro in the earth!" she muttered to herself. "Noo's for me to prove the trowth o' Scripture! Whether he'll flee or no, we'll see: I'll resist him. It's not me that'll run, onyway!"

His lordship had been standing by his lodge on the lookout, and when he saw Grizzie approach, he started out to encounter her. As she drew near he stopped and stood motionless in the middle of the path. On she came till she was within a single pace of him. He did not move. She stopped.

"I don't doobt, my lord," she said, "that I'll hae to make the road a bit wider. There's hardly room for yer lordship an' anither. But I'm gettin' on fine!"

"Is the woman an idiot?" exclaimed his lordship.

"Muckle sichlike yersel', my lord!" answered Grizzie; "—no wi' that muckle wit but I might hae more to guide my steps through the wilderness ye would make o' what was no an ill world."

"Are you aware, woman, that you have made yourself liable to a heavy fine for trespassing? This field is mine!"

"An' this footpath's mine, my lord—made wi' my ain two feet, an' I coonsel ye to stan' aside, an' let me by."

"Woman, you are insolent."

"Troth, I needna yer lordship to tell me that! Nonetheless might one auld wife say t' anither."

"I tell you there is no path here."

"An' I tell you there *is* a path here, an' ye hae but to will the trowth to ken that there is. There was a road here long before yer lordship's father was married t' yer lordship's mither, an' the law—what o' it yer lordship hasna remade—is dead again' ye: that I can prove. Hae me up in coort! I can take my oath as weel's onybody when I'm sure o' the right."

"I will do so, but in the meantime you must get off my property."

"Weel, stan' aside an' I'll be off o' 't in less time than yer lordship."

"You must go back."

"Hooly an' fairly! Bide till the gloamin' an' I'll go back—never fear. In the meantime, I'm gaein' off o' yer property the nearest way—an' that's straight after my nose."

She tried, for the tenth time or so, to pass, but turn as she might, he confronted her. She persevered. He raised the stick he carried, perhaps involuntarily, perhaps thinking to intimidate her. Then the air was rent with such an outcry of assault as shook his lordship's nerves.

"Hold your tongue, you howling jade!" he cried—and the epithet sufficed to destroy every possible remnant of forebearance in the mind of Grizzie.

"There's them that tells me, my lord," she said with sudden calm, "that that's what ye called Annie Fyfe, poor lass, when she came after ye, fifty year ago, to yer father's hoose, an' gotna one copper to hold her an' her bairn frae the roadside! An' you the father o' it! Na, ye needna snarl at me like that, my lord! Spare yer auld teeth for the gnashin' they'll *hae* to do. Though ye fearna God nor regard man, yer hoor'll come, an' yer no like to bid it welcome."

Beside himself with rage, Lord Lickmyloof would have grabbed her, but she yelled an even louder cry than before—so loud that James Gracie's deaf collie heard her, and having a great sense of justice, more courage than teeth, and as little regard to the law of trespass as Grizzie herself, came, not bounding, but tearing over the land to her rescue as if a fox were at one of his sheep. He made straight for his lordship.

Now this dog was one of the chief offenses of the cottage in the mind of the lord, for he had the moral instinct to know and hate a bad man, and could not abide Lord Lickmyloof. He had never attacked him, for the collie cultivated self-restraint, but he had made his lordship aware that there was no friendship in his heart toward him.

Silent as swift, he was nearly on the enemy before either he or Grizzie saw him. His lordship staggered from the path and raised his stick with a trembling hand.

"Doon wi' ye! doon, Covenant! doon, ye tyke!" cried Grizzie. "Hold yer teeth if ye would keep the few ye hae! De'il a bite but banes is there underneath the trowsers!"

The dog obeyed, and now crouched, loving her with his tail while with his eyes he watched the enemy and his stick.

"Hark ye, Covenant," she went on, "he's sold his sowl to the deevil, and he told him that never more should he turn a hair at cry or moanin' or groan o' despair. Hold frae him, Covenant, my fine fellow, hold frae him."

When Grizzie at length lifted her eyes from talking to the dog, Lord Lickmyloof was beyond the hollow, hurrying as if to fetch help. In a few minutes she was safe in the cottage, out of breath, but in high spirits; and even the dying woman laughed at her tale of how she had served his lordship.

"But ye ken, Grizzie," suggested James, "we're no to return evil for evil, nor scolding for scolding."

"Call ye that scolding?" cried Grizzie. "Ye should hear what I didna say! We'll be tried by what we *can* do, no by what we canna! An' as for returnin' evil, did I no hold the dog frae the death-shanks o' him?"

Meanwhile, the laird and Cosmo had spent a quiet and happy Sunday as usual. It was now halfway through the gloamin' toward night, and they were sitting together in the drawing room, the laird on the sofa and Cosmo at one of the windows. The sky was a cold clear calm of thin blue and translucent green, with a certain stillness that will more or less forever be associated with a Scotch Sunday. A long low cloud of dark purple hung over the yet glimmering coals on the altar of sunset, and the sky above it was like a pale molten mass of jewels that had run together with heat, and was still too bright for the stars to show. They were both looking out at the sky, and a peace as of the unbeginnings of eternity was sinking into their hearts. The laird's thoughts were with his Marion in the region beyond the dream; Cosmo's were with Joan in the dream that had vanished into itself. If love be religion, what matter whether its object be in heaven or on the earth! Love itself is the only true nearness. He who thinks of his Savior as far away can have made little progress in the need of him; and he who does not need much cannot know much, any more than he who is not forgiven much can love much.

They sat silent, their souls belonging rather to the heaven over their heads than the earth under their feet, when suddenly the world of stillness was invaded with a hideous yelling, above which almost immediately rose the well-known voice of Grizzie in fierce opposition.

They rushed outside. Over the gate and new wall they saw several heads, in-distinct in the dull light. Hurrying there, they found Grizzie in the grasp of Lord Lickmyloof's bailiff, and his lordship looking on with his hands in his pockets and a smile on his face. But it was not for her own sake that Grizzie cried out; there were two more in the group—two of the dog-kind, worrying each other with all the fierceness of the devotion which render's a master's quarrel more than the dog's own. They were, however, far from equally matched, and that was the cause of Grizzie's cry, for one was the somewhat ancient collie named Covenant, whose teeth were not what they once had been, and the other a mastiff belonging to Lord Lickmyloof, young and mean, loosed from the chain that night for the first time in a month. It looked bad for Covenant, but he was a brave dog, in-capable of turning his back on death itself when duty called him, and what more is required of dog or man! Both the dogs were well-bred each in its kind; Covenant was the more human, Dander the more devilish, and the battle was fierce.

The moment Cosmo saw who the combatants were, he knew that Covenant had no fair chance. In an instant he was over the wall and had thrown himself in their midst to part them; whereupon the bailiff, knowing his master desired the death of Covenant, let Grizzie go and made as if to rush upon Cosmo. But now it was Grizzie's turn, and she grabbed the bailiff and clung to him. He cursed and swore and even hit at her, but she got hold of his collar and did her best to throttle him.

Cosmo did the same for the mastiff with less effect and had to stun him with a blow on the head with a rock. He then grabbed up Covenant in his arms and handed him over the wall and gate to his father. The same moment the bailiff got away from Grizzie and rushed him, calling to their dog. But the animal, only half recovered from the effects of Cosmo's blow, either mistaking through bewilderment or moved by some influence not explicable, instead of attacking Cosmo, rushed at his master. Rage recalls dislike, and it may be he remembered past irritations and teasings. Suddenly aware of his treacherous intent, in a moment his lordship had jumped over the wall and gate and stood panting and shaking beside the laird, in his turn the trespasser. The dog would have been over after him had not Cosmo, turning his back on the bailiff, knocked the dog to the earth again.

"Hold him! hold him! hold the devil, you brute!" cried his lordship.

"It's yer ain dog, my lord," said the bailiff, whatever consolation there might be in the assurance as he took him by the collar.

"Am I to care whether the dog's my own? Hold him the tighter. He'll be beyond mischief by morning!"

"He's the true dog that sides wi' the right; he'll be in bliss afore his master," said Grizzie as she descended from the gate and stood on her own side of the fence.

But the laird was welcoming his lordship with the heartiness of one receiving an unexpected favor in the visit.

"Come in an' rest yersel' a bit, my lord," he said, "an' I'll take ye back to yer ain property an easier way than ower a dry-stane dyke."

"If it *be* my property," returned his lordship, "I would be obliged to you, Laird, to keep your folk off it!"

"Grizzie, woman," said the laird, turning to her, "ye surely dinna want to bring me to disgrace! The land's his lordship's—bought an' paid for, an' I hae no more right ower it than James Gracie's collie here, poor beast!"

"Ye may be right aboot the lan', Laird, the more's the pity!" answered Grizzie. "But the footpath, beggin' the pardon o' both lairdship an' lordship, belongs to me as much as to either one o' ye. Here I stan', alone for mysel'! That road's my neighbor, an' I'm boun' to see to it, for it would be a sore thing to many a poor body like mysel' to lose the right o' it."

"You'll have to prove what you say, woman," said his lordship.

"Surely, Grizzie,' said the laird, "his lordship must un'erstan' affairs o' this nature better'n you or me."

"As to the un'erstan'in' o' them, Laird, I make nae doobt," returned Grizzie, "an' I make jist as little doobt that he's on the wrong side o' the wall this time."

"Na, Grizzie—for he's upon *my* side o' it noo, an' I welcome him."

"He's jist as welcome to the path I made wi' my ain feet through the roughest plowed land ever crossed."

With the words Grizzie, who hated compromise, turned away, and went into the kitchen.

"Come this way, my lord," said the laird.

"Take the dog home," said the lordship to the bailiff. "Have him shot the first thing tomorrow morning. If it weren't the Sabbath, I'd have it done tonight."

"He's a good watch, my lord," interceded the man.

"He may be a good watch, but he's a bad dog," replied his lordship. "I'll have neither man nor dog about me that doesn't know his master. You may poison him if you prefer it."

"Come, come to the house, my lord!" said the laird. "This is, as you said, the Sabbath night, and the thought of it should make us merciful. I have nothing to offer you but a chair to rest in, and then we'll take to the road like neighbors, and I'll show you the way home."

His lordship yielded, for his poor thin legs were still trembling with the successful effort they had made under the inspiration of fear, and now that the canine incentive was gone, the dyke seemed a rampart insurmountable.

"What are you keeping that cursed dog there for?" he said as he turned, catching sight of Cosmo holding Covenant by the back of the neck.

"I am only waiting till your lordship's mastiff is out of the way," answered Cosmo.

"So you may set the beast on me again, as that old hag of yours did this morning?" As he spoke they had neared the kitchen door, open as usual, and Grizzie heard his words.

"That's as big a lie as ever yer lairdship heard tell in the coort!" she cried. "It's the nature o' dogs to loathe a tyrant. They see past the skin. Fetch the beast in here, Cosmo. I'll answer for him. The poor animal can't stand his lordship."

"Hoot, hoot, Grizzie," began the laird anew, with displeasure in his tone. But already the dog was in and the kitchen door closed.

"Leave her alone, Mr. Warlock, if you don't want to have the worst of it," said his lordship, trying to laugh. "But seriously, Laird," he went on, "it is not neighborly to treat me like this. Oblige me by giving orders to your people not to trespass on my property. I have paid my money for it, and must be allowed to do with it as I please."

"My lord," returned the laird, "I have not given, and will not give you, the smallest annoyance myself. I hope yet to possess the earth," he interjected, half-unconsciously, to himself, but aloud. "But—"

"Hey! hey!" said his lordship, thinking the man was sending his reason after his property.

"But," continued the laird, "I cannot interfere with the rights of my neighbors. If Grizzie says she has a right of way—and I think very probably she knows what she is about—I have no business to interfere."

"Confound your can't!" cried his lordship. "You care no more for your neighbors than I do. You only want to make yourself unpleasant to me. Show me the way out, and be damned."

"My lord," interrupted Cosmo, "if you weren't an old man I would show you the quickest way out! How dare you speak so to a man like my father!"

"Hold your tongue, you young fool! *You* stand up for your father!—idling about at home and eating his food and sending him to the poorhouse! Why don't you work like a decent young man? With your education you could work your way up. I warn you, if you fall into my hand, I will not spare you. The country will be better to live in when there are fewer sluggards about like you."

"Cosmo," said his father, "do not answer him. Show his lordship the way out, and let him go."

As they went through the garden, Lord Lickmyloof sought to renew the conversation, but Cosmo maintained a stern silence, and his lordship went home more incensed than ever with the obstinate paupers.

But the path in which Grizzie gloried as the work of her own feet, hardened and broadened. The following week Mistress Gracie died, and the day after she was buried, the old cottar came to the laird and begged him to yield the contested point and sell the bit of land he occupied. For all the neighbors knew Lickmyloof greatly coveted the Gracie's tiny croft, though none of them were aware what a price he had offered for it.

"Ye see, sir," he said, "noo that *she's* gone, it matters nothin' t' Aggie or me whaur we are or what comes o' us."

"But what would come o' yersel' an' Aggie wi'oot a place t' lay yer head? We're no to make oorsel's sae ill off as was the Maister; we must leave that to his will. Ye wouldna hae *her* look doon an' see ye in less comfort than when she was wi' ye!"

"Weel," rejoined James, "on that veery point I hae a word o' proposal to make ye. Ye had nae men noo aboot the place. Why shouldna Aggie an' me come an' bide in the men's quarters, an' be at han' t' lend a hand when it was wanted? Aggie an' me would help t' get mair oot o' the garden. I would hae mair time for weavin'. An' ye would get a heap o' money for the bit o' grund frae Lickmyloof."

The laird saw that they might at least be better accommodated at the castle than the cottage. He would consult his son, he said. Cosmo in his turn consulted Aggie, and was satisfied. In the winter the wind blew through the cottage bitterly, she said.

As soon as it was settled, Cosmo went to call on his lordship, and was shown into his library.

His lordship guessed his errand, for his keen eye had that same morning perceived signs of change about the cottage. He received him with politeness, and asked to know how he could serve him. From his changed behavior Cosmo thought he must be sorry for the way he had spoken to the laird.

"My father sent me," he said, "to inform your lordship that he is now at length in a position to consider your lordship's proposal to purchase James Gracie's croft."

"I am greatly obliged to your father for his consideration," replied Lord Lickmyloof, softly wiping one hand with the other, "but I no longer have any desire to secure the land. It has been so long denied me that I have finally grown in-different to it. That is a merciful provision of the Creator, that the human mind should have the faculty of accommodating itself on circumstances which have become a positive nuisance."

Cosmo rose.

"As soon as you have made up your mind," added his lordship, rising also, "to part with what remains of the property, *including the castle*, I should be glad to make an offer on that. It would make a picturesque ruin from certain points of view on the estate."

Cosmo bowed, and left his lordship grinning with pleasure.

38

....

Harvesttime Again

The summer came again, and then the harvest, and with it once more the op-portunity for Cosmo to earn a pound or two. But he determined this time not to go so far from home to find work, for he could see that his father's spirits and energy were better the more he was with him. Left alone, he began at once to go home the faster—as if another dragging anchor were cast loose, and he was drawn the more swiftly where the tides of life originate. To the old and weary man the life to come appeared as rest; to the young and active Cosmo it promised more work.

But it is all the same—what we need for rest as well as for labor is *life*; it is more life we want, and that is everything. The eternal root causes us to long for more existence, more being, more of God's making, less of our own unmaking. Our very desire for rest comes of life, life so strong that it recoils from weariness. The imperfect needs to be more—must grow. That sense of growth, of ever-enlarging existence, is essential to the created children of an infinite Father; for in the children the paternal infinite goes on working—recognizable by them, not as infinitude, but as growth.

The best thing in sight for both father and son seemed to Cosmo a place in Lord Lickmyloof's harvest—to reap with the other workers the fields that had so recently been his own. He would then almost be within sight of his father the whole day. Therefore he applied to the *grieve*, the same bailiff with whom he had all but fought on that memorable Sunday of Trespass. But the man, though of a coarse nature, was not spiteful, and that he had quarreled with another was not to him reason for hating him ever after. But he dared not hire a man his master counted his enemy without his leave. And inside he could hardly help a twinge of pleasure at the thought of what he called poor pride being brought to the shame of what he called beggary—as if the labor of a gentleman's hands were not a good deal further from beggary than living upon money gained by one's ancestors.

Lord Lickmyloof smoldered in silent rage a while before giving an answer. The question was, which would most gratify the feelings he cherished toward the man of old blood, high station, and poor fortunes—to accept or refuse the offered toil? His deliberation ended in his orders to the bailiff to hire the young laird, but to be careful that he did not pay the wages of an experienced workman for the tender hands of a gentleman—an injunction the bailiff allowed to reach Cosmo's ears.

The young laird, as they all called him, was a favorite with his enemy's men—partly that they did not particularly love their master; partly because they admired a gentleman who could so cheerfully descend to their level, showing not the least condescension, and was in all simplicity friendly with them; and partly because some of them had been to his evening school the last winter and had become attached to him. No honest heart, indeed, could be near Cosmo long and not love him—for the one reason that humanity was in him so largely developed. To him a man was a man, whatever his position or calling. He honored in his heart every man as, if not already such in the highest sense, yet destined to be one day a brother of Jesus Christ.

In the arrangement of the mowers, the grieve placed Cosmo last, presuming him the least capable, so that he would not slow down the rate of the field. But it did not take long for Cosmo, bringing up the rear in the line of mowers but rapidly catching up, to make his neighbor in front a little uneasy about his legs. When the man turned to Cosmo jokingly and said he objected to having them cut off, he then asked him, for the humor of the thing, to change places with him. The man at once agreed, and as Cosmo worked still closer to the front, the rest behaved with equal courtesy, showing no desire to contest with him the precedence of labor. And before the end of the long bout, Cosmo was swinging the leading scythe, and many were the compliments he received from his companions as they stood sharpening their tools for the next round, in which they were all of one mind that he must take the lead. Some begged him, however, to be considerate in his pace, as they were not all so young as he, while others warned him that, if he kept going as fast as he had begun, he would never be able to keep it up, and the first would be last before the day was over. Cosmo listened and thereafter restrained himself for the sake of his companions. Nevertheless, by the time the day's end came, he was nearly exhausted from the exertion. Even in the matter of work a man has to learn that he is not his own, but has a Master, whom he must not serve as if he were a hard one. When our will goes hand in hand with God's, then are we fellow workers with him in the affairs of the universe—not mere discoverers of his ways, watching at the outskirts of things, but laborers with him at the heart of them.

The next day Lord Lickmyloof's shadow was upon the field, and there he spent some time watching how things went.

Now Grizzie and Aggie, irrespective of Cosmo's hiring, had put their heads together and decided that, although they could not both be away from the castle at once, they might between the two of them, with the agreement of the bailiff, do a day's work and earn a day's wages. And although the grieve would certainly have listened to no such request from Grizzie in person, he was not capable of refusing it to Aggie.

Hence it came about that Grizzie, in her turn that second morning, was gathering the fallen grain into bunches behind Cosmo's scythe, hanging her labor on that of the young laird with as devoted a heart as if he had been a priest at the altar, and she his loving acolyte. I doubt if his lordship would have just then approached Cosmo had he noted who the woman was that went stooping along behind the late heir of the land, now a laborer upon it for the bread of his household.

"Well, Glenwarlock!" said the old man, giving a slap to the palm of his right hand as he stopped in front of the nearing mower, "you're rather a famous hand at the scythe! The grain bows down before you like the stocks to Joseph."

"I have a good arm and a sharp scythe, my lord," answered Cosmo cheerily.

"Whisht, whisht, my lord!" said Grizzie. "If the corn hear ye, it'll stan' up again an' cry oot. Listen t' it."

The morning had been very still, but that moment a gust of wind came and set all the grain rustling.

"What! *you* here!" cried his lordship. Then looking round, he yelled, "Crawford, you rascal! Turn this old cat out of the field!"

But he looked in vain; the grieve was nowhere in sight.

"The de'il sew up yer lordship's mouth wi' a beard o' barley!" cried Grizzie. "Haith, if I was a cat, ye'd hear me curse!"

His lordship thought to himself that she would certainly disgrace him in the hearing of his workers if he provoked her further, for their former encounter had revealed that she knew things not to his credit. They were all working away as if they had not heard a thing, but most of them had heard every word.

"Hoots, woman!" he said in an altered tone, "can't you take a jest?"

"Na; there's too many o' yer lordship's jests has turned fearsome earnest to them that took them!"

"What do you mean, woman?"

"Woman! he says? My name's Grisel Grant. Who doesn't ken auld Grizzie, who's never turned her back on frien' or foe? But I'm no gaein' to affront yer lordship wi' the sight o' yersel' in front o' yer people—sae long, that is, as ye hold a quiet tongue in yer mouth. But give the yoong laird there any o' the dirt ye're aye lickin' oot o' yer loof*, an' the auld cat'll be cryin frae the hoosetop!"

"Grizzie! Grizzie!" cried Cosmo, stopping his work and coming back to where they stood, "ye'll ruin all!"

"What is there to ruin that he can ruin more?" returned Grizzie. "When yer back's to the wall, ye canna fall. An angry chief will call up the de'il, but an angry wife'll make him run for his life. When I'm angert, I fear not even his lordship there!"

Lord Lickmyloof turned and went, and Grizzie set to work like a fury, probably stung by the sense that she had gone too far. Old woman that she was, she had soon

---

*Hand.

overtaken Cosmo, but he was angry and did not speak to her. After a while, when the heat of wrath was eased, Grizzie could not endure the silence, for in every motion of Cosmo's body in front of her she read that she had hurt him grievously.

"Laird!" she cried at last, "my strength's gone frae me. If ye dinna speak to me I'll drop."

Cosmo stopped his scythe in mid-swing, and turned to her.

"Grizzie," he said, "I winna deny that ye hae vexed me—"

"Ye needna. I wouldna believe ye. But ye dinna ken the man as I do, or ye wouldna be sae angert at anything woman could say to him. If I was to tell ye what I ken o' him, ye would be affrontit afore me, auld wife as I am. Haith, ye wouldna work another stroke for him!"

"It's for the money, not for *him*, Grizzie. But if he were as bad as ye call him, all the same, as ye weel ken yersel', the Lord makes his sun to rise on the evil an' on the good, an' sends rain on the just an' the unjust!"

"Ow, ay! the Lord can afoord it!" remarked Grizzie.

"An' them that would be his must afford it too, Grizzie," returned Cosmo. "Whaur's the good o' callin' ill names, woman?"

"Ill's the truth o' them that's bad. Why not set ill names to ill doers?"

" 'Cause a Christian's bound to destroy the works o' the evil one. An callin' names raises more o' them. The only thing that destroys evil is the man himsel' turnin' against it, an' that he'll never do frae ill names bein' thrown at him. Ye would never make me repent that way, Grizzie. Hae mercy on the auld sinner, woman."

The pace at which they were making up for lost time was telling upon Grizzie, and she was silent. When she spoke again it was upon another subject.

"I could jist throttle that grieve there!" she said. "To see him the night afore last come home to the very gate wi' Aggie was enouch to anger the saint that I'm not."

Jealousy sent a pang through Cosmo's heart. Was not Aggie one of the family—more like a sister to him than any other could ever be? The thought of her and a man like Crawford was unendurable.

"She couldna weel help hersel'," he rejoined; "an' whaur's the harm, sae long as she has naethin' to say to him."

"An' who kens hoo long that may be?" returned Grizzie. "The heart o' a woman's no deceitful as the Book says o' a man, an' sae is a heap the easier deceived. The child's no ill-lookin'! An' I don't doobt that he's no sae rough wi' a yoong lass as wi' an auld wife."

"Grizzie, ye don't think that oor Aggie's one to be taken wi' the looks o' a man!"

"Why not—when it's all the man she has! A woman's heart's that soft sometimes, she'll jist take him, so as no to hurt him. I wouldna keep that frae any lass. If the fellow carry a fair face, she'll swear her conscience doon that he must hae a good heart."

Thus Grizzie turned the tables on Cosmo, and sheltered herself behind them. Scarcely a word did he speak the rest of the morning.

At noon, when work gladly made way for dinner, they all sat down among the stooks to eat and drink—all except Grizzie, who appropriated the oatcake she and Aggie had a right to between them, took it home, and set the greater part aside. Cosmo ate and drank with the rest of the laborers, and enjoyed the homely repast as much as any of them. By the time the meal was over, Aggie had arrived to take Grizzie's place.

It was a sultry afternoon, and from the heat and the annoyance of the morning from Grizzie's tongue, and her talk about Agnes, the scythe hung heavy in Cosmo's hands. Aggie did not have to work her hardest to keep up with him. But she was careful to maintain her proper distance, for she knew that the least suspicion of relaxing effort would set him off like a thrashing machine. He led the field, nevertheless, at a fair speed. His fellow laborers were content, and the bailiff made no remark. But Cosmo was so silent, and prolonged silence was so unusual between them, that Aggie was disturbed.

"Are ye no weel, Cosmo?" she asked.

"Weel enough, Aggie," he answered. "What makes ye ask?"

"Ye're holdin' yer tongue sae quiet. And," she added, for she caught sight of the bailiff approaching, "ye hae lost the last inch or two o' yer stroke."

"I'll tell ye aboot it as we go home," he answered, swinging his scythe in the arc of a larger circle.

The bailiff came up.

"Don't wrestle yourself to death, Aggie," he said.

"I must keep up wi' my man," she replied.

"He's a hot man at the scythe—too hot! He'll be fit for nothing before the week's out. He can't keep on at this rate!"

"Ay, he can! Ye dinna ken oor yoong laird. He's worth two ordinar' men. An' if ye dinna think me fit to gather to him, I'll let ye see ye're mistaken, Mr. Crawford."

And with the words Aggie went on gathering faster and faster.

"Hoots!" said the bailiff, going up to her and laying his hand on her shoulder. "I know well enough you have the spunk to work till you drop. But there's no need to now. Sit down and take your breath a minute—here in the shadow of this stook. When Glenwarlock's at the other end, we'll set out together and be up with him before he's had time to put a fresh edge on his scythe. Come, Aggie! I've been wanting to have a word with you for a long time. You left me before I knew where I was the other night."

"My time's no my ain," answered Aggie.

"Whose is it, then?"

"Sometimes it's the laird's, an' sometime's my father's, an' noo it's his lordship's."

"It's your own so long as I'm at the head of his lordship's affairs."

"Na, that canna be. He's bought my time, an' he'll pay me for it, an' he shall hae his own."

"He's been no friend to you or yours."

"What's that t' the point?"

" 'Cause I'm here to make it right for you now where he might not."

"Call ye that makin' it right to temp' me to wrong him?" said Aggie, going steadily on at her gathering, while the grieve kept following her step by step.

"You're awfully short with a body who's trying to help you, Aggie!"

"I may weel be, when a body would hae me neglec' my paid work."

"Well, I reckon you're right after all, so I'll just fall in and lend you a hand."

He had so far hindered her that Cosmo had gained a little, and now in pretending to help, he managed to hinder her yet more. But still she kept near enough to Cosmo to prevent the grieve from saying too much of a personal nature, and by and by he left her.

When they quit work for the night, he would have accompanied her home, but she never left Cosmo's side, and they left together.

"Aggie," said Cosmo as soon as there was no one within their hearing, "I dinna like that man hangin' aboot ye—glowerin' at ye as if he would eat ye."

"He wouldna do that, Cosmo. He's civil eneuch."

"Ye should hae seen hoo rough he was to Grizzie!"

"Grizzie's some rough hersel' sometimes," remarked Aggie quietly.

"That's true," assented Cosmo. "But a man should never behave like that to a woman."

"Say that to the man," rejoined Aggie. "The woman can take care o' hersel'."

"Grizzie, I grant ye, is more than a match for any man. But ye're not so long in the tongue, Aggie."

"An' do ye think that a long tongue is a lass's safety, Cosmo? I dinna believe 'tis so! But what's taken ye tonight that ye speak to me sae? I ken no occasion."

"Aggie, I wouldna willingly say a word to vex ye," answered Cosmo; "but I hae noted an' heard that the best o' women sometimes take unaccountable fancies to men no fit to hold a candle to them."

Aggie turned her head aside.

"I would ill like ye, for instance, to be drawn to yon Crawford," he went on. "It's eneuch to me that he's long been the chief assistant to such an ill man."

A slight convulsive movement passed across Aggie's face, leaving behind it a shadow of hurtless resentment yielding presently to a curious smile.

"I micht make a better man o' him," she said, and again looked away.

"They all think that!" returned Cosmo with sad bitterness. "An' so they will to the world's end. But, Aggie," he added after a pause, "ye ken ye're no to be unequally yoked."

"That's what I hae to heed, I ken," murmured Aggie. "But what do ye un'erstan' by it, Cosmo? There's nae worshipers o' idols noo as in Bible days."

"There's idols visible, an' idols invisible," answered Cosmo. "There's heaps o' idols among them that coonts themsel's Christians."

A silence followed.

"You an' me's aye been true to one anither, Aggie," resumed Cosmo at length, "an' I would ask to hae a promise frae ye—jist to content me."

"What aboot, Cosmo?"

"Promise, an' I'll tell ye, as the bairnies say."

"But we're no bairnies, Cosmo, an' I darena—even to you that I would trust like the Bible. Tell me what it is, an' if I may, I will."

"It's not between you an' me, Aggie. It's only this—that if ye ever fall in love wi' anybody, ye'll let me ken."

Agnes was silent for a moment. Then with a slight tremble in her voice, which in vain she tried to smooth out, and again turning away, she answered: "Cosmo, I darena. The thing ye require o' me might be what a lass could tell to the Father o' her—him that's in heaven. But to none else."

Cosmo was silenced, as indeed it was time and reason he should be, for he had no right to make such a request, though he did it in all innocence. He might well have asked her to tell him, but not to promise to tell him. He did not yet understand that he had gone too far, however, and felt as if, for the first time in their lives, that he and Aggie had begun to be divided.

They entered the kitchen. Aggie hastened to help Grizzie lay the cloth for supper. Her grandfather looked up with a smile from the newspaper he was reading near the window. The laird, who had an old book in his hand, looked up.

"Here, Cosmo!" he called. "Jist listen to this bit o' wisdom, my man—frae a heart doubtless praisin' God this many a day in higher worlds: 'He that would always know before he trusts, who would have from his God a promise before he will place his confidence in him, is the slayer of his own eternity.' "

The words mingled strangely with what had just passed between him and Agnes. Both interchanges gave him food for thought, but could not keep him awake after the day's labor.

The bailiff continued to haunt the goings and comings of Agnes, but few thought that his attentions were acceptable to her. Cosmo, however, continued more or less uneasy.

At length the harvest was over, and the little money the household had earned was laid aside for the sad winter, once more on its way. But no good hope dies without leaving a child behind it—a younger and fresher hope. The year's fruit must fall that the next year's may come, and the winter is the only way to the spring.

39

● ● ● ● ● ● ● ● ● ● ● ● ● ● ● ● ● ● ●

The Final Conflict

*W*hen the work in the fields was done, and as there was no more weekly pay for teaching and no extra hands needed for farm labor, Cosmo, hearing there was a press of work and a scarcity of workmen in the building trade, offered his services to Sandy Shand, the stonemason, who was then building a house in the village for a certain Mr. Pennychik. His offer was accepted, and so Cosmo found himself working in town, now doing the work of a mason, now a carpenter, and receiving fair wages, until such time when the weather put a stop to all but indoor work of the kind.

But instead of his readiness to turn his hand to any honest work reaping him a good opinion in the eyes of his neighbors, Cosmo became the object of blame and ridicule. That a young man of his abilities, with a college education, should spend his time—*waste* it, people said—at home, puttering about at work that was a disgrace to a gentleman, instead of going away and devoting himself to some so-called honorable calling—the thing was unheard of for a man who might be "getting on" in the world.

"Look at Mr. Pennychik!" they said. "See how he has raised himself in the social scale. There he stands, a rich man and employer of others, while the lazy gentleman whose ancestors were lairds of the land, is nothing but one of his hired laborers." Such is the low idea most men have of the self-raising that is the duty of man! They put ambition in the place of aspiration. Not knowing the spirit they were of, these would have had Cosmo abandon his father. They knew nothing of, and were incapable of taking into account the refined moral nature of that son as a result of life with his father, such as could never have allowed him to gather riches or possessions like many others. Like his father he had a holy weakness for purity. If there is one thing a Cosmo soul recoils from, it is lowness—of action, of thought, of judgment. Cosmo would not have left his father to make a fortune, even in the most honorable way.

As the severe weather came upon them, things did not look promising. But they had a fair stock of oatmeal laid in, and that was the staff of life. There was also a tolerable supply of fuel which neighbors had lent them horses to bring in from the peat fields.

With the cold weather the laird again began to fail and Cosmo began to fear that this would be the last of the good man's winters. As the best protection from the cold he spent most of the time in bed, and Cosmo spent almost his entire life in the room, reading aloud to his father when the old man was able to listen, and to himself when he was not.

The other three of the household were mostly in the kitchen, saving fuel, and keeping each other company. And thus the little garrison awaited the closer siege of beleaguering winter, in their hearts making themselves strong to resist the more terrible enemies which all winter armies bring flying on their flanks—the haggard fiends of doubt and dismay—which can even creep through the strongest walls. To trust in spite of the look of being forgotten; to keep crying out into the vastness whence comes no voice, and where seems no hearing; to struggle after light, where there is no glimmer to guide; to see the machinery of the world grinding on as if self-moved, caring for no life, not shifting a hairsbreadth for all the begging against it, and yet believe that God is awake and utterly loving; to desire nothing but what comes meant for us from his hand; to wait patiently, willing to die of hunger, fearing only lest faith should fail—such is the victory that overcomes the world, such is faith indeed.

After such victory Cosmo had to strive and pray hard. It was difficult for him, sometimes sunk deep in the wave, while his father floated calm on its crest: the old man's discipline had been longer. A continuous communion had for many years been growing between him and the heart from which he came.

"As I lie here, warm and free of pain," he said once to his son, "expecting the redemption of my body, I cannot tell you how happy I am. I cannot imagine how ever in my life I feared anything. God knows it was my obligation to others that oppressed me, but now, in my utter incapacity, I am able to trust him with my honor, and my duty, as well as my sin."

"Look here, Cosmo," he said another time; "I had temptations such as you would hardly believe, to try to better my worldly condition and thus redeem the land of my ancestors. And the world would have commended, not blamed me, had I yielded. But my God was with me all the time, and I am dying a poorer man than my father left me, leaving you a poorer man still, but praised be God, an honest one. Be very sure, my son, God is the only advisor to be trusted, and you must do what he tells you, even if it lead to a stake to be burned by the slow fire of poverty.—O my Father!" cried the old man, breaking out suddenly in prayer, "my soul is a flickering flame of which you are the eternal, inextinguishable fire. Because you are life, I live. Nothing can hurt me, because nothing can hurt you. To your care I leave my son, for you love him as you have loved me. Deal with him as you have dealt with me. I ask for nothing, care for nothing but your will. Strength is gone from me, but my life is hid in you. I am a feeble old man, but I am dying into the eternal day of your strength."

Cosmo stood and listened with holy awe and growing faith. For what can help our faith like the faith of the one we most love when it is sorely tried and yet proves sound and strong?

But there was still one earthly clod clinging to Cosmo's heart. There was no essential evil in it, yet it held him back from the freedom of the man who, having parted with everything, possesses all things. The place, the things, the immediate world in which he was born and had grown up had a hold of his heart that savored of idolatry. The love was born in him and had a power in him. And though it had come down into him from generation after generation of ancestors, and he was therefore not accountable for its existence, as soon as he became aware of its existence he knew that he alone was accountable for its continuance. For Cosmo was not one of those weaklings who find in themselves certain tendencies toward wrong, which perhaps originated in the generations before them, and who say to themselves, "I cannot help it, so why should I fight it?" and at once create new evil, and make it their own by obeying the inborn impulse. Such inheritors of a lovely estate, with a dragon in a den which they have to kill that the brood may perish, make friends with the dragon, and so think to save themselves trouble.

It is not that Cosmo loved his home too much. I only think he did not love it enough in God. To love a thing divinely is to be ready to yield it without a pang when God wills it. But to Cosmo the thought of parting with the house of his fathers and the rag of land that yet remained was torture. Instead of sleeping the perfect sleep of faith, he would lie open-eyed through half the night, hatching scheme after scheme to retain the house. The bad dream of its loss haunted him, and he felt that, if it came true, he would rather live in the dungeon wine cellar of the moldering mammoth tooth than forsake the old stones to live elsewhere in a palace. The love of his soul for Castle Warlock was like the love of the Psalmist for Jerusalem: when he looked at a stone of its walls, it was dear to him. But the love of Jerusalem became an idolatry, for the Jews came to love it no longer because the living God dwelt therein but because it was *theirs*. And then it was doomed, for it had become an idol.

The thing was somewhat different with Cosmo: the house was almost a part of himself—an extension of his own body, as much his as the shell of a snail is his. But he had yet to learn to leave the care of it to him who made it, for his castle of stone was God's also. The idea of the old house had not yet been quickened within him to the feeling that God was in it with him, giving it to him. Not yet possessing the soul of the house—its greatest bliss, which nothing could take from him—he naturally could not be content to part with it. It seemed an impossibility that it should be taken from him—a wrong to things, to men, to nature that a man like Lickmyloof should gain the lordship over it. As he lay in the night in the heart of the old place, and heard the wind roaring about its stone-mailed roofs, the thought of losing it would sting him almost to madness. Sometimes he would jump out of bed to pace the floor, like one of the children in the fiery furnace, only the furnace was of worse fire, being the wrath which worketh not the righteousness of God.

Suddenly one night he became aware that he could not pray. It was a stormy night. The snow-burdened wind was raving, and Cosmo would by now have been pacing about the room except that now he was in his father's and dreaded disturbing him. He lay still, with a stone in his heart, for he was now awake to the fact that he could not say, "Thy will be done." He strained to lift up his heart, but could not. Something had arisen between him and his God and beat back his prayer. A thick fog was about him! In his heart not one prayer would come to life.

It was too terrible! Here was a schism at the very root of his being. The love of things was closer to him than the love of God. Between him and God rose the rude bulk of a castle of stone. He crept out of bed, lay on his face on the floor, and prayed in an agony. The wind roared and howled, but the desolation of his heart made it seem as nothing.

"God!" he cried, "I thought I knew you, and sought your will. And now I am ashamed before you. I cannot even pray. But hear my deepest will in me. Hear the prayer I cannot offer. Be my perfect Father to fulfill the imperfection of your child. Be God after your own nature, beyond my feeling, beyond my prayer. You know me better a thousand times than I know myself—hear and save me. Make me strong to yield to you. I have no way of confessing you before men at this moment, but in the depth of my thought I would confess you and yield everything but the truth, which is yourself. And therefore, even while my heart hangs back, I force my mouth to say the words—*Take from me what you will, only make me clean, pure, divine.* To you I yield the house and all that is in it. It is yours, not mine. Give it to whom you will. I would have nothing but what you choose shall be mine. I have you, and all things are mine."

Thus he prayed, with a reluctant heart, forcing its will by the might of a deeper will that *would* be for God and freedom, in spite of the cleaving of his soul to the dust.

Then for a time his thoughts ceased in exhaustion.

When thought returned, all at once he found himself at peace, in the midst of an unspeakable calm. How it came he could not tell, for he had not been aware of its approach. But the contest was over, and in a few minutes he was fast asleep, one with him whom all men in one could not comprehend, whom yet the heart of every true child lays hold upon and understands.

It was not that after the passing of this crisis on this particular night there was no more stormy weather. Often it blew a gale—often a blast would come creeping in—almost always in the skirts of the hope that God would never require such a sacrifice of him. But he never again found he could not pray. Recalling the strife and great peace, he would always at such times make haste to his Master, compelling the slave in his heart to be free and cry, "Do your will, not mine." Then would the enemy withdraw, and again he breathed the air of the eternal.

When a man comes to the point that he will no longer receive anything except from the hands of him who has the right to withhold, and in whose giving alone lies the value of possession, then is he approaching the inheritance of the saints in light, those whose strength is made perfect in weakness. But some, for the present, can in no way comprehend such matters any more than the chickens in the yard. Their hour will come; in the meantime, they are counted the fortunate ones of the earth.

40

· · · · · · · · · · · · · · · · · ·

A Forced Winter's Rest

*J*ames Gracie fell sick. They took him from the men's quarters, and gave him Cosmo's room so they could better attend to him. Cosmo put a bed for himself up in his father's room, and Grizzie and Aggie slept together. So now the household was gathered literally under one roof—that of the kitchen tower, as it had been called for centuries.

James's attack was serious, requiring much attention as well as expenditure. Cosmo said that as long as his money lasted, it should go to nurse him, though James objected bitterly to such waste, as he called it, saying what remained of his life was not worth it. But learning the mood the old man was in, the laird rose and went to his bed, and said to him solemnly, "James, who are ye to tell the Lord it's time he should take ye? What kin' o' faith is it to refuse a sup 'cause ye see na anither spoonful upon the road behind it?"

James hid his old face in his old hands. The laird went back to his bed, and nothing more was ever said on the subject. The days went on, the money ran fast, no prospect of more appeared, but still they had enough to eat.

One morning in the month of January, still and cold, and dark overhead, a cheerless day in whose bosom a storm was coming to life, Cosmo was sitting at his usual breakfast of *brose*, the simplest of all preparations of oatmeal. For the first time in a long while, he thought about the cabinets in the drawing room and found himself wondering whether some of the old family curiosities might not, with the help of his friend the jeweler, be turned into some badly needed funds. Not waiting to finish his breakfast, he rose and hurried at once to examine the family treasures in the newly thought-of light of necessity.

The drawing room felt freezing, dank like a tomb, weary of its memories. It was so still that it seemed as if sound would die in it. Not a mouse stirred. The few pictures on the walls looked perishing with cold and changelessness.

But Cosmo did not stand gazing for long. He crossed to one of the shrines of his childhood's reverence, opened it, and began to examine the things with the eye of a seller. Once they had seemed to be priceless treasures; now he feared they might bring him nothing in his sore need. He felt scarcely a sorrow at the thought of parting with them as one by one he set certain ones aside and put them on a table. He was like a miner searching for golden ore, not a miser whom hunger had overpowered. When he had gone through the cabinet, he turned to look at what he had found. There was a dagger in a sheath of silver of raised work, with a skillfully wrought hilt of the same; a goblet of iron with a rich pattern in gold beaten into it; a snuff-box with a few diamonds set round a monogram in gold in the lid. These, with several other smaller things that had an air of promise about them, he decided to pack up and send to Mr. Burns as a trial to see what they might be worth. But when he went back to his father, he found he had been missing him, and put off his walk into Muir o' Warlock till the next day.

As the sun went down the wind rose, and the storm came to life—the worst of the winter. It reminded both father and son of the terrible night when Lord Mergwain went out into the deep. The morning came, fierce with gray cold, a tumult of wind and snow. There seemed little chance the postal carrier would be able to go for days to come. But the storm might have been more severe in their particular part of the hills than in the open country, and Cosmo determined to go into town to see. Besides, there were certain items he needed to get for the invalids.

With a great deal of difficulty he made his way through the snow to the village. And there also he found it so deep that the question about the carrier's going anywhere would have been how to get the cart out of the shed, not whether the horses were likely to get it through the Glens o' Fowdlan: of that there was no possibility whatever. Therefore, he left his parcel with the postman's wife, and proceeded to spend the last of his money, which amounted to half a crown. Having done so, he set out for home, the wind blowing fierce, and the snow falling thick.

He had not gone far outside the village, battling with wind and snow above and beneath, before he began to feel his strength failing him. It had indeed been failing for some time. Grizzie knew, although he himself did not, that he had not been eating so well lately. And now for the first time he began to find his strength unequal to the elemental war. He laughed at the idea and held on. The wind was right in his face, and the cold was bitter. But it was not long before his breath grew short and his head began to ache. He longed to be home so that he could lie down and breathe, but a long way and a great snowy wind were between him and rest. He fell into a reverie, and seemed to get on better when not thinking about the exertion he was making. The monotony of it brought on an almost dreamy state in which he lost all notion of time and distance, and after a while began to wonder whether he must not be near the place where the parish road turned off. He stopped and stood still, and looked about, but nothing was to be seen through the drifts except more drifts behind them. Was he even on the road at all? He looked this way and that, but could find neither ditch nor dyke he recognized.

He was lost!

But he well knew the danger of sitting down, yet knew that even now, as he was nearing exhaustion, he might well be wandering away from the abodes of men, lessening with every step the likelihood of being found. He turned his back to the wind and stood—how long he did not know. But while he stood thus, almost between waking and sleeping, he received what seemed like a soft blow on the head. It dazed him, and the rest was like a dream in which he walked on and on for ages, falling and rising again, following something, he never knew what. Slowly his consciousness ceased, and when he next came to himself, he was in bed.

Aggie was the first to get anxious about him. They had expected him home in time for dinner, and when it began to grow dark and he had not come, she could stand it no longer and set out to meet him. But she did not have to go far, for she had barely left the kitchen door when she saw someone leaning over the gate. Through the gathering twilight and the storm, she could distinguish nothing more, but she never doubted it was the young laird, though whether in the body or out of it she did doubt quite fearfully. At first she thought he was dead, for there came no answer when she spoke. But presently she heard him murmur something about conic sections.

She opened the gate gently. He would have fallen as it swung in, but she held him. Her touch seemed to bring him a little to himself. She supported and en-couraged him. He obeyed her, and she finally succeeded in getting him into the house. It was a long time before Grizzie could make him warm in front of the kitchen fire, but at last he came to himself sufficiently to walk up the stairs to bed, though afterward he remembered nothing of the entire proceeding.

He was well on the way to recovery before they let the laird know in what a dangerous plight Aggie had found him. But the moment he learned that his son was ailing, the old man seemed to regain a portion of his strength. He rose from the bed, and for the two days and three nights during which Cosmo was feverish, he slept only in snatches. On the third day Cosmo persuaded him to return to his bed.

The women now had their hands full—all three of the men in the house were laid up! Now it all fell to them! Almost without saying a word between them, they understood each other. Each had saved a little money—and now no questions would be asked! Aggie left the room and came back with her little store of coins, which she put into Grizzie's hand. Grizzie laid them on the table, then went to her box, brought out hers, laid them on the other side and shook them together. " 'Tis oors nae mair," she said, "but belongs t' whate'er befall us." Thence for a time the invalids had all their moderate needs supplied.

When Cosmo came to himself on the third day, he found he was possessed by a wondrous peace. His soul was calm and trusting, like that of a bird on her eggs who knows her one grand duty in the economy of creation is repose. His only concern was his father, and the cheerful voice that invariably answered his every inquiry was sufficient reassurance.

For three more days he lay in a kind of blessed lethargy. He dreamed he could not recover, and did not even desire to. In his half slumbers he seemed always to be floating down a great gray river, on which thousands more were likewise floating, each by himself, some in canoes, some in boats, some in the water without even an oar. Every now and then one would be lifted and disappear, none saw how, but each knew his turn would come when he too would be laid hold of. In the meantime all floated helpless onward, some afraid at the unknown before them, others indifferent, and some filled with solemn expectation.

On the seventh day he began to regard the things around him with some interest, and began to be aware of returning strength, and the approach of duty. Before long he would have to rise and do his part to keep things going!

Still he felt no anxiety, for the alarm of duty had not yet called him. And as he lay passive to the influences of restoring strength, his father would, from his bed, tell him old tales he had heard from his grandmother. And sometimes they made Grizzie sit between the two beds and tell them stories she had heard in her childhood. Her supply never seemed exhausted. Every once in a while one or the other of them would say, "There, Grizzie! I never heard that before!" and Grizzie would answer, "I daresay no, sir! Hoo should ye? I had forgotten it mysel'!"

One of the stories Grizzie told, in English rather than the old Scots of her tongue, went as follows:

In a cold little valley, far among the hills, where the winter was a sore thing, there lived an honest couple, a man that had many sheep, and his wife—folk well off in respect of this world's things. They were looked up to among the neighbors, but not to be envied, seeing they had lost a whole bonny family, one after the other, till there was not one left in the house but just one laddie, the bonniest and the best of all, and as a matter of course, the very apple of their eye. "Among the three o' us, Laird," here Grizzie paused in her tale to remark, "ye'll be the only one 'at can fully un'erstan' hoo the heart o' a parent must cleave t' the last o' his flock." Then she continued.

Whether it was that their hearts were too much wrapped up in this one human creature for the growth of their souls, I don't know—there must be some reason for it—this last one began in his turn to dwindle away like the rest. And wherever the two poor folk turned themselves in their sadness, there stood death, glowering at them out of his black eyes. Pray they did, you may be sure, and cry when it was dark, but neither prayers nor tears made no difference. The bairn was sent for, and away the bairn must go. And when at length he lay stretched out in his last clean clothes till the robe of righteousness that needs no washing would be put upon him, what could they think but that the world was done for them!

But the world must go on, though the heart may sag. And the friends and neighbors gathered from near and far till there was a heap of folks in the house, come to the burying of the bonny bairn. And folk must eat and live nonetheless that the matter they come upon be death. And so the night before the funeral, their dinner the next day when they came back from the grave had to be prepared.

It was in the springtime of the year, late in those parts. Most of the lambs had come, but the storms were reluctant to leave the laps of the hills, and long after the weather had begun to be lighter lower down, the sheep couldn't be let out to get their own feed for themselves but still had to be kept in the pen. So to the pen the gudeman had to go, to fetch home a lamb for the friends' and the neighbors' dinner. And as it fell out, it was a fearsome night of wind and driving snow—worse, I would reckon, than anything we have nowadays. But he didn't turn aside for the wind or snow, for he cared little what came to him with such an emptiness in his heart. On the contrary, the storm was like a friendly cloak to his grief, for on the road he fell to crying and complaining and lamenting aloud, judging no doubt, if he thought at all, that he might do whatever he liked with nobody nigh. To the sheep pen, I say, he went wailing and crying aloud after his bonny bairn, the last of his flock, now taken from him.

Half blind with the night and the snow and his own tears, he came to the door of the shelter where they kept their sheep. And what should he see there but a man standing in front of the door—straight up and still in the dark! It was most fearsome to see someone there, so far from any place—not to say on such a night! The stranger was robed in some kind of plaid, like the gudeman himself, but whether a Lowland or a Highland plaid, he couldn't tell. But the face of the man—that was not to be forgotten—and that for the very friendliness and kindness of it. And when he spoke, it was as if all the voice of them that had gone before were made up into one, for the sweetness and the power of the tone of it.

"What brings ye here in such a storm, man?" he said. And the sound of his voice was aye softer than the words of his mouth.

"I come for a lamb," answered the gudeman.

"What kind of lamb?" asked the stranger.

"The very best I can lay my hands on in the pen," answered he, "for it's to put before my friends and neighbors. I hope, sir, you'll come home with me and share it. Ye'll be welcome."

"Do your sheep make any resistance when you take the lamb? or when it's gone, do they make any outcry?"

"No, sir—never."

The stranger gave a kind of sigh, and said, "That's not how they treat me! When I go to my sheepfold and take the best and the fittest, my ears are deafened and my heart torn with the clamors—the bleating and bawling of my sheep—my own sheep! complaining loud against me—and me feeding them, and clothing them, and keeping evil and foxes from them, all their lives, from the first to the last! It's some kind of ungratefulness, and hard to abide."

By this time the man's head was hanging down, but when the voice ceased, he looked up in amazement. The stranger wasn't there. Like one in a dream where he knew not joy from sorrow or pleasure from pain, the man went inside and wept over the heads of the creatures that came crowding about him. But he sought the best lamb nonetheless and carried it away with him. And the next day he came home from the funeral with a smile on his face where had been none for many a day. And the next Sunday they heard him singing in the kirk as nobody had ever heard him sing before. And never from that time on was there a moan or a complaint to be heard from the lips of either of the two of them. They had no bairn to close their eyes when their own turn to look at death came, but where there's none behind, there's all the more to find.

Grizzie ceased, and the others were silent, for the old legend had touched the deepest in them.

"It's sometimes in the storm, sometimes in the desert, sometimes in the agony, an' sometimes in the calm, whaure'er he gets them right by themselves, that the Lord visits his people—in person, as a body might say," remarked the laird, after a long pause.

Cosmo did not get well as fast as he had begun to expect. Nothing very definite seemed the matter with him; it was rather as if life itself had been checked at the spring, therefore his senses dulled, and his blood made thick and slow. A sleepy weariness possessed him, in which he would lie for hours, motionless, desiring nothing, fearing nothing, suffering nothing, only loving. The time would come when he would have to be up and doing, but now he would not think of work; he would imagine himself a bird in God's nest—the nest into which the great brother would have gathered all the children of Jerusalem. Poems would come to him—little songs and prayers—spiritual butterflies, with wings whose spots matched. Sometimes humorous little parables concerning life and its affairs would come to his mind. But the pity was that none of them would stay, and he had to comfort himself with the thought that nothing true can ever be lost; if one form of it goes, it is that a better may come in its place. Happy is the half-sleeper whose brain is a thoroughfare for lovely things—all to be caught in the nets of Life, for Life is the one miser that never loses, never can lose.

When Cosmo was able to get up for a while every day, the laird was placed in Aggie's care, Grizzie having yielded a portion of her right of nursing him. Now for the first time the laird began to discover how much there was in Aggie. Expressing his admiration of her knowledge and good sense, her intellect and insight, he was a little surprised that Cosmo did not seem so much struck with them as he was himself. Cosmo, however, explained that her gifts were no new discovery to him; he had been aware of them from childhood.

"There are few like her, Father," he said. "Many's the time she's held me up when I was ready to sink."

"The Lord reward her!" responded the laird.

All sicknesses are like aquatic plants of evil growth; their hour comes, and they wither and die, and leave the channels free again. Life returns—in slow, soft ripples at first, yet in irresistible tide, and at last in pulses of mighty throb through every pipe. Death is the final failure of all sickness, the clearing away of the very soil in which the seed of the ill plant takes root and grows.

By degrees Cosmo recovered strength and did not leave behind him the peace that had pervaded his weakness. But now the time for action was at hand. For weeks he had been fed like the young ravens in the nest, and, knowing he could do nothing, had not troubled himself with the useless *how*; but it was time once more to understand, that he might be ready to act.

Mechanically he began again to consider what he must do to keep the family's ship from sinking. He went to his bureau and opened it, but there was not so much as a penny. He knew there could not be unless some angel had visited it as he lay. There was no work available that he knew of and even had there been any, at present he would have had no strength with which to do it. As the spring came on there would again be labor in the fields, and that he would keep in his mind, but the question was of the present and its need.

One thing only he would not do. There were many in the country around on very friendly terms with his father and himself. But his very soul revolted from any attempt to borrow money when he could see no prospect for repaying it. He would carry the traditions of his family no further in that direction. He would quite rather die. But so that his father might not suffer in want, he would beg. "Where borrowing without hope of repayment is dishonest," he said to himself, "begging may be the most honorable course. It is possible that the man who has no way of earning the day's bread has something of a divine right to beg."

In Cosmo's case, however, there was this difficulty with such reasoning: he could easily make a living of some sort if he would but leave his father. And that was the one thing he was determined not to do. Before absolute want could stare them in the face, they must have parted with everything. No, he was not ready yet to take to making the rounds of the neighboring farmhouses to try to receive from each a dole of a handful of meal. Something must be possible before it would come to that! But what?

Once more he fell to thinking, but again it was only to find himself helplessly afloat in a sea of nonpossibilities. He could see nothing in the immediate future but beggary. Could it be that God indeed intended to bring upon him this last humiliation of all? In the mire of his thoughts the immediately practical vanished, lost in reasoning, and once more he tried to return to it. But it was like trying to see through a brick wall. To write again to Mr. Burns before he heard from him would be too much like the begging, which he had not yet resolved to do. He never suspected that the parcel he had left at the carrier's house was still lying there—safe under one of his wife's summer shawls. Neither could Cosmo go to

Mr. Simon, for he was too poor and had now for some time been far from well himself; the doctor had acknowledged some fear about his lungs.

All at once the thought came to him: why shouldn't he pledge the labor of his body for the coming harvest, in exchange for a partial present payment? He would have nothing to be ashamed of in making the offer to any man who knew him enough to be friendly. He would but ask a part of the fee in advance. True, when the time came he might well be as much in need of money as he was now, and there would be little or none to receive from his work. But on the other hand, if he did not have help now, he would never even be able to reach that future day at all. And when he did, there might by then have come other help that he could not at this moment foresee.

Better beg then than now! He would make the attempt, and do so on the first day he was strong enough to get out and walk the necessary distance. In the meantime he would have a look into the meal-chest.

It stood in a dark corner of the kitchen, and he had to put his hand in to learn its condition. He found a rather substantial layer of meal in the bottom. How there could be so much after his long illness, he scarcely dared imagine. He would have to ask Grizzie, he said to himself, but he hesitated in his heart to question her.

There then came a spell of warm weather, and all the invalids improved. Cosmo was able to go out, and every day had a little walk by himself. Naturally he thought of the only other time in his life when he first walked out after an illness. Joan had been so near him then it hardly seemed that anything could part them. And now she seemed an eternity away. For months he had heard nothing of her. She was no doubt married by now, and, knowing his feelings for her, must have decided it kinder not to write.

Then the justice of his soul turned to the devotion of the two women who had tended him in this trouble, though the half of it he did not yet know. And from that he turned to the source of all devotion, and made himself strong in the thought of the eternal love.

41

Help

*C*osmo had reached the decision to take his request first to the farmer in whose fields he had labored two seasons earlier. The distance was rather great, but he tried to convince himself he would be able to walk home every night. In the present state of his strength, however, he found it a long trudge indeed; and before the house came into sight he was very weary.

"I was almost as ill-off," he said to himself, "when I came here for work the first time, yet here I am—alive, and likely to work again! It's just like going on and on in a dream, wondering what we are coming to next."

He was shown into the parlor and had not waited long before the farmer came. He scarcely welcomed him, but by degrees his manner grew more cordial. Still the coldness with which he had been received caused Cosmo to hesitate, and a pause resulted. The farmer was the first to break it.

"Ye didna give us the favor o' yer company last hairst!" he said. "I would hae thought ye might hae foun' yersel' more at home wi' the like o' us than wi' that ill-tongued miser, Lord Lickmyloof! None o' us took it ower weel that ye didna give us the chance o' yer company."

This explained his reception, and Cosmo quickly explained his conduct.

"You may be sure," he answered, "that it went some against my grain to seek work from *him*, and I had no reason on earth for not coming to you first but that I didn't want to be so far from my father at night. He's not as strong as he was."

"Very natural!" responded the farmer heartily, wondering in himself if any of his sons would have considered him so much. "Weel," he went on, "I'm relieved to un'erstan' the thing, for the lasses would hae persuaded me I had given ye some offense wi' my free-spoken ways, when nothin' could hae been farther frae the thought o' my heart."

"Indeed," said Cosmo, "I assure you, Mr. Henderson, I would never imagine offense from you. You have always treated me most kindly. And I could not give you a better proof of what I mean by coming to you first, the moment I was able to walk after a lengthy recent illness, with the request I now have to make of you. Will you engage me for the coming harvest, and pay me a part of the fee in advance? I know it is a strange request, and if you are unable to oblige me I doubt if there is another man to whom I would venture to make it. I have been very ill, but I am now well on the mend and there is a long time to recover my strength before the harvest. To tell you the truth, we are greatly in need of a little money at the castle. We are not greatly in debt, but we have lost all our land; and a house, however, good, won't grow oats. But we want to hold on as long as we can. I am sure if you were in our place, you would not want to part with the house a moment before you were absolutely compelled to."

"But, Laird," said the farmer, who had listened with the greatest attention, "hoo can the thing be, that among all the great fowk ye hae kent, there should be none to whom ye can turn? I canna un'erstan' hoo the last o' sich an auld family should na hae a hand held oot to help them!"

"It is not so very hard to explain," replied Cosmo. "Almost all my father's old friends are dead or gone, and a man like him, especially in hard times, does not readily make new friends. Almost the only person he has been intimate with in late years is Mr. Simon, whom I daresay you know. And my father has what many people consider peculiar notions—so peculiar, indeed, that I have heard of some calling him a fool behind his back because he paid them money his father owed them. I believe if he had rich friends, they would say it was no use trying to help such a man."

"Weel!" exclaimed the farmer, "it jist puzzles me to ken hoo there can be any trowth in the Bible when a good man like that comes sae near to beggin' his bread!"

"He is very near it, certainly," assented Cosmo. "But why not he as well as any other?"

" 'Cause they tell me the Bible says the righteous man shall never come to beg his bread."

"Well *near* is not *there*. But I'm sure there must be a mistake. The writer of one of the psalms—I do not know whether David or another—says he never saw the righteous forsaken or his seed begging bread; but though he may not have seen it, another may."

"Weel, I fancy if he had, he wouldna hae been long in puttin' a stop to it! Laird, if a small matter o' fifty pound or sae would tide ye ower the trouble— weel, ye could pay me when ye liked."

It was a moment or two before Cosmo could speak. A long conversation followed, rising almost to fierceness on the part of the farmer, because of Cosmo's refusal to accept the offered loan.

"I do see my way," persisted Cosmo, "to paying for my wages with my work, but nothing more. Lend me two pounds, Mr. Henderson, on the understanding that I am to work it out in the harvest, and I shall be in debt to your kindness forever. But more than that I simply cannot accept."

Grumbling, the farmer at length handed him the two pounds, but obstinately refused any written acknowledgment or agreement.

Neither of them knew that all the time the friendly altercation had been proceeding, there was Elsie listening at the door, her color coming and going like the shadows in a day of sun and wind. When it was over, she entered and asked Cosmo to stay and have tea with them, to which the farmer himself added his enthusiastic agreement. Cosmo accepted the invitation, and indeed was glad to have a good meal. The time passed with pleasure to all, for the relief of having two pounds in his pocket and the genuine kindness shown him put Cosmo in great spirits. The old farmer was admiringly curious at the spirit of the youth who could yet afford to be merry in the midst of such hardship.

Cosmo sat with his neighbors till the gloaming began to fall. When he rose to go, they all rose with him and accompanied him fully halfway home. When they left and turned back, and he was again alone, his heart grew so glad that, weak as he yet was, and the mists rising along the path, he never felt the slightest chill, but trudged cheerily on, praying and singing, until at length he was surprised to find how short the way had been.

For a great part of it, after his friends had left him, he had glimpses now and then of someone in front of him that looked like Aggie, but the distance between them gradually lengthened, and before he reached home he had lost sight of her. When he entered the kitchen, Aggie was there.

"Was ye upon the road afore me, Aggie?" he said.

"Ay."

"What for didna ye bide for me?"

"Ye had yer company the first half o' the road, an' yer songs the last, an' I didna think ye wanted me."

So saying she turned and went up the stair.

As Cosmo followed, he turned and put his hand into the meal chest. It was empty! There was not even enough for another day! He smiled in his heart and said to himself, *The links of the story hold together yet!*

Going up to his father, he had to pass the door of his own room, now occupied by James Gracie. As he drew near it, he heard the voice of Aggie speaking to her grandfather. What she said he did not know, but he heard the answer.

"Lassie," said the old man, "ye can never see past the Lord to ken whaur he's takin' ye. Ye may jist as weel close yer own eyes. His garment spreads over the road, an' what we hae to do is to hold a tight grip o' it—not try to see beyond it."

Cosmo hastened the rest of the way up and told his father what he had over-heard.

"There's naethin' like faith for the makin' o' poets, Cosmo," said the laird. "James never appeared t' me t' hae more o' what's called intellect than ordinar'. But ye see the man that has faith is aye a growin' man, an' sae will always be comin' t' somethin' more, even in this warl'. An' when ye think o' the ages to come, truly it would seem to matter little what intellect a man may start wi'. I knew mysel' one that in ordinar' affairs was counted little better than an idiot, but who turned t' a prophet when he gaed doon upon his knees. Ay! fowk may laugh at what they haena a glimpse o'."

Here Cosmo heard Grizzie come into the kitchen, and went down to her. She was sitting in his father's chair by the fire and did not turn her face when he spoke. She was either tired or vexed, he thought. Aggie was also not in the kitchen again.

"Here, Grizzie!" said Cosmo, "here's two pounds, an' ye'll need t' make it go farther than it can, I'm thinkin', for I dinna ken whaur we're to get the next."

"Ken whaur ye got the last?" muttered Grizzie, and then hastily tried to cover her words. "Whaur got ye that, Cosmo?" she said.

"What if I dinna tell ye, Grizzie?" he returned, willing to rouse her with a little teasing.

"That's as ye see proper, sir," she answered. "Naebody has a right t' say to anither, 'Whaur got ye that?' 'cep' they doobt ye hae been stealin'."

It was a somewhat strange answer, but there was no end to the strange things Grizzie would say: it was one of her charms! Cosmo told her at once where and how he had got the money, for with such true comrades, although not yet did he know how true, he felt almost that a secret would be a sin.

But the moment Grizzie heard where Cosmo had engaged himself, and from whom he had borrowed the two pounds on the pledge of that engagement, she jumped from her chair and cried, with clenched and outstretched hand, "Glenwarlock, young sir, ken ye what ye're doing? The Lord preserve us! He's an innocent!" she added, turning with an expression of despair to Aggie, who was watching the two with a strange look.

"Grizzie!" cried Cosmo, astonished. "What on earth makes ye look like that at the mention o' one who has jist helped us oot o' the worse straits we was ever in?"

"If there had been naebody nearer home t' help ye oot o' worse straits, it's worse straits ye would be in. An' it's worse ye'll be in yet if that man gets his will wi' ye."

"He's a fine, honest man! An' for worse straits, Grizzie—arena ye at the verra last wi' yer meal?"

As he spoke, he turned and, in bodily reference to fact, went to the chest into which he had looked a few minutes before. To his astonishment, there was enough meal in it for a good many days! He turned again and stared at Grizzie. But she had once more seated herself in his father's chair with her back to him, and before he could speak she went on.

"Shame fall t' him, say I, that made his money as a flesher in the west end o' Howglen, to try to get a gentleman o' a thousand year for one o' his queens! But, please the Lord, we'll hold clear o' him yet!"

"Hoot, Grizzie! Ye surely canna think any man would regard the likes o' me as worth lookin' to for a son-in-law! He wouldna be sich a gowk!"

"Gowk here, gowk there! He kens what ye are an' what ye're worth—weel that! Hasna he seen ye at the scythe? Doesna he ken there's ten times more to be made o' one gentleman like you, wi' money at his back, then ten common men sich as he's like to get for his daughters? Weel kens he it's nae yer fault that ye're no freely sae weel off as some that ought an' will be worse off, if it be the Lord's will, before all is done! Doesna he ken that Castle Warlock itsel' would be a world's honor to any leddy—no to say a lass brought up over a slaughter-hoose? Shame upon him an' his!"

"Weel, Grizzie," rejoined Cosmo, "ye may say what ye like, but I dinna believe he would hae done what he has done—"

"Ha!" interrupted Grizzie. "What has he done? Doesna he ken the word o' a Warlock's as good as gold? Doesna he ken yer work, what wi' yer pride an' what wi' yer ill-placed gratitude, will be worth to him that o' two men? The man's nae daft! He kens what he's aboot! Haith, ye needna spend much gratitude upon such benefactions!"

"To show ye, Grizzie, that ye are unfair to him, I will tell ye that he pressed on me a loan o' fifty pounds."

"I tell ye sae!" cried Grizzie, jumping to her feet. "God forbid ye took him at his offer!"

"I did not," answered Cosmo; "but all the same—"

"The Lord be praised for his abundant an' great mercy!" cried Grizzie, more heartily than devoutly. "We may contrive t' win ower the two poun', even should ye no work it oot. But *fifty*!—the Lord be aboot us an' keep us frae ill! So sure's death, ye would hae had to take the lass! Cosmo, ye canna but ken the auld tale o' the muckle-mouthed Meg?"

"Weel I ken it," replied Cosmo. "But ye'll aloo, Grizzie, times are altered since the day when the laird could give a choice atween a wife an' the gallows! Mr. Henderson canna weel hang me for two pounds. But, Grizzie, whaur did that meal in the kist come frae? There was none in it an hour ago."

With all her faults of temper and tongue, there was one evil word Grizzie could not speak. In the course of a not very brief life, she had tried a good many times to tell a lie, but had never been able to. And now, determined not to tell where the meal had come from, she naturally paused unprepared. It was but for a moment. Then out came the following utterance:

"Some fowk says that the age o' miracles is past. For mysel' I dinna pretend t' any opinion; but sae long as the necessity was the same, I wouldna want t' think Providence wouldna be consistent wi' itsel'. Ye must mind the tale, better than I can tell it, concernin' yon meal-girnel—much like, I daresay, oor own, though it be called a barrel in the Book. Eh, but a happy woman was she that had but t' take her bowl an' go t' the girnel, as I might take my pail an' go t' the wall! An' why mightna the Almighty make a meal-wall as weel's a water-wall, I would like t' ken! One thing must be jist as easy t' him as anither—jist as one thing's jist as hard t' us as anither. Eh, but we're helpless creatures!"

"In yer way, Grizzie, ye would keep us as helpless as ever, for ye would hae everything kept away frae oor hands, even what we can do oorsel's, like we was bairnies in oor mither's lap! It's o' the mercy o' the Lord that he would make men an' women o' us—no keep us bairns forever!"

"It may be as ye say, Cosmo. But sometimes I could almost wish I was a bairn again, an' had t' look to my mither for everythin'."

"An' isna that as the Lord would hae o' us, Grizzie? We canna aye be bairns to oor mithers—but we can an' must aye be bairns to the great Father o' us."

"I hae an ill heart, I don't doobt, Cosmo, for I'm too hard t' content. An' I'm too auld noo, I fear, to make mysel' much better. But maybe some kindly body like yersel' will take me in han' when I'm dead, an' put some sense int' me."

"Ye hae sense enough, Grizzie, an' to spare, if only ye would—"

"Guide my tongue a wee better, ye would say! But little ye ken the temptation o' one that has but one weapon to make use o'! An' the gift ye hae ye're no to despise, ye must turn everythin' t' acoont."

Cosmo did not care to reason with her further and went back to his father.

Grizzie had gained her point, which was to turn him away from questions about the meal. Indeed, she had exercised more sense in the drift of the conversation than even Cosmo knew!

For a little while they now had enough to live on. And if it seems that the horizon of hope was narrowing around them, it does not necessarily follow that it seemed so to them. For what is the extent of our merely rational horizon at any time? But for faith and imagination it would be a narrow one indeed! Even what we call experience is but a stupid kind of faith. It is a trusting in impetus instead of love.

More eternal growth and good was going on than outward circumstances could have revealed; indeed, what was happening of an everlasting nature was partially a result of the collapse of all worldly hope. Those days were fashioning an eternal joy to father and son, for they were loving each other a little more before each day's close, and were thus putting time—utterly independent of worldly or financial gain—to its highest and most sacred use.

42

A Visit to Mr. Simon

Until he was laid up, Cosmo had gone often to see Mr. Simon. The good man was now beginning to feel the approach of age, but he was cheerful and hopeful as ever, and more expectant. As soon as he was physically able, Cosmo renewed his visits, but seldom stayed long with him, both because Mr. Simon could not bear too much talking, and because he knew his father would be watching for his return.

One day it had rained before sunrise, and a soft spring wind had been blowing ever since, a soothing and persuading wind that seemed to draw out the buds from the secret places of the dry twigs, and whisper to the roots of the rose trees that their flowers would be wanted before long. And now the sun was near the foot of the western slope, and there was a mellow, tearful look about earth and sky. Grizzie entered the room where Cosmo was reading to his father, as he sat in his easy chair by the fireside, and told them that Mr. Simon had had a bad night and was worse. The laird asked Cosmo to go at once and ask about him, to see if they might help in any way.

The wind kept him company as he walked, flitting softly about him, like an attendant that needed more motion than the young man's pace would afford. The breeze seemed so full of thought and love that he found himself wondering if all things having to do with the earth might not—in the true eternal reality—be in fact spirit rather than what we call *matter*. Then came the thought of the infinitude of our moods, of the hues and shades and endless kinds and varieties of feeling, especially in our dreams. And he said to himself how rich God must be, since from him we become capable of such differences and depths of conscious life.

How poor and helpless, he said to himself; *what a mere pilgrim and stranger in this world must be he who does not have God one with him! Without God life cannot be free. In no other way can we move in harmony with the will and life of all that is about us!*

As he walked up the hill thinking, the stream was by his side, tumbling out its music as it ran to find its eternity. And the wind blew on from the moist west, where the gold and purple had fallen together in a ruined heap over the tomb of the sun. And the stars came thinking out of the heavens, and the things of earth withdrew into the great nest of the dark. And so he found himself at the door of the cottage, where lay one of the heirs of all things, waiting to receive his inheritance.

The news he heard at the door was that the master was better, and the old woman showed Cosmo at once to his room, saying she knew he would be glad to see him. When he entered the study—where, because of his long illness and need of air, Mr. Simon lay—the room seemed to grow radiant, filled with the smile that greeted him from the pillow. The sufferer held out his hand almost eagerly.

"Come, come!" he said; "I want to tell you something—a little experience I have just had—from my illness, no doubt. Outwardly it is nothing, but to you it will not be nothing. It was blowing a great wind last night."

"So my father tells me," answered Cosmo, "but for my part I slept too soundly to hear it."

"It grew calm with the morning. As the light came, the wind fell. Indeed, I think it lasted only about three hours altogether.

"I have lately been suffering a good deal with my breathing, and it has been worst when the wind was high. Last night I lay awake in the middle of the night, very tired, and longing for the sleep which seemed as if it would never come. I thought of Sir Philip Sidney, how, as he lay dying, he was troubled because, for all his praying, God would not let him sleep. It was not the want of sleep that troubled him, but that God would not give it to him. And I was trying hard to make myself strong to trust in God whatever came to me, sleep or waking, weariness or slow death, when all at once the wind rose with a great roar, as if the Prince of the power of the air were mocking my prayers. And I thought to myself, *It is then the will of God that I shall neither sleep nor lie at peace tonight* and so I said, 'Thy will be done!' and laid myself out to be quiet, expecting that my breathing would begin to grow thick and hard, as it has on previous such occasions, with the end result that in the end I would have to be struggling for every lungful. So I lay waiting. But still as I waited, I kept breathing softly. No iron band ringed itself about my chest; no sand filled up the passages of my lungs!

"The cottage is not very well sealed, and I felt the wind blowing all about me as I lay. But instead of beginning to cough and wheeze as I usually do, I began to breathe better than before. Soon I fell fast asleep, and when I woke I seemed a new man almost, so much better did I feel. It was a wind of God, and had been blowing all about me as I slept, renewing me! It was so strange, so delightful! Where I dreaded evil, there had come good. So perhaps will it be when the times which the flesh dreads draws close—we shall see the pale damps of the grave approaching, but they will never reach us. We shall hear ghastly winds coming from the mouth of the tomb, but when they blow on us they shall be sweet—the waving wings of the angels that sit in the antechamber of the hall of life, once the sepulchre of our Lord. And when we die, instead of finding we are dead, we shall have waked into all the more clarity of life!"

It was an experience that would to most men have meant nothing beyond mere physical relief. But to Peter Simon it was a word from the eternal heart, which, in every true and quiet mood, speaks into the hearts of men. When we cease listening to the cries of self-seeking and self-care, then the voice that was there all the time enters our ears. It is the voice of the Father speaking to his child, never known for what it is until the child begins to obey it. To him who has not ears to hear, God will not reveal himself: it would be to slay him with terror.

Cosmo sat a long time talking with his friend, for now there seemed no danger of hurting him with too much exertion. Therefore it was late when he rose to return home.

43

• • • • • • • • • • • • • • • • • • • •

Suspicions

Aggie was in the kitchen making the porridge when he entered.

"What's come o' Grizzie?" asked Cosmo.

"Ye dinna like my parritch sae weel as hers?" returned Agnes.

"Jist as weel, Aggie," answered Cosmo.

"Dinna tell Grizzie that."

"Why?"

"She would be angered first, an' then her heart would be like t' break."

"There's no reason to say it," conceded Cosmo. "But what's come o' her tonight?" he went on. "It's some dark, an' I doobt she'll—"

"The road atween this an' the Muir's no easy to lose," said Aggie.

Almost the instant the words were out of her mouth, her face flushed hotter than fire or cooking could make it. What she had said was in itself true, but what she had not said, yet meant him to assume, was not true, for Grizzie had gone nowhere near Muir o' Warlock. Aggie had never told a lie in her life, and almost before the words were out of her mouth, she felt as if the solid earth were sinking from under her feet. She left the wood spoon sticking in the porridge and dropped into the laird's chair.

"What's the matter wi' ye, Aggie?" said Cosmo, rushing over to her in alarm, for her face was now white.

"Oh, Cosmo—I telled ye a lie!"

"Aggie!" cried Cosmo in dismay, "ye never told me a lie in yer life."

"Never afore," she answered. "But I hae told ye one noo! Grizzie's no gone to Muir o' Warlock."

"What do I care whaur Grizzie's gone!" rejoined Cosmo. "Tell me or not, as ye like."

Aggie burst into tears.

"Hold yer tongue, Aggie," said Cosmo, trying to soothe her, feeling her trouble himself. For he was sorry she should *almost* have told him a lie, and his heart was sore for her misery. He knew the suffering it must cause to have done a thing so foreign to her nature. "It *could* be little more," he went on, "than a slip o' the will, seein' ye made such haste to set it right again. For mysel', I banish the thought o' the thing."

"I thank ye, Cosmo. Ye would always do like the Lord himsel'! But there's more in it. I dinna ken what to do or say. It's a sore thing t' stan' atween two an' no ken what to do without doin' wrong. There's somethin' it almost seems to me ye hae a right t' ken, but I canna be sure. An' yet—"

She was interrupted by the hurried opening of the door. Grizzie came staggering in, with a face of terror.

"Close the door!" she cried, almost speechless, and sank into a chair, gasping for breath and dropping her canvas bag at her feet; it was about the size of a pillowcase.

Cosmo closed the door, and Aggie quickly got her some water, which she drank eagerly. After a time of panting and sighing, she seemed to come to herself, then rose and said as if nothing had happened, "I must see to the supper."

Cosmo tried to pick up her bag to help her with it, but she pounced on it and carried it with her to the corner by the fireplace. In the meantime the porridge had begun to burn.

"Eh, sirs!" she cried, "the parritch'll be all scorched—not to mention the waste o' good meal! Aggie, hoo could ye be sae careless!"

"It was enough t' make anybody forget the pot, t' see ye come in like that, Grizzie!" said Cosmo.

"An' what'll ye say to the tale I bring ye?" rejoined Grizzie, as she turned the porridge into a dish, careful not to scrape too hard on the bottom of the pot.

"Tell us all aboot it, Grizzie, an' bena too lang either, for I must go to my father."

"Go to him. There's naebody here would keep ye frae him!"

Cosmo was surprised at her tone, for although she took abundant liberty with the young laird, he had never known her to be rude to him.

"Not till I hear yer tale, Grizzie," he answered.

"An' I would fain ken what ye'll say to it, for ye never would alloo 'at ye believed in kelpies*; an' there's me been followed by a sure one, this last half-hoor—or it may be less!"

"Hoo kenned ye it was a kelpie. It's dark as pitch."

"Kenned! he says? Didna I hear the deevil ahind me—the tramp o' his four feet as if they had been four an' twenty!"

"I wonder why he didna catch up wi' ye, Grizzie," suggested Cosmo.

---

*A *kelpie* is a mythical Scottish beast, or water demon, which resembles a horse and is said to haunt rivers and peat bogs and Highland lakes and lures the unwary to their deaths.

"God kens hoo he didna. I won'er mysel'. But I ran, I tell ye, all the way till ye shut the door!"

"But they say," objected Cosmo, who could not fail to perceive from what Aggie had said that there was something going on which he should know, "that the kelpie only lives by some water-side."

"Weel, didna I come by the tarn o' the tap o' Stieve Know?"

"What on earth was ye doin' there after dark, Grizzie?"

"What was I doin'? I said na I was there after dark, but the cratur might hae seen me pass weel enough. Wasna I ower the hill to my ain fowk in the How o' Hap? An didna I come home by Luck's Lift? An' wouldna the guidman o' that same place hae me do what I haena done but twice in twenty year—take a dram o' whiskey? An' didna I take it? An' was I no in need o' it? An' didna I come home all the better for it?"

"An' get a sight o' the kelpie in the bargain—eh, Grizzie?" suggested Cosmo.

"Hoots! go away up t' the laird, an' leave me to get my breath an' yer supper t'gither," said Grizzie, who saw to what she had exposed herself. "An' I wish the next kelpie on you! Only whate'er ye do, Cosmo, dinna turn yer back on it, for he'll carry ye straight home t' his master, an' we all ken who *he* is."

"I'm no gaein," said Cosmo, "till I ken what ye hae in that pack o' yers."

"Hoot!" cried Grizzie, snatching up the pack and holding it behind her back, "ye would never try to' look int' an auld wife's pack! What ken ye what she mightna hae there?"

"It looks to me neither more nor less than a meal-pock," said Cosmo.

"Meal-pock!" returned Grizzie with contempt. "What next?"

He made another attempt to seize the bag, but she caught the large spoon up from the empty porridge pot and showed the posture of fight with it, in genuine earnest beyond any doubt for the defense of her pack. Whatever the secret was, it looked as if the bag were somehow connected with it. Cosmo began to grow very uncomfortable. So strong were his latent suspicions that he dared not for a time allow them to take shape in his brain lest they should spring at once into the life of fact.

His mind had, for the last few days, been much occupied with the question of miracles. Why, he thought to himself, should one believing in an almighty and loving Power at the heart of all affairs find it impossible that, in their great need, their meal-chest should be supplied like that of the widow of Zarephath? If he could believe the thing was done then, there could be nothing so difficult in hoping the thing might be done now. If it was possible once, it was possible in the same circumstances at some other time. And in the meantime it was a fact that they had all had their daily bread supplied.

But now this strange behavior of Grizzie set him thinking of something very different. And he could not get the question out of his mind as to why the jeweler had not made some reply to his request concerning the things he had sent him. His only conclusion in the whole matter was that it must be the design of Providence to make him part with the last clog that fettered him; he was to have no ease in life until he had yielded the castle.

If that were so, then the longer he delayed the greater would be the loss. To sell everything in it first would but put off the evil day, whereas if he were to part with the house at once, and take his father where he could find work, they would be able to still have some of the old things about them to ease the strangeness of a new home. The more he thought about it the more it seemed his duty to put a stop to the hopeless struggle, and to at last consent in full to the sorrow to which it seemed the will of God to bring them. Then with new courage he might begin something new, no more on the slippery slope of descent, but with the firm ground of the Valley of Humiliation under their feet. They could not continue on much longer as things now stood, and he was ready to do whatever was required of him. His only wish was that God would make it plain.

The part of discipline he liked least—a part of which doubtless we do not yet at all understand the good or necessity—was uncertainty of action, the uncertainty of what it was God's will he should do. But on the other hand, perhaps the cause of that uncertainty was the lack of perfect readiness. Perhaps all that was needed to make duty plain was absolute will to do it.

These and other such thoughts went flowing and ebbing for hours in his mind that night until at last he thought to himself that his immediate duty was plain enough—namely, to go to sleep. He yielded his consciousness, therefore, to him from whom it came and within a short time was in a deep slumber.

44

. . . .

Discovery and Confessions

In the morning Cosmo woke wondering whether this might be the day when God would let him know what he was to do. He was certain he would not have him leave his father. But anything else by now he could believe possible.

The season was approaching the nominal beginning of summer, but the morning was very cold. He went to the window. Air and earth had the look of a black frost—the most unfriendly, the most killing of weathers. And his father's bronchitis was worse! Quickly he fetched fuel, lit the fire, then left him still asleep, and went downstairs. He was earlier than usual, and Grizzie was later. Only Aggie was in the kitchen. Her grandfather was worse also. Everything pointed to a more severe tightening of circumstances around them, and stronger necessity at the same time: this must be how God was letting him know what he had to do!

He sat down and suddenly, for a moment, felt as if he were sitting on the opposite bank of the Warlock River, looking up at the house where he was born and had spent his days—now the property of another and closed to him forever.

Within those walls he could not so much as order the removal of a piece of straw, could not chop a piece of kindling for a fire to warm his father! "The will of God be done!" he said, and the vision was gone.

Aggie was busy getting his porridge ready—which Cosmo had by this time learned to eat without any accompaniment—and he thought to himself that here was a chance of questioning her before Grizzie should appear.

"Come, Aggie," he said abruptly, "I want to ken why Grizzie was in sich a terror aboot her bag last night. I'm thinkin' I hae a right t' ken."

"I wish ye wouldna speir," returned Aggie, after a brief moment's pause.

"Aggie," said Cosmo, "gien ye tell me it's none o' my business, I winna speir again."

"Ye *are* good, Cosmo, after the way I behaved to ye last night," she answered with a tremble in her voice.

"Dinna think o' it nae mair, Aggie. To me it is as gien it had never been. My heart's the same to ye as afore—an' justly. I believe I un'erstan' ye sometimes, most as well as ye do yersel'."

"I hope sometimes ye un'erstan' me better," answered Aggie. "Sore do I mourn that the shadow o' that lie ever crossed my min'."

"It was but a shadow," said Cosmo.

"But what would ye think o' yersel', gien it had been you that sae near—no, I winna nibble at the truth any mair—gien it had been you, I will say't, that lied that lie—sich a one that it was?"

"I would say to mysel', that wi' God's help I was the less likely ever to tell a lie again. For that noo I un'erstood better hoo a temptation might come upon a body all at once, no giving him time to reflect—an' sae my responsibility was the greater."

"Thank ye, Cosmo," said Aggie humbly, and was silent.

"But," resumed Cosmo, "ye haena told me yet that it's none o' my business what Grizzie had in her bag last night."

"No, I couldna tell ye that, 'cause it wouldna be true. It is yer business."

"What was in the bag then?"

"Weel, Cosmo, ye put me in a great difficulty. For though I never said to Grizzie I wouldna tell, I made nae objection—though at the time I didna like it—when she told me what she was gaein' to do. An' sae I canna help fearin' it may be some false to tell ye. Besides, I hae let it gae sae lang wi'oot sayin' a word that the good auld body could never accept't if I was t' turn on her noo an' tell."

"You are dreadfully mysterious, Aggie," said Cosmo, bringing his English to bear on what was becoming a more serious situation than he had thought at first. "And in truth, you make me more than a little uncomfortable. What can it be that has been going on so long, and had better now be told me? Have I a right to know or do I not?"

"Ye hae a right to ken, I do believe, else I wouldna tell ye," answered Aggie. "I was terrified, frae the first, t' think what ye would say t' it! But ye see, what was there left t' do? You, an' the laird, an' my gran'father was all laid up t'gether, heaps o' things were wanted, the meal was gone, an' life depended on fowk haein' what they could eat an' drink!"

As she spoke the truth began to dawn more fully on Cosmo. He asked no more questions, but sat waiting the worst.

"Dinna be ower hard upon Grizzie an' me, Cosmo," Aggie went on. "It wasna for oorsel's we would do sich a thing. An' maybe there was none but them we did it for that we would hae been able to do it for. But praise, gien there be any, she has it all. For, that worst mightna come to the worst, at the last she took the meal-pock," said Aggie, and burst into tears as she said it, "an' went oot wi' it."

"Lassie," he said after a few moments of staring at her as one dumb, "didna ye ken in yer own soul that we would rather hae died?"

"There it is! That's jist what for Grizzie wouldna hae ye told! But dinna think she gaed to anyplace whaur she was kent," sobbed Agnes, "or appeared to any t' be other than a poor auld body that went aboot for hersel'. Dinna think either that she ever told a lie or said a word t' make fowk pity her. She had aye before her the possibility o' bein' called to account someday. But I'm thinkin' if ye had asked her an' not me, ye would hae heard a stronger defense than mine! One thing ye may be sure o'—there's nobody a hair the wiser aboot it!"

"What difference does that make?" cried Cosmo. "The fact remains."

"Hoot, Cosmo!" said Agnes with a revival of her old authority over him, "ye're taking the thing in a fashion no worthy o' a philosopher—not to say a Christian. Ye take it as if there was shame in it! An' gien there wasna shame, I dare ye t' prove there can be any disgrace! If ye come to that wi' it, hoo was the Lord himsel' supported when he went aboot cleanin' oot the world? Wasna the women that went wi' him providin' all things?"

"True; but that was very different! They all knew him and loved him—knew that he was doing what no money could pay for; that he was working himself to death for them and their people—that he was earning the whole world. Besides, there was no begging there. He never asked them for anything."—Here Aggie shook her head in unbelief, but Cosmo went on.—"And those women, some of them anyhow, were rich, and proud to do what they did for the best and the grandest of men. But what have we done for the world that we should dare look to it to help us?"

"For that matter, Cosmo, arena we all brothers an' sisters? Everybody's brothers an' sisters wi' everyone. It's but a kin' o' some mean pride that wouldna be obliged to yer ain fowk after ye hae done yer best. Cosmo! every handful o' meal given in this or any hoose by them that wouldna in like need accept the same is an affront frae brother t' brother. Them that wouldna take, I say, has no right to give."

"But nobody kent the trowth o' where their handful o' meal was goin'. They thought they were giving it to a poor auld woman, when they were in fact giving it to men with a great house over their heads. 'Tis a disgrace, an' hard to bear, Aggie!"

" 'Deed, the thing's hard upon us all! But whaur the disgrace is, I will not condescend to see. Men in a big hoose! Two o' them auld, an' all three in their beds no fit t' move! Do ye think there's one o' them that gave meal to Grizzie—though what less than the handful o' meal, which was all she ever got, it would be hard to imagine—that would hae given less had they kent it was for the life o' auld Glen-warlock, a name respected, an' more than respected, whaurever it's heard? Or for the life o' the yoong laird, brought t' death wi' laborer's work an' then almost killed in a storm? Or for auld James Gracie, that's led a God-fearin' life till he's almost too auld to live any longer? I say nothin' aboot Grizzie an' me, who could take care o' oorsel's gien we hadna three dowie men t' look after. We did oor best, but when all oor ain money was away after the rest, we couldna leave oorsel's to earn mair. If you three could hae done for yersel's, we would hae been sendin' ye home somethin'."

"You tell me," said Cosmo, as if in a painful dream, through which flashed lovely lights, "that you and Grizzie spent all your own money upon us, and then Grizzie went out and begged for us?"

" 'Deed, there's no anither word for it—nor was there one other thing to be done!" Aggie drew herself up and went on with solemnity. "Do ye think, Cosmo, whaur head or heart or fit hand could do anythin' to ward off want or trouble frae you or the laird, that Grizzie or mysel' would not do what came to us? I beg ye won't lay to oor charge against us what we were driven to. As Grizzie says, we were jist one step frae desperation."

Cosmo's heart was full. He dared not speak. He came to Aggie, took her hand, looked her in the face with eyes full of tears. She had been pale as sun-browned skin could be, but now she grew red as a misty dawn. Her eyes fell and she began to pull at the hem of her apron. Grizzie's step was on the stair, and Cosmo, not yet quite prepared to meet her, walked out.

The morning was neither so black nor so cold as he had imagined it. He went into the garden, to the nook between the two blocks of the castle, there sat down, and tried to think. The sun was not far above the horizon, and he was in the cold shade of the kitchen tower, but he felt nothing and sat there motionless. The sun came southward, looked round the corner, and found him there. He brought with him a lovely fresh day. The leaves were struggling out, and the birds had begun to sing. Ah! what a day was here, had the hope of the boy been still swelling in his bosom!

But the decree had gone forth! No doubt remained! There could no longer be the least uncertainty. The house must follow the land! Castle Warlock and the last foothold of soil must go that wrong should not follow ruin! Were those divine women to spend money, time, and labor that he and his father should hold what they had no longer any right to hold? Or in beggary were they to hide themselves in the yet lower depth of begging by proxy, in their grim stronghold, living upon unacknowledged charity, as their ancestors had lived on plunder?

He dared not tell his father what he had discovered until he had at least taken the first step toward putting an end to the whole falsehood. To delay action was of all things what Cosmo dreaded. And as the loss mainly affected himself, the yielding of the castle must primarily be his deed and not his father's. He rose at once to do it.

The same moment the weight of Grizzie's meal-pock was lifted from his heart. The shame was, if there was indeed any shame in the thing, that they should have been living in such a house while the thing was done. When the house was sold, let people say what they would! In proportion as a man cares to do what he ought, he ceases to care how it may be judged. Of all things why should a true man heed the unjust judgment?

With his decision, he stood, climbed over the gate and wall, and took his way along Grizzie's path—once more, for the time at least, an undisputed possession of the people.

But while he had been thinking in the garden, Grizzie, who knew from Aggie that her secret was such no more, was in dire distress in the kitchen, fearing she had offended the young laird beyond reconciliation. In great anxiety she kept going every minute to the door to see if he were coming back to have his breakfast. But the first she saw of him was his back, as he leaped from the top of the wall. She ran after him to the gate.

"Come back," she cried, "come back! an' I go doon upon my auld knees to beg yer pardon!"

Cosmo turned the moment he heard her and went back.

When he reached the wall, over the top of the gate he saw Grizzie on her knees upon the round paving stones of the yard, stretching up her old hands to him as if he were some heavenly messenger just descended, whose wrath she feared. He jumped over wall and gate, ran to her, and lifted her to her feet.

"Grizzie, woman," he said, "what are ye aboot? Bless ye, Grizzie, I would almost as soon fight wi' my ain mither whaur she shines in glory as wi' you!"

Grizzie's face began to work like that of a child in an agony between pride and tears, just before he breaks into a howl. She gripped his arm hard with both hands, and at length faltered out, gathering composure as she proceeded.

"Cosmo, ye're like an angel o' God! Eh, sich an accoont o' ye I'll hae t' gie yer mither when I see her! For surely they'll let me see her, though they may weel no think me good enough to bide wi' her up there, for as long as we was t'gether doon here! Tell me, sir, what would ye hae me do. But jist one thing I must say: gien I hadna done as I did do, I do not see hoo we could hae got through the winter."

"Grizzie," said Cosmo, "I ken ye did all for the best, an' maybe it was the best. The day may come, Grizzie, when we'll go t'gether t' call upon them that put the meal in yer pock, an' return them thanks for their kindness."

"Eh, na, sir! That would never do! Why should they ken anything aboot it! They were jist kind, like at large, an' to naebody in particular, like the man wi' his swearin'. They gave t' me jist as they would to any auld beggar wife. It was to me they gave't, no to you. Let it lie upon me."

"That canna be, Grizzie," said Cosmo. "Ye see, ye're one o' the family, an' whatever ye do, I must hold my face to."

"God bless ye, sir!" exclaimed Grizzie, and turned toward the house, entirely relieved and satisfied.

"But eh, sir!" she cried, turning again, "ye haena broken yer fast yet today."

"I'll be back in a few minutes, an' make a breakfast o' it out o' the ordinary," answered Cosmo, and hastened away again across the field.

45

·······················

It Is Naught, Saith the Buyer

When Cosmo reached the gate of his lordship's estate, he found it closed, and although he rang the bell and called loudly to the gatekeeper, no one appeared. He put a hand on the top of the gate and jumped over it. But just as he landed, who should come round a bend in the drive a few yards off but Lord Lickmyloof himself, out for his morning walk. His irritable cantankerous nature would have been annoyed at the sight of anyone treating his gate with such disrespect, but when he saw who it was that thus made nothing of it—clearing it with as much contempt as a lawyer would a quibble not of his own devising—his displeasure grew immediately to indignation and anger.

"I beg your pardon, my lord," said Cosmo, taking the first word that apology might be immediate. "I could make no one hear me, and therefore took the liberty of describing a parabola over your gate."

"An ill-fashioned one, in my judgment, Mr. Warlock! I fear you have been learning to think too little of the rights of property lately."

"If I had put my foot on your new paint, my lord, I should have been to blame. But I vaulted clean over it, and touched nothing more than if the gate had been opened to me."

"I'll have an iron gate put in!"

"Not on my account, my lord, I hope. For I have come to ask you to put it out of my power to offend anymore by enabling me to leave Glenwarlock."

"Well?" returned his lordship, waiting.

"I find myself compelled at last," said Cosmo, not without some tremor in his voice, which he did his best to quench, "to give you the first right of refusal, according to your request, of the remainder of my father's property."

"House and all?"

"Everything except the furniture."

"Which I do not want."

A silence followed.

"May I ask if your lordship is prepared to make me an offer? Or will you call on my father when you have made up your mind?"

"I will give two hundred pounds for the lot."

"Two hundred pounds!" repeated Cosmo. He had not expected a large offer, but was unprepared for one so small. "Why, my lord, the bare building material would be worth more than that!"

"Not to take it down. I might as well blast it fresh from the quarry. I know the sort of thing those walls of yours are! Vitrified and rotten and moldy with age, by George! But I don't want to build. And left standing, the place is of no use to me. I should but let it crumble away at its leisure!"

Cosmo's dream rose again before his mind's eye. But it was no more with pain. For if the dear old place was to pass from their hands, what other end could be desired for it?

"But the sum you mention, my lord, would not, after paying the little we owe, leave us enough to take us from the place."

"I should be sorry for that. But you have my offer, take it or leave it. You'll not get half as much if it come to trying to dismantle it. To whom else would it be worth anything, bedded as it is in the midst of my property? If I say I don't want it, see if anybody will!"

Cosmo's heart sank anew. He dared not part with the place on such terms; he would have to consult with his father. For the moment his power of action was exhausted. He could do no more on his own—not even to spare his father.

"I must speak to the laird," he said. "I doubt if he will accept your offer."

"As he pleases. But I do not promise to let the offer stand. I make it now—not tomorrow, or even an hour from now."

"I must run the risk," answered Cosmo. "Will you allow me to jump the gate?"

But his lordship had a key and preferred opening it.

When Cosmo reached his father's room, he found him not yet thinking of getting up. He sat down and told him everything—to what straits they were reduced; what Grizzie had felt herself compelled to do; how his mind and heart had struggled with the castle; and where and on what errand he had been that morning. He ended with the result of his interview with Lord Lickmyloof. He had fought hard, he said, and through the grace of God had overcome his weakness. But now he could go no further without his father. He was up to no more and did not know what to do.

"I would not be willingly left out of your troubles, my son," said the old man cheerfully. "Leave me alone a little. There is one, you know, who is nearer to each of us than we are to each other. I must talk to him—your Father and my Father, in whom you and I are brothers."

Cosmo bowed in reverence and withdrew.

After about half an hour he heard the signal with which his father usually called him and hastened to him.

The laird held out his old hand to him.

"Come, my son," he said, "an' let us talk together as two o' the heirs o' all things. It's easy for me to regard calmly the loss o' a place I am on the point o' leavin' for the home o' all homes, whaur, once I'm there, all things doon here must dwindle outworthied by reason o' the glory o' that place. But gien I've ever had anythin' to call an ambition, Cosmo, it has been that my son should be one o' the wise, wi' faith to believe what his father had learned afore him, an' sae start further on upon the narrow way than his father had started. My ambition has been that my efforts an' my experience should in such measure avail for my boy, is that he should begin to make his own efforts an' gather his own experience a little nearer that perfection o' life to which oor divine nature groans an' cries, even while unable to know what it wants. Blessed be the voice that tells us we must forsake all, and take up oor cross, an' follow him, losing oor life that we may find it! For whaur would he hae us follow him but to his ain home, to the very bosom o' his God an' oor God, there to be one with him!"

Such a son as Cosmo could not listen to such a father saying such things and not drop the world as if it were no more important than the burnt-out cinder of the moon.

"When men desire great things, then God is ready to hear them," he said; "and so it is, I think, Father, that he has granted your desires for me. I desire nothing but to fulfill my calling in God—the calling you planted within my heart, even before I was born, with the upward quest of your own life."

"Then ye can part wi' the auld hoose without weepin'?"

"As easy, Father, as wi' a piece o' bread when I wasna hungry. I do not say that another mood may not come, for you know the flesh lusts against the spirit as well as the spirit against the flesh. But in my present mood of light and peace, I rejoice to part with the house as a victory of the spirit. Shall I go to his lordship at once and accept his offer? I am ready."

"Do, my son. I think I have not long to live, and the money, though little, is large in that it will enable me to pay the last of my debts and die in the knowledge that I leave ye a free man. Ye will easily provide for yersel' when I am gone, and I know ye willna forget Grizzie. For James Gracie, he must have his share o' the siller frae the sale because o' the croft. We must calculate it fairly. He'll no want much more in this world. Aggie'll be as safe as any angel, anyway. An', Cosmo, whatever God may mean to do wi' ye in this world, ye'll hae an abundant entrance ministered to ye into the kingdom o' oor Lord an' Savior. Who dares look for a better fate than that o' the Lord himsel'? But there was them that obtained kingdoms, as weel as them who by faith were sawn asunder: they were both martyrdoms; an' whatever God sends, we shall take."

"Then you accept the two hundred for croft and all, Father?"

"Dinna argue for a penny more; he might go back upon't. Regard it as his final offer."

Cosmo rose and went, strong-hearted and without a single thought that pulled back from the sacrifice. There was even a certain pleasure in doing the thing just because in another and lower mood it would have torn his heart: the spirit was rejoicing against the flesh. To be rid of the castle would be to feel, far off, as the young man would have felt had he given all to the poor and followed the master. With the strength of a young giant he strode along.

When he reached the gate, there was Lord Lickmyloof leaning over it.

"I thought you would be back soon! I knew the old cock would have more sense than the young one. And I didn't want my gate scrambled over again," he said, but without moving to open it.

"My father will take your lordship's offer," said Cosmo.

"I was on the point of making a fool of myself, and adding another fifty to be certain of getting rid of you; but I came to the conclusion it was a piece of cowardice, and that, as I had so long stood the dirty hovel at my gate because I couldn't help it, I might just as well let you find your own way out of the parish."

"I am sure from your lordship's point of view you were right," said Cosmo. "In any case, we shall content ourselves with the two hundred."

"Indeed you will not! Did I not tell you I would not be bound by the offer? I have changed my mind, and mean to wait for the sale when your debts force it to the auction block!"

"I beg your pardon. I did not quite understand your lordship."

"You do now, I trust!"

"Perfectly, my lord," replied Cosmo, and turning away left him grinning over the gate. But the grin soon turned to a curious look, almost as if he were a little ashamed of himself—as if he had only been teasing the young fellow, and thought perhaps he had gone too far. Cosmo, in total peace of heart, was not even angry with the man.

On his way home the hope awoke, and once again began to whisper itself, that they might not be able to sell the place at all, that some other way would be provided for their leaving it, and that when he was an old man he would be allowed to return to it to die in it. But then up jumped his conscience, jealously watchful lest hope should undermine submission, or weaken resolve. God *might* indeed intend that they should not be driven from the old house! But he kept Abraham going from place to place, and never let him own a foot of land, except as much as was needed to bury his dead.

And there was our Lord. He had not a place to lay his head, and had to go out-of-doors to pray to his Father in secret. The only things to be anxious about were that God's will should be done and that it should not be changed by any lack of faith or obedience or submission on his part. Then it would be God's very own will that was done, and not something composite, in part made necessary by his opposition. If God's pure will was done, he must equally rejoice whether that will took or gave the castle!

And in such a frame of mind he returned to his father.

When he told him the result of his visit, the laird expressed no surprise.

"He makes the wrath o' a man to praise him," he said. "This will be for our good."

The whole day after this there was between them not another allusion to the matter. Cosmo read to his father a ballad he had just written. The old man was pleased with it, and when he had done the first reading, immediately asked for a second that he might the better absorb the truths therein. This was the ballad, in great part the result of a certain talk with Mr. Simon.

The miser he lay on his lonely bed,
    Life's candle was burning dim,

His heart in his iron chest was hid
   Under heaps of gold and a well-locked lid.
And whether it were alive or dead,
   It never troubled him.

Slowly out of his body he crept.
   Said he, "I am all the same!
      Only I want my heart in my breast;
      I will go and fetch it out of the chest."
Swift to the place of his gold he stepped—
   But he was dead and had no shame.

He opened the lid—oh, hell and night!
   For a ghost can see no gold;
      Empty and swept—not a coin was there!
      His heart lay alone in the chest so bare!
He felt with his hands, but they had no might
   To finger or clasp or hold!

At his heart in the bottom he made a clutch—
   A heart or a puff-ball of sin?
      Eaten with moths and fretted with rust,
      He grasped but a handful of dry-rotten dust:
It was a horrible thing to touch,
   But he hid it his breast within.

And now there are some that see him sit
   In the tomb-like house alone,
      Counting what seems to him shining gold,
      Heap upon heap, a sum ne'er told:
Alas, the dead how they lack of wit!
   What he counts are not even bits of bone!

Another miser has got his chest,
   and his painfully hoarded store;
      Like ferrets his hands go in and out,
      Burrowing, tossing the gold about;
And his heart too is out of his breast,
   Hid in the yellow ore.

Which is the better—the ghost that sits
   Counting shadowy coin all day,
      Or the man that puts his hope and trust
      In a thing whose value is only his lust?
Nothing he has when out he flits
   But a heart all eaten away.

That night as he lay thinking, Cosmo decided to set out in the morning for the city, on foot, begging his way if necessary. There he would tell Mr. Burns of the straits they were in, and ask him his best advice how to make a living for himself and his father and Grizzie. As for James and Agnes, they might stay at the castle, where he would do his best to send them enough to supply their need. As soon as his father had had his breakfast, he would let him know his resolve, and with his assent, would depart at once.

His spirits rose as he considered it. What a happy thing it was that Lord Lick-myloof had not accepted their offer! All the time they saw themselves in a poor lodging in a noisy street in the city, they would know they had their own strong silent castle waiting to receive them as soon as they were able to return to it! Then the words came to him: "Here we have no continuing city, but we seek one to come."

The special discipline for some people would seem to be that they shall never settle down, or feel as if they were at home, until they are at home in very fact in the quiet of their heart, no matter what their outward condition.

"Anyhow," said Cosmo to himself, "such a castle we have!"

To be lord of space, a man must be free of all bonds to place. To be heir of all things, his heart must have no *things* in it. He must be like him who makes things, not like one who would put everything in his pocket. He must stand on the upper, not the lower side of them, where he controls rather than is controlled. He must be as the man who makes poems, not the man who gathers books of verse. He must be as the man who absorbs the truths of a book and brings its principles into his daily life, not the man who collects books for their fine bindings. Only so do the *things*, the *poems*, the *books* become truly his eternal possession.

God, having made a sunset, lets it pass, and makes such a sunset never again. God has no picture-gallery, no library, no collections, no monuments to the past. What if in heaven men shall be so busy growing that they shall not have time to write or read!

How blessed Cosmo would live with his father and Grizzie in the great city— in some such place as he had occupied when at the university! The one sad thing was that he could not be with his father all day; but so much the happier would be the homecoming at night! Thus imagining, he fell fast asleep.

He dreamed that he had a barrow of oranges, with which he had been going about the streets all day, trying to sell them without success. He was now returning home, the barrow piled as high with the golden fruit as when he had set out in the morning. He consoled himself, however, with the thought that his father was fond of oranges, and now might have as many as he pleased. But as he wheeled the barrow along, it seemed to grow heavier and heavier, and he feared his strength was failing him and he would never get it back to his father. Heavier and heavier it grew until at last he could hardly push it along. It was the dead of night, and at last he reached the door, and having laboriously wheeled it into a shed, pro- ceeded to pick from it a few of the best oranges to take up to his father. But when he came to lift one from the heap, lo, it was a lump of gold!

He tried another and another: every one of them was a lump of solid gold—it was a dream-version of the golden horse. Then all at once he said to himself without knowing why, "My father is dead!" and woke in misery.

It was some time before he could persuade himself that he had but been dreaming. He rose, went to his father's bedside, found him sleeping peacefully, and lay down comforted, and did not that night dream again.

"What would money be to me without my father?" he said to himself.

Some shrink from making plans because experience has shown how seldom they are realized. But the plans of those who make them infrequently are just as subject to overthrow as those who order every day by the most exacting of schemes. It had been a long time since Cosmo had made any definite plans, and the resolve with which he now fell asleep was as modest and reasonable as a wise man could well cherish.

Nevertheless, the morning went differently from his planned intent and expectation.

46

·················

An Old Story

He was roused before sunrise by his father's cough. After a bad fit, he was very weary and restless. Now, in such a condition Cosmo could almost always get him to sleep by reading to him. Therefore he got out a short story and began to read. At first it had the desired calming effect, but in a little while he woke, and asked him to go on. The story was of a king's ship so disguising herself that a pirate took her for a merchantman. Cosmo, to whom it naturally recalled the old captain, made some remark about him.

"You mustn't believe," said his father, "all they told you when a boy about that uncle of ours. No doubt he was a rough sailor fellow, but I do not believe there was any ground for calling him a pirate. I don't suppose he was anything worse than a privateer, which, God knows, is bad enough. I imagine, however, for the most of his sea life he was captain of an East Indiaman, probably trading on his own at the same time. That he made money I do not doubt, but very likely he lost it all before he came home and was too cunning, in view of his probable reception, to confess it."

"I remember your once telling me an amusing story of an adventure—let me see—yes, that was in an East Indiaman. Was he the captain of that one?"

"No—a very different man—a cousin of your mother's that was. I was thinking of it a minute ago; it has certain points, if not of resemblance, then of contrast with the story you have just been reading."

"I should very much like to hear it again when you are able to tell it."

"I have got it all in writing among my Marion's papers. You will find, in the bureau in the book closet, in the pigeon hole farthest to the left, a packet tied with red tape. Bring that and I will find it for you."

Cosmo brought the bundle of papers, and his father handed him one of them, saying, "This narrative was written by a brother of your mother's. The Captain Macintosh, who is the hero of the story, was a cousin of her mother, and at the time of the event related must have been somewhat advanced in years, for he had now returned to his former profession after having lost largely in an attempt to establish a brewery on the island of St. Helena!"

Cosmo unfolded the manuscript and read as follows:

An incident occurring on the voyage to India when my brother went out, exhibits Captain Macintosh's character very practically, and not a little to his professional credit.

On a fine evening some days after rounding the cape of Good Hope, sailing with a light breeze and smooth water, a strange sail of large size hove in sight and apparently was bearing down directly upon the *Union*, Captain Macintosh's ship; evidently a ship of war but showing no colors—a very suspicious fact. All English ships at that time were obliged to carry armaments proportioned to their tonnage, and crew sufficient to man and work the guns carried. The strange sail was nearing them, "the big stranger" as the seamen immediately named her. My brother, many years afterwards, more than once told me that the change, or rather the "transformation" which Captain Macintosh underwent, was one of the most remarkable facts he had ever witnessed; more bordering on the supernatural than anything else. When he had carefully and deliberately viewed "the big stranger" and laid down his glass, his eyes seemed to catch fire, and his whole countenance lit up. A new spirit seemed to possess him, while he preserved his utmost coolness. He advanced deliberately to what is called the poop railing, steadily looking forward, then called—"Boatswain! Pipe to quarters. Muster roll call. Now, my men, we shall *fight!* I know you will do it well! Clear ship for action!"

I have only my brother's word and judgment upon the fact, who had never been under fire, but his opinion was that no British ship of war could have been more speedily or more completely cleared for action, both in rigging, decks, and guns—guns double shotted and run out into position. "The big stranger" was now coming near—no ports opened, and no colors showing—everything about it increasing the cause of suspicion that there was some ill intent in the wind—and it was very evident, from the size of "the big stranger"—nearly three times the size of the little *Union*—that one broadside from the former might send the latter at once to the bottom.

The whole crew, including my brother, were in the highest spirits, more as if preparing for a dance than for work of life and death. Suddenly the captain gave the command: "Boarders, prepare to board! Lower away, boarding boats"—and no sooner said than it was done.

The stranger was now at musket shot. It was worthy of the courage of a *Nelson* or a *Cochrane* to think of boarding at such odds—a mere handful of men to a full complement of a heavy frigate's crew! The idea was altogether in keeping with the best naval tactics and skill. Foreseeing that one broadside from such an enemy would sink him, he had to anticipate such a crisis. Boarding would at least divert the enemy from their guns, and he knew what British seamen could do, in clearing an enemy's decks! There was British spirit in those days! Let us hope it shall appear again, should the occasion arise. The captain himself was the first in the foremost boarding boat—and the first in the enemy's main chains, and to set his foot on the enemy's main deck! But then a most magic-like scene saluted the boarders, yet it did not yet allay suspicion—there was not a single enemy on deck! Here, a characteristic act of a British "tar," the *Union's* boatswain, must not be omitted—an old man of war's man, no sooner had his foot touched the enemy's deck, than he ran toward the ship's stern—to the wheel, where he encountered the only man on the deck—a big, lubberly looking man standing at the wheel. In less than a moment the *Union's* boatswain had his hands on the enemy steerman's throat, and with one fell shove, sent him spinning, heels over head, all the full length of the ship's quarterdeck, where he landed on the main deck—one may suppose he landed rather astonished!

The manly boatswain himself was the only man actually hurt in the affair. His boarding pistol, by some accident, went off—its double shot running up his forearm and lodging in the bones of his elbow. Amputation became necessary, and the dear old fellow soon afterwards died.

But what did the whole strange affair come to? "The big stranger" turned out to be nothing but a large, heavily armed Portuguese frigate! Actually the only warship of the Portuguese navy then afloat—a fine specimen of Portuguese naval discipline no doubt, without a watch even on deck! They had known immediately upon seeing her that the *Union* was English, and a merchant ship—which a practiced seaman's eye can do at once; and they had quietly gone to take their siesta, after their country's fashion—Portugal at that time being one of Britain's allies, and not an enemy; a grievous disappointment to the crew of the *Union*.

"My uncle seems to have got excited as he went on," said Cosmo, "to judge by the number of words he had underlined!"

"He entered into the spirit of the thing pretty well for a clergyman!" said the laird.

47

·················

A Small Discovery

*W*hen they had had a little talk over the narrative, the laird asked Cosmo to replace the papers and he rose to obey. As he approached the closet, the first beams of the rising sun were shining upon the door of it. The window through which they entered was a small one, and the mornings of the year in which they so fell were not many. When he opened the door they shot straight to the back of the closet, lighting with rare illumination the little place, commonly so dusky that in it one book could hardly be distinguished from another. It was as if a sudden angel of light had entered a dungeon.

When the door fell shut behind him, as it did of its own, the place felt so dark that he seemed to have lost memory as well as sight, and hardly could discern where he was. He opened it again and, having put a stopper against it, proceeded to replace the papers. But the strangeness of the presence there of such a light took so great a hold on his imagination, and it was such a rare thing to see what the musty dingy little closet—the treasure chamber of the house—was like, that he stood for a moment with his hand on the cover of the bureau, gazing into the light-invaded corners as if he had suddenly found himself in Aladdin's cave. Old to him beyond memory, it yet looked new and wonderful to have much that had before only been known to his hands now suddenly revealed to his eyes also. Among other facts he discovered that the bureau stood not against a rough wall as he had imagined, but against a plain surface of wood. In mild surprise he tapped it with his knuckles, and almost jumped at the hollow sound it returned.

"What can there be behind the bureau, Father?" he asked, turning and re-entering the room.

"I dinna ken o' anything," answered the laird. "The desk stan's close against the wall, doesna it?"

"Ay, but the wall's wood, an' soun's hollow."

"It may be but a wainscoting; an' if there was but an inch atween it an' the stones, it would soun' like that."

"I would like t' pull the desk oot a bit, an' hae a nearer look. It fills up the space, an' I canna weel get at it."

"Do as ye like, laddie. The hoose is mair yers than mine. But noo that ye hae put it in my head, I mind my mither sayin' that there was once a passage atween the two blocks o' the hoose. Could it be there? I thought it had been atween the kitchen an' the dining room. My father, she said, had it closed up."

"It seems to go farther back than the thickness o' the wall," said Cosmo, who had been looking at the closet from where he stood by the bedside. He went and looked out of the western window, then turned again toward the closet. "I canna think," he resumed, with something like annoyance in his tone, "hoo it could be that I never noticed that afore! A body would think I had nae head for what I prided mysel' on—an un'erstan'in' o' hoo things are put together. The closet runs right into the great blind wall atween the two houses! I thought that wall had been nothin' but a kind o' curtain o' defense, but there may weel be a passage in the thickness o' it!"

So saying, he reentered the closet and proceeded to move the bureau. The task was not an easy one. The bureau was large, and so nearly filled the width of the closet that he could attack it nowhere but in front, and had to drag it forward, laying hold of it where he could, over a much-worn oak floor. The sun had long deserted him before he got behind it.

"I would like to break through the boards, Father!" he said, going again to the laird.

"Anythin' ye like, laddie! I'm growin' curious mysel'," he answered.

"I'm afraid of makin' too much racket, Father."

"Nae fear, nae fear! I haena a hurtin' head. The Lord be praised, that's a thing I'm seldom troubled with. Go an' get what tools ye want an' go at it. If the hole should let in the wind, I'm thinkin' ye'll be able t' patch it again if need be. What kind o' timmer is it?"

"Only pine, sae far as I can judge."

Cosmo went and fetched his tool box, and then set to work. The partition was strong, of good sound pine boards, neither rotten nor worm-eaten—inch-thick boards matched with tongue and groove, not the easiest to break through. But having a center-bit and brace, he bored several holes near each other, and then knocked out the pieces between them. Then came a saw with which he was able to make a large enough opening to creep through. A cold air met him, as if from a cellar, and on the other side he seemed to be in another climate.

Feeling with his hand, for there was scarcely any light, he discovered that the space he had entered was not a closet. There was no shelf or anything in it whatever. It was certainly most like the end of a deserted passage. His feet told him the floor was of wood, and his hands that the walls were of rough stone without plaster, cold and damp.

With outstretched arms he could easily touch both walls at once, and he advanced thus a few paces until he struck his head against wood. He felt panels, and concluded he had reached a door. There was a lock, but the handle was gone. He went back a little, then turned again and threw himself against it. Lock and hinges and everything gave way, the door fell right out before him, and went crashing to the floor.

He went staggering on with it, and was brought up by a bed, half-falling across it. Quickly he regained his feet with an involuntary shudder.

He was in the guest room, the gruesome center of legend, the dwelling of ghostly awe!

Its presiding spirit seemed not to have yet forsaken it, for a thrill passed through him at the discovery. From his father's familiar room to this was like some marvelous transition in a fairy tale—the one was home, a place of daily use; the other a hollow in the faraway past, an ancient cave of time, full of withering history. Its windows being all to the north and long unopened, it was lusterless, dark, and musty with decay.

Cosmo stood motionless a while, gazing about him as if, from being wide awake, he suddenly found himself in a dream. There lay the door, and there was the open passage!

He lifted the door. The other side of it was covered with the same paper as the wall, from which it had brought with it several ragged pieces. He went back, crept through the hole he had made, and rejoined his father.

In eager excitement he told him of the discovery he had made.

"I heard the din frae the fallin' door," his father said quietly. "I should not wonder noo," he added, "if we discovered a way through to the third block."

"But what could have made gran'father close it up?"

"There was, I believe, some foolish ghost story connected wi' it—perhaps the same one old Grannie told you."

"I wonder Gran'mamma never spoke of it!"

"My impression is she never cared t' refer t' it."

"I daresay she believed it!"

"Weel, I daresay! I wouldna won'er!"

"Why do ye call it foolish, Father?"

"Jist for thoughtlessness, I don't doobt. But who could hae imagined to keep a ghost oot by paperin' ower a door, when, if there be any trowth in sich tales, the ghost goes through a stone wall jist as easy as open air! But surely o' all fools, a ghost must be the worst o' things aboot the place!"

"Maybe it's to hold away frae a worse. The queer thing to me, Father, would be that the ghost, frae bein' a fool in his life, should grow a wise man the minute he was dead! Mightna it be a part o' his punishment to be made to see hoo things go on after he's dead! What could be harder, for instance, upon a miser, than to see his heir go to the devil by scattering what he went to the devil for tryin' all his life t' gather?"

" 'Deed ye're right enough there, my son!" answered the old man. Then after a pause he resumed. "It's aye siller or bones that fetches them back. I can weel un'erstan' a great reluctance to take their last leave o' their fortunes, but for the bones—ey, but I'll be only too pleased to be rid o' mine!"

"But whaur bones are concerned, hasna there aye been false play with their death?" suggested Cosmo.

"Would it be revenge, then, think ye?"

"Most o' the stories o' that kind end wi' bringin' the murderer t' justice. But the human bein' seems in all ages t' hae a great dislike to the thought o' his bones bein' left lying aboot. I hae heard Gran-mamma say the dirtiest servant was aye clean two days in her life—the day she was born an' the day she died."

"Ye hae thought mair aboot it than me, laddie! Anyway, it must be a fine thing to leave as little dirt as possible ahind ye, an' take none wi' ye."

"If anybody will go clean an' leave clean, Father, ye will."

"I look t' the Lord, my son. But noo, when a body thinks o' it,' he went on after a pause, "there would seem somethin' curious in those tales concernin' the auld captain! Sometime we'll take Grizzie into oor counsel, an' see hoo many stories we can gather, an' what we can make o' them when we lay them all together. Gien the Lord has it in his mind t' keep us in this place, yon passage may turn oot a great convenience."

"Ye dinna think it would be worthwhile opening it up noo?"

"I would wait for warmer weather. I think the room's jist some colder already from it."

"Jist think what a comfort this door would have been so often with such a passage between the blocks o' the hoose. An' noo, jist as we are likely t' leave the house forever, we first discover it!"

"But how weel we have got along wi'oot it!" returned his father.

"I'll close it up for now," said Cosmo.

In a few minutes he had screwed a box-lid over the hole in the partition and shut the door of the closet.

"Noo," he said, "I'll go back an' set up the door on the other side."

Before he went, however, he told his father what he had been thinking of, saying that he would like to go the next day, if he approved and was well enough.

"It's not a bad idea," said the laird; "but we'll see what the morn may be like."

When Cosmo entered the ancient bedroom of the house from the other side, he stood for a moment staring at the open passage and the fallen door as if he saw them for the first time. Then he proceeded to examine the hinges. They were broken; the half of each remained fastened to the doorpost, the other half to the prostrate door. New hinges would be necessary. But in the meantime he would prop it up.

He did so, and before he left the room, as it was much in need of fresh air, he opened all the windows.

His father continued to be better all through the day, and he went to bed early so that he might start for Aberdeen at sunrise.

48

·············

A Greater Discovery

In the middle of the night Cosmo was awakened by a loud noise.

He had been too sound asleep to recognize its nature; he only knew it had awakened him. He sprang out of bed, was glad to find his father undisturbed, and stood for a few minutes wondering.

All at once he remembered that he had left the windows of the old bedroom open; the wind had risen and was now blowing what sailors would call a gale. Probably something had been blown down! He would go and see. Taking a scrap of candle, all he had, he crept down the stair, outside, and out to the great door.

As he approached the room from the side by which he had always known it, the faint horror he felt of it when a boy suddenly returned upon him as fresh as ever. For a moment he almost thought he was dreaming. Was he actually there, in the dread place, in the middle of the night?

But with a concerted effort he dismissed the folly, came to himself again, and entered the room, if not with indifference yet with composure. There was just light enough to see the curtains of the terrible bed waving wide in the stream of wind that followed the opening of the door. He shut the windows, lit his candle, and then saw the door he had set up so carefully flat on the floor. The chair he had put against it for a buttress had not been high enough, and it had fallen down over the top of it. He placed his candle beside it, and proceeded once more to raise it.

But as he cast his eyes up to mark the direction, he caught a sight which made him lay it down again and stand up without it. The candle on the floor shone halfway into the passage toward the room where he had left his father sleeping. It lit up a part of one wall of it, and showed plainly the rough edges of gray stones of which it was constructed. Something in the shapes and arrangement of the stones drew and fixed Cosmo's attention. He took the candle, examined the wall, came back out of the passage with his eyes shining.

Of course! He remembered now!

With his lips firmly closed in eager determination, he left the room, and went up a story higher to that over it, which was still called his room. There he took from his old secretary the unintelligible drawing hid in the handle of the bamboo cane. With a beating heart he unfolded it.

Certainly its lines *did* more or less correspond with the shapes of the stones in the passage! He must bring the two face to face!

Down the stair he flew. It was the dead of the night, but every remnant of childhood's awe and terror was gone in the excitement of the anticipated discovery. He stood once more in the passage, the candle in one hand, the paper in the other, and his eyes going and coming steadily between it and the wall, as if trying to read the rough stones by some hieroglyphic key. The lines on the paper and the joints of the mortar corresponded with almost absolute accuracy.

But another thing had caught his eye as well, a thing yet more promising.

He delayed examining this new phenomenon until he was fully satisfied of the correspondence he sought to establish between the paper and the stone joints. But now he gave it his full attention. On one of the stones, one remarkable neither by position or shape, he saw what seemed to be the rude drawing of a horse. But as it was higher than his head, and the candle cast up odd shadows from the rough surface, he could not see it well.

He got a chair, stood on it, and saw that it was plainly enough a horse, like one a child might have made who, with a gift for drawing, had had no instruction in its finer points. It was scratched on the stone. Beneath it, legible enough to one who knew them so well already, were the lines:

Catch yer naig an pu' his tail:
In his hin' heel caw a nail;
Run his lugs frae ane' anither;
Stan' up, an' cal' the king yer brither.

How these instructions were to be followed with such a horse as the one on the flat before him would be something he would have to investigate during the day. Probably the wall must be broken into at that spot. In the meantime he would set up the door again and go to bed.

But as he turned to leave he found himself alarmed at the turmoil the sight of these signs caused within him. He dreaded possession by any spirit but the One. Whatever he did now he must do calmly and not give the enemy a foothold by his imagination.

Therefore, to bed he went. But before he gave himself up to sleep, he prayed to God to watch him, lest the commotion in his heart and the giddiness of hope should make something rise that would come between him and the Light Eternal. The man in whom any earthly hope dims the heavenly presence and weakens the mastery of himself is on the byway through the meadow to the castle of Giant Despair.

In the morning he rose early and went to see how the stone could be removed. He found it, as he had feared, so close-joined with its neighbors that none of his tools would serve to dislodge it. He went to Grizzie and got from her a thin old knife; but the mortar had gotten so hard since those noises the servants used to hear in the old captain's room that he could not make much impression upon it, and it looked like the job was likely to be a long one. He said to himself it might be the breaking through of the wall of his father's prison and his own, and therefore a joyous though a difficult one.

As soon as his father had had his breakfast, Cosmo told him what he had discovered during the dark hours. The laird listened with the light of a smile, not the smile itself, upon his face, and made no answer. But Cosmo could see by the all but imperceptible motion of his lips that he was praying.

"I wish I were able to help you," he said at length.

"There isna room for mair than one at a time, Father," answered Cosmo. "An' I hope to get the stone oot afore I'm tired. You can be Moses praying while I am Joshua fighting."

"An' prayin' again' worse enemies than ever Joshua wrestled wi'," returned his father. "For whan I think o' the rebound o' the spirit, even in this my auld age, that couldna but follow the mere liftin' o' the weight o' debt, I feel as if my soul would be tumbled aboot like a ball, an' its auld wings take to long slow flaggin' strokes in the over-thin air o' joy. The great God protect us frae his ain gifts! Wi'oot him they're ten times worse than any wiles o' the deevil's own. But I'll pray, Cosmo; I'll pray!"

Cosmo went back to his work. He soon tired of the old knife—it was not tool enough, and had to fashion on the grindstone a screwdriver into a special implement. With that he got on better.

The stone—whether by the old captain's own hands, his ghost best knew— was both well fitted and fixed, but after Cosmo had worked at it for about three hours, his tool suddenly went through. It was then easy to knock away from the edge gained, and on the first attempt to pull it out, it yielded enough that he could get a hold with his fingers. And the rest was soon done. It disclosed a cavity in the wall, but the light was not enough to let him see into it, and he went to get a candle.

Now Grizzie had a curious dislike to any admission of the poverty of the house even to those most interested, and having but one small candle end left, she was unwilling to yield it and confess that it was her last one.

"Them that burns daylight, soon they shall hae nae light!" she said. "What would ye want wi' a candle? I'll get a fir-candle for ye, gien ye like."

"Grizzie," repeated Cosmo, "I want a candle."

She went grumbling, and brought him the miserable end.

"Hoot, Grizzie!" he exclaimed, "dinna be sae stingy. Ye wouldna, gien ye kenned what I was aboot."

"Eh! what are ye aboot, sir?"

"I'm no gaein' to tell ye yet. Ye must hae patience, an' I must hae a candle."

"Ye must take what's offered ye."

"Grizzie, I'm serious."

" 'Deed, an' sae am I! Ye shall hae nae mair than that—not if it was to scrape the girnel—an' that's been used long already, an' twice over."

"Grizzie, I'm afraid ye're aboot t' anger me."

"Ye'll get nae mair!"

Cosmo burst out laughing.

"Grizzie," he said, "I dinna believe ye hae an inch mair candle in the hoose!"

"It needs no Warlock t' tell that! Gien I had it, why shouldna ye hae it? Ye hae the best right to it."

Cosmo took his candle and was as sparing of it as Grizzie herself could have wished.

49

A Great Discovery!

The instant the rays from the candle end were thrown into the cavity, Cosmo saw what, even expectant as he was, made him utter a cry. He seemed to be looking through a small window into a toy stable—although a large one for a toy. Immediately in front of him was a stall, in which stood a horse with his tail toward the window he had made. He put in his hand and felt it. For a toy it was certainly large, not much smaller than a rocking horse. It was covered with a hairy skin. More stones would have to be removed before it could be taken from its prison stall, where, like the horses of Charlemagne, it had been buried so many years.

He extinguished the precious piece of candle, and set to work once more with a will and what light the day afforded. The task was not much easier than before. Every one of the stones was partly imbedded in the solid of the wall. The old captain must indeed have worked hard! For assuredly he was not a man to ask for help in a matter for which he desired secrecy—though undoubtedly it was his sudden death, and the nature of it, that prevented him from disclosing the matter to someone before he left the world. The rhyme, the drawing, the scratches on the stone all indicated his intention. Cosmo took pleasure in thinking that, if indeed his ghost did walk about, as Grannie and others believed, it must be more from the desire to reveal where his money was hidden than from any gloating over the imagined possession of it.

But it was now dinnertime and he had to rest, for he was tired as well as hungry. And no wonder! The work had been awkward as well as hard and steady. He locked the door of the room, went first to tell his father what he had found, and then quickly ate his meal, for the night was coming and there were no candles. Persistently he labored, and at length was able to lay hold of the animal by the hind legs. He tried to draw it gently from the stall. But it would come a little way only, and then no farther. Again he lit the candle and peeped into the stall where he perceived a chain attached to its head stretching to the far end. He dared not try to break it, lest he might injure the mechanism he hoped to find in it. But clearly the horse could not have been fastened as it was as the stall then stood. The stall must have been completed and built up after the horse was thus secured and in place.

He now needed a candle more than ever, and one held for him by another. But he was not yet prepared to take Grizzie into his confidence, or to hurt her by seeming to prefer Agnes. Therefore, he fell to examining the two stones forming the sides of the stall, and led by the appearance of one of them, he proceeded to attempt to remove it in the dark. He seemed to make little or no progress, for most of the time he could not even see the proper spot to set his tool before striking it.

But at length the stone moved, and in a minute he had it out. For the last time he lit his candle. There was just enough of it left to show him how the chain was fastened. With a pair of pincers he detached if from the wall.

And now the horse was in his arms and his first thought was to take it straight to his father, in whose presence it must be searched. But he did not want to go down through the great door and thus through the kitchen where Grizzie would see him. So he would have to go to the other end of the passage and try to open the hole into his father's room that he had boarded up with the box-lid.

The laird was seated by the fire when Cosmo burst through, and carrying the horse, he placed it on a chair beside him. They looked it all over, wondering whether the old captain could have made it himself. Cosmo thought his father prolonged the inquiry from a wish to still his son's impatience. But at length he spoke.

"Noo, Cosmo, in the name o' God, the giver o' every good an' perfect gift, see gien ye can get into the entrails o' the animal. It canna be full o' men like the Trojan horse, or they must be enchanted an' small. But what's in it may carry a heap worse danger to you an' me than any nummer o' armed men!"

"Ye mind the rhyme, Father?" asked Cosmo.

"No sae weel as the Twenty-third Psalm," replied the laird with a smile.

"Weel, the first line o' it is, 'Catch yer naig, 'an pu' his tail.' Wi' much difficulty we hae caught him, an' noo for the tail o' him!—There! that's done—though there's no muckle to show for it. The next direction is, 'In his hin' heel caw a nail.' We shall turn up his four feet together, an' noo let's see the proper spot whaur to caw the said nail!"

The horse's shoes were large, and the hole where a nail was missing had not to be looked for more than a moment. Cosmo took a fine bradawl and pushed it gently into the hoof. A loud whirring noise followed, but with no visible result.

"The next direction," said Cosmo, "is, 'Rug his lugs frae ane' anither.' Noo, Father, God be wi' us! an' gien it please him we be disciplined, may he give us grace to bear it as he would hae us bear it."

"I pray the same," said the laird.

Cosmo pulled the two ears of the animal in opposite directions. The back began to open, slowly, as if through the long years the cleft had begun to grow together. He sprang from his seat. The laird looked after him with a gentle surprise. But it was not to rush from the room, nor to perform any frantic dance of joy over what they had found.

One of the windows looked westward into the court, and at this season of the year the setting sun looked in at that window. He was looking in now; his rays made a glowing pool of light in the middle of the ancient carpet. Beside this pool of light Cosmo dropped on the floor like a child with his toy, and pulled harder at the ears of the horse.

All at once into the pool of sun began to tumble a cataract as of shattered rainbows, only brighter, flashing all the colors visible to human eye. Then it ceased.

Cosmo turned the horse upside down, and a few stray drops followed. He shook it and tapped it, like Grizzie when she emptied the basin of meal into the porridge pot. But the cataract had not vanished. There it lay heaped and spread, a storm of conflicting yet harmonious hues, with a foamy spray of spiky flashes, and spots that ate into the eyes with their fierce color. In every direction shot the rays from it, blinding. It was a mound of stones of all the shapes into which diamonds are fashioned. The heaviest of its hues was borne light as those of a foam-bubble on the strength of its triumphing radiance. There pulsed the mystic glowing red, heart and lord of color; there the jubilant yellow, light-glorified to ethereal gold; there the loveliest blue, the truth unfathomable: there the green, that haunts the brain with nature's soundless secrets—all together striving, yet atoning, fighting and fleeing and following, parting and blending, with illimitable play of infinite force and endlessly delicate gradation.

Scattered here and there were a few of all the colored gems—sapphires, emeralds, and rubies. But they were scarce of note in the mass of ever newborn, ever dying color that gushed from the fountains of the light-dividing diamonds.

Cosmo rose, left the glory where it lay, and returned to his father where he sat down beside him. For a few moments they regarded in silence the shining mound, where, like an altar of sacrifice, it smoked with light and color. The eyes of the old man as he looked seemed at once to sparkle with pleasure, and yet at the same time to quail with some kind of fear.

He turned to Cosmo and said, "Cosmo, are they what they seem?"

"What do they seem, Father?" asked Cosmo.

"Bonny bits o' glass," answered the old man. "But," he went on, "I canna but believe them something better, since they come to us in such a time o' sore need. But, be they this or be they that, the Lord's will be done—noo an' forever."

"I ken somethin' about such things, Father," said Cosmo, "frae bein' sae much in Mr. Burns' shop. An' I tell ye, they're mostly all diamonds; an' frae the number o' them they must be worth a thousan' pound gien they be worth sixpence. But I darena guess."

"They'll be enough to pay oor debts anyway, ye think, Cosmo?"

"Ay, they will—an' many a hundred times ower. They're mostly good size, an' no a few o' them large."

"Cosmo, we're too long on givin' thanks. Come here, my son. Go doon upon yer knees, an' let's say to the Lord what we're thinkin'."

Cosmo obeyed and knelt at his father's knee. His father laid his hand upon his head so that they might pray more in one.

"Lord," he said, "though nothing a man can take in his hands can ever be his own, not being of his nature—that is, made in thy image; yet, O Lord, the thing that's thine, made by thee after thy holy will and pleasure, man may touch and not be defiled. Yea, he may take pleasure both in itself and in its use, so long as he handles it in the hollow of thy hand, not grasping at it to call it his own, like a rough bairn seeking to snap it away that he may have his fool will with it. O God, they're bonny stones and full of light. Forbid that their light should breed darkness in the heart of Cosmo and me. O God, rather than we should do or feel one thing in consequence of this thy gift that thou wouldn't have us do or feel, we would have them take the gift back. And if in thy mercy, for it's all mercy with thee, it should turn out after all that they're not stones of thy making but counterfeit glass, the product of art and man's devices, we'll lay them altogether and keep them safe. We'll look upon them as a token of what thou would have done for us if it hadn't been that we weren't yet to be trusted with so much, and that for the safety of our souls. O God, let not the sunshiny Mammon creep into my Cosmo's heart and make all darkness. Let not the light that is in him turn to darkness. God have mercy on his wee bairns, and let not the playthings he gives them take their eyes off the giving hand! May the light now streaming from the heart of the bonny stones be the bodily presence of the Spirit, as once was the dove that descended upon the master, and the bush that burned with fire and wasn't consumed. Thou art the father of lights, and all light is thine. Make our hearts burn like them—all light and no smoke! And if any of them came in at a wrong door, may they all go out at a right one. Thy will be done, which is the purifying fire of all things and all souls! Amen."

He ceased and was silent, praying still. Nor did Cosmo yet rise from his knees: the joy, and yet more the relief at his heart filled him afresh with fear, lest, no longer spurred by the same sense of need, he should the less run after him from whom help had so plentifully come. Alas! How is it with our hearts that in trouble they cry, and in joy forget, that we think it hard of God not to hear, and when he has answered abundantly, we turn away as if we wanted him no more!

When Cosmo rose from his knees, he looked his father in the face, his eyes wet.

"Oh, Father!" he said, "how the fear and oppression of ages are gone like a cloud swallowed up of space. And are not all human ills doomed thus to vanish at last in the eternal fire of the love-burning God? And now, what'll we do next?" he added, turning his eyes again on the heap of jewels. The rays of the sun had now left them, and they lay cold and almost colorless, though still bright: even in the dark some of them insisted on shining! "Eh, but I wonder hoo he got them."

"Hooever they were gotten," rejoined the laird, "there can be no question but the only way o' cleansin' them noo is to put them to the best possible use we can."

"An' what would ye call the best use, Father?"

"Whatever makes o' a man a neighbor. A true pursuin' after God's notion is the sorest blow to Satan. But we'll hae t' wait t' see what work the Lord lays oot for us. In the meantime, hadna ye better bury yer dead again? They must lie in the dark, like human souls, till they're brought to do the deeds o' light."

"Dinna ye think," said Cosmo, "that I might set oot in the mornin' after all, though on a different errand, an' go straight to Mr. Burns? He'll soon put us in the right way to turn them to account. They're o' small avail as they lie there."

"Ye canna do better, my son," answered the old man.

So Cosmo gathered the gems together into the horse, lifting them in handfuls. But, peeping first into the hollow of the animal, to make sure he had found all that was in it, he caught sight of a bit of paper that had got stuck, and found it a Bank of England note for five hundred pounds. This in itself would have been riches untold an hour ago—now it was only a convenience.

"It's funny to think," said Cosmo, "that though we hae all this siller, I must tramp like any vagrant tomorrow to the city. Who is there in Muir o' Warlock that could change it, an' who would I go to wi' it gien he could?"

His father replied with a smile.

"It brings to my mind the words o' the Apostle: 'Noo I say, that the heir, sae long as he's but a bairn, differs naething frae a servant, though he be lord o' all.' Eh, Cosmo, but the word admits o' curious illustration!"

As soon as he had finished giving him his supper of diamonds, Cosmo set the horse again in his old stall, and replaced the stones that had shut him in as well as he could. Then he wedged up the door of the captain's bedroom, and having nothing to make paste, glued the wallpaper again to the wall that it had torn off when it fell.

He then went to the kitchen to seek Grizzie.

50

A Visit to Mr. Burns

*G*rizzie," Cosmo said, "I'm gaein' on a long tramp in the morning, an' I'll need a great pouchfull o' oatcakes."

"Eh, sirs! An' what's takin ye from home this time, sir?" returned Grizzie.

"I'm no gaein' t' tell ye tonight, Grizzie. It's my turn to hae a secret noo! But ye ken weel it's long since there's been anything to be gotten by bidin' at home."

"Eh, but, sir! Ye're never gaein' to leave the laird! Bide an' die wi' him."

"God bless ye, Grizzie! Hae ye any coins?"

"Ay, I hae six shillin's, four pennies, an' a farthin' coin!" answered Grizzie in the tone of a millionaire.

"Weel, ye must jist len' me half a croon o' it."

"Half a croon!" echoed Grizzie, staggered at the largeness of the demand.

"Haith, sir, ye're no bashful when ye make yer request!"

"I dinna think it's too much," said Cosmo, "seein' I hae to walk thirty five miles t' Aberdeen tomorrow. But bake ye plenty o' bread, an' that'll hold doon the expense. But if he can help it, a body shouldna be wi'oot a coin in his pocket. Gien ye had none t' give me, I would set oot bare. But as ye like it, Grizzie. I could beg—noo that ye hae shown me the way," he added with a gentle laugh, so that she might not be hurt.

"Weel, I'll give ye eighteen pence, an' considerin' all that's t' be done wi' what's left, ye'll hae to grant it's no an unfair portion."

"Weel, weel, Grizzie! I'm thinking I'll hae to be content."

" 'Deed, an' ye will, sir! Ye'll hae nae mair."

That night the old laird slept soundly, but Cosmo was the whole time just on the brink of unconsciousness from his gladness at heart. The morning came golden and brave, and his father was well enough to be able see him go. So he set out, and in the strength of his relief walked all the way without spending a half-penny of Grizzie's eighteen pence. Two days before he would have come to consult his friend about how to avoid the bitterest dregs of poverty—now he had to ask him how to make his riches most readily available!

He did not tell Mr. Burns, however, what his final object was—he only begged him, for the sake of friendship and old times, to go with him for a day or two to his father's.

"But, Mr. Warlock," objected the jeweler, "that would be to take an unnecessary vacation, and we've got to be diligent in business."

"The thing I want you for is business," replied Cosmo.

"But what's to be done with the shop? I have no assistant I can trust."

"Then shut it up and give your men a holiday. You can put up a notice informing the public when you will be back."

"Such a thing was never heard of!"

"It is quite time it should be heard of then. Why, sir, your business is not like a doctor's, or even a baker's. People can live without diamonds."

"Don't speak disrespectfully of diamonds, Mr. Warlock. If you knew them as I do, you would know they had a thing or two to say."

"You never heard me speak of them disrespectfully, Mr. Burns."

"I confess you are right. I was only talking from the diamond side of the question. Like everything else, they give to us according to what we have. To him that hath shall more be given. The fine lady may see in her fine diamonds only victory over a rival; the philosopher may read embodied in them law inexorably beautiful; and the Christian poet—oh, I have read my Spenser, Mr. Warlock!— will choose the diamond for its many qualities, as the best and only substance wherein to represent the shield of the faith that overcometh the world. Like the gospel itself, diamonds are a savor of life unto life, or a savor of death unto death, according to the character of them that look on them."

"That is true enough. Every gift of God is good that is received with faith and thanksgiving, and whatsoever is not of faith is sin. But will you come?"

At length Mr. Burns consented to close his shop for three days and go with Cosmo.

In the meantime things went well at Castle Warlock, with—shall I say?—one exception: Grizzie had a severe fit of repentance, mourning bitterly that she had sent away the youth she worshiped with only eighteen pence in his pocket.

"He's sure to come to grief for the want o' jist that one shilling mair!" she said over and over to herself, "an' it'll all be only my fault! What gien we never see him again? Eh, sirs! It's a terrible thing to be made wi' such a contrary disposition! What'll come o' me in the next worl', it'll be hard for anybody to say!"

On the evening of the second day, however, while she was washing up in the gloomiest frame of mind, in walked Cosmo, with a gentleman behind him.

"Hoo's my father, Grizzie?" asked Cosmo.

"Won'erful weel, sir," answered Grizzie, with a little more show of respect than usual.

"This is Grizzie, Mr. Burns," said Cosmo. "I have told you about how Grizzie takes care of us all!"

"How do you do, Grizzie?" said Mr. Burns, shaking hands with her. "I am glad to make your acquaintance."

"Here, Grizzie!" said Cosmo. "Here's the eighteen pence ya gae me for expenses. But I didna need it."

As he was speaking he drew her aside to the corner where the meal-chest stood, and now continued.

"Jist a word wi' ye, Grizzie! Look here! Only dinna tell!"

He drew out of his pocket and now showed her a bunch of bank notes. She had never seen so many scattered over all her life—not to say in a bunch! He took from among them ten pounds and gave it to her.

Grizzie stood gaping at the money as if such a sum could not be believed, but the next moment, like one suddenly raised to dignity and power, she began to order Aggie about as if she were her mistress, and an imperious one at that. Within ten minutes she had her bonnet on and was setting out for Muir o' Warlock to make purchases.

Oh, the pride and victory that rose and towered in Grizzie's mind as she walked to the village with all that money in her pocket! The dignity of the house of Warlock had rushed aloft like a sudden tidal wave, and on its very crest Grizzie was borne triumphing heavenward. From one who begged at strange doors for the daily bread of a decayed family, all at once she was the housekeeper of the most ancient and honorable castle in all Scotland, steering the great ship of its fortunes!

With a reserve and a dignity as impressive as provoking to the gossips of the village, from one shop to another she went, buying carefully but freely, rousing endless curiosity by her look of mystery, and her evident consciousness of infinite resource. But when at last she went to the Warlock Arms and bought half a dozen bottles of port at the incredible price of six shillings a bottle, there was not a doubt left in the Muir that "the auld laird" had at last and somehow come into a great fortune.

Grizzie returned with as much as she herself could carry, and driving before her two boys carrying a large basket between them. Now she was equal to the proper entertainment of the visitor, for whom, while she was away, Aggie, obedient to her orders, was preparing the state bedroom—thinking all the time of that night long ago when she and Cosmo got it ready for Lord Mergwain.

Cosmo and Mr. Burns found the laird seated by the fire in his room. There Cosmo recounted to their friend the whole story of the finding of the gems, beginning far back with the tales concerning the old captain, as they had come to his knowledge, just touching on the acquisition of the bamboo cane and the discovery of its contents, and so descending to the revelations of the previous two days. But all the time he never gave the jeweler a hint of what was coming. In relating the nearer events, he led him from place to place, acting his part in them, never once mentioning stone or gem. Then suddenly he poured out the diamonds on the rug in the firelight.

The resulting reaction on the part of Mr. Burns can well be imagined. Meanwhile, while Cosmo was away in the city, another event of importance had taken place.

51

· · · · · · · · · · · · · · · · · ·

Too Sure Comes Too Late

The same day Cosmo left, Lord Lickmyloof sent to the castle the message that he wanted to see young Mr. Warlock. The laird returned the answer that Cosmo was away from home and would not be back till the following day.

In the afternoon his lordship appeared, desiring an interview with the laird. Though it was a little against his liking, he granted it.

"Sit ye doon, my lord," said Grizzie, "an' rest yer shins. The road atween this an' the lodge must be slippery."

His lordship yielded and took the chair she offered, for he would rather propitiate than annoy her, seeing he was more afraid of Grizzie than anything in creation except dogs. And Grizzie, appreciating his behavior, had compassion on him, and spared him her tongue.

"His lairdship," she said, "mustn't be hurried gettin' dressed. He's no used to see anybody these days. I'll go an' see gien I can help him. He never would hae a man aboot him 'cept the yoong laird himsel'."

Relieved by her departure, his lordship began to look about the kitchen, and seeing Aggie, asked about her grandfather. She replied that he was getting on rather poorly.

"Getting old!"

"Surely, my lord. He's making ready to go."

"Poor old man."

"What would yer lordship prefer? Ye wouldna go on in this worl' forever?"

"Indeed, I would have no objection—so long as there were pretty girls like you in it."

"Suppose the lasses had a choice too, my lord?"

"What would they do?"

"Go, I'm thinkin', rather than stay with such men."

"What makes you so spiteful, Aggie? I never did you any harm that I know of."

"Ye ken the story o' the good Samaritan, my lord?" said Aggie.

"I read my Bible."

"Weel, I'll tell ye a bit mair o' it than ye'll get there. The Levite an' the Pharisee—naebody ever said yer lordship was like either o' them—"

"No, thank God! nobody could!"

"—they went by on the ither side an' let him lie. But there was one who came up an' took him by the legs, 'cause he lay upon his land, an' he would hae pulled him off. But jist in the nick o' time by came the good Samaritan, an' set the greedy lan'owner rinnin'. Sae it was soon a small matter to anybody but the ill neighbor, who couldna weel go straight to Paradise when he died. Abraham would hae a fine time o' it wi' sich a selfish bairn in his bosom!"

Blast the women! Young and old, they're too many for me! said his lordship to himself. Just then Grizzie returned and invited him to walk up to the laird's room, where he made haste to set forth the object of his visit.

"I said to your son, Glenwarlock, when he came to me the other morning, that I would not buy."

"Yes, my lord."

"However, I have, lawyer though I be, changed my mind, and am now come to renew my offer."

"In the meantime, however, we have changed our minds, my lord, and no longer wish to sell."

"That's very foolish of you."

"It may seem so, my lord. But you must allow us to do the best with what modicum of judgment we possess."

"What can have induced you to come to such a fatal resolution? I am thoroughly acquainted with the value of the land all about here, and am convinced you will not get such a price from another, be he who he may."

"You may be right, my lord, but we do not want to sell."

"Nobody, I repeat, will make you a better—I mean an equal offer."

"I could well believe it might not be worth more to anyone else—so long, that is, as your lordship's property shuts it in on every side. But to your lordship, it might well be worth—"

"That is my affair! What it is worth to you is the question."

"It is worth more to us than you can calculate."

"I daresay, where sentiment sends prices up! But sentiment is not in the market. Take my advice and a good offer. You can't go on like this, you know. You will lose your position entirely, and every scrap of anything that goes with it. Why, what are you thinking of!"

"I am thinking, my lord, that you have scarcely been such a neighbor as to induce us to confide our plans to you. I have said we will not sell—and as I am something of an invalid—"

Lord Lickmyloof rose, feeling fooled—and annoyed—with himself and everybody in "the cursed place."

"Good morning, Glenwarlock," he said. "You will live to repent this morning."

"I hope not, my lord. I have lived nearly long enough. Good morning."

His lordship went softly down the stair, hurried through the kitchen, and walked slowly home, wondering whether it might not be worth his while to buy up Glenwarlock's remaining debts.

52

·······················

The End of a Life Well Rounded

𝒫irate or not, the old gentleman was a good judge of diamonds!" said Mr. Burns as he set down one of the largest. "Not an inferior one in all I have looked at! Your uncle was a knowing man, sir; diamonds are worth much more now than when he brought them home. These rough ones will, I trust, turn out well—we cannot be quite so sure of them. But there are many, many thousands of pounds involved here!"

"How much suffering the earlier possession of them would have prevented!" said the laird. "And now they are ten times more welcome that we have the good of that suffering in our characters first. To have had them twenty years ago might have relaxed the suffering and prevented the discipline."

"Sapphires and all of the finest quality!" continued Mr. Burns, in no mood for reflection. "I'll tell you what you must do, Mr. Cosmo. You must get a few sheets of tissue paper and wrap every stone separately—a long job, but the better worth doing! There must be hundreds of them in all!"

"How can they be hurt, being the hardest things in the world?" said Cosmo.

"Put them in any other company you please—wheel them to the equator in a barrow full of gravel, or line their box with sandpaper, and you will leave them unscratched and naked as they were born. But, bless your five wits! Did you never hear the proverb, 'Diamond cut diamond'? They're all of a sort, you see. I'd as soon shut up a thousand gamecocks in the same cellar. If they don't scratch each other, they may, or they might, or they could, or they would, or at any rate they should scratch each other. It was all very well so long as they lay in the wall of this your old diamond mine. But now you'll be forever playing with them! No, no! wrap each one up by itself, I say."

"We're very unlikely to keep fingering them, Mr. Burns," said Cosmo. "Our chief reason for wishing you to see them was that you might, if you would oblige us, take them away and dispose of them for us!"

"Ah!" rejoined Mr. Burns. "I fear I am getting too old for a transaction of such extent! I should have to go to London—to Paris—to Amsterdam—who knows where?—to make the best of them—perhaps to America! And here was I thinking of retiring!"

"Then let this be your last business transaction. It will not be a bad one to finish up with. You can make it a good thing for yourself as well as for us."

"If I undertake it, it shall be at a fixed percentage."

"Ten?" suggested Cosmo.

"No. There is no risk, only labor in this. When I took ten for that other diamond, I paid you the money for it, you will remember: that makes a difference. No, ten would be far too much. Perhaps five, but even that—"

"Then we'll make it eight," interrupted Cosmo, "and that is my final word on it. I shall hear of not a percent less. You have been very good to us, and this is the least we can do."

"I wish you would come with me," said Mr. Burns. "I could help you to see a little of the world."

"I should like that a great deal. But I could not leave my father."

After all the arrangements had been made, the next day Mr. Burns prepared to leave the ancient glen called Warlock. He was a little nervous about the safety of the portmanteau that held such a number of tiny parcels in silver paper, and would not himself go inside the coach even though it was raining. He took a place outside, in sight of his luggage.

What the diamonds brought, I will not say. I would not have my book bristle with pounds like a French novel with francs. Suffice it to say they more than answered even Mr. Burns's expectations.

When he was gone, and all hope for this world vanished in the fruition of assured solvency, the laird began to fail—not out of despair, but out of the utter peace that God was over all and in all. He had grown not so much weary of this world but ready for the next.

While Cosmo was still on the way with Mr. Burns and the portmanteau to meet the coach, the laird said to his faithful old friend, "I'm tired, Grizzie. I'll go to bed, I think. Gien ye'll give me a hand, I winna wait for Cosmo."

"Eh, sir, what for should ye be in sich a hurry to sleep awa' the bonny daylight?" remonstrated Grizzie, shot through with sudden fear, not daring admit to herself that she was afraid. "Wait till the yoong laird comes back. He winna be long."

"Gien ye haena time, Grizzie, I can manage for mysel'. Go yer way, lass. Ye hae done yer best for him that yer Marion left!"

"Eh, sir! Dinna speak like that! It's terrible t' listen to! In the very face o' the providence that's been takin' sich pains t' make up to ye for all ye hae gone through—noo, when all's weel, an' like to be weel, to turn roond like this an' speak o' gaein' to yer bed! It's no worthy o' ye, Laird!"

He was so amused with her admonition that he laughed heartily, brightened up, and did not go to bed before Cosmo came—kept up, indeed, a good part of the day, and retired with the sun shining in at his western window.

The next day, however, he did not rise at all. But he had no suffering to speak of, and his face was serene as the gathering of the sunrays to go down together. A perfect yet deepening peace was upon it.

Cosmo scarcely left him, but watched and waited, with a cold spot at his heart, which kept growing bigger and bigger, as he saw his father slowly drifting out on the ebb-tide of this earthly life. Cosmo had now to go through that most painful experience of all—when the loved ones seem gradually withdrawing from human contact and human desires, their cares parting slowly further and further from the cares of those they leave—a gulf ever widening between, already impassable as lapsing ages can make it. But when final departure had left the mind free to work for the heart, Cosmo said to himself, *What if the dying, who seem thus divided from us, are but looking over the tops of insignificant earthly things? What if the heart within them is lying content in a closer contact with ours than our dull fears and too-level outlook will allow us to share? But we shall go after them, and be taught by them. In the meantime, let us so live that it may be the easier for us in dying to let the loved ones know that we are loving them all the time.*

The laird ceased to eat, and spoke seldom, but would often smile—only there was in his smile, too, that far-off something which troubled his son. One word he often murmured—*peace.* Two or three times there came what seemed a check in the drift seaward, and he spoke plainly. On one of these occasions, he said:

"Peace! peace! Cosmo, my son, ye dinna ken hoo strong it can be! Nobody can know what it's like till it comes. I have been troubled all my life, and now the very peace is almost too much for me! It's like as if the sun would put out the fire. I just seem to be lying here sometimes waiting for you to come into my peace and be one with me. But ye hae a lang this world's life afore ye yet! Eh! Winna it be gran' whan it's weel ower, an' ye come! You an' me an' yer mither an' God an' all! But somehow I dinna seem to be leaving ye either—not half so much as when ye went away to the college, even though you're ten times closer to me now than you were then. Death can't well be much like anything we think about it. But there must surely be a heap of folks altogether dreary and visionless in the world death takes us to. And the more I think about it, the more likely it seems we'll have a heap to do with them—a hard work it may be trying to let them know what they are, and where they came from, and how they must go to get home—for death can no more be your home than a fall on the road can be your bed. There may be many ones there we called old here, that we'll have to take like a child on our knees and bring up.

"I see not another way of it. The Lord may know better, but I think he's shown me this. For them that are Christ's must have work like his to do, works of love and redemption and growth, and why not personal ministration to them that are dead, that they may come into more life by knowing him better? Auld bairns as weel as yoong hae t' be fed wi' the spune."

The day before he went, the laird seemed to wake up suddenly, and said, "Cosmo, I'm not inclined to make a promise wi' regard t' any possible communication wi' ye frae the other world, nor do I the least expect t' appear or speak to ye. But don't conclude me away frae ye alt'gether. Fowk may have a heap o' communication without either o' them knowin' it at the time, I'm thinkin'. Remember this anyway: God's oor home, an' if ye be at home, an' I be at home, we canna be far apart!"

As the sun was going down, closing a lovely day of promise, the boat of sleep, with a gentle wind of life and birth filling its sail, bore the old pilgrim softly gliding across the faint border between this world and that. Perhaps for a time, like a babe newborn, he needed careful hands and gentle nursing. And if so, his wife was there, who must surely by now had had time to grow strong.

Cosmo wept and was lonely, but not brokenhearted; for he was a live man with a mighty hope and great duties ahead of him, each of them ready to become a great joy. Such a man not even diamonds could hurt, although where breathes no wind of life, those very crystals of light are among the worst in Beelzebub's army to blow a soul into a thing of hate and horror.

And so the mantle of "the lairdship," as Grizzie called it, was passed from Glenwarlock the elder to Glenwarlock the younger, a man of twenty-six now, and for the first time in his life with only one Father to help guide his steps.

53

A Breaking Up

*C*osmo settled himself in his father's room, and read and tried his hand at writing. Mr. Simon was himself preparing to go to the world he had always considered his true home. Realizing his master's imminent departure, with renewed grief Cosmo spent many hours alone in the hills, contemplating the lives of these two, his closest teachers, pondering, aspiring to faithfully carry on the legacy they had left him.

For some time, things in the castle went on in the same quiet way as before. The household led the same homely simple life, only faring better. The housekeeping was in Grizzie's hands, and she was a liberal soul—a true bread-giver.

James Gracie did not linger long behind his friend. His last words were, "I won'er gien I hae a chance o' catchin' up wi' the laird!"

On the morning that followed his funeral, as soon as breakfast was over, Aggie sought Cosmo, where he sat in the garden with a book in his hand.

"Whaur are ye gaein', Aggie?" he said, as she approached prepared for walking.

"*My* hour's come," she answered. "It's time I was away."

"I dinna un'erstan' ye, Aggie," he returned.

"Hoo should ye, sir? Everybody kens, or should ken, what lies to their own hand. It lies to mine to go. I'm not needed noo. Ye wouldna hae me eat the bread o' idleness?"

"But, Aggie," remonstrated Cosmo, "ye're one o' the family! I would as soon think o' seein' my own sister, if I had one, go frae home for nae reason at all!"

The tears rose in her eyes and her voice trembled.

"It canna be helped. I must go," she said.

Cosmo was speechless for many moments. He had never thought of such a possibility; and Aggie stood silent before him.

"What hae ye in yer head, Aggie? What think ye o' doin' wi' yersel'?" he finally asked, his heart swelling so that he could scarcely bring out the words.

"I'm gaein' to look for a place."

"But, Aggie, if it canna be helped, an' if ye must, ye ken I'm rich, an' I ken there's naebody in the world wi' a better right to share in what I hae. Wouldna ye like t' go to a ladies' school an' learn a heap o' things?"

"No, I wouldna. It's hard work I need to hold me to the right road. I can aye learn what I hunger for, an' what I dinna desire I'll never learn. Thanks to yersel' an' Mister Simon, ye had put me in the way o' that. It's no knowin' things—it's knowin' the road ye're travelin' that's o' consequence to ye. The rest I make nothing o'."

"But a time might come when ye would want many a thing ye might hae been able t' learn afore."

"When that times comes, I'll learn them then, wi' half the trouble an' in half the time, no to mention the pleasure o' learnin' them. Noo, they would but take me frae the things I can an' must make use o.' Na, Cosmo, I'm bound to do somethin' wi' what I hae, an' no bide till I get more. I'll be aye gaein'."

"Weel, Aggie, I dare not tempt ye to stay if ye ought to go. An' ye would but despise me if I was fool enough to try it. But ye canna refuse to share wi' me. That wouldna be like one that had the same Father an' the same Master. Take a thousand poun' to begin wi', an' go an'—an' do anything ye like, only dinna work yersel' to death with rough work. I canna bide to think o' it."

"A thousand poun'! No one coin! Cosmo, I would hae thought ye had mair sense! What would a pussy cat do wi' a silk goon? Ye can gie me the two poun' ten I gae t' Grizzie to help hold the life in us. A body must hae somethin' in their pouch if they can, an' if they canna, they must do wi' nothin'. It's won'erful hoo little's really needed!"

Cosmo felt miserable.

"Ye winna go ohn seein' Master Simon!"

"I tried to see him last night, but auld Dorty wouldna let me near him. I would like t' say farewell to him."

"Weel, put off yer gaein' till the morn, an' we'll go t'gither tonight an' see him. Dorty winna hold *me* oot."

Aggie hesitated, thought, and finally consented. Leaving Cosmo more distressed than she knew, she went to the kitchen, took off her bonnet, and telling Grizzie she was not going till the morrow, sat down and proceeded to pare the potatoes.

"Once more," said Grizzie, clearly resuming an unclosed conversation, "why ye should go's clean beyond me. It's true the auld men are gone, but here's the auld wife left, an' she'll be a mither to ye, as weel as she kens hoo, an' a lass o' yer sense is easy t' mither. In the name o' God I say it, the worl' might as weel object to two angels biding in heaven together as you an' the yoong laird in one hoose! Say what they like, ye're but a servant lass, an' here am I ower ye! Aggie, I'm some auld mysel', an' hardly fit t' make a bed by mysel'—no to mention scourin' the floor. It's no considerate o' ye, Aggie!—jist cause yer father—hoots, he was but yer gran'father!—is dead o' a good auld age, an' gathered t' *his* Father, to go an' leave me alone! Whaur am I to get a body I could bide t' have in my sight, an' you gone—you that's been like bone o' my own bone t' me! It's no good o' ye, Aggie! There must be some o' yer temper in it! I'm sure I ken no cause I ever gae ye t' want t' leave."

Aggie said not a word. She had said all she could say, over and over; so now she pared her potatoes and was silent. Her heart was sore, but her mind was clear and her will strong.

Up and down the little garden Cosmo walked, revolving many things in his mind. "What is this world and its ways," he said, "but a dream that dreams itself out and is gone!"

The majority of men worship solidity and fact. But even a fact may be a mere shred for the winds of the limbo of vanities. Everything that *can* pass away—however solid it may temporarily be—belongs to the same category with the dream. The question is whether the passing body leaves a live soul; whether the dream has been truly dreamed, the life lived aright. For there is a reality beyond all facts of suns and systems, wealth and lands, houses and possessions. Solidity itself is but the shadow of a divine necessity, and there may be more truth in a parable than in a whole biography. Where life and truth are one, there is no passing, no dreaming more. To that waking all dreams truly dreamed are guiding the dreamer.

But the very last thing anyone need regard—and this was the conclusion to which Cosmo's meditation finally led him—is the judgment of others, whether it be their judgment of his dreams, his visions, his aspirations, or his life's goals.

The all-pervading, ill-odored phantom called Society is but the ghost of a false god. The fear of man—trust in man, deference to the opinion of man—is the merest worship of a rag-stuffed idol. The man who seeks the judgment of God can well smile at the unsolicited approval or condemnation of self-styled society— even Christian society, if such a term can be used. There *is* a true society—quite another thing. No doubt the judgment of the world is of some moral value to those capable of regarding it. To deprive a thief of the restraining influence of the code of thieves' honor would be to do him irreparable harm; so with the trades-man whose law is the custom of the trade. But God demands an honesty, a dignity, a purity, a beauty of being altogether different from that demanded by man of his fellow. And he who is taught of God is out of sight above such law as that of thieves' honor, trade-custom, or social recognition—he is subjected instead to a law of God which, when obeyed, brings utter liberty, and disobeyed is a hell deeper than all of society's slums.

The evening was Mr. Simon's best time, and therefore Cosmo and Aggie let the sun go down before they left the castle to visit him. On their way they had a pleasant talk about old things, now the one, now the other bringing some half-faded event from the store-closet of memory.

"I doobt ye'll remember me takin' ye oot o' the Warlock one day when there was a bit o' a flood on?" said Agnes at length looking up into Cosmo's face.

"Eh, I never heard o' that, Aggie!" replied Cosmo.

"I canna think to this day hoo it was ye fell in," she went on. "I hadna the charge o' ye at the time. Ye must hae run oot o' the hoose, an' me after ye. I was very near taken away wi' ye. Hoo we struggled oot o' the water I canna un'erstan'. All that I ken is that when I came t' mysel' we were lyin' grippin' one anither upon a piece o' the bank."

"But hoo was it that naebody ever said a word aboot it afterward?" asked Cosmo.

"I never told anybody, an' ye wasna auld enough to remember it."

"Why didna ye tell?"

"I was feart they would think it my fault, an' no let me take charge o' ye anymore. But I kent ye was safer wi' me than wi' any other aboot the place. Gien it had been my fault, I couldna hae held my tongue. But as it was, I didna see I was bound to tell."

"Hoo did ye hide it?"

"I ran wi' ye home to oor ain hoose. There was naebody there. I took off yer wet clothes, an' put ye int' my bed till I got them dry."

"An' hoo did ye dry yer ain?"

"By the time yers was dry, mine was too."

When they arrived at the cottage, Dorty argued against letting them in, but her master heard Cosmo's voice and rang his bell.

"I little thought your father would have gone before me," said Mr. Simon. "I think I was aware of his death. I saw nothing, heard nothing, and was not thinking about him at the moment. But he seemed to come to me, and I thought to myself,

He is on his way home. I shall have a talk with him by and by."

Agnes told him she had come to bid him goodbye; she was going in search of a new place.

"Well," he answered after a thoughtful pause, "so long as we obey the light in us, and that light is not darkness, we can't go wrong. If we should mistake, he will turn things round for us; and if we be to blame, he will let us see it."

He was weak, and they did not stay long.

"Don't judge my heart by my words, my dear scholars," he said. "My heart is right toward you, but I am too weary to show it. God bless you both. I may not see you again, Agnes, but I shall think of you there, and if I can do anything for you, be sure I will."

When they left the cottage, the twilight was halfway toward the night, and a vague softness in the east prophesied the moon. Cosmo led Agnes through the fields to the little hollow where she had so often gone to seek him. There they sat down in the grass and waited for the moon. Cosmo pointed out the exact spot where she rose that night she looked at him through the legs of the cow.

"Ye mind Grizzie's rhyme," he said.

" 'What the coo loups ower the mune,
The reid gowd rains intil men's shune'?

I believe Grizzie took the queer sight for a good omen. It's so strange hoo fowk'll mix up God an' chance, seein' there could hardly be two more contradictory ideas! I mind once hearin' a man say, 'It's almost a providence!' "

"I don't doobt most fowk would say 'There's almost a God,' " said Aggie. "For my part I see nae room atween no believin' in him at all, an' believin' in him alt'gither an' lettin' him do what he likes wi' ye."

"I'm o' yer mind there, Aggie, oot an' oot," responded Cosmo.

As he spoke the moon came peering up, and turning to Agnes to share the sight with her, Cosmo saw the yellow light reflected from tears.

"Aggie! Aggie!" he said in much concern, "what are ye cryin' for?"

She made no answer, but wiped away her tears and tried to smile. After a little pause, she said, "Anybody would think, Cosmo," she said, "That if I believe in a God, he must be a small one! Why shouldn't anybody cry that has but a far-away notion o' such a God as you an' the laird an Master Simon believes in!"

"Ye may weel say that, Aggie!" rejoined Cosmo—yet sighed as he said it, for he thought of Lady Joan. A long pause followed, and then he spoke again, seriously.

"Aggie," he said, "there canna well be two in this world that ken one another better than you an' me. We hae been bairns together; we hae been to the school together; we've had the same master; we've come through dour times together— I doobt we hae been hungry together, though ye said no word; we hae wrestled wi' poverty, an' maybe wi' unbelief; we love the same fowk best; and above it all we both set the will of God. It would be terrible to us both to part—an' for me an awful thing, besides, to know that the first thing wealth did for me was to take ye away. It would almost break my heart to think that her that came through the land of drought wi' me—ay, took me through it, for without her I would hae fallen to rise nae more, that she should go climbin' the dry hill-road, an' me lyin' in the bonny meadow grass at the foot of it. It canna be reason, Aggie! What for should ye go? Marry me, Aggie, an' stay—stay an' call the castle yer ain!"

"Hoots! Would ye marry yer ain mither!" cried Agnes, and to Cosmo's renewed dismay burst into laughter and tears together.

Cosmo looked at her speechless. It was as if an angel had made a poor human joke! He was much too bewildered to feel hurt, especially as he was aware of committing no folly.

But Aggie was not pleased with herself. She choked her tears, crushed down her laughter and conquered it. She took his hand in hers.

"I beg yer pardon, Cosmo," she said. "I shouldna hae laughed. Laughin', I'm sure, is far enough frae my heart! I kenna hoo I came to it! But ye're such a bairn, Cosmo! Ye dinna ken what ye would hae! An' bein' a kind o' mither to ye all yer life, I must show ye what ye're aboot—I wouldna make too much o' the years atween us. It was no small matter when we was bairns, but 'tis not even quite two years, an' it seems like no sae much noo. Still, 'tis no a small matter. But surely ye haena to be told at this time o' day that for fowk to marry that dinna love each other is no a good thing for them t' do."

"I *hae* aye loved *you*, Aggie," said Cosmo, with some reproach in his tone.

"Weel do I ken that. An' an ill heart would be mine if I didna tell ye that! But, Cosmo, when ye said the word, didna *your* heart tell ye that ye meant somethin' not jist the very same as ye intended me to un'erstan' by it?"

"Aggie, Aggie!" sighed Cosmo, "I would try to love ye better an' better."

"Ay, ye would, if ye could, Cosmo. But ye're too honest to see through yersel'. An' I'm no sae honest but I can see through you. Ye would marry me 'cause ye're no willin' to part wi' me, likin' me better than any but one, an' her ye canna get! If I was a leddy, Cosmo, maybe I might not be ower proud to take ye upon those terms, but no bein' what I am. Bein' the one ye *almost* love, the one perhaps ye loved second best, might lead ye t' a sad time o' repentance! An it might lead me to the same! Once married to ye, if I were to take it into my head that I was one hair in yer way, or that ye would be one hair freer wi' me oot o' yer sight, I would be like to run to the very back wall o' creation!

"Na, it was weel enough the way it has been between us—but *married!* Ye would be good to me, aye, I ken that, but I would be aye wantin' to be dead, that ye might love me a wee better. For ye're no in love wi' me, Cosmo. And I say nothin' o' what the world would say to the laird o' Glenwarlock marryin' his servant lass; for ye care as little for the world as I do, an' we're both some wiser for it. But after all, Cosmo, I would be oot o' my station—wouldna I noo? The hen-birds nae doobt are aye the soberer to look at, an' haven't the grand colors nor the grand ways wi' them that the cocks have. But still there's a measure in all things: it would ill set a common hen to hae a peacock for her man. My soul, I ken, would go hand in hand, in a humble sort o' way, wi' yours, for I un'erstan' ye, Cosmo. An' the day may come when I'll look fitter for yer company than I do noo. But who like me could help a sense o' unfitness, if it were but gaein' to the kirk side by side wi' you? Look at the two o' us noo in the moonlight t'gether! Dinna ye see that we dinna match?"

"All that would be nothing if ye loved me, Aggie."

"If *ye* loved *me*, ye should say, Cosmo—loved me enough to be prood o' me. But that ye dinna. Examine yer own heart, an' ye'll see that ye dinna. An' why should ye?"

Here Aggie broke down. A burst of silent weeping, like that of one desiring no comfort, followed. Suddenly she ceased and rose, and they walked home without a word.

When Cosmo came down in the morning, Aggie was gone.

54

•••••••••••••••••••

Reflection

*C*osmo had no need of a very searching examination of his heart to know that it was mainly the wish to make her some poor return for her devotion, as well as the sincere desire to retain her company, that had influenced him in the offer she had been too wise and too genuinely loving to accept. He did not fall into any depths of self-blame. For whether his love was the marrying kind or not, it was of a quality pure and true. The only sadness his offer carried with it was its justification of Aggie's departure.

But Grizzie saw no justification of it anywhere.

"What I'm to do wi'oot her, I dinna ken. *No becomin'* he says, *for a lass like her to live under the same roof wi' a bachelor like himsel'!*

"Who ever heard o' sich stupid rubbish! As gien she had been a lady indeed! I might jist as much object to bidin' wi' him mysel'! But I'll do what I like, an' let fowk say what they like, sae long as I'm no fool in my ain eyes!"

But by degrees Cosmo grew to regret having addressed Agnes as he had. He saw in the thing a failure in respect, a wrong to her dignity. Seeming at the time to himself to be going against the judgment of the world, he now began to ask himself if there had not been in him a vague condescension operating all the time. Had he not been all but conscious of the feeling that perhaps his position made up for any lack there might be in his love? Had she been conventionally a lady, instead of an angel in peasant form, would he have been so ready to return her kindness with an offer of marriage?

Now that he understood this, had he not been brought up with her from childhood as with an elder sister, she might even now have begun to be a formidable rival to the sweet memories of Joan's ladyhood. For he saw in her that which is at the foot, not only of all virtue, but of all beauty, of all grandeur, of all growth, of all attraction. Every charm—in its essence, in its development, in its embodiment, is a flower of the tree of life, whose root is the truth.

The shallow philosopher would ridicule such a statement, thinking of a certain lady to him full of charm, who had no more love for the truth than a mole for the light. But that lady's charm does not spring out of her; it had been put onto her, and she will soon destroy it. It comes not from within her, and will therefore one day leave her naked and not lovely. The truth in one like Agnes was supreme for itself. To have asked such a one to marry him for reasons lower than the highest was good grounds for him to feel ashamed. But even then he was not *painfully* ashamed, for he felt safe with Agnes, as with the elder sister who pardons everything.

When they next heard news of her, it was that she had rented Grannie's cottage from her own aunt in the village, and was going to have a school there for young children. Cosmo was greatly pleased, for the work would give scope to some of her highest gifts and best qualities, while it would keep her serving.

Cosmo turned his attentions heartily to study. He not only read but wrote regularly every day in the hope of more thoroughly shaping and testing his thoughts and ideas. The room over the kitchen, which had first in his memory been his grandmother's, then became his own, and then for a time James Gracie's, he made his study. And from it to the drawing room, with the assistance of a village mason, he excavated a passage—for it was little less than excavation—in the wall connecting the two blocks under the passage in which had lain the treasure.

The main result Grizzie's new command of money found was in a torrent of cleaning. If she could have had her way, I think she would have put up scaffolds all over the outside of the house and scrubbed it down from chimneys to foundations.

On the opposite side of the Warlock River, the laird rented a meadow, and there Grizzie had the long-awaited satisfaction of seeing two cows she could call her own, the finest cows in the country, feeding with a vague satisfaction in the general order of things. The stable housed a horse after Cosmo's own heart, on which he made excursions into the countryside, partly in the hope of coming upon some place not too far off where there was land to be bought.

All that was known of the change in his circumstances was that he had come into a large fortune by the death—date not mentioned—of a relative with whom his father had not communicated for many years, and Cosmo never had. Lord Lickmyloof, after his repeated endeavors to get some information about this relative, was perplexed and vaguely suspicious.

How the spending of the money thus committed to him was to change the earthly issues of his life, Cosmo had not yet learned, and was waiting for light on the matter. For a man is not bound to walk in the dark, but only to wait until the light comes. Neither must he act, merely for the sake of doing something, and thus run the risk of doing wrong. He that believeth shall not make haste. He had nothing of the common mammonistic feeling of the enormous importance of money, and did not feel that it laid upon him a heavier weight of duty than any other of the gifts of God. And if a poet is not bound to rush into the world with his poem, surely a rich man is not bound to rush into the world with his money. Rather set a herd of wild horses loose in a city! A man must first know how to *use* his money before he begins to spend it. And the way to use money is not so easily discovered as some would think, for it is not one of God's ready means of doing good. The rich man as such has no reason to look upon himself as specially favored. He does have reason to think himself especially tried. In loving a certain youth, Jesus did him the greatest kindness he had in his power by telling him to give his wealth to the poor, and then to follow him in poverty.

The first question is not how to do good with money, but how to keep from doing harm with it. Whether rich or poor, a man must first of all do justice, love mercy, and walk humbly with his God. Then, if he be rich, God will let him know how to spend. Cosmo was in no hurry. It is not because of God's poverty that the world is so slowly redeemed. Not the righteous expenditure of money will save it, but that of life and soul and spirit—and that of nerve and muscle, blood and brain. All these our Lord spent—but no money. Therefore of all means for saving the world, or doing good, as it is called, money comes last in order, and far behind.

Out of the loneliness in which his father left him, grew a great peace and a new strength. More real than ever was the other world to him now. His father could not have vanished like a sea bubble on the sand. To have known a great man such as he, is to have some assurance of immortality. One of the best of men said once that he did not feel any particular longing for immortality, but, when he thought of certain persons he had known, he could not for a moment believe they had ceased to be. He had beheld the lovely and believed, therefore, in the endless.

Castle Warlock was scarcely altered in appearance. In its worst poverty it had always looked dignified. There was now more life and activity about it, and freedom. But not so much happiness. The diamonds had come, but his father was gone, Aggie was gone, Mr. Simon was going, Joan had never answered their letters, and he would probably never see her again!

Cosmo had scarcely a hope for this world. Yet nonetheless did he await the will of The Will. What that was, time would show, for God does his work through time, which is also his creation.

55

· · · · · · · · · · · · · · · ·

The Third Harvest

*A*s the days went by, Cosmo's engagement to Mr. Henderson drew near. No doubt the farmer would have let him out of it at once, but not for a moment did Cosmo consider trying to back out of it because he was now in plenty. He would never have considered a thing disgraceful only because he was a rich man. No true man will ever ask of a fellow creature, man or woman, the doing of a thing he himself would feel degraded to do. There is nothing like Christianity to make all men equal, to level such distinctions—but it levels by lifting to a lofty tableland, accessible only to humility. Only he who is humble can rise.

So Cosmo's thought was not to gain respect by thus holding to what he had undertaken, but simply to honorably and gratefully fulfill his contract. Not only would it have been a poor return for Mr. Henderson's kindness to treat his service as something beneath him now, but, worst of all, it would have been to accept ennoblement at the hands of Mammon, as of a power able to alter his station in God's world. To change the spirit of one's way because of money is to confess oneself a born slave, a thing only with an outside and no heart, a Knight of Riches with a maggot for his crest.

Therefore, when the time came Cosmo presented himself. With a look of astonishment the worthy farmer held out his hand.

"Laird," he said, "I didna expect *you!*"

"Why shouldn't you?" returned Cosmo. "Haven't I been your hired man for months?"

"But fowk tellt me ye had fallen heir to a sight o' siller!"

"But how should that affect my bargain with you, Mr. Henderson? Money in the pocket can't take an obligation from the back."

"Drivin' things to the wall, nae doobt," returned the farmer. "An' though the law might hae been on my side, what's that among frien's?"

"A bargain's a bargain," answered Cosmo. "With no reason not to come, it would have been ill-mannered, not to say dishonest and ungrateful. But if you have spoken to anyone else about my place, he can have the fee, and I'll have the work. Let things stand, Mr. Henderson."

"Laird!" answered the farmer, not a little moved, "there's no a man I would rather see at my work than yersel'. All o' them, men an' women, work the better when ye're among them. They'd be affronted not to keep up wi' a gentleman! Sae come away, an' ye're welcome! Ye'll take somethin' afore we fall to it?"

Cosmo accepted a jug of milk, half cream, from the hand of Elsie.

The girl was much improved, having partially unlearned a good deal of the nonsense gathered at school, and come to take a fair share with her sisters in the work of the house and farm. She was neatly dressed and handsome, with a smile on her mouth showing the whitest of teeth, and her eyes glowed in obvious admiration of Cosmo. To one more knowledgeable in such things than Cosmo, there would also have been apparent the flash of design in those same eyes; she too had heard of the new Warlock wealth, and as a result Cosmo stood higher than ever in her estimation as a prize to be won.

They went to the fields, and without having to start off in last position, the other workers immediately deferred to him as their leader. When Cosmo reached the end of the first bout, and stood to sharpen his scythe, he was surprised to see, a little way off, gathering after one of the other men, a form he could never mistake. *She* had known he would keep his bargain and would be here! She did not look up, but he knew her figure and every motion of it too well to mistake Aggie for any other in the world.

Aggie well knew that she was exposing herself by thus coming to work in Mr. Henderson's fields. But she did not care what anyone might think. She was far above heeding such dangers, feeling confident of how things stood between her and Cosmo. Those who do the truth are raised even above defying the world. Aggie gave herself no more trouble about the opinion of the world than of a dog.

She had refused Cosmo's offer to marry her, but she was not therefore prepared to allow him to go about undefended to anyone else who might try to grab him. She had been his mother once, and she felt it her duty, for love of him and devotion to his family, to look out for him still. And she knew one who would be hampered by no scruples in trying to win him. Indeed, Agnes might well have thought it better he should marry her as the cottar's than the farmer's daughter!

Anyhow, she had resolved to keep an eye on the young woman so long as Cosmo was within her swoop. He was chivalrous and credulous, and who could tell what Elsie might not dare! Her own refusal to be his wife did not deprive her of antecedent rights. And it was a good thing—for there was Elsie gathering behind Cosmo, biding her time!

The instant the day's labor was done, Aggie set out for home, not having exchanged a word with Cosmo all day. But she intended to linger on the way in the hope of his overtaking her. The Hendersons would have had him stay the night, but he had given his man orders to wait for him with his horse at a certain point on the road; and Aggie had not gone far before he caught up with her.

Aggie had largely got over the pangs of her heart; she knew what she had done was for the best. Therefore she was nowise annoyed at the cheery unembarrassed tone in which he called out when he saw her. Perhaps neither of them would forget the awkwardness of the exchange at their last parting, but each loved the other too much not to look forward to the day when they could again be friends as brother and sister—maybe even more deeply than before. She turned and greeted him with the same absence of constraint, sending a smile to him which said, *All is well!*

"An so ye're gaein' to take the bairnies under yer wing, Aggie!" said Cosmo, as they walked along. "They're lucky little things that'll go to yer school! What put it int' yer head?"

"Mr. Simon advised it," answered Aggie. "But I believe I put it in his head first, sayin' hoo little was done for the bairnies jist at the time they were easiest t' guide. Rough work makes the han's rough, an' rough words make the heart rough."

"The whole countryside'll be grateful to ye, Aggie. Ye'll let me come an' see ye sometimes?"

"None would be sae welcome," answered Aggie. "But will ye be bidin' on, noo that ye haena yer father? Winna ye be gaein' away to write books an' make fowk fin' oot what's the matter wi' them?"

"I dinna ken what I'm gaein to do," answered Cosmo. "But for writin' books, I could do that better at home than any ither place, wi' anythin' remindin' me o' my father, an' wi' you nearby to give me coonsel."

"I hae aye been yours to command, Cosmo," replied Aggie, glancing down for one moment, then immediately up again in his face.

"An' ye're not angered wi' me, Aggie?"

"Angered at ye, my bonny lad!" cried Aggie, and looked up at him with a world of tenderness in her eyes and a divine glow of affection in her honest handsome face. Hers was the love so sure of itself that it cannot be ashamed. She threw her two strong, shapely arms round his neck. He bent his head, and she kissed him heartily on the mouth, and burst into tears. "It was only that ye didna ken what ye were aboot," she went on, half laughing, half crying. "An' bein' yoonger than mysel', I was bound to take care o' ye. For a woman as weel's a man must be her brither's keeper." Surely but for that other love that lay patient and hopeless in the depth of Cosmo's heart, he would now have loved Aggie in a way that might have led to love of a kind which could justify him in saying he loved her. And to that it might have come in time, but what is the use of saying what might have been when all things are ever moving toward the highest and best for the individual as well as for the universe! "Ye see yersel' I was right," concluded Aggie.

"Ay, ye was, Aggie," answered Cosmo, ashamed at having to make the confession in the knowledge that this latest only proved all the more what a lovely woman she was. "Ah, but ye're a good woman, Aggie! An' bound to make some honest man the best wife in the Muir!"

"But," said Aggie, not to be diverted from the purpose of her desire to meet Cosmo on the road, "all lasses mightna ken sae weel what was best for them, nor care sae much what was good for you. Naebody livin' can ken ye as I do, an' if ye were to let some ither lass think ye cared aboot her—it might be but as a friend, she might be taken wi' ye all the same, sae much that—that maybe she might make ye think as hoo she couldna live wi'oot ye—an' then what would ye do, Cosmo?"

Cosmo could hardly imagine himself in such a situation and looked at Aggie a little perplexed.

"I dinna quite un'erstan' ye," he said.

"Na, I reckon no! Hoo should ye! Ye're jist too simple for this world, Cosmo! But I'll put it to ye plainer. What would ye do if a lass was to fall a cryin' an' a wailin' an' fling hersel' at ye—what would ye do wi' her, Cosmo?"

" 'Deed, I dinna ken," replied Cosmo, with some embarrassment. "What should I do, Aggie?"

"I would hae ye set her doon where ye stood; if it be on the road, then upon the nearest dyke; if it be in the hoose, then upon the nearest chair, an' then take to yer legs an' run. Wait na even to pick up yer bonnet, but run an' run till ye're more than sure she can never catch up wi' ye. An' specially if the name o' the lass should begain wi' an *E,* I would hae ye run as if the auld captain was after ye."

"I hae had small occasion," said Cosmo, "to run frae *him.* "An' if the lass didna fling hersel' at me, Aggie, but was as good as ye yersel', what would ye hae me do then?"

"Wait t' see what yer heart tellt ye," answered Aggie.

And therewith, partly to change the subject, for Cosmo understood perfectly well her meaning with respect to the family of his present employer, and partly because he had long wanted an opportunity of telling her, he began to acquaint her with the facts of his recent history which he had felt bound to keep to himself until now. He gave her the whole history of the discovery of the diamonds, omitting nothing, even where the tale concerned Lady Joan. Before he got to the end of it, they were at the place where the man was waiting with his horse, and as that was the place where Aggie had to turn off to go to Muir o' Warlock, there they parted.

56

"Luik To Yer Hert"

The next day things went much the same. Aggie and Cosmo met and spoke to one another during the breaks between bouts around the field when Aggie's mower completed his round close enough to Cosmo that their times coincided. The subject of Elsie did not come up again. They also partook of their midday meal together, laughing and talking like the old times, resolving many a theoretical difficulty between them, about which one would usually conclude, "Mr. Simon would aye hae an answer t' gie us!"

Elsie again gathered for Cosmo, attempting on several occasions to wile him into conversation. Cosmo was friendly, but on his guard. And after the midday break, Elsie was noticeably quiet, thinking what she must do to eliminate the bothersome Aggie. No doubt some means could be contrived to make her father think her work not worth her wages.

Immediately when the strenuous labor of the day was past, Cosmo and Aggie fell in together to begin the walk home, Aggie to the Muir, Cosmo to his waiting groom. They talked as they hadn't for months, and for Cosmo the restoration of his relationship with Aggie gave once more the glow of vitality to his life. He laughed as he hadn't since the death of his father.

When they were about halfway to the point where they must part, the figure of another country girl could be seen approaching on another road which joined the one they were on, but they took little heed of her. They continued on and passed the point where the two dirt roads met. But as they were walking slowly and deep in conversation, the young woman who had been nearing them, scarcely observed, readily made up the distance between herself and the two laborers. When Aggie stopped for a moment, the better to make a point to Cosmo, the stranger caught up with and joined them.

She was a young woman in the garb of a peasant. But there was something about her not belonging to the peasant. To the first glance she was more like a superior servant out for a holiday, but a second glance was bewildering. For then she did not look like a servant at all. She stopped with a half timid but quiet look, then dropped her eyes as her face flushed slightly.

"Will you tell me, please, if I am on the way to Castle Warlock," she said, with a quiver about her mouth that made her look like a child trying not to smile.

Cosmo had been gazing at her. She reminded him very strangely—but it could not be! What could *she* be doing *here*! But the moment he heard her voice, which was as different from that of a Scottish peasant as Tennyson's verse is from that of Burns, he gave a cry.

"Joan!" he gasped, and seizing her hand, drew it to his lips, and held it there.

She made no sound or movement. The color filled her face, then left entirely and it looked as if she was about to faint. Cosmo took her, as one might a child in his arms, and began to walk swiftly homeward.

Aggie had a momentary fierce struggle with her rising heart. But she spoke to the Lord, succeeded in mastering it, and fell back to follow some twenty or thirty yards behind. Who could tell but that she might be needed? But she would otherwise not interfere with Cosmo's treasure, for hers truly was the love of God's woman for another of his servants.

In a few moments Joan was herself again. Cosmo set her down and they walked side by side.

"Where have you come from!" asked Cosmo, still bewildered in the first overwhelming joy-wave, but endeavoring to make his words and thoughts resume their normal operations.

"From Cairntod, the place I came from that wild winter night," answered Joan.

"But you are . . . when were you . . . how long . . . have you been married?"

"*Married!*" echoed Joan. "Cosmo, how could you?"

She looked up in his face, wild and frightened.

"Well, you never wrote! and—"

"It was you who never wrote!"

"I did not, I confess. We thought it best. But my father did—many times—and got no answer."

"I wrote again and again, and *begged* for an answer," said Joan, nearly in tears, "but none came. If it hadn't been for the way I dreamed about you, I don't know what would have become of me!"

"The devil has been at his old tricks, I fear, Joan."

"Doubtless—with my brother as his agent."

"And Dr. Jermyn?" said Cosmo, with a look half shy, half fearful, as if after all some bolt must be about to fall from his heaven.

"I can tell you very little about him. I have scarcely seen him since he brought me the money."

"Then he didn't. . . ?"

"Didn't what?"

"Didn't he ask you to marry him?"

Joan laughed.

"I had begun to be afraid he had something of the kind in his head when all at once I saw no more of him."

"Why was that?"

"I can only guess. He probably spoke to my brother, and that was enough."

"Didn't you miss him?"

"Life *was* a little duller."

"If he *had* asked you to marry him?"

"Well?"

"Would you?"

"Cosmo!"

"You told me I might ask you anything!"

She stopped, turned to the roadside, and sat down on the low earth dyke. Her face was white.

"Joan! Joan!" cried Cosmo, "what is it?"

"Nothing, only a little faintness. I have walked a long way and am getting tired."

"What a brute I am," said Cosmo, "to let you walk. Do you think you could ride on a man's saddle?"

"I think so, if only I were not so tired."

They were approaching the place where Cosmo's horse would be waiting him. He ran to take him, and to send the groom home on foot with a message.

To Joan it was a terrible moment. Had she been acting on a presumption that had no foundation? She had come to a man whom she hadn't heard from in well over a year. She had taken so much for granted! What if she had misunderstood everything!

When Joan sat down, Agnes stopped. Several times she started to run to her, fearing something had gone wrong, but checked herself lest she should cause more mischief by interfering: till she knew she was needed she would do nothing. When she saw her sink sideways on the dyke, she started forward, but seeing Cosmo hurrying back only a few moments after, she stopped again.

Before Cosmo reached her Joan had sat up. The same faith, or rather hope, which had taken shape in her dreams, now woke to meet the necessity of the hour. She rose as Cosmo came near, saying she felt better, and let him put her on the horse.

But now Joan was determined to face the worst, to learn her position and know what she must do.

"Has the day not come yet, Cosmo?" she said. "Can you now tell me why you left me so suddenly?"

"It may come with your answer to the question I put to you," replied Cosmo.

"You are cruel, to be so ambiguous!"

"Am I? How? I do not understand?"

It was getting worse and worse. Joan found herself growing almost angry. It is so horrid when the man you love *will* be so stupid!

She turned her face away and was silent a moment. A man must sometimes, even at the risk of presumption, suppose a thing he knows not for sure, that he may know whether it be or not. But Cosmo was indeed something of the innocent Aggie took him for.

"Joan, I don't see how I am in the wrong, after the permission you gave me," he persisted, too modest. "Agnes would have answered me straight out."

"How do you know that! What have you ever asked her?"

For one who refused an answer, Joan was tolerably exacting in her questions.

"I asked her to marry me," replied Cosmo.

"You asked her to marry you!"

"Yes, but she wouldn't."

"Why wouldn't she?"

Joan's face was now red as fire, and she was biting her lip hard.

"She had more reasons than one against it. Oh, Joan, she *is* so good!"

"And are you going to marry her?"

Instead of answering her question, Cosmo turned and called to Agnes, some thirty yards behind them:

"Come here, Aggie."

Agnes came quickly.

"Tell Lady Joan," he said, "what for ye wouldna marry me."

" 'Deed, my lady," said Agnes, her face also like a setting sun, "ye may believe anythin' he tells ye, jist as if it were gospel. He doesna ken hoo to make a lie."

"I know that as well as you," replied Lady Joan.

"Na, ye canna do that, 'cause ye haena kent him sae long."

"Will you tell me why you would not marry him?"

"For one thing, 'cause he loved you better than me, only he thought ye was married, an' he didna like lettin' me go frae the hoose."

"Thank you, Agnes," said Joan with a smile nothing less than heavenly.

And with that she slipped from the saddle, threw her arms round Aggie's neck, and kissed her.

Aggie returned her embrace with simple truth, then drawing gently away, said, putting her hand before her eyes as if she found the sun too strong, "It's very well for you, my lady; but it's some sore upon me. For I told him he shouldna marry his mither—meanin' mysel'—an' ye're full as auld as I am."

Joan gave a sigh.

"I am a little older, I believe," she answered, "but I cannot help it. Nor would I if I could, for three years ago I was still less worthy of him than I am now."

Here Cosmo set Joan up on the horse again, and a full explanation followed between them, neither thinking of being any less honest because of Aggie's presence. She would indeed have fallen behind again, but Joan would not let her, so she walked side by side with them, and amid the rest of the story heard Cosmo tell how he had yielded Joan because poor Jermyn loved her. Agnes both laughed and cried as she listened, and when Cosmo ceased, threw her arms once more around him, saying, "Cosmo, ye're worth it all!" Then releasing him, she turned to Joan.

"My lady," she said, "I dinna grudge him to ye a bit. Noo that he's yours, an' all's come round as it should, I'll be mysel' again. But I'm sure ye'll un'erstan', my lady, for ye hae a true hert. An' ye must know that when a woman sees a man bearin' all things true an' unselfish, almost like a god, not thinkin' he's doin' anythin' out o' the ordinary, she can't help lovin' him. An' more, my lady, I mean to love him yet, but as the two o' ye that God has joined t'gether. An' when I think o' the one o' ye, it'll be t' think o' ye both. Noo, ye'll go on t'gether again, an' I'll come ahind."

57

· · · · · · · · · · · · · · · · ·

The Future of the Glen Called Warlock

Joan had gone to visit distant relatives who had all at once begun to take notice of her. She had come with them more gladly than they knew, on a visit to Cairntod. There such a longing seized her to see Cosmo that, heedless of consequences of presumption, she donned a peasant's dress and set out on foot for Castle Warlock. She had lost her way and was growing both weary and very uneasy when suddenly she saw Cosmo and Aggie on the road before her.

"But what am I to do now, Cosmo?" she said. "What explanation can I make of myself to my people?"

"You can tell them you met an old friend, and finding him now a rich man, you immediately fell in love, and like a prudent woman consented at once to marry him."

"I must not tell a story."

"Who is asking you to tell a story?"

"You do, telling me to say I have a rich lover."

"I do not. I am rich."

"Not in money?"

"Yes, in money."

"Why didn't you tell me before?"

"I forgot. How could I think of riches with you filling up all the thinking place!"

"But what am I to do tonight?"

"Tonight? Oh! I hadn't thought of that! We'll ask Aggie."

So Aggie was once more called and consulted. She thought for a minute, then said, "It wouldna do for her to stay at the castle. Cosmo, as soon as ye're home, sen' yer man on the horse to let my lady's fowk ken. Then she can write them a letter an' tell them she's fallen in wi' an auld acquaintance, a lass called Agnes Gracie, a decent yoong woman, an' haein' lost her way an' bein' tired, she's gaein' home wi' her for the night; an' the laird o' Glenwarlock was sae kind as t' sen' his man on the horse to carry the letter. That way there'll be nae lies told, an' no ower much o' the truth."

When they arrived at the castle, Grizzie was not a little scandalized to see her young master with a country lass on his horse, and making so much of her. But when she came to understand who she was, and that she had dressed up as she had to get to Castle Warlock more easily, she was filled with approbation, even to delight.

"Eh, but ye're a lass to make a man prood!" she said. "Sit ye doon, my leddy, an' be right welcome! eh, but ye're bonny, as ever was ony! An' eh, but ye're steady as never was a leddy! May the Lord bless ye, an' the laird kiss ye!"

Joan laughed merrily, being happy as a child.

They had supper, and then a cart came rumbling to the door, half full of straw, into which Joan got with Aggie. A few things Aggie had borrowed from Grizzie to make her guest comfortable were handed in, and they set out for Muir of Warlock. In the morning Joan declared she had never slept better than in old Grannie's boxbed.

They were married almost immediately, and nobody's permission asked. Cosmo wrote to acquaint Lord Mergwain with the event, and had in return, from his lordship's secretary, an acknowledgment of the receipt of his letter.

Of what they had to tell each other, of the way they lived, of how blessed they were even when not altogether happy—of these matters I say nothing, leaving them to the imagination of him who would speculate about how much Cosmo got for his diamonds, and whether, if Lord Mergwain should not marry, Cairncarque would come to Lady Joan.

After a few years more, Lord Lickmyloof fell into serious financial default by reason of several dubious investments into which his greed had led him. With great anguish of spirit, he came hat in hand to call upon "the laird" to inquire whether he might be in the market to redeem some of the land that had so unfortunately fallen out of the family estate during his father's time. Grizzie was cordial, but her heart glowed with the hot coals of vengeance satisfied.

Cosmo greeted his antagonistic neighbor with such open-armed absence of resentment as to make one think his lordship was in fact one of the closest of friends. He listened attentively to his lordship's offer, asked what he would take for the entire lot, with the exception of his house, ten acres which adjoined it, and a thoroughway to the main road. He heard the figure, said he would consult with his counselors, as he called them, thanked his lordship for coming, and promised to return his call the following afternoon.

That same day Cosmo discussed the matter with Joan and Grizzie first of all, then Aggie and Mr. Burns, who had retired to Muir o' Warlock, so attached had he become to the young laird, as he still called him, and was now living off his percentage from the diamonds. They all agreed that Cosmo should buy the property his lordship had offered, but in the white heat of righteous indignation Grizzie declared that "the auld thief's askin' dooble what he could frae any ither body!" Joan, Aggie, and Mr. Burns all agreed.

The following morning Cosmo spent alone, walking the fields, hills, and streambeds of his youth. Never since the death of the two old men had he desired the advice of his father and Mr. Simon so greatly, nor felt their presence so keenly. All morning he walked, heedless of the boundaries between his and his neighbor's land, asking himself over and over, "Lord, what wilt thou have me to do?"

At length he returned, and met Joan halfway up toward Mr. Simon's, where he had taken her that first winter after her father's death. She smiled at him, and he silently took her hand and they descended back toward the house.

"Grizzie's right," he said at length, "he is asking double what the land would bring on the market."

'But you know what you must do regardless?" said Joan. "That's what you're about to say, is it not?"

"Yes, I think I do," Cosmo replied.

That afternoon Cosmo walked Grizzie's well-worn battle-path toward the Gracies', and thence up the hill to Lord Lickmyloof's, where he delivered a check to his lordship for half again above the price he had asked.

Grizzie was speechless when she heard what had taken place, but before she had the chance to vent incredulity at what "the innocent cratur" had done, Cosmo silenced her.

"Ye ken what he tellt us, Grizzie, that we must gie t' him that asks, an' when a man would hae yer sairk aff yer back, gie him yer jaicket besides. He would always hae us gie mair than we must, Grizzie. An' besides, the money's na oor's. 'Tis the Lord's! 'Tis the Lord who's given us oor inheritance, both the land an' the life within us."

Aggie's little school thrived. She became not only one of the most loved women in the village but also one of the most respected—a lady in all the ways that matter, and only lacking the title in the one way that mattered least of all. When she was thirty-two, the old schoolmaster died and was replaced by a young man from Dufftown. He loved learning and truth almost as much as she, and it could hardly be helped that he and Aggie would love one another. They were married a year later, and it was not long before the standards in all the right modes of education were in Muir o' Warlock the highest of any part of the region.

As a wedding gift, the laird presented Aggie and her new husband the old Gracie croft where Aggie had been raised, along with twenty acres of land that stretched down to the Warlock. He also lent his laborers, when work in the fields was slow, to the task of building a new house for "the twa schulemaisters," as they were called in the village. The old cottage stood next to it for many years, and Aggie's and Cosmo's children played together in it every summer, and over all the hills around and between their two homes.

Grizzie lived yet many years, finally attaining to the age of ninety-seven before being taken home. To all the children of the village she was known, as had been many before her, simply as "Grannie."

Cosmo and Joan had three sons and one daughter. As they grew, though earthly poverty was not one of their concerns, Cosmo nevertheless worked strenuously to fill them with the same values of righteousness, truth, and spiritual blessing as had been passed into him by his own father. With each of his sons, as his father had done with him, he took them aside on their birthdays to tell them—for the story never grew old—how the land and everything on it was a gift from the hand of the Lord, to be used for his purposes rather than their own. With each one alone, once a year, he walked hand-in-hand into the hills, there to remind them of their true and lasting inheritance, an inheritance not of earthly possessions, but—as his own father had built so strongly into him:—a *true* inheritance, in which the true business of life is not to get what you can, but rather to give what you can, and to do justly, to love mercy, and to walk humbly before your God.

Cosmo wrote a little poem a week after he and Joan were married. Joan treasured it all her life, and when she was old, gave the original of it to her daughter, saying, "I know you have heard the words many times before, but I want you to have this copy of the poem, for it is your father's legacy—the cry of his heart after our God. There is no more lasting heritage I can give you than that!"

> All things are shadows of thee, Lord:
>   The sun himself is but a shade;
> My soul is but the shadow of thy word,
>   A candle sun-bedayed!
>
> Diamonds are shadows of the sun;
>   They drink his rays and show a spark:
> My soul some gleams of thy great shine hath won,
>   And round me slays the dark.

All knowledge is but broken shades—
    In gulfs of dark a wandering horde:
Together rush the parted glory-grades—
    And lo, thy garment, Lord!

My soul, the shadow, still is light,
    Because the shadow falls from thee;
I turn, dull candle, to the center bright,
    And home flit shadowy.

Shine, shine; make me thy shadow still—
    The brighter still the more thy shade;
My motion by thy lovely moveless will!
    My darkness, light delayed!